INTRODUCTION

First published in 1977, Tegel Manor is the oldest of "Haunted House" adventures in fantasy roleplaying. The Manor is a sprawling edifice of 250+ rooms filled with tricks, traps, puzzles, monsters, and situations both humorous and horrific. Like the classic haunted house, not much of Tegel Manor makes logical sense, but it's still as dangerous as adventuring can get. The huge manor house has been the curse of its owners, the Rump family, for generations – no matter how many times they have tried to get rid of it, the ownership manages to come back to them. This intertwined and sinister relationship between the house and its chosen family is a history of horror, evil, and greed. There is a lot for the characters to learn about the curse, and their knowledge might just keep them alive long enough to tell the tale.

If you've already seen the 1977 version of the Manor, there's a lot more for you to learn in this updated and expanded version of the classic. This printing contains expanded descriptions of the rooms, new areas, new monsters, new magic items, and much more, all with spectacular color illustrations.

A fun fact: In 1981 Judges Guild was contacted by a little-known foreign company called Konami who wanted to produce a game based on our Tegel Manor. Konami noted that their game was ready and all they needed was the Tegel Manor title for American release. Judges Guild turned the offer down, but five years later, Konami released the popular video-game Castlevania. So it's not impossible that, at some level, Tegel Manor forms some of the conceptual basis for Castlevania as well as for the countless D&D haunted house adventures that would follow it over the course of decades.

Welcome to the thrills and chills of the granddaddy of all haunted house adventures — the quirky and terrifying masterpiece that is Tegel Manor!

HOW THIS BOOK IS ORGANIZED

Chapter 1 contains the description and key to Tegel Village, because after all, every good old school adventure starts in a tavern… We recommend the Bark and Byte. After all, you will *sleep* well there.

Chapter 2 describes the wilderness areas surrounding the manor, including random encounters, a pirate base, and the Rump Family graveyard.

Chapter 3 details the Sanctum of Madness, the Temple of Frigga and the dungeons below both. This area has been significantly expanded over any previous version because, after all, the evil priests here worship *Frog God Game's* icon.

Chapter 4 contains all of the Rampaging Rooms of the Manor itself. Please note that we have taken pains to expand these rooms beyond their previous one-line entries and have added a few new twists and turns to the empty closets and traps. We have also tried hard to detail the specifics of the pictures and statues, as well as the traps present in each. This chapter is where, we expect, the bulk of adventuring will take place.

Chapter 5 describes the dungeons below the Manor itself (there are 4 distinct levels). While deeper usually means more difficult, it's our experience that these dungeons make an excellent place to rest and recover (at least with respect to the manor itself!).

Appendix I contains the descriptions and names of the Rump Family members. Please get to know the family well, as they represent what is perhaps the most dangerous denizens present in the manor.

Appendix II contains stat blocks and other information about all creatures and non-player characters appearing in the book. After all, when **Sarthoggus** casts *caustic burst* on the head of the wizard, you need to know what is does. Please note that we assume you will have a monster manual or other reference for standard monsters. We just could not find it in our hearts to make Chuck lay out another Zombie stat block.

Appendix III details a list of possible actions or powers for the numerous Startling Statues that abound in the Manor. The random

effects of these (and the paintings) were always one of the most interesting part of adventuring here.

Appendix IV give a ready reference for a GM to invent or alter one of the many traps present throughout the Manor (or anywhere else we suppose). In the spirit of *Tome of Adventure Design*, we strive here to create a handy way to mix things up a bit.

Appendix V contains a list of Eldritch experiments that could occur if the player characters fool around with any of the alchemy labs present in the manor. It's really just here to add a bit of spice in the event that they get cocky while messing around in the Wizard's Tower.

Appendix VI details the new magic items and spells that are contained within this work. Please note that while many of the magic items are indeed potent, most have significant drawbacks if used. After all, this is a haunted house.

Finally, a note about the maps. We are including a poster map of both the wilderness and the Manor inside the covers of this book. In addition, we have scattered sections relevant to the area of the Manor throughout Chapter 4 to allow the GM to easily see the connections between rooms without flipping back and forth between the poster map and the text. That being said, the poster maps are wonderfully detailed and should be used (and admired!) by the reader.

THE HISTORY OF THE GUILD AND OF THE MANOR, FROM BOB BLEDSAW II

If I remember correctly, Dad's gaming group started into Tegel Manor in February of 1976, and did not leave until nearly Easter-time. It was not really a play-test of a potential product, for Judges Guild was not founded for another 3 months; it was just a fun place to run the players through. After the success of our subscription service launch in August of 1976, though, it was put in a folder as a definite possible project. At the time, we called these "Installments," because it was all about our Guildmember subscription service. The idea of a stand-alone module was not tested. That was new ground. It may have been in Dad's mind as a possibility, though. He was a dreamer and often creative.

With the summer of 1977, Judges Guild had just completed its first year of business. Having anchored a growing subscription service, we were providing fantasy gamers with a steady flow of fresh material for their campaigns; the bulk of which centered at Rhamsanderah, the City State of the Invincible Overlord, and was fleshing out the world beyonde (which we titled the Wilderlands). Our world was growing, as was our business. In July, plans began for our fall releases, and Dad wished to make something special for the Halloween Season.

Halloween was always well-celebrated by our family. In his teens, Halloween led to Dad's only run-in with the law. He was pushing over outhouses (still a common sight in our neighborhood) when he slipped and fell into the dung-pit. His band of hooligans abandoned him when the owner emerged from his house with a shotgun. Dad was arrested for vandalism and had to ride to the police station on the fender of the squad car (a sickening embarrassment he never forgot).

Tegel Manor has its share of pits.

Tegel, like the City State, began as a small booklet and a few loose maps as "Installment Material." Dad, of course, placed it into his Wilderlands world-setting, but in time it grew to stand on its own as an adventure module. The same was true with others that followed; Modron for example, and soon TSR too saw the value in producing stand-alone adventure modules placed in their own world-setting. Tegel was really the first to break away from the City State, and had a distant location, far to the East on the first continental Campaign Map the Guild was to publish.

Once it was decided to make Tegel the October 1977 Installment (still called a "City State Installment"), Dad asked me to create a cover for it, and asked for some art to include in it. At the time I was a pencil-artist. I was very accomplished with a pencil, but wary of ink and pens. That is why the Flying Turkey (the Company Logo) had to be inked over by my father. The same became true for the Tegel cover. Dad inked over my very detailed pencil drawing to make it print-ready: this explains the oddities of the details in that first cover, which was really a half-cover or thick banner taking nearly half of the booklet top.

The instruction from Dad was, "I need a drawing of a Haunted House this size," and gave me the dimensions. The drawing did little to illustrate the enormous castle-like complex that became Tegel, but it did have a Halloween feel. My own inspiration came from the opening credits of Saturday-Morning's Scooby-Doo with bats flying by, but I had nothing but memory to draw from (video tape being a rare commodity in 1977). It became my first product cover, of the several I did that followed.

Just as it was liked by the gaming group at home, Tegel was received well by the subscribers, and by 1978 had grown into a stand-alone module that went through several printings and editions by 1985. Like with most Guild products, each printing saw some changes and revision. In Dad's view a product such as Tegel (number JG-27) was much like a vehicle model... if you bought the Chevy Impala of 1963, then the same model in 1968, the differences between the two are staggering. The same was true for a Guild product. We did not think to create a different vintage number to each edition, and while the Guild staff was always working on new products (or the latest Wilderlands installment), sometimes as much as half the crew was revising the past modules for the next printings.

Maps aside, we never sent a printer the same thing twice. When stock of a certain product began to run low, the masters were sent to the light-tables for revisions and any newly written content was pasted in. That was one of Dad's rules "It can always be improved upon prior to printing." The first print-run of Tegel Manor manifested in the form of 12 boxes of un-collated sheets which were stacked in my bedroom and the adjacent hallway of our home. Also in my bedroom was a standing saddle-stapler, and I was soon at work putting the booklets together. It was with some pride that I brought one of the first finished booklets to school, showing my Art teacher, Mrs. Dunn.

In 1985 the Guild went into self-imposed hibernation, but interest in Tegel resurfaced. Colonel Lou Zocchi (of Avalon Hill and Gamescience fame) loved the module, and partnered with Dad to release a revised and expanded version through Gamescience in 1989. Lou had been one of the Guild's earliest distributors, and he and my Dad had shared a long mutual respect. Dad contributed little to this project, as Zocchi employed the skills of author Niels Erickson (Wizard's Realm) for the expansion. As previous versions of Tegel had all been for D&D, Erickson stripped out the mechanics to conform to a Universal or Generic System. Mechanics aside, the Erickson material was very good, and the Gamescience edition is still sought-after by fans.

Over the next decade, the Gamescience Version was the last word on Tegel, but then shortly before Dad's death in 2008, fans began coaxing out a Tegel for the D20 game system, and the online bulletin boards began to drum up interest in seeing it come together. Dad passed away in April of 2008, and after a month of grieving, I reluctantly stepped into his shoes. One of the first things I had to do was find out what was owned, what could be published (with or without royalty agreements) and the status of each title. Three of Dad's longtime friends, each a little worried for what might become of the Guild, offered personal assistance and advice: Bill Owen (Dad's longtime friend and Guild founding partner), Dave Arneson (author of Blackmoor and First Fantasy Campaign), and Colonel Lou Zocchi.

In the Guild's archives was two partial manuscripts on Tegel, both from the Guild's Sunnyside Days. One was a play-tested Tegel II, which seemed more of an expansion to the story line, while the other was a cruder more humorous (with adult content) pitch with the working title Rump Romp. As Lou had published the last version of Tegel, I asked him what he thought might be added or revised. He said there were some mechanical problems with the portals in his Gamescience version, and that he and my father wished to expand to include the rooftop. They had agreed on the use of four imps to be encountered there, named Aquis, Fortis, Gingis, and Vitus... and several jokes followed. Lou has long been an accomplished magician, but he has real talent at comedy too.

Dave Arneson too had some input on a Tegel Sequel. He told me Dad had devised a storyline (possibly shooting for a Christmas release) wherein Tegel would be encountered but all doors and windows blocked as if by magic, the manor aglow in a strange light. The only way to enter was via the roof and chimney (the chimney working as a time-portal) shooting you back in time, the soot tagging your date from which you came). The goal was to free a certain Elf named Kringle who had mistakenly come down the wrong chimney, landing amid the fiendish Rumps of Tegel Manor. This I tied to the folder Dad had the materials in, on which he had written the title Night of the Living Rumps.

For a time I tried to piece together a working version of a Tegel sequel from both manuscripts, but my heart was not in it, and I did not feel up to the task. Night of the Living Rumps has some interesting elements, though. The premise is that as a wedding gift to the Rumps, the wizard Swayne enchanted the very walls of the Manor to protect them from the elements, and enchanted loadstones within the chimney to create a portal which would bring peoples from the future or past into the Rump parlor... the Rumps love having unexpected guests drop in. Free Santa from the brig or not, returning to your own time requires you make your way back to the rooftop and drop into the chimney again. Dave Arneson especially liked the idea that this mechanism could be used to explain the presence of modern weaponry in Tegel, taken from the new arrivals.

I still see Lou at conventions when I can, and I always bring him a little something from my Dad. Dave has passed away too, and I cannot help but feel he and my father would have done greater things if they had collaborated more. It was not until after my father passed and I got access to his computer files that I discovered that he had done some work with Dave Arneson on one of my own game ideas concerning the steamboat era (where one starts as a cub pilot and builds until he owns a small fleet of riverboats, competing against the encroaching railroads).

In 2017, I was at the North Texas RPG Con speaking with Bill Webb, who was instrumental in keeping the Guild alive over the last two decades. He brought some of the Guild's best works to glorious hardback grandeur, keeping Judges Guild in the ears of the industry, while introducing our line to a new generation of gamers. I mentioned that I had read a manuscript for a Tegel Manor revision by Gabor Lux and it was a shame that a D20 version was never completed. Bill then let me know how much Tegel meant to him personally, and so we agreed on the title Tegel Complete. I sent the original Tegel Playtest Map to the Webb Family as a gift to Tegel's biggest fan, and for all he has done to help the Guild along. Judges Guild has always been blessed with great fans.

Way back in 1977, this little kid discovered the realms of wonder that are Fantasy Roleplaying while travelling to camp in a motor home. Years later, that little kid started has written or produced hundreds of books to support the game. That little kid was me, and 41 years later, I still remember the magic that Tegel Manor inspired.

Tegel Manor was where, for me at least, it all began. First as a player, and shortly afterwards as the Game Master. I will never forget that first session—my poor, 1st level cleric was the only one who made his saving throw for some fear effect, and was left alone to face a dozen skeletons. I made my turn roll—and managed to finish off the final two undead horrors that could only in my mind be the terrible creatures that I remembered from Jason and the Argonauts.

Later that session (after my comrades returned to find me victorious), I recall clearly moving the right arm of a statue and it spitting out a magic scroll! It was all fun and games for me until I was robbed by

Tegel Manor
The Judges Guild Classic Reborn

Authors
Bill Webb & Thom Wilson with additional material by Gabor Lux

Producers
Bill Webb & Zach Glazar

Project Managers
Bill Webb & Zach Glazar

Fantasy Grounds Conversion
Michael G. Potter

Editors
Jeff Harkness & Edwin Nagy

Art Director
Casey W. Christofferson

Layout and Graphic Design
Charles A. Wright

Cover Design
Jim Wampler

Front Cover Art
Artem Shukayev

Interior Art
C.J. Marsh, Terry Pavlet, & Artem Shukayev

Cartography
Alyssa Faden & Robert Altbauer with additional design elements from Ainsley Christofferson and Raven Metcalf

FROG GOD GAMES IS

CEO
Bill Webb

Creative Director
Matthew J. Finch

Production Director
Charles A. Wright

Chief of Operations
Zach Glazar

Special Projects Director
Jim Wampler

Customer Relations
Mike Badolato

ADVENTURES WORTH WINNING

FROG GOD GAMES

ISBN: 978-1-62283-735-9

Table of Contents

Roughneck Rump the Rotund on the way back to town. "Stand and Deliver" he said. We were far outmatched by him and his icky goblins with bows…ah well, we survived (except Richard's magic-user).

That Christmas, all I wanted was this game. My parents obliged me by purchasing a white box set (at of all places Nordstroms!). I returned a couple of sweaters I got that year and used my Christmas money to get two sets of dice (I still have them!), a copy of Outdoor Survival (yep—still have it too), and a single module—Tegel Manor. Being the youngest of the group, I was immediately elected Game Master (so the older guys could be players). They thought they could take advantage of the little kid…well, they quickly learned from that mistake.

For the past 41 years, I have been running the same campaign, set in a mix of the Wilderlands and my own creation. Tegel Manor figured prominently in the foundations of my game. I still pull it out now and again and run it for my kids, at conventions (3 TPKs at one convention two years ago).

Over the years, I was fortunate enough not to just meet, but actually work with, Bob Bledsaw Sr. While at Necromancer Games, we were able to complete the Wilderlands of High Fantasy, the City State of the Invincible Overlord and even Caverns of Thracia. We had just started working on Tegel when Bob fell ill, and the project was never completed. I had even figured out how to make a map (impossibly big for 2007 technology) that would accommodate 28mm figures for the entire manor itself.

I was grief stricken when we were unable to continue with the first love of my roleplaying life.

Then, two years ago, a mutual friend helped broker an agreement between Frog God and Judges Guild to revise and revisit Tegel Manor. I took charge of the project myself, and with help from several friends, we have created what I believe is an expanded version worthy of the modules legacy. No longer are the Monastery and Temple just boxes on a map. The single lines of the town are revised and expanded to detail each location, and the wilderness areas are filled out as well. Lots of those "blank rooms and rat tunnels" now have contents and lead places. After all, I spend 41 years running this module—I added a great deal of content in that time.

That being said, the whole remains true to the snarkiness and tongue-in-cheek puns of the original. This book is to me, canon, and all revisions were checked to ensure they met my standards for the look, feel and smell of the historical book.

Chapter 1: Tegel Village

Introduction

Less known for its fertile fields and stout farmers, the village of Tegel is the site of the infamous manor. All manner of evildoers moved to its vicinity since the lamentable but timely downfall of the Rump family, threatening the simple lives of its inhabitants. Indeed, between the cultists of Tsathoggus, the Dearth Monster of Derfingel Marsh, brigands, pirates, and undead, it is a small wonder they still till their farms as if nothing had happened! Though the harvests remain good and the rich grains still find their market, many are reconsidering their residence. After all, what is a full purse good for if one isn't alive to appreciate it?

Mayor Ternelmor and his aides have their hands full. They have to deal with monsters and other assorted menaces, all the while making sure that Sir Runic the Rump — the last of his line — doesn't regain his holding by some miracle. On the other hand, it wouldn't hurt if some of the nearby problems were solved, by sword or by deceit, and they are willing to pay handsomely to this end. Adventurers seeking their fortune who are not afraid of a gruesome and untimely death should find what they are looking for!

A. Ranold Rax

Once known as the "Defiler of Dearthwood," Ranold Max (**bandit lord**[II] with AC 19 chainmail and *+1 shield*, replace greatsword with heavy mace — damage is bludgeoning) is a former reaver retired from his pirating days to enjoy the simple country life. Much of the gold he gained fighting orcs and plundering ships on the perilous estuary of the Roglaroon went down with his ship and crew. The remaining 753 gp is safely hidden in the cellar below his modest stone house. The buried iron chest holding his treasure also contains a broken *+1 scimitar* and the colorful outfit he wore as a captain. Ever the opportunist, Ranold struck a deal with the Evil High Priest Sarthoggus and became a willing informer, which, given his eloquence and good relations with Ternelmor, is invaluable to the frog cultists.

Possessions: +1 small metal shield, chainmail, heavy mace, 6 throwing daggers (ivory handles, worth 40 gp each), 28 gp, 300 sp, *potion of superior healing* (cursed, hit points are lost again in 1d10 minutes — a present from Sarthoggus).

B. Brinna Birgit

This blunt, enterprising spear-maiden hails from the village of Sea Rune to the southeast. She is a skilled mercenary but her gruff manners and open dislike of men haven't endeared her to most prospective employers; in fact, she had to turn to farming to make a living. Brinna (as **burglar**[II] with AC 17 chain shirt and shield, and the ability to cast *speak with animals* 1/day, replace light crossbow with longbow) is willing to join a group for an equal share and to take part in the fighting, but refuses to risk her life unnecessarily. If expeditions prove lucrative, she can find an additional 2d4 Amazons for hire (as **burglar**). She holds Sir Runic Rump in contempt, having been approached by him on various occasions to "get some personal belongings from the manor." These forays all ended before even crossing the manor's gates; Sir Runic usually beat a hasty retreat as soon as he lost sight of the village.

Possessions: chain shirt, large metal shield, longbow, engraved iron horn (a family heirloom), three spears at home, 26 gp.

C. Temple of Thor

An old, moss-covered statue of a valkyrie stands before the village shrine. Beyond the iron reinforced door lies the sanctum of Thor; a solemn, cold, and empty place. Sixteen round shields hang on the bare stone walls. If a ritual is in progress, they clang and resound as if beaten by invisible sword hilts (this dweomer grants any cleric of Thor inside the walls +3 to their spell attack roll and spell save DC, and the ability to cast one fifth-level spell per fortnight). One of the shields is engraved with a map to some lost treasure haul. The altar, not unlike an anvil, holds two censers and a font of holy water (five doses per week).

A young priestess named Arnthora (**priest**) administers the temple and sees to the spiritual needs of the villagers. Arnthora is losing attendance to Sarthoggus' temple on the hill; thus, she is grateful for any help in clearing them out. Her room is sparsely furnished, and contains a cot, a book with heroic songs in runic script, a chest with personal belongings, and a bearskin.

Possessions: chainmail, heavy mace, ceremonial staff (masterwork), 58 gp, 400 sp, *spell scroll* of *cure wounds* and *hallow*.

D. Abandoned House

The acolytes of Sarthoggus kidnapped the inhabitants of this large dwelling and turned them into cauldron-born zombies. Both entrances are boarded shut, and a thick coat of dust covers everything inside. The house and its contents — mundane belongings and farming implements — may be had for a mere 120 gp, paid to Ternelmor. The farm itself costs an additional 100; it is weedy and not very profitable.

E. Rothald the Twice-born

Knives and daggers of all sorts hang on Rothald's walls; he practices with them constantly. Rothald (as **spy** with AC 13 from leather armor, Strength 15, add dagger attack at +4 to hit, 1d4 + 2 piercing damage and replace shortsword with longsword at +4 to hit, 1d8 + 2 slashing damage) used to work at the manor, but has since been reduced to a commoner, as he points out lamentingly. Since money is tight, he is prepared to part with items in his collection: 30 common daggers (2 gp each), 4 gold-etched daggers (260 gp each or 900 gp for the whole set), and a *cursed −1 dagger* (400 gp).

Possessions: leather armor, longsword, 4 gold-etched daggers, 9 sp, bottle of rotgut.

F. Bark & Byte

The dwarf Cretin Nodcock (as **captain** with AC 12 from studded leather armor, replace longsword with greataxe at +6 to hit for 1d12 + 4 slashing damage), the incredibly ugly owner of this fine-dining establishment, is known for providing unusual entertainment in the evening: a dancing band of three "houris" is well appreciated by the mostly male clientele. Leaving little to the imagination, these three ladies dress in a provocative attire and seduce patrons with considerable ease. The fact that some paramours never return from the resulting dalliance is usually attributed to monsters. Few, however, suspect that the monsters are the ladies themselves.

Ronda, Rusnya, and Otromba are all **jackalweres** (with Charisma 14 and Deception +6), inhuman therianthropic monsters who crave human flesh and blood — preferably fresh and alive! They use their sleep-inducing gaze while still in human form. If their partner fails his saving throw, they change into their hybrid form, slit his throat, and devour his body in a frenzy. Note that the jackalweres prefer to target outsiders who won't be missed by anyone of consequence.

Skills: Craft (cook) +5; *Feats:* Toughness (x2), Endurance.

Cretin Noddock's Possessions: studded leather armor, dagger, dwarven waraxe, 85 gp.

Jackalweres' Possessions: suggestive attire, chainmail bikini, cheap jewelry worth 2d4x5 gp each, 104 gp.

G. Neptune's Trident

An inn with a marine theme, Neptune's Trident is run by Quinta Demetria (**footman**[II]), a venerable fisherman who likes to bore his customers with stories of unlikely sea monsters. The fare is simple, mostly consisting of fish, fish, and even more fish, but at least the rooms are clean — five are available for 2 sp per day. Quinta Demetria knows a good deal about the pirates on the coast from having observed their camp while fishing.

Possessions: studded leather armor, shield, spear, unkempt clothing, 50 gp gold ring, 14 gp.

H. Mordacity Maghoula

Ternelmor's righthand man, Mordacity Maghoula (**bandit lord**, replace greatsword with *+1 greataxe* at +6 to hit for 1d12 + 4 slashing damage) is the leader of Tegel's meager militia. His stingy and unpleasant nature hasn't endeared him to the militia members, despite his unquestionable fighting prowess. Mordacity carries a whip in addition to his magical battleaxe and uses it frequently on the four slaves working his land. An ironbound chest in his house contains his wealth: 330 gp, 480 sp, a bronze statuette of a vrock demon, and a set of eight ivory dice worth 60 gp.

Possessions: breast-plate, *+1 greataxe*, whip, 45 sp, *potion of haste*.

I. Mayor's House

The house of Ternelmor, Tegel's mayor, is the most prosperous in the village. Two **guards** stand by the front door day and night, preferring not to let in any of the rabble. The inside rooms are clean and well maintained. A long oak table (an old present from the Rump family) seats no fewer than 12 people, although most of the time, only Ternelmor, Mordacity Maghoula, and a few guards use the furniture, as the village council was disbanded some time ago. The rooms of the house are cramped; they contain various valuables retrieved from the manor for "safekeeping." Among the assorted furniture, tableware, and tapestries stands a rusty suit of full plate armor that may still be

made serviceable. The mayor's room holds two large chests. One contains the village treasury while the other holds his own personal wealth. Both are locked and can be opened with a successful DC 18 Dexterity check with thieves' tools.

Chest #1 contains 1600 sp, 400 gp, 65 pp, and a large gold bar worth 300 gp.

Chest #2 contains 700 sp, 600 gp, six silver goblets worth 20 gp each, a masterwork chain shirt, and a masterwork small metal shield.

Ternelmor (as **captain** with *+1 longsword*) is an overweight, balding man in his fifties. Very good with administration and organization, he quickly seized and consolidated power after the downfall of the Rump family. Since then, he has more-or-less been successful in retaining Tegel's attraction as a market for the surrounding farms, even if this meant occasionally bribing bandits and pirates to stay away. Despite the great undertaking, he commissioned the construction of a great citadel a few miles northwest of the village center. At the moment, only the foundations and a few walls stand, but the ready supply of free labor ensures that work progresses smoothly.

Ternelmor's foremost concern is Sarthoggus and his cultists. He wouldn't mind seeing them eliminated and offers an interested party the treasures the frog-priests possess as a reward for driving them out. He has mostly given up on ever retaking Tegel Manor; in fact, he wouldn't mind if the Rumps never regained their importance and power.

Ternelmor's Possessions: chainmail armor, metal shield, *+1 longsword*, golden signet ring (60 gp), 48 gp.

Guards' Possessions: leather armor, small wooden shield, shortspear, warning horn.

J. Shrine of Molna

This simple edifice houses an altar and a clay statue dedicated to Molna, God of Travelers. Those who can't afford a room at an inn may rest here in safety. The shrine is maintained by the villagers and occasionally visited by a wandering cleric. A small offering bowl holds 5d4 cp and 1d4 sp. Taking these coins invites divine retribution in the form of more frequent random encounters until the offender atones for the transgressions.

K. Altharontha's Boarding House

Altharontha's inn is the most expensive in Tegel and mostly caters to wealthier wayfarers. The establishment is quiet and decent; order is kept by Altharontha's two sons, Shark Mersin and Vinca One-eye. These lads are in good humour but don't hesitate to throw out an unruly customer. Accomodations are 15 sp per night, while meals are 1 gp per day (or you can try the exclusive Rump Roast, only 7 gp per serving). The cashbox behind the counter holds 50 gp, 23 sp, and 14 cp. Stairs lead to a well-stocked cellar with wine and various smoked meats. Altharontha and her sons have the stats of a **guard** with AC 12 (leather armor). Replace spear with other weapons, but use same stats.

Altharontha's Possessions: dagger, various kitchen utensils.

Shark's Possessions: leather vest, mace.

Vinca's Possessions: leather vest, shortsword, shortbow.

L.-M.-N. Deserted Houses

These three buildings are empty. All inhabitants have fled the village for greener pastures. Like building D, these houses are also available for sale at the price of 60 gp, 50 gp, and 45 gp, respectively. The farms belonging to them have already been sold.

O. White Horse Sleigh Bar

A small and crowded pub for tired farmers, the Sleigh specializes in White Wassil drink. This beverage costs 2 sp per cup and causes almost instant intoxication. A DC 12 Constitution saving throw is required to avoid getting intoxicated on the first cup, and the DC increases by 2 for each additional cup within an hour. The patrons are usually rowdy, and the jovial bartender, Hasnovar (as **bandit**), doesn't mind a little action himself. At any given time, there is a 60% chance 2d6+6 inebriated patrons (**commoners** or **hardy commoners**) are here, and another 60% chance that they are aggressive. The drinks are kept under a padlocked trapdoor, and only a small barrel is brought forth every evening. The lock on the trapdoor can be opened with a successful DC 14 Dexterity check with thieves' tools.

Possessions: dirty clothes, 2 sp, bottle of White Wassil drink.

P. Ep Stroten

A cunning litigation trickster from the City State of the Invincible Overlord, Ep Stroten (**assassin**[II]) traveled to Tegel to find a way to get his hands on the infamous Tegel Manor. With his extensive knowledge of legal matters (and his extraordinary skills in forgery), he can produce all sorts of documents proving his rights to the building, its treasures, and even its undead inhabitants, accompanied by the necessary bribes if necessary.

Fortunately, several people stand in his way: The first of them is Runic Rump, who, by the right of blood, still has the claim on his inheritance. The second is Ternelmor, who doesn't want anyone to become his new lord. The third group is the Rump clan itself; after all, this upstart isn't even on their family tree! Thus, Ep Sroten is seeking worthy hirelings to set matters straight — that is, eliminate all competition and clear out at least parts of the manor. He can pay in gold, which his employers, the cult of Orcus, can supply in abundance.

Ep Sroten's dwelling is a prosperous family home he purchased from Ternelmor a few months ago. He shares it with three **guards**, all of them Orcus worshippers adept at fighting dirty. The guards are named Lanarr, Xor, and Molthran. The house is reasonably well furnished and includes a locked study holding his paperwork, several forged documents, deeds, and proclamations, not to mention an iron lockbox. The door can be unlocked with a successful DC 20 Dexterity check with thieves' tools.

The box is trapped with a *glyph of warding* (explosive runes — lightning) trap placed by a priest of Orcus that only he can bypass. It has a DC of 16. It contains 65 pp, 150 gp, a *potion of sleep*[VI], a *potion of greater healing wounds*, seven doses of basic poison, and an *amulet of proof against detection and location*.

Sroten's Possessions: leather armor, three daggers, *potion of gaseous form*, *potion of resistance* (poison), 97 sp, 8 gp, well-hidden Orcus symbol.

Guards' Possessions: chain shirt, large wooden shield, 2d6 sp, well-hidden Orcus symbol; Xor has a *potion of invisibility* he uses to escape if things go wrong.

Exotic Items

Antique longsword[1]	96 gp
Bejeweled cup	210 gp
Book, travelogue[2]	80 gp
Book, religious[3]	100 gp
Carpet	50 gp
Potion, green[4]	150 gp
Potion, steaming[5]	200 gp
Small statuette, monstrous[6]	65 gp
Small statuette, triton	35 gp
Tapestries, set of three	180 gp

[1] Needs minor repairs.

[2] Contains mostly accurate maps of the isles east of the continent, with brief descriptions. May be out of date.

[3] Contains hymns to Mitra, and a *spell scroll* of *heal* folded neatly between two pages.

[4] *Potion of superior healing.*

[5] *Potion of resistance* (fire).

[6] Depicts a humanoid figure with the head of a ram, clutching a wicked looking staff. Secret compartment holds a dose of Death Dust and a small silver key. A creature who inhales the dust must succeed on a DC 16 Constitution saving throw or take 3d6 necrotic damage and be incapacitated for 1 minute. An incapacitated creature can repeat the saving throw at the end of each of its turns ending the effect on itself with a success.

Q. Halaf Fec's Trade Monopoly

Catering mostly to the needs of the village farmers, the monopoly also serves travelers. Most general goods are available, up to Tegel's 200 gp limit. A few exotic wares (see sidebox) are also for sale; these were recovered from the manor by a thief who later succumbed to some trap or monster.

Halaf Fec (**scout**) is willing to buy more items as far as his wealth allows. He pays 40% of the market value, more for especially desirable goods (golden utensils, etc.), which he sells at 80% for a tidy profit. He keeps his money in a hidden wooden box that can be found with a successful DC 16 Wisdom (Perception) check. The box contains 140 sp, 745 gp, a set of four electrum rings with small rubies in an ebony box (600 gp), two matched mountain crystal figurines (90 gp each), a fine pearl necklace (320 gp), and a *spell scroll* of *lesser restoration*.

Possessions: leather armor, silver-worked dagger, 60 gp.

R. Residence of Sir Runic the Rump

Dimwitted owner of Tegel Manor, Sir Runic (**holy knight**[II] with AC 23 from *+3 plate armor* and shield, *+3 longsword* at +8 to hit for 1d8 + 6 slashing damage, who automatically fails any saving throws against fear and automatically succeeds on all other saving throws) has been reduced to living among his subjects — something no nobleman should ever have to endure! Nevertheless, Sir Runic perseveres, especially since he feels at least marginally safe within the confines of the village. In addition to being a dullard, he is renowned for his poltroonery — possessing morals on par with the lousiest lily-livered lackwits. He constantly attempts to sell his inheritance, often for unbelievably cheap prices. Being nearly penniless, he has hopes for getting something out of his feared family home. Also, twice lost in card games, the manor's new owners have always returned asking for their money back — often at the threat of violence!

Sir Runic is distraught over his various relatives' and ancestors' corrupt modes of living and begrudgingly agrees to help a buyer clear the house out, thus putting many to rest; however, he is frightened by most family members, especially Ruang Rump the Ripper. Most of the time, he has to pass a successful Wisdom saving throw merely to venture beyond the village perimeter, another to enter the manor proper, and yet another for every hostile/frightening encounter inside. The DC is 10 for the first roll, increasing by 2 every time afterward. Once he fails a save, Sir Rump turns tails and flees shrieking. Fortunately for him, his relatives still consider him a part of the family — sure, he's a lamentable weakling, but blood is thicker than water, so they leave him alone unless Sir Runic directly engages them in melee.

Sir Runic shares his abode with four servants who accompany him all the time. Not the brightest bunch, these are all who are still loyal to him. The first of them is Lascini (**footman**[II] with darkvision 60 ft.), an elven spearman fond of courtship, romance, and little else. He remains hopeful that one way or another, the manor may be regained. The second is Enar the Proper (**captain**[II] with darkvision 60 ft.), a dour and serious dwarf. Enar's loyalty is unquestionable, and his courage is commendable as well. The other two are the brothers Afring and Hrinar (**guards**). Elderly retainers, they have nowhere else to go and thus stay by Sir Runic's side; after all, he is so weak and defenseless! In battle, they follow Sir Runic's example, which means they usually run like hell.

Sir Runic's Possessions: +3 *plate*, large metal shield, +3 *longsword*, +1 *ring of deflection & protection* (adds to AC and saving throws), 255 gp, 160 sp, and 24 cp.

Lascini's Possessions: leather armor, two shortspears, mandolin, foppish clothing, decorative dagger.

Enar the Proper's Possessions: chainmail, large metal shield, longsword, horned helmet, *potion of cure light wounds.*

Afring's Possessions: chainmail, greatsword, tabard with the Rump coat-of-arms, wineskin.

Hrinar's Possessions: chainmail, longbow, dagger, tabard with the Rump coat-of-arms, *everfull bottle of brandy.*

S. Home of Baladar the Ranger

Baladar the Ranger[II], woodsman and sworn enemy of Sir Runic, lives here. He is found in his cottage in the wilderness (location **GG.**) 90% of the time. The door to the house is locked but there is little of value to be had here anyway. It can be unlocked with a successful DC 13 Dexterity check with thieves' tools.

T. Dotho the Stout

Dotho (**greater commoner**[II]), a halfling pipeweed farmer, inhabits this simple cottage. Dotho's rafters are usually full of dried pipeweed, which he sells to Halaf Fec the merchant. He is often seen puffing on his pipe or enjoying a beer at the Bark & Byte, an establishment he recommends to everyone. All in all, he is the archetypal halfling — lazy, cheerful, and annoying.

Possessions: hand axe, shortbow, 12 arrows, pipe, pouch of pipeweed, 9 sp, 5 gp.

U. Marash-ar's Fine Horses

A wooden carving of a horse adorns Marash-ar's house. His wares, four horses, may be seen grazing on the field nearby. All four are average draft horses, but Marash-ar's gushing enthusiasm makes them seem much more wondrous ("I swear them's have pegasus blood, just a drop, mind yah, but they have it, just look at those beautiful eyes!"). The wily merchant (**bandit**) is willing to part with any of the "fine creatures" for 50 gp, or he can "get an actual war-beast" for 130 gp in a few days, which, in the end, is just like the others. Other items for sale include saddles for 12 gp, bags of feed for 5 cp, "miracle feed" for 2 sp, and a decorative harness for 35 gp.

Possessions: rusty scimitar, wide-brimmed leather hat, copper medallion, 110 gp, 5 sp, small Tharbrian round shield (throws it away in combat).

V. Lookout Tower

This tall, round stone tower reaches a height of 60 feet. Arrow slits enable the defenders to shoot at anyone in the central square, and a small ballista is suitable for larger opponents. The tower door is locked, barred, and reinforced by thick iron bars. It can be unlocked with a successful DC 18 Dexterity check with thieves' tools. Ten soldiers (**guards** with long bow at +3 to hit for 1d8 + 1 piercing damage and replace spear with handaxe) stand watch or play dice all day long. They occasionally practice shooting at birds or to scare innocent passers-by. A subterranean room contains provisions sufficient for eight days and a secret escape tunnel leading to hex 1415. The tunnel can be found with a successful DC 18 Wisdom (Perception) check. An alcove with a lantern and a tinderbox is 30 feet down the tunnel.

Possessions: leather armor, handaxe, longbow, dice, warning horn.

W. Grain Storage

This is the communal grain storage. Two floors with stacks and stacks of sacks, all of them containing grain. Traces of faded murals on the wall remain, but what they depicted — or what kind of purpose this place originally served — is not known.

Chapter 2:
The Lands About Tegel Village

Introduction

Beyond the fertile fields which surround Tegel village lies the wilderness. The lands to the north and south are reasonably peaceful, dotted by small farmsteads whose inhabitants sell their wares on the village markets. Apart from the occasional goblin raid or wolf pack, they have little to fear. On the other hand, the area between Tegel and the seacoast is extraordinarily dangerous due to monsters, brigands and worse.

The most prominent of these dangers is the **Temple of Tsathoggus**, in plain sight of the village. Sarthoggus, the foul high priest, commands an army of undead and fanatical worshippers from here and engages in bizarre experiments in his underground laboratory. Thus far, no one has succeeded at driving them out.

To the south, beyond Boiling Brook, rises a rocky hill, empty and desolate Savant Scarpe. The **Monastery** on the hill was inhabited by an order of benevolent monks. Since their disappearance, it has been rumored that invisible monsters lurk beyond its open gates, and so does a magical relic of some significance.

Derfingel Marsh to the southwest is rarely visited, and it is well known for a lumbering man-eating monstrosity that dwells in its shallows. The monster usually feeds on fish and giant frogs, but is known to prowl the land at night in search of human prey.

Recently, pirates have arrived at the seacoast and erected a small base, complete with a lookout tower. They occasionally make forays into the rest of the wilderness, planning overland escape routes and assessing the strengths and weaknesses of the village militia.

Finally, there is **Tegel Manor**, standing on a high plateau over the sea. With the exception of the family graveyard, it is described in the next chapter. In any case, it is shunned by sane people.

Random Encounters

All outdoors movement outside of the village is subject to an encounter roll every 20 minutes. If the party is resting, decrease the frequency to three rolls per night, unless they draw attention to themselves, in which case roll hourly. A roll of 1 on a six-sided die signifies an encounter has occurred. Consult the tables and apply the results as appropriate. The following exceptions should be noted:

- On the hill near the Temple east of Tegel village, all encounters are with 2d4 **cauldron-born zombies** (60%), 2d4 **acolytes** of Sarthoggus (30%) or both (10%).
- There are no random encounters on Savant Scarpe. In fact, the entire area is devoid of animal life.
- In and near Derfingel Marsh, all encounters are with 3d6 **killer frogs** (80%) or the Dearth Monster of Derfingel Marsh (**black dragon wyrmling**) (20%).
- On the seacoast north of Boiling Brook, all encounters are with 3d6 pirates (**scouts**).
- And finally, on the plateau of the manor, there are no encounters in the daytime; roll as inside manor during the night. Family members so encountered don't pursue fleeing characters.

Daytime

1d8	Encounter
1	Roughneck Rump the Rotund (**NPC #96**) and 12 **goblins** (with 12 hit points)
2	2d4 **cauldron-born zombies**[II]
3	2d4 **acolytes** of Sarthoggus (**X.**)
4	3d6 pirates (**CC.**)
5	3d10 **stirges** (TAKE COVER!)
6	3d10 **goblins**
7	Baladar the Ranger (**GG.**)
8	Lost villager (use **commoner**)

Nighttime

1d8	Encounter
1	Ruang the Ripper (**NPC #81**)
2	1d4 dire bats (use **giant bat**)
3	Dearth Monster of Derfingel Marsh (**AA.**)
4	**Carrion beetle**
5	3d10 **skeletons**
6	2d12 **ghouls**
7	Athrane the Druid (**FF.**)
8	Rump family member[I] and 2d10 **skeletons**

Roughneck Rump the Rotund: see Rump Family Tree (APPENDIX I.). Roughneck Rump is accompanied by 12 tough goblins (as **goblin** but with 12 hit points). A feared highwayman, he and his band have waylaid many a traveller, greeting same with a shrill "Stand and deliver!" If possible, the bandits ambush characters. They don't engage a clearly superior foe. If defeated, they retreat to the goblin caves (area **BB**) and bring in reinforcements.

Cauldron-born zombies: see APPENDIX II. These specially enchanted undead have one defect — they lose 1 hp for every hex distant from their creator.

Acolytes of Sarthoggus: these robed fanatics travel the countryside, forcefully gaining new converts to Tsathoggus the frog-god. They dye their skin green and perform certain facial alterations to please their harsh master. Once engaged, they fight to the death. **Acolytes** killed this way don't decrease their numbers at the temple. Once three groups are defeated, they don't venture outside anymore, but Sarthoggus prepares plans to do away with the party.

Pirates: pirates from the coast are usually careful in their encounters. They'd rather retreat to their coastal base and return with a larger force than be senselessly slaughtered. If they attack, they try to open with a volley of missiles. Use **scouts** for these.

Stirges: the swarm of stirges in the area is a nasty encounter for low level parties. It is clear that they pose a mortal threat, which you should emphasize for inexperienced groups. Hiding in the grasses, under leaves or any kind of shelter is protection enough. Once 30 stirges are defeated, they are considered wiped out. They have a nest in the deepest woodlands.

Goblins: as above, but without Roughneck Rump. Absent his leadership, the goblins are both disorganized and cowardly, fleeing as soon as they take a few losses. Goblins slain in random encounters do not decrease the numbers found at their cave.

Baladar the Ranger: this woodsman is described at area **GG**. Baladar is friendly to travellers, unless they are accompanied by Sir Runic Rump.

Lost Villager: unless encountered on farmland or close to the village, this **commoner** is considered to be lost. There is a 30% chance of major wounds and 25% of severe mental trauma — babbling about horrible monsters and foul undead.

Ruang the Ripper: see Rump Family Tree (APPENDIX I.). This skilled assassin follows parties silently and only attacks isolated members. If confronted by more than two people, he flees at once to return at a later date. Ruang lives in the Manor (room **B12.**) and despises Sir Runic (even though he won't kill him).

Dearth Monster of Derfingel Marsh: this **black dragon wyrmling** is described at area **AA**. It attacks from the air or ambush with its breath weapon, thereafter moving in to kill.

Ghouls: once they subdue their opponents, ghouls carry them back to the cemetery south of Tegel Manor.

Athrane the Druid: a sworn foe of Sarthoggus, Athrane lives near the manor at area **FF**. He is suspicious of groups, but helpful if they prove themselves to be champions of good. If traveling with the party, all animal encounters (including the dragon and the stirge swarm) are considered neutral or friendly. Use the **druid** stat block.

AA. Derfingel Marsh

The mucky marsh is swarming with 3d6 **killer frogs**[II] who attack people without hesitation. 3d6 are encountered at one time. Derfingel Marsh is also the home of the Dearth Monster of Derfingel Marsh, a **black dragon wyrmling** (but with Intelligence 8) that stalks the countryside at night. This creature lairs in a small cave (hex 2618). Thus far, it has amassed 1700 sp, 200 gp and 4000 cp in its hoard. A plugged glass bottle is also found in the pile. It contains rum and nothing more. The dragon doesn't talk, and neither does it cast spells, being an extraordinarily dumb specimen.

BB. Goblin Burrows

Six small caves on both sides overlook the road. They are inhabited by a goblin tribe under the leadership of **Roughneck Rump the Rotund**[I], feared highwayman. There is a 25% chance Roughneck is here (60% at night). Otherwise, only the 60 **goblins** are present. Roughneck has collected 200 gp, 610 sp, an ebony statuette of a blackbird (gemstone eyes, 250 gp), plus he still has a spare courtier's outfit. These goblins are hostile to those living under the manor and vice versa.

CC. Pirate Base

These seagoing scoundrels have established a base on the coast and erected a tower to observe and intercept seagoing traffic. There are 60 pirates (as **scout** but with weapons as follows: 60% are equipped with scimitars, 30% with light crossbows and shortswords, and 10% with heavy crossbows and shortswords. The latter group also wears chainmail armor [AC 16]) at the base, two **pirate lieutenants**[II] (Lucion and Key) and their leader, Gonthmain (as **bandit captain**). There is a 20% chance that their vessel is also nearby, with an additional 120 of the same cutthroat scum, four lieutenants and Lord Mornard ("the Symmerian"), their leader (use **gladiator**).

Since the pirates aren't here to get senselessly slaughtered, they usually observe or even talk first and attack later, preferably in large numbers. They may be reasoned with and if placated with valuable gifts, they may become neutral or friendly towards the group. They are always looking for more men to join their band. Naturally, they are untrustworthy and rotten to the core.

Each pirate has: leather vest/chainmail, scimitar/shortsword, light/ heavy crossbow, 2d6 sp, 1d6 gp. Each lieutenant has: chain shirt, scimitar, light crossbow, dagger, bottle of spirits, 12 gp. Gonthmain has: chainmail, falchion (as longsword), gold earrings (6 gp each), four gold rings (40 gp each), gaudy gold necklace (80 gp), gold bracers (70 gp), 110 gp. Lord Mornard has: *+2 breastplate*, large metal shield,

+1 longsword, *potion of greater healing*, ruby ring (700 gp), 135 gp.

The pirates have two small boats anchored on the northern beach. These are guarded by two men.

CC1. Barracks

Both of these barracks house 20 pirates, although there is space for as much as 30 per house. Furnishings are simple: two story bunk beds, a few wood tables and chairs. The pirates usually play games of chance (since they all cheat, there is no harm done to anyone), do woodcarving or anything else to alleviate their boredom.

CC2. Supplies

A good amount of foodstuffs, from smoked meats to kegs of cheap ale are kept in the locked, windowless house. Unlocking the door requires a DC 12 Dexterity check with thieves' tools. It can be broken down with a DC 18 Strength check.

CC3. Prison

Another locked house, this one is reserved for captives captured on raids, held for ransom or detained for insubordination. There is a 60% chance for 1d3 captives. Determine type by rolling 1d100: 01-30 **commoner**, 31-50 merchant/minor **noble**, 51-70 disciplined pirate (as **bandit**), 71-85 adventurer (choose as desired), 85-95 slave girl (**commoner**), 96-00 special (major noble, wizard, princess, wererat, etc.). The lock on this building requires a DC 15 Dexterity check with thieves' tools to pick, and the secured door requires a DC 20 Strength check to break open.

CC4. Kitchen

Smoke and the smell of cooking food fills the kitchen. Rusty Rold (as **bandit**) the cook and two attendants attend to the fireplace and the big cauldron of meat stew that's boiling over it, chop wood or do other assorted kitchen-related tasks. Rusty Rold is an expert with his kitchen knife, and happy to prove it. He has a white hat, greasy clothes, 4 kitchen knives, and a scimitar

CC5. Officers' Quarters

Lucion, Key and Gonthmain sleep here. Unless they are present, the door is locked. Opening it requires a DC 18 Dexterity check with thieves' tools. The officers' quarters contains a single table, three desks, animal skins hanging from the walls or lying on the floor. Additionally, there are four trunks. Three contain miscellaneous clothing, personal belongings and are unlocked. The fourth is the community chest, locked securely to prevent theft. It can be opened with a DC 22 Dexterity check with thieves' tools. It has 300 sp, 1100 gp, two opals (90 gp each), a bag of golden nuggets (70 gp total), a letter with orders from some faraway overlord (with instructions on which ships to attack and which to leave alone) and Gonthmain's *potion of heroism* which he doesn't dare to drink unless in dire straits.

CC6. Tower

This three-story overlook is well defended. Twenty pirates (as **scout**) man the tower; ten as lookouts and ten on the first floor. They sound their alarm if attacked, peppering attackers with missile weapons and vile insults. The door to the tower is always locked. The lock can be picked with a DC 14 Dexterity check with thieves' tools, or the door smashed open with a DC 20 Strength check.

CC7. First Floor

Salvaged floorboards from a derelict ship have been used in the construction of the tower floor, the helmsman's wheel turned into a wooden chandelier. The pungent smell of stale lamp oil clings to the wood. Ten pirates (as **scout**) pass the time in boredom. They are all armed with heavy crossbows (7 [1d10 + 2] piercing damage) instead of longbows.

CC8. Cellar

Like **CC2.**, this place is a storeroom. Preserved food, oil, firewood and spare oars are all found here.

CC9. Second Floor

Twenty simple cots and other odds and ends.

TEGEL MANOR
Each hex is 30 yards wide.

Ten lookouts (**scout**) stand watch with heavy crossbows (7 [1d10 + 2] piercing damage). They have a barrel of oil at their disposal (for setting missiles aflame) and a horn to signal their companions with.

DD. WARLORD'S ISLAND

A steep rock outcropping in the sea. Even from the shore, it is easy to see the man-made steps in the cliffside, leading up to the top. The waters about Warlord's Island are very treacherous. A character piloting a boat has to succeed at a DC 18 Dexterity check with Vehicle proficiency (water) or the vehicle is smashed to the rocks, taking 10 (3d6) bludgeoning damage.

The stairs lead to a small ledge with an ancient, weatherworn stone stele. The following words written in ancient Orichalan may be deciphered with a bit of work (DC 20 Intelligence check for somebody who speaks Orichalan, or *comprehend languages* or similar magic): *"It is I, Strabonus, Lord of the Middle Seas, who raised this stone. Defeating the Small Kings, I piled their heads on the earth and left no man of theirs standing. Such were my deeds after the skies became red and the Blood Star was over us no more."* Nothing else but harsh winds and dead stone are to be found here.

EE. BEACH

Driftwood and logs have washed on the shore. The figurehead of a ship depicting a mermaid is found among them. A thorough search and a successful DC 18 Wisdom (Perception) check uncover a soggy, ironbound chest containing 600 unstamped gold coins. The gold is false.

FF. ATHRANE THE DRUID

Detested by villagers for his arrogance, Athrane the **Druid** lives here alone, only sharing his simple home with a **wolf** companion, Fangs. Athrane is a foe of Sarthoggus, considering his influence harmful, but is too weak to root him out. Athrane knows quite a bit about the wilderness, including the location and general attributes of all areas previously described. He is also familiar with the secret coastal entrance to the manor dungeons, having spied on the goblins living there before.

Athrane is distrustful of strangers until they prove themselves. He will gladly join a respectful and good-aligned group, however, staying in their company as long as they are working towards clearing the land of the taint of evil! If traveling with the party, all animal encounters are considered neutral or friendly. He has no treasure, caring not for such trifles, but desires to own the *cauldron of Keridwen*, which he knows is found inside the manor somewhere.

Athrane has hide armor, a quarterstaff, a golden sickle, mistletoe, assorted herbs, a *potion of healing*, and a *potion of resistance* (fire).

GG. BALADAR THE RANGER

Champion of good and dumb as a rock, **Baladar** is also a declared enemy of the cowardly Runic Rump, who once left him in a tight spot with a specter in the manor. Unlike Athrane (whom he is on good terms with), he is friendly to travelers unless they are accompanied by Sir Runic. Baladar's cottage in the woods is a simple shack; a few animal skins, firewood and cooking utensils are found in it in addition to his rickety bed. Baladar is happy to help against any group of evildoers, except the beasts in the Monastery and the manor itself.

Baladar doesn't associate with half-orcs, whom he considers members of the giant-class and, thus, enemies.

Baladar has a chain shirt, a longsword, a longbow, 28 arrows, one vial of antitoxin, 30 ft. of rope, 55 sp, and 40 gp.

HH. Rump Family Graveyard

Being the burial site for the Rump family and their servants, this place is emptier than one would think. Limestone and marble headstones list names and a line or two about the deceased. The graves themselves are empty: simple depressions in the cold, damp earth — after all, their inhabitants are on the loose! Besides the graves, there are two small mausoleums. Both are constructed of pure white marble and overgrown with moss and creeping vines. Reliefs with bucolic scenes have been carved into the stone; a coat of arms commemorate the family and other noble lineages it is related to.

Inside the mausoleums, stairs lead down into shallow 30 foot by 60 foot crypts where the most important family members were buried under the watchful gaze of statues depicting solemn warriors and mirthful maidens. Each crypt is inhabited by 3d10 **skeletons**, 1d10 **zombies** and 1d10 **ghouls**. These undead are the soldiers of the lich, Ridwik[1] (**NPC #85**). Crypt #1 has been looted, but #2 has a small (fake) diamond ring, lying forgotten in an abandoned casket. It can be found with a DC 22 Wisdom (Perception) check. The ring is worth 1200 gp, or 120 if the forgery is recognized.

Beyond the graveyard, a hidden, steep trail meanders down the cliff face to hex 4931. The trail can be located with a DC 14 Wisdom (Survival) check or DC 18 Wisdom (Perception) check. This is the concealed entrance to the second level of the dungeons and an exit for the goblins in room **DL2M**.

Terrible Tombstones

1. Here lies Rithiena Rump/Stuck in her head/Pulled back a stump.
2. This is Rolf/His life was full/Till he tried/To milk a troll.
3. Rupture learned with great regrets/Syannggs don't make good pets.
4. Reckless Rump R.I.P./Tried to dance with a chimerae.
5. Racey hitched his wagon to a dragon/Now he does no more braggin'.
6. Roget's gullet went awry/While eating at the Balor's Eye.
7. Razzle met his term/Hacking at a purple worm.
8. Roderick – quite a cager/Till he failed to pay a wager.
9. Ramie wished he hadn't been born/Hanging on a gargoyle's horn.
10. Ravenbeard – insulted a Roc/Showed no fear/Broke an egg/Wound up here.
11. Rook wound up on a fork/Buried him with belching orc.
12. Here rests Riddles Rellwood/Once in a feisty mood/Stranded by a roper/Failed to give an answer.
13. Rinsel the Ravishing/All vital bits missing.
14. Raoul the Reformer/Rogue and Rascal/Renegade Romantic.
15. Last in the fight/First in the flight/Retreat Rumplast was killed by a wight.
16. Reciting Ralfrid played his lyre/Always in element/We burned him on the pyre/Appreciating his talent.
17. Never miss Rallick/His life has gone by/Ate so much garlic/Made a troll cry.
18. Felled by a giant wasp's sting/Reviled Randolph didn't see it coming.
19. Retort Rowanter/Fell down the well/His crazy banter/Turning into a yell.
20. As well travelled as the road/Rosienna the Romancer was turned into a toad.

CHAPTER 3: SANCTUM OF MADNESS

Sanctum of Madness has been designed for 4 to 6 Tier 3 characters, and takes place near the infamous Tegel Manor. Seasoned adventurers are called to assist the leaders of Tegel Village in their investigation of missing farmers and travelers along the south and west roads close to the hamlet. What starts as a simple inquiry into the disappearances slowly turns into a brewing plot of intrigue, deception, and violence, leaving the characters with no one to trust and enemies hiding within every shadow.

ADVENTURE BACKGROUND

Many years have passed since the ruined temple of Tsathoggus east of Tegel Village housed the vile cultists of the demonic frog-god. After holy warriors of Thor and Frigga destroyed the wicked temple, the sinful worship of the old god was thought to be finally driven from the region. Reduced to rubble, the temple was cleared of all living things and left barren for what was hoped to be all time. A new temple to Frigga was erected nearby to maintain vigilance over the area and to prevent the recurrence of evil worship. In time, a monastery was built, originally for the purpose of training new members of their order, but eventually it was abandoned when Frigga's favor among the people waned.

Finding the well-made monastery empty, monks of the order of Garm took residence within the structure, removing all signs of Frigga and replacing them with symbols of their guardian of the Hel-Gate. Although the monks have kept to themselves over the many years since taking over the monastery, their grounds are stalked by dire wolves, the living aspects of their god. At times, nearly a dozen of the large beasts may be seen roaming through the tall grass surrounding the holy compound.

Frigga's temple remains in its original location, serving Tegel Village since it was erected shortly after Tsathoggus' temple was razed. The hamlet remains faithful to their goddess and often seeks the priests' assistance in matters of importance or times of indecision. In recent months, however, the high priests of Frigga have not been seen, relinquishing their duties to the acolytes and initiates who remain connected to the village elders and daily worshipers.

Neither religious group is fond of the other, although both factions prefer to avoid one another instead of engaging in public verbal sparring or tumultuous conflict. In fact, both groups fear that the other is up to no good or is in some way secretly trying to undermine the other. Both orders are correct in their assumptions, but neither suspects the full truth of the other's plans.

ADVENTURE SYNOPSIS

Around the same time that the high priests of Frigga sequestered themselves within the bowels of the temple, villagers and travelers on the regional roads near Tegel Village began to disappear. Suspicious of the strange monks and their large pets, the villagers fear the missing are victims of the guardian to Hel, the goddess of death. Surprisingly, the lawful evil monks of Garm are not to blame for the missing villagers.

The Friggan priests, after accidentally discovering the old tunnels of the ruined temple beneath their own, reawakened the old god Tsathoggus from his perpetual slumber, and were forced into servitude. At first unwilling to abandon their faith, the clerics became enthralled by power as they restarted the old god's original plan of demonic possession and complete domination over the region. While the high priests sought the forgotten rituals of permanent transmogrification, they left their initiates in charge of the ruse to continue serving Frigga and to keep the majority of the villagers unaware of their new plans.

The new priests of Tsathoggus are trying to accomplish two goals: First, they are working toward a transformational process that converts frog eggs to frog warriors. Their idea of a fully morphological cycle includes a fifth stage, the humanization of frogs into walking aspects of Tsathoggus. Second, they hope to please the frog-god with a frog warrior army to get his attention and to bolster his desire to return to the Material Plane once again. Unfortunately, the only thing standing in the way of their plans is the missing *Book of Madness*[VI], an artifact that can provide the last incantation to complete the fifth morphological step.

Led by the former high priest of Frigga, Sarthoggus has fully shifted his absolute faith to the demonic frog-god, even impressing several minor demons and fiends of the lesser planes with his power and ruthlessness. To assist and accelerate his plan to find the *Book of Madness*[VI], the high priest has enlisted the help of several planar beings by promising nearly limitless rewards in wealth and power found in the Tegel region. Although the promises are outright lies, Sarthoggus believes he has fooled a small contingent of demons who signed on to his evil plan. The high priest is not worried about paying the final rewards for their servitude, hoping that Tsathoggus and his army of frog warriors will protect him from the deceit in the end. The fiends are well aware of his deceit, however, but are assisting the human priest for their own gain. They believe the *Book of Madness* may actually be one of their own sought-after *Books of Keeping*, and are willing to stick around long enough to find the book and take it for themselves if it's one of their own tomes.

While a small number of priests and their hired minions search for the lost artifact needed to complete the ritual, the high priests continue to test the individual steps of transmogrification on kidnapped villagers and unwary travelers. Although they have been successful in the first few stages of the transformation spells, all victims perish in the final stage without the critical and necessary artifact. Members of Tsathoggus' new order have scoured much of the old tunnels and are unknowingly close to finding the lost spellbook.

Fooling the town with their feigned faith, the priests have kept the region in the dark about their new plans. They quickly implicate the monks in the disappearances, even offering support and a reward to characters if they eliminate the monks. If consulted, the village elders support the temple priests' suggestion of driving the monks from the area, believing they are the reason for the missing townsfolk.

STARTING THE ADVENTURE

Elders of Tegel Village are on the lookout for capable adventurers traveling through the area, and offer a powerful artifact as a reward for solving the mystery of the disappearing townsfolk. Additionally, the town leaders may increase the reward by adding a special reserve of gold bars if they are close to convincing an enterprising band of travelers to help. The area is known for its abundant riches; Tegel Manor is close by, and the legends of its endless halls filled with unclaimed treasures are well known.

Ternelmor, the mayor of Tegel Village, embraces any offers of help, especially from outsiders without an interest in the region's political or religious disagreements so prominently argued by residents and merchants. In fact, the mayor and any member of the town council, when spotting newcomers in the area, approach veteran adventurers with a plea for help. Although the town council cannot pay the adventurers in coin, they are willing to give the group a powerful artifact if they can solve the disappearances. The high priestess Arnthora has an ancient item of great power stored within Thor's temple in a secret vault location that only she and one other priestess know about. A paladin used this item in the battle many years ago to drive a terrible evil from the land. The relic has been stored away until this day. Although Arnthora is reluctant to give away the item, it is one

of the few things of great value the village has left to offer as a reward to solve the mystery of the recent disappearances.

The priestess will not divulge the true details of the item until the group gets to the bottom of the lost inhabitants and travelers. If questioned, she says that the item has incredible powers that benefit its wearer. Although she prefers that at least one adventurer from the group be a devout follower of Thor or Frigga, she relinquishes the item to a group that delivers on its promise to help. See **Appendix VI** for more details about the powerful artifact, the *golden plate armor of Thor*[VI].

After consulting the unknowingly false priests of Frigga, the town leaders suggest that the characters start with an investigation of the monastery. Of course, the evil monks will not allow visitors; entry into the monastery will have to be a clandestine endeavor. However, the monks are known to capture trespassers and feed them to their dire wolves or worse.

If the characters wish to meet with the Frigga priests first, the elders arrange a meeting in the village, inviting several initiates to a small banquet. There, the characters have a chance to ask questions and begin their investigation. The low-level acolytes that attend this meeting are unaware of the true events happening below their temple, and answer questions to the best of their ability.

Hooks

Most characters likely are visiting the area in and around Tegel Village while preparing to take a run at Tegel Manor. This scenario offers a shorter but no less deadly adventure, suitable before or after their attempts at the massive manor-fortress on the sea. Successfully discovering the growing re-emergence of evil under the temple and learning the secret of the disappearing villagers gains the trust of Tegel villagers, potentially unlocking a few secrets helpful in navigating the large manor.

Tsathoggus' Return

The ancient frog-demon cares little for the mortal pawns in his endless game for possession and domination of the Material Plane. Awakened from his forced sleep, he eagerly awaits the priests' completion of the transmogrification ritual, and accepts nothing other than complete success. After using the high priest and his minions to complete the final spells, he emerges from his prison to unleash his wrath upon the area, utterly devastating all living things, including his own devoted followers.

Town leaders, including the mayor and several prominent residents, have already begun secretly worshipping the frog-demon and are looking for a group to remove the Garm monks from the area. Arnthora, the priestess of Thor, has noticed that several village residents have changed their behavior recently. Initially thinking that their altered demeanor was a byproduct of their apparent worry for the missing villagers, she now suspects that something else, something more sinister, is afoot. She spends much of her free time watching several residents, looking for clandestine meetings and sideways glances. None of the secret Tsathoggus converts realize they are being watched so carefully.

Frog-God Followers

The following is a list of Tegel villagers who secretly worship the frog-god:

Ternelmor — Mayor
Churlish — Leader of Militia
Halaf Fec — Merchant
Cretin Nedcock — Owner of Bark & Byte, dinner establishment

The new followers of Tsathoggus have no intention of rewarding the characters for eliminating the frog-god's high priests or destroying the precious artifact. They wish only to continue their ruse, shifting blame and fault to the evil monks of Garm. Hoping to get the characters to eliminate some or all of monks of the order, or at least distracting them from the real threat until the final spell can be cast, is the secret council members' primary purpose when they recruit the characters. If any of the characters or Arnthora begin to unravel the council's secret plans, they take steps to neutralize any who oppose them.

THE BOOK OF MADNESS

Buried by the ruination of the former demon-god temple, the black *Book of Madness*[VI] holds the secrets to the final spells needed by Tsathoggus and his mortal minions. Within five days of the characters' arrival in the area, the searching priests discover the buried tome. After another two days, High Priest Sarthoggus has enough information to attempt the final ritual, succeeding where all other efforts failed. For information about the events that unfold after the ritual's success, see more details under **Ending the Adventure**.

BANQUET AT TEGEL VILLAGE

After the group agrees to help, Ternelmor and Arnthora arrange for the Frigga priests to meet with the adventuring group in town at an impromptu banquet the following day. Although their invitation is extended to the Frigga high priest and his chosen advisors, only three initiates arrive for the meeting. The priestess of Thor finds this extremely odd, but the other town leaders seem to be less concerned with the change in attendance.

The three initiates claim that the priests of their order are extremely busy researching a new spell and the lost history of their order, and have sequestered themselves deep within the temple until their completion. This explanation satisfies the council members, but further confuses Arnthora. She has not heard of any unknown history of Frigga nor is she aware of any new spells needed by the order. If the characters try to magically determine if the initiates are telling the truth or pass a DC 18 Wisdom (Insight) check, they find that the initiates are truthful. The acolytes have been given the direction by the sequestered high priests; the initiates follow their leaders' orders completely and without question.

The initiates and the town leaders, except for Arnthora, quickly direct the group to the temple of Garm, indicating that the evil monks and their vile beasts are likely the cause of the disappearances. Arnthora remains silent during the meal, carefully watching the wordless exchanges between several of the council members.

The Frigga acolytes propose a cautionary and secret investigation within the monastery. They tell the characters that it would be best if they infiltrate the facility at night and sneak through the building in search of clues about the recent disappearances. They urge the characters to take care in their mission; the monks are especially ruthless with respect to trespassers.

Before the group leaves for the monastery, Arnthora chooses the most trustworthy character for a hurried and discreet conversation. She believes that many of the town leaders are acting strangely and cannot be fully trusted. Additionally, she finds it bizarre that the high priest of Frigga did not join them for the dinner — he is not known to turn down excellent food and drink, or a chance to discuss the merits of Frigga and the lady's rewards.

THE MONASTERY OF GARM

Although evil, the monks aren't responsible for any of the current issues in the area. They treat the problems in Tegel Village with indifference, preferring to avoid any direct contact with the villagers and priests of Frigga. The missing villagers are not their dilemma, and they really don't care if people are disappearing. They are interested in what the Frigga priests are doing under their temple, having felt a change in power from their area in recent weeks. They suspect that the once-good priests are involved in the disappearances but have no intention of doing anything about it.

Master Kandasto[II], the head of their order, interrogates the characters if the monks catch them trying to infiltrate their monastery. Kandasto seeks to uncover who enlisted their services, and if he discovers that the priests of Frigga are implicating the order of Garm in the disappearances, he likely offers a counterproposal to the group: investigate the temple of Frigga for a special reward. Although they dislike the priests of Frigga, they have learned to coexist with their small temple for a number of years. However, the recent shifts in cosmic power, coinciding with strange changes in the Friggan priests' behaviors, have the head monk wondering if something foul is soon to come. Paying the characters to eliminate the priests under the temple of Frigga is a necessary step for the order of Garm to preserve its place in the religious pecking order in the region, especially if the priests changed deities or uncovered a terrible evil.

The monks treat their dire wolves as important members of the order of Garm; if the characters killed one or more of their beasts, Master Kandasto[II] is less generous with a reward. Instead of offering the group a powerful magical weapon, they spare their lives in exchange for their investigation of the temple and the eradication of anything out of the ordinary. A failure to accept the counterproposal may create an extended stay for the group within the dire wolf cells below the initiate tower (**Area M-3**) while they think over the request.

Either way, the intruders must pass the Tests of Garm before leaving the monastery. Master Kandasto lets the shade of Garm far below the central temple determine the trespassers' future in the affairs of any religious conflicts within the Tegel region, including their part in this latest treachery. If the characters survive the test, they are allowed to leave to continue their investigation at the Temple of Frigga. If the group decides to flee the area without completing their new task, Garm repeatedly sends various forms of dire wolves, real and dead, to haunt them to the end of their days.

While captured, the characters are tattooed with a special Garm rune. The rune is temporary and can be removed by the chief monk at any time. Master Kandasto[II] removes the rune from characters if they survive the Tests of Garm. However, at any time during their captured stay at the monastery that the characters attack the monks or dire wolves, or try to escape, Master Kandasto or one of his trusted advisors activates the rune. The rune explodes, dealing 105 (10d10+50) necrotic damage to the affected character.

THE MONKS OF GARM

There are 40 initiate[II] level monks in the monastery, watched over by 10 disciples[II] as trainers. Master Kandasto[II] runs the monastery, keeping the monks busy with day-to-day tasks, planning long-term schedules, and working with Garm's temples throughout the region for permanent placement opportunities. Master Lofutu (mendicant[II]) is Kandasto's second in charge and implements many of the plans and schedules created by the monastery leader.

Each trainer wears a *monk's colored sash*[VI] imbued with a specific magical power. The sash can be found in three colors: red, yellow, or blue. When removed from the waist, the sash can be used like a whip or a lasso to ensnare a foe's limbs or neck as needed.

APPROACHING THE MONASTERY

The road south out of Tegel Village splits after the Boiling Brook bridge, creating a secondary path that leads in a southeasterly direction away from the main road. The dirt trail climbs a steep hilltop and leads directly to the monastery. The plateau has a few small tree groups on the monastery's west and east sides, but is mainly clear of large vegetation besides the 3- to 4-foot-tall grass covering the entire area. The monks keep the grass tall on purpose; their dire wolves are able to hide and stalk trespassers much easier under the cover of the thick meadow. There is a 50% chance that 1 or 2 **dire wolves** will be encountered for every 15 minutes spent on the grassy plateau. Any noise in the area, including combat and spellcasting, brings additional dire wolves to its source. Additionally, the sounds of combat likely reach the ears of one or more Garm monks who patrol the outer walls of the monastery (daytime only).

AREA M-1: MONASTERY ENTRANCE

At the north end and front of the monastery, a set of oak doors banded with iron strips and bolts remains closed at all times. At night, these doors are locked and barred, but are unlocked during the day. A pair of low-level monks wait just inside the doors during daylight hours, prepared to receive guests or engage with the uninvited. A wide brass bell can be seen atop the wall over the doors; a twisted rope hanging from the device within the entry allows the monks to summon additional members of their order with a single pull.

With the doors secured after nightfall and several dire wolves patrolling the exterior, the monks leave the front entrance unguarded. The exterior wall is more than 20 feet tall and requires a DC 20 Strength (Athletics) check to climb without a rope (change to DC 15 if a rope is used). If quiet, the characters will likely be unseen during this approach.

AREA M-2: MONASTERY EXERCISE YARD

During the day, dozens of monks practice their skills within the wide yard. At least one **disciple**II instructs the **initiates**II as they train. Training temporarily pauses if dignitaries or high priests of Garm visit the monastery; trainees line up along the inner walls of the yard until officials enter the temple area (**area M-6**). At night, this area is empty.

AREA M-3: INITIATE BUNKHOUSE

This circular, two-story building is reserved for the newest initiates of the order. At least a dozen **initiates**II have simple bunks on the upper two floors of the building. In times where more initiates are needed or an increased interest in the order occurs, six additional bunks can be added. Both floors are empty during the day as the initiates will be training, working, or praying. They are rarely in this tower until night.

Just inside the entrance, several racks of quarterstaffs and slings line the walls along the stairs to the upper and lower levels.

AREA M-3A: DIRE WOLF CELLS

An underground floor below the initiate quarters is accessed by a wide, sloping walkway found inside the entrance to the tower. Below, ten cells for the monks' cherished dire wolves encircle the bottom floor. Half the beasts are always found outdoors; the monks rotate the outdoor patrols, changing the creature's shifts to keep them fresh and interested in their duties. Each dire wolf is superbly trained, responding to verbal commands and whistles, and is magically bound to the grassy plateau. Any wolf that tries to leave the monastery hill feels agonizing pain until it returns to its patrol area.

Five **dire wolves** are almost always here, along with at least 1 **disciple**II trainer. At night, the trainer sleeps upon a straw mat in the middle of the room. Dire wolves, detecting the unfamiliar scent of adventurers, howl and bark viciously, loud enough to wake the sleeping trainer and the initiates above.

A key on the trainer's belt opens individual cells. However, a series of levers on the central column in the area can open groups of cells; moving individual cell levers into position and throwing the master lever opens all the selected cells at once. The trainer may attempt to free all available dire wolves if overwhelmed by the player characters.

AREA M-4: VISITING GUEST QUARTERS

Important guests of the monastery are given special quarters during their stay. Several private rooms with plush beds, fresh clothes, and meals served to an open, common area are found in the upper portion of this structure. Although guests are rare, the occasional Garm high priest or wealthy patron may stop here while traveling through the region. The monastery's kitchen and dining hall are found at ground level.

If the characters are caught but subsequently agree to Master Kandasto's counterproposal, they are given several rooms here until they are ready to start their investigation of the temple of Frigga. They are allowed to stay for no more than two nights before they are escorted out of the monastery.

AREA M-5: GENERAL QUARTERS

Ten to twenty monks use the large sleeping and study quarters within these structures as their permanent quarters during their lengthy stays at the monastery. Most monks spend their entire life here, never leaving but instead working and training other monks for their service to Garm. A small number of monks leave the monastery each year to further their service to the guardian of the Hel-Gate elsewhere in the realms. Many stay, never receiving the call to leave the monastery, satisfied with their service to their god by protecting the monastery and training initiates for a lifetime.

Much like the initiate bunkhouse (**area M-3**), the area is quiet and empty during the day. Initiates II and disciples II are busy training, working, praying, and teaching elsewhere in the facility until nightfall.

AREA M-6: TEMPLE OF GARM

Dominating the monastery in sheer size and impressive decoration, the central structure beyond the exercise yard is dedicated to teaching the ways of Garm to all who desire to learn. Monks spend several hours of the day teaching new recruits or praying to Garm in the tall temple. A massive marble sculpture of the wolf-god fills the southernmost portion of the temple, standing upon five raised steps and staring down on the rest of the space with intent and all-seeing eyes.

A pit, 15 feet wide and 10 feet deep, opens before the sculpture. The pit is the entrance to the Tests of Garm (see **area G-1**). At any time, a monk or visitor to the monastery may undertake the test to prove worthiness to the guardian of the Hel-Gate. Master Kandasto also uses this pit to punish non-believers or threats to the monastery, letting Garm's aspect mete out the appropriate justice to the test's victims or survivors. Most who enter are unworthy and never return.

Several dozen cushions in five ordered lines are seen on the floor. Incense from hundreds of small lamps burns day and night, faithfully replenished by devout monks on a rigorous and unfailing schedule. Although it isn't unusual for the occasional monk to be found here late at night in deep prayer, the area is generally empty during the evening hours until sunrise.

A relic of great power, *bracers of the master pugilist*VI, has been stored in a secret compartment at the top of the sculpture in the skull of the great wolf. A DC 25 Intelligence (Investigation) check discovers the well-hidden compartment and the magical wrappings within. If the compartment is opened without using the proper sequence of hidden button presses, a loud chime rings within the temple, alerting all in the monastery to potential thievery. When Master Kandasto opens the compartment, no chimes rings. The sequence can be discovered with a successful DC 30 Intelligence (Investigation) check or by acquiring the knowledge from one who knows. Simply noting the existence of the alarm can be done with a successful DC 20 Intelligence (Investigation) check once the compartment has been located.

Monastery of Garm

AREA M-7: CHIEF MONK OF GARM, MASTER KANDASTO

Tucked into the southeast corner of the monastery, the master of the order of Garm has two small rooms dedicated to running the monastery. The front room is used for meetings and monastery business with important guests. **Master Kandasto**[II] prefers to hold religious discussions within the temple, but in matters of business, finance, or dispersing punishment to the occasional initiate, he uses this small area. A simple wooden table, six chairs, and several tapestries reveling in the wondrous power of Garm fill the room.

Beyond the meeting room, Master Kandasto keeps a small, frugal bedchamber. A writing desk, chair, straw bed, and wardrobe barely fit into the tiny space. Two books are stacked neatly upon the master's desk. A book of initiates with their monastery start and end dates sits atop the pile. A quick read of the book indicates that the monastery currently has 11 initiates[II], 23 disciples[II], and 10 dire wolves. The second book on the pile is Master Kandasto's private journal, and references the strange shifts in religious energy in the area. Multiple passages clearly mention the disappearances, but all lack opinion and any deeper interest in the problem. He casually notes in one of the latest entries that he wonders if the Temple of Frigga is close to the source of the missing villagers.

During the day, Master Kandasto moves about the monastery according to his own rigorous schedule. He is most often found in the temple, assisting with teaching, or in the exercise yard demonstrating his exceptional martial arts skills. The head of the order is often the last to leave the temple, praying into the late night before retiring to his chambers.

Observant characters may see the signs of floor scratches near the wardrobe's feet with a successful DC 15 Wisdom (Perception) check. If the wardrobe is pulled into the center of the room, the characters find a hidden floor compartment. Within, Master Kandasto keeps a chest of gold and silver (775 gp, 1389 sp) used primarily to pay for food and services his monks are unable to provide. Much of the treasure has been donated to the order throughout the years, replenished only when patrons visit the monastery or visitors require Master Kandasto's or Garm's advice.

TESTS OF GARM

If the characters are to take the Tests of Garm as punishment for their intrusion or injury to the monk's honored pets, then they are brought to the temple (**area M-6**) and lined along the edge of the pit. All who are to take the test are treated justly and fairly, leaving the judging to the tests below the monastery. They are told of four tests, each of which evaluates, in a different way, their worthiness to the mortal world. Very few survive the tests; those that do are changed forever. (After each test described below is a table for assigning points based on the characters' success or failure.)

Characters are allowed to take any and all of their possessions with them in the test. Master Kandasto likely says that some of their physical possessions will be of little help to what they will soon face. No answers are given to character's questions, but they are urged to begin the tests immediately. All available monks circle the characters and the pit, ready to use their quarterstaffs to push the adventurers in if they hesitate.

AREA G-1: TEST OF FEAR

The characters must blindly jump into the pit; they are not allowed to use ropes or to climb down along the edge of the pit. Those who delay are forcibly shoved into the hole. If the characters resist and fight back, Master Kandasto activates the necrotic Garm rune tattoos (as mentioned in the **Monastery of Garm** section). Under their master's commands, the monks continue to push the characters into the pit, even ones who are unconscious or dying.

Once the characters are falling within the pit, they may attempt to use magic or skills to slow down their fall or to grab onto the side of the pit. The pit walls are perfectly smooth and are extremely difficult to grab while falling. A DC 20 Strength (Athletics) check may be attempted; a successful check merely slows down the drop unless the check is passed three consecutive times, indicating the character has stopped falling and is clinging to a small ledge or crack.

A character imagines falling at least 500 feet before reaching the bottom, but actually fall only 100 feet, five consecutive times. A character who doesn't pass a DC 20 Intelligence (Investigation) check at least once out of five tries (at each reset point) take 37 (10d6) bludgeoning damage when landing at the bottom. A character that passes the check once takes half damage from the fall. More than two passes negates all damage, unveiling the illusion; the character realize that the fall isn't truly what it seems, and begins to slow down, settling upon the floor. Since all the characters are falling together (unless other characters have managed to hang onto the side or slow their descent somehow), they aren't able to tell others in their group of the illusion until the test is over.

The remains of dozens of humanoid forms in various stages of decomposition are found sprawled across the floor, their limbs and spines broken and skulls pulverized. Many forms are still clothed in the robes of the monks of Garm, obviously failing their first test. Other clothing and gear can be discovered if the remains are thoroughly searched. Two usable suits of leather armor, a backpack, three daggers, a longsword, a mace, two torches, and a tinderbox are all easily found amid the corpses.

On the east wall of the pit, a single rounded archway leads away into complete darkness. An ancient, indecipherable language covers the stones around the arch. If a DC 20 Intelligence (Investigation) check is passed, the writing can be interpreted. It reads, "Enter your future without examining your past." A successful DC 15 Intelligence (Investigation) check reveals that the writing repeats itself on every stone.

Damage Taken	Points
0 hit points	2 points
Half damage	1 point
Full damage	0 points

AREA G-2: TEST OF SPEED

A 20-foot-wide straight and level passage leads east for several hundred feet. The entire length of the tunnel is completely dark, and no exits can be found along the smooth walls throughout its stretch. Nothing remarkable happens to the characters until they pass the first 100 feet. At this first invisible mark, the sound of slipping and sloshing steps is heard behind the group, seemingly far away yet close enough to feel as if the moving being will soon overcome the characters.

Garm has created a vile creature for this test, placing it at the start of the tunnel once the characters enter it. A cross between an ooze and a medusa, this shapeless, bubbling mass initially moves as quickly as the characters, but increases its speed such that it overcomes the group if they delay or slow down. As long as the group keeps moving as fast as possible, they are likely to reach the end of the hallway and pass the test.

The characters should heed the words from the previous room; they should run forward, ignoring what's behind them until they reach the exit of the tunnel. Once the surviving members of the group reach the last 10 feet, the **medooza**[II] retreats. Any characters returning to the tunnel to retrieve fallen or injured party members start the pursuit over again.

Several stone forms are in the tunnel, as previous monks and challengers failed to avoid the medooza[II]. A character running through the tunnel at full speed without a light source or darkvision has a 1-in-10 chance of running into a stone form every 100 feet. Any collision deals 5 (1d10) bludgeoning damage to the character and costs the character 10 feet of movement.

Event	Points
Character never looks back	2 points
Looks back but not turned to stone	1 point
Engages the creature or is turned to stone	0 points

AREA G-3: TEST OF COMBAT

Another archway, this time in the north wall, leads to a large room beyond. Faint etchings of weapon and armor silhouettes are found on the stones around the doorway and can be depressed to light up the outside line of the crude image. An image for every common weapon and armor type is found along the hundred stones set into the archway, but only five images may be depressed at one time. If more than five are pressed, the images reset to their unlit state. The items depressed are the only weapons and armor that may pass through the archway into the next room. Any item carried by the characters that isn't part of the list of depressed items are magically transported to the opposite side of the chamber, more than 100 feet away, just beyond the opening of yet another archway.

Besides the standard weapons and armors, other items are also found on the stones: wands, staffs, shields, boots, gauntlets, and other item types that may have a normal and magical category are represented. Simple items such as backpacks, belt pouches, common clothing, and non-protective gear are not shown and are permitted within the chamber.

Any item type not selected is magically removed upon entry into the chamber. Once a character enters the chamber, she or he cannot exit through the same archway. However, the character can speak to the characters on the other side of the archway and relay details about the chamber without issue. A character who leaves the 10-foot space near the door and moves into the room immediately initiates the start of the encounter. Characters can try to move to their transported gear but find their way blocked much like the entry into this room; a magical forcefield prevents any exit from the room until the test in this area is completed.

Any item selected that is now within the chamber (carried within by a character) cannot be unselected from the depressed images on the archway. However, items not carried into the chamber can be unselected by characters who have not yet entered the chamber, who are free to select different items by pressing any of the remaining silhouettes.

Once the encounter begins, with any number of characters leaving the location adjacent to the archway and moving farther into the chamber, a **gargantuan dire wolf of Garm**[II] materializes in the center of the room. On the first combat round, the huge creature spends its turn constituting, completing the transformation from mist to flesh and blood. The creature is more than 40 feet long, and its mouth is capable of swallowing a person whole with a single bite.

When the dire wolf reaches 0 or fewer hit points, it returns to its misty form and disappears into small holes found within the floor in the center of the chamber. Once the wolf is defeated, the magical one-way barriers on each archway are reversed, allowing characters to exit. Note that once a character exits the chamber, re-entry starts the combat sequence with the gargantuan wolf again, transporting the unselected items to the opposite archway, and preventing any exit from the room until the creature dies.

Event	Points
Character survives the encounter	1 point
Character is slain	0 points

AREA G-4: TEST OF HONOR

The archway from the previous chamber opens into a 50-foot-long hall, with four pairs of pillars through the center, found every 10 feet. Each pillar is made of a highly-polished glass that returns a reflection like a full-length mirror. At first, there appears to be no exit from the room. However, a successful DC 20 Wisdom (Perception) check of the north end of the hall displays a fine silver bead outlining the shape of an archway. No magic or skill opens this sealed portal; the test in this room must be passed by at least one character for the archway to open.

TEST SCENARIOS

Scenario 1: The character sits within a room where an official is judging a stranger accused of murdering a local merchant. The character knows that he or she actually committed the murder, but can only watch as the official finds the stranger guilty, punishable by death. As the stranger is led away, he looks at the character in desperation. If the character says nothing to the stranger or officials before the stranger leaves the room, he or she fails the test and it ends. If the character admit to the crime, the scene ends and the character is freed from the pillar-mirror.

Scenario 2: The character is being praised for finding and dispatching a local bandit group, knowing full well that a different adventurer died completing the task. As a local official heaps praise and monetary rewards on the character, the adventurer's friends look at the character with disgust. If the character stops the official and admits the dead adventurer was the true hero, he or she passes the test. Otherwise, the character fails and the test ends.

Scenario 3: A pair of brazen guards is harassing a woman in a dimly lit tavern. They are making remarks about the girl's looks and her reputation, both of which are untrue. Getting urged on by other patrons, the guards continue their barrage of filthy remarks, pushing the girl to tears. The character knows the statements are false. She looks at the character to see what they will do. A character who speaks on her behalf, telling the guards to back off or to quit their insults, passes the test and exits the scenario. A character who doesn't intercede allowing the girl to break down in tears fails the test.

Scenario 4: The character watches as a rogue removes the purse from an oblivious merchant on a busy street. A customer points to the thief, indicating that he's just robbed the merchant. Just before he's surrounded by guards, the thief promises to split the bag of large rubies with the character if he or she implicates someone else on the street. A character who agrees and redirects the guards to some other person fails the test. A character who validates the accusation by saying that the thief indeed stole from the merchant passes the test and ends the scenario.

Scenario 5: The character watches as a building rages with fire. Screams for help are heard from within but the character is alone on the street. He or she can see through one of the windows to where a man, woman, and child are trapped in a corner of a room, unable to exit their burning chamber. The child sees the character and reaches her hand out, screaming for assistance. A character who jumps through the window to help passes the test. A character who leaves or watches the people die fails the test.

Scenario 6: Guards run up and ask the character to assist in rescuing people from a sinking ferry in the harbor. The character is on the way to an important meeting with a patron with a lucrative adventure. Seeing that the guards number too few to rescue all the ferry customers, the character must decide whether to help or to continue to the meeting. A character who offers to assists passes the test. One who ignores the request and continues fails

A character that gazes into one of the pillar-mirrors is immediately captivated by his or her own reflection, trapped until the subsequent test is completed. No spell or device frees the character from this unblinking stare and transfixed gaze. Each character locks the pair of pillars so that only four tests may be attempted concurrently. A character that looks into the opposite pillar while a character is transfixed is able to watch the events of the test as they unfold. The trapped character must complete the entire test or it is considered failed.

One of the scenarios presented in the sidebar below is presented to each character who takes the test. You can choose a test randomly or by choice, and you may alter its elements as desired. The scenario should be explained to the character as if the character was present in the event. The player should be made to believe that the character has been transported into the pillar and is present for the "real" scenario as it occurs. Other characters know that the character has not left the room, but are unable to communicate with the trapped character. At the end of each short test, the character is freed from the transfixed state.

If more scenarios are needed, you are urged to create them.

You should run each scenario for each transfixed character without providing the results until each character chooses the end to his or her test. If any other characters begin a test before the end of any other character's test, you should run a scenario for them as well, holding the results until every character has gone. If any character passes, the hidden portal opens, revealing the exit. No character may retake a test. If all the characters fail, the exit portal opens.

Event	Points
Character passes a scenario	1 point
Character fails a scenario	0 points

G5: Judging Room

After the characters leave the pillar-mirror room, they enter a massive chamber that spans hundreds of feet in every direction. When they look back toward the portal they just used, it is gone, replaced with more of the new chamber stretching away into darkness. A scroll floats in the air in the center of room, illuminated by a single beam of light emanating from the floor below it. If searched, the entire chamber is found to have no exit.

Spells and devices that detect magic directed at the scroll register strongly. Any character that opens and reads the scroll invokes the final scoring from the tests. As the scroll is touched, the glowing face of Garm lights up the entire chamber with intensely bright light, seemingly emanating from everywhere all at once. As the image's wolfish mouth moves, a voice speaks in each of the character's heads. Garm indicates the results of the tests to each character individually yet simultaneously. He uses one of two simple words: "Passed" or "failed." The voice should be overwhelming and fill the character with dread and awe.

Use the table below to determine the results of the character's tests by total encounter scores.

Points	Result	Details (permanent)
5+	Boon	Add 1 point to an attribute of the player's choice and 1 point to a random attribute
4	Boon	Add 1 point to a random attribute
3	Change	Alignment changes to Lawful Evil
2	Penalty	Subtract 1 point from a random attribute
1 or less	Penalty	Subtract 1 point from a primary attribute, 1 point from a random attribute

Once the instant boons and penalties are applied, the scroll disappears and the room turns instantly dark. At the south end of the room, an open lit portal appears. When characters exit the area through the open portal, they are transported back to the temple at the monastery of Garm, instantly appearing before the statue of the great wolf on their knees in supplication.

Master Kandasto considers any character that survives the tests to have "passed," regardless of how they were judged by his god. If Garm allows the character to return to the monastery, he must see something of value within the character. All returning characters are escorted to the guest quarters (**area M4**) and healed by the temple priests. They are reminded of the next part of the agreement, the infiltration of the Temple of Frigga.

Temple Ruins

The remains of Tsathoggus' temple are found adjacent to the new holy place of Frigga. Although the original structure was burned to the ground leaving only rubble and remnants of the building, access to the lower tunnels of the evil complex remain. The holy fire, lightning, and powerful spells of the army of Thor and Frigga devastated the area, but not every inch of the collapse was thoroughly searched. Two sets of stairs, initially impassable, are now open enough to allow a single Medium creature to pass into the subterranean depths.

As the characters approach, they may discover a small wisp of smoke drifting up from behind the ruins. A young boy (**sneakthief**[1]), no more than 12 years old, has made his temporary home within the remnants of the temple. He and his faithful dog (**mastiff**), after traveling here from a western realm, have been venturing into the lower levels in search of valuable trinkets to sell at the market. The boy, Lenrall, has discovered only several mundane items to this point. Although his searching has kept him fed, he's still looking for a big score.

His dog, Chomper, is almost as big as he is and is protective of his master. Unless the characters are superbly quiet and stealthy, the dog alerts Lenrall to approaching strangers. Chomper does not attack the characters unless they make a sudden move toward Lenrall or unless the boy commands him to engage. If the boy flees, so does the dog.

Lenrall has recently discovered a small cache of gold and silver temple utensils and plans to return for them soon. However, his delving has unnerved him; he has heard noises deep within the levels and knows that something evil and violent has awakened there. With his courage failing, he plans one more descent to the cache to grab all he can, before leaving the region forever.

Lenrall does not share his knowledge of the stash with adventurers, but can direct the group to one or both of the two tunnel openings deep within the ground for a small fee. For 10 gp, he tells them how to get to one of the openings, or both for double the price. For 100 gp, he takes them there himself.

If the adventurers plan to explore the ruins, Lenrall and his dog wait aboveground until 24 hours pass or they return sooner. After that, Lenrall makes his final descent to grab all he can before leaving the ruins for good. If he has escorted the group to one or both of the tunnel openings, he leaves after doing his part. He immediately heads to the stash, then exit the ruins.

Both tunnel openings require several hours of digging to gain access to the area beyond.

Area R-1: Ruins Exterior

Even decades after the ruination of the vile temple that once occupied the hill east of Tegel Village, the signs of a furious battle between Law and Chaos are still evident. Foundational stones scattered from lightning strikes are found broken in various places around the site. Holy fire from the gods has scorched patches of earth where no grass has grown since. The temple's exterior walls can be imagined from the what's left of the structure's cornerstones and broken pillars.

Old Temple
Temple Ruins
R9
R8
R7
N
R3a
R10
S
R11
R2
R1
1 Square - 10 Feet
R3b
R4
R6
R5
R12
R13
R15
R14
a
b
c
d
e
f
R16

Two sets of stairs still access the lower level of the former temple. However, only one set of stairs leads to an unobstructed tunnel below (see **area R-12**). Lenrall has explored several rooms and tunnels in both areas, but with the unnatural sounds he's heard below, his trips have been quick and his searches incomplete.

AREA R-2: GATHERING ROOM

The main stair descends into a large chamber once used for gatherings of priests, acolytes, and temple visitors. Dark, pungent water fills the area, pooling here from somewhere beyond the chamber. Remnants of furniture have been piled into the northeast and southeast corners of the chamber. Common rats scuttle about the floating debris, hiding in the piles when the water is disturbed. Two western exits lead into darkness until they reach two tunnel collapses (**areas R-3a** and **R-3b**).

Dark magic from the spells of the evil priests of the new temple permeates the water, reaching even this area of the ruins from their subterranean origin far beyond the westernmost tunnels. Prolonged contact with the murky water is dangerous, its effects often causing madness and mental collapse. A creature must make a DC 18 Wisdom saving throw for each hour spent within the watery depths of the western ruins, losing 1 point of Wisdom on a failure. A character who is completely submersed must succeed on a DC 18 Wisdom saving throw or temporarily lose half their current Wisdom. When a character's Wisdom ability score reaches zero, the character goes insane. While insane, a character forgets associations with his or her group, purpose, and most abilities. The insanity is cured when the character regains at least 3 points of Wisdom. Wisdom points may be regained at a rate of 1 point per 12 hours while outside the ruins and the water within or through the use of magic.

As the character's Wisdom reduces from the maddening curse of the foul water, the character begins to experience terrifying hallucinations, eventually leading to an inability to perceive the difference between reality and illusion. A character who has lost 3 points of Wisdom suffers from effects like the *Confusion* spell until at least one point of Wisdom has been restored.

The corrupted water also has affected the embalmed priests in this part of the temple ruins. Dark energy from the ensorcelled water brought the dead priests back to a state of undeath, neither living nor truly dead. Their wrapped forms now roam the wet tunnels as **mummies** (with no vulnerability to fire damage) when they are unable to rest, or slumber fitfully upon their deathbeds.

The greatest of their kind, once the most powerful priest in the land, has also been reawakened in his burial chamber. Unlike the others, he retains much of his former power and has gained additional benefits from the water's dark magic. He is now a **mummy lord** (with advantage on saving throws against fire and no vulnerability to fire damage), a dreadfully powerful creature who quietly guards one of the most powerful artifacts of his former order: the *Book of Madness*[VI]. His very presence in the ruins brings strength to the other mummies found throughout, making this area extremely dangerous for unprepared adventurers.

AREA R-3A: NORTH TUNNEL COLLAPSE

With the utter destruction of the temple, several tunnels have partially collapsed throughout the underground complex. This area has received a complete undoing, however, with the walls and ceiling sealing the tunnel with hundreds of tons of stone and earth. The area is impassable unless the characters spend several days of effort to clear the collapse. A close inspection reveals that water does pass under and through the debris, seeping into the tunnel and **area R-2**.

AREA R-3A: SOUTH TUNNEL COLLAPSE

Thousands of pounds of earth and stone filled this tunnel when the old temple above was destroyed. However, years of settling and shifting has created a small pocket at the top of the old passage, creating enough room for a Small character to squeeze through. Two characters working eight hours, or four characters working four hours, should clear enough rubble to create a passable space for a Medium creature.

Noise from digging likely draws several of the ruin's fallen from various burial chambers: the recently reawakened mummy priests. As characters squeeze through the opening to gain access into the darkened tunnels beyond the collapse, there is a 50% chance that 2–5 **mummies** (with no vulnerability to fire damage) may be seeking the origin of the noise. Although the priests of the original temple were already evil, the vile magic within the water has twisted their spirits further, infesting the embalmed creatures with hatred and malevolence without regard to whom they once served. They now seek to destroy anything they find, killing all who invade their damp tomb, without a need to serve their old god.

Note that there are no more than 12 mummies in the ruins. Mummies encountered in this area have come from **areas R-4** through **R-7**. Remove mummies from some of these chambers if a few are encountered at the collapsed tunnel entrance. Continued noise from battle in the tunnel may empty the burial chambers of all mummies, leaving those chambers empty. The mummy lord in **area R-11** does not leave its chambers, slumbering until the secret door is opened and the room is entered.

AREA R-4: BURIAL CHAMBER OF HIGH PRIEST VORKOST

Sodden tapestries hang on each of the walls, straining on their fixtures as the bottoms absorb the rising water. Faint visages of vile and unspeakable acts are still seen within the cloth under close examination. A character who studies the tapestries for more than a few minutes has a chance to understand the event's details and may suffer temporary effects from the horrifying images; A character who studies the tapestries must succeed on a DC 15 Wisdom saving throw or temporarily lose 1 point of Wisdom.

A single marble slab in the center the room is the final resting place for High Priest Vorkost, a once reverent and respectable priest of the former temple. He rises from his death sleep at the slightest noise, seeking the death of any who enter his chambers. Carrying a magical sickle and golden dagger, the **mummy** (with dagger and *charismatic sickle*[VI], and no vulnerability to fire damage) attacks clumsily with the weapons for one round, before dropping them in favor of his rotting fists and dreadful glare attacks thereafter.

A heavy bronze chest sits submerged in one corner of the room, barely seen through the murky water. It can be detected with a successful DC 15 Wisdom (Perception) check. It takes a total Strength of 20 to lift the chest out of the water. The chest is air-tight and contains several old parchments of historical importance; if opened underwater, the scrolls are instantly destroyed. If removed out of the water, characters discover that the scrolls contain several references to Arch Priest Gornax (**area 11**), the highest of their order, who guards a great and powerful treasure even after his death. This, of course, is a reference to the *Book of Madness*[VI]. Unfortunately, the writing is in an ancient, forgotten language; characters can make a successful DC 20 Intelligence (Religion) check to decipher the key elements of the writing.

Mixed in with the scrolls are 1,000 sp and 500 gp. Additionally, four plain red candles in wax paper wrappings are actually *candles of invocation* attuned to the god Tsathoggus and the Chaotic Evil alignment.

Area R-5: Resting Place of High Priest Hoorvort

Blackened marble walls, dulled with time, intensify the darkness within this chamber, even when torches and lanterns are used. Only magical light sources seem to permeate the unnatural darkness within the area. Tapestries once hung on the walls but are now found in clumps along the edges of the room, fully submerged within the brackish water. Broken fixtures suggest that the weight of the waterlogged tapestries caused them to break away years ago. The tapestries themselves are ruined and useless.

Although the slab in the middle of the room appears empty when the characters enter, the remains of High Priest Hoorvort are floating face down on the opposite side of the area. When the water within the area is disturbed (assuming the characters are trudging through the filthy pool), the **mummy** (with no vulnerability to fire damage) pulls itself up over the slab, looking for and moving toward the nearest enemy. However, several pieces of its wrappings are caught on the corner of the slab, limiting its range. It primarily relies on its dreadful stare attack while ensnared.

A bronze shortsword lies on the slab, previously laid next to the priest during his funeral ceremony. The mummy has no interest in the weapon, its mind fully focused on rending the characters' flesh with its rotting hands and foul teeth. However, characters should immediately recognize the value of the ancient weapon, as ten rubies have been set into the hilt, and its handle is wrapped with a woven lock of golden hair. The weapon is a *flametongue* (shortsword), and the lock of golden hair is an *endless rope*[VI].

A secret drawer in the base of the slab well under the water can be found with a successful DC 20 Intelligence (Investigation) check. It contains ten bars of gold, each worth 1,000 gp.

Area R-6: Remains of High Priest Guldugat

Several boulders have shaken loose of the ceiling and have crashed into the tunnel making navigation challenging. Characters must climb around and over debris to reach the room beyond. You may elect to require Strength (Athletics) or Dexterity (Acrobatics) checks here to avoid falling fully into the water; remember, submersion from a fall into the water can have very devastating effects. Within the chamber, on a low-lying black slab, the group can see a voluminous **mummy** (with no vulnerability to fire damage, Speed 15, and 90 hit points) slumbering on its side. The wrappings can barely hold its rotting skin and bone in place, as putrid flesh bulges through the old linen in dozens of areas. At the first sound of noise, the mummy turns and slides off its slab, and moves toward intruders.

Once an overweight, gluttonous priest, Guldugat has been reduced to a mess of extra skin that flaps loosely when the creature moves. The mummy moves at half rate as it struggles to maintain its fleshy, loose form.

Six broken wooden chests line the western wall, their contents either swept away by the current or found under the water throughout the room. If characters spend 15 minutes searching the floor of the room under the water, they have a 50% chance of finding 1d4 x 10 coins of various types.

Northern Tunnels

Water in the northern parts of the ruins is deeper than elsewhere, reaching nearly two feet in the outermost chambers. The tunnels were designed to slope toward **area 9** where a pit could wash away any excess water in the underground passages. However, the constant seeping of water from the west coupled with the corpse blockage within the pit has made the water rise throughout.

Area R-7: Burial Room of High Priest Jhorl

A faint murmuring can be detected as the group travels through the tunnel to this area. The sounds of low voices, repeating a pattern of foreign words in musical cadence, can be clearly heard when adventurers are within 30 feet of the chamber opening. Once they are within sight of the inner portion of the room, they see 4 bloated **zombies** (with Speed 10 feet) standing around a stained white marble slab. A **mummy** (with no vulnerability to fire damage and see below for additional information), adorned with ornate wrappings, a silken skirt and golden jewelry, lies unmoving upon the flat stone.

Although noise awakens the slumbering form on the slab, the bloated zombies do not cease their chant or engage the characters until the form fully rises. Even then, they retreat to the rear of the chamber, preferring to chant or sing prayers to their high priest as it engages the group. Each bloated zombie gives its energy to the mummy. Each zombie that has at least one remaining hit point grants a +1 bonus to the mummy's melee attacks. Also, the mummy starts with temporary hit points points equal to the total hit points of the zombies. Each time a zombie uses its undead fortitude skill successfully, the mummy regains one temporary hit point.

One of several important Tsathoggus priests who died before the battle between the gods, High Priest Jhorl was a tall, sadistic man who thrived on others' pain and torment. He was known for torturing victims for information and fun, often drinking their blood and eating their organs after they bled out. His current form is impossibly thin, making his wrapped form look absolutely fragile. However, he is anything but weak and, using the energy from the chanting zombies, is tougher than the typical mummy.

A careful inspection of the funeral slab and a successful DC 15 Intelligence (Investigation) check reveal a hidden compartment, accessible from the top of the device. High Priest Jhorl's instruments of torture are found within a bag inside. Any who take the instruments from the bag are instantly cursed, unable to remove the instrument from their hand(s) without magical assistance. A DC 18 Charismas saving throw can prevent the curse from taking effect. The torture items are worth 100 gp.

Twenty silver bars line the rest of the compartment, each worth 1,000 sp.

Area R-8: Embalming Room

Six stone tables form a circle in the middle of this room. Each is stained red from years of embalming and other forbidden rituals, their previous use apparent by the crimson silhouette blemishes on their tops. If the water around the tables is searched, several rusty embalming instruments are likely found.

Wooden tables line the walls, each holding dozens of jars, tubes, and clay pots. Most are empty, their contents dried or evaporated long ago, but a couple of well-stoppered containers hold the remnants of organs. Bits of a human brain, liver, and kidney are found within the old vessels. A nondescript clay pot holds a single raw cut diamond, round in shape. It is worth 5,000 gp.

Area R-9: Pit of Undeath

Acolytes of the evil temple sought refuge here when the battle between the frog-god and his enemies raged, dying when holy fire descended into the temple's lower chambers. Black scorch marks are seen on several walls, intermingled with streaks of crimson. Several inanimate skeletons are slumped against walls and behind broken furniture. Dozens of the acolytes jumped into the drainage pit at the far side of the room, hoping to avoid the intense fire that raged throughout the underground chambers. As the acolytes died in the water, their bodies blocked more and more of the pit's grate until water no longer drained from the area. Although this was not a problem during the period that followed the temple's initial inactivity, in the years that followed when water from the western chambers filled the area, the water had nowhere to go and began filling the tunnels.

Affected by the water's dark magic, the corpses within the pit have recently animated (as **zombies** with Speed 5 feet). If the characters look in the hole, they see hundreds of corpses underwater crawling over each other trying to find a way out of the watery pit. The force of the underground draw still remains, pulling the corpses toward the grate. However, if the corpses catch sight of the adventurers, several pull themselves from the pile to claw up to the top of the hole. Any who fall into the pit is drawn to the grate and remaining corpses; characters must pass a DC17 Strength check to avoid getting pinned to the pile or grate. Corpses have advantage underwater when attacking trapped characters. A character may try to break free of the underwater pull by using an action to attempt a DC17 Strength check.

If more than a dozen corpses exit the pit, water noticeably begins to lower in the area, the grate now free of its former blockage. The water in the entire tunnel system lowers about an inch per hour, until only a few small pools of water remain in lower areas. With the water blockage cleared and the watery pull gone, the remaining hundred or so corpses climb out of the hole and wander the underground tunnels. Within 48 hours, any remaining mummies regain their vulnerability to fire damage.

Several dozen silver coins, rusty knives, and rotted wooden clubs are found on the dead acolytes. If the water drains from the room, more coins and weapons are found amid the debris in the room. A total 2d3 x 10 gold pieces worth of coins can be found.

Area R-10: Tunnel Opening

A major collapse of the tunnel blocks the entire area. However, water still flows underneath the collapse, indicating that there may be a way underneath. If Lenrall is with the group, he reveals that there is enough room under the collapse to swim to the other side. It is a long distance and only the strongest adventurers may make the swim. The young boy says that he has done it only once and it was difficult. He took the chance to swim back only because of the horrifying sounds he heard on the other side. Lenrall will not make the attempt again. The only information he can relay is that the tunnel continues on for a great distance on the other side. After his horrifying swim, Lenrall spent several days in the ruins above regaining his wits and courage.

Attempting the swim requires three ability checks; each takes place at a third of the distance, and they get progressively harder as the characters squirm and squeeze through small openings under the collapse. At first, they fight the rising fear of swimming through narrow places in darkness. Then, they use their strength to move through challenging areas. Finally, they struggle to hold onto that last remaining moment of their breath to make the last stretch of the swim. Those who make it to the other side find a dark, long tunnel leading into absolute darkness.

First Check	DC 15 Wisdom	FAIL: Panic, lose 1 point Wisdom (temp), return
Second Check	DC 17 Strength	FAIL: Take 3 (1d6) bludgeoning damage from collapse
Third Check	DC 20 Constitution	FAIL: Lose 7 (2d6) hit points from loss of breath
Drowning Check		If second and third check are failures, retry the third check. Failure reduces the character to 0 hit points, leaving its unconscious body to clog the tunnel for other swimmers.

This tunnel leads west without any exits or rooms along its length until it reaches the second level under the Temple of Frigga (**area DT-7**). Note that characters who survive the long and dangerous swim may surface on the other side of the rubble amid several Stone Delvers and Hellbenders working to clear the area.

Area R-11: Secret Chamber of Arch Priest Gornax

A well-concealed door hides the burial chamber from the hallway, its advanced mechanism a challenge to even the most talented rogue. A successful DC 25 Intelligence (Investigation) check discovers the secret door and unlocking mechanism, while a passed DC 25 Dexterity check with thieves' tools opens the portal. The door slides into the wall, allowing water from the tunnel to pour into the otherwise dry room, unless the blockage in the pit grate in **area R9** has been cleared. Hundreds of dried scarab beetles covering the floor are reconstituted by the onset of water, returning them to life. Riding the rushing water backward into the chamber, the small insects grab onto the back and side walls to escape drowning under the deluge. Once on the walls, the tiny insects await their master's awakening before moving again.

Five black and red tapestries line the north and south walls, showing images of physical and spiritual transformations, both of willing worshippers and unwilling victims. A single pedestal stands before each tapestry, holding a simple clay pot. Nine of the ten clay pots contain the heart of a former high priest of the order. The clay pot on the southern wall closest to the sarcophagus contains the heart of Arch Priest Gornax, now a mummy lord. The destruction of the arch priest's heart ensures that the mummy lord cannot reform after its death.

Large piles of bones in the northeast and southeast corners are the remains of Gornax's private guard. While alive, the arch priest kept 20 well-trained soldiers nearby at all times. Upon Gornax's death, the men willingly gave up their lives to die with their master, knowing that his reawakening would mean their return to the world of the living as more powerful warriors. If summoned by the mummy lord, 1d4 **black skeletons**[II] form out of the piles in one combat round. They rush to their master's aid after they have formed, attempting to shield him from melee attackers by standing in their way.

Arch Priest Gornax rests in his standing sarcophagus, awakening when water splashes against his container or the lid is pried open.

Standing more than 7 feet tall, the **mummy lord** (AC 19 from magic sash, advantage on saving throws against fire, no vulnerability to fire damage, and see below for magic items) reigns supreme over the ruins, lending his power to all undead creatures within. He exits his sarcophagus with his *scepter of agonizing torment*[VI] in one hand and a *glove of exsanguination*[VI] covering the other. A solid gold headband encrusted with black onyx gems adorns his wrapped forehead, and a magical silver sash with shimmering silk hangs over his bony hips. Unless he is beset as he exits his tomb, he immediately targets the first spellcaster he sees with a torturous blast from his scepter.

Each turn, Arch Priest Gornax attacks characters within melee range with his *glove of exsanguination*, and use one of his scepter's powers. . He can also command any number of the scarab beetles to attack as a swarm (as **swarm of insects** but with immunity to poison damage, exhaustion, and being poisoned).

If the room has been flooded with water, the mummy lord cannot use either of its legendary actions, blinding dust or whirlwind of sand. As long as he is holding his magical scepter, he will not use his rotting fist attack, preferring to use the device's power or his glove attack for nearby foes. Once he uses his glove attack, he turns to using one of his legendary actions, his dreadful stare or rotting fist attacks. The water's maddening properties have no effect on the mummy lord. If Gormax is brought to 0 hit points, his scepter vanishes and reappears XXXXX

The silken sash is magically enchanted to remain perfectly clean at all times, even when wet or exposed to dirt, blood, or grease.

Although non-magical, the gold and onyx headband is worth 10,000 gp. The arch priest's sarcophagus is filled with silver and gold coins; there are 5,575 sp and 1,250 gp within small pots in the standing funerary box. Five bags of one hundred gems are within the containers. Rubies, emeralds, diamonds, sapphires, and topazes are in the bags, each worth 100 gp (total value of 50,000 gp).

A large, black tome hovers close to the 10-foot-high ceiling, spotted only when characters look in its direction. The foul leather tome is the *Book of Madness*[VI], a unique and legendary tome of incredible destructive power.

Dozens of Tsathoggus acolytes and their demon work force are scouring the underground levels below the new temple, searching frantically for the *Book of Madness*[VI]. It is needed for Sarthoggus, the new high priest of the frog god, who plans to finalize the transmogrification ritual with the lost spell found within. See **Area DT-13** for more details on the final ritual and lost spell.

Area R-12: Eastern Stairs

Lenrall and his faithful dog ventured farther in this area of the ruins, and the tunnels are both dry and safe compared to the western section. The young boy searched the three largest rooms fairly thoroughly (**areas R-13, R-14,** and **R-16**) and found many small trinkets to sell at market. However, with the smaller rooms inaccessible and no other places to search, he began scouring the western tunnels. After a few close calls with the foul undead in the flooded tunnels, he returned to the eastern section, hoping to find a few more treasures before leaving the area for good.

Strange noises within a few of the smaller rooms along the main tunnel in this section made Lenrall reluctant to force many of the doors open to get inside. He tried a few of the quieter areas and came away with several nice baubles, and would like to get several more. He would welcome the characters' assistance in opening the rest of the doors to get inside, offering a share of the treasure found within. Of course, they would have to take care of whatever is still lurking in the locked rooms.

Area R-13: Storage Room

The slippery steps drop the characters down into a wide underground area filled with a mixture of destroyed furniture, barrels, crates, and natural debris. Leaves and sticks from aboveground have been swept down the stairs and into the large room after heavy rains and strong winds. Lenrall has looked through the area several times and nothing of value remains.

Area R-14:

Senior Acolyte Chamber

Lenrall pulled the rotted door to this room off its rusty hinges weeks ago as he searched the area for treasure. Broken furniture, decaying clothing, and spoiled wine are found amid the clutter. It is clear that the young boy searched under piles, within furniture, and around every inch of the room.

Hundreds of dusty old tomes and disintegrating scrolls litter the floor, pulled down from shelves during dozens of thorough searches. Although the young boy has searched the area well, he cannot read and skipped over several valuable tomes and journals. A lengthy search of 4 to 8 hours should reveal at least two interesting books. Each passed DC 15 Wisdom (Perception) check should find one of the two valuable journals. Other successful checks beyond the first two attempts should find valuable items for sale; these will have little information about Tsathoggus or the *Book of Madness*[VI], but will have interesting notes about rituals, general prayer, and clerical practices that are valuable to those seeking these types of antique materials.

Although the first journal has been damaged from fire, smoke, and time, several legible pages in the first part of the book reference the story of the Arch Priest Gornax and his failed attempts to use a magical artifact (the *Book of Madness*[VI]) in his possession. The name of the artifact is never mentioned within the journal, although it is referenced often. The journal's owner, a high priest of Tsathoggus, questions the arch priest's loyalty to the order, instead supposing his greedy lust for individual power. Most of the middle of the book is destroyed, but the last entries in the journal theorizes that the arch priest hid the artifact away before his death so that no other priest would be able to use it. The high priests suspect it is hidden somewhere under the temple but even the arch priest's burial chamber is a secret, unknown to the order.

The second critical find is but a single page tucked into a rather unimportant book. A map of the burial chambers in the western portion of the old temple's tunnels details several areas that were thoroughly checked for the artifact. **Areas R-2, R-4, R-5** and **R-6** are crossed off on the parchment, leaving **areas R-7** through **R-9** "unchecked." Of course, the priests did not know about the existence of the arch priest's burial chamber (**area R-11**); the map does not show this area.

Area R-15: Acolyte Rooms

Before the warriors of Frigga and Thor destroyed the old temple, it was the home of fourteen priests. Two high priests and twelve acolytes staffed the temple, spending their evenings resting in the dark chambers belowground. Six rooms for twelve acolytes are found in this hallway; four of the doors are open and lead to rooms Lenrall has searched. The doors to **areas R-15c** and **R-15f** remain closed and locked, and unsearched.

Each of the open rooms has the remnants of a bunk bed, a broken table and chairs, and fragments of rotted robes or travel clothing. It is possible that searchers may find pieces of deteriorating parchment or damaged writing utensils. After Lenrall's last few weeks of investigation, little is left to find in the four accessible areas.

Area R-15c: Locked Room

A sophisticated and rusted lock and thick wooden door kept this area unexplored for many years. The door can be opened after passing a DC 17 Dexterity check with thieves' tools. Like the rest of the acolyte rooms, a bunk bed, a table, and two chairs are within. The furniture is in decent shape, however, having been locked away all this time. An exhaustive search may reveal a few trinkets of value, but the area reveals nothing of importance to the characters' current mission.

A few normal rats occasionally visit the room using several cracks in the stone walls and tunnels in the earth. These pose no threat to the party and are probably what Lenrall heard behind the closed door when he explored the hallway rooms.

Area R-15f: Ritual Room

When the followers of Frigg and Thor attacked the temple, many acolytes and worshippers fled into the east and west tunnels. Those who fled to the eastern section realized they were trapped in an underground dead-end, and tried to find a place to hide until the battle ended. As the holy warriors searched the tunnels for remaining followers of Tsathoggus, the dozen huddled within this room made one final plea to the frog-god for protection. The evil god demonstrated his power — and his twisted humor — and killed them all, piling them into a pile of bloody bones. Assuming the bodies of the followers were dead, the triumphant warriors continued their search elsewhere. However, Tsathoggus reanimated his followers as a single, foul being; a **bone swarm** [II]. All the bones, blood, and hatred were lumped into one new creature, still waiting here, searching for an exit.

The lock can be opened with a successful DC 17 Dexterity check with thieves' tools or a successful DC 20 Strength check. When the door is finally opened, the bone swarm leaps out into the hallway, attacking the nearest characters. The mindless creature is seething from its long imprisonment, and seeks only to kill any organic being it finds.

Before he was slain by his god, one of the acolytes hiding in this room stashed a box under the bunk bed. It contained several vials of a special salve that was needed in the planned raid of the arch priest's burial chamber. One of the high priests had uncovered the burial room and knew that the arch priest prolonged his "life" with a mummy lord ritual. Suspecting that the arch priest had buried the artifact in his chamber, several acolytes and the priest planned to enter and search Gornax's burial room (**area R-11**). However, the attack on the temple came just before the planned attempt. Their answer to the mummy's deadly rotting disease was a special concoction that would negate the mummy's infectious attack. The acolyte responsible for the vials was in this room when Tsathoggus decided to "protect" his followers. Details of the plan can be found in **area R-16**.

Of the eight vials, only five have survived. When the salve is applied to the skin, it negates two mummy rot attacks. It no longer protects the skin after it negates the two attacks, leaving the character susceptible to the mummy lord's diseased ability. Each vial contains enough for one Medium creature or two Small creatures.

A successful DC 15 Intelligence (Investigation) check reveals the black box under the lower bunk bed. Three vials are unstoppered and dry; the other five are sealed with wax and contain a glittery, viscous liquid. The vials' contents smell like wildflowers. If consumed, the liquid provides the imbiber with the benefits of a *lesser restoration* spell.

Area R-16: High Priest's Chambers

Lenrall searched this room, removing all valuable trinkets and treasures for his trips to market. Much like the room at the north end of the underground tunnel (**area R-14**), he threw books and scrolls to the side as he searched for gold and silver. Drawers have been emptied, the bed mattress has been opened up, and tapestries torn down to search for hidden areas in the walls.

Most of the written work references service to the frog-god; simple rituals, daily prayers, important calendar dates, and acolyte performance notes are found in hundreds of tomes and scrolls in the room. Much of the work however, has been ruined by time's decaying hand. A long search of the area (4 to 8 hours) reveals one important book: the high priest's diary. A thorough read of the legible pages reveals the plan to infiltrate the arch priest's burial chamber to search for the artifact. The diary describes how a trusted few acolytes and the high priest, with the aid of a special concoction made for the trip, would be entering the recently found chamber. Instructions to cover their skin with the special salve are clear, but the vials cannot be found within this room (they are instead located in **area R-15f**).

The diary does not mention the location of the burial chamber or the artifact. All the characters will be able to glean from the few surviving pages is that the small group of priests was on the verge of possibly finding the lost artifact within the secret chamber. An exceptionally perceptive character with a successful a DC 20 Intelligence check may be able to determine that the secret chamber of the arch priest mummy is somewhere in the western portion of the underground tunnels.

Optional Encounter

If you feel as though the players need additional information at this point in the adventure, you may use this optional encounter to reveal one or more pieces of useful background. This optional encounter is unnecessary if the group has already explored the underground caverns of the current high priest of Tsathoggus.

At some point while the characters are exploring the old ruins, they encounter two robed figures in the area, preferably in a location making it difficult to escape the group. Identifying the holy symbols on the robes, it is apparent that the two men are acolytes of Frigga. One of them is wearing a strange mask that covers his entire face and neck. The mask is made of a green-hued ceramic, and frog-like in design. Bumps in the ceramic resemble warts and overly exaggerated widely spaced eyes make the frog's face both grotesque and pained in expression. Although horrible, the mask is mild in comparison to the priest's true features underneath. Warped, sagging skin covers small fissures seeping greenish pus around the priest's eyes, nose and mouth. Various-sized green blotches cover the priest's skin, giving him an amphibious appearance. One orbital socket seems to be out of place, moved farther to the side of his head, and the eye within it roams in random directions.

Arrogant and devout in his faith of the frog-god, the masked acolyte demands the characters leave the area to avoid Frigga's wrath. The characters notice that he drags out the goddess's name, almost as if unwilling to say it. Characters should quickly come to realize that the acolyte is unlikely to serve the goddess; his demeanor and rude behavior are unfitting an acolyte of Odin's wife. If insulted, the **preacher** [II] of Tsathoggus attacks the group.

The unmasked, younger priest seems nervous and confused, and allows the masked man to answer all questions. He avoids verbal and physical conflict, preferring to negotiate for his life with the limited information he has. If his partner attacks the group, the young acolyte recoils from battle, cowering in the safest area he can find. If questioned about his purpose in the area, he trades his knowledge for his safe release.

He first tells the group that he is new to the order of Frigga, having joined the temple in the last few weeks. When he arrived, he found that the notoriously caring priests were anything but that; the acolytes rarely spoke to each other and treated one another with distrust and suspicion. Only low-level acolytes were running the temple, and all other priests were belowground researching newly found artifacts and writings. The lowest-level acolytes were not allowed under the temple, and any who tried to gain access were sent back aboveground by newly hired temple guards. Several of the young acolytes caught brief glimpses of the priests below the temple, and noticed that they all were wearing variations of the frog mask.

The two acolytes were sent to the old ruins from the Frigga temple to search for lost writings, in the form of ancient scrolls or personal journals. Neither priest knew where to search but were instructed to search every inch of the underground tunnels for any writing from before the old temple's fall. The masked priest had been sequestered underground for some time, and volunteered for a quick trip aboveground to search the ruins. Being the most recently recruited acolyte, the young man was forcibly volunteered to accompany the masked man, to assist in digging, lifting, and any other physical task required. When the characters find the two priests, they were just beginning their search of the ruins. They do not have any scrolls or journals in their possession.

With a successful DC 15 Charisma (Intimidation or Persuasion) check, the young man reveals that the area under the Frigga temple connects to the underground tunnels of the old ruins. The pair were instructed to start their search aboveground after it was discovered that the connecting tunnel was blocked by several yards of rubble and deemed impassable.

The young acolyte plans to leave the temple of Frigga, fleeing the region after his encounter with the characters.

Temple of Frigga

To most, the Temple of Frigga is a holy and lawful place, proudly serving the surrounding area near Tegel Village since the defeat and destruction of the old temple many years ago. For those who prefer serving Odin's wife over her son Thor, the Temple of Frigga provides housewives, maidens, and those seeking marriage a place to pray and seek wisdom. However, the temple has undergone a quiet and yet unnoticed transformation from serving the loving goddess to an unholy and wicked worship of the grotesque frog-god Tsathoggus.

Services at the temple remain dedicated to the goddess, at least in appearance. Regular worship hours have been maintained and most of the congregation has been excluded from the changes underway underneath the temple. A select few Tegel villagers have been secretly included in the return to the foul god; those who have rejected the offer of a new life under Tsathoggus have been included in the list of "missing." All who rebuked the offer perished in the transmogrification vats deep under the temple. Additionally, many of the acolytes, refusing to change their faith to the frog-god, became test subjects in the earlier rituals deep under the temple. Most died in the early tests, but a few survived as mindless, mutated humanoids who now roam the dark tunnels in the lowest level.

While acolytes maintain appearances aboveground, higher-ranking priests have delved deep under the temple in search of necessary components and artifacts to complete the rituals of the frog-god. Sarthoggus has been instructed by his new deity to complete the unfinished ritual, failed by his predecessors buried below the old temple. Tsathoggus wishes to transform humans to sentient forms of himself, retaining knowledge of their human lives while gaining the benefits of the evil demon. Unfortunately, Sarthoggus cannot find the last spell, hidden within the *Book of Madness*[VI]. The former Arch Priest Gornax hid the book away before his death, ensuring that no other cleric could complete the ritual until his eventual return.

Sarthoggus and his minions have thoroughly searched the levels below the Friggan temple and are beginning to recheck the tunnels below the destroyed ruins. Although the human priests searched the ruins previously, they're sure they've missed something. Hordes of demons, stone delvers, and hellbenders clear the rubble-strewn tunnel between the two areas, and investigate every inch of the ruins until they find the secret door (**area R-11**) and regain the lost book. They find the room and book within five days of the characters' arrival.

To ensure that his plans remain secret, Sarthoggus hired a small band of six mercenaries to keep nosy villagers and travelers out of the temple. They have been instructed to keep the Frigga acolytes out of the lower levels and temple exterior, and to help preserve the appearance of normal temple operations. However, any inquisitive visitors should not be allowed entrance into the temple nor should they have any interaction with the remaining disciples within. Force has been authorized for those unwilling to follow the guards' rules. The hired thugs work in groups of two, rotating between three eight-hour shifts in the temple.

One of the six hired mercenaries leads the small band. His garb is indistinguishable from the rest of the group but he stands out when he commands the others during encounters with the player characters. You should determine which two-man group he is in at the time the characters arrive (**areas T-1, T-3** or **T-7**). The leader has better armor and weapons than his band; both his chainmail armor and longsword are +1.

Area T-1: Approach to the Temple of Frigga

Until recently, the approach to the temple was a well-tended path winding through a trimmed grassy hill. Acolytes cleared the path of debris, meticulously raking errant stones out of the grass back into the walkway. Wooden signs with Frigga's wisdom, faithful encouragement, and reminders of the goddess's promises to her people were always maintained with fresh paint and wiped clean of nature's damaging effects. As the characters approach, they see a path that is now disheveled, with stones scattered throughout the lawn, and find the signs either fading from the sun's rays or covered in moss and dirt. It is obvious the once dutiful acolytes have given up their notorious cleaning duties.

Acolytes would once rush forward to welcome visitors and the faithful as they approached, but now only 2 armed temple guards (**veterans**) stand outside the closed entrance, watching nearing travelers with suspicion. For simple townsfolk, the guards open the doors to the temple without question. However, advancing armed characters are refused entry unless they leave their weapons outside. Guards ring a nearby bell to summon more of their kind if the characters become unruly. Neither guard wears a Frigga holy symbol or the typical colors favored by her followers.

Area T-2: Temple of Frigga

The largest area of the temple is dedicated to the goddess. Dozens of marble benches are grouped throughout the area, either facing flawless sculptures or situated around reflecting pools with intricate patterns made from bright mosaic tiles arranged in the form of Frigga's face. Eight symmetrically placed pillars extend from the floor to the towering roof. The eastern wall of the temple displays a masterfully woven tapestry of incredible beauty and value, showing Odin's wife surveying all aspects of a woman's life, from birth through death. Exits are visible to the north, south, and east. A temple guard is stationed in each of the eastern doorways and will not allow anyone through without an escort, even the acolytes.

A quick examination of the area reveals that the temple interior matches its exterior: Debris floats in the reflecting pools, the floor is dirty with sand and dirt tracked in from the outside, and much of the

Temple of Frigga
Ground Floor

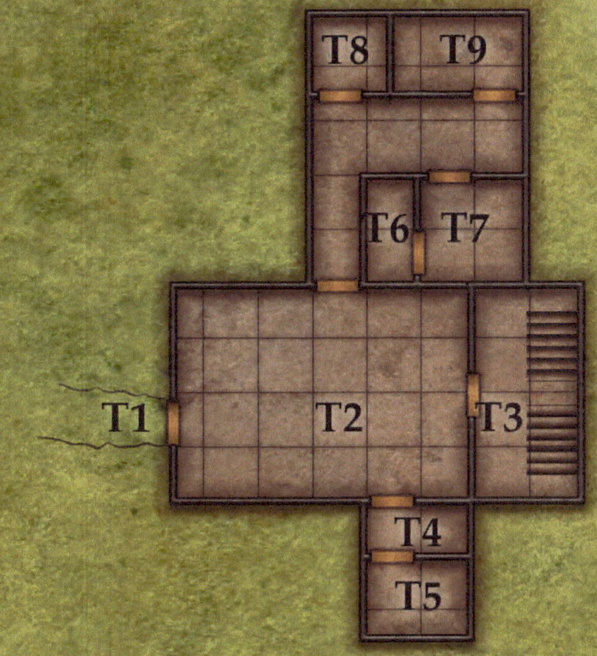

1 Square - 10 Feet

shine of the marble surfaces is missing. Even within the temple of Frigga, the acolytes have resigned their duties.

During most days, several women and a few men (**commoners**) sit on the marble benches in quiet contemplation, or seek advice from one of the many **acolytes** in the temple. Often, devoted townsfolk would sit for hours in hopes of receiving Frigga's inspiration or assistance. Most stay but a few minutes now, quickly asking the goddess for help or rapidly making their donation. It may be noticed that many worshippers avoid the acolytes, instead keeping to themselves and leaving abruptly when priests approach.

Acolytes serving in the temple all wear the same simple robes, displaying their symbol of Frigga proudly. Although they seem to behave as any zealous young acolytes newly acquainted with their god should, a careful eye (DC 17 Perception) may detect a level of distrust with others of their order. The interactions between acolyte and worshipper seem normal enough, but acolytes seem to intentionally avoid the other holy servants of Frigga.

A golden urn set below the magnificent tapestry of the goddess overflows with dead flowers. Acolytes were responsible for burning the daily and weekly floral donations but have apparently stopped performing the important ritual. Few fresh floral arrangements are found in and around the urn.

After the sun drops below the distant hills and darkness creeps into the temple, the remaining acolytes of the temple sequester themselves in **areas T-5** and **T-9** to avoid the strange events within the main temple. Each night, the 4 sculptures of Frigga (as **clay golems**) awaken and stalk the temple and its halls. Except for the mercenaries and the occasional priest passing through the temple to the outdoors, any who are found in the open are subject to the wrath of the possessed marble creatures. The once lovely and peaceful features of the All-Father's wife on each stalking statue are replaced by twisted expressions of hate and malevolence. Although they slide through the temple slowly and silently, they quickly charge any who do not belong.

Area T-3: Storage and Staircase

Temple guards will not allow any worshipper or temple visitor past **area T-2**, keeping all but a few acolytes from entering this area. Two sets of stairs descend under the temple out of sight. Several casks of spices, salted meat, and charcoal line the western wall. In the center space between the two staircases, a huge burning urn sits unused. Careful inspection and a successful DC 15 Intelligence (Investigation) check reveal that it looks to have not been used for many days, perhaps weeks.

Like those from **area T-1**, the temple guards' uniforms lack any insignia or holy symbol. Any characters attempting to enter this area are first warned, then escorted from the temple. The guards (**Veterans**) use force if necessary, even within the holy temple itself. They never use force with the acolytes, instead preferring to summon a higher-level priest from below the temple to ascend to ground level to discipline the acolyte. If necessary, the guards call to other off-duty mercenaries in **area T-8**.

The stairs in this area descend to what was once the study and sleeping quarters of many of the priests and acolytes of Frigga. However, in their twisted and evil state, the new followers of Tsathoggus rarely rest or stop to eat, ever pursuing the final goal of their leader's mission.

Area T-4: Private Council Area

Followers in need of further advice or wisdom can arrange an appointment with an acolyte or priest, using this area for a private discussion away from the main temple. A simple chalkboard on the wall by this room's door often lists the names and times of appointments. However, a simple, hastily scrawled message is currently displayed, "No appointments at this time."

A small table with four comfortable chairs fills the center of the room. A tall bookcase on the east wall contains dozens of old books and scrolls that are filled with the wisdom and teachings of the goddess. A wooden serving tray holding four simple metal cups and pitcher is on a corner stand. A thin layer of dust covers the table and serving tray, indicating little use over the last few weeks.

A curtained archway in the south wall leads to a simple bedchamber that is reserved for evening acolytes who are responsible for receiving travelers and worshippers during off hours.

Area T-5: Sleeping Area

This area was often used by one or two slumbering acolytes who awaited late-night visitors to the temple. When the entry bell was rung, one or both would rush to receive those in need, providing refuge, healing, or advice as necessary. During less chaotic times, this area would be empty during the day as the acolytes bustled about their daily tasks. With many of their underground rooms now off limits, the remaining acolytes cram themselves into the only two sleeping chambers aboveground (this area and **area T9**). A quick look in this room indicates that at least four **acolytes** are sharing the living space. There is a 25% chance that one of acolytes may be resting here during the day.

A set of double bunks have been pushed up against the south wall, and several blankets lie crumpled on the floor in the center of the area. A dozen books and scrolls have been piled between the blankets and bunk beds, with the top book flipped open. A quick check of the temple book shows that the manuscript is open to a chapter titled, "Purging Your Temple of the Unfaithful." A loose parchment tucked behind the open page in the book lists several names with all but one crossed out; the only uncrossed name is Arvid.

Arvid is the last acolyte who entered the lower levels to investigate the strange events below the temple. Arvid hasn't returned and is feared lost to the growing evil underground. In fact, Arvid was captured sneaking around and dropped into one of the transmogrification vats. The young acolyte did not survive the painful process.

Area T-6: Private Room

Women who were unwelcome in Tegel Village or who were passing through the area were allowed to stay at the temple for as long as they needed, using this private room until they were ready to move on. Single pregnant women, the homeless, or traveling maidens were given a soft bed and warm meals until their eventual departure. Although small, the two sets of bunk beds in this room could hold four women in need. A simple washbasin, four drawer dresser, and two stools fill the tight space.

The room is not currently used by any wayward women, and is instead filled with the extra gear of the newly hired temple guards. When the mercenaries arrived several weeks ago, the two women who were using this room were asked to leave. Both women, nearly ready to give birth, may be found in Tegel Village temporarily staying with the resident midwife.

Travel backpacks, patched cloaks, and dirty bedrolls are piled up in the center of the room. Broken weapons and spoiled food are found amid the hastily discarded items. At the rear of the room, several dismembered bodies of murdered acolytes and late-night visitors are found thrown into a thoughtless pile. These are the remains of the unfortunate few who encountered the possessed statues of **area T-2** late at night. The mercenaries tossed their bodies into the small room the following morning.

Area T-7: Priest's Chambers

One evangelist[II] was responsible for the daily schedules and temple tasks, and used this room as his temporary quarters when his turn came up in the rotating schedule. The priest directed the acolytes' training and studies, and observed their duties each day. Additionally, the priest conducted general worship services in the main temple and met with followers to give advice or to dispense Frigga's wisdom. At night, the priest retired to these quarters to study and rest.

After the shift in the faith occurred, the role of head priest of daily worship was abandoned. No priests have used this room since Sarthoggus called the mid- and high-level disciples to the lower level. The last priest locked the door as he departed for the underground; no one has entered the room since. Although the mercenaries discussed breaking in and looking around, their fear of the high priest's wrath keeps them out of the forbidden area. The remaining acolytes are too busy trying to maintain their faith in the failing temple to enter the priest's quarters.

The lock on the door is fairly simple, requiring a DC 15 Dexterity check with thieves' tools to unlock.

The last priest left the room as if he was returning to it at some point. A plate of moldy food sits upon the wooden table, with a half-filled cup of spoiled wine nearby. Three candles have guttered long ago, leaving a large pile of wax at each of their bases. A pair of dusty spectacles sits in the crease of an open book on a side table.

A search of the room and a successful DC 15 Intelligence (Investigation) check should reveal the message from the high priest, summoning all his priests to a special meeting in lower level. The parchment with the short message is found under the wooden table in the room. In Common, it reads, "To all those with three summers of service, assemble below in the open library today at noon for an important discovery of faith and truth. — Sarthoggus"

No identifying details are found within this room, making it impossible to determine which priest used this room last and where he may be at this time. However, with a successful DC 15 Wisdom (Survival) check it is apparent that no one has returned to this room in several weeks.

Area T-8: Mercenary Quarters

Four beds line the walls of the room, and a single table with two chairs clutter its center. Once a room for one or two acolytes, the area has been retrofitted to fit four guards and their gear. At any time, two mercenaries (**veterans**) are resting here during their time off, with the other four of their band watching the temple entrance and guarding the stairwell to the lower levels. Each pair of guards rotates through the 16-hour duty, split between the two guard posts, returning here for an eight-hour rest period.

Any intrusion into their sleeping quarters by anyone other than an acolyte bringing food instantly aggravates the mercenaries. They jump up and grab their weapons and attack the intruders.

The small band of mercenaries are a talented bunch, skilled in combat and fighting in close quarters. Although cornered in the small area, the two off-duty warriors fight together to gain advantage on their attacks until one falls. Neither guard surrenders, knowing that a fate worse than death awaits traitors.

Area T-9: Acolyte Chamber

Six **acolytes** share this room, resting here at night to avoid the lurking statues in the main temple. Makeshift bunks from seat cushions, old blankets, and soiled mats cover the entire floor. Although a half dozen acolytes use the room currently, the number of beds suggest that more than a dozen once spent their nights here. During the day, the room is empty while the temple acolytes continue to serve their goddess in the main temple, attempting to reassure the local populace that the temple remains strong in faith. At night, the acolytes huddle in the room, whispering in hushed tones, and hoping that the statues or mercenaries leave them be for just one more pass of the moon. Several of their number have tried to leave the temple or sneak into the lower levels; none has returned.

A poorly fashioned door bar has been constructed on the inside of the portal and is thrown across the door at night to keep the evil out. Although it gives the young priests a small measure of comfort, it likely would fail to withstand a strong push from the other side. One or two strong individuals could push the door inward, breaking through the wood bar and flimsy door with a successful DC 15 Strength check.

Guessing that many of their order have either been taken away or worse, the acolytes defend their only safe location if pinned down, fighting with clubs, cudgels, and staffs if forced into battle by intruders. However, characters offering assistance are well received, likely drawn into the room to discuss matters in hushed voices. If asked about the state of the temple, the acolytes tell the characters that their order is compromised by evil, instigated by higher-ranking officials at the core of their group. They say that many of the younger brethren have either fallen victim to the growing evil below the temple or have gone missing.

The help they seek does not include their rescue from the temple. They wish to continue to serve the village during the day, reassuring the farmers and settlers of the region that Frigga still protects her people. Continuing the daily services is their duty, and they will not fail the goddess's flock. However, the characters may assist the acolytes and their goddess by ridding the lower levels of the unknown evil that seeks to destroy the temple. They can point the group to the stairs that lead to the lower levels and to a few of the rooms below. Unfortunately, they have not been below the temple in several weeks and are unaware of the vast exploration and tunneling by summoned demons and otherworldly creatures.

Temple Tunnels

Two small areas were created by craftsmen below the Friggan temple long ago, primarily built for study and to house the large contingent of priests of the order. Each area was separated by two different stairs: The northern staircase led to a section reserved for the leaders of the temple, while the south steps led to an area for the main group of veteran priests. Acolytes were housed aboveground in several small rooms within the temple itself. Private chambers, study rooms, and open libraries were found in both sections.

When High Priest Sarthoggus discovered ancient texts referencing a defeated temple nearby and its foul deity within the topmost and dusty shelves of one of the open libraries, he began a journey seeking knowledge. He was interested in the history of the ruined temple and its corruption, which led to its eventual demise. At first, his interest was purely academic, but his pursuit of details led to the discovery and lure of the frog-god's power. Unable to withstand the desire for extreme power, he secretly converted his faith to Tsathoggus and began his campaign to transform the Friggan temple to the frog-god.

Over the last few months, Sarthoggus enlisted the support of dark forces to help tunnel the areas beyond the original space below the temple. Using hellbenders and stone delvers, the high priest has dug in several directions in his search for the lost arcane items of his new god. Illusionary walls maintain the original appearance of the small under chambers, but the temple tunnels have been expanded to nearly double their size. The new areas now house many of the foul creatures who work to help bring the vile deity back to the material plane. Many of the priests have also been converted to Tsathoggus and now serve in roles of taskmasters and explorers, leaving their divine studies in the past.

Bullywugs have been the largest group of supporters, flocking to the high priest in the hundreds. Leaving their swampy homes in the Derfingel Marsh and farther west, they've migrated to the dark

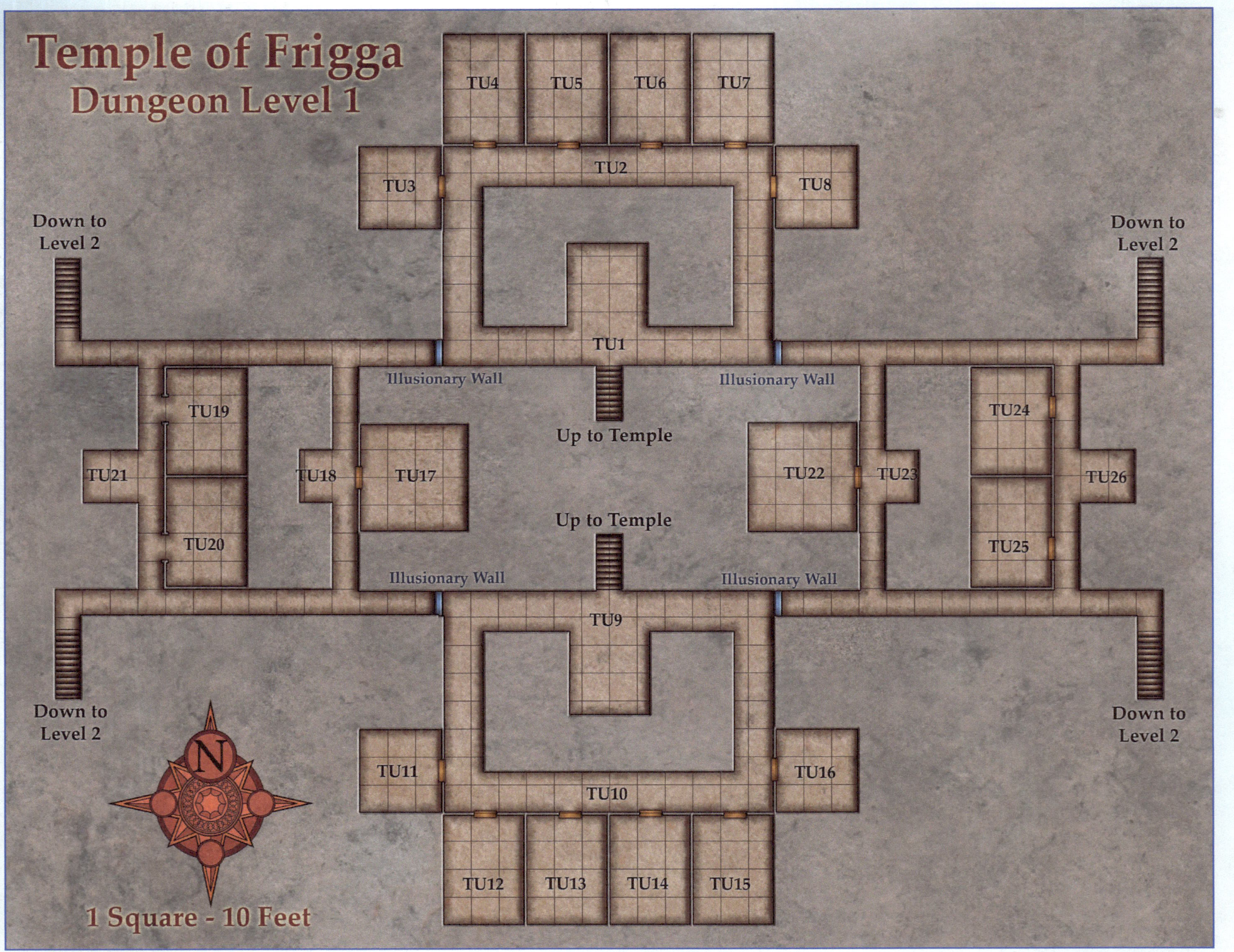

Temple of Frigga
Dungeon Level 1
Down to Level 2
Down to Level 2
Down to Level 2
Down to Level 2
Up to Temple
Up to Temple
Illusionary Wall
Illusionary Wall
Illusionary Wall
Illusionary Wall
TU1
TU2
TU3
TU4
TU5
TU6
TU7
TU8
TU9
TU10
TU11
TU12
TU13
TU14
TU15
TU16
TU17
TU18
TU19
TU20
TU21
TU22
TU23
TU24
TU25
TU26
N
1 Square - 10 Feet

tunnels below the temple by swimming upstream in the Boiling Brook and into the main chamber below the temple. Each bullywug has volunteered for as many transformations as needed, both to prove their devotion to Tsathoggus and for a chance to transform into a more powerful creature, the sacerdotal bullywug. The majority of the surviving bullywugs exit the transformation pools crippled, deformed, and grotesquely misshapen. These bullywugs are put to work as slaves and workers throughout the tunnel complex.

Sarthoggus has abandoned safe and precise tunnel work, instead preferring that his workers dig faster and farther as he seeks the last piece of his goal. Dozens of converted townsfolk and misled priests now search new levels even lower than the original tunnels, seeking the black *Book of Madness*[VI]. A great reward awaits the one who finds it, driving explorers into unsafe areas and in some cases to their death.

Several different evil creatures roam the halls, either freely or led by human priests who usher workers to new areas of work. Most of the creatures are now in the lowest level of the temple but many return to the original tunnels to receive new tasks or to dig through old texts, hoping for a bit of information missed by others. The hallways are wet, the floors and walls covered in a strange oily substance that has been tracked to the outer areas from the transformational vats. Many of the creatures below the temple have either been to the vat cavern (**area DT-13**) to work or have survived one of the failed transformations in one of the surrounding chambers. Creatures track the foreign substances on their feet as they move through the tunnels, or their aberrant wounds spit grotesque fluids on the walls and floor. Characters likely encounter the filmy substance throughout their journey in the tunnels. Any running, dashing, or charging actions are made at disadvantage throughout the tunnels.

Wandering Monsters

1d20	Result
1–10	Nothing encountered
11–14	1d4 tsathar[II] slaves
15–16	1d6 geruzous
17	1 kytha[II]
18	2 kythas[II]
19	1 kimaris[II]
20	1 masked priest of Tsathoggus (evangelist[II])

Former Friggan priests who travel the under chambers all wear the mask of the frog-god, hiding their failed transformation mutations from each other by order of Sarthoggus. Each priest has suffered the painful test, proving their worthiness to Tsathoggus while offering the high priest a subject to further his experimentation. Although each mask has a unique expression of horror, pain, or evil laughter, they all have a similar design, with a frog-like appearance and made of the same ceramic and clay material. The faces beneath the masks are all hideous, with various mutations and twisted transformations. You are encouraged to describe the unmasked priests as awfully and disgustingly as possible.

Those that survive the transformations are blessed with unnatural powers. Each surviving priest and villager found within the tunnels below the temple has advantage on saving throws versus effects that cause psychic or necrotic damage, and are resistant to these types of damage. All creatures found in the underground can speak the special language of Tsathoggus, a confusing series of croaks and clacks that befuddles even the most intelligent listeners. Passing a DC 25 Intelligence check allows a listener to pick up a few repeating patterns, giving them a 50% chance to understand simple conversations.

Several mid- to higher-level priests have also been bestowed special spell abilities from Tsathoggus after their failed transformation. At a minimum, each priest may cast one extra spell per capable level each day. The highest of the order have been granted even more spells; these are listed with their statistics in their corresponding sections.

Area TU-1: Northern Staircase

A wide stone staircase drops the characters 25 feet below the temple into an old, foot-worn tunnel. A small open chamber at the foot of the stairs was once a private latrine for the venerable priests housed in the northern section, but has now been widened into a public toilet for all manner of creatures of the area. Both the smell and appearance of the area makes its purpose immediately apparent.

There is a 1-in-10 chance that one of the denizens of the area is using the latrine as the characters descend the stairs. Unless the group is noisy, they gain surprise over the occupied creature. Use one of the creatures from the wandering monster table to determine which foul foe is found here.

Unless a successful DC 20 Intelligence (Investigation) check is made, the eastern and western portions of the tunnel appears to be corners that turn the passages north toward the private chambers of the priests beyond. However, those that pass their checks at either corner realize that the tunnel also continues straight, leading deeper into newly created sections of the underground. A successful DC 15 Wisdom (Survival) check reveals that the tunnel beyond the simple illusion is rather new, likely mined within the last six months.

Area TU-2: Library of the High Priests

The entire south wall of this large stone chamber has been carved into a long, five-shelf bookcase. Books that are often used occupy the middle three (second to fourth) shelves, while massive old tomes fill the lowest (fifth) shelf. Ancient tomes and dusty scrolls fill the top (first) shelf. The stone bookcase is very strong, holding thousands of pounds of books, statuettes, and other small idols.

This is the location that started High Priest Sarthoggus on his evil journey to reawaken the frog-god. A small tome tucked into the corner of the highest shelf was discovered by the old priest several months ago, forever changing his faith to Frigga and his view of the old pantheon of gods. The high priest carries the small book with him at all times, often thumbing through its ancient pages when he searches for answers to his questions.

Characters could spend several weeks searching through the shelves, finding dozens of valuable books and scrolls. Each character has a cumulative 5% chance to find a valuable item here for every four hours searched. All but a few valuable books are focused on religion, history, or regional geography, and range in value from 100 gp to 1,000 gp. Not a single book or scroll in this area gives the location of the *Book of Madness*[VI]; the Arch Priest Gornax made sure that its location was not documented.

Several priests enter the area throughout the day, searching through tomes for clues to the location of the *Book of Madness*[VI]. There is a 1-in-10 chance that a masked priest (evangelist[II]) enters the library while the characters are in the room.

TU-3: Study Chamber

Used only by the occasional priest searching through library books in private, the former study chamber was once filled with priests tutoring acolytes or studying ancient texts. Three tables and six chairs fill the small room. Oil sconces are found on each wall, and dozens of candle stubs are scattered about the tabletops and floor. A single book lies open on one of the tables, left behind by a priest scurrying off to check a new location in the tunnels. If the open pages are examined, it will be clear there is nothing relevant or important about the content or the book itself.

A careful search of the area and a successful DC 18 Intelligence (Investigation) check, specifically on one of the tables, reveals an interesting charcoal pattern on its top. If a character places a parchment on the table and presses down on it firmly, it creates a simple map of the main transmogrification cavern below this level. Apparently, a priest had drawn the area on the top of the table for someone, perhaps to give directions to one of the vat rooms. The charcoal drawing was well done and is accurate. Note that a parchment pressing will be reversed from the drawing on the table.

AREA TU-4: PRIVATE CHAMBER

High-ranking priests once used the private rooms in this section of the level; however, any priest or villager surviving the transformation tests below may use any of the living quarters in the north or south sections. Several of the rooms are shared by multiple individuals, using the space for brief periods of rest between long shifts of exploration and work. A priest or worshipper who finds a room occupied chooses a different one. Ownership of space is unimportant to the followers of Tsathoggus — only the discovery of the lost artifact to return the frog-god to power matters.

The private chamber has two small beds, a table and stool, a writing desk, and small dresser. Various religious objects of their previous faith are found tossed aside or in pieces on the floor. A thorough search of the room and a successful DC 15 Intelligence (Investigation) check reveal a small leather bag tucked in the back of the bottom drawer. A single, large ruby wrapped in a piece of burlap hides within the bag. It is worth 5,000 gp.

TU-5:
PRIVATE CHAMBER OF THE DYING

Unlike the other private room doors of this section, a lock secures the door of this room. The device can be opened with a successful DC 15 Dexterity check with thieves' tools, and once opened reveals a ghastly sight if the characters provide a light source for the dark area beyond. Several mattresses have been laid side by side on the floor, filling the entire area; no other furniture is found within the room. Several priests and villagers lie upon the soiled mattresses, left here to slowly die. Every doomed individual, suffering from a failed transformation, spends his or her last moments in compete darkness and incredible agony, without any aid from the rest of the frog-god's cult. The dead are removed only to make room for more of the dying.

The characters get a clear view of the mutations and failed transformations, seeing several grotesque alterations to the human form. Fluids spill from open wounds, limbs are bent in impossible directions, and facial disfigurations make all but the strongest willed characters violently ill. Each character must pass two saving throws or suffer the effects of what they see here. Failing a DC 15 Constitution saving throw puts the characters at disadvantage for all actions for one hour. Failing a DC 20 Wisdom saving throw causes 17 (5d6) psychic damage and reduces the character's Wisdom by half for one hour.

None of the dying can be healed enough to return them to a worthwhile state; the transformations are too devastating and the magic from the failed tests is too strong to reverse.

AREA TU-6:
PRIVATE CHAMBER AND THE THIEF

As the characters approach the door to this room, they notice that the entry is open slightly. If the characters briefly listen and pass a DC 20 Wisdom (Perception) check, they may hear what sounds like a quick search of the area beyond. Within, a drow (**master spy**[II] with Charisma 14, darkvision 120 ft., innate ability to cast *dancing lights* at will and *darkness* and *faerie fire* once per day each, spell save DC

13, and an *amulet of the planes*) is tossing the contents of the room, searching for any clues to the location of the *Book of Madness*[VI].

Attempting to use the *Book of Madness*[VI] as a gift to gain the favor of the Spider Queen, the drow thief hopes to find the book before Sarthoggus or his minions. When not hiding and lurking in the tunnels listening for information, she is searching each room thoroughly for further clues. If caught by the characters, she attempts to negotiate her way free, first using absurd lies before attempting to convince the group to help. If the characters refuse to assist her or let her go, she uses her *amulet of the planes* to return to the Abyss. She is saving the ring's ability to return to the Queen's plane with the *Book of Madness*[VI]; returning prematurely without the artifact will surely irritate the Queen of Spiders.

She is unaware that Sarthoggus recently stole an artifact (the *wand of painful anguish*[VI], **area DT-19**) from a drow priestess. If the rogue learns that this wand is within the tunnel complex, she may try to obtain it and use it as leverage with or to gain a reward from one of the many drow families of the underworld. Sarthoggus is actively being hunted by drow assassins who are tasked with retrieving the wand and eliminating the meddlesome priest.

The room is currently a mess from the drow's quick search. Two beds, a table, and a high-backed chair, and tall wardrobe are found within the small chamber.

AREA TU-7:
PRIVATE CHAMBER OF THE COLLECTOR

As the door to this room opens inward, the characters view a bizarre and awful sight. Hundreds of glass containers filled with different humanoid body parts floating in a greenish, eerie liquid have been placed on tables, desks, and shelves throughout the chamber. External parts as well as internal organs are in the containers, each labeled in Common identifying the creature, organ, and date cultivated. The containers vary in size, from small tubes holding eyes, tongues, or teeth, to large canisters with entire heads, limbs, or full but tiny humanoids. A successful DC 15 Intelligence check reveals that the glass storage vessels are arranged by creature type.

A narrow path weaves through the stacks of glass containers, leading to the back of the room to a small cot and a stack of old tomes. Dozens of unlit candles are found throughout the room, lit to illuminate sections of containers as needed. Each book found in the pile focuses on the subject of humanoid anatomy, and lists both common and uncommon features of a wide array of creatures.

The Collector (as **commoner**) (as he is known throughout the tunnels) uses this area for his personal quarters and study area. Charged by Sarthoggus to research the organs of the creatures that die from failed transformations, the Collector dissects and catalogs every part of each new creature. He either pulls their bodies directly from one of the transformation vats or from the death room nearby (**area TU-5**). Using the large room found at **area TU-17**, the Collector and his helpers dismember creatures and test the organs for various results. The short, disfigured human has not been subjected to the trials of the frog-god; Sarthoggus spared him from the tests to ensure he remains functional to test the failed experiments. The Collector's physical appearance is purely genetic, being born stunted and deformed. Shunned by the villages in the region, the old man was an undertaker before coming to help the high priest.

There is a 1-in-20 chance that the Collector is here, either resting or dropping off newly cataloged organs. He is almost always found in **area TU-17**, working tirelessly to help Sarthoggus reach his ultimate goal. The containers in this room are his prized possessions; he does almost anything to preserve them. Any threat to the damage or destruction of the glass vessels forces the Collector to beg for their safekeeping. He trades information or his hidden stash of gold coins to ensure the jars remain intact. However, the Collector is dedicated to the high priest and likely gives the characters false information, luring them to their doom.

A small chest under the Collector's cot contains 1,250 gp. The small wooden box has a false bottom that hides an agreement from Sarthoggus. The secret compartment can be found with a successful DC 20 Intelligence (Investigation) check. The parchment details the arrangement between the high priest and the Collector, promising that the former undertaker would be spared from the mandatory trials of the frog-god for his service to the high priest. A special clause in the "contract" states that the Collector may keep any parts of the test subjects after their examination.

Area TU-8: Former Chambers of the High Priest Sarthoggus

Although the door to this room looks similar to the rest in the area, it has the addition of a worn brass name plate that reads "High Priest of Frigga." The goddess's name is barely legible, having been scratched out some time ago. When the door is opened, all creatures within 10 feet of it must make a DC 20 Dexterity saving throw as the door discharges necrotic energy. Failure results in 18 (4d8) necrotic damage to the one grasping the handle and 9 (2d8) necrotic damage to anyone within 10 feet of the door. The trap can be found before discharge by passing a DC 20 Intelligence (Investigation) check, and disabled with a DC 17 Dexterity check with thieves' tools. The magical trap resets once after its initial discharge, allowing for a second and final blast.

The high priest of Frigga was afforded a luxury room; this spacious area is filled with fine furniture, a private library, and dozens of gold and silver personal possessions. When the characters enter the room, it is apparent that the room has not been used in some time. In fact, the high priest no longer sleeps, and never leaves the lower chambers while he toils endlessly with new transformational attempts. It does look as if the high priest left the room with the intention of never returning, leaving personal items of his old human form no longer needed.

A neatly made canopy bed sits near the south wall, with bright white lace hanging between the posts. A small table next to the bed holds six small books and a silver candelabra. Five barely used wax candles sit in the polished holder (1,000 gp value). The bottom five books are common temple references, independent of specific pantheons, that discuss and detail worship practices, congregational motivations, and tithe management. The top book in the pile is Sarthoggus' journal, which details temple events, interesting regional meetings and gatherings, and the high priest's daily musings. However, the last two pages have the ramblings of a mad man, as Tsathoggus took hold of the priest's mind. A read of the pages reveals that Sarthoggus struggled for weeks to fight the frog-god's return, but failed in the end. His final message, scribbled in a shaky hand, acknowledges his need to confront the evil deity's simulacrum at the ruins and drive him out of the mortal plane as his predecessors did before. Based on the current state of the Firggan temple, it is apparent that Sarthoggus failed.

Two eight-foot-tall dressers sit against the east wall, their double doors closed. One holds formal robes and clerical garb used by the high priest when he served his former deity. The other contains travel gear, including hooded cloaks for inclement weather and leather pants and boots. A study desk and a high-backed chair have been pushed up against the west wall. A gold inkwell, two feather quills and a stack of parchment sit unused on the desk. The inkwell is dry but is worth 500 gp. A successful review, indicated by passing a DC 17 Intelligence (Arcana) check, of the quills discovers that one of the writing instruments is magical. The *quill of accurate writing*VI allows the user to write mistake-free messages, increasing writing speeds by 25%.

A small dinner table with two plush chairs sits in the middle of the room, holding six neatly stacked silver plates and matching cutlery. Two silver goblets embedded with rings of small sapphires stand next to the dishes. The total value of the set of silver is 5,000 gp. A search of the goblets reveals the initial "S" (in Common) on the bottom of each.

If the large canopy bed is slid away from the wall, the group finds a trapdoor in the floor. The complex lock in the small door can be opened with a successful DC 20 Dexterity check with thieves' tools. The shallow space below the trapdoor contains four small wooden chests of equal size. The first chest holds 10 gold bars, each stamped with the likeness of the frog-god Tsathoggus. The second chest holds two unmarked vials, both filled with a red and silver swirling fluid. Each vial is a *potion of supreme healing*. The third box contains the *spear of Frigga*VI. The last chest holds a fully charged *rod of resurrection*VI. A short rest is required for attunement to the rod by a cleric, druid, or paladin.

Area TU-9: Southern Staircase

In better times, acolytes and visitors to the temple were allowed to use these stairs to access the public latrine found at the bottom. Now, acolytes may use the toilet with an escort from one of the mercenaries, and visitors are not permitted beyond the storage room (**area T-3**) upstairs. Acolytes who attempt to slip away from mercenaries are harshly punished or worse, given to the priests below to be test subjects within the transmogrification vats.

Human priests are allowed to use the latrine, but non-humans are not permitted in this area of the tunnels. There is a 1-in-20 chance that a human priest (**evangelist**II) is occupying the latrine as the adventurers enter the area from the stairs. The illusionary walls are the same as in **area TU-1**.

Each of the private living quarters' doors in this section are locked, opened by the same key held by many who wander in the area. Unless specified, each door lock can be opened with a successful DC 17 Dexterity check with thieves' tools.

Area TU-10: Open Library

The acolytes and lesser priests of the order were allowed to borrow and study any of the books found on the long wooden shelf on the north wall. Spanning the entire wall, the wooden shelf is fairly empty, having but a few books on it. Most of the books are uninteresting, detailing regional plant life, historical climate patterns, simple sewing methods for robes, and the proper way to polish marble sculptures. Several books have been damaged by an oily substance (from the hands of surviving priests who search for the location of the *Book of Madness*VI).

A successful DC 17 Intelligence (Investigation) check reveals that the wooden bookcase has been built in front of a carved stone shelf in the wall. A single, long stone shelf was likely replaced with the bigger book rack, making more space for the priests' tomes and scrolls. If the bookcase is slid away from the wall (requiring two characters with a combined Strength of 30), a dusty ledge can be found. A meticulous search and a successful DC 20 Intelligence (Investigation) check discover a frail parchment in the shadowed corner of the shelf. The paper is extremely old and crumbles unless care is taken in its handling. Several lines have been scrawled upon the parchment, in a trained and steady hand: "… and so, the Arch Priest hid the artifact in his tomb under our struggling temple, had it sealed and the masons slain and burned. This was the last we ever saw of the hateful Gornax and the cursed Book, although he promised to return someday to return the Unspeakable back to our world. May the gods keep him dead forever."

Moving the bookcase is a noisy endeavor, likely attracting inquisitive priests and creatures from the tunnels beyond the living quarters. There is a 25% chance that one of the tunnel wandering monsters enters the area to search for the source of the noise.

Area TU-11: Study Room

Several overturned tables and dozens of broken chairs fill the room, giving the appearance that the area was destructively searched. Someone or something tossed the room without regard for any of the items within. Torn books have been thrown into piles, their removed pages scattered about, and bent brass candelabras lie in various parts of the room. At first glance, the room appears to have been thoroughly searched. However, if the characters perform an exhaustive investigation and make a successful DC 18 Intelligence (Investigation) check, they may find a few interesting items. One of the hundred torn pages found at the bottom of a pile on the floor details the complete morphological cycle of a frog. Five crude drawings, each with a few words in Common, are illustrated on the page, using a circle to show the evolutionary steps: The process begins with eggs, moves to tadpoles, then two-legged frogs, and finally to full frogs. Where the fully formed frog should be shown as the final stage before laying eggs to start the cycle again, a fifth stage depicting a humanoid frog-man, bent and wicked, is instead listed as the new last step in the process.

Additionally, a small leather pouch is found strapped to the underside of a chair. Although it seems to contain a pinch of ordinary sand, the bag actually holds a single use of *dust of disappearance*.

AREA TU-12: PRIVATE QUARTERS

When the door to this small room is opened, the characters' nostrils are immediately assaulted with the stench of burned flesh and charred bone. Smoke drifts from the room through the open door, floating into the hallway behind the characters. Within, four bloodstained bunks, stacked two high, are pushed against the east and west walls. A three-foot-high pile of burned bodies of various sizes and conditions smolders in the middle of the room. Humans and unrecognizable large humanoid forms are bent and twisted upon the old pyre. Bodies closer to the bottom are blackened and partially disintegrated while those piled upon the top of the grotesque stack are more lightly burned. Bone ash and charred bits of leather and cloth are found along the edges of the fire ring. A small pile of simple weaponry is haphazardly stacked near the south wall.

Bodies of the dead found in **area TU-5** and the transformation pool rooms are often brought here to be burned. At the same time every day, two human priests transport several bodies from the tunnels and vats to the room. After searching the bodies for valuables, they pile them upon the growing pyre, and burn the remains for four to six hours before dousing the fire with sand. Any gold, silver, or gems found on the dead are returned to the altar of Tsathoggus. Weapons and armor are piled along the south wall to be sorted at a future time.

Two **masked priests of Tsathoggus**[II] may be here (50% chance) tending the fire when the characters arrive. One priest aggressively attacks temple intruders without regard for his safety while his cohort casts one of his spells before also launching into combat.

Most of the weapons and armor in the pile are simple common items, but a successful DC 15 Intelligence (Investigation) check reveals that one of the short swords is a *blade of two sides*[VI].

AREA TU-13: PRIVATE QUARTERS OF THE BLIND PRIEST

If characters attempt to pick the lock of the door to this area, an old, bent man on the other side opens the portal before they finish their work. Unlike most of the human priests in the tunnels, the elderly man is unmasked, displaying the ravages of the transformation tests across his features. His eyes are milky white, glazed over with an oozing film that slowly drips down his scarred cheeks. A crooked, toothless mouth moves silently, his distorted lips parting enough for the characters to see he lacks a tongue. He beckons the characters inside with a wave of his fingerless hand, but resorts to telepathic communication to ask the nearest character to step inside if the group halts at the door. The targeted character hears the crisp words of the old priest clearly in his or her head, and may respond with thoughts in return.

The old man cares little for Sarthoggus and his search to return the frog-god to this world, having suffered through several failed transmogrifications with little reward. He seeks only a few moments of companionship, and a dialogue with intelligent and sane individuals. If he persuades the characters to enter his small room, he shuffles to a nearby oversized chair, settling into the plush seat slowly and gingerly. He probes the minds in the room, looking for the most likely candidate to answer his questions about the outside world (you should pick the player character most fit to answer his questions honestly). In return, he answers questions about the temple and the high priest's plans, and although his answers may often be misleading or incomplete, they are never false.

He questions the characters about the state of the Friggan temple above, the residents of Tegel Village, and the time of year in the region. He has lost track of time within the windowless and dark tunnels, and knows he can't leave to see the world above as he expects to die soon. He is especially interested in news of Arnthora, the priestess of the temple of Thor, and her viewpoint on the change in power within the pantheon (with Frigga abandoning her temple).

After several minutes of questioning, the old man becomes visibly exhausted and begins to fall asleep in his chair. Before drifting into unconsciousness, the old man gives one of the characters a mental warning: "Beware the planar servants of the high priest, especially the winged ones, who enslave others for their evil purposes!" Accompanying the warning is a series of horrific imagery depicting insect-like creatures and winged fiends assaulting the weak, teleporting away from one place only to reappear somewhere else. Additionally, a towering creature is quickly shown, carving through rock with massive, fiery claws. These are of course the fiery hellbenders, a product of the experiments performed by the head priest.

There is very little in the room of interest. Besides his chair and an empty side table, a few wooden crates and boxes are piled in a corner, and a ragged blanket is stuffed behind his chair.

AREA TU-14: PRIVATE QUARTERS

This room has the typical trappings of priest quarters, with beds to sleep four men. The room is used by any who are looking for a brief rest between long hours of work. There is 25% chance that 1d4 **priests** may be here resting, reading, or praying.

AREA TU-15: TEMPORARY STORAGE ROOM

An overabundance of unused and broken furniture fills the space from wall to wall, haphazardly and precariously stacked to the ceiling. There is still five feet of open space just inside the door, allowing one or two characters an area to stand and move within the room. Any adjustment to the dangerous stack of chairs, tables, cots, and dressers may cause an avalanche of furnishings to fall upon any within the tight space. A character making a successful DC 17 Wisdom (Perception) check may notice a glass-topped case in the rear of the room surrounded by broken furniture and empty crates. The container looks out of place with the rest of the items in the room; the ornate wooden box is engraved with the runes of Frigga.

Characters who have carefully examined the stack of furniture may be able to remove less dependent pieces to reduce the chance of a total collapse. A successful DC 15 Intelligence check for every five feet of clearing negates a collapse, otherwise there is a 50% chance that the entire stack slides into the open space and into the hallway. Any characters under the pile within the room takes 5 (2d4) bludgeoning damage from the weight of the avalanche of furniture.

In order to clear the area, much of the excess furniture must be moved into the hallway. Each five feet of cleared space must be relocated to another open five-foot square within the room or hallway. Each five feet of furniture removal takes 15 minutes.

When the characters reach the rear of the room, they see the wooden case more clearly. A golden mace lies within a red velvet-lined case under a clear class lid. The lid, case, and mace are all perfectly clean, absent of any dirt or grime normally found throughout the tunnels. Holy runes are both on the interior and exterior of the case, decipherable by any who follow Frigga or pass a DC 17 Intelligence (Religion) check. The runes repeat, declaring the item within the case is called *Frigga's Influence*[VI], a magical mace once used by high priests of her order in times of battle.

AREA TU-16: PRIESTS' MEAL AREA

Many surviving villager test subjects have been made the slaves of the tunnels, providing meals and basic services for the priests, the fiends that serve Sarthoggus, and hellbenders. Although the hellbenders avoid the north and south sections of the priests' quarters, only passing through when necessary, the human slaves travel to their locations to serve the beings as needed. Powerful fiends travel throughout the complex unhindered and unquestioned.

Four human slaves (**commoners**) are busy within this chamber, cleaning up empty plates and cups, and discarding uneaten meals. They are under the watchful eye of the horrific and terrible Taskmaster (as **ogre** but resistant to bludgeoning, piercing, and slashing damage from nonmagical attacks and add remove greatclub and javelin and replace with *whip*: +6 to hit, reach 10 feet, one creature. *Hit:* 11 [3d4 + 4] slashing damage), a mutated human villager that survived more tests than any of his kind. The large man lashes out at the slaves with his barbed whip even when the slaves work hard, tearing skin from their scarred backs and arms with each strike. The Taskmaster is a grotesque and foul creature, with much of his memory of his previous life lost during the painful transformation tests. He thrives on hate, pain, and suffering, for the slaves under his charge as well as for himself.

Although the Taskmaster stands roughly five feet tall in a bent-over state, he can straighten up to his full seven-foot frame when encountered by the characters. He blows a whistle found around his thick, bulbous neck when intruders enter the room, hoping to summon nearby priests to his aid. The slaves cower in the corner until the battle ends, fleeing the area as soon as they can. If questioned, the characters find that the slaves' minds are nearly empty of useful information.

There is a 25% chance that 1d4 **masked priests**[II] may already be in the chamber, seated at tables eating a disgusting meal made from the remains of failed transformation victims. The priests aid the Taskmaster in battle but clearly care little for the failed experiment, ordering him to engage the characters directly while they cast spells from afar.

In the rear of the chamber, a small kitchen is used to prepare the foul meals for the priests. Large pots filled to the brim with a greenish liquid and chunks of torn flesh are stacked three high in several places. A washbasin with brown water contains dozens of unwashed metal dishes, bowls, and cups. If examined, the characters may be able to find several different types of creatures' flesh within the pots.

AREA TU-17: DISSECTION CHAMBER

The hallway near this area is always busy, with slaves, geruzous, and other creatures continuously transporting the remains of failed experiments to the Collector for his tests. Priests often visit the Collector for his latest analysis on recent failed transformations, hoping for news or a breakthrough. There is a 50% chance that the hallway is empty when the characters arrive at either end. Use the **Hallway Encounters Table** below to determine possible encounters in the hallway.

1d20	Result
1–2	1 **geruzou**[II], leaving the Collector's dissection chamber (north)
3–5	2 **geruzous**[II] carrying four halves of humans (north to south)
6–10	1 **priest**, checking in with the Collector (**commoner**) (south to north)
11–16	2 human slaves (**commoners**) carrying a full human body into the dissection chamber
17–19	2 human slaves (**commoners**) exiting the dissection chamber (south)
20	The Collector (**commoner**) exiting his work area, heading toward **area TU-7** (north)

The door to the work area is always unlocked, as partial remains and full bodies are brought in and out at all times of the day. Unusable portions of dissected remains are dumped into the hole found across the hall (**area TU-18**).

Eight metal tables are in the room, four adjacent to the north wall and four near the south edge. All but one has a body on it, each in various stages of dissection. Four low-level **acolytes** turned assistants prepare the bodies for the Collector (**commoner**) by performing the first stages of dissection. The body, depending on the anatomy, is split open with each organ removed but left connected (if possible). The remains of three humans, one hellbender, one geruzou, one priest, and one stone delver are on the tables, in different stages of organ removal.

When the characters arrive, the assistants are busy with their work and ignore any who enter unless threatening noises or actions are made. Although the assistants are human, the failed transformational side effects have made them perfect for the tasks in the dissection room. They are single-minded in purpose and task, working on each body until it is ready for the Collector to examine. If the Collector is within the area when the characters arrive, he scrambles to a lever on the eastern wall. If allowed to pull the lever, he summons a squad of 10 **geruzous**[II] that arrive within five rounds. Until the supporting soldiers arrive, the Collector begs for his life, attempting to delay the characters. He confesses that he does his work in exchange for being spared the transformations below the temple. When asked specifically of locations and further details of the transformation, he ceases to communicate, preferring the character's wrath to that of High Priest Sarthoggus. However, if the characters praise the Collector's work and feed his ego, he more than likely divulges information while he describes his findings and analysis.

The acolytes assistants will not fight, preferring to hide behind bodies until the characters leave. For every 30 minutes the characters are in the area, there is a 50% cumulative chance that one of the hallway encounters occurs (use the Hallway Encounters table above, not including the Collector leaving); there is a 100% chance after 60 minutes.

Two bins are lined up next to each table, marked "Keep" and "Discard." Organs and flesh that can be used to make food for the transformed priests are placed in the "Keep" bin. Unusable flesh, destroyed organs, and bones are placed in the "Discard" bin, then dumped into the disposal chute across the hall when filled. Several tables throughout the room are covered in glass bottles, jars, and vials. Although most are empty, at least a dozen are tagged and filled with a full organ cultivated from a failed transformational experiment. The Collector's work notes are found on a table, filled with thousands of entries on his findings. Although most are unintelligible ramblings of an untrained madman, a few tidbits of information can be discovered.

A thorough check (60 minutes) of the book reveals that High Priest Sarthoggus is still seeking the final spell to complete the transmogrification process. Another 60 minutes of review discovers that the high priest seeks a lost book that likely contains the spell he needs. A final 60 minutes of review (3 hours total) reveals that the high priest plans to transform all the residents of the region by adding transformational powers into the local water supply.

Area TU-18: Disposal Chute

A recess in the hallway contains a wide, slippery hole that leads into darkness. This hole is used to discard unusable remains from the dissection across the hall. Anything thrown into this hole slides down a steep chute into **area DT-2** below. Months of rotten and bloody remains have been dumped into this hole, making it incredibly slippery. Characters who decide to descend into the hole unaided need to pass three DC 20 Dexterity (Acrobatics) or Strength (Athletics) checks or fall into the churning pool below, taking 14 (4d6) bludgeoning damage.

Area TU-19: Hellbender Nest

An open entry to this area provides a clear view into the hellbender nest from the hallway. In the room are 3 **hellbenders**[II]; one slumbers while two are feeding on the remains of a stone delver. In the back of the room, an unconscious human **acolyte** bound to the wall by hand and foot slowly squirms in intense pain. The area reeks of death and rotten meat.

The acolyte has not undergone any transformation from below. This is Arvid, mentioned on a list in the temple (**area T-5**). He was caught sneaking around in the tunnels by the two hellbenders, who decided to infect him with a hellbender tadpole as they captured him. A hellbender tadpole is maturing in his belly and is nearly ready to eat its way out. He can be roused and questioned one time, as he suffers from five levels of exhaustion, before passing into permanent unconsciousness and death within 12 hours. Arvid tells the characters that he ventured down the stairs just southwest of this chamber and into two subsequent chambers beyond (**areas DT-3** and **DT-5**) before being caught. He briefly describes the horrific areas and the creatures he hid from while he searched for a way out. Arvid lasts no more than 10 minutes before succumbing to the pain and drifting into unconsciousness. Within several hours, the red hellbender tadpole eats its way out of the acolyte's stomach and begins to consume the remainder of the body.

The three hellbenders are confident that they can best mere mortals. They do not call for aid and try to infect as many of the characters with one or more hellbender tadpoles as possible.

Area TU-20: Feeding Pool

A shallow pool overfilled with abnormal and deformed tadpoles fills most of this room, leaving but a narrow ledge that allows characters to complete circumnavigate the depression. The tadpoles are of various sizes, colors, and stages of the morphological transition of a frog. Two, four- and no-legged varieties of tadpole swim within the brackish waters, bumping into each other frequently with the lack of space. The failed transformation tests below often result in an overabundance of tadpoles, which are perfectly suited for hellbender and demon meals. Several times per day, humans slaves transport large buckets of frog tadpoles to the chamber, depositing dozens of the large creatures into an already overflowing pool. Dead tadpoles are consumed by living frog spawn within the pool or tossed aside by the hellbenders when found.

One out of every five tadpoles has unnaturally developed razor-sharp teeth that are capable of rending the skin from an arm or hand thrust into the pool. If a character feels brave enough to reach into its relatively shallow depths, a swarm of deformed tadpoles (as **swarm of quippers**) attack much like a school of piranha. Their attack is swift and vicious, with each tadpole satisfied with a small chunk of flesh. The swarm can reduce an arm to bone in mere seconds.

A character who passes a DC 15 Wisdom (Perecption) check may see a shiny object at bottom of the pool. A mindless slave accidentally collected a silver rod along with a batch of tadpoles, and dumped it into the pool. It appears as a simple, plain metal rod made from or covered in silver. However, when fetched from the pool, the finely engraved runes and patterns spanning its entire length will be seen immediately. The wondrous and valuable item is a *rod of the protector*[VI]. Priests and servants of High Priest Sarthoggus are actively searching the tunnels for the missing item, which has been lost for several days.

Area TU-21: Healing Pool

A small alcove in the western side of the hallway contains a sculpted fountain within its dark and shadowed confines. The chiseled face of a wide-eyed demon slowly drools a green, foamy liquid into the basin under its short chin. A drain at the bottom of the basin gathers unused liquid, recycling it back into the demon's mouth. Smelling like an infected wound, the liquid emits a slight glow as it drips down the stone features of the monstrous demon face. Very little of the strange fluid pools at the bottom of the basin before draining away. A successful DC 17 Intelligence (Religion) check reveals that the demon face closely resembles that of Tsathoggus.

Any non-believer of the frog-god that consumes the fountain's fluids may suffer one of three ill effects. Three checks must be made when swallowing the secreted fluids. First, a successful DC 15 Constitution saving throw avoids 14 (4d6) poison damage. Second, a successful DC 15 Wisdom saving throw prevents the character from falling victim to a 30-minute bout of insanity. During this period, the character talks loudly to nobody, fights imaginary foes, and is unable to use abilities or cast spells. Failing a DC 15 Strength saving throw means the character loses 1d4 points of Strength for one hour.

Any character passing all three checks the first time the liquid is imbibed is immune to the liquid's effects for 24 hours. Additionally, any saving thows made against the fluids from the transformational vats below are halved (DC halved, rounded up) during this period. This bonus can be gained only once by each character.

Believers of the frog-god can use the fluids from this fountain to recover energy and health each day. Just a mouthful of the foul goo heals a creature for 2d6 hit points or restores 1d4 statistic points once per 24-hour period. Although many creatures drink from the fountain several times each day, they receive the boon from its powers only once each healing period.

Area TU-22: Holding Cell

Captured villagers, rebellious priests, and insubordinate servants are brought to this large holding cell before being transported to their next destination. Human villagers are brought to the transformation vats for testing or discarded into the sewer pits below the disposal chute (**area DT-2**) if they are too unruly. Worthy priests are given a second chance after suffering a long imprisonment within the cells. Those unable to reorient themselves to Sarthoggus' master plan return to the transformation vats for a second round of painful testing. Most fail to survive the extra trip through the pools. The priests who emerge from the vats still breathing are deemed special and given more authority and responsibility; they are considered to be one of the frog-god's chosen few. Finally, any of the humanoid servants that have been locked in the holding cell are re-evaluated for service by one of the priests after their lengthy confinement. Those who pass their evaluation are returned to duty to serve the priests or Sarthoggus. The majority of defiant servants fail their review and are given to the demons, hellbenders, or stone delvers to do with as they wish; they are generally never seen again.

When the characters arrive, five humans (**commoners**), one **priest** and two **svirfneblins** (deep gnomes) are here. Three of the five humans are recaptured tunnel slaves being held until enough slaves are available for more transformation tests. The mercenaries recently captured two humans skulking around the Friggan temple at night. The lone priest is near death, having been beaten severely by his brothers after he was caught stealing from them. After refusing to dig a new tunnel for their masters, the two deep gnomes were thrown into the cell for an attitude adjustment.

All but the two villagers ignore the characters as they approach the latticework of iron bars that make up the exterior of the holding cell. They rush to the bars and scream for assistance, likely attracting the Number Keeper or the torturer in the eastern section of the tunnels. Distraught and terrified, the husband and wife duo do not silence their pleas until freed or until the characters leave their line of sight. Any continued wailing has a 50% chance of infuriating the snivfneblins, who may beat them into silence and possibly to death.

A massive padlock and wrapped chain keep the door to the holding cell secure. The keeper of the key to the lock, a bloated and lazy astral ronin known as the Number Keeper, is either in his office in **area TU-24** or assisting the torturer in **area TU-25**. The lock can be picked with a successful DC 20 Dexterity check with thieves' tools. Unless a DC 20 Dexterity saving throw is made after it is opened, it is also noisy. As the large-linked chain unravels from the bars, it cascades to the floor in a thunderous crash.

Both the priest and deep gnomes have little to say to the intruders, instead smirking knowingly at their queries. Only the human slaves answer questions from the characters. They give vague directions and provide simple answers to basic questions. Any challenging requests are too complicated for the slaves, as their minds are nearly destroyed from their dark surroundings and constant, tortuous work.

Area TU-23: Blood Fountain

The twisted form a young human child, bent backward as if its back has been broken, has been carved into a shallow alcove in this hallway. The human child's face is wracked with horrific pain, and its tiny arms seem uncontrollably thrown back. A red liquid spews from the ruptured stomach of the stone statue, splattering against the interior of the alcove before sliding into a metallic bowl. A slow stream of the same liquid seeps from the child's eyes, also eventually trickling down into the bowl.

Sampling the red liquid confirms that it is blood. A successful DC 15 Wisdom (Medicine) check also indicates that the blood is a mixture of several different races and creatures; there are too many variants to clearly identify any particular strains, although human and dwarf are prominent.

A detailed investigation of the mechanical workings of the fountain with a successful DC 17 Intelligence (Investigation) check indicate that the blood is pumped to it from the east. A slow-moving drain at the bottom of the bowl prevents it from overflowing, redirecting excess blood back into the statue where it again exits, draining slowly from its eyes.

Although the bloody substance spewing from the fountain contains no special properties, it amuses Sarthoggus to provide a drink to his faithful, drained from the many slain slaves and servants of the tunnels.

Area TU-24:
Office of the Number Keeper

Sarthoggus recruited an **astral ronin**[II] to assist in keeping track of the tests and the numbers of races who failed or survived the initial transformations. The fat, lazy mercenary left Gehenna with dozens of demons, answering the call to raise the frog-god from his slumber on the Prime Material Plane. He spends most of his time behind an oversized, bloodstained desk counting the eyeballs of the dead. Hundreds of glass jars line the shelves of the room, grouped by race and week. A massive book lies atop the desk, open to a page with thousands of marks, scribbles, and notes. Red liquid in an inkwell and a long feather quill sit next to the book. A wonderful silver greatsword rests on a wall rack at the far side of the room.

There is a 1-in-3 chance that the Number Keeper is here, his head deep within the book as he tallies the results of more victims of the transformation vats. If he is not present, he is likely to be in the adjacent area (**TU-25**) or down below gathering more numbers from High Priest Sarthoggus. He first considers the intrusion of the characters to be a welcome break from his laborious workload, making sarcastic remarks about their appearance, the futility of their endeavor, and their lesser breeding. However, he gets bored of the banter, and wants to get back to his work. Dismissing them with a wave of his hand and expecting them to leave, he returns to counting eyeballs and writing notes in his book. If they do not leave, he immediately becomes enraged, viciously and mercilessly attacking the group with such vigor that it is likely heard in the next room.

Three drow (as **captains**[II] with darkvision 120 ft. and innate ability to cast *dancing lights* at will and *darkness* once per day) assistants help the astral ronin with his work, rechecking counts, organizing jars, and finding missing eyeballs. The Number Keeper adores the three female drow helpers who willing left their home to aid in the mission to awaken Tsathoggus and wreak havoc in the region. Each of the drow are elite warriors trained to defend their houses but in this case, to defend the Number Keeper at all costs. They have grown equally fond of the generous mercenary and do all they can to save him from intruders.

A painstaking count of the Number Keeper's book reveals that there have been 444 tsathar, 252 humans, 134 hellbenders, 77 deep gnomes, 46 dwarves, 12 elves, 11 geruzous, 7 stone delvers, 4 halflings, and 1 kytha lost to the transformation vats since the tests began. A single eyeball from each and every creature is found within the glass jars in this room, except for a single eye of each race stored in the containers in the private chambers of the Collector (**area TU-7**). An additional exhaustive check of the book indicates a rough estimate of the number of surviving creatures. The unsubstantiated numbers are about double the dead.

A note in the back of the book mentions that a large group of goblins is being recruited for assistance, using the promise of ransacking and pillaging nearby towns to entice the small humanoids. However, the note details their eventual "sacrifice" to the transformation vats.

The greatsword on the far wall was owned by the first astral ronin the Number Keeper dispatched in battle many years ago. He keeps the prized item in sight as a reminder of the race's struggle and to validate his prowess to visitors. The silver blade is a *+3 greatsword*. It is fixed in place and takes 2 rounds to remove from the secure rack. The Number Keeper cannot use the greatsword created by his defeated nemesis; he merely appreciates it upon his wall.

In a lower desk drawer, a lock box holds the Number Keeper's payment for his dedicated work. The metal box holds 2,500 gp and a *spell scroll* of *lightning bolt*. A successful DC 17 Dexterity check with thieves' tools opens the lock box.

Area TU-25: Torture Room

Two **chain devils** are hard at work torturing a Tegel villager (**commoner**) as the characters near the door to this area. The work is being supervised by the torturer, a disgraced **cambion**[II]. Using shovels and buckets, 3 **tasathar**[II] slaves gather blood and organs from the floor, depositing it all in a wall chute in the western wall. Three tables are found in the room with only one in use at the moment. A worktable nearby holds dozens of cruel-looking instruments covered in coagulated and dried blood. The walls of the room are stained a dark maroon, hinting at patterns typically produced by violent evisceration and forceful bludgeoning.

At the characters' arrival, the two chain devils immediately rush the group, using their chain attacks to slow down the first through the door. The torturer uses its control spells from a distance until he needs to wade into combat with his spear or cast one or more spells. The bullywug slaves hide behind a table, avoiding combat unless they are directly threatened.

The cambion and his assistants were torturing the Tegel villager for pure pleasure, requiring nothing from the frightened human. The poor adolescent is near death after nearly an hour of meticulous cutting and slicing. He is able to answer one or two basic questions about his capture and imprisonment before expiring.

Blood and organs are separated after they are dropped into the wall chute; a slanted screen filters fleshy material away from a funnel below. Organs and flesh slide along the screen until they drop into a chute, taking them to parts unknown. The blood flows down a slight decline through a clay pipe in the wall until it reaches a reservoir adjacent to the blood fountain (**area TU-23**). As the reservoir fills, a magical pump forces it through the fountain in dramatic fashion.

Area TU-26: Rinsing Station

The sound of trickling water emanates from the dark alcove at the east side of the hallway. A sneering face made from darkened marble appears as the group nears the shadows of the alcove. It has two long-fingered hands cupped under its chin that form a small bowl. Brown water spills from the mouth of the stone face, filling the wide hands of the fountain basin. Although it smells musty and earthy, the water is fairly clean. Under the hands, a wider bowl takes spilled water and any overflow back underground away from the fountain.

When the cambion or Number Keeper desires to wash after a particularly bloody session in the torture room, they use this fountain to rinse the mess from their hands and faces. Remnants of dried blood are found on the walls and floor of the alcove, left behind by the otherworlders from previous washings. Slaves and servants passing by the area may occasionally drink from the fountain.

Final Notes on the Level

Servants on errands from below the level use all four staircases to access areas of the tunnels. Characters may encounter slaves, servants, and patrolling guards along the two main tunnels (the long routes stretching from staircase to staircase), especially if they remain in these areas for too long. Although the group may bump into servants and slaves along the cross tunnels and in rooms throughout the level, most of the guards rarely patrol outside their main routes.

Deep Tunnels Under the Temple

Abandoning the square angles and perfectly formed tunnels above, Sarthoggus has instructed his servants to mine the deeper tunnels quickly to make room for the growing masses of his minions. Using stone delvers and hellbenders instead of the deep gnomes he previously enlisted to make tunnels, Sarthoggus has seen the distance and number of tunnels increase dramatically. The natural tunneling abilities of the stone delvers and the rock-melting claws of the hellbenders have produced an array of twisting and interconnected passages throughout the level. Natural caves have been found and connected to the new tunnels, and most importantly, the large beasts have found the underground stream that the high priest has been seeking for months.

Coursing deep below the surface, the unusually warm waters of the underground stream have been harnessed and redirected to five large pools in a massive cavern in the north end of the complex. Sarthoggus uses these manmade pools to test his transmogrification spells, attempting to create likenesses of the frog-god through unnaturally forced morphological transformations. Without the *Book of Madness*[VI], however, the high priest lacks the spell to complete the process. Each and every transformed humanoid dies in the last pool.

Regardless of his failures, Sarthoggus continues his work in hopes that the book will be found. As the characters arrive at the Friggan temple, his priests are narrowing down the location of the lost artifact, guessing that it may be in one of the overlooked areas of the old temple. If the characters take too long delving under the temple, Sarthoggus' minions finally discover and obtain the book. The repercussions of the book falling into the high priest's hands are immeasurable. With the last spell for the transformation process known, Sarthoggus begins his population of frog-god "aspects," hoping to gain the favor of Tsathoggus himself and awaken him from his deep slumber.

Increasing the number of willing and unwilling servants for the new subterranean temple required that the stone delvers and hellbenders boost their work speed. New tunnels have been started throughout the area, with many abandoned as work is constantly needed elsewhere. The tunnelers are continually redirected to new areas to satisfy the high priest's desires. Several large chambers have been carved out to house hundreds of slaves and mining servants. Dozens of deep gnomes, bullywugs, and humans toil endlessly to meet the priest's requests. The number of demon guards has been increased to keep the servants and slaves on task. The area is teeming with dedicated minions.

Recently, Sarthoggus secretly began the formation of a new escape chamber below the Tsathoggus altar in **area DT-19**. The high priest hired 10 deep gnomes to build the secret chamber, promising their families thousands of gems and bars of gold for their service. The gnomes understand that they are to be slain upon completion of the hidden area. The high priest will use this area to escape or travel from the region as necessary, using a unique teleportation device he has magically relocated to the unfinished chamber. He keeps priceless artifacts and his personal effects within the chamber, away from the distrustful hands of his priests and minions.

The deeper tunnels are lit only in areas where human slaves and priest must travel. Chambers where darkvision-enabled creatures work or live are usually not lit. Commonly traveled tunnels and passages are periodically lit with sconces, providing just enough light between light sources to navigate the treacherous terrain in relative safety. If the area description lacks lighting details, use the creature types in the area and frequency of travelers to determine if light sources exist.

The encounters of this level are extremely challenging. Each large chamber is filled with large numbers of minions, and demon[II] patrols are large and plentiful. Geruzous[II] make up the bulk of the guards' ranks, supported by several kythas[II] and a few kimarisses[II].

Area DT-1: Northwest Entry Chamber

The 10-foot-wide stairs descend from the tunnels, forming two right angles to alter the direction of travelers 180 degrees. At the point where the last stairs end and a long tunnel extends to the entry chamber, the characters can see light and movement in the distance. The remains of discarded servants can be found along the tunnel, likely unable to prove to the guards their need to travel through the area.

A group of 4 **geruzous**[II] and a **kytha**[II] are stationed in the large chamber, charged to stop every servant, slave, and priest as they enter the area from either direction. Any who travel through the room are questioned as to their purpose; unsatisfactory answers are met with rejection or an attack, depending on the mood of the guards. The bodies of the dead are either tossed into the western hallway as a warning to others or discarded in **area DT-2**.

There is a 50% chance that a **kimaris**[II] is present, checking in on the lesser creatures. If present, the faceless fiend naturally leads the geruzou guards, directing them in battle as needed.

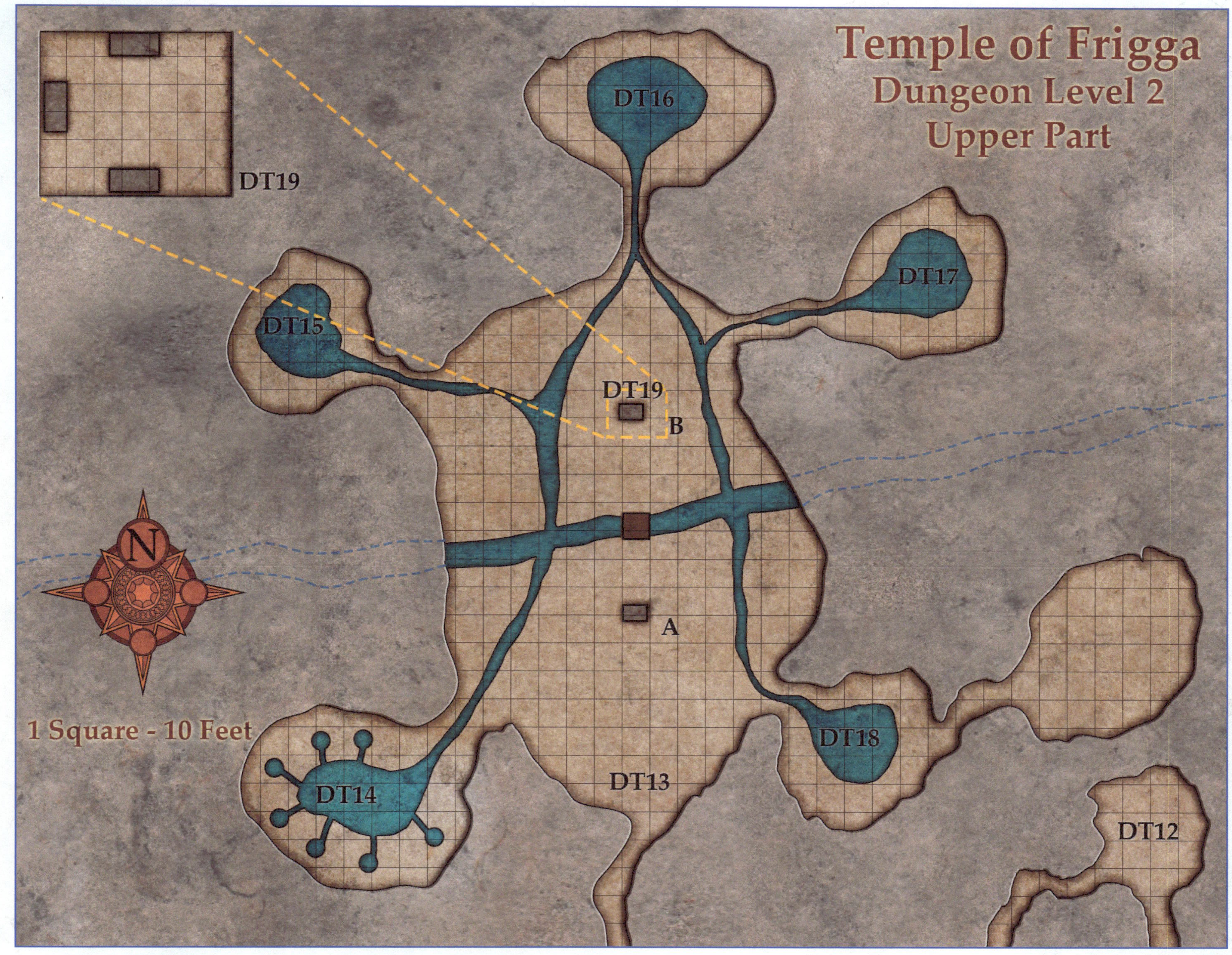

Temple of Frigga
Dungeon Level 2
Upper Part
DT19
DT16
DT15
DT17
DT19
B
A
1 Square - 10 Feet
N
DT14
DT13
DT18
DT12

Area DT-2: Walkway

When the naturally formed ravine was discovered by the svirfneblin miners, they preserved a narrow, stone walkway that arched over the deep depression. The arching bridge is just over 10 feet wide at its center, and closer to 15 feet in width at both ends. Slaves and passive servants usually wait at one end, allowing others to pass over the bridge before continuing across. However, natural adversaries and new rivalries between groups that encounter each other at this area often use the bridge as a dueling area. There is a 10% chance that the characters arrive here as a duel between two combatants is taking place. It will likely be between a **drow** and a **deep gnome** or two different **demons**[II], but other racial combinations may be found.

Remains discarded through the disposal chute above (**area TU-18**) periodically fall into the depression below the walkway but occasionally splash along the stone bridge itself. Areas of the bridge may become slippery and although slaves are charged with cleaning the walkway each day, spots may develop that require a DC 15 Dexterity saving throw to avoid slipping off.

The bottom of the recess can be found 50 feet below the walkway, although it is covered with more than 10 feet of rotting remains. Any descent into the area is likely to cause a character to become diseased; for every ten minutes spent in the disposal pit under the bridge, the character must pass an increasing Constitution saving throw to avoid becoming dangerously ill. The DC starts at 15 and increases by 1 for every ten consecutive minutes in the area. You can pick from any known diseases or just make each failed check result in a cumulative −1 penalty to actions for the next 12 hours.

There is a 50% chance that characters encounter 2 **otyughs** in the disposal pit, who are happily immersed in the endless supply of carrion. The two creatures likely ignore movement in the pit unless they are close by, assuming its more falling organic matter from above. However, communication between characters or extreme movement within the pit gets their attention.

All but a few bodies within the pit are stripped slaves, failed transformation test subjects, or dissection chamber remnants. The occasional duel or fight on the bridge has sent drow and deep gnomes into the hole with their gear. There is a 10% chance that searching characters may find a fresh body still wearing armor and weapons and carrying treasure.

Area DT-3: Demon Lair

The southwestern staircase empties into a freshly bored tunnel of intermittent widths and heights that twists and turns until it reaches this large chamber. Stone delvers have recently created this tunnel that eventually ends in the central chamber (**area DT-5**). Total darkness envelops the area, hiding several **demons**[II] who lounge or rest between shifts of supervising slaves. Several niches at varying heights within the roughly hewed chamber make for excellent resting spots and defensible positions. Only characters with a successful DC 20 Wisdom (Perception) check and darkvision see the total number of demons resting at various heights in this chamber when they arrive. Any light source instantly alerts the demons to intruders; human slaves, servants, and priests rarely use this entrance to the tunnels.

If the characters are lucky, only **geruzous**[II] are encountered here. Use the **Tunnel Encounters Table** below to determine what other foul creatures may be found.

Tunnel Encounters

1d20	Result
1–3	1 kimaris[II], 3 kythas[II], and 6 geruzous[II]
4–7	2 kythas[II], and 8 geruzous[II]
8–12	1 kytha[II], and 10 geruzous[II]
13–18	12 geruzous[II]
19–20	20 geruzous[II]

A total of 6 **kimarisses**[II] are in the tunnels; if one is found here, it should be removed from other encounter areas accordingly. The higher positions within the chamber are generally reserved for more powerful demons; kimarisses and kythas will be in the higher niches above the lesser geruzou variant and remain there during combat, casting spells and using ranged abilities to harass the characters. Geruzous try to teleport behind characters each round, making surprise attacks on defenseless and weaker characters.

This area is one of two demon lairs found within the subterranean labyrinth, the other being found at **area DT-11**. The demons desire little rest while on the Prime Material Plane, preferring to spend their time tormenting slaves and servants. They have no treasure, instead awaiting the fulfillment of Sarthoggus' promise of widespread mayhem and chaos and wealth in the region after the frog-god's return.

Area DT-4: Chamber of Slaves

A dim light can be seen from either entrance, casting shadowy silhouettes on the tunnel walls just beyond the chamber. Hundreds of slaves use this many-tiered chamber for brief rests between long hours of servitude. Humans (**commoners**), gnomes (**svirfneblin**), and **bullywugs**[II] all share the tight space, often fighting for a small patch of open area for a brief nap. Fights between races break out frequently, usually resulting in one or more slaves falling to their death in the center of the deep cavern. Their captors care little for their squabbles, often letting the slaves work out their own issues.

The cavern has been dug out in a spiraling pattern, with a thin ledge that winds downward into a deep pit. A shallow alcove has been carved out along the inside portion of the ledge, providing space for resting slaves. Looping around the cavern ten times, the ledge finally ends at the bottom of the cavern in a small depression filled with stagnant water. Bodies of the dead that have fallen or been pushed from the upper ledges are dragged out of the pool and placed to the side to decompose. Dozens of partially rotted remains and humanoid bones can be found opposite the ledge ending at the bottom. Although the slaves drink from the pool, characters may become ill if they sample the water. A character who drinks from the water must succeed on a DC 15 Constitution saving throw or be poisoned for one hour. When unable to swim in the run-off pools near the transformation vats, bullywug slaves may be found washing in the brackish pool.

Guarding each entrance are 8 **geruzous**[II] and 1 **kytha**[II] who watch over the slaves, ensuring that none linger too long in the chamber. Slaves are permitted only a few hours of rest, and are roused from their naps by the demons when they oversleep. There is a 50% chance that a **theurgist**[II] is present in the chamber, looking for a missing slave.

If the characters attempt to free the human slaves after the demons are killed, they refuse to leave the tunnels unless escorted to the surface. Otherwise, they hide in the sleeping holes with the gnomes and bullywugs, preferring slavery to being captured while trying to escape. The gruesome stories of those caught while trying to flee the tunnels have made the notion of escape an impossibility to the minds of the weakened slaves.

Area DT-5: Central Chamber

Always a bustle of activity, the well-lit central chamber is an intersection of several tunnels where slaves, servants, priests, and guards pass through on their way to their next errand. The wide chamber has four possible exit points that simplify travel to three of the stairwells and to the main transformation chamber. At any time, dozens of different races move through the area. Slipping through the chamber unnoticed requires a successful DC 25, Dexterity (Stealth) check.

Excess water from the transformational vat chamber stream (**area DT-13**) flows through the tunnel and into this chamber, eventually spilling into the sloping tunnel that leads to **area DT-10**. All who walk through the northern and eastern edges of this area trudge through quick-flowing, shin-deep water. A steady stream of water pours down into the lower tunnel, following the natural slope that eventually feeds the tunnel to the old temple (**areas DT-7** and **R-10**).

The exit to the north passage is the only guarded location, where **2 kythas**[II] and a masked priest of Tsathoggus (**apostle**[II]) ensure that no unwanted visitors access the transformation vats and rooms beyond. A low wall made of empty casks and crates barricades the northern tunnel entrance. Only masked priests, recognizable assistants to High Priest Sarthoggus, or specially branded slaves are allowed past this sentry point. Any who try to sneak by are instantly attacked. If necessary, the masked priest uses a specially tuned whistle hanging about his neck to summon stone delvers and hellbenders (**area DT-10**) for assistance. In two rounds, 1d4 **stone delvers**[II] and 1d4 **hellbenders**[II] arrive, with more following every four rounds thereafter.

Battle in the chamber scatters non-combatants; slaves and servants flee to any open exit, scattering into darkness and safer chambers until the fighting ceases. There is a 50% chance that 1d6 **geruzous**[II] or 1d2 **apostles** are traveling through the chamber at the time the characters enter the area. The additional foes may detect sneaking characters or join the fight if battle between the tunnel guards and intruders ensues.

Two sloping tunnels dip below the central chamber, taking travelers to **areas DT-3** and **DT-11**.

AREA DT-6:

NORTHEASTERN STAIRCASE

A short staircase from the upper tunnel ends abruptly in a well-lit chamber filled with recently arrived recruits to Sarthoggus' cause. A dozen encamped **trolls** await new orders from the high priest, ready to serve the returning frog-god's will with the promise of man-flesh and unending treasure. All but one or two are asleep or resting on rotting fur mats and are easily surprised if the area is entered quietly. An especially large and cruel **troll warlord**[II] leads the group.

Feeling that the emergence of player characters is a test by the high priest, the trolls engage the group without seeking aid from other creatures of the tunnels. They fight to the last, willing to prove their worthiness to Tsathoggus by killing and dying in his name. Not a single troll flees or grants mercy to its foes during the fight to hold their position in this chamber. Although they do not seek aid from others, the sounds of battle may alert and draw creatures from **areas DT-11** and **DT-12**.

A massive chest filled with the trolls' tribute to the high priest can be found in the northeastern corner of the room. The 8-foot-long chest is wrapped with a several chains, which are secured together with a rusty padlock. Although the lock can be picked with a successful DC 17 Dexterity check with thieves' tools, it can also be opened with a key that the leader carries around his neck. Picking the lock on the chest triggers a magical fire trap that explodes for 21 (6d6) fire damage in a 20-foot radius. The trap can be discovered with a successful DC Wisdom (18 Perception) check and disarmed with a successful DC 20 Dexterity check with thieves' tools.

Hundreds of books written by several different races are piled on top of thousands of gold coins. The trolls heard that Sarthoggus was looking for a book and, not knowing exactly what he was seeking, they decided to bring every book they could find. Most of the books are mundane in nature, but a thorough examination of the pile of tomes should reveal a couple of useful items. A full read of a magical tome titled *The Way of the Warrior*[VI] gives any Fighter-based class a boon of 10,000 experience points. A spellbook with two remaining pages holds the spells *chromatic orb*, *hold person*, *slow*, *wall of fire*, and *wall of stone*.

Under the books are 15,000 gold coins, each minted with the profile of a drow priestess.

AREA DT-7:

TUNNEL TO THE OLD TEMPLE

Sarthoggus' latest command to the stone delvers and hellbenders is to clear the rubble in the collapsed tunnel that leads to the old temple. Several groups of tunneling creatures take shifts clearing the rubble to provide simpler access for the high priest's minions. Sarthoggus is intent on finding the *Book of Madness*[VI] and has directed his searching priests to recheck the old temple. He'd rather keep the masked priests belowground for now; clearing the long tunnel keeps the priests hidden from prying eyes aboveground and provides direct access to the old temple crypts.

Excess water from the rinsing station above (**area TU-26**) trickles down through the ceiling of the watery tunnel.

The large creatures are a few days from clearing the tunnel completely. They clear the large stones and piles of earth from the tunnel, loading large bags that are periodically hauled away by numerous slaves. The bags are emptied in various empty chambers and dead-end tunnels found throughout the subterranean labyrinth. Waiting to transport bags are 1d6 **bullywug**[II] or human (**commoner**) slaves.

AREA DT-8:

SOUTHEASTERN STAIRCASE

Hundreds of pieces of broken furniture and debris fill the room at the bottom of the staircase from the upper tunnels. A narrow path winds between precariously piled furnishings, eventually leading to a secret door in the west wall. The dangerously piled bed frames, chairs, tables, and wardrobes are held in place by a thick blanket of webs. Just wide enough for a single Medium creature to navigate, the weaving path itself is free of webs, indicating that it may be used somewhat frequently.

Characters see hundreds of tiny, harmless spiders throughout the webs and piles. However, a large **demon spider**[II] lurks in one of the corners of the dark room, waiting to spring on the characters as they travel through the area. It prefers to target the last character on the path as the group exits the room on either side. Although the spider is only 3 feet in length, its demon gaze and steely exoskeleton make it a challenging foe. It may be detected if the characters stop to listen in the area and succeed on a DC 18 Wisdom (Perception) check.

Sarthoggus has placed the demon spider in this area to guard the stairs from intruders and to prevent slaves from escaping. Occasionally, the torturer from **area TU-25** deposits a misbehaving servant or dying slave in the room for the spider. The foul creature prefers to feast upon healthier victims, making it more apt to attack a character in the group, risking detection to get to its target. Its nest is in the southeastern corner of the room, well-hidden and difficult to get to. It can be noted with a successful DC 20 Wisdom (Perception) check. It takes characters 4 hours to move and stack the room's contents to get to the nest. A ceiling nest contains several dried husks of dead humanoids, including a half-orc wearing leather armor. A careful examination of the body reveals two magical items stuck within the web wrappings. His bony fingers still grasp the scabbard of a *scimitar of speed*, indicating that he was unable to free the magical blade in time to fight the demonic insect. He wears *+2 studded leather armor* that adds. A thorough search of the nest also leads to finding 1d100 gp and 1d100 sp amid the belongings of various victims.

The narrow path through the debris pile seems to lead to a dead-end at the west wall. A poorly disguised secret door leads to **area DT-9**. It can be noted with a successful DC 15 Wisdom (Perception) check.

Area DT-9: Storeroom

Dozens of casks, barrels, crates, and boxes of food and drink are stacked in this area for the human denizens of the lower tunnels. The high priest and his trusted minions have little time to break from their work to sit down to a meal, so servants fetch supplies from this chamber for Sarthoggus and his priests in the transformational chambers. Servants prepare light meals for their masters once per day, using ingredients from the storeroom. When supplies run low, additional food and wine are brought down into the storeroom by servants in the upper tunnels.

As Sarthoggus and his masked priests continue their transformation, their need for human food lessens. The storeroom will be used for other purposes when food supplies are no longer needed.

Area DT-10: Stone Delvers

Water flows into this chamber constantly from the central chamber (**area DT-5**) above, moving on to the long tunnel to the old temple (**area DT-7**). Ledges along the edge of the chamber have been carved out by forceful claws, providing wide sleeping platforms above the waterline for slumbering stone delvers. Half the large beasts rest in this chamber while the other half of their tunneling group works in the long tunnel beyond. Resting here until their shift begins are 1d4 **stone delvers**[II]. Additionally, there is a 50% chance that slaves (**commoners** or **tsathar**[II]) carrying bags of rock and dirt are trudging through the chamber, heading up to the central chamber before depositing their heavy loads in other areas of the complex.

Sarthoggus first recruited the creatures to quickly tunnel under the Friggan temple to find the underground stream for his transformational vats. After the stream was discovered, they were instructed to continue their rapid excavating to create room for the high priest's growing number of servants and guards. They were recently redirected from creating tunnels and chambers to clearing out the collapsed tunnel to the old temple.

The high priest is compensating the creatures for their hard work with large quantities of rare gems and precious metals discovered during their tunneling. A secret niche in the chamber holds a large stash of gems and chunks of gold. After discovering the hidden compartment in a rock wall with a DC 18 Wisdom (Perception) check, characters find 147 rubies, 122 emeralds, 88 diamonds, 47 sapphires, 33 topazes, and 21 black opals. Each gem is worth 2d20 gp. Several chunks of raw gold are piled within the niche, each worth 500 gp in weight.

Unlike the stone delvers, hellbenders require little to no sleep and are rarely found in this chamber. They toil endlessly, melting rock with their intensely heated claws as their tunneling counterparts rest.

Area DT-11: Demon Lair

Narrow at the base but widening at its top, this chamber has several ledges at various heights along the walls up to the ceiling more than 30 feet from the floor. The area smells of old excrement and rotting flesh. Characters may detect the foul smells from as far as 50 feet away from the area with a successful DC 17 Wisdom (Perception) check.

Crammed into this small chamber are 20 **geruzous**[II] awaiting instructions from their superiors in **area DT-12**. Stationed at a crossroad chamber between the staircase to the upper level (**area DT-6**) and the central chamber (**area DT-5**), the insect warriors are in a prime position to assist different areas of the tunnel complex when trouble manifests. There is a 50% chance that half the demons have been summoned to a different area of the tunnels, leaving only 10 geruzous here.

When idle, the geruzous harass the occupants in **area DT-6** by throwing excrement and dead bodies into the staircase chamber. The tension is rising with the trolls currently residing in the area, and soon escalates into a light skirmish between the creatures. If the kimaris masters in **area DT-12** don't soon intercede, a full battle eventually occurs.

Area DT-12: Demon Masters

Preferring not to mix with the lesser varieties of their kind, kimarisses use this area to organize their group and to plan for the eventual invasion of the village and region aboveground. While contemplating their attack on the surface, they direct the geruzous and kythas in daily activities within the tunnel complex. Unlike other demon nests and chambers, the vastly superior kimarisses use humanoid furnishings and tools. Regional maps adorn the walls of the chamber with markings indicating primary attack points and rally locations. Tables are covered with dusty tomes and writing utensils, as well as glass jars and vials filled with unknown liquids. Four dozen bare and bloody skulls from several different races sit upon narrow ledges that circle the chamber, each turned to stare at the western and southern entrances into the room. Characters may recognize the skull shapes as human, dwarf, orc, gnome, and demons with a successful DC 15 Intelligence (Medicine) check. Interestingly, the most numerous of the cranial trophies are of geruzous.

Usually in deep conversation about the upcoming invasion, 3 **kimarisses**[II] are always found here. There is a 50% chance that one additional kimaris will be here in between work shifts in the tunnels. Each of the demons in the room is a veteran of several campaigns wreaking havoc on various planes throughout the multiverse. They fearlessly attack intruders, using their spells and innate abilities to quickly thwart characters, or call for the geruzous in **area DT-11** to assist them if overwhelmed.

Characters recognize the wall maps as Tegel region and village locations with a successful DC 15 Intelligence check. The tomes on the table are roughly written in the illegible language of the kimarisses. Only the brightest characters may glean information from the dusty journals with a successful DC 20 Intelligence check. Most of the writings contain the ramblings of arrogant demons declaring their victories over the humans in advance. All but one of the vials and jars on the tables are foul concoctions from unknown fluids. With a successful DC 20 Intelligence (Investigation) check, a character can determine contents are bodily fluids from different races. One vial is actually a *potion of invulnerability*[VI]; the kimarisses have no idea that this container holds the magical fluid.

A hidden chest under a pile of discarded leather cloaks and capes contains a bag of gold (750 gp), a small box of uncut diamonds (10, each worth 500 gp), and a *cube of force*. The kimarisses are unaware of the power of the cube and stashed it in their chest for further examination later. One of the cloaks in the pile has a *brooch of shielding*.

Area DT-13:
Main Transformation Cavern

Only the northern passage from the central chamber (**area DT-5**) leads to the main transformation cavern. Water flows unchecked through the tunnel, forced outward by the rushing stream in the large cavern. Characters tramp through surprisingly warm water as it rushes past their shins and knees. Uncoordinated player characters may get knocked over by the strong flow of water; any adventurer with a Dexterity score lower than a 9 must make two DC 10 Dexterity checks while traveling through, falling prone on a failure.

When the tunnel ends, the group get its first clear view of the massive cavern at the northern end of the complex. It is more than 200 feet long and 100 feet wide, with a ceiling nearly 50 feet above their heads. A narrow but fast-moving stream cuts through the middle of the cavern, running east to west in a slightly diagonal line. Five sections of the stream have been channeled to allow water to veer off to five smaller chambers along the outside of the cavern. The force of the underground river coupled with the sloppily carved diversion channels sends excess water over the edges and into the chamber. The entire floor of the cavern is under a thin layer of warm water.

Hundreds of short stalactites and stalagmites cover the floor and roof of the large chamber, obstructing various parts of the area from the group's view. Thousands of inverted skeletons hang from rusty chains, intermixed with the rock formations of the roof. Suspended by bony ankles or cracked pelvic bones, the skeletal remains of humanoids of all different shapes and sizes lightly swing on their bulky chains overhead. Many are missing arms or heads, but those who still have their upper appendages have them wired to point their hands and fingers in various directions, suggesting they are hinting at different locations in the chamber. Skeletal remains with intact skulls have had a *continual flame* spell cast within their empty craniums, An eerie light shines from their eye sockets, providing a dim light to the cavern. Occasionally, a breeze from an unknown source drifts through the cavern, causing hundreds of skeletal mandibles to clatter in a cacophony of eerie chatter.

The characters may be able to use the stalagmites to hide and move through the cavern unseen. Many of the natural rock formations provide enough cover for one Medium creature. The rushing river adds a constant noise that drowns out light footfalls and whispers. the guards have disadvantage on their Wisdom (Perception) checks to notice sneaking characters.

Dozens of **bullywug**[II] slaves bustle about the chamber, carrying full barrels or pushing wooden carts filled with watery contents. They take little notice of the characters, intent on performing their assigned tasks to avoid the lash of the whip. Demon taskmasters circle the chamber, watchful of lazy slaves or unauthorized visitors, ever ready with their barbed whips and sharp knives. If seen, humans, dwarves, and elves in the group are immediately attacked by 12 **geruzous**[II] and 3 **kythas**[II]. Gnomes, half-orcs, or other races may be able to avoid immediate assault.

At least 2 masked priests of Tsathoggus (**apostles**[II]) are present in this chamber, scurrying from side chamber to side chamber, taking water samples, and casting minor spells to keep the pools warm and viable for the transforming creatures within. If a battle begins in the watery chamber, the masked priests join, supporting the demon taskmasters to repel intruders.

Two raised platforms in the center of the cavern (marked A and B on the map) provide a higher vantage point for viewing the work within the main chamber and the smaller side rooms. One of the **unmasked priests of Tsathoggus**[II], Gorask or Forgnast may be standing upon the platforms supervising and assisting the other priests as needed. A roll of 11–20 on 1d20 indicates that neither is present; however, a result of 6–10 suggests one of them stands watch over the area. A roll of 1–5 means that both of the dreaded priests are within the cavern.

An arched wooden bridge crosses the rushing stream at the middle of the chamber, providing safe access between the northern and southern halves of the large cavern. The stream may be jumped if a successful DC 15 Dexterity (Acrobatics) check is made. The fast-moving stream likely pulls any who fall into it out of the chamber quickly, unless a successful DC 20 Strength saving throw is made. The current draws swimmers into a subterranean river that eventually merges with the Boiling Brook to the southwest. You must determine if those trapped within the swift-moving stream can survive the lengthy ride through the underground river.

Somewhere to the east of the chamber, the stream is heated as it passes through a volcanic subterranean lake. The temperature of the water was perfect to initially heat the transformation pools. Priests use their magic to keep the pool temperatures at the required levels that best suit the growth and production of the eggs, tadpoles, and froglings. By the time the water merges with the Boiling Brook a mile later, the water has changed to match the average temperature of underground rivers.

If the group arrives after the high priest finds the *Book of Madness*[VI], Sarthoggus[II] is present within the main chamber. He is preparing the final spell needed for full transformation of the grotesque beings in the fourth morphological chamber (**area DT-17**) before they are moved into the last chamber (**area DT-18**) for maturation. If the high priest is beginning the long incantation to complete the challenging process, most of the slaves will be moving frog-like creatures into the fourth

chamber for maximum effect. Additionally, the guards and priests will likely be watching the magical process and may miss the characters as they enter the area.

During the dark ritual recreated from the *Book of Madness*[VI], Sarthoggus alternates between sacrificing Tegel villagers on the raised platform (B) and speaking the unholy words of the lengthy incantation. His gaze is fixed upon the fourth chamber as he performs his grizzly work, awaiting visual confirmation that the evil spell is taking effect. At the incantation's midway point, a green hue emanates from the chamber, bringing a murderous grin to the high priest's face and confirming imminent success. The entire process should take two hours to complete, imbuing the transformation pool with the magic needed to complete the transmogrification. Within ten days, any creatures from the fourth pool moved to the last vat mature into magical frog men with unnatural powers and abilities (see **Appendix B**).

However, if the characters arrive before the book is found, the high priest will either be in his newly fashioned chamber below the cavern or in one of the transformation vat areas. The **Sarthoggus Location Table** below provides possible locations for the high priest (with and without the *Book of Madness*).

1d20 (without book)	1d20 (with book)	Location
1	1–7	Main Cavern (**area DT-13**)
2	8	Transformation area (**DT-14**)
3–4	9	Transformation area (**DT-15**)
5–6	10	Transformation area (**DT-16**)
7–10	11–14	Transformation area (**DT-17**)
11–14	15–19	Transformation area (**DT-18**)
15–20	20	Secret chamber (**DT-19**)

Sarthoggus is so intent on finding the *Book of Madness*[VI] that he can sense its location if it comes within 50 feet of him, even if he is belowground in his secret chamber (**area DT-19**). If the characters have the book with them and come close to the high priest, he immediately rushes to its location, attacking any who stand in his way to get the artifact. The high priest summons every guard and priest within range to find the book and to destroy its current possessors. Sarthoggus may call on the hundreds of flying frog-bat creatures (as **swarm of ravens**) who nest in the stalactites above the cavern, using a magical device that hangs around his neck. A slight squeeze of the pendant causes the hideous failed transformations to swarm any targets the high priest indicates.

The character carrying the book is drawn to Sarthoggus' power once the high priest is nearby, and is inclined to hand it over without hesitation. The high priest avoids targeting the current possessor of the book with any damaging effects, instead choosing to destroy their companions while the character struggles with the book's willful impact. A character with the book must pass a DC Wisdom saving throw to avoid losing their sanity and handing the book over to the high priest. A character who fails the saving throw may attempt it again immediately upon taking damage. Even after a character hands over the book to Sarthoggus, the character is severely penalized, temporarily losing half his or her Wisdom score (rounded up) for 24 hours. The book has other effects on the character that carries it; review **Appendix VI** for more details about the *Book of Madness* and the dangers of possessing the vile artifact.

The top of the platform labeled B on the map can be raised to provide ladder access to the high priest's secret chamber below. Sarthoggus prefers to use a *teleportation circle* spell to access his hidden chamber to keep the physical entrance a secret from the prying eyes of lesser minions and slaves within the cavern. A successful DC 20 Intelligence (Investigation) check while searching the platform reveals the secret entrance. The complex mechanism to open it can be operated with a successful DC 18 Dexterity check. The interior of platform has been magically altered with a *programmed illusion* spell, making it look like an empty interior. Any who look into the platform after the top is raised see a bare storage container unless they pass a DC 20 Intelligence (Investigation) check.

If the high priest begins to lose his battle with characters here, he uses his *teleportation circle* to flee to his secret chamber (**area DT-19**). Any guard or priest protects their high priest to the death, ensuring his escape above all other actions. Sorcerer or Wizard characters likely recognize the spell Sarthoggus uses to escape the fight.

Area DT-14: Egg Chamber

A narrow channel funnels the stream's warm water into this dark chamber. Meshed metal screens cover an iron barred gate entrance. The door is unlocked, but a bell above the entrance rings loudly when it is opened. Characters with a successful DC 15 Wisdom (Perception) check notice this bell before opening the door and can disable it by opening the door slightly and moving the bell before it rings. A ringing bell brings **bullywug**[II] slaves from within the chamber to the entrance.

Tens of thousands of green frogs cling to every viable surface, with many engaged in egg production or mating. Although most of the frogs are normal-sized amphibians, more than a hundred **giant frogs** are engaged in the same activity. Bullywug slaves try to keep the larger frogs from the smaller varieties, but the task is nearly impossible. A small percentage of the little frogs are eaten by the larger versions if they venture into their small area.

As females deposit the fertile eggs into the pool, the bullywug slaves move the newly laid eggs into sections of the pool to keep track of the egg maturity cycle. As eggs hatch into tadpoles, dozens of slaves transport them into the next chamber (**area DT-15**). This process of moving eggs and tadpoles occurs night and day; new eggs are deposited all the time, and tadpoles emerge dozens of times throughout the day. Eggs and tadpoles from the giant frogs are tracked separately in smaller pools away from the main egg pool.

Several dozen screened nests hang from the ceiling of the chamber, each filled with various insects. Moths, grasshoppers, beetles, and gnats of different sizes are raised in the nests and are released periodically to feed the hungry frogs. During feeding times, the chamber is a chaotic scene of thousands of frogs feasting on insects. After releasing the insects, the bullywugs quickly exit the chamber, only returning after the feeding subsides. There is a 1-in-10 chance that the slaves and archpriests are waiting outside the entrance for the feeding frenzy to end when characters reach this area.

Six **sacerdotal tsathar**[II] believe that Tsathoggus is their true god and volunteered to support the high priest in his efforts to reawaken him. They watch over the pools, blessing them dozens of times each day. They defend the pools as if they were filled with their own offspring. Fanatical bullywug slaves throw themselves at intruders, willing to lose their lives to defend the bullywug priests, whom the slaves believe are the extensions of deities.

One of the tsathar priests carries a *sacerdotal scepter*[VI]. A green frog head with two glowing eyes sits atop the short, black scepter.

Area DT-15: Tadpole Chamber

Fluorescent lichen covers the ceiling and walls of this chamber, making it well-lit compared to the other areas of the tunnel complex. Strangely misshapen fungi grow along the outer edges of the floor, bending toward the light source they crave. A soft moss grows around the pool, covering the floor of the chamber throughout. Three racks of long poles with nets at their end are found on the north, west, and south sides of the chamber.

Viable tadpoles surviving the birth process in the egg chamber (**area DT-14**) are transported to the deep pool in this chamber. The area is watched over by at least 10 bullywug slaves who monitor the pool

from its exterior and occasionally from within if necessary. Several times a day, slaves transport tadpoles and their yolk sacks from the egg pool by bucket or barrel, dumping them into the dark water. The bottom of the pool is filled with green vegetation and algae, providing a healthy diet for the growing tadpoles. Although the water is clear, the pool is more than 50 feet deep, making the bottom hard to see from its exterior. Thousands of tadpoles swim rapidly throughout the pool, feeding on vegetation and yolk sacks. If larger tadpoles of the giant frog variety begin to feed on the smaller tadpoles, they are removed and given to the hellbenders in the upper levels.

Each bullywug slave wears a special, tight-fitting necklace made of multicolored corral and seashells that protects it from the guardian of the pool, a **water weird**[II]. Sarthoggus bound the creature to protect the pool from any who enter it unless they are wearing the specially attuned necklace.

Tadpoles that begin to grow back legs are removed from the pool by the slaves using long pole nets found throughout the chamber. Using buckets and barrels, the tadpoles are shifted to **area DT-16** to continue their morphological process. Any tadpoles that are found to have begun to grow both front and back legs simultaneously are instead moved to **area DT-17**.

In the southernmost part of the chamber, a small cluster of fungi appears to be dying; the mushrooms' color has drained, leaving them gray and shriveled in appearance. A keen character with a successful DC 15 Wisdom (Perception) check may notice a **brown mold**[II] growing behind the fungi, covering the wall and floor in and around the mushroom patch.

Area DT-16: Legged Tadpole Chamber

The northernmost chamber has the widest and deepest pool of the five areas used for frog transformation. It is here that Sarthoggus begins using magic to enhance the growth of the tadpoles, in both speed and size. He accelerates the growth of the froglings so that he can have more test subjects in the later steps of transformation. Unfortunately, his magic causes about a 50% fatality rate in the tadpoles. Dead tadpoles are discarded in **area DT-2**, given to the hellbenders, or eaten by other tadpoles. Between the high priest's magic and cannibalism, the number of tadpoles is reduced drastically.

Tadpoles with back legs change their diets from plant-based to protein-based. Giant frog tadpoles would eat the smaller version if they weren't separated into a special section in the pool. A section of the pool is screened off from the rest, and used to hold giant frog tadpoles who are now close to a foot in length.

Six bullywug slaves tend the two sections of the pool at all times, separating aggressive or giant tadpoles and feeding them the remains of failed test subjects or other tadpoles. Once tadpoles begin to grow front legs, they are moved to **area DT-17**.

Area DT-17: Frog Pool Chamber

The entrance to the most important transformation chamber is magically trapped to ensure that nothing enters and disrupts the high priest's work within. A nearly invisible rune trap has been set in the first ten feet of the short tunnel into the area. Only those who know the command word may pass though the trap unharmed. However, any who pass without speaking the phrase "The frog-god returns" activates the powerful trap. It explodes outward into the main cavern, dealing 55 (10d10) force damage, spread evenly between all within the tunnel at the time of the explosion. The runes may be noted with a successful DC 20 Wisdom (Perception) check and removed with a successful DC 22 Intelligence (Arcana) check. The exploding trap alerts every creature in the main cavern and side chambers to the presence of intruders. Only Sarthoggus, his two unmasked priests Gorask and Forgnast, and the two bullywug slaves allowed to work in the chamber know the password phrase.

Sarthoggus' test spells and incomplete incantations are directed at the four-legged tadpoles in the small pool in this chamber. Without the *Book of Madness*[VI], he continues to struggle to complete the last spell that changes the froglings to humanoid beings. Only a few tadpoles have survived the transformation spells tested on the pool. Those that somehow survive are transformed into grotesque, misshapen creatures that look nothing like the high priest desires them to be. These horribly failed test subjects are discarded or given to the hellbenders.

Occasionally, Sarthoggus tests a new spell on a batch of humanoids, hoping to find an alternative to the missing incantation. The results of the test have all been failures, either killing everything within the pool or leaving a few survivors horribly deformed and maimed. Survivors who pledge their lives to the high priest after their test are allowed to live and are put to work somewhere within the tunnel complex. The disfigured believe their survival of the transformation test means they are part of the "chosen," the first group worthy to be a part of Tsathoggus' army of believers. Surprisingly, many who survived their test eagerly volunteer for another transformation experiment, often begging the high priest to be included in the next attempt.

Only two **bullywug**[II] slaves are allowed to work in this chamber, attending the tadpoles in their struggle to survive the latest transformation spell. The slaves report progress or changes to the latest batch of test subjects to the high priest directly. Each of the two slaves have undergone three separate tests; they are revered by other bullywug slaves and are fully trusted by Sarthoggus' priests who see their devotion to the cause as pure and true. The two slaves only rest between tests, spending every waking moment watching over the pool during active transformation tests. Sarthoggus starts the next test when he has a new idea or spell, sometimes taking up to two or three days to prepare.

When Sarthoggus is testing with tadpoles, the pool is filled with 400 to 500 froglings. When he periodically tests with slaves, captured villagers, or unruly minions, less than a dozen victims are secured within the pool. When the characters arrive here, use the **Pool Occupants Table** below to determine the current occupants of the pool. Note that if the high priest possesses the *Book of Madness*[VI] and is casting the lost incantation, thousands of froglings will fill the pool.

POOL OCCUPANTS

1d20	Details
1	1d10 humans (villagers, captured travelers, acolytes, etc.)
2–3	10 disobedient slaves (bullywugs, gnomes, etc.)
4–18	1d6x100 four-legged tadpoles
19–20	Empty pool

The bullywug slaves have sleeping mats near the pool that are used only when the pool is empty. Two racks of tools for maintaining the pool and its occupants are against the southern wall.

AREA DT-18:

FINAL TRANSFORMATION CHAMBER

Unless Sarthoggus has been actively using the lost incantation from the *Book of Madness*[VI] for several days, this chamber is vacant. The channel from the main stream that leads to the small pool within the center of the chamber trickles water into the half-filled pool. No life is found within the pool itself; no creatures have survived or successfully transformed in the previous chamber (**area DT-17**) to be moved to this area for the final maturation process.

However, if the high priest possesses the artifact and has cast the lost incantation on the creatures in the pool in **area DT-17**, it is likely that dozens of four-legged froglings are maturing into medium-sized humanoid creatures, losing their tails and growing to 4 feet tall.

This area is extremely active with slaves and priests entering and exiting throughout the day. Sarthoggus spends much of his time here, watching his little creatures grow into full bipedal warriors. The pool can hold only about 50 froglings, limiting the final morphological process to 40 or 50 froglings every seven days. Many of the successful transformations in the previous pool (**area DT-17**) die before they can make the final move into this chamber. Sarthoggus allows the occupants of that pool to fight for survival, reducing the count to the strongest 50 froglings before moving them to the final pool. (Note that the effects of the maturation pool work only for a small number of creatures. If Sarthoggus increases the pool size, only 40 or 50 frog warriors mature, regardless of the width and depth of the pool.)

Once Sarthoggus completes the last step of the transformation process, he redirects the stone delvers to this chamber and has them extend the chamber north and east to make room for the new frog warriors. The burrowing creatures create a massive area beyond the pool to house and train the new frog warrior army.

After a few weeks, the matured froglings learn to speak and use weapons. Once Sarthoggus raises 400 to 500 warriors, he initiates his plan to attack Tegel Village and surrounding towns (see details under **Ending the Adventure**).

AREA DT-19: SARTHOGGUS' SECRET ROOM, SANCTUM OF MADNESS

Trustworthy svirfneblins mined a large space below the main cavern, creating a secret chamber for the high priest to rest, study, and escape threats from above. Their craftsmanship is instantly recognizable; perfect corners, equally spaced stone blocks, and flawless floor patterns differentiate this area from the rest of the tunnel complex. Floor to ceiling tapestries depicting the four morphological cycles of the frog cover the four walls. A bronze ladder at the east end of the room leads up to the raised platform in the main chamber (**DT-13**, area B on the map). Twenty floating light bubbles hover equidistantly throughout the room, providing illumination for the priest to work and read. Simple commands turn them on and off, or dim them as desired.

Glass beakers, clay pots, and iron bowls cover a large table on the north wall. **Sarthoggus**[II] tests new transformation spells with various ingredients and small creatures found within the containers on the bench. Deformed tadpoles, dead frogs, and misshapen creatures float in forgotten containers or lie dissected on the table. Anatomical tomes and old spellbooks are piled in various places on the long table, left behind by the frustrated priest. Small bowls of crushed ingredients, including organic matter and crystals, are found scattered across the work area.

A giant idol of Tsathoggus stands on a black marble pedestal near the south wall. The golden statue stands 4 feet tall and has two red eyes that seem to glare at intruders with a strange and uncanny hatred. Made from two large rubies, the eyes of the frog god are extremely valuable, each worth 10,000 gp. However, their removal causes a poisonous cloud to release from the idol's sneering mouth, filling the entire area within two rounds. Every character in the room must make a DC 20 Constitution saving throw against the gas to resist the urge to worship the frog-god. Those who fail their saving throw see other characters as threats and may turn on them. A character getting a successful of DC 15 Wisdom saving throw is confused (per the spell) for 1d4 + 1 rounds, while, failure causes the character to attack others for the same duration.

The stone pedestal is hollow and accessible by a secret panel at the rear of the fixture. A successful search and use of the hidden mechanism releases the contents of the compartment, causing 5,000 pp to pour out of the back. The secret door can be located with a successful DC 15 Wisdom (Perception) check and the mechanism understood with a successful DC 15 Intelligence (Investigation) check. If the large idol is lifted from the pedestal, a small slot is found at the top of the stone platform. The idol can be lifted with a successful

DC 22 Strength check.

Set upon a tall, single step dais, the high priest's large bed sits near the west wall of the chamber. Black linen hangs from the four posts of the canopy bed. The bed looks to be little used by the hard-working priest. A secret area in the dais stores the high priest's most sacred and important devices. A successful DC 18 Intelligence (Investigation) check while searching the stone dais reveals a wide drawer that pulls out from the platform. A black wand and gnarled green staff are found within the drawer. The black wand is a unique artifact, especially created for a drow priestess and just recently stolen from her underground city by Sarthoggus. It is the *wand of painful anguish*[VI], a device created to maximize the torment of injured targets.

The green staff is a *staff of the frog*[VI], an item Sarthoggus created to prove his devotion to Tsathoggus. The frog god's likeness has been carved into the head of the staff.

If Sarthoggus teleported to this area during a battle with characters, he is found at the dais quickly drawing out the staff and wand. If he is surprised in his chamber, he tries to get to the dais to get his powerful items.

Sarthoggus is usually engaged in spellcasting and monitoring the morphological cycles of the froglings, and rarely carries his *staff of the frog*[VI] or *wand of painful anguish*[VI] with him as he works. The high priest feels relatively safe in his subterranean lair and sees no need to carry them most of the time. However, you can elect to have the high priest found with one or both items if desired.

The high priest is tall and gaunt, and appears exhausted most of the time. His skin is scaly and damp, much like a wet toad. Having survived several transformation tests himself, his face and hands are horribly disfigured. Large pieces of skin peel from his body constantly, only to grow back within a few days. He is clothed in a simple dark-green robe without any markings. He often covers his head and face with the hood of the robe, except when he is examining the transformation pools or casting spells.

If Sarthoggus is encountered alone, either within his secret chamber or elsewhere in the complex, he first casts protection type spells before he tries to obtain his magical devices. He uses his defensive spells to ward off effects while he gets into a better position to retrieve his wand and staff before handling the intruders.

If the high priest is surrounded by demon guards or other priests, he tends to be more offensive in nature, trying to eliminate his foes quickly and efficiently. He switches between direct damaging spells, targeting the greatest threat, and area of effect spells to weaken the entire group of opponents.

Sarthoggus' simple-looking robe is actually a powerful magical item, the *robe of the devoted*[VI].

ENDING THE ADVENTURE

If Sarthoggus obtains the *Book of Madness*[VI] and completes the unnatural morphological process, he embarks on a violent plan of regional dominance and tyranny in the name of his new god, Tsathoggus. Using a minimum of 400 or 500 frog warrior troops supported by dozens of demons (assuming they have remained behind to help) and bullywug priests, Sarthoggus starts by overrunning the monastery of Garm and Tegel Village. It takes eight to ten weeks to produce enough frog warriors before the high priest is ready to attack the surface dwellers.

However, if the characters remove the *Book of Madness*[VI] from the area, Sarthoggus is not be able to create the last needed incantation for several months. He eventually develops a solution to the lost incantation without the book; removing the artifact from the region only prolongs the timeline.

If the characters eliminate Sarthoggus and leave at least one masked priest alive, the surviving frog-god worshipper takes over Sarthoggus' role as high priest. All priests of the frog-god order must be destroyed to eliminate the threat of war. If no priests survive their battles with the player characters, the demon, hellbender, bullywug, and stone delver minions leave the area.

Dozens of demons signed on as mercenaries to assist Sarthoggus in hopes that the *Book of Madness*[VI] is one of the tomes that have every demon name recorded within. Unfortunately for the planar mercenaries, the artifact is not one of the books they seek. Upon this discovery, the fiends immediately leave the material plane, abandoning the high priest and his evil plan.

CHAPTER 4: RAMPAGING ROOMS

INTRODUCTION

Tegel Manor stands on a flat plateau overlooking the sea and the surrounding lands. With the exception of few clutches of windswept and leafless trees, only the sturdy wooden walls and brick facades of the manor break the harsh winds blowing from the east. The age of the structure is apparent on the first look, and despite the spells that protect it, a few cracks and fallen bricks are already apparent. Strangely enough, most of the narrow windows are still intact.

Inside the manor, the party is free to roam the corridors and rooms as they will. With the exception of a few more out-of-the-way places, there is really no area here that cannot be reached in some way — although not *always* through an apparent one.

RANDOM ENCOUNTERS

Roll a six-sided die to check for random encounters in Tegel Manor. A result of "1" indicates an encounter with a family member. Roll 1d100 and consult the Rump Family Tree (**Appendix I**) for results, treating characters already dispatched as "no encounter." Check for random encounters every 20 minutes while the characters are exploring the manor's labyrinthine passages and spacious rooms. Also roll if they make too much noise or if a melee develops that lasts for more than 6 rounds. Attempting to harm family portraits or statues automatically attracts 1d4 + 1 family members in 2d6 rounds. Secluded spots, including rooms with closed or locked doors, are safe to rest in (roll only once per hour), and so are well-barricaded rooms. If certain very powerful family members — liches or vampires — are looking for the characters (very likely if they do too much damage), don't decrease encounter frequency. Also, these more intelligent NPCs do their best to organize other family members against the party, setting up ambushes and hunting down intruders with massed undead. Under no circumstances will family members "kill" (well, most are already dead) one another.

GENERAL GUIDELINES

Rooms and Doors. The text indicates the general dimensions of each room, including their height. Empty rooms are considered to contain dust, small amounts of fallen debris, probably smashed and unrecognizable furniture (unless, of course, you deem it fit to populate them with creations of your own!). The floors are covered by rough stones or by marble slabs or exotic wood in more exquisite locations such as the Great Hall, the Master Gallery, or the Throne Room. Personal quarters tend to have wooden boards.

Doors are likewise made of sturdy wood, mostly intact despite the passage of time. Most doorways are considered to have doors in them, unless you prefer them not to have one. Secret doors, unless specified otherwise, open by pushing a stone, moving a torch holder, or manipulating a similar fixture nearby. General statistics follow:

Standard Wooden Door. They are 2 inches thick and can be broken with a successful DC 18 Strength check or by doing 18 points of damage against an AC 15. Doors are immune to psychic and poison damage. Locked doors can be opened with a successful DC 18 Dexterity check with thieves' tools unless noted otherwise.

Secret Door. The doors can be found with a successful DC 20 Wisdom (Perception) check. They are 6 inches thick and can be broken with a successful DC 24 Strength check or by doing 30 points of damage against AC 15. Secret doors are immune to poison and psychic damage.

Protective Enchantment. In bygone days, a powerful charm was placed on Tegel Manor to protect it from the ravages of time and human occupation. This ward also includes fire resistance for the manor's timbers. Walls and beams are unharmed by non-magical fire and have a damage threshold of 30 against magical fire damage. They are resistant to damage from non-magical attacks. Note that the protection doesn't extend to the *contents* of the rooms or even their doors. New construction (walled up doorway, etc.) is also fair game. Finally, anyone actually attacking the structural portions of the manor (with axes, fire, etc.) is attacked by the manor itself after 1 minute of such activity. The manor does not defend doors, paintings, or statues in this manner. The manor makes two melee weapon attacks each at +10 to hit, range 10 ft. from any surface of the manor, against one creature. On a hit, it does 16 (3d6 + 6) bludgeoning damage.

Continuous Effects. Rump family members cannot be destroyed or commanded by channel divinity, although they can be turned.

Magic Portraits. Since family history meant so much for the Rumps, it is no wonder they built a veritable temple to their ancestors in the form of an extensive picture gallery. Once space ran out, they put the rest of the pictures in the throne room, and then later, in dining rooms, foyers, private apartments and elsewhere. The whole manor was slowly but surely buried under the weight of half-forgotten memories, traditions, and legends. Over the ages, several portraits have gained a limited consciousness, the personalities of their models manifesting in one way or another.

Portraits are regular-looking oil paintings with a wooden frame and a metal plate bearing the name of the personality depicted. If magical, it is triggered on specific conditions — usually by touching the picture or upon examination. This is described in **Appendix I**.

Harming pictures is a hazardous undertaking. Like the timbers and walls, the portraits benefit from the protective enchantment placed on Tegel Manor, although to a lesser extent. They are resistant to acid, cold, fire, and lightning, and from bludgeoning, piercing, and slashing from non-magical attacks. A portrait has 15 hit points and AC 16. If the characters destroy enough portraits, this results in swift and merciless retribution by Ridwik of the Relic, Count Radu Rumpula, or Rasping Rashuak — after all, these *nobodies* are threatening family legacy!

Statues. As generous patrons of the arts, the Rumps amassed a large statue collection during their glory days. Some statues bear potent spells, others are just decorative. Most statues are described in the room writeups. Those statues not described may be generated randomly using the tables in **Appendix III**. If the PCs destroy enough statues, this results in swift and merciless retribution as described for portraits.

Pits and Traps. In their last decades of doomed decadence, the Rumps constructed well-concealed pits and insidious traps to harm and destroy trespassers. The traps were easy to bypass and neutralize in days of peace with hidden mechanical triggers. Alas, these triggers have mostly been damaged beyond repair or willfully sabotaged.

Pits are 20 feet deep and have hinged lids constructed from material identical to the floor around it. Pits close on their own 50% of the time in 1d6 minutes. Others are too rusted or decayed to function more than once, sending their victim crashing down along with broken bits of wood and metal and inflicting 7 (2d6) bludgeoning damage. A successful DC 18 Wisdom (Perception) check discerns an absence of foot traffic over the section of floor that forms the pit's cover. A successful DC 18 Intelligence (Investigation) check is necessary to confirm that the trapped section of floor is actually the cover of a pit.

Shafts are basically open pit traps and pose little danger to a careful party. Some of them may contain a few interesting odds and ends, a monster, or just the body of a former victim.

Those traps that aren't described in the text of the work may be generated randomly or chosen from the list provided in **Appendix IV**.

Hallowed Hallways. Whether it is the loud banging in the Knocking Hall, the disembodied hands trying to trip intruders on the Spectral Staircase, or the sounds of merrymaking ghosts in the Singing Swordsman hall, the manor's passages are anything but ordinary. The Judge is encouraged to use these noises, apparitions, or smells as a

source of wonderment and distraction for his group — for example, the sobbing in Crying Hall could lead the party into the pit trap at the end, or the mirages of Apparition Hall could warn of real or imaginary dangers.

Rat Holes. Most giant rat holes are 3 feet in diameter and all have a 20% probability of blockage by a rock or cave in. Removing the rock usually requires a successful DC 14 Strength check; digging takes 2d4 x 10 minutes (remember those random encounters?).

A – Servants' Wing

This wing is characterized by spacious dining rooms and kitchens and was once bustling with activity and the quarters of the numerous servants, maids, butlers, and lackeys serving at Tegel Manor. Now it consists of the rotten remains of these things, as well as a few of the servants who have transformed into something less than human. The entrance to **A1** has inlaid brick and cobblestones. Two withered trees and two statues stand guard next to a horse tie station. One statue is of a female Viking warrior, and is nonmagical. The other is of a halfling-headed troll with its arms outstretched. If its left arm is pushed toward the center, it pops its mouth open to reveal a *spell scroll* of *sleep*. Subsequent attempts have a very different effect. A second attempt causes it to open its mouth and cast a *suggestion* spell to "Go Away!" A third attempt causes it to cast *hold person*. The fourth attempt casts *fear*, and the fifth casts *lightning bolt*. The spells require a DC 16 saving throw and are cast at the lowest possible level. The sixth pops a *spell scroll* of *suggestion*, and then the sequence repeats (casts *sleep*, *hold person*, *fear*, *lightning bolt*, *spell scroll* of *hold person*, etc.). Several scrolls could be gained this way; however, remember that wandering monsters apply here, and that the *lightning bolts* are aimed at held characters.

A1. Master Foyer

Beyond the twin statues guarding the path leading to the gravel-paved courtyard, a dire warning greets travelers: three moldering corpses are slumped against the wall by the outside door, possibly former heroes, as they still bear rusty arms and wear torn and rotten leather capes with corroded armor underneath. If the doors are approached, the statue to the west erupts in maniacal and triumphant laughter. The corpses are jerked upward by an unseen force, take a few stumbling steps forward and fall down, lifeless once more.

The arched gates open with a sigh, exhaling staleness and corruption to reveal the first of Tegel Manor's many rooms. A high, vaulted ceiling is supported by six thick, sturdy stone columns. Small holes in the roof above let in beams of light to fall on dust, hardened guano, and the bare stones of the tiled floor. Ten portraits hang on the walls, each covered by thin, wispy cobwebs. Underneath them lie comfortable seating arrangements ready to accommodate anyone and to fall apart immediately in a shower of sawdust and moldy fabric.

After anyone takes a few steps into the foyer, Butler Bertalan, a balor ghost (use the statistics of the **greater ghost**[II], except the balor ghost also has the balor's Fire Aura trait. At the start of each of his turns, he decides if this trait is active or not), appears in front of the party, peering at them through eyes of molten fire. He spends a moment in quiet contemplation and finally asking them politely for their cloaks. If refused (or attacked), he stretches his wings, exhales a stream of soot and sparks, and leaves indignantly through the western wall. Bertalan is among the few creatures in our uncouth and degenerate days who really know his manners, which should be evident to anyone who converses with him. He is knowledgeable but discreet: He gladly tells anyone which direction to go if they are looking for a place

Game Room
A21 Secret Study
A20 Bed Room
A19 Bed Room
A6 Mead Hall
Stale Smell
Bakshon
Maid's Room
A8 Maid's Room
Grand Dining Hall
Mice
Maid's Room
A9 Butler's Room
Mumbling Hall
A5 Master Foyer
A3 Bed Room
Raucous Laughter
Screaming Hall
Bedroom
A2 Room of Fear
Singing Sword enon Hall
A12 Scullery Maid
Growing Hall
A10 Kitchen
A11 Bakery
A1 Great Hall
Scullery Maid
B3 Room
B1 Bedroom
A17 Scullery Maid
A13 Cook's Room
A14 Cook's Room
A16 Scullery Maid
Flanking Hall
Cortage Hall
Laughing Hall

One-way Teleport To
One-way Teleport From
Two-way Teleport
Giant Rat Hole
Magical Statue
Non-magical Statue
Spectral Staircase
30   Numbered Paintings

Curtain or Tapestry
Two-way Secret Door
One-way Secret Door
Covered Pit
Trap Door in Ceiling
Shaft
Large Shaft
Fireplace (shaft)

to sleep, to meet his masters, or to visit the pleasant inner court — just nothing that would compromise the Rumps. Thus, for example, asking about the undead would result in a disapproving glance and something along the lines of "*But sir, I am not aware of these **things** you are inquiring about.*" Bertalan, like all good butlers, is an expert at rationalizing the irrational ("*You said dusty? Certainly, I am afraid the maids must have forgotten about that particular corridor. It will be corrected immediately.*"), dodging allegations ("*By my word, that is a mistake! I have to deny the scurrilous **gossip** that Count Radu is a vampire. No such thing, sir, no such thing.*"), and frustrating any inquisitive questioner.

The large wooden door to the Grand Hall is decorated with a huge carving depicting the Rump coat-of-arms. Riotous laughter and singing may be heard from the other side.

A2. GREAT HALL

As large as a great temple, this hall is a spectacle to behold even in its current state. Thick wooden beams between massive columns support the roof over a chamber that reaches the width of 110 feet from the north to the south and almost one and a half that from the east to the west. Six long tables surrounded by dozens of chairs fill the room in between. Two large fireplaces have benches in front of them for those who wish to warm their bones by the fire — if they don't mind that it went out many years ago. Chandeliers with extinguished candles hang on long iron chains, hardened streams of wax frozen in midair.

Twelve **skeletons** (with AC 17 from chain shirt and shield and no bow) sit by one of the long tables, singing, banging on their shields, dancing on tables, and raising silver goblets in grotesque toasts. Upon seeing intruders, they draw blades and attack. The skeletons wear the uniforms of men-at-arms. The 30 goblets are worth 12 gp each.

Useless and rusty trophies won in forgotten battles hang on the walls: swords, maces, daggers and polearms, chainmail, rotted leather and shields. The crown of this collection, a 30-foot-long halberd, hangs on the western wall. A large marble plaque reading "The Halbard of Broll" [sic] hangs under the immense weapon. The plaque below the halberd conceals a hidden compartment with a lever. The compartment may be found with a successful DC 19 Intelligence (Investigation) check. Pulling the lever teleports everyone in a 20-foot range to **DL1B** (a room in the rat tunnels between the twin levels of the Southwest Wing!). The teleport is one way.

On the eastern wall, a moldy, 110-foot-long embroidered tapestry decays in silence. The tapestry depicts the ancient history of the Rumps — incorrectly, with lots of slain dragons and not that many pirates, assassins, and robber barons. The tapestry and the southern fireplace conceal a total of three badly hidden secret doors (Search DC 12).

One of the statues by the southern exit (an older gentleman) nods almost imperceptibly as someone passes it. If this character fails to stop and examine the statue, it shouts, "*Did you know that 'if' is the middle word in life?*" as soon as the character moves more than 60 feet away from it. It does this only once per week.

A3. BEDROOM

This was once the room of a servant, perhaps a footman or a maid. The furnishings remain, and are humble if functional looking. Although still soft and comfortable, the furnishings are decayed and have a musty smell. Enchanted rose petals covering the bed crumble to dust if touched. Anyone within 5 feet of the petals when one crumbles must succeed on a DC 14 Constitution saving throw against poison or fall into a slumber lasting 1d6 minutes. A bejeweled sword (380 gp) hangs on the northern wall in a decorative scabbard. Six **stirges** have made a nest in the rafters. These nasty bloodsuckers prefer to prey on sleeping or isolated characters, draining their blood to sate their hunger, and do not attack unless fewer than 3 awake Medium-sized creatures are in the room.

A4. GRAND DINING ROOM

A large wooden table set with tarnished silverware, a motheaten tablecloth, and burning candles bears remains of food and dishes, platters of bones, and cracked crystal goblets. As the players enter, 16 ghostly figures seated around the table disappear, fading back into oblivion.

The fireplace hides a metal lockbox under a large heap of ash with 560 gp in assorted gems and 450 sp. The box may be found with a successful DC 18 Intelligence (Investigation) check. A **specter** in the form of an older gentleman remains asleep, mumbling softly to himself in a comfortable chair by the hearth. If the fireplace is disturbed or if the intruders make too much noise, he attacks.

Hundreds of mice have taken up a nest in the southern pantry storage. They explode in a tidal wave (harmless) if the door is opened.

A5. KITCHEN

Twin fireplaces (one is a bread oven) identify this as a kitchen. Seemingly still in use, the knives, pots, and platters in the kitchen are in meticulous order. A large pot of soup boils over the southern fireplace. Small jars with spices and herbs stand on a long counter by the south wall.

Five butcher knives (as **animated swords** but doing 4 [1d4 + 2] slashing damage on a hit) animate and fly at intruders. The boiling pot flies off the stove and hurls itself at the largest party member. The target must make a DC 15 Dexterity saving throw, taking 10 (3d6) bludgeoning damage on a failure or half as much on a success. Six **giant rats** pour forth from the western room, maddened by feral hunger. A locked cabinet holds 10 silver platters worth 36 gp each. The lock can be opened with a successful DC 14 Dexterity check with thieves' tools. The rat tunnel in the back room leads to **Dungeon Level 1**.

A6. MEAD HALL

From the hallway, raucous singing can be heard coming from this room. This emanates from the zombies (see below).

A strange cackling sound can be heard coming from the northwest corner of the hall (see the trap description below).

This drinking hall is overrun by two **swarms of insects** (spiders) and delicate cobwebs hang in thin sheets from the blackened beams, cover the fireplace, and coat the colorful flags taken in many battles and the six corroded suits of full plate armor standing guard. These webs make the area difficult terrain. The inlaid wooden floor creaks under the steps of intruders. Six **zombies** (with great clubs, +3 to hit, *hit:* 2d6 + 1 bludgeoning damage), loudly singing drinking songs and clad in mold-covered liveries, stand over a dead rat to the north, thumping on it with large sledgehammers.

The spiders lurk in the webs among the beams. They jump down on the backs of characters, preferring Small targets. The zombies are so absorbed in their gruesome activity that they don't join the fray until the party gets within 20 feet. Setting the webs aflame causes 2d4 points of damage to all caught within.

All but one of the corroded suits of plate armor are worthless, although the colored flags are not. Each of the flags is woven of fine gold and silver, interspersed with cloth thread. Each is worth 100 gp intact, and only 5 gp each if the webs are burned.

The plate armor on the southeast wall is enchanted. While it appears to be old and rusted, it is in fact *+1 plate mail of ugliness*. This armor functions as normal *+1 plate*, but the wearer has disadvantage on all Charisma checks while it is worn.

The secret door behind the plate mail on the west wall can be found with a successful DC 19 Wisdom (Perception) check and opens by pushing a loose brick on the fireplace. The loose brick may be found by explicitly pressing on them, or a successful DC 20 Intelligence

(Investigation) check. Failure to locate the mechanism means a knock spell or some other magical means must be used to open it.

The fireplace itself has a permanent fire inside (illusory), and no wood or fireplace implements are present. Two loose bricks at the edge of the mantel push inward to open and close the secret door. The brick on the right (facing the fireplace) is currently slightly depressed (closed). Pushing the brick on the left opens the door, returning the right brick to its position flush with the rest of the mantelpiece. The illusory fire radiates heat, but is itself not flame, as is evidenced by the myriad of webs present within the "flames." To the west of the fireplace is a horrible trap.

A stuffed teddy bear lies abandoned next to the fireplace. Careful examination notes that it is not web-covered, and that not even zombie footprints are near it. This bear is a trap. If touched, it becomes apparent that the bear is the source of the cackling, as it transforms into an **Annis Hag**[II] in one round! The hag attacks until slain, then returns to teddy bear form. The summoning trap functions once per week, and the teddy bear is nearly indestructible (immune to elements, has 200 hp and resistance to bludgeoning, slashing, and piercing damage).

A7. MAID'S ROOM

Humble furnishings including a bed, a smashed dresser, and a rack of maid's clothing identify this as a servant's quarters. A broom, feather duster, and dustpan hang on the wall. The bedding is rotten and covered with bloodstained clothing. Hidden in the bedding is a pearl brooch (140 gp) with a silver stickpin.

Characters with sharp ears and a successful DC 14 Wisdom (Perception) check may pick up almost inaudible sighs. The noise becomes normal breathing in 1d3 rounds and the walls quiver. A loud panting begins 1d3 rounds later as the walls start to move in and out 2 feet. After an additional 1d3 rounds, the breathing noise becomes deafening, with the movement of the walls increasing to 10 feet. Finally, after another 1d3 rounds elapse, it becomes so unbearable that characters take 4 (1d8) force damage and have to succeed on a DC 17 Constitution saving throw or be stunned for 1d6 rounds. Stunned characters are in for a world of trouble; in another 1d8 rounds, the walls slam together and suffocate all inside the room, crushing the bed and the chest, as well as any items excluding thick metal bars and the like. Creatures caught in this final crushing blow die.

A8. MAID'S ROOM

This room contains humble furnishings that include a bed, a dresser, an iron and ironing board, and a small locked trunk. The bedding appears to be strangely clean and free of dust and detritus. It is perfectly made. The dresser contains several sets of perfectly folded sheets and pillowcases (5 gp). The bed appears intact but collapses under any amount of weight. The trunk is locked and trapped with a poison needle hidden in its latch. It contains 1,080 cp, 10 sp, 2 gp and an opal necklace (580 gp). Finding the trap requires a successful DC 17 Intelligence (Investigation) check and can be disabled with a successful DC 17 Dexterity check with thieves' tools. The lock can be picked with a successful DC 17 Dexterity check with thieves' tools. If the lock is opened before the trap is disabled, or if the check to disable the trap fails by 5 or more, the trap is triggered. When triggered, the needle makes a ranged attack at +10 to hit one target within 5 feet. On a hit, the target takes 1 piercing damage and must succeed on a DC 16 Constitution saving throw or take 10 (3d6) poison damage and be paralyzed for 2d6 x 10 rounds. A paralyzed creature takes 10 (3d6) poison damage at the start of its turn and may attempt the saving throw at the end of its turn, ending the effects on a success.

Every 20 minutes, a ghostly young girl wearing a maid's clothes appears in a random corner of the room, screams in mortal terror, and disappears. There is no game effect from this, other than to make the players nervous.

A9. BUTLER'S ROOM

This room is more lavishly furnished than most of the other bedrooms in this wing. The entire room is immaculately clean and neat. Furniture consists of a bed with perfectly made bedding (square corners and everything), a 10-foot-tall wardrobe, and a desk covered with wine bottles, a decanting set, and cheesecloth.

A large, thick red rug with a greenish, oily puddle in the middle (**green slime**[II]!) covers the floor of this room. A **severed hand**[II] crawls on the sheets and scampers for cover if someone attempts to catch it. It deftly avoids the green slime.

The wardrobe contains seven balor-sized tuxedos, six giant-sized sets of wingtip shoes, and a large cloak. The wine bottles on the desk are of fine vintage (5 bottles worth 10 gp each). The decanting set is crystal and worth 40 gp.

A backpack with 180 gp, 55 sp, 225 cp and a small assortment of miscellaneous items seemingly collected in a hurry hangs from a peg on the wall, just by a clean and intact livery.

The adjacent room (with a fireplace), while not connected to the butler's chambers, was used as a wine storage room. Within it are several hundred empty wine bottles and kegs, as well as a few full ones. Six of the bottles are old vintage and still good (10 gp each); however, one (randomly determined) is poisoned (DC 14 Constitution saving throw or die). The rat tunnel leads to **Dungeon Level 1**.

A10. KITCHEN

A surreal scene greets anyone entering the kitchen. Fifteen fine ceramic plates (Tiny paraphernalia **animated objects**[II]) float in the air, lazily drifting across the room. Three jars (Tiny paraphernalia **animated objects**[II]) spin around an empty, gently swaying rocking chair. Unwashed dishes, including frying pans and a large covered soup bowl made of silver, lie in a basin of brackish, filthy water.

The three jars and the 15 plates are animated objects. They hurl themselves at the party as soon as they enter. Since they are fragile, a hit or a miss both indicate they deal damage to themselves as well! The silver soup bowl is worth 200 gp if cleaned. If someone shakes it before opening, angry thrashing and hissing is heard from the inside. The bowl contains spoiled, oily soup and three furious cottonmouth snakes (as **poisonous snake**).

A11. BAKERY

This room contains rolling pins, old, moldy sacks of flour, large mixing bowls and spoons, and is obviously a bakery. Howling winds and monstrous growling may be heard from the chimney above the large oven. A **giant stag beetle**[II] has wandered inside the bakery and lives in the large chimney. It is feasting peacefully on a rotted table.

On a simple examination, the characters uncover an upturned pot weighted down with heavy stones. Hissing breathing is audible. A **flying skull**[II] is trapped under the pot. Upon its release, it takes to the air, cackles maniacally, breathes a shower of sparks on the party, and flies away (up the chimney), still cackling.

A strange clanking sound (metal on metal) can be heard outside the southern door. The source of this is unknown (though it could be a wandering monster). The secret door in the hallway leads to a 3-foot-wide secret entrance to second story M areas of the manor. The secret door is detected with a successful DC 19 Intelligence (Investigation) check and is opened by poking a series of nail heads (2, 3, 5, 7, 11, 13, 17, and 19) out of the 21 nails in the boards on the wall. All the prime number nail heads must be pushed in to open the door.

The rat tunnel leads to **Dungeon Level 1**.

A12. Scullery Maid

This room, or rather series of rooms, used to house the scullery maids (lower tier, junior level maids). Each room in the dormitory complex contains a simple bed, a chamber pot, clothing, and implements of "maid destruction" such as brooms, mops, and dusters. The entire complex is a mess. Everything looks like a tornado hit it. Sheets and clothes are strewn about; dust and garbage are everywhere. In the center of the main room is a large wooden chest. It seems to be untouched by the rest of the chaos.

The lid of the chest has a hidden compartment that contains a golden whistle. The compartment can be found with a successful DC 20 Intelligence (Investigation) check. The whistle, while worth 70 gp in itself for its delicate craftsmanship, is magical, enabling its user to control statues depicting dogs (such as the giant foo dog in the vestibule [area **Q6**]). A tiny inscription engraved on the whistle reads, *"Canis Minor Movens."*

A13. Scullery Maid

These are the quarters of the head maid. As opposed to the rooms across the hall, this room is well kept and orderly. It contains a bed, a dresser, and a small table with a single chair, upon which sit a dozen neatly folded napkins. The closets to the east of the room contain shelves of fine linens and clothing. Against the south wall is a 10-foot-wide mirror.

The mirror seems to emit a faint breeze. If the mirror is touched, the head of a monstrous **purple worm** emerges from whatever netherworld to which the mirror leads. The purple worm is too large to exit the room, but it can attack anyone inside (plus its roars may attract monsters.) Fortunately, there isn't enough room to use its stinger. Destroying the mirror requires *dispel magic* cast successfully against a 6th-level spell, although a *banish* spell sends the purple worm back whence it came.

Hidden in the closet linens is a lead-lined, 5-foot-long wooden fishing rod case. Inside is a rather strange looking rod and reel that is somehow just too thick for a fishing rod. This item is equivalent to a *staff of frost*.

One of the closets has a pair of secret doors leading to the head maid's very dangerous private rooms beyond. The doors can be found with a successful DC 19 Wisdom (Perception) check. This is where the maid herself still resides. Also note that the rat tunnel in the maid's private quarters leads to **Dungeon Level 1**.

The maid, once a witch who controlled the lesser maids through witchcraft, has been transformed into a **pennagalen**[II]. The back rooms are meticulously kept, and upon entrance, a strange, old woman can be seen sweeping the area with a broom and muttering quietly to herself. She appears to be an ancient crone with withered limbs and a hunched back. Her skin is creased with age and she is nearly toothless, at least in a literal sense. She is dressed in a pink cloak and wears white slippers.

If approached or spoken to, she appears confused, and mutters strange words and random phrases at those she encounters. She asks strange questions such as *"What color is the sky?"* and *"Why do the birds eat worms?"* After 30 seconds or so, she gets frustrated and becomes upset and even more confused. After 1 minute, she falls to the ground weeping, then explodes in a fountain of blood.

Out of this rises her head and entrails separated from the rest of her body, leaving the lifeless husk of her torso and limbs on the ground. She flies around the room attacking until slain. She does not follow anyone who passes through the secret door and leaves the area. The corpse portion of the body wears a gold brooch worth 200 gp inlaid with mother of pearl in the shape of a cat.

Bear Trap

Bear Trap. Discovering the trap without setting it off requires a successful DC 20 Intelligence (Investigation) check. Failing the check by 5 or more while looking through the detritus triggers the trap. A creature that steps on the plate or otherwise triggers it must succeed on a DC 14 Dexterity saving throw or take 7 (2d6) piercing damage and stop moving. Thereafter, until the creature breaks free of the trap, its movement is limited by a 3-foot length of chain securing the trap to the floor. A creature can use its action to make a DC 14 Strength check to free itself or another creature within its reach on a success. Each failed check deals 1 piercing damage to the trapped creature.

A14. Cook's Room

Fresh bloodstains dot the beds, the floor, the walls, and the doors. Laughter grows in intensity while the party is in the room, culminating in a hysterical crescendo followed by gurgling noises and gasps for air. A shelf above the simple bed holds a candle that lights itself when the party approaches, and a zircon signet ring worth 150 gp that also has a hidden chamber with one dose of an ingestible poison. The secret compartment can be found with a successful DC 18 Intelligence (Investigation) check. A creature that consumes the poison must succeed on a DC 18 Constitution saving throw or take 22 (4d10) poison damage and be poisoned for one hour. A broom in the southeast corner is animated by otherworldly forces. It slams its handle into the gut of the first character entering the room and immediately falls back on the floor lifeless.

Broom. *Melee Weapon Attack:* +8 to hit, one creature within 5 ft. *Hit:* 7 (1d6 + 4) bludgeoning damage.

The room to the north is filled with detritus that is two feet deep. Beneath this is a bear trap that is almost impossible to detect due to the piles of junk in the room.

A15. Cook's Room

This appears to be a simple bedroom. Hanging on the wall above a bed is a glinting and sharp-looking scimitar. This is a *+1 scimitar* that the chef who lived in the room used for chopping meat. It possesses a simple intellect and a LE alignment, and has Intelligence 7, Wisdom 9, and Charisma 8. The weapon communicates by limited telepathy, usually broadcasting such thoughts as *"Kill ... kill ... killlll ..."*

A pair of shiny black boots (Tiny paraphernalia **animated object**[II]) lies under the table. They are animated and follow intruders around like a happy puppy, stamping angrily if their "companions" dally around too much. In combat, however, they get underfoot, tripping and kicking. Lurking under a chair (having previously chased the boots) is a **killer shrew**[II]. This miniature but tough little murderer leaps on the backs of small characters, going straight for the jugular. He lives here and hunts rats as the rat tunnel leading to **Dungeon Level 1** is full of food.

A16. Scullery Maid

This is another simply adorned maid's room that contains a bed, a wardrobe, and a small table. Sleeping in the bed (well, not really sleeping) is a beautiful **zombie** in a maid's outfit. It attacks mindlessly if disturbed.

On the table, a teacup covered by a rotting napkin is full of white crystalline powder (*dust of appearance*[VI], 4 doses).

A17. Scullery Maid

A strange growling noise can be heard from this room before characters open the door. This room also appears to be a maid's room. It contains a bed and a sewing table and has a stack of tapestries in one corner. A cobweb-covered silver cross (estimated value 180 gp — it's a large one) hangs on the east wall. Blood covers the floor in distinct footprints leading through the room complex toward the Minor Gallery (**A18**) and up to the Bedroom (**A19**). They disappear into a wall at the secret door (making it very easy to find). The door can be opened by spinning it centrally. A catch can be located by pushing on the wooden planks along the wall next to the door.

Every 40 minutes, a screaming, bloody, and obviously mortally wounded woman in a thin white gown, holding a leather bag, runs across the room screaming. She is either headed to the Bedroom (**A19**) or coming back from there. Any interaction short of simply ignoring her causes her to fly into a rage and attack intruders. She is a **bloody bones**[II].

A18. Minor Gallery

This corridor is the northern terminus of the hall housing the Rump family portraits. The venerable old-timers are biding their time here chatting and frightening the occasional outsider, oblivious to the illusory inferno that envelops the place with its heatless flames every 50 minutes. Comfortable armchairs line the portrait gallery. The floor is made of exotic inlaid wood, the endless rows of geometric patterns broken by the occasional historical scene. Iron chandeliers provide illumination. A female **wraith** chops meat with a *+1 dagger* on a small round table; this bloody bit is a human arm, still fresh! The young fellow it belonged to may still be found on the bottom of the pit to the north, sans his arm, of course. Apart from a leather vest, a short sword and the silver locket he wears around his neck (the painted portrait of a woman is inside it — quite similar to the she-wraith!), he has no valuables. With a successful DC 21 Wisdom (Perception) check, characters thoroughly examining the gallery may catch a glimpse of something glinting up among the supporting beams. This item is a *potion of greater healing*.

To the south, a staircase leads up to the playroom. A statue of a creepy clown with a nameplate that reads "Pennywise" rests in the corner of the stairs at the bottom.

A19. Bedroom

Once a lavish bedroom, this area now appears to be all chewed up and nested in. Just by the rat hole leading downstairs to **Dungeon Level 1** lies a huge pile of gnawed bones and offal. The bones are mostly from rats. There is an 80% chance of encountering 2d6 **giant rats** here. In the southwest corner of the room is an invisible suit of *Rump armor*. The armor becomes visible when worn. The rat tunnel leads to **Dungeon Level 1**

> ## Rump armor
>
> *Armor (plate), vettry rare*
>
> This suit of *+1 plate armor* bears the name of Ribbonsor Rump the Rider, a famed jousting champion, etched into the insides of the greaves. When riding a horse, you cannot be unseated or fall off a steed while wearing this armor.

A20. Bedroom

This room is covered in red: drapes, rugs, the bedsheets on the canopied and curtained bed, even the walls and the thin layer of dust on the floor. This red is broken by a huge silver shield mounted with the Rump coat-of-arms (value 250 gp).

A beautiful woman lies in the bed. Her hair is unkempt but her bright yellow skin is unmarred and beautiful. She signals the party by ringing a bell. If they approach the bed and pull apart the curtains, she motions with her hand, beckoning them closer. She doesn't speak but tries to communicate in sign language. Occasionally, she produces a small comb and tries to rearrange her wild hair. This activity stirs up a cloud of the yellow dust, which falls in an endless supply from her head. The woman is an animated colony of deadly **yellow mold**[II], and she is stirring up her spores to infect and destroy the characters. Fortunately, much of the stuff is inert, only the fresh yield being effective. The poisonous effects of the spores are noticeable in 2d4 rounds. A single point of damage destroys the woman, blowing her into a 20-foot-diameter deadly spore cloud.

Three closets are present to the east. The southern closet is full of old, musty, and worthless clothing and contains a secret door to the Mead Hall (see **A6** for details) that can be opened just by pushing on it from this side. The center closet contains 12 empty buckets that appear to be stained with blood. They are neatly stacked in sets of 6, and the bottom bucket in one stack contains a mummified human hand wearing a *ring of warmth*. The closet to the north is locked and trapped with a scything blade that swings out toward the room at a 4-foot-high arc when the door is opened. The trap can be noted with a successful DC 15 Intelligence (Investigation) check and disabled with a successful DC 17 Dexterity check with thieves' tools. The lock opens with a successful DC 19 Dexterity check with thieves' tools. If the trap is triggered, all creatures within 5 feet of the door must succeed on a DC 17 Dexterity saving throw or take 14 (1d8 + 8) slashing damage. This closet leads to a long hallway containing areas **A21**, **A22**, and the entrance to the Brothers Tower.

The secret door in the hallway that accesses area **A21** requires a successful DC 23 Wisdom (Perception) check to find and is *arcane locked*.

A21. Secret Study

This room appears to be an alchemist's laboratory. Shelves of old books and scrolls line the walls, and laboratory equipment is piled on tables throughout the room. The northeast corner has a round, white stone disc 6 feet in diameter. A button is on the wall near this disc. Anyone on the disc when the button is pushed teleports to area **E9**.

Faint, chaotic organ music permeates the room, creating an atmosphere of unease. This uncertain, almost inaudible sound is mixed with a regular buzzing noise from the northeast corner that seemingly rises out of thin air (or, more accurately, the arrival position of the teleport from **E9**).

In addition to the alchemy gear (worth 500 gp) are several items of interest. The first is right there on a reading podium: the *Ordinal of Alchemy*, a heavy leather-bound tome containing parchment pages of

ORDINAL OF ALCHEMY

This tome of knowledge gives its reader a +2 bonus to Intelligence (Arcana) checks made to understand or create alchemical substances for as long as it is available for consultation. An interested character may learn how to make the following concoctions. The DC listed after the substance is for an Intelligence (Arcana) check to create the substance.

Necrotic Dust (DC 20): Requires incense worth 50 gp per dose mixed with mummy dust. Once sprinkled on corpses, it animates them as zombies as per *animate dead*. Each dose is good for one hit die worth of undead.

Blade Venom (DC 18): A creature who takes piercing or slashing damage from a weapon coated with this poison must succeed on a DC 18 Constitution saving throw or be poisoned. While poisoned, a creature takes 7 (2d6) poison damage each round. A poisoned creature may repeat the saving at the end of each of its turns, ending the effect on a success. Cost: 200 gp.

The Great Transformation (DC 20): Using this formula, an alchemist can convert up to 1,000 cp to 1,000 gp with a dose of basilisk powder. Note that the extraction of the powder itself requires a reasonably intact basilisk. A single specimen yields 1d6 doses. If cockatrice is substituted, the DC is 24 and 1d10 x 10% of coins are defective.

TABULA SMARAGDIANA

This small folio is a potent tool in dealing with "enchanted" monsters, including most constructs, fiends, and elementals summoned by spells or magic items. A character may recite aloud from its passages to force said monsters to roll a Wisdom saving throw. The DC for the save is 10 + character's Charisma modifier. A creature that fails its saving throw must flee from the character's sight. The effects are generally identical to turning undead, and last for as long as the character is reciting. If the creature succeeds at the save, it is immune to the book's effects for 24 hours.

alchemical symbols, equations and arcane diagrams — a treasure trove of eldritch recipes. The second is a metal tube propped against smaller volumes. It contains a sealed *spell scroll* with *antimagic field* and *geas* penned by the wizard Rasping Rashuak, as should be evident from the old, blocky letters on the sealing wax. Breaking the seal without first speaking the name of Rashuak releases a curse. If the character who opens the scroll fails a DC 17 Wisdom saving throw, the character can speak only in a rasping whisper until the curse is removed. There is a 20% chance that any spell cast by this character that has a verbal component fails. The third item is a seemingly regular folio closed by a miniature lock (stuck, but may be removed with a single snap): the *Tabula Smaragdiana*, prized by conjurers for its use in the dismissal of hostile summoned monsters.

A22. GAME ROOM

This room appears to be some sort of living room mixed with a casino and bowling alley. An organ by the west wall plays wild music constantly, its levers pounded by an unseen force. The only things visible are two old slippers working the pedals. In addition to the musical talents of the mysterious maestro, the Game Room provides many means of entertainment.

A small bowling alley is occupied by a disproportionately large, 2-foot-diameter bowling ball (Tiny paraphernalia **animated object**[II]) that tries to roll over approaching characters, upturning and crushing furniture just to get them.

A card table in the middle of the room is full of scattered and torn playing cards and spare change (14 cp). A ghostly hand deals three cards to each character present. A single assembled deck (*deck of many things*) sits at the head of the table.

The room contains various board games, games of chance, and other means of tabletop entertainment as well as dice, cards, and a roulette wheel. Spinning the roulette results in a small black vertigo above the table, from which 4 shrieking **shadows** emerge, attacking in a frenzy.

The corner by the rat hole, conveniently separated by a wooden folding screen painted with bright and gaudy colors, is full of children's toys, including a wooden toybox with a *bag of tricks* (green) hidden under an assortment of wooden building blocks.

The rat tunnel leads to **Dungeon Level 1**.

B – SOUTHWEST WING, FIRST STORY

This wing of the manor was used by the family. In fact, Ruang the Ripper, one of the few "living" family members, maintains a hideout beyond the southeastern secret door. He sleeps in room **B12** by day and prepares poisons in the Secret Laboratory (**B16**) by night.

B1. RED ROOM

Red wall coverings and bedsheets, as well as a woven wool red carpet (200 gp), adorn this chamber. A crimson skull facing the door lies on a large, wooden chest. It asks an endless stream of questions from the party, but answers none itself. It sprouts wings and flies away if disturbed or if it goes unanswered for too long. If opened, the chest emits a loud gong, the doors slam shut, and a spectral skull rises and casts *gust of wind* (spell save DC 16) in the room.

B2. NANNY'S ROOM

This appears to be another servant's room. It contains a simple bed with nursery rhyme patterns sewn into the old, moth-eaten quilt, a cradle, and a small table and chair set consisting of three chairs, two of which are child-sized. Finally, a large, lit fireplace warms and illuminates the room.

The flames change color every two minutes. Blue flames heal 2 (1d4) hp per round of contact, red causes 3 (1d6) fire damage, orange absorbs magic from characters touching it, erasing prepared spells first, highest to lowest level (all spells of a level are gone in one round), thereafter moving on to potions, scrolls, and other magic items, one per round. Finally, yellow flames don't affect flesh but are otherwise intense enough to melt steel plate. Molten metal causes 7 (2d6) fire damage every round until removed. An iron ladder in the chimney leads up to the playroom. A soft lullaby from the southwest corner nearest to the cradle is a *sleep* spell (with a 1st-level spell slot) cast every 40 minutes.

Giggling Hall
B2 Nanny's Room
B1 Bedroom
Scullery Maid
B3 Corner Gallery
A16 Scullery Maid
Storeroom
B6 Bedroom
Playroom
Second Story
B20 Playroom
Altar Nook
B7
Scampering
Thunderclap
B19 Bedroom
B8 Bedroom
B18 Bedroom
B9 Bedroom
Master Gallery
B10 Trophy Room
B4
B17 Bedroom
B11 Butler's Room
B15 Armory
B12 Butler's Room
B16 Laboratory
B13 Bedroom
B14 Bedroom
KEY
Curtain or Tapestry
Two-way Secret Door
One-way Secret Door
Covered Pit
Trap Door in Ceiling
Shaft
Large Shaft
Fireplace (shaft)
Trap
One-way Teleport To
One-way Teleport From
Two-way Teleport
Giant Rat Hole
Magical Statue
Non-magical Statue
Spectral Staircase
30 Numbered Paintings

B3. Corner Gallery

Dozens of mice inhabit this hallway, creating a strange, scampering sound in certain areas. Four portraits hang in the low arched passage connecting the minor and master galleries. These paintings are blackened by some kind of moldy decay. A corroded suit of full plate stands in the corner of the stairs leading up to the playroom. The armor falls apart on a mere touch with a loud clang, releasing its heavy iron mace and large metal shield. A **giant water bug**[II] crawls on the wall. It is harmless as long as it is left alone.

B4. Master Gallery

Candles light the way for the party as they venture forth into the master gallery. They automatically go out 20 feet behind them. This hallowed hall has seen better days. A layer of dead insects covers the onyx-inlaid floor tiles and crunches underfoot. Thick sheets of cobwebs hang from the ceiling every 60 feet. Piles of gnawed human and canine bones lie by the walls here and there including an impressive pile in an otherwise empty side room. A **swarm of insects** (spiders) still bide their time among the webs of the ceiling, dropping on careless characters. They cry out in childlike human voices as they approach. Setting the huge amounts of webbing aflame destroys the spiders and does 10 (4d4) fire damage to all others and draws the ire of the portraits hanging on the walls. They hurl insults at the party and summon the guards to "remove this rabble." In 2d6 rounds, 1d4+1 family members (see **Appendix I**) arrive to investigate the commotion. If Ruang the Ripper is in his room, he also learns of the characters and prepares to get them, one way or another.

B5. Storeroom

Dozens of large urns lie in rows in this room. Ten large glass urns contain monsters preserved in stale oil. The monsters include a baby bulette, two orcs, a five-headed hydra, three bugbears, a scorpion, and two apes. These ten are identical and 5 feet in size. The rest of the urns are of varying size and hold anything from pickled olives to wine or honey. A short trail of 5 cp on the floor leads to three piled jars of blood. A quiver holding 30 arrows hangs from a peg in the wall, in the company of four hatchets, a rusty rapier, and an empty leather bag. Finally, a fat ceramic crock in the northwest corner is full of **gray ooze**, still alive and hungry.

B6. Bedroom

This side chamber is a larder for the monstrous spiders in the master gallery. Two dead gnomes in cocoons hang from the ceiling. The door opens and slams shut every 30 minutes. Apart from the gnomes, only a double bed and a dresser are found here.

B7. Altar Nook

Thin, crudely engraved copper sheets hang in two rows from the walls, supplemented by the odd flint-tipped spear and primitive wooden shield. The crown jewel of this collection is the copper griffon idol standing in the northern recess, flanked by two large drums, and a collection of large, man-sized reed baskets. Three copper masks lie on a marble sacrificial stone, with recognizable animal features: a falcon, a tiger, and a wolf. If the idol is approached, invisible hands beat on the drums, increasing their pace as the intruders draw closer and closer — stopping abruptly just as one of them steps into the recess. The idol is worth 1,000 gp to a collector. The masks are worth 10–15 gp each.

Their loathsome nature becomes apparent upon a cursory examination: wicked hooks on the insides are intended to tear into human flesh, thus affixing them to one's face permanently (and requiring a *remove curse* spell to remove).

B8. Bedroom

A 20-foot-by-10-foot oil painting on the south wall depicts a living battle scene. Horses charge and stumble, halberdiers advance toward a squadron of mace-wielding knights, trumpets blare, and banners fall. A company of archers launches volley after volley at the knights. An arrow flies out of the picture every 4 rounds, making an attack at +6 to hit against a random target within the room. On a hit, the arrow does 3 (1d6) piercing damage. Obviously, arrows are stuck everywhere in the room.

B9. Bedroom

This room appears to be a mix of a bedroom and some sort of bizarre trophy room. In addition to a rotted bed and old, moldy clothing, several poor taxidermy specimens are strewn randomly about, including a giant ant, two giant lizards, the head of a dire wolf, and assorted smaller beasts. The dire wolf's head has a copper nose-ring: a *ring of animal influence*, but the head makes a single bite against anyone examining it.

Bite. *Melee Weapon Attack:* +5 to hit, one creature within 5 ft. *Hit:* 7 (1d8 + 3) piercing damage.

B10. Trophy Room

With the protective spell over Tegel Manor fading, the weather and time have begun to take their toll here. A huge metal shield and a two-headed axe of a giant rust peacefully on the wall. The skeleton of what might have been a giant snake lies coiled in the northwest corner (an impressive specimen, too — twice as thick as a human leg, with corresponding length). A petrified dwarf brandishing a warhammer has had his head knocked off. The head lies on the floor, with a shiny, metal dagger hilt protruding from it. The *+1 dagger* can be removed with a successful DC 16 Strength check. An iron holy symbol of Thor still hangs around his neck, unaffected by the basilisk that claimed this cleric's life — but not by rust, which has turned it brittle and useless.

A 10-foot-diameter glass bowl holds a strangely preserved giant octopus. Anyone examining the bowl within 5 feet is attacked by 1d3 tentacles of the **giant octopus zombie**[II].

A large rug in the northern portion of the room seems to undulate slightly if approached. It also appears to have something in it. If uncovered or disturbed, 2 **giant bombardier beetles**[II] emerge and attack.

B11. Butler's Room

This is a bedroom of one of the lesser butlers in training. It contains a bed, a neatly stacked set of old papers that turn to dust if touched (they are bills related to kitchen wares, etc.), a wardrobe containing butler suits, and 4 **giant rats**, and a mold-covered corpse of the room's former occupant. The mold completely covers the head and face of the corpse except for its white skullet hair that pokes through the green fungi.

The mold and the dead butler pose no hazard. The rat tunnel leads to **Dungeon Level 1**.

B12. Butler's Room

The former room of the head butler, this place has been converted into the hideout of **Ruang Rump the Ripper**[I]. In fact, there is a 70% chance during the day that he is around here *somewhere*, no doubt aware of the party and well prepared.

This room appears recently used and "occupied." A small table contains freshly eaten remains of a chicken. The wood fireplace is warm and contains coals, and a small keg of ale stands next to the bed, which has clean sheets and covers.

On a shelf are 6 small bottles labeled "healing," "invisibility," "control undead," "invulnerability," "flying," and "extra healing." Each is actually a deadly poison brewed by Ruang, and disguised to look like the potion in question. The switch can be determined with a successful DC 20 Intelligence (Arcana) check or by casting *detect magic* or *identify* (since they are not magical). A creature who drinks one of the vials must succeed on a DC 17 Constitution saving throw or instantly be brought to 0 hit points.

The bed is simple but intact and clean. The left foot bedpost contains a secret compartment containing 400 gp, a small key (see area **B14**) and a real *potion of invisibility*. The compartment can be found with a successful DC 18 Intelligence (Investigation) check.

Ruang's retreat is not without its own haunting. A burst of screams and choking noises comes from the fireplace. Unfastened helmets and hats float up to the ceiling. Climbing up the chimney, characters can also enter the Wolves Run through a less known way — emerging in the Seance Room (**M10**).

A pile of papers lies on the table. Each appears to be a contract between Ruang and himself, with gold piece rewards for a successful assassination of several people (he is delusional, of course). Names appearing and the gold rewards are: Ternelmor, 200 gp; Sir Runic Rump, 100 gp; Ridwik the Relic, 500 gp; Arnthora, the priestess of Thor, 1,000 gp; Sarthoggus, 5,000 gp; and at the end of the list in large, carefully penned letters, the Invincible Overlord, 1 gp.

B13. Bedroom

This room was once a bedroom, but now just smells like a fetid swamp. The roof has leaked here, and puddles of algae and water have rotted everything away, except for a single bedpost that stands upright and untouched. Mushrooms and toadstools cover everything organic in the room. A **swarm of tiny green frogs**[II] swarm on the rotting carpet of this bedroom. A single **giant frog** has regurgitated three partially eaten dead rats for the tiny frogs to eat. The frog doesn't attack unless provoked. Four thin perfume vials (25 gp each) sit on a small round table, untouched by the mold.

A secret door leads to a 3-foot-wide corridor running to the west. The secret door opens by pulling on the intact bedpost (as a lever). It is made of copper, not wood.

B14. Bedroom

The ominous portrait of Ruang the Ripper hangs on the walls of this otherwise unremarkable bedroom. Its eyes seem to follow intruders with a calculated, cold expression. Every 1d6 x 10 minutes, an **invisible stalker** passes through the secret door leading outside and crosses the room, accompanied by a cold, harsh wind and the sounds of incoherent mumbling. It attacks if it is delayed or followed.

A secret door to outside is difficult to discover, requiring a successful DC 22 Intelligence (Investigation) check, and is *arcane locked*. It can be opened only by its key (owned by Ruang the Ripper) or a *knock* spell.

B15. Armory

All the doors to this room are locked. Once entered, this room is obviously an armory of some sorts. Racks and tables hold weapons and armor. Rusted suits of armor and shields hang from pegs and on mannequins around the room. Rump crests decorate all of these.

Sitting on weapon racks are 36 swords, 52 spears, 23 shields, four halberds, six daggers, two longbows, and a small bundle of 10 arrows (the rest of the quivers, all eight of them, are empty). All of the equipment and armor are mundane except one — a *dancing longbow*.

Dancing Longbow

Weapon, very rare (requires attunement per below)

If touched by a creature that is not attuned to it, the bow animates as an **animated object: flying sword** except that it makes ranged weapon attacks (150/600 ft.) instead of melee and does piercing damage on a hit. The bow can be grasped with a successful DC 20 Dexterity check. Once grasped, it stops attacking, attunes to the creature that grasped it, and behaves as a *dancing longbow* until a creature that is not attuned to it touches it.

While attuned to the dancing longbow, you may use it as a *dancing longsword* except that it makes ranged weapon attacks (150/600 ft.) instead of melee, does piercing damage on a hit, and will not move more than 5 feet from you. While dancing, it magically pulls arrows from your quiver.

B16. Secret Laboratory

This room can be accessed only if one first locates the secret door beyond the other secret door from area **B13**.

This well-kept and orderly laboratory contains various alchemical and chemical components and equipment (700 gp). Shelves and tables are arranged so neatly that only someone in a manic state could have ordered them. A magical alarm above the entrance sounds loudly for 10 minutes or until the command word ("Count Rumpula") is spoken.

An *ophite amulet* is in a box on one shelf.

Ophite Amulet

Wondrous item, common

This tiny greenish stone amulet depicts two serpents coiled around each other. While wearing it, you have advantage on saving throws against snake venom.

B17. Bedroom

Painted walls depict remarkably well-preserved scenes of farming, harvest, and feasting. Some locations are clearly recognizable as Tegel Village in its heyday some 200 years ago. The peacefully bucolic scenes are in stark contrast to the contents of the room itself; noxious vapors emanate from the decaying remains of an orc shackled and

chained to a hook in the ceiling. The chandelier formerly hanging there has been carefully placed in the closet. A *magic plough* with a long agate blade (785 gp) is hidden carefully under a double bed. This item is magical and doubles crop yields when used to prepare the soil for planting. The side rooms to the north contain a dressing boudoir and a privy.

B18. Bedroom

A dark mass of some tarry, black substance lies in a shallow pit below corroded floorboards. While the contents of the room look intact save for the 5-foot-diameter hole, this is in fact not so. The **black pudding** that ate away that section of the floor has weakened the remaining boards as well. With a successful DC 18 Intelligence (Investigation) check, observant characters may detect this structural weakness. The not-so-observant who would investigate the stone statue on the opposite side are in for a rude shock. They must succeed on a DC 15 Dexterity saving throw or fall into the slimy monster waiting below, automatically suffering an attack!

A magic statue of a beautiful, bat-winged female stands along the east wall of the room. It is finely detailed, and even the veins seem to show through the skin. If touched, it quietly whispers *"Beware the Vestibule"* and hisses, sounding strangely like a cat.

A trap is in the closet attached to this bedroom. On its floor lies a broken wooden chest, with gold coins spilling out of it (75 gp). If the coins are touched, the removal of their weight releases a thin wire that holds a 200-pound rock in the ceiling of the closet. The trap may be noted with a successful DC 19 Wisdom (Perception) check and disarmed through any appropriately clever ruse. If the trap is triggered, each creature within the closet must make a DC 16 Dexterity saving throw, taking 21 (6d6) bludgeoning damage on a failure or half as much on a success.

B19. Bedroom

This room had served as a bedroom. A comfortable rotted leather chair by an oak dresser still bears a neatly folded blood-covered sheet. A hole in the back of the dresser serves as an ingress/egress point for 2 **giant rats** that emerge to investigate (and flee back unless only one or two characters are present).

The rat tunnel leads to **Dungeon Level 1**.

B20. Playroom

Stairs lead up from the gallery below into the playroom. An old, creaky rocking horse rocks to a child's song. Once colorful and lively tapestries depicting fables with knights, unicorns, and the Small Folk have faded in this shadowy attic that once accommodated four small infants, but the scattered toys still await the curious child eager to explore a world of wonder and fascination. Just for example, a brightly painted wooden "mystery box" hides a delightful surprise in the form of a black mamba (as **giant poisonous snake**). A doll (Tiny possessed **animated object**[II]) sits on a tiny couch, sipping tea from its very own little silver cup (1 gp) and playing with its very own little fork and knife, which it is very, very proficient with. A cuddly teddy bear (Tiny possessed anamalistic **animated object**[II]) is just waiting to be hugged (no reason to mention those long, pointed teeth). A brave band of 9 toy soldiers (Tiny humanoid **animated object**[II]) are undertaking a drill exercise. This gallant squadron guards an impressive war cache of pretty marbles (rubies and emeralds, 40 pieces at 200 gp each!). A piggy bank on the mantelpiece has 52 gp, 170 sp, 312 cp, and 2 ep. This fireplace also conceals a chute and an iron ladder to the Nanny's Room (**B2**), no less. Watch for the flames, though; and adults, beware: You might get stuck in there with your pants on fire. Medium creatures must make a successful DC 14 Dexterity (Acrobatics) check to squeeze through the chimney without getting stuck. A stuck creature can be freed with a successful DC 12 Strength check, but takes 2 slashing damage. Watching over the room is the statue of a jovial old dwarf. This is one of the manor's many enchanted statues, and its powers are for you to determine.

C – Rooms of Renown

These rooms and hallways are dark and dreary, even by Tegel Manor standards. No windows and less light are the standard of the C Wing, along with even more dust and detritus. Strange, eldritch noises fill these halls, the sounds of lost souls and long-forgotten members of the family, seeking attention from any who would listen.

C1. Mess Hall

Strange whispers echo through the hallway outside this room, and a faint hissing sound can be heard to the south of the adjacent western passage. The doors to this room swing loosely on hinges like the doors on a salon in the Old West being blown by the wind (but no wind is present here). This large room appears to be a dining area for the servants and guards of the manor, and contains a long table and 12 chairs, half of which contain **skeletons** in chainmail (AC 16) eagerly gnawing on old, desiccated bones of some animal. The only "food" remaining is a chunk of moldy bread. Pewter mugs and plates lie on the table (worth 40 gp). The skeletons gesture for intruders to join them, gesticulating greetings and trying to talk with no tongues or vocal cords. They attack only if violently disturbed.

The skeletons are oblivious to the half-starved **giant rat** in their midst, which greedily munches on the bread — the rat runs away immediately and exits through the northeast room to the tunnel down to **Dungeon Level 1**.

The low, arched recesses surrounding the main room hold empty beer kegs and wine barrels, boxes of moldy foodstuffs, and ruined and moldy linens and table wares. In the large room in the southeast corner are several barrels of water. Ten giant gnats (as **stirges**) drink from the body of a halfling lying by a barrel of stale water. If they sense fresh blood nearby (within 20 feet), they swarm and attack.

C2. Bedroom

This room is a bedroom like so many of the others nearby. It contains a bed, a dresser, and a simple trunk. Strangely though, everything here appears intact and fresh, with the exception of the rat tunnel dug into the floor in the southwest. The dresser and trunk contain mundane items (men's clothing, a shaving set, and two pairs of boots).

The door to the west wall leads to a storage area containing several boxes of clothing and papers. One of the boxes has a hidden compartment in its base that contains a lead-lined wooden case with a *tome of thievery*. The only problem with this is, of course, a strange purple drape (as **lurker above**[II]) that floats above the boxes.

The drape undulates in an otherworldly dance along the ceiling, and drops two rounds after the room is entered, covering any inside.

C3. Bedroom

This bedroom smells like stale urine and musty cloth. Another bedroom, it contains a bed and dresser, along with several scattered loose items that indicate a woman lived here. A silver hair comb (2 gp) and small hand mirror (4 gp) lie on the dresser. The rest of the contents of the room are old, moldy, and worthless. Dust-covered bones lie covered in a blanket upon the bed. The skeleton wears a heavily jeweled necklace (appears to be worth 500 gp) stretched tightly around the vertebrae of its neck. This is a *cursed necklace of strangulation*[VI].

The inner room holds a single rocking chair and a small chest with knitting needles, thread, scissors, golden thimble (1 gp), and other kinds of sewing equipment. A painting easel sites in front of the rocking chair. An oil painting of an old woman is being painted with an animated brush by some unearthly force. The paintbrush completes the painting every 24 days, then paints over the existing painting again and again. If disturbed or destroyed (the brush has 1 hp), the powerful **noble skeleton**[II] animates and attacks!

C4. Bedroom

Strange panting noises haunt the hallway outside of this room, fading to nothing as the door is opened. Scenes of battle cover the walls of this bedroom, most prominently featuring a 7-foot-tall man wielding a greataxe, chopping up everything in his path. A bed and a rat-gnawed dresser made of wood contain nothing of value. The air is quite cold due to the **brown mold**[II] present in the dresser. Opening the dresser exposes the mold. A suit of rusty (but usable) Medium plate armor rests on a stand in the northeast corner of the room. Bits of it seem to move 2 rounds after the room is entered. It quivers and shakes, acting as if it might animate. A **giant rat** is inside the armor. It attempts to flee to the rat tunnel in the northwest corner the armor is attacked or otherwise disturbed. A two-headed greataxe lies concealed under the bed. It can be found with a successful DC 14 Wisdom (Perception) check.

C5. Bedroom

This bedroom contains a large canopy bed with heavy, velvet curtains. An unstrung harp lies on the floor in the southern alcove (worth 120 gp if repaired). The air is slightly chilly (no doubt due to the frosty room to the north), yet the fragrance of herbs still lingers. Of this collection, only two items are magical: a set of two *harmonious jars* sitting in two circles of a chalk-drawn diagram. A ceramic decanter of water sits next to them.

The chair by the writing desk runs across the room if it (or the desk) is touched, and flips upside down as it hits the wall with a thud. If touched again, it changes into a **wight** and attacks!

✝	One-way Teleport To	
✝	One-way Teleport From	
✝✝	Two-way Teleport	
○	Giant Rat Hole	
⬤	Magical Statue	
⬤	Non-magical Statue	
←▯▯	Spectral Staircase	
30	Numbered Paintings	

∿	Curtain or Tapestry	
S	Two-way Secret Door	
S→	One-way Secret Door	
⊠	Covered Pit	
▫	Trap Door in Ceiling	
▪	Shaft	
●	Large Shaft	
▭	Fireplace (shaft)	

Artemesia Amulet

Wondrous item, uncommon

The amulet is a simple flower-shaped lucky charm made of brass that grants advantage on all Constitution saving throws to resist the effects of exhaustion while you wear it.

C6. Guards' Room

Accessed — strangely enough — through the large bath, the lounge and quarters of the guards are situated in convenient proximity to the Great Hall and the Throne Room. Two long tables, empty weapon racks, and a multitude of stools are found here; the individual cells have two two-story bunks each, and a 50% chance of a wooden chest with miscellaneous items and 3d6 cp or the like. One of the chests contains the *Artemesia amulet*, a minor magic item. The long tables are empty, except for two kegs of arsenic-laced wine and a battleaxe stuck in one of the tables. A creature who drinks the wine must succeed on a DC 13 Constitution saving throw or become poisoned for 10 minutes and lose 3 points of Strength while poisoned. The **battleaxe** hurls itself at the ceiling, and after a moment, one of the player characters, thereafter ceasing animation. Two rat tunnels lead down to the dungeons from rooms in the northwest and southeast corners of this room complex.

Battleaxe. *Melee Weapon Attack:* +6 to hit, one creature within 30 ft. *Hit:* 7 (1d8 + 3) slashing damage.

C7. Bedroom

Crying can be heard from the hallway to the south (see the Maid's Room, **C9**). This bedroom appears to have been smashed and torn to pieces by something. Oddly intact is a floating table that mutters curses and insults in a matronly voice at any who enter. Set into the table are ten 10 gp amber gems and in the center of the table is set a 650 gp siderite stone. The siderite is the source of the voice, and bears a curse that makes it extremely desirable to everyone hearing it and causes discord (per *symbol of discord* spell). Resisting its effects requires a successful DC 16 Constitution saving throw.

C8. Bedroom

This bedroom is spotlessly intact, and contains a bed, a dresser, and a table and three chairs, on one of which sits a corpse wearing a *necklace of fireballs* around its neck. The dresser contains nothing but normal clothing (strangely, they smell sweet and freshly washed) and a small brass key. Touching the skeleton causes moans overhead that get stronger and stronger by the second. Red drapes adorn the east wall. The secret door leading to area **D8** behind the drapes closes on its own unless propped open. It requires the key from the dresser or a successful DC 18 Dexterity check with thieves' tools to open. Opening it triggers a *glyph of warding* trap in the process.

The *glyph of warding* (explosive runes) can be detected with a successful DC 18 Intelligence (Investigation) check. If triggered, each creature within a 20-foot-radius sphere must make a DC 18 Dexterity saving throw, taking 27 (6d8) thunder damage on a failure or half as much on a success.

C9. Maid's Room

This room, like area **C8**, is strangely clean and intact. It's obviously a bedroom, and the ghostly figure of a maid cries softly on the bed. A small, unlocked footlocker rests at the end of the bed. Unless the door is quietly closed immediately, any intrusion draws the ire of the animated bed (Large paraphernalia **animated object**[II]) which rushes to knock over and trample its victims. Her rest disturbed, the crying **wraith** maid also attacks intruders. A broom standing in the northwest corner is a *broom of flying*, with a command word of "Rupark."

C10. Bath

This bath is kept strangely warm by some unknown magical force. Boxes along the edges contain bars of soap and oils and perfumes worth 20 gp, and the water is "living" (e.g. it moves and does not become stagnant). Sitting on its edge is a large raven that squawks and disappears with a loud snap, leaving behind a single black feather (sharp and metallic, and usable as *+1 dagger*). Two comely, naked phantoms of bathing ladies immediately emerge from the water and float through the glass-domed ceiling, jabbering away at each other in a gossiping tone. The magic statue by the pool depicts a naked, big-nosed man whose marble left hand is missing. The limb is found in the bottom of the pool under a foot-deep layer of muck and sediment, and if replaced, the statue comes to life and serves the character as a **berserker** for 1d20 days.

C11. Bedroom

A long, jagged crack crosses the wooden floor of this bedroom from the east to the west. If someone is foolish enough to cross, it opens, revealing a disembodied maw trap (see sidebar) with sharp teeth.

Disembodied Maw Trap

When a creature steps within 5 feet of the jagged crack in the room, the crack widens and the floorboards slant toward the crack. Each creature within 10 feet of the crack when it opens must succeed on a DC 15 Dexterity saving throw or fall into the crack in the floor. A creature in the crack is restrained and it has total cover against attacks and other effects outside the crack, and it takes 11 (2d10) piercing damage at the start of each of its turns as broken floorboards inside the crack impale the creature. A creature, including the trapped creature, can take its action to pull the trapped creature out of the crack by succeeding on a DC 15 Strength check. If the check to free the trapped creature fails by 5 or more, the creature takes 5 (1d10) piercing damage. If the trap is triggered and no creatures fall into the crack, 1d4 rounds later, the crack emits noxious swamp gas that lasts for 2d4 rounds. Each creature breathing the gas must make a DC 15 Constitution saving throw, taking 11 (2d10) poison damage on a failed save, or half as much damage on a successful one. The DC to spot the crack is a 10. A successful DC 20 Intelligence (Investigation) check determines the floorboards near the crack are lined up in such a way as to allow them to swing downward toward the crack without marring the surface of the floor. The trap can be prevented from triggering with anything magical or mechanical that would prevent the floorboards from moving or being stepped on, such as a long plank of wood or the *web* spell.

Outside the room, ghostly figures sometimes flit from room to room if magical light is present. They are harmless.

C12. Bedroom

The door to this room, while apparently oiled and in good shape, emits a loud creaking sound when opened or closed. Twenty eyes on the back of the eastern door open and peer at intruders, following their every move. The room has blue walls and a red ceiling, all painted with an extremely vibrant shade. The bed and dresser are both rotten and broken down and contain nothing of value. A secret door leads to the south. Any noise here could draw the rakshasa from area **C14**.

C13. Bedroom

This room smells badly of cat urine. Someone or something has shredded the bed cloths in this room, stuffing the torn remains into a large basket in the northeast corner. The western door bears large cat-like scratches. The bundle contains four round, wet giant ant eggs, one of them only a few days from hatching (requires warm environment). Four large glass jars on a shelf above a writing desk contain a moldy liquid. Suspended in one is a glass eye that peers outside and knocks on the glass surface to draw the attention of the party. A round tin container has a *rhododendron amulet* wrapped in linen and covered with a thick layer of wax.

> ## Rhododendron Amulet
>
> *Wondrous item, rare*
>
> This pink soapstone amulet depicts a small dog. While wearing it, you can control 4d6 normal dogs as a *dominate beast* spell (spell save DC 18) or force a single larger canine once per day to succeed on a DC 18 Wisdom saving throw or run away in fear for 1 minute.

C14. Butler's Room

Torture implements hang along the walls and dangle from the ceiling in this once-elaborate bedroom. Chained to the north wall before the secret passage is a dwarf woman clad in nothing but a chainmail bikini and similar loincloth. She claims to have been kidnapped and brought here by a depraved sadist nicknamed "The Follower of Gore" and urges the party to free her before this monster returns. Characters succeeding on a DC 16 Wisdom (Perception) check may note that contrary to the claims of the lady, no signs of physical harm are apparent, and the torture implements are dusty and unused. She is in fact a **rakshasa** who wishes to infiltrate and do away with the party. An ongoing melee is joined by the bugbears in area **C15**, who rush to aid their "mistress."

The rakshasa uses its *illusion*, *charm*, and *suggestion* spells to get the party to go along with its will, and certainly attempts to escape if it feels that it might be killed.

C15. Antechamber

Two **bugbears** (one with a potion that allows it to cast *acid arrow* once with a +5 spell attack bonus) serving the rakshasa next door inhabit this antechamber/guardroom. They spend their time playing dice (stakes are slices of human ham), beating on four dead giant ants, and sleeping on their filthy rags. Two deer head trophies pierced by numerous iron-tipped quarrels look upon the scene in disapproval.

D – Noble Suites

This area is all obviously for the "higher classes" and is where the noble family members live(d). The tapestries are finer, the furniture higher end, and the hallways meticulously kept clean by some strange magic. The area near the Throne Room (**D1**) is the prowling grounds of two family vampires. Count Radu Rumpula inhabits a single, well-appointed bedroom (**D5**), whereas his wife, Rank Rumpula, has a whole suite at her disposal (**D2–D4**). There is a 25% chance that either vampire is home — and if a lengthy or loud melee develops in the area, they are certainly going to investigate!

D1. Throne Room

Massive green and white serpentine pillars support the carved, bas-relief stonework of the arched ceiling. Strange devil and god-like faces are carved into this stonework, and if watched, seem to move slightly and babble to one another. Light shines through a dome above, shedding light on the center 30 feet of the room. A huge purple curtain hangs from the southeast passageway, totally obscuring it. Behind the curtain, a cranking sound, similar to the winding of a gigantic crossbow, can be heard if the throne dais is stepped on (this is the trap in area **D8** arming itself). A large marble throne sits in the east, covered in dusty cobwebs (strange for this area). These webs are unbelievably sticky and strong. Anyone touching them is stuck (per a *web* spell with DC 16 spell save).

A thick red curtain covers the northeastern exit from this room, and leads to the choking hall. The gagging and strangling sounds emitted here are disturbing to any who hear them. Passing this curtain exposes one to a horrid sight: Hanging from the walls of this hallway are the wriggling and desiccated corpses of victims of the vampires. Six bodies hang from neck manacles with their feet inches off the floor. While long dead, each of these is now a **coffer corpse**[II], although a helpless one (unless released). These undead horrors grasp alternatively at their throats and any living creatures in view. They attack only if released or if approached within 3 feet (they are immobilized by the strangling manacles).

Three **giant spiders** wait patiently in the empty fireplace, where they have created a hidden lair. The spiders wait until someone is caught in a web, and try to trap those who are still free thereafter.

Two secret doors and two traps exist in this room. Both secret doors are normally hard to locate and open. The west door leads to a secret hallway terminating in area **A2** (in the fireplace) and the east secret door to a narrow hallway leading to area **D7**. The staircase beyond the secret door to the west is also trapped. The first person stepping on the stairs triggers a dozen darts to fly from a panel in the ceiling. Each creature within the 20-foot section of corridor at the base of the stairs must succeed on a DC 17 Dexterity saving throw or take 3 (1d6) piercing damage. The trap can be detected with a successful DC 17 Intelligence (Investigation) check and disarmed with a successful DC 17 Dexterity check with thieves' tools.

The throne itself is trapped. Anyone bold enough to sit on the throne itself must succeed on a DC 16 Wisdom saving throw or suffer a curse that gives them disadvantage on all saving throws until removed.

D2. Bedroom

Satin and silk dominate the boudoir of Countess Rank Rumpula (**vampiric wizard**[II]) (25% present, 50% sleeping); shades of red and blue mingle with the blackness of the dusty velvet carpet. A **severed hand**[II] drums its fingers constantly on a round oak table — if touched or approached, it goes straight for the whip on the dressing cabinet (this latter item is a valuable itself: ruby-inlaid ivory handle, 998 gp). The dressing cabinet contains the usual articles for a noblewoman's bedroom — expensive perfumes, makeup, exotic powders, and well-made combs and brushes fill the cabinet drawers.

Servant's Quarters
Q6 CO
Roaring
Choking Hall
D5 Bedroom
D6 Bedroom
D7 Sitting Room
K3 Plant Roo
Rattling Hall
K4 Bedroo
K10 Bedroo
K11 Bedroom
D2 Bedroom
D3 Study
D4 Bedroom
D1 Throne Room
C8 Bedroom
T
D8 Vault
Cranking Hall
D9 Bedroom
D10 Chapel
D11 Bedroom
D12 Bedroom
D13 Bedroom
D14 Sanctum
Cobwebs
E3 Stockroom
One-way Teleport To
One-way Teleport From
Two-way Teleport
Giant Rat Hole
Magical Statue
Non-magical Statue
Spectral Staircase
30   Numbered Paintings
Curtain or Tapestry
Two-way Secret Door
One-way Secret Door
Covered Pit
Trap Door in Ceiling
Shaft
Large Shaft
Fireplace (shaft)

Two closets are found beyond the western wall of the spacious bedroom. The northern closet may have once stored luxurious clothing and shoes, but now serves as Rank Rumpula's fake sleeping chamber. A fancy coffin has been placed within this room to appear as the countess's resting place; however, her true abode is cunningly hidden below the device. A well-hidden tunnel under the piled chunks of earth within the coffin leads to Rank Rumpula's genuine abode. The tunnel can be found with a successful DC 15 Intelligence (Investigation) check. The tunnel entrance is trapped with *Dust of Sneezing and Choking*. A creature that passes through it and fails a DC15 Constitution saving throw is incapacitated for 2d4 rounds. A thorough search with a successful DC 14 Intelligence (Investigation) check of the coffin dirt leads to finding a 480 gp ruby ring (*ring of evasion*).

Deteriorating gowns, dresses, and shawls fill the other closet. The once-expensive clothing is no longer of any value; however, if a character carefully removes all the expensive beading, gems, and pearls from the clothing, they may be able to sell the lot of materials for 150 to 200 gp.

D3. STUDY

Known mainly as an accomplished wizard, the countess was also a reputed and notorious sadist. While far from the magical might of the lich Ridwik (or Rasping Rashuak, the Man in Scarlet!), she could stand on her own, especially where charms were concerned. This study contains her collection of arcane texts, most of them rotted and illegible. To add insult to injury, a cup of rancid wine resting on the writing desk hurls itself at the intruder with the cleanest attire.

Although most of the books appear destroyed and long since usable, a salvageable volume may be discovered among the rotting pile of tomes with a successful DC 15 Intelligence (Investigation) check. The plain-looking book is actually an unused *Manual of Gainful Exercise*. A successful DC 17 Intelligence (Investigation) check while searching the area behind the bookshelf in the south wall should reveal a hidden niche that contains the countess's treasured spellbooks. Unfortunately, unwitting searchers may also discover a deadly *Glyph of Warding* (*Explosive Runes*) spell-trap placed upon both spellbooks. To make matters worse, one of the spellbooks is invisible, making the trap almost nearly impossible to detect until it is accidentally triggered. The *glyph* can be found with a successful DC 20 Intelligence (Investigation) check. If triggered, each creature within a 20-foot-radius sphere must make a DC 20 Dexterity saving throw. Those who fail take 27 (6d8) thunder damage while those succeeding take half this amount.

Spellbook 1 — Cantrips: *Dancing Lights, Light, Ray of Frost*; 1st level: *Burning Hands, Charm Person, Detect Magic, Identify, Magic Missile, Silent Image*; 2nd level: *Darkness, Detect Thoughts*; 3rd level: *Dispel Magic, Fireball*; 4th level: *Greater Invisibility*.

Spellbook 2 — Cantrips: *Light, Mage Hand*; 1st level: *Alarm, Shield, Unseen Servant*; 2nd level: *Gust of Wind, Levitate, Locate Object*; 3rd level: *Dispel Magic, Glyph of Warding, Protection from Energy, Slow*; 4th level: *Confusion, Fire Shield*.

D4. BEDROOM

Once, this room used to be just as lavishly decorated as area **D2**. Alas, the presence of Rufus, Rank Rumpula's pet **owlbear**, has contributed much to its current sorry state. Although the countess usually keeps Rufus under the influence of a regularly renewed *charm monster* spell, its occasional periods of freedom always result in further destruction. Right now, for example, the damned thing is shredding ancient and apparently valuable papyrus scrolls to use as bedding in its lair, at least until it is done away with. If the scrolls don't fall prey to the owlbear or the fury of the melee, one of them may point to the location of a hidden desert tomb, or a lost city, or maybe bear a beneficial clerical spell — up to you, as always.

D5. BEDROOM

Count Radu Rumpula[1] (25% present, 40% sleeping) has made sure that his bedroom remains undisturbed. The locking mechanism of the single iron door has been jammed beyond repair — it is impossible to pick; in fact, a Dexterity check with thieves' tools under DC 14 results in broken lockpicks! Count Radu uses the keyhole himself, wafting through it in his gaseous form. As an alternative to forcing the door, which requires a successful DC 25 Strength check or 20 points of damage against AC 15, one may also use the rat tunnels from below. No matter how the characters gain access to Radu's sanctum, they are greeted by a jovial, mocking voice that asks, *"What uncouth peasants dare enter the count's bedroom?"* as the shadow of a huge bat flickers across the walls.

An exquisitely decorated bedroom is found beyond the secured entry, with wall hangings of rich drapes, portraits of the Rumpula family, and a pair of dueling blades (one of the blades is a *+2 rapier*). A nearby couch is being used as a base for Radu's coffin, and several other furnishings are found neatly situated within the room. A table holds a decanter filled with a small amount of red liquid (old wine) and four gilded, copper candelabras (20 gp each). Additionally, a gold key sits upon the desk in plain sight (it opens the liquor cabinet). A lavish writing desk and large trunk with folded clothes are pushed against the north wall, and a large liquor cabinet is found adjacent on the opposite wall. After unlocking the cabinet with the gold key found nearby, characters find four elven goblets (440 gp) and four crystal flasks, each filled with a rare brandy. Those with a nose for fine liquors quickly realize the brandy is of the utmost quality (worth 160 gp per flask) and has aged so well that it has gained healing properties; the contents of three of the flasks heal as a *Potion of Superior Healing*. However, one flask has been tainted with an exotic and tasteless poison, and instead deals 28 (8d4 + 8) poison damage or half as much with a successful DC 18 Constitution saving throw.

D6. BEDROOM

This small bedroom used to be a side chamber of Radu's suite, but the northern archway has been walled in. Currently, only a dusty bed and a large writing desk are here. A huge parchment with meaningless mystical symbols crumbles to dust as soon as light shines on its surface.

D7. SITTING ROOM

Comfortable couches, plush chairs, and low tables once served family and guests during everyday visits and special occasions. Heads of hunted creatures hang on the darkened wood walls, their eyes staring down upon characters with disdain and disgust. Although the eyes of the dead creatures won't ever be seen moving no matter how long the characters watch them, they will be looking in a different direction each time the group looks back at them. Several of the creatures appear freshly slain with droplets of blood still found around their noses, eyes, and mouths.

Three sculptures of the same large and attractive woman line the east wall, each shaped into a suggestive and flirtatious pose. If any of the characters makes a lewd comment or mentions something distasteful in her presence, all three sculptures animate and move toward the offending characters, chastising them with silent words and pointing fingers. Upon the character's sincere apologies, the sculptures return to their petrified state along the east wall, changing their poses to those more becoming of a proper lady.

A thick book lies upon one of the tables of the room, containing hundreds of pages of detailed hunting excursions that include dates, locations, and creatures captured or killed. Count Radu took copious notes during his trips, and proudly displays his accomplishments here for all to see.

D8. VAULT

Heavy, impenetrable iron doors seal the treasure vault. Only the knowledge of the long-lost proper combination allows entry under normal circumstances. However, an extraordinary burglar may be able to sabotage one of the delicate mechanisms with a successful DC 28 Dexterity check with thieves' tools, and there is also the secret passage from area **C8**. Adventurers hoping for riches beyond their imagination are in for disappointment, however, as the vault was looted long ago. Only a pile of 15,480 cp, 53 sp, and 7 gp remains. The pile is covered with sticky, moldy syrup. A different band of burglars — black ants — has burrowed inside the no-longer-airtight vault, drawn by the lure of the sugary goodness.

D9. BEDROOM

This bedroom was reserved for the holy man who tended the small chapel nearby (**D10**) although it appears as though the cleric's tastes were non-traditional. Instead of a meager bedroom as would be expected, the old man preferred luxurious surroundings that included a large canopied bed, exquisite tapestries depicting scenes unbecoming of a devoted and pious man, and several personal effects made of silver and gold laid upon a well-made table at the end of the bed. A large painting of the cleric hangs on a wall near the bed, with the figure's longing eyes gazing upon the comfortable bed.

The table has a false bottom that can be found with a successful DC 18 Intelligence (Investigation) check. It contains four large quartz gems (50 gp each) and 35 gp.

The bed is an insidious trap that causes drowsiness in observers. Anyone who lies down to take a short nap is in for an unpleasant surprise as the top descends quickly to suffocate the sleeper. Getting off the bed before being trapped requires a successful DC 18 Dexterity saving throw. A creature caught under the top cannot breathe and requires a successful DC 16 Wisdom saving throw each round they are awake on the bed to avoid falling into a deep and lasting sleep. The canopy can be destroyed by doing 10 points of damage against AC 11, but a sleeping character takes half of any damage inflicted. Once the canopy is destroyed, the magic of the bed is lost. Noting the trapped nature of the bed before lying on it can be accomplished with a successful DC 20 Intelligence (Arcana or Investigation) check. The Arcana check reveals the sleep dweomer, while the Investigation check reveals the canopy trap.

A short passage from the room leads to one of the vault's iron doors. The partially decomposing body of the cleric lies slumped next to the iron doors of the vault, his outstretched hands reaching for the large opening ring. Any noise causes his head to swivel in the direction of the source. As the cleric's eyes come to rest upon approaching characters, his head slowly falls from his shoulders and rolls across the passage until it comes to rest against the opposite wall. The eyes remain aware for a few more seconds before they film over, the life lost from them for all eternity.

D10. CHAPEL

A singular block of black stone stands against the southern wall of the room, its square edges showing no sign of chipping or wear. Nearly reaching the ceiling of the room, the ebony, featureless block seems out of place for what appears to be a chapel; rows of kneeling cloth and several stools are arranged in a clear pattern suggestive of practicing worship. Weaker-willed or exceptionally perceptive characters will see through the magical guise covering the block, which conceals the true form of an alien creature unknown to this world. Even the briefest sight of the idol is enough to make the unprepared onlooker temporarily insane. However, the characters that fit neither group see nothing but a block of jet-black stone.

A creature with a Wisdom below 6 or anyone who succeeds on a DC 20 Wisdom (Perception) check sees the true nature of the alien and suffers the effects of a *confusion* spell for one minute.

A small **spider** lurks behind the idol and leaps on solitary characters.

D11. BEDROOM

A **rust monster** in this room feasts on an iron-frame bed that jumps about moaning and crying for help. If the monster is dispatched, the bed refuses to answer further inquiries and doesn't react to any further damage either (has it been slain?).

D12. BEDROOM

A five-candled candlestick sits upon a small table in this dark, undersized bedroom. Most of the furniture is of low value or worthless. The candlestick eludes grasping hands by quickly floating to the ceiling, lighting its wick with a crackling purple spark and releasing a cloud of laughing gas. The gas fills the whole room in 1d4 rounds and has a good chance of incapacitating party members. Each creature in the room must succeed on a DC 16 Constitution saving throw or be incapacitated with laughter. An incapacitated creature may attempt the saving throw again at the end of its turn and end the effect on a success. At your option, the roaring laughter may attract a few critters who are waiting just for this happy occasion.

D13. BEDROOM

This simple yet functional bedroom is far from the well-traveled parts of the manor; hence, it hasn't been disturbed in ages. The spectral figure of a grumbling dwarf paces across the floor constantly. If the dwarf is disturbed, the translucent form turns glowing red, runs up the wall, across the ceiling, and down the other wall, leaping at the party and exploding in a flash of red light. Each creature in the room takes 1 (1d3) force damage and must succeed on a DC 12 Constitution saving throw or be deafened for 1d10 x 5 minutes. The only treasures in the room are the contents of the dwarf's chest: a set of well-oiled chainmail armor, a dwarven waraxe, and a small metal shield resting on a layer of plain white pebbles.

D14. SANCTUM

A brazier at the eastern end of the room burns slowly, releasing a thick, sweet-smelling smoke that dances within the characters' nostrils. Raising two of its four arms to the archways to either side, a tall statue behind the brazier gazes upon those who enter the room from the west. Upon taking a single step into the room, a mangy dog appears out of the smoke and growls menacingly at the characters. This is a mere illusion: If the dog is "slain" (AC 11, 4 hit points), it just splits into two dogs of equal size. All disappear when 13 exist or if they are ignored for more than five minutes. They fade back into thin wisps of incense smoke. They don't attack.

The statue's four arms are all that differ from general human anatomy; otherwise, it appears as if the figure was modeled after a middle-aged acolyte. Closer inspection of the statue reveals that its right eye and right nostril are closed. As characters approach either archway in the room (on either side of the statue), the brazier begins burning hotter, producing more smoke.

If characters step through the right archway, the color of the brazier smoke turns purple and becomes toxic and poisonous. Characters in the sanctum must succeed on a DC 14 Constitution saving throw or fall incapacitated to the floor as they writhe in agony and pain. An incapacitated character takes 2 (1d4) poison damage at the beginning of its turn and may make a new saving throw at the end of its turn to end the effect on a success. Those in the small room behind the statue feel no ill effects. Entering the left archway does not alter the color or toxicity of the smoke. The next character who exits the small room through the right archway causes the smoke to return to normal; however, the archway is activated each time a single living creature moves through the portal. The smoke does not leave the sanctum, and the room east of the statue is empty.

E – SOUTHERN QUARTERS

Before the nobles of the manor house moved to the newly constructed Southwest Wing, their sleeping chambers were found in this older part of the great house. Rasping Rashuak once had his laboratory in this part of the house but has since abandoned its use since turning into a lich. The area is sparsely populated, but by no means is it safe. Disgusting insects and undead silently roam the halls in this, the quieter part of the manor.

E1. LAUNDRY

Steam rises from a giant hole in the floor, drenching the room in thick humidity and obscuring the stench of rotting flesh from four deceased creatures. Sagging bedclothes hanging from fraying clotheslines hide a portion of the large room (and the dead bodies) from view. This open pit is 5 feet deep; the boiling water within is fed by the heated pool in area **DL3K**. Immersion causes 21 (6d6) fire damage per round.

A **giant leech**[II] is attached to the back of a wet sheet. A giant metal pot filled with steaming, brackish water simmers near the opening, a metal device suspending the vessel over the heat. Cleavers, forks, and a large ladle sit upon a nearby table, stained with years of use. A look at the utensils reveals that they are warm to the touch, possibly used recently to test the contents of the metal pot. If characters use the cooking device to reel in the pot, they find it filled with poorly-made broth and chunks of slug meat. Traces of other dead flesh, possibly human, are found within the stew if closely inspected.

E2. STOCKROOM

Thick cobwebs stretch across the entry of this storeroom, barring entry unless characters are willing to slash or burn through the sticky strands. Thousands of tiny spiders skitter mindlessly across the webs, crawling directly into fire or to safety without purpose or understanding. If characters leave their appendages within the webs long enough, dozens of the tiny spiders scurry up their arms or legs and into their clothing. Although they are not painful, the little spiders hide themselves in the characters' clothing and gear until removed (after hours of careful inspection).

The stockroom contains two boxes full of snake foam, one crate of dead crickets (labeled, appropriately enough, *"Dead Crickets"*), a glass jar of tiny mole teeth, a keg of thick basilisk blood, and a pouch of crab eyes. A ledger full of scribbled notes and shipping manifests rests on an empty barrel.

E3. BEDROOM

A pile of broken furniture in the center of the room is all that remains of the servants' bedchambers. Once a neatly organized room for six servants, the room was partially cleared out and its contents piled for

Crying Hall
Bedroom
C10 Bath
Rolling
Laundry
L2 Stockroom
D9 Bedroom
Chapel
Cobwebs
D8 Bedroom
Bedroom
C15 Antechamber
Apparition
L8 Utility
L7 Bedroom
E6 Bedroom
E5 Bedroom
Stockroom
D1 Boudoir
Musty
Creaking Corridor
L11 Chapel
Quarreling
Kitchen
D4 Bedroom
50
51
D5 Bedroom
Snapping Hall
L12 Bedroom
E4 Bath
E15 Bedroom
E10 Bedroom
Laboratory
E13 Bedroom
F1 Bedroom
F2 Bedroom

One-way Teleport To
One-way Teleport From
Two-way Teleport
Giant Rat Hole
Magical Statue
Non-magical Statue
Spectral Staircase
30   Numbered Paintings
Curtain or Tapestry
Two-way Secret Door
One-way Secret Door
Covered Pit
Trap Door in Ceiling
Shaft
Large Shaft
Fireplace (shaft)

removal. Although the room appears empty, an **enormous centipede**[II] has made its home within the pile of broken beds, tables, and chairs. It can be heard moving about the pile but is unlikely to come out unless the characters set the pile ablaze.

The large insect is fond of shiny baubles and has accumulated many coins, jewelry, and fashion accessories it has found throughout the deserted wing. If the characters coax the large, poisonous centipede out (possibly with a successful DC 14 Wisdom [Animal Handling] check) and can get into its nest, they find 1d100 sp, 1d10 gp, 1d4 silver bracelets and earrings, 1d2 gold bracelets, a ruby ring, an ivory comb, and a silver mirror.

E4. BOUDOIR

Smashed vases, overturned furniture, and emptied containers fill the darkened room. A low, mournful moan emanates from a silk-covered cage at the western edge of the room. Sitting with its knees pressed against its chest, a covered figure within the cage rocks back and forth as it sobs. No attempt to communicate with the cloaked figure succeeds, but if the door is unlatched and opened, the figure suddenly springs forth to attack its would-be saviors. The former handmaiden of Lady Rubienna Rumpula is now a mindless **ghoul**! Caught wearing the lady's dress, the handmaiden was long ago placed within the cage to die. Long strands of dried blonde hair were once braided but now cover her hideous face from view.

E5. BEDROOM

Adventurers carefully mapping this wing of the manor may detect this concealed space between the other bedrooms. No apparent entrance to the forgotten room can be found, but the northern, eastern, and southern walls are thin enough to allow access if enough time is spent demolishing the old plaster and lathe. Age-old, stale air rushes out to greet those who peek into the darkened room, giving the impression that this room has been sealed for quite some time.

A lone figure slumbers upon a long block of marble, its skin stretched taught from years of dry air. It slowly rises as characters enter the room, shambling erratically toward the first foe it sees. The **pyre zombie**[II] explodes fire when first struck, igniting the dry debris and brittle furniture found throughout the room. Within a few rounds, all items in the room should be ablaze; however, the lack of air in the room slowly snuffs out all but the most intense fires.

E6. BEDROOM

A loose tapestry showing a large family banquet under orchard trees in summer runs along the open, northern portion of this bedroom. The wall hanging easily slides aside — the top edge of the ornate tapestry is lined with hoops that slide along a metal bar attached to the ceiling. Beyond, a four-post bed with silken draperies has been pushed up against the south wall. A silver tiara with dozens of bright sapphires sits upon a nightstand adjacent to the bed.

Unbeknownst to adventurers, a **medusa** lies in wait behind the green, silk curtains of the large bed. Characters approaching the bed or nightstand likely see the medusa all too late.

E7. BEDROOM

Four **severed heads**[II] roll across the dusty floor of this bedroom, butting and hurling vile insults at each other. The heads are so absorbed in their little row that they don't take notice of the characters unless they are directly interrupted. Once this happens, they either try to flee or beg for mercy in whiny, high-pitched voices (although it is only a matter of time before they resume their argument!). The heads know a little about the place, and one of them has heard about the secret door in Snapping Hall to the southwest.

E8. UTILITY

Two hallways access this important utility room, one from the west and one from the south. An elaborate system of mechanical boilers pop and groan as they supply boiling steam and melted materials to various parts of the manor. Among other rooms, the Laboratory (**E9**) and the Bath (**C10**) both require constant heat from the utility room and cease to function without it. Three **strangling zombies**[II] are all that remain of the former utility worker team who toiled tirelessly over their precious contraptions. Each ghost darts between machines, fixing both real and imagined issues, trying to keep everything running for their masters. If interrupted from their work, they attack trespassers but only to drive them from the utility room — they return to work once adventurers enter either hallway outside the area.

Most of the boiling steam and melted materials enter a complex system of magical tubes in the northeastern corner, exiting the room to areas of the manor that need intense heat. If opened, release valves on the machines and the magical tubes squirt boiling steam or melted iron into the room. Creatures who come into contact with the materials or steam must make a DC 15 Dexterity saving throw or take 35 (10d6) fire damage on a failure or half as much on a success. If the machines are turned off for more than a few hours, denizens of the manor house come to inspect the utility room and to question the workers.

E9. LABORATORY

All undead, including other family members, avoid the former laboratory of the lich Rasping Rashuak. Although the old master is rarely here, not even the most powerful dare to enter its iron door. The western entry into the room is locked with a complex mechanism that requires a skillful hand to open and a successful DC 22 Dexterity check with thieves' tools. Each door to the room is trapped with a *glyph of warding* that releases a *flame strike* spell when activated. Another *glyph of warding* has been placed on the stone in front of the open northern doorway and releases a *dispel magic* spell when triggered. Spotting the glyphs requires a successful DC 18 Intelligence (Investigation) check. If the *flame strike* glyph is triggered, each creature within a 10-foot radius, 40-foot-high cylinder centered on the nearest creature within 60 feet must make a DC 18 Dexterity saving throw. A creature that fails takes 14 (4d6) fire damage and 14 (4d6) radiant damage on a failed save, or half as much on a successful one. If the *dispel magic* glyph is triggered, the creature makes an ability check with a +5 modifier against the nearest magical effect.

The interior of the laboratory is in meticulous order, as *unseen servants* regularly dust off all items and surfaces, clean up spills, and do basic maintenance. As with all laboratories, the room is filled with various pieces of scientific equipment such as beakers, bottles, and bowls stacked on numerous tables and all fed by tubes of boiling steam and molten steel from the utility room (**E8**). Much of the equipment and steam power supports a central work station where a glass dome-shaped transparent force field protects Rashuak's most valuable lab items. A collector of scientific equipment or active researcher would value this equipment at around 5,000 gp. However, removing the pieces and parts to the complex subsystems without damaging them or misplacing critical sections makes this a laborious task, taking between two or three days of careful cataloging and packaging.

The force field contains the guardian of this place: a thick crystalline glass case full of feeding fluid wherein floats the purplish-blue **brain of an imprisoned demon**[II] — Rashuak's able assistant in his experiments. The brain is psionically active and after a brief observation period assaults unrecognized intruders mercilessly. It always initiates a *mental blast* first, then moves on to *greater concussion* and *brain lock* until its foes are dead. The brain dies as soon as the feeding fluid

is drained. This may be accomplished by cracking the glass case, breaking the glass tubes transporting the stuff inside the force field, by contaminating said stream, or simply by destroying a significant portion of the lab equipment. The glass case and tubes have a damage threshold of 5, 20 hit points, and AC 16. Alternately, either can be smashed with a successful DC 22 Strength (Athletics) check. The last method is not advisable, as the resulting reaction generates a deadly poisonous gas that fills the entire laboratory in 1d4 rounds, and seeps outside in another 1d6. A creature within the area when the reaction first starts must succeed on a DC 17 Constitution saving throw or gain one level of exhaustion and become poisoned. In addition, a creature must do the same for each minute that it spends in the wretched air. The poisoned condition lasts until the creature takes a long rest or is magically cured. Exhaustion is recovered at normal rates. The reaction stops after 1d6 x 10 minutes, but a full day must elapse before the air becomes breathable.

Several tables, an unlit brazier, and a small book stand can be found within the protective dome. Extra lab equipment, a mortar and pestle, five small metals bowls, and a recently deceased imp are on the tables. Each of the five bowls has the beginnings of an independent experiment — a knowledgeable crafter of potions (one trained in alchemist's supplies, for example) would recognize each started potion as: a *potion of clairvoyance*, a *potion of gaseous form*, a *potion of heroism*, a *potion of invisibility*, and a *potion of mind reading*. An empty book on the stand is a magical spellbook. Although empty, it has been enchanted to copy spells cast by others as they are cast. Each day, it has a cumulative 10% chance to copy a cast spell. Once a spell has been written into the book, it does not try again until the next day.

In addition to the force field, there is also a teleport in the room. It is operated with a large lever in the southwest corner. If it is pulled, all sentient beings within 10 feet are transported to area **A21**, and all sentient beings in area **A21** are brought here. Note that the demon brain is **not** in range.

Finally, the two rooms to the east are holding cells for experimental subjects. Four human skeletons are inside. The skeletons exhibit strange deformities — bony spikes on the skull, a pair of curled horns, and cloven feet. Bits of shaggy fur are also found.

E10. Bedroom

The crackling of lightning is heard periodically from within the room. Inside, a corner of a modest sleeping chamber has been cleared to accommodate a large iron cauldron and a huge copper jar. This is the *cauldron of Keridwen*, a sacred druidical artifact. It is filled with a heated, moss-green sludge (foul but otherwise harmless water). The crackling comes from the copper jar, which is surrounded by a halo of electricity. Every three rounds, a bolt of lightning snaps from the jar to the cauldron or any metal item within 10 feet. A creature in the way must succeed on a DC 17 Dexterity saving throw or take 10 (3d6) lightning damage. A creature that touches the copper jar takes 17 (5d6) lightning damage. The jar may be neutralized by grounding the current or spilling out the mildly acidic mixture inside. Touching the acid causes 10 (4d4) acid damage.

Cauldron of Keridwen

Wondrous item, very rare

This artifact is sacred to druidical orders, who will stop at nothing to get it. Once per week, pure spring water poured inside turns into an enchanted potion — equivalent to the spell *regenerate*.

E11. Chapel

The headless statue of a female goddess, slightly reminiscent of the mother of the old gods, stands triumphantly near the south wall of this small, unused chapel. Dozens of wooden stools are found within the dusty room but many have been cast aside to allow foot traffic from the north and south doors. A natural pool bubbles in the northwest corner. At first, the clear liquid appears as spring water; testing it reveals its healing properties. Each cupful of the enchanted water heals 1 hit point of damage. The pool is drained after 20 cups of water are removed but refills after 24 hours. Soon after characters enter, mumbling becomes chanting as a robed priest appears and suddenly crumbles to dust.

E12. Bedroom

The heat from the adjoining bath keeps this room overly warm and humid, drenching the bedsheets, draperies, and table linen. Water drips from candelabras, furniture, and wall hangings, creating small pools of stagnant water in various areas of the room. The humidity has soiled the many paintings in this room, streaking the walls with colorful water as it seeps away from the damaged masterpieces. Rust has formed on most of the iron dresser handles and on the hinges on wardrobes, chests, and doors.

Three small closets in the northeastern corner once held hundreds of wonderful outfits for a fashionable young woman but have been slowly destroyed by heat-loving black moths. Thousands of the tiny creatures live within the closets, feasting on gowns, corsets, and travel clothes. Noise in the closets causes the moths to panic and burst from their nests within the clothes, creating a darkened cloud of fluttering insects. A character surprised by the black moth swarm must succeed on a DC 17 Dexterity saving throw or accidentally inhale one or more of the creatures. Consuming a black moth causes hallucinogenic behavior for 1d4 hours.

E13. Bedroom

Gilded wallpaper peels from the walls and ceiling as heat from under the floor makes this room unbearably warm. A broken heating pipe below the adjacent bath chamber has been sending heat into the bedroom for some time, turning this bedroom into a sauna-like space. Water drips from everything in the room, and several varieties of fungus grow unchecked throughout the space. The southern windows are swollen shut and are covered in a black film that blocks out all sunlight. All but a single painting has turned into a mess of seeping colors. The lone painting that seems unaffected by the heat shows a trio of seated elderly men who seem to gaze at the entrance to the cesspit (southeast of the room). One chair among the aging gentlemen is strangely empty. If the cesspit chamber is searched, the body of an old man can be found at the bottom of the disease-laden pit. The old man rejoins his friends in the painting after his body is found.

A small closet that joins this bedroom and another nearby (**F1**) contains a single, wooden box. If opened, a golden centipede jumps from its prison, and makes a melee weapon attack against the nearest character within 10 feet at +4 to hit. If bitten, a character must succeed on a DC 15 Constitution saving throw to avoid an injection of golden poison. The magical poison turns the fingernails, toenails, and teeth of the affected character a golden color (removed by a *remove curse* or similar spell). After making 1d4 bites or after being reduced to 0 hit points, the centipede turns into a solid gold statuette worth 1,500 gp and loses its magical properties. The centipede has AC 15 and 20 hit points.

E14. Bath

The utility room (**E8**) pumps boiling steam into this bath chamber to keep the water in the central pool hot. Dripping with water, the decaying ceiling bows dangerously low over the heated pool. Stone benches surround the pool on all sides, providing a seat for those who needed a break from the heat of the bath. A thick film of green algae has formed on the surface of the pool, preventing characters from seeing anything within the large bath. A corrupted **water elemental** slumbers below the surface but is awakened by any who enter the bath.

One of the long stone benches seems wider than the rest and can be found to be hollow if checked. Within, the headless vampire **Rapid Rithiena**[1] rests until disturbed. She wears six silver rings (20 gp each) and two golden bracelets (50 gp each). Her stone bench coffin is filled with the dried leaves of several rare plants; characters who are knowledgeable in plant lore may detect several healing herbs and spell components in the mix of old vegetation.

E15. Bedroom

A small band of three elven swordsmen has made camp in the relatively well-preserved bedroom. These travelers, by their own admission, entered the manor through the secret door in the linen closet to the south and are seeking the fabled *rod of Ragnar* lost long ago to elvenkind and supposedly kept in a sitting room somewhere near the Throne Room (**D1**). The "elves" are in fact **doppelgangers** who have merely adopted the likeness of the elves. They seek to join a party and attack once characters are properly weakened. One of the doppelgangers even shares a *potion of healing* with a wounded character to gain their trust.

F – Corner Quarters

The seven rooms in this corner of the great manor have been secured by the Lady Rubienna Rumpula and her devoted minions. Male guests are often lured to her bedchamber, all too late realizing her true intentions. A vampire must feed after all, but why not have a little fun first?

F1. Bedroom

Unlike many of the decaying bedrooms of the manor, Lady Rubienna's bedroom is meticulously clean and pleasant smelling. Ghostly servants frequently clean the room, preferring to arrive and depart while the lady is elsewhere. Not a speck of dust or dirt can be found anywhere within the lavish quarters of the vampire mistress. Couches, tables, chairs, and her extravagant bed are absolutely clean of all foreign materials, even blood. A magical aura rests on the room — if dispelled, the ghostly servants never return, and the room begins to fall into ruin as it was once before.

When **Lady Rubienna Rumpula**[1] is present, she spends much of her free time preparing potions to attract new lovers, crafting exotic perfumes to keep her smelling wonderfully, or designing new poisons to immobilize her latest pet. She is a masterful alchemist and crafter of poisons, skillful in measurements and balance in her brews and tonics. No fewer than a dozen of her special concoctions are present upon the shelf over her bed. Characters can find vials of otyugh saliva, a toxic vial of nightshade, three love potions, and *potions of paralysis*[VI] among the containers. She stores most of her crafting utensils and raw materials in a hidden compartment in the back of one of her wardrobes.

A table near her bed has several golden goblets and a pitcher (1,000 gp) and three crystal containers of a rare red wine infused with noble blood (100 gp each). Her dresser and wardrobe contain only the finest gowns and courtesan clothes, each bedecked with hundreds of tiny rubies, Lady Rubienna's favorite gem (275 gems in total, each worth 5 gp). An ivory and platinum hairbrush and comb (500 gp) sit upon her night table.

F2. Bedroom

A grim sight awaits those who enter this little-used bedroom — six women (**vampire spawn** with half hit points) wearing nothing more than tight corsets and burlap sacks as tight-fitting dresses hang upside down, their ankles wrapped with rusty chains fixed to the ceiling. Each woman has been drained of most of her blood and is in a state of vampirism. These were the lady's rivals at some point before Rubienna's cunning and skill caught them unawares. The lady plans to let them hang here for all eternity, starving but never dying, forever hungry.

Each of the women pleads to be rescued, claiming that the lady of the manor captured them in a fit of jealously. However, any who are freed are overcome with hunger and soon turn on their rescuers.

A large **rug of smothering** on the floor below the suspended women grabs any character who steps upon it.

F3. Kitchen

Burning meat, smashing pots, and the occasional thud of a heavy cleaver are all signs that the characters approach a staffed kitchen. This large room is busy with 10 ghoulish servants as they mindlessly prepare meals for imaginary guests. Grunts, shouts for ingredients, and uttered curses create a cacophony of noise that can sometimes be heard in other wings of the manor. The kitchen is well supplied with fresh meat of unknown origin lying on every table and rotting vegetables and foul spices being added to every pot. The cookware is old and rusty, and many of the utensils are bent and broken.

Characters in the room are ignored unless the get in the way of the cooks and butlers as they work. **Ghouls** attack intruders only to push them out of the busy kitchen, and return to work after successfully removing unwanted guests. If the characters persist in getting underfoot, one of the ghoul chefs whistles for a **flesh golem** that emerges from one of the pantries in a few rounds to escort the characters out.

Several pantries surround the kitchen proper, and are filled to the brim with rotting food, spoiled wine, and useless ingredients. A careful search of the pantry in the northeast part of the kitchen reveals a fine wooden box filled with six crystal spice containers (750 gp).

F4. Bedroom

Grotesque, creamy yellow worms writhe on the floors of the bedroom. If it were not for their gruesomeness, their color would nicely complement the beige of the drapes, the floral paintings on the wall, and the tan ceramic tiles of the small bedroom to the west. If they are stepped on, the worms scream in high, disturbingly human screams.

F5. Bedroom

An abandoned bedroom appears to have belonged to a small child, presumably the offspring of one of the former ladies of this wing. A bassinet, crib, a small dresser full of baby clothes, and several trunks of infant and toddler toys fill the unused room. A periodic baby's cry can be heard in various places of the room by one or two of the characters — none of the other characters hear the cry and may well assume their compatriots are slowly going mad in the large manor. Following the faint cries, a ghostly image of a baby appears to the same confused adventurers, floating from bassinet to crib to changing table. A painting of a stoic husband standing close to his saddened spouse as she holds a deceased baby hangs over the crib. Any uncouth remark made about the painting or the painting's content causes 3 **will-o'-wisps** — one noticeably smaller than the other two — to squeeze through the cracks in the floor and attack the characters, targeting the remark-maker first.

† One-way Teleport To		∿∿∿ Curtain or Tapestry
↓ One-way Teleport From		S Two-way Secret Door
†† Two-way Teleport		S→ One-way Secret Door
○ Giant Rat Hole		⊠ Covered Pit
⬭ Magical Statue		□ Trap Door in Ceiling
⬯ Non-magical Statue		▪ Shaft
⬅▯▯ Spectral Staircase		● Large Shaft
30 Numbered Paintings		⬒ Fireplace (shaft)

F6. Bedroom

Only the northern entrance to this room is unbarricaded; both the western and southern exits have been blocked with wardrobes, dressers, oversized chairs, and wide tables. A large canopied bed is the only piece of furniture not being used to block an entrance. The ghostly image of a young nanny paces back and forth in the room, continually returning to the northern entrance to peer into the child's room beyond. Nothing short of powerful spells or magic dispels the ghostly form from her watchful duty.

Any attempt to move the furniture that blocks the exits summons two illusionary butlers who try to hurriedly return items back to the doorways. If an exit is cleared, the butlers flee into the revolving door beyond the southern exit, spinning the old, creaking portal around as they depart. Once the doorway is clear of debris, a steady stream of ghosts pours into the room, most dressed as courtesans and servants of the manor house: 1d8 ghosts enter the room each round for 10 rounds or until the debris is returned to the doorway. The line continues to the northern door, and the ghostly procession disappears into thin air after reaching the northern room (**F5**). However, every fourth ghost is actually a well-dressed **ghast** that jumps out of line to attack the nearest character.

If characters follow the butlers into and through the revolving door, they may be transported to various locations within the wing. Use the table below to determine if the characters (independently) are teleported elsewhere.

Random Room Teleportation

1d10	Location
1	F1
2	F2
3	F3
4	F4
5	F5
6–10	No teleport occurs

F7. Linen

At one time, servants of the wing stored fresh linens and towels for the masters of the manor here. Most of the shelves on the walls are empty, their contents used and never replaced years ago. Several empty gown and hat boxes have been cast to the floor to rot in the damp corners of the closet. A single mannequin (Medium humanoid **animated object**[II]) stands by itself on the south wall, apparently unscathed by the wet filth that covers everything else in the room. When touched, the mannequin animates, attacking characters with metal hangers and scissors, and lashing out with measuring tapes and ribbons.

On a top shelf, out of sight by anyone except very tall characters, is a small box that contains fur-lined gloves, a hat, and a scarf. Although nicely made and warm, they are worth less than 5 gp. However, a character who searches the interior of the left glove finds a diamond ring caught in the middle finger hole. The large gem and platinum band is worth 5,000 gp.

The mannequin hides a well-hidden exit to the outside of the manor. Although nearly impossible to find from the exterior, the narrow door opens inward into the closet to reveal a small garden beyond.

G – Torture Chambers

Guests searching for the nearest bathroom occasionally wandered into the manor's torture chambers, which are oddly located too close to the northern front entrance. Whether the Rumps designed it this way on purpose or if it was a small area that slowly grew larger over time, no one knows for sure. Those entering the manor today through this front door can hear the faint screams of departed and lost guests.

G1. Bedroom

A dusty bedchamber is situated far too close to the main torture chamber to attract any attention from treasure hunters. Besides a few trinkets and common items, little is left to attract the attention of those who peek into the room. A large oily stain has eaten itself into the floorboards in the middle of the room. It shrinks, coagulating into a **mudbog ooze**[II] as it flows forward toward the closest party member.

G2. Room of Fear

If the dread of the Torture Chamber proves inefficient, this sanctum of grotesque and horrid paintings should do the job. The scenes depicted are so gruesome that onlookers must succeed on a DC 17 Wisdom saving throw or panic. A panicked creature drops whatever it is holding and leaves the room as soon as possible and must move away from the room at full speed on its turn. Even characters who make their saves become shaken, suffering disadvantage on all ability checks. Both effects last 10 rounds, but a character who has failed must succeed on a second saving throw or be unable to willingly enter the room. Additionally, characters who start their turn in the room must succeed on a DC 18 Constitution saving throw or be nauseated for as long as they remain in the room and for 10 minutes afterward.

For those able to withstand the oppressive onslaught of terror, a rich reward of unique and valuable trinkets can be found throughout the room. A silver pitcher encrusted with chocolate diamonds (1,000 gp) and four silver shot glasses (100 gp) sit upon a platinum tray (250 gp) on a table in the southwestern corner. A set of six crystal decanters (750 gp) are filled with blood-infused wine (variable value) on a centrally located table. A painting that initially displayed a horrific scene of unrelenting torture instead depicts a scene of the very room the characters are in. The painting shows a glowing spot in the floor under the table in the center of the room. If the area is searched, characters find a secret niche with a bag of mixed gems (2,500 gp total). The painting is magical and can be used once per week to detect 1d4 hidden locations within a room of maximum size 50 feet x 50 feet.

If the painting is removed from the wall, a **shadow** hidden within the frame exits to attack characters. If the shadow takes more than 50% of its maximum damage, it flees to another painting in the room to hide.

G3. Torture Chamber

Haunting screams of agony and fading scenes of tortured victims vanish as the characters arrive in this room. Ancient mechanisms of torture fill the large space, many stained with bile, blood, and vomit. Iron spiked coffins, nailed chairs, stretching tables, boiling vats, brazen bulls, and hanging cages are found throughout. Skeletons are chained to walls and fill many old cages, their bones forced to spend eternity in the Tegel Manor torture chamber.

Most of the equipment is too rusty or old to work properly; however, if the statue at the southern end of the room is activated (see below), the devices magically begin working again. Most machines show shadowy images of victims within them, each silently screaming in

G6
Bedroom
G7
Den
G11
Temple of
Harmikis
F
G9
Alcove
40
41
42
G5
Cells
Moaning Hall
Crack in the Wall
oyer
Screaming Hall
Whining Hall
43
44
G4
Bedroom
G2
Room of Fear
G3
Torture
Chamber
G10
Bedroom
H1
Bedroom
H2
Par
Laughter
G8
Sitting Room
T
Wails
G1
Bedroom
Q6 COURT
Roaring

One-way Teleport To
One-way Teleport From
Two-way Teleport
Giant Rat Hole
Magical Statue
Non-magical Statue
Spectral Staircase
30   Numbered Paintings
Curtain or Tapestry
Two-way Secret Door
One-way Secret Door
Covered Pit
Trap Door in Ceiling
Shaft
Large Shaft
Fireplace (shaft)

agony as ghostly torturers perform their grisly work. Mist replaces water, oil, and fire in various devices, replacing the element that would normally slowly kill their intended victims. Characters touching the mist feel the original element without it actually harming them.

An 8-foot central shaft is surrounded by coiled chains (Medium ensnaring **animated object**[II]) that animate to grapple and throw anyone within 10 feet of the pit into the depths. The pit is 30 feet deep and leads to area **DL2B** where a hungry ogre awaits tasty morsels arriving from above.

An 8-foot-tall marble statue of a two-faced man stands at the southern end of the room, his left arm raised and his right arm close to his side. The left side of his face is burned and angry, and the opposite side is pleasant and smiling. The statue holds a chain that dangles three feet below his clenched left hand. When pulled, the left arm lowers and activates the torture equipment (see above). As the left arm lowers, the right arm raises and magical blue flames erupt from its outstretched fingers. Each flame travels to an open portal, sealing it with a powerful *arcane lock* spell, coupled with a *glyph of warding* (invoking a temporary *flesh to stone* effect). The *glyph* can be noted with a successful DC 15 Intelligence (Investigation) check. The *flesh to stone* requires DC 15 Constitution saving throws to avoid its effects.

As the characters wait for the right hand to slowly fall back into its original position (after 30 minutes), some of the ghostly torturers try to force them into various devices. Although the torturers cannot be killed or dispelled, their forceful actions can be resisted with successful DC 15 Strength saving throws. Any character who fails to resist being captured and dragged to a torture device is strapped in and takes 1d4 slashing, bludgeoning, or piercing damage (your choice, depends on torture device) each round until freed. A creature can free itself by using an action and succeeding on a DC 15 Strength (Athletics) or Dexterity (Acrobatics) check, or they can be freed by another character using an action to make a Strength (Athletics) check. Once the statue's right arm returns to its side, the effects of the room and doors cease.

G4. Bedroom

As terrifying as the room before was, this one is a step beyond. Although the sable cougar skins covering the floor and the coal-black banners offer no threat and the ivory-yellow marble throne provides a welcome change of color, it is the strangely alluring aura of total darkness in the southwest quarter that fills even the most stalwart hero with silent dread (roll a saving throw against this fear).

The dark aura is extremely cold and, upon touch, erupts with a chill orange flame that sheds no light (on the contrary, it seems to increase the darkness and exhales a breath of frosty air). Within a few heartbeats, a large figure sheathed in the same unnatural glow emerges — a demonic apparition the height of two men with large, folded bat wings, cloven hooves, and a horned head. The figure holds a fiery whip in one hand and a smooth black blade in the other. The **lesser balor**[II] is just an illusion, but it *is* effective unless immediately disbelieved or dispelled. The illusion can be seen through with a successful DC 18 Intelligence (Investigation) check.

G5. Cells

Those responsible for guarding the prisoners in the two cells to the west are long gone, leaving their charges to suffer and die here after their departure. Only a wooden table and two broken chairs are found in this simple guardroom. Both doors to the western cells are still locked, their mechanisms and hinges rusted and nearly inoperable. The old bars can be ripped from the failing masonry with a successful DC 18 Strength check.

A total of three skeletal prisoners are found in the cells, two in the northernmost cell and one in the adjacent cell. The two male skeletons in the northern cell were gentlemen imprisoned for outstanding "debts." One of the gentlemen had a hidden pocket in his pants.

After the garment rotted, the gold coins within fell to the cold floor. Characters can find 25 gp under one of the skeletons.

The solitary prisoner in the southern cell was an old wizard who wronged one of the Rumps. His eyes, hands, and tongue were removed to prevent him from casting spells, but in a vicious act of spite, he was locked up with his spellbook. Although many of the topmost pages have decayed, several pages near the back of the book are still legible, protected by its waning magic.

Spellbook — 4th: *Arcane Eye, Dimension Door*; 5th: *Dream, Passwall*; 6th: *Move Earth*.

G6. Bedroom

This room is a mess. Debris litters the floor from a terrific struggle, and smashed bits of wood mingle with torn fabric, broken clay shards, snapped polearms, and bent swords. The extent of the destruction is such that the remaining splinters still twitch! Amid the chaos is the only item remaining unbroken or unbent: a padded coffer with a blackish bottle of Old Derfingel Red wine (labeled).

Although the wine is within a poorly-made vessel, its full potency remains. A single cup of the rare wine provides the same benefits as a *potion of resistance* (roll randomly each time). The opaque bottle holds four cups of the intoxicating liquid. If all four cups are consumed in one sitting, it also acts as a *potion of supreme healing* but puts the imbiber in an unconscious state for 12 hours.

G7. Den

This narrow room off the adjacent bedchamber may have once been a place for the Rumps to relax and retell stories of their past triumphs, but it has now been reduced to an abysmal and useless space. Water has seeped in from the outside of the manor to pool in low spots in the floor and to rot any furniture that stands on the slick floor. Musty and moldy animal trophies hang from walls, water dripping from noses, tusks, and ears. Wooden chairs have collapsed after their legs rotted, while others barely stand, ready to pitch a seated guest to the floor.

A low table still smells of the tobacco it once held but now contains only remnants of wet pipeweed and bits of ash. Two tapestries on the south wall show groups of fat men hunting from horseback in front of a forest. The bottoms of the tapestries have rotted, their soaked lower half straining their fixtures near the ceiling — they look like that may fall at any time. Six etched steel cups and a matching decanter sit upon a table in the center of the room. Unfortunately, the steel cupware is rusty and useless.

At 5 p.m. each day, an unseen clock chimes and several ghostly, overweight Rumps enter the room to sit, drink, and tell stories. Although no words can be heard from the shadowy visions, the jovial nature of the conversation is quite apparent. If the characters wait long enough, one of the ghosts gets up from his chair and retrieves a wondrous pipe from a hidden niche in the east wall. The item is made of gold and platinum and is studded with sapphires and rubies. When the clock strikes 6 p.m., the ghosts exit the room and do not reappear until the next day. Before the Rumps leave, the pipe is returned to the hidden niche. Characters searching that area of the wall find an actual pipe worth 750 gp as revealed previously. Without this clue, finding the niche requires a successful DC 17 Wisdom (Perception) check.

The two closets beyond the den are filled with broken furniture, debris, and refuse from other rooms, stashed here by current denizens. Characters may find a small locked box amid the piles of worthless junk. A bag of silver tokens is found within the box, presumably chips for some long-forgotten card game. The 100 slim tokens are worth 5 sp each due to their unique, ornate carvings, and purity. Unlocking the box without breaking it requires a successful DC 13 Dexterity check with thieves' tools.

G8. Sitting Room

Ladies of the manor would often gather in this out-of-the-way sitting room to gossip away afternoons and to giggle while listening to their suitors "enjoying" their visit to the nearby torture chamber. The Rump ladies had strict rules with respect to men entering this forbidden chamber; men who persisted in entering were hauled away to the torture chamber or worse. Of course, the ladies tried to entice newcomers into the room with a brief show of leg or shoulder.

Large, soft sofas and plush, oversized chairs are now stained and dusty, but still offer a comfortable seat to anyone brave enough to sit in them. The five pieces of furniture (two sofas, three chairs) are actually **mimics** that lie in wait for their next victim. Any character sitting upon one is attacked by one, then all five in the next round. However, the mimics are equally satisfied with turning on each other as their ferocity increases.

Several chairs surround a gilded table in the southwest corner of the sitting room. Eight dainty drinking glasses and a matching crystal carafe are all stained red, pink, and purple with old lipstick. One of the chairs is a bit taller than the rest, presumably designed and designated for the high lady of the family. Strapped underneath the oval table near the unique chair is an ivory-handled, silver dagger studded with masterfully-cut diamonds. A hint of blood is found upon its tip. The dagger is not magical but is worth 1,250 gp.

A room to the east can be accessed through parted curtains. Two small tables covered with dozens of tiny bottles, cases, and containers stand side by side along the south wall. Each table has a mirror that the ladies used when they sat to reapply makeup and fix their hair. However, the mirror now reveals no image when used. Instead, a prolonged stare into the mirror has a 20% chance of summoning a **dretch** demon who exits the mirror to attack the offending character.

A beautiful silver handmirror can be spotted amid the perfume bottles, foundation containers, and lipstick cases. The well-crafted item is worth 250 gp.

G9. Alcove of Agony

Detailed wall carvings depicting the decapitation of hundreds of commoners line the walls of this room and long hallway. Executioners swing large axes and two-handed swords, performing the grisly work in front of dozens of Rump onlookers. At its northern end, characters see a lit brazier that burns with an unholy flame. A black mace floats above the brazier, suspended by the rising heat. As soon as the mace is touched, it disappears, breaking the illusion. Seeing the illusion before touching it requires a successful DC 20 Intelligence (Investigation) check. Once the illusion ends, the room erupts in cries of agony and pain as the executioners begin their work again. Most of the executioners in the wall continue their work on invisible victims; however, four stone **gargoyles** dressed in executioner garb leave the walls to engage the characters at the north end of the hallway. Each executioner is as strong as the others — hit points reduced from one are reduced from all. Each creature attempts to behead its foe with a large halberd or two-handed sword. Gargoyle executioners delivering a critical hit have a 5% chance of beheading their foe.

G10. Bedroom

Gold and silver cover every object in this gaudy bedroom. Tables, chairs, dressers, cabinets, and the large bed are covered or trimmed in gold, silver, or both. Even the smallest object in the room has some gilding or silver-trim. However, as characters begin to examine the trappings of the room, they find that the silver and gold is merely paint. Common items have been painstakingly painted with fine colors to fool most observers. A successful DC 12 Intelligence (Investigation) check discerns the truth.

Although most of the items are fakes, a few items of note are within the awful room. A comb on a dresser is made of real gold, worth 125 gp. A painting of a proud hunting dog over the bed has a paint-gilded frame but the work itself is actually quite valuable (150 gp). Searching the bottom drawer of a dresser reveals a bag of 20 raw silver chunks, each worth 10 sp.

Peering into the southern closet will shock all but the most stalwart characters — a torso of a man hangs from a rope from the closet ceiling. No head, arms, or legs are found on the torso, and no sign of blood can be found anywhere. Surprisingly, the body has not rotted while in this closet. A character who sees this for the first time must succeed on a DC 18 Wisdom saving throw or be stunned for one round.

G11. Temple of Harmakhis

Darkness is unnaturally intensified by the onyx marble stone of the ceiling, walls, and floor. Non-magical light sources are at half strength here — the god of death prefers the room dark. A large idol depicting the wretched god rests upon an altar at the northern end of the room. Next to the altar slab, an 8-foot-diameter copper ball (worth 210 gp for the metal alone) rests precariously on the edge. Affixed to the ball is a length of silver chain (53 gp) that is in turn connected to a shining gold collar worth 210 gp. There is an 80% chance that disturbing the items brings down the ball, which rolls toward the entrance, crushing everything in its path, and possibly smashing the secret door off its hinges as well. The precarious stability of the ball may be determined with a successful DC 12 Intelligence (Investigation) check. If triggered, each creature in its 8-foot-wide path must succeed on a DC 16 Dexterity check or take 21 (6d6) bludgeoning damage. An enormous clay pot before the altar contains the body of a dead orc and a helm with a bloodstone embedded over three stars. This item is worth 100 gp.

H – Rooms of Revelry

This part of the manor has survived the test of time better than other wings, showing fewer signs of decay, deterioration, and flooding. Windows are larger and cleaner, and let in more light. Most areas are free of unpleasant and unwanted guests; however, not every room is a welcoming place.

H1. Bedroom

Adjoining area **G10**, this bedroom is decorated in the same manner — gilded and trimmed furniture are painted with the same decorative paint. A low, murmuring chorus of gruff voices chants, *"Betwixt the meadow, Under the bone; Are scrolls of wonder, Beware the Clone."* The sound of the voice seems to emanate from the southern wall where a secret door may be found with a successful DC 14 Intelligence (Investigation) check. A narrow secret tunnel leads to the servants' quarters (**H7**). Rounding the corner, characters see a faint, ghostly image flee into the room beyond.

H2. Parlor

By day, the room is well-lit as the sun streams through exquisite ceiling panes made of ornate and colorful glass. At night, however, the room is illuminated by a single light source: the dancing flames of a large copper brazier supported by a man-sized stone toad. As light slowly creeps back into the room at sunrise, the brazier somehow burns low, its coals nearly extinguished.

A dark silhouette of a man sits in a large leather chair as it ponders the words in an old tome. He ignores characters until they try to directly interact with him, either by touch or with questions. Interrupted, the man's true form is revealed: He is a **wraith** (that can innately cast *hypnotic pattern* 3x/day with a DC 14 spell save)! Angered, he jumps up to engage the characters in combat. At the same time, six wooden balls start to juggle themselves.

A wide assortment of comfortable chairs, long couches, and lavish tables fill the parlor. If two or more characters sit upon the couches and chairs, a ghostly reverie begins; dozens of imaginary guests begin to fill the room, drinking, laughing and socializing. Characters who fail a DC 13 Wisdom saving throw believe it to be real, even interacting with the ghostly partygoers. Those who fail their check refuse to leave for 1d4 hours while they enjoy the wonderful event.

H3. Bedroom

A bedroom off a parlor seems a strange architectural design but a closer look reveals that it once was a private room for parlor guests who needed a private place to discuss business or family matters. The bed and nightstand look out of place with the rest of the furnishings, likely added later to accommodate party guests who had enjoyed the festivities in the other room a little too much. In a corner, fiery yellow eyes peer out of a pile of bones and tendons. A moment later, tufts of coarse black hair appear; this creature is a **goblin** (with 18 Strength, +6 to hit and 7 [1d6 + 4] damage with its scimitar) who has been driven insane by the horrors of the manor. The goblin has gained extraordinary strength from the experiments Ridwik of the Relic has subjected it to, but this great ability isn't reinforced by any courage; the wretched little thing merely tries to run away and hold on to its *potion of healing*.

H4. Store

As builders and renovators worked to update this wing of the manor, many finishes were placed in this centrally-located storeroom. Tapestries, rugs, draperies, and tall vases were left here until the work was complete. Forgotten or unused, much of the materials is damp with moisture, ruining the exotic fabrics and masterful weaves. All but a few ceramic vases are cracked or chipped.

A **ghost** takes inventory of the room, counting rugs and tapestries and checking off totals on its long scroll. Unless the characters attempt to remove something from the room, it never takes notice of the characters, being too busy with its important work. Under a moldy rug in the southeast corner, the characters may find a small velvet case that contains an onyx stone on a gold chain worth 160 gp.

H5. Bedroom

This room — and the other ones nearby — were once used by Resplendent Rambert, one of the last of the later Rump line. Known for his chivalrous attitude, womanizing, and martial prowess, Rambert was very much a man of the family. The most striking feature of his erstwhile domain is the blood-red pennant hanging from a lance on the south wall. Three meticulously polished metal shields glint, hanging from steel hooks. Each of them is well used but in good shape.

The same can't be said of the mossy couch (Large monstrous **animated object**[1]) by the east wall; its decaying state is a marked contrast to the other items here. As the PCs leave the room, a gruff voice yells *"Dastard-hearted coward hinds!"* and the couch animates to attack!

H6. Ballroom

Wild chamber music continues to play as 36 ghosts disappear upon entering. The unseen orchestra's tunes get progressively more disjointed and disharmonious by the second. As characters move

H11
Stateroom
H10
Salon
H12
Smoking Room
Gnawing Hall
H7
Office
H13
Music Room
Incense Smell
110
Domo's Room
57
58
T
H8
Bedroom
H9
Bedroom
19
Dancing
H6
Ball Room
S
59
H14
Tea Room
17
Bedroom
16
Harem
Alcove
H4
Store
Damp
13
Greenhouse
H5
Bedroom
H15
Bedroom
Crack in the Wall
Whining Hall
Knocking Hall
H1
oom Bedroom
H2
Parlor
H3
Bedroom
12
Hothou
G1
Bedroom
H16
Bath
H17
Servant's
Quarters
Roaring
Bony Hall
Meowing Hall

One-way Teleport To
Curtain or Tapestry
One-way Teleport From
Two-way Secret Door
Two-way Teleport
One-way Secret Door
Giant Rat Hole
Covered Pit
Magical Statue
Trap Door in Ceiling
Non-magical Statue
Shaft
Spectral Staircase
Large Shaft
30
Numbered Paintings
Fireplace (shaft)

across the ballroom dancefloor, finely dressed ghosts attempt to pair up with each one, leading them toward the middle of the finely decorated room. Characters must succeed on a DC 15 Wisdom saving throw to resist the intense stare of their ghastly partner — those failing their check believe the dance and their partner to be real, and allow their partner to whisk them about the area as the invisible orchestra slowly speeds up the tune. Just as a character steps on the square marked **H6**, the music suddenly stops and the huge crystal chandelier crashes down on the character who had just regained its senses. The character must succeed on a DC 18 Dexterity check or suffer 21 (6d6) bludgeoning damage from the falling chandelier. The music immediately restarts. Characters who were dancing may attempt a second saving throw at this point.

After 2d20 minutes, the music finally ends, and the ghosts slowly fade into the curtains as they leave the ball. The invisible orchestra members momentarily reveal themselves around the outer edge of the room, take their bows and quickly disappear into the walls.

The remaining bits of the chandelier, even in their damaged state, are worth some 70 gp. Two wonderfully-made violins are mounted on both sides of the fireplace; each is worth 100 gp.

H7. Office

So close to the Ballroom (**H6**), this was one of the manor's more elegant offices. The huge coffin desk standing on a velvet carpet is full of inkpots and giant feather quills. Each of the desk items is hurled at the party by an unknown force, seemingly tossed in their general direction without decent aim. However, if the party leaves and returns to this room later, the items are hurled at them once again, this time with incredible force and deadly accuracy.

The first time the desk is triggered, each character in the room must make a DC 12 Dexterity saving throw. A character who fails takes 1 bludgeoning damage for each point she or he failed by. The second time, the DC is 16 and a failure results in 1d3 bludgeoning damage for each point of failure.

With a successful DC 18 Wisdom (Perception) check, one or more members of the group may notice that one of the quills does not leave its inkwell during the chaotic bombardment. This quill is an exceptional writing instrument, capable of making any hand appear steady and well-trained in penmanship. It is worth at least 50 gp to writing sages and wizards.

H8. Nursery

An overwhelming smell of alcohol permeates the room. An empty cradle by the southern wall rocks rhythmically to the soft lullaby of an invisible woman's voice. Occasional whimpers emerge from within. A storage closet to the south of this room holds broken and worn-out cradles and bassinets. Several are splashed with a red substance, presumably blood. Something silver glimmers from a cradle near the bottom of one of the piles. Halfway under a rotting bedsheet, the group may find a silver locket containing the silhouette of plump woman. It is worth 100 gp.

H9. Bedroom

This bedroom's cheerful, plum-colored decor exudes a faint, drafty odor of jasmine mixed with dust and decay. Looking at the empty west wall, the **ghost** of a petite woman wearing plum-and-white velvet sobs softly in a chair. The lady's disturbance is over the terrible old man in area **H10**, who smells up the place; she requests that he be driven out of the house. Should this deed be accomplished, the plum of the room turns ghost-gray and only a heap of ashes will be seen on the chair — accompanied by the glint of a beautiful diamond bracelet (1,800 gp).

H10. Salon

An old, kindly beggar reclines on a soiled and filthy couch that matches his appearance — the old man is absolutely grungy. He looks like he hasn't seen a bath in years, his hair is matted and greasy, and his skin is stained and blotchy from malnutrition and a squalid lifestyle. The beggar asks for a few gold coins from each character but is never satisfied with what he is given. His demeanor quickly changes to obstinate and rude if his requests (or demands) are refused or ignored. Unless placated with a sum of at least 600 gp, he polymorphs into his real form of a **glabrezu** demon. The demon starts combat with *confusion* before wading into melee. The monster accepts surrender only for the soul of at least one of its attackers, which he claims upon the point of the character's death.

H11. Stateroom

Originally reserved for accommodating notable dignitaries, the worm-eaten, throne-like chairs, enameled metal shields, and tattered banners of the stateroom have seen better days. A curious sight greets the intruders. Four **zombies** are bowing to a fat white **giant rat** seated on one of the thrones, wearing a pink cape and a red plumed hat. One of the thrones has been cursed to *polymorph* anyone who sits upon it into a rat. The effect is permanent unless someone other than the victim removes the polymorphed rat from the throne. This garbed rat is actually a fanciful **zombie** (with 45 hit points) that somehow became seated upon the cursed throne. If the rat is removed from the seat, it returns to its undead zombie form.

A character who sits upon the cursed throne must succeed on a DC 15 Wisdom saving throw or be polymorphed into a rat. A *remove curse* spell reverses the effect, assuming the rest of the group can catch their friend if he or she flees the room.

H12. Smoking Room

Overwhelming smoke and the stench of tobacco envelop the smoking room. Within the grayish haze, smoky profiles of men form in the leather armchairs, then disappear. A copper spittoon in the northeast corner is worth 6 gp if properly cleaned of the accumulated unwholesome sludge.

H13. Music Room

The dusty, closed-in smell here reveals the room hasn't been visited in ages. Nevertheless, a concerto of erratic music is in progress, as a large organ and a graceful harp try to harmonize their tunes without much success. Yellowed sheets of paper with musical notes are scattered on the floor. Although both instruments are close to falling apart, some parts are still valuable; the 42 ivory keys of the organ are worth 10 gp each. Although the strings of the harp are golden in color, they are merely gilded — underneath the gold paint, the strings are found to be made of a simple metal, typical to this type of instrument. Neither invisible musician allows their instruments to be torn down for pieces without a fight, with each casting proper insults and slapping characters across the face with unseen, silk gloves. The musicians can do no damage, however.

H14. Tea Room

The intoxicating aroma of roses lingers over the gaudy, lavish decor — flower and vine wallpaper covers the walls and ceiling. Although peeling in several places, the bulk of the ornamental but garish

wallpaper still hangs on the plaster walls. The small round table is set with a stunning silver tea service (475 gp) and a large silver bowl (205 gp) containing the main course: a **black pudding** that quickly flows out to devour its would-be devourers.

H15. Bedroom

The Rump coat-of-arms dominates the fine woven carpet in the middle of the room. Occasionally (50% chance every 10 minutes), the furniture in the room slides to one side as if the room was in a listing boat. Interestingly, vases, old picture frames, and washbasins stay in their places as the furniture slides about the room. The drawers of a large bureau by the north wall open and expel clothing at the party if they come too close, then slam shut. Heaving sounds are heard from within.

H16. Bath

Images of beautiful mermaids attending Rump family members cover the walls of this warm and well-kept bath chamber. Steam rises from the seemingly hot water, creating a thin fog near the ceiling as the warm and cold air meet. Water ripples as if there is movement within the dark waters of the wide pool. If all the sconces of the room are lit, the bathwater lightens to a blue-green hue that makes it easy for onlookers to view the 3 swimming **swarms of miniature mermaids**[II] within. The bright light signals for their emergence — 2-foot-long mermaids swim to the edge of the bath, beckoning characters to enter with waving hands, oval eyes, and perfect smiles.

However, if the characters enter the pool, the mermaids recognize that they aren't Rump descendants (likely, by scent). Instead of bathing the characters, the mermaids tear into them with fangs as they try to pull them into the deeper section of the bath.

Several other victims have met their final moments in the deeper section, leaving their bones and a few trinkets behind. Three silver rings (10 gp each), one gold bracelet (25 gp), and a ruby necklace (75 gp) are found intermingled with the bones.

H17. Servants' Quarters

It is apparent from the moment characters enter this room that it was the servants' quarters for this wing at one time. None of the lavish and extravagant gilding, polish, or finery of the other rooms is present in this spacious yet boring room. Several pieces of broken furniture are piled in a heap in the center of the room, presumably the beds, dressers, and chairs of the servants from long ago. A search of the pile of debris reveals nothing of interest; however, a single portrait of a red flower that hangs askew on the northern wall has a gold and platinum necklace fastened to its back. The well-made necklace was likely stolen from one of their masters and forgotten here when the servants left. Platinum is interwoven into the gold braids of the necklace, making it worth 750 gp.

I – NORTHEAST QUARTERS

No section of the manor has as much sprawling vegetation and rampant plant-growth as the northeastern wing. Floors and walls of rooms and hallways are bursting with vines, weeds, and thorny bushes that seem to reach for characters as they pass by. It's almost as if the plants have minds of their own.

I1. BEDROOM

A pungent incense coalesces at the doorway, warning characters with a burning irritation of the eyes, nose, and throat as they enter. Those who linger within the room for a minute must succeed on a DC 16 Constitution saving throw or suffer blindness (50%) or incapacitating illness (50%) for 2d6 rounds. The strange, misty smoke follows characters that are initially unaffected, seemingly trying to get the better of resistant trespassers.

Somehow unaffected by the thick smoke of incense, a black cat perches on a ledge behind a tapestry hanging on the eastern wall. If any character gets within five feet of the large cat, it leaps to the floor and mysteriously disappears in a flash of fire and ash! The strange feline leaves behind a clump of black hair on the floor after it departs. When held, the clump of hair provides 120 ft. darkvision.

If the room is entered again within an hour of exiting it, the cat returns to its perched position behind the tapestry. When it repeats its disappearing act, again leaving the clump of hair on the floor, the previous hairball mysteriously vanishes.

I2. HOTHOUSE

A thick humidity overwhelms those entering who are unaccustomed to the warmth of a dense jungle. As soon as characters enter, the fireplace begins billowing waves of steam that cascade over rows and rows of closely planted vegetation; rare flowers fight to survive, outnumbered by strangling vines and tall weeds 10 to 1. Colorful flower petals hide the dangerous poisons of leafy plants and venoms of thorny vines. Characters failing a DC 10 Dexterity saving throw bump into something that they shouldn't, resulting in one of many maladies — sleeping, sickness, and deadly toxins abound in this room.

Hundreds of silver and coral coins have been placed near the stems of many of the plants. Characters spending an hour or more in the room find 785 gp worth of coins. However, many are still coated with a strange toxin that begins a 24-hour illness resulting in a painful and explosive death. Determining which ones are coated requires a successful DC 18 Wisdom (Perception) check. Each character that touches a coated coin must succeed on a DC 16 Constitution saving throw or fall ill. Ill creatures gain one level of exhaustion every 3 hours until dead or cured. Approximately 30% of the coins of coated.

A tall **grotesque plant**[II] near the fireplace extends its long vines at approaching characters, hoping to pull them close enough to "bite"; the plant has a strange beak at its center that can pluck skin from an unprotected arm or face with ease. The plant recoils at fire, letting go of any held characters and wrapping itself up in its long vines and large leaves to avoid injury.

The room to the east contains a deteriorating pile of mulch and fertilizer left here some time ago. Grub-seeking **giant fire beetles** are living in the pile and may look upon the characters as a better meal than the meager grubs and worms infrequently found in the area.

I3. GREENHOUSE

Unique and magical plants continue to grow in this warm and stuffy greenhouse, long after Rump gardeners abandoned their work. A lack of ventilation makes this room oppressive — water drips from every leaf and vine, pot, and shelf. The floor is covered in a thin layer of water that makes any quick movement within the walkways a treacherous exercise.

An exotic plant in the center of the room has six tiny pods that hang from its thick stem. If touched, the pods open to reveal 6 tiny **plant goblins**[II]! Although they are fierce for their size, they prefer to run and hide within the dense fauna within the room. However, they fight if cornered, working together silently to attack a single foe at a time.

A well-hidden, rare plant in the southwest corner mysteriously grows thin, gold leaves. When removed, these paper-thin leaves can be used for gilding or as fancy parchment.

I4. SAUNA

Fed by the same vents as areas **I2** and **I3**, the sauna is likewise filled with steam. The billowing cloud heavily obscures anything beyond 5 feet and conceals a **giant crab** that waits patiently by the secret door. The tunnel it guards leads to a dead end — or does it? A step of the Sighing Staircase may be pushed out from below to grant access to the East Wing. The step can be found with a successful DC 14 Intelligence (Investigation) check.

I5. BEDROOM

This place is an extension of the Harem (**I6**), and just as well appointed. Two **wereboars**, appearing as twin sisters in chainmail bikinis, are pinned to the west wall by silver chains (they are so fine — and so heavy — that they would fetch 41 gp apiece). They plead for their release, and if this is done, they immediately revert to their porcine forms, still female, but not quite as fetching.

I6. HAREM

Large pillows, opaque silk curtains, and thick rugs fill this oddly-shaped room. The cushions are set in a circle around a low-burning brazier in the middle of the room, and provide a comfortable respite from the incessant conflict elsewhere in the manor. Thin wisps of incense waft from the brazier, filling the room with a strong aroma that is hard to identify. If characters sit upon the cushions, invisible imprints upon nearby cushions hint at ghostly harem girls that may try to interact with them every 1–2 rounds. Faint giggling and seductive whispers seem to be just at the edge of the characters' hearing, keeping them on the constant lookout for visitors. All dreams in the room are pleasant, the drinks and snacks are automatically replenished, and no undead bother to check on the location. However, after spending the third night here, the characters awake in the prison (**DL2K**) stripped of all belongings. Upon their return, they find everything in the room has disappeared save for a single rose petal.

Incense Smell
H13 Music Room
18 Temple of Quetzalcoatl
56
T
110 Domo's Room
111 Lounge
H9 Bedroom
19 Dancing Room
J1 Den
H14 Tea Room
17 Bedroom
16 Harem
15 Bedroom
Damp
H15 Bedroom
55
13 Greenhouse
14 Sauna
J5 Foyer
12 Hothouse
T
11 Bedroom
KEY
Curtain or Tapestry
Two-way Secret Door
One-way Secret Door
Covered Pit
Trap Door in Ceiling
Shaft
Large Shaft
Fireplace (shaft)
Trap
One-way Teleport To
One-way Teleport From
Two-way Teleport
Giant Rat Hole
Magical Statue
Non-magical Statue
Spectral Staircase
Numbered Paintings

17. Bedroom

The odor of burning wax fills the room. A bed bearing a coffin, surrounded by 33 thick candles, occupies the center of the place. Three silver crosses hang on each wall (5 gp each). Upon entry, all the candles ignite, only to go out one by one individually. The small coffin requires two characters with a combined 30 Strength to open. It is completely empty. If the lid is raised to its full height, a strong wind blasts through the western exit, extinguishing all non-magical light sources. A silk-paper kite under the bed somehow remains in a pristine state while the rest of the room slowly decays.

18. Temple of the Serpent

This place of peaceful contemplation is dedicated to Quetzalcoatl in his more benevolent aspect. The fragrance of exotic flowers wafts through the air as sitar music plays somewhere far away. A large brocade pillow floating 2 inches off the floor is a *carpet of flying*. Dozens of folded paper dolls of a colorful, feathered serpent hang from the ceiling, spinning when the slightest of breezes circulates through the room. Each paper doll of the Quetzalcoatl provides a temporary boon to a character when removed (once per 7-day period); one randomly-chosen primary statistic gains a +1 bonus until the character takes a long rest if the paper doll is attached to clothing and proudly worn. Note that the paper doll must be affixed to clothing while in this room to gain the bonus. Paper dolls are magically replenished within 24 hours of their removal.

A strange boundary marker is placed in each corner of the room at mid-height. Any character who is primarily in the upper half of the room (with more than 50% of their body in the space between the midway point and the ceiling) is magically transported outside the manor.

The altar of Quetzalcoatl is a great furnace used to burn sacrificial offerings. It is flanked by two rainbow-like serpent statues (couatls) and its own enameled surface is adorned with vibrant tones. *Continual flames* burn within. Sacrificing colorful plumes, silks, or even multicolored sand on this altar brings good luck — advantage on the character's next saving throw. If the shrine is desecrated in any way or inappropriate items are sacrificed, the couatl statue to the right animates as a **stone golem**.

19. Dancing Room

Chairs face the west wall in three orderly rows. Any clapping sounds cause 30 ghostly dancing girls and musicians to appear for a performance that lasts two hours. At the end of their recital, the ghostly dancers invite remaining characters to play musical chairs — enough chairs for the dancers and characters (minus one) slide across the room into a wide circle. Rousing marching music begins as the shadowy ballerinas circle the chairs. Each round, a chair is removed before the music starts. Each participating character should make a Dexterity check. The ghostly dancers make their checks with a +3 modifier. The character or dancer with the lowest check is eliminated. If a character wins the last seat in the final round, they are showered with 10d100 gilded rose petals (each worth 1 gp). However, if a ghostly dancer wins, the characters are forcefully removed from the room while the musicians play a proper finale tune.

110. Domo's Room

A steady drizzle of red liquid showers the room from a thousand tiny holes in the ceiling. A sample of the pooling liquid reveals that it's the bloody mixture of a multitude of species. A velvet rug, as bloody as the rest of the room, slowly crawls across the floor, its two huge feelers twitching nervously. The rug is harmless. The rug-creature seeks out pools of blood to soak itself in, constantly moving from an emptied depression to one recently filled from the draining ceiling. Oddly, the rug is never fully saturated by all the blood-soaking and is unnervingly and inexplicably dry to the touch.

Any prodding of the ceiling has a cumulative 10% chance per attempt to rupture the thin and weakened ceiling, sending a wave of blood washing over the group. Each character must succeed on a DC 20 Dexterity or Strength check (player's choice) or get washed out of the room in either exit. The rushing blood-wave forces characters out of the room but does not spill into the hallway or room beyond. The blood instead curls up the walls and drains back into the ceiling. The ruptured ceiling mysteriously repairs itself and the room returns to its previous state.

If the characters wait long enough (once per day at a random hour), they see the velvet rug deposit a large, blood-red ruby in an empty floor depression before it moves on to another pool. The flawless ruby is worth 10d100 gp.

111. Lounge

Rows under rows of decorative arabesque on the walls turn out to be the illuminated chronicle of the Rump family. The wall inscriptions detail mostly fictitious deeds of daring while omitting the less savory aspects of the family's history. This means that little here is factual — or even tangentially related to the truth.

An intricately carved chest with detailed inscriptions that match the walls of the room looks to be extremely valuable, especially to any surviving Rump family member (worth 100 gp, double to triple that to a Rump). A large golden handle on the chest beckons to characters. The chest's occupant is a miniature red dragon (Small anamalistic monstrous **animated object**[II]), which looks like a very elaborate and finely carved statuette but turns out to be alive and extraordinarily belligerent. Next to the dragon is a crystal container sealed with beeswax. It seems to contain metallic blue flies. These little beasts are equivalent to an **insect swarm** and animate if the container is unstoppered. They obey spoken commands. If no command is given, they attack whoever is closest (most likely the character who opened their prison).

J — East Wing, Ground Floor

The ground floor of the three-story East Wing is secluded, accessible only through narrow rat holes (the largest found in area **J4**), a secret door (from the Sauna, area **I4**) or by knocking down several of the fragile walls along the western portion of the wing. Monsters wandering through the manor cannot enter the wing unless they have the ability to move through solid walls. A two-way teleporter in area **J4** provides access into the wing from the fourth story of Brother's Tower (**O3**) at the opposite side of the manor.

J1. Den

Bright light pours in through windows on the east wall each morning, illuminating the once-relaxing den of the wing. Large couches and high-backed, plush chairs encircle a great mahogany table covered with silver candlesticks, rotting books, and several discarded pipes. At night, the room is submerged in total darkness, allowing the former denizens to return to their favorite haunt to retell stories and discuss family matters. No fewer than a dozen shadowy images are found resting upon the furniture here after sundown. They ignore the characters for the most part, acknowledging their presence only when magical light is used to illuminate the room. Even then, their engagement with the living consists only of side-glances, the occasional disdainful stare, and a few snide remarks.

If the silver candlesticks or old books are removed from the room, they disintegrate to dust within seconds. The pipes, however, are relatively worthless but can be removed from the den.

A keg of delicious golden wine on the table heals 1d4 hp per mug, but the imbiber ages 1d6 x 10 years after a three-hour delay for every mug consumed. A successful DC 16 Constitution saving throw prevents the process, as does a *lesser restoration* or *remove curse* spell.

J2. Chamber of Reptile

A weathered statue of a human male still stands to one side of the room, surrounded by a vast pile of leaves, branches, and rotting vegetation. The putrid heap moves if prodded, and the scaly body of a **spirit naga** (replace *water breathing* with *hypnotic pattern*) slithers forth. The naga offers advice for treasure, but gives none, instead using his charming gaze and spells to snare and eliminate his foes, preferably by compelling them to enter the room to the north. If heavily wounded, the serpentine seducer uses his *hypnotic pattern* spell to escape, or bargains for his life in exchange for his "treasure" conveniently hidden in room **J3**. As the shambling mound there engages the characters, he flees to safety, planning bloody revenge.

J3. Bedroom

Moss has overgrown the wooden paneling and furniture of this small bedroom. Light shines through the gaps in the ceiling, casting beams of light on the green carpet. A greenish mass of moss, leaves, and vines is a **shambling mound** that attacks as soon as a character is within its reach. Note that the exit to the west is boarded up.

J4. Hunter's Room

Dozens of hunting trophies line the walls of the room, from small innocent creatures of the forest to large, exotic beasts of faraway and

One-way Teleport To
One-way Teleport From
Two-way Teleport
Giant Rat Hole
Magical Statue
Non-magical Statue
Spectral Staircase
Numbered Paintings

Curtain or Tapestry
Two-way Secret Door
One-way Secret Door
Covered Pit
Trap Door in Ceiling
Shaft
Large Shaft
Fireplace (shaft)

mysterious locales. Characters passing a DC 12, 15, or 18 Nature check can identify some to all (your choice on a 12 or 15) of the mounted heads. A few of the faded plaques under the trophies are still barely legible and may hint to the associated creature and its origin.

Only one trophy is not mounted on the wall but poses fully assembled in the center of the room. An intact **giant lizard skeleton**[II] stands in the northeast corner. Disturbingly, its two green eyes are still in their sockets, peering menacingly on intruders. The creature demands dew worms in Abyssal, and if it doesn't get any, it attacks!

A massive stone seat resembling an ancient throne can be seen in the southeastern corner of the room. Any who sit upon it are instantly teleported to the fourth level of the Brother's Tower (**O3**) and those using the two-way teleporter there arrive here, seated.

The attached rooms to the south were used to prepare trophies for mounting, for storing taxidermy supplies, and to discard the unwanted parts of the hunted animals. Countless bones for hundreds of prepared animals are found scattered throughout the two rooms. A careful search of the area may reveal a small silver knife that cuts through animal skin, muscle, and tendon with ease.

J5. Foyer

The dusty portrait of Radded Rufus (**NPC#55**), bored out of his mind, rambles on to his only conversation partner for centuries, a dust-covered stuffed ape with turquoise gem eyes (10 gp each). He pleads to be taken somewhere else — anywhere but this place. Behind the portrait is a bricked-up doorway. Removing the bricks reveals that there are *two* walls, and a skeleton wearing a leather apron and still holding a mason's trowel in his hand is trapped in between.

J6. Bedroom

It is obvious to see that this small room was a young lady's bedroom; a single canopy bed with pink lace, a dressing table, and several mannequins draped with old ballgowns give away the previous occupant's gender and approximate age. Although the tiny gowns were once beautiful, time has been cruel to the silk, satin, and crinoline garments. A trunk at the foot of the small bed is curiously empty.

A search of the bed reveals a bow, several arrow shafts, and a bag of 36 silver arrowheads placed between the two mattresses. Searching the dressing table uncovers a hidden note secured under the bottom drawer. It reads, "Our dance was magnificent. I hope you agree. Until next time, my lady. — RR".

J7. Refectory

It must have been mostly servants who had used this place, as evidenced by the simple craftsmanship of the huge dining table in the middle. The table swarms with thousands of flies that cover vaguely human-shaped lumps of rotted meat. Movement causes the fly swarm to envelop the characters, blinding them until they are somehow destroyed. The swarm is gross but harmless, and so are the putrid corpses crawling with white maggots in the west room (this place looks like it could have been a kitchen once … probably). A sooty chute in the fireplace leads to the Dining Room above metal rungs make climbing easier.

K – Staff Quarters

Manor life was not grand for all inhabitants at Tegel. Cooks, blacksmiths, gardeners, and other craftsmen spent much of their time performing tasks or running errands for the Rumps. What little remaining time they had after their work was completed was spent praying in their own temple, sleeping, and, occasionally, bathing. This section of the manor was reserved for the poor souls who served their masters. They had little more than basic necessities — the rooms in this area prove that clearly.

K1. Temple of Odin

A disapproving frown seems to sit on the All-Father's brow as he looks upon the morbid scene in his simple sanctuary: cobwebs and filth cover the wooden pews and the rusted iron altar. Nine **ghouls** feast on the grisly remains. Once they notice intruders, they attack, cackling in glee. The spirit of the All-Father awakens within the statue if the characters stand their ground against the ghouls, animating the statue's eyes, head, and arms during the fight. Characters hear the statue whisper encouragement during the fight, urging them to eradicate the foul creatures. If the ghouls are destroyed, the statue returns to its previous pose; however, instead of a disapproving frown, it appears satisfied. It also has a *javelin of lightning* in its hand, which it offers as a gift to the group for clearing out the room.

K2. Carriage House

A loud snort or whinny sounds every sixth round from a random stall. The pale outlines of long-dead steeds waiting for their turn to pull invisible carriages can be seen in several empty stalls. Shouts from ghostly coachmen who are cursed to spend eternity preparing carriages for forgotten Rump family members occasionally interrupt the silence of the building. A top hat hanging from a hook appears to have weathered the time well; it is in fact a *hat of disguise* that cannot be removed once placed upon the head of a living being (it fails to work on undead). A black, velvet-lined carriage with drawn curtains stands before the rusted iron doors. It contains an empty casket with dirt inside.

The carriage doors are rusted shut, and require a successful DC 20 Strength check to open them.

K3. Plant Room

An overwhelming wave of scents and odors, both pleasant and strange, washes over characters as they enter a room filled with hundreds of species of flowers and plants. A multitude of colorful flowers with intense fragrances tests olfactory organs and the knowledge of even the most seasoned botanist. Several common and rare ingredients may be discovered throughout the room. For sickly characters (Constitution less than 9), the area is a toxic, unpleasant place — unless a successful DC 15 Constitution check is made, these characters spend every minute within the room sneezing and coughing. These characters have disadvantage on skill checks and attack rolls while in the room.

A **giant wasp** has made a paper nest in the southeast corner. The lair can be spotted with a successful DC 14 Wisdom (Perception) check. It emerges after the lotus has taken its toll and tries to paralyze as many victims with its venom as possible. The nest is empty, save for six doses of lotus pollen inside. Disturbing the nest also disturbs the pollen, and the investigating character must immediately make a successful DC 16 Constitution saving throw or suffer the ill effects of the yellow lotus (see sidebox).

KEY
Curtain or Tapestry
Two-way Secret Door
One-way Secret Door
Covered Pit
Trap Door in Ceiling
Shaft
Large Shaft
Fireplace (shaft)
Trap
One-way Teleport To
One-way Teleport From
Two-way Teleport
Giant Rat Hole
Magical Statue
Non-magical Statue
Spectral Staircase
30 Numbered Paintings
I1 Bedroom
Iron Door
K2 Carriage House
54
D6 Bedroom
K3 Plant Room
K7 Bedroom
K1 Temple of Odin
D7 Sitting Room
Rattling Hall
K4 Bedroom
K5 Gardener's Room
K10 Bedroom
K9 Bedroom
K6 Bath
K8 Store
K11 Bedroom
K12 Smithy
52
53
Cranking Hall
L3 Bedroom
L5 Rumpus Room

Yellow Lotus

These exotic plants grow only in hot, humid environments such as jungles or (for instance) the Plant Room (area **K3**) of Tegel Manor. Yellow lotus is a potent poison. A character inhaling yellow lotus pollen must make two DC 16 Constitution saving throws, one to prevent the primary effect and the other to prevent the secondary effect. Its primary effect is a light slumber that follows 3 rounds after the pollen is inhaled. Its secondary effect is 1d8 points of Constitution damage. The Constitution damage is recovered after a long rest. Generally, each plant has 1d2 doses of lotus dust that may be recovered and used or sold for about 1,600 gp.

K4. Bedroom

Although mostly shielded from the fragrance of the yellow lotus in the Plant Room, some aspect of that place still lingers, creating a dreamlike, hazy environment. The current occupant of the dark apartment is a yellow **flying skull**[II] (with the ability to grant wishes) in a long scarlet robe. It asks if the party has seen the "Keeper."

A negative answer permits each character one *wish* each (*"Then what is your wish?"*). The wish must be declared immediately and without hesitation or the skull moves on to the next character. After all characters have had their chance or if the skull is attacked, the apparition disappears in a flash of orange light. If the characters answer "yes" to the skull's question, it mumbles *"No need for me, then"* as its form fades into nothingness.

Sleeping in the room is not advisable; characters doing so suffer 1d2 points of permanent Constitution loss due to lung damage — after all, some of those lotus pollens *do* get in here!

K5. Gardener's Room

A disheveled room filled with pots, gardening supplies, old dirt, and burlap sacks at first appears to be nothing more than a workroom for gardeners. However, a longer look reveals it was also the bedroom of the gardener. Several boards have been placed upon a small bed so it may be used as an extra worktable. One of the burlap sacks contains a mysterious dust that when sprinkled, turns whatever it touches to a dark green hue. A well-preserved coil of rope hangs from a hook next to the bed. Closer inspection reveals that it is a *rope of climbing*. Interestingly, a box under the bed contains a handful of petrified seeds. A note within the box claims they are magical, capable of growing trees that bear gems as fruit. This is false, of course. As for the compost, it seems to be full of bone shards, some disturbingly humanlike.

K6. Bath

The small servants' bath is a mere closet with a single wooden tub. The large nostrils of a reptilian creature peek out from the still waters within the large tub. If the water is disturbed, a malformed **crocodile** lifts its head from the water and bears its jagged teeth in warning. Characters may spot several odd differences with the beast, including its short size, uniquely human eyes, and its apparent dislike of the water. The group may be able to determine that the creature is a polymorphed **centaur** who fell prey to a cruel trick. The centaur serves his saviors if turned back to normal. He knows of the traps protecting the Lich's Laboratory (**L6**) and has heard that an evil spirit lives within the silver bell of the Wizard's Tower.

K7. Bedroom

The wooden table in the middle of this room was made from the huge shield of a hill giant. Runes etched into its surface spell out the title "Lord of Telgarn." Several wooden mugs lie on its surface, and a small cask of mead stands next to the previous occupant's bed. A holy symbol of Odin hangs over the bed, next to an enormous helmet that could easily double as a cauldron. A wide leather strap affixed to the underside of the table is a *belt of giant strength* (fire).

K8. Store

Various animal skins lie in chaotic piles. These shaggy pelts include lion, bear, wolf, jaguar, and leopard skins. They are too decayed to be of value; furthermore, they have been infested by ticks, including a **giant tick**[II]. The tick tries to crawl on the back of a smaller character and suck it dry before falling off and scurrying back to its nest.

K9. Bedroom

This bedroom that once housed several stable hands has been restored to look almost decent. Even the usual dust and cobwebs are absent. Living in this room is a spectacularly ugly gnome (**Vali**[II]) who usually sits by his large oak table and carves arrow shafts with a rusty knife. This fellow introduces himself as "The Fletcher" and gifts each character carrying a bow with an arrow — two if they are exceedingly polite. He refuses to answer further questions and will not be encountered on any later visit.

Despite his humble appearance, the gnome is none other than the god Vali, Norse deity of the Eternal Light, the best bowman in nine worlds. Vali's gifts are special *arrows of lightning* (see sidebox). He doesn't care for much talk at the moment, and if he is attacked or threatened, he teaches his challengers a painful lesson. Vali enjoys combat as much as any of his divine companions. That is, a *lot*.

Arrows of Lightning

Ammunition (arrow), legendary

Supercharged cousins of your garden variety *lightning arrow*, you gain +3 on your attack roll and inflict 1d6 piercing plus 7d6 lightning damage on a hit. However, even a miss means the arrow is consumed!

K10. Bedroom

The furnishings of the room clearly convey the area's original purpose although the items found at its center are strangely out of place for a servant's bedroom. Additionally, the room has an unnatural feeling of vertigo that causes less-dexterous characters to become unsteady or to fall. Characters must pass a DC 15 Dexterity (Acrobatics) check to remain standing within the room. The sharp smell of ozone comes from a pewter tankard brimming with acid. Touching the liquid causes 14 (4d6) acid damage. The table it rests on also holds an ornate walking stick. The brass head may be twisted off to reveal a cavity with 23 10 gp amber gems. The removable head can be noticed with a successful DC 18 Intelligence (Investigation) check. The walking stick seems to be attracted to the tankard. Touching the items together results in a tremendous electrical burst that destroys both items. All creatures within 10 feet must make a DC 15 Dexterity saving throw, taking 17 (5d6) force damage on a failure or half as much on a success.

K11. Bedroom

This room once belonged to the dread pirate Rummy Rory (**NPC #24**), who preferred the company of the servants to his insane relatives, whereas they were happy to avoid a deranged lunatic like Rummy. Mounted fish, a sailor's hammock, old ocean maps, and a porthole that opens to reveal a wall give the impression of a ship captain's quarters. Statuettes from faraway lands line wooden shelves on the walls and several traveling diaries filled with fantastical stories of sea battles are piled high on a small captain's desk. Two dozen empty bottles of cheap rum are found scattered about the floor (Rummy never cared to pick them up!). Cabinets in the west wall are groaning under the weight of yellowed documents. These are of little interest, but a leather-bound tome, the log of the Seaborn Saber, has a description and vague directions to the "Wondorous Isles" [sic] where a mountain of amethyst is located.

K12. Smithy

Even though no human smith has worked here since time immemorial, the forge is still hot. Sparks fly and iron ingots float above the fire pit. A large iron hammer (Tiny paraphernalia **animated object**[II]) pounds on the anvil in an endless monotone. It hurls itself at intruders entering the workshop as the asthmatic wheezing of the bellows rasps vile insults. The hammer falls down after the first successful hit but reanimates as soon as the characters think they are safe!

Crude iron objects lie about in disarray. They include nails, iron sheets, horseshoes, a fire poker, and two metal flasks. Four of the horseshoes are *horseshoes of speed*.

L – Lich's Lair

Ridwik of the Relic, a lich of incredible prestige and great power, long ago claimed the Wizard's Tower for himself as his new lair. He added several rooms to the manor that now connect to the tower before setting his minions to the task of protecting the new wing. The area is mostly silent; however, the occasional footfall or low moan may be heard when the characters stop to listen.

L1. Stable

A furious contest of wills takes place in this otherwise empty stable, whose main entrance was walled up ages ago. A noble **ki-rin**[II] is cornered by an **intellect devourer**[II], who advances menacingly toward its psionically weakened prey unless, of course, the characters turn the tide of the battle. The ki-rin is thankful to his rescuers but prefers to

Solarium
N9
Loft
N10
L1
Stable
T
L2
Barracks
L3
Bedroom
S2
S3
L5
Rumpus Room
Chiming Hall
T
Q4
Crypts
L4
Armory
L7
School Room
L6
Liche's
Laboratory
KEY
Curtain or Tapestry
Two-way Secret Door
One-way Secret Door
Covered Pit
Trap Door in Ceiling
Shaft
Large Shaft
Fireplace (shaft)
Trap
One-way Teleport To
One-way Teleport From
Two-way Teleport
Giant Rat Hole
Magical Statue
Non-magical Statue
Spectral Staircase
Numbered Paintings

be escorted out of the manor and present a reward later. The intellect devourer just attacks anybody it can.

A secret door in the back of one of the stalls leads to a long, dark hallway hidden between a bedroom (**L3**) and the barracks (**L2**). About halfway down the narrow passage, it appears a bag was hastily discarded or possibly thrown from the stall into the hidden space. Opening the bag disturbs the glow-bugs within, which scatter throughout the tunnel. Most are caught within the ceiling of webs, illuminating a massive nest of thousands of harmless spiders. Anyone willing to reach into the bag finds a golden horse comb that magically untangles manes or tail hair instantly. It is worth 250 gp.

L2. BARRACKS

A skeleton in full plate armor hangs upside down from the rafters while half a dozen **skeletons** armed with spears (replace short sword with spear and add ranged attack at +2 to hit for 1d6 piercing damage) try to stab their suspended target. Dozens of shelves contain various bits and pieces of armor, weaponry, and gear taken from foolish interlopers. Most of the items are useless, either rusted or damaged, but a few helms, daggers, and short swords are passable. Other useless or mundane items are crammed upon the shelves.

If the suspended skeleton is dropped, the characters find that he wears an *amulet of health* under its armor.

L3. BEDROOM

Only a former bedroom, a company of 4 **zombies** are busy converting this place into a storeroom. The tireless undead are currently stacking barrels of sparrows, frog legs, and snakes preserved in a saline solution. Not all barrels contain the strange combination of avian, reptilian, or amphibian organs and body parts; one barrel contains a strange mixture of water and red, viscous liquid that smells awfully. Anyone brave enough to search the barrel finds thousands of tiny bone shards at the bottom of the container. However, a false bottom in the barrel contains a waterlogged silk pouch of diamonds (100 tiny gems, each worth 10 gp). The secret stash can be found with a successful DC 18 Intelligence (Investigation) check.

L4. ARMORY

Two **ghouls** guard the lich's spare arsenal. Most of the weapons have already been distributed to the ever-growing undead horde, but 10 battleaxes, 23 spears, 13 longswords, and 27 daggers remain. The ghouls are busy polishing the weapons when they are interrupted.

L5. Rumpus Room

Long hallways pass by the west and east sides of the servants' quarters to end in this large, unused gathering place. Although tidy and well kept, no one is ever seen cleaning the room at any time during the day or night. The decorations and furnishings of the room — much of it seemingly chosen to meet the tastes of adults, children, huntsmen, nobles, and ladies — appeal to most anyone. Historical tomes, including those that detail much of the Rump family history and the geography of the Tegel area, line shelves along the southern wall between windows facing the crypts. Suits of armor, mounted trophies of age-old hunts, and paintings of royal ladies are found along the western and northern walls. A massive tapestry spanning the entire eastern wall depicts several continuous scenes of Rump soldiers triumphing over threatening and fantastical creatures and evil-faced men. A box overflowing with puzzles and wooden toys sits under a center table. Comfortable couches and simple chairs are arranged pleasingly throughout the room.

Every 1d3 minutes, crashes and thuds come from random quarters of the room, and unattended items — wooden mugs, tin plates, etc. — are hurled in random directions. The fireplace belches sparks every 4 minutes. Anyone standing in the way is affected as if by *burning hands* cast at 1st level with a DC 14 spell saving throw (3d6 fire damage or half as much with a successful Dexterity saving throw). This haunting is the work of Ramatic Rumpula (**NPC #52**), whose portrait hangs to the right of the fireplace. Threatening the picture with harm provides a short relief in the chaos.

L6. Lich's Laboratory

Within the massive foundation of the monstrous Wizard's Tower lies Ridwik's laboratory. Unlike the alchemical treasure trove of his brother, Rasping Rashuak (**E9**), the lich's laboratory is a room of half-completed experiments, bizarre creature dissections, and other undreamed of grisly deeds. Ridwik's fascination with death and undeath borders on insanity.

Steel doors covered in the skin of fallen enemies and insolent servants keep unwanted guests from the laboratory. Each open archway is trapped with a *glyph of warding* that teleports living creatures to either the Crypts (**Q4**) or the Torture Chamber (**G3**) when triggered. The glyphs can be noted with a successful DC 19 Intelligence (Investigation) check. Doors are locked with complicated mechanisms that require a successful DC 19 Dexterity check with thieves' tools to open.

To ensure intruders are kept from reaching his laboratory machinations or other rooms in the Wizard's Tower, Ridwik placed five pits near the entry of the room. Using magic and long-dead masons, the lich masterfully created invisible floor coverings to the pits. Noting the first one requires a successful DC 20 Wisdom (Perception) check. A character who finds one has advantage to find subsequent ones. Falling victims are quickly grabbed by a dozen long, bony hands with clawed fingers that pull the unlucky fool down to the bottom where hungry, unseen creatures frantically feed. Only a successful DC 17 Dexterity saving throw saves a character from certain death. A character takes 5 (3d4) piercing damage from being bitten each round within one of the pits. Escaping the pit requires a successful DC 17 Strength (Athletics) check, but the DC increases by one for each round a character is stuck in the pit.

Making matters worse, a well-trained **mummy** (immune to fire damage) hides here. It was instructed to steer characters closer to the pits or to push them into the discovered holes. It abandons this task only to protect the stairs from those looking to access the upper levels.

A massive hanging candelabra suspended by thick chain links provides just enough light to see the room's contents. The round laboratory has several experiments or studies in progress although the dust built up on the equipment makes it seem as if they were started long ago. Glass jars with grotesque bits of unidentifiable creatures stand next to half-started dissections on bloodstained tables. Boiling green liquid bubbles over the sides of crystal beakers, burning holes into smudged parchments and wooden counter tops. On a small table near the western wall, dozens of glass tubes, bottles, and jars separate liquids from fleshy masses. An open spellbook on a reading stand is turned to a blank page that has but a single word inscribed, "*Power.*" Although it appears like an ordinary feather, a token tucked into the back of the book is actually a *feather token* (whip).

Much of the equipment is valuable, although the sheer weight of everything that appears to have value may make removing it a worthless endeavor. It is possible that an adept eye discovers a magical glass beaker currently not in use on one of the many tables in the room. When the command word "*Hot*" is spoken within 5 feet of the device, it begins to warm up until, after 10 minutes, it reaches 250° Fahrenheit. Using the alternate command word "*Cool*" reduces the temperature 10°, while using the command "*Off*" shuts it off. It takes 30 minutes to cool to room temperature. This device is worth between 250–500 gp to almost any wizard.

A small box on a side table nearby contains four *ioun stones* — they are *awareness*, *protection*, *reserve* (with *vampiric touch* stored), and *sustenance*. Lifting the false bottom of the small box also reveals a hidden *brooch of shielding*.

Dozens of alchemy and wizardry practice books are piled haphazardly on a narrow bookshelf near the southern wall. Most are worth between 5–10 gp; however, one tome titled, "*Dragon Anatomy, a Primer*" is worth 50 gp or more. The trained eye of a seasoned wizard should quickly find a spellbook filled with 10 spells (*acid splash, chill touch, alter self, crown of madness, gaseous form, magic circle, blight, locate creature, creation, dominate person*) and an untitled book with Ridwik's disorganized notes on his lich transformation.

Disturbing any of the experiments in progress chimes a loud bell several times that brings ghoul servants and other undead from various parts of the wing to check on the laboratory.

L7. School Room

As insane as the rooms of Tegel Manor can be, this orderly school room takes the cake. Sitting in orderly rows of desks are 15 **zombies** that study choking under their instructor, a **wight** clad in the black robes of academia. A dummy by the lectern serves as a demonstrative object, and helpful diagrams on the blackboard offer further insights into human anatomy. Alas, all this work is for naught, for when the professor instructs his disciples to go forth and practice on the characters, they just answer with a guttural growl of "*Braaaains*" as they shamble toward the assailants.

M – Wolves Run

The ghostly Spectral Staircase ascends to a mostly isolated level above the Southwest Wing. Anyone discovering the secret door in the Clanking Hall and braving the grasping, disembodied hands that try to trip intruders on their way (see **Appendix IV**, trap 11), can enter this place — flight or scaling the walls and entering through a window is another alternative, and so is climbing the chimney in the Butler's Room one level below (**B12**). There are also the teleporters from the Wizard's Tower or the Great Hall. No matter how they arrive, however, the characters must confront the werewolf pack dwelling in these quarters. The werewolves and their lupine companions are well organized and mercilessly hunt down intruders. They are occasionally aided by **Pandemule the Pandemagisticator**[II], the insane wizard of the library. There are no random encounters here. Any undead has already been chewed up or torn to putrid bits by the wolf pack.

M1. Waiting Room

A slimy trail in the inch-thick layer of dust leads to one of the couches by the north wall. The skeleton sitting on the couch looks disturbingly like aspic; the glistening, glassy pile covering its bones is a **gray ooze** that is busy consuming the remaining flesh. Visible through the jelly is a golden brooch worth 215 gp.

To Attic
Spectral Staircase
KEY
Curtain or Tapestry
Two-way Secret Door
One-way Secret Door
Covered Pit
Trap Door in Ceiling
Shaft
Large Shaft
Fireplace (shaft)
Trap
One-way Teleport To
One-way Teleport From
Two-way Teleport
Giant Rat Hole
Magical Statue
Non-magical Statue
Spectral Staircase
Numbered Paintings
M8 Store
M1 Waiting Room
M2 Bedroom
M9 Bedroom
M3 Study
Whispering Hall
M4 Bedroom
Howling Hall
M11 Bedroom
M5 Sitting Room
M7 Bedroom
M10 Seance Room
M6 Maid's Room
M12 Library
Wiz's Belfry P6
Master Gallery
B4
B12 Butler's
B16 Laboratory
23
22
21
20
19
18
17
16
8
9
10
11
13
14
15

M2. Bedroom

The windows of the comfortable bedroom overlooking the Vestibule (**Q6**) are shuttered, casting long shadows on the canopied bed, the dressing screen, and the broken mirror on the south wall. As soon as a character enters the room, the looking glass shatters, only to mysteriously restore itself in 1d3 minutes. Upon a closer examination, it is apparent that blood seeps from underneath the jagged shards.

The guardians of the room are 2 **shadows** hiding behind a rotting drape that billows suspiciously. If slain, they disappear screaming into the mirror, and the flow of blood increases to a steady trickle.

M3. Study

A sickly-sweet stench greets anyone opening the door to this abandoned study. The grotesquely butchered bodies of nine goblins are piled about a writing desk. They were members of the goblin tribe from **DL1M** who were ambushed by the werewolves on a hunting trip. They have no items of interest.

Dusty bookshelves stacked with miscellaneous works line the walls. These shelves expel their contents periodically, hurling volume upon volume on the floor or at intruders (+1 to hit against one target within 20 ft. for 1 bludgeoning damage).

M4. Bedroom

A banner proclaiming the *"Brotherhood of the Skulls"* hangs on the north wall. Skulls of all types from the human to the monstrous sit on the shelves, the bed, and anywhere there is a bit of room. A purple **flying skull**[II] sitting on a small cabinet by the king-sized bed shrieks and floats into an open wall cabinet to the east, which then shuts. Investigation reveals that the elusive undead has disappeared without a trace.

M5. Sitting Room

The howl of a wolf sounds from the direction of the northwest corner, then ceases. Six pillows surround a small table set with tea service, one of them palpitating periodically. If punctured, the pillow takes off like a deflating balloon, and releases sweet-smelling sleep gas all over the room. Creatures in the room must succeed on a DC 16 Constitution saving throw or fall into a deep slumber for 1 minute or until another character takes an action to shake the character awake or until the character takes damage.

The small, hard bed to the north doubles as a chest. It contains a plum-colored robe and a **shadow** that quickly fills the robe and attacks, preferring to drain sleeping opponents as it murmurs to itself absentmindedly.

M6. Maid's Room

Growling sounds and playful yips come from the room. Inside, 4 **young werewolves**[II] play with their 3 **wolf** companions under the supervision of their nurse, a female **werewolf** wearing an old nightgown. The cubs, their matron, and the wolves attack in a fury of gnashing teeth and howling. If the young are threatened, the female gains a +3 bonus to her attack and damage rolls.

M7. Bedroom

Barring some excavation, the room may be entered only through the attic above **M11**. Tapestries have long since rotted, falling to the floor to reveal cracked plaster walls and a multitude of reddish stains of unknown origin. A voluptuous maiden (a **werewolf**) struggles to climb out of a jagged crack in the floor (a disembodied maw trap — see sidebar). Curiously, her ripped dress remains unstained by blood, and her face twists with frustration more than pain. Helping this lady in distress *may* better relations between the characters and the wolf tribe, provided no more than three wolves have been killed so far.

M8. Store

The leader of the pack, a grizzled old **werewolf**, lives here amid wrecked furniture and shards of smashed pottery with his **wolf** companion. He usually is found sitting on a makeshift throne. The werewolf wears a black robe embroidered with silver sigils that signify his position. He hides behind a moldering cupboard if he expects visitors, and springs forward with a loud growl. If the battle goes poorly, he leaps out the window and flees into the woods.

M9. Bedroom

A tall pile of broken furniture and plaster clutters the southern entrance to the room, prohibiting a clear view of the area until it is circumnavigated. Large chunks of the ceiling have fallen into the room, either shaken loose or fallen after years of moisture damage. The floor is a mess of debris and counts as difficult terrain. A **werewolf** is perched on a sturdy oak chest containing a hawk-crested helm. It is extremely protective of its treasure and attacks if approached. The rectangular alcove to the north is a small shrine dedicated to Harmakhis. Six sacrificial daggers glint on an altar stone.

M10. SEANCE ROOM

The darkness of the inky drapes hanging from the walls is made even more striking by the ghostly blue light swirling in a crystal ball. A disembodied woman's head in the crystal allows questions once per week (70% of knowing, 80% of veracity). Only questions regarding Tegel Manor and its surroundings are answered. She can also summon one Rump of choice every day.

A black-clad **wight** lurking behind the velvet drapes to the northeast guards the crystal oracle. A secret door in its lair opens into a secret storeroom where mystical paraphernalia is stored: a prestidigitator's cape hangs next to an iron brazier and boxes of dowsing rods, candles, chalk, and similar materials. Only the five doses of holy water in a large glass decanter are of any value here.

Searching the fireplace and getting a successful DC 10 Wisdom (Perception) check reveals rungs descending the chimney to **B12**. A *deck of many things* rests on the mantelpiece in an elegant ivory box (valued at 120 gp).

M11. BEDROOM

The figurehead of a ship — a leering shark — is watching over this suite. Cargo nets cover the ceiling, each sagging under the weight of fallen plaster and broken ceiling lath. A half of a ship's mast has been bolted to the western wall and filled with various rusty steel hooks and pins hung with deteriorating sailors' garb. The ceiling netting has been rigged to collapse on unsuspecting victims; characters must make a successful DC 15 Dexterity saving throw to avoid getting caught in the netting and crushed by the weight of its contents. Those failing take 14 (4d6) bludgeoning damage. The trap can be spotted with a successful DC 16 Intelligence (Investigation) check.

Two **werewolves** are arguing over a table of looted riches: a casket full of silver chains (124 gp total) and a tiger eye necklace (592 gp). They are almost at blows as the characters approach, but quickly forget their quarrel as they wade into combat.

The room to the east is similarly decorated, but the mold is even more unpleasant. An open trapdoor in the ceiling leads into a small attic area where a gap in the floor allows access into a bedroom (area **M7**). The attic is littered with dusty crates full of moldy trash. Four long boxes secured by sturdy padlocks contain beheaded corpses that are green-gray from the mold. The padlocks can be opened with a successful DC 15 Dexterity check with thieves' tools.

M12. GREATER LIBRARY

Bookshelves are pushed close to both northwestern entrances of the room, making it extremely difficult for Medium-sized creatures to enter without knocking books off of shelves or getting their equipment caught on chairs, tables, or reading stands. Large creatures must move shelves out of the way, likely knocking over hundreds of books and creating excessive noise. Books are piled precariously, creating leaning stacks of decaying tomes and swaying towers of brittle manuscripts. The sounds of chirping may be heard by characters who succeed on a DC 19 Wisdom (Perception) check — these are the sounds of bookroaches, an insect that destroys books at an incredible rate. A battle is being waged here between the insect population and the library's protector ...

The sole inhabitant of this place is the deranged librarian, an insane wizard who calls himself **Pandemule the Pandemagisticator**[II]. Old Pandemule is totally deranged, having been driven insane by solitude and age. Roaming the labyrinth constantly, he is on very good terms with the wolf pack, which provides him with nourishment in exchange for his foolish advice that the werewolves believe to be prophetic. Unless his mind is restored by a *heal* or similarly powerful spell, Pandemule behaves in a chaotic fashion. He is as likely to help his visitors as to blast them into atoms. Any sort of spell that harms his precious books results in swift and extraordinarily brutal retribution. Pandemule has a dusty robe, a gnarled staff, a *potion of greater healing*, a *potion of gaseous form*, a *spell scroll* with *magic missile* x3, *teleport*, and *greater invisibility*.

Pandemule uses a small space atop one of the bookshelves along the south wall as his sleeping and private reading room. He has arranged larger books on alternating shelves to act as a simple staircase to gain access to his nook at the top of the back bookshelf. Along with a simple sleeping mat and a two magical candles (unlit wax candles with a *continual flame* spell cast upon each), he keeps a stack of his prized books: several insignificant works by amateur authors that contain mindless drivel and outlandish ideas. Only one who is quite insane would find this work either fascinating or useful. In his spare time, he searches the library for a tome on bookroaches, hoping to find the answer to eradicating the destructive insects. There is a 1-in-100 chance that a character may find the lost tome, but only after spending a full day searching for the plainly bound, thin book. Pandemule rewards the character who finds the tome with the knowledge of the werewolf den and, if pressed, with one or both of his magical potions.

A tapestry on the east wall depicts a tall tower-spire. Next to it, the outlines of a door are traced on the wall. Stepping through the portal, one finds oneself in the Wizard's Belfry — the peak of Wizard's Tower. There are also two statues in the library. The northern statue near one of the library's entrances depicts an old sage who holds an open scroll. The statue is hollow and contains one of the three nests of bookroaches in the library (the second is in the west wall, and third is under the centermost bookshelf). Any disturbance of the statue flushes the entire nest, sending thousands of the vile little bugs into the library. This surely causes the insane librarian excessive agitation.

Cut from white marble, the southeastern statue is that of a beautiful woman. Her angelic face is carved into a look of intense scrutiny as she ponders the contents of an open tome. Although the book has been carved from the same piece of marble, several stone pages have been added to the center of the tome. Characters find that they can flip these additional pages forward and back. Once every 12 hours, when a page is turned, a random effect occurs.

1d8	Details
1	A book flies from the shelf and strikes a character in the face for 2 (1d4) bludgeoning damage
2	A character coughs up 1d4 bloody and partially-chewed bookroaches
3	One of Pandemule's prized books falls from a character's pocket to the floor (loudly and noticeably!)
4	A character feels a piece of metal in his boot; it turns out to be a gold coin!
5	The next spell that Pandemule cast automatically fails
6	The statue smiles briefly, and a character is healed for 1d8 hit points
7	A non-magical weapon that a character carries is enhanced with a +1 bonus lasting 12 hours
8	A book drops from the top of a bookshelf — there is a 25% chance that it is a *Tome of Understanding*.

KEY

 Curtain or Tapestry
Ş Two-way Secret Door
Ş→ One-way Secret Door
⊠ Covered Pit
□ Trap Door in Ceiling
■ Shaft
● Large Shaft
⌑ Fireplace (shaft)
T Trap
† One-way Teleport To
⊥ One-way Teleport From
‡ Two-way Teleport
○ Giant Rat Hole
Magical Statue
Non-magical Statue
←▯▯ Spectral Staircase
30 Numbered Paintings

N – East Wing

Just beyond the Sighing Staircase, characters find the second and third floors of the East Wing, a portion of the manor that rises high above the first level and surrounding grounds. Nearly a self-sufficient manor unto itself, the upper floors of the East Wing had a small library, a prison, a solarium, and a veranda that stretched the length of the eastern side of the structure. As Rump family members sipped their coffee, many a breaking dawn was witnessed from this fine deck. Unfortunately, the upper floors are now in the later stages of ruination.

N1. Lesser Library

A mere shadow of the Greater Library (**M12**), this comfortable reading room beyond the secret door is mostly dedicated to lighter reading: romance, adventurous yarns, some pamphlets with rather lurid tales, travelogues, and poetry are commonplace. A stuffed smilodon (Huge analmalistic **animated object**[II]) guards the collection. The enchanted beast snarls if the shelves are approached and attacks if a single book is touched.

A thorough search of the library for interesting items (after the smilodon has been dealt with, of course) reveals a book of lewd poetry that magically replaces each poem's name with the reader's name when spoken aloud, and a small tome with 13 pages that radiates strong magic.

N2. Studio

Nearly every square inch of the walls is covered in abstract paintings. Two dozen easels of various heights fill the room, making navigation through the area difficult without bumping or knocking over one or more wooden stands. A **skeleton** (replace short sword with paint bucket attack at +2 to hit for 1d6 bludgeoning damage; remove shortbow) in a beret and rotting smock studies a portrait of a kobold intently, palette and brush in hand. If others view this masterpiece, it melts, the colors flowing down the white surface. Infuriated by their uncouth behavior, the faux painter tries to smear his paintbrush in the face of the uncivilized onlooker. None of the paintings is worth more than a few gold pieces in their current moldy or smeared states.

N3. Bedroom

Old, yellowed bedsheets with large rust-brown stains cover a bed. The still intact body of a handsome young man in his twenties lies below. If someone lifts the sheets, an apparition of an obese matron screams *"Villain! Sorcerer, 'tis thou hast slain my son!"* as she charges through the wall, screaming.

N4. Dining Room

The scent of a fine-cooked meal lures characters into the eastern room — tantalizing aromas of exotic spices meshed with mouth-watering fragrances of cooked beef and pork surely summon hungry characters to the richly decorated dining room table. An impossibly white tablecloth covers a table suited for six, with silver plates and cutlery (total value of 100 gp) laid out for important guests. A single silver bell inlaid with colorful gemstones sits at the middle of the table. No food can be found anywhere within the room. A large gold candelabrum worth 515 gp is set with four fine wax candles. However, soon after the characters enter, the cabinet by the fireplace levitates to the ceiling and numerous plates fall out and shatter. Taking the candelabrum attracts its protector, a decaying **mummy** — the source of the spicy smell. Ringing the bell accomplishes the same.

N5. Prison

Thick chains bind a great warrior in this dark chamber. The bonds allow only 10 feet of movement away from the wall. A plate of stale bread and a jug of stale water are his sole sustenance, and a flimsy blanket his cover. The warrior, a powerful **werebear**, is dying, clutching his last remaining treasure: a helm surmounted with the snarling head of a bear. Only 1d6 minutes of his life remain before he shuffles off the mortal coil. When he expires, his manacles (Tiny ensnaring **animated object**[II]) release the corpse and advance toward the nearest character while snapping open and shut.

N6. Cook

Green moss and lichen have turned the floor and walls of this chamber into a plush carpet. Three **giant rats** lurk near the rat hole. Most areas of the floor are benign, merely a spongy carpet that provides a quiet and soft walking surface. However, several mossy clumps offer a chance to ensnare feet and ankles within a bony trap. A unique organism living within the moss has transformed parts of itself into rudimentary traps to catch rats and other small creatures in the manor. A foot or hand is easily snared, pinning the limb to the floor until freed. There is a 33% base chance (minus 1% per point of Dexterity) that a character "accidentally" find one of the moss-traps. A character who does can avoid the snare with a successful DC 18 Dexterity saving throw and can use an action to attempt a DC 18 Strength (Athletics) or Dexterity (Acrobatics) check to break free once ensnared.

N7. Kitchen

A pot of bouillon simmers on a low fire on an untended stove, stirred by a tireless wooden spoon. Sampling the stew has a random permanent effect on individuals, per the table below. However, enjoying the ghoulish repast may have other, unintended consequences as you deem appropriate.

1d8	Effect
1	Increase height 2 inches
2	+1 to Dexterity
3	−1 to Charisma
4	+1 to Constitution
5	−1 to Constitution
6	+2 to Intelligence
7	+1 to Wisdom
8	+2 to Strength

A garbage chute in the northeast corner dumps remains unceremoniously into the Dining Room (**N4**), greatly upsetting the mummy if it hasn't been encountered already. A keg of bitter ale and a barrel of sour wine complement sacks of moldy flour and two huge rolls of still edible cheese.

N8. Dormitory

The aroma of hyacinth mingles with a hint of decay. The room must have been used by young ladies: rows of bunk beds stand next to vast closets on the west wall containing exquisite costumes. The decomposed corpse of a model still wearing a topaz diadem (510 gp) sits in a chair, looking vainly upon her own reflection. The diadem seems strangely affixed to the skull and must be removed with extreme force, likely shattering the skull into thousands of fragments when separated. Each fragment transforms into a small moth that floats away while the faint scream of a young girl is heard, trailing off into silence.

N9. SOLARIUM

A gross, shin-deep pool of sludgy goo fills this dark room. Glass ceiling panels are covered in a thick film, preventing the sunlight from entering the large space. Once filled with rare plants, vegetables, and fruit-bearing trees, the area now has nothing but rot and decay. The slimy pool of decaying organic matter is ripe with disease and fungal risks.

Searching through the slimy muck with a successful DC 20 Wisdom (Perception) check yields two items — a black, chaotic evil, magical longsword named *Darkslayer* and a huge key inscribed *"Dragon Caves — Ruby Throne Room."*

DARKSLAYER

Weapon (greatsword), legendary
(requires attunement by an evil character)

Black as obsidian, this magical greatsword emanates Evil (CE to be exact). It calls out to those it deems worthy of holding it, generally picking a weak-willed, evil character from the group. It is highly intelligent and sentient, capable of manipulating its wielder's emotions to do its bidding. Darkslayer can hear and see invisible creatures up to 50 feet and often incites it wielder to attack them, even when the target is unseen. Each critical fumble rolled with an attack with Darkslayer ages the character 1d4 years. A character who dies from old age while holding Darkslayer returns as an undead being appropriate to their level and power.

You gain a +2 bonus to attack and damage rolls with this weapon.

N10. LOFT

Clouds of dust and sawdust billow as footsteps kick up the filth on the floor. The smell of guano is both unnatural and overwhelming. Four huge vats of dye, originally used to color clothes, have developed a leathery layer atop the still fluid. Two kegs of paint accompany the vats. Four large **vampire bats**[II] hang near a hole in the south wall, dozing until their next mealtime. Any loud noise awakens the massive bats, causing them to attack immediately.

N11. BEDROOM

Greeting the party in this sensuous boudoir of silken curtains and plush beds is a loosely dressed beauty with strings of diamonds and sapphires wound in her hair. This mysterious lady casts a *geas* at the first character through the door with a DC 20 spell save. She then changes into a black arrow and flies through the ceiling. A sparkling gold energy shield absorbs all missiles and spells directed at her.

The affected character is tasked with collecting an arm bone of a ghoul, a leg bone of a vampire, a skull of a skeleton, and a spine of a freshly slain zombie. When these items are brought before the

mysterious lady, they are turned into 1d4 doses of *Dust of Undead Protection*[VI]. Additionally, the room can be searched without repercussion. A box of gold coins (125 gp) is found under the bed, a wooden box with four *potions of greater healing* sits under a small side table, a set of silver hairpins (100 gp value) in a small pouch sits on a dressing table, and a strange robe hangs on a wall hook — this is a *robe of eyes*.

O – BROTHER'S TOWER

An old crumbling tower known as the Brother's Tower, stretching upward five stories, shadows the western portion of the manor. There are some who say that the tower was the first building constructed, with the manor added on over time. The tower has dozens of entry points from the outside, after man-sized chunks of stone and mortar have fallen away from the structure over the years. Climbing the exterior of the tower is easy in some places but dangerous in others — it is possible to loosen a massive section of the tower with a poorly-placed foot or hand.

O1. SECOND STORY: GUARDROOM

Only small, shuttered arrow slits — and a doorway leading to the single balcony overlooking distant Tegel Village — illuminate what used to be a well-stocked guardroom. Weapon racks (12 heavy crossbows, 14 short bows, 10 longswords, 25 daggers) by the walls surround plain bunk beds with 34 sleeping **skeletons** (AC 15 from leather and a small steel shield) still clad in rotting leather armor, weapons at the ready. Two shambling figures in blue tabards move back and forth between the bunks, checking on the skeletal guardsmen, while a third similarly dressed figure checks off names on a worn wood-backed parchment in his bony hands. Unlike the skeletons on the rotting bunks, the three moving creatures have decaying flesh that hangs from old bones. Once the characters proceed into the room, the 3 **wight** sergeants and the skeleton guards spring into action.

Although there is no apparent way to ascend any further, with a successful DC 14 Strength (Athletics) check it is possible to scale the walls on the outside of the tower to reach the third story. Failure results in a 30-foot fall and 10 (3d6) bludgeoning damage. Six 1-foot steel rods driven into the stones seem to provide a safe route; however, with the exception of the first two, they are loose and don't support anyone heavier than a thin halfling. Note that once up there, the characters must still brave a treacherous and crumbling ledge (1 foot wide) leading to the eastern window that allows access to the third story, as all others are blocked by heavy bars. The ledge can be traversed with a successful DC 13 Dexterity (Acrobatics) check.

O2. THIRD STORY: BEDROOM

Thick, 30-foot-long chains drag constantly across the ceiling of this bleak prison. A thick layer of dust covers the floor of the third level of the tower. A careful examination of the floor reveals smallish footprints near the center of the room (the homunculi hiding in the ceiling trapdoor occasionally drop down to hunt). The wide area is relatively bare — there is only a small bed with rotting sheets, a broken dresser missing all its drawers, and a chair with torn caning. A single window on the eastern side of the tower is barred although the rust and corrosion of the old metal looks to have made them weak and vulnerable. It can be pulled out with a successful DC 12 Strength check. Three other windows on the northern, western, and southern sides of the tower were sealed years ago and their brickwork still looks to be fairly strong and intact.

A hollow, stuttering voice intones from a glowing and spinning scroll (*Moonwort Scrowle*) levitating above a reading stand. If someone approaches the ceiling trapdoor, 3 **homunculi** armed with tiny,

Guardroom
Tegel's Arcade
One-way Teleport To
One-way Teleport From
Two-way Teleport
Giant Rat Hole
Magical Statue
Non-magical Statue
Spectral Staircase
30   Numbered Paintings
Curtain or Tapestry
Two-way Secret Door
One-way Secret Door
Covered Pit
Trap Door in Ceiling
Shaft
Large Shaft
Fireplace (shaft)

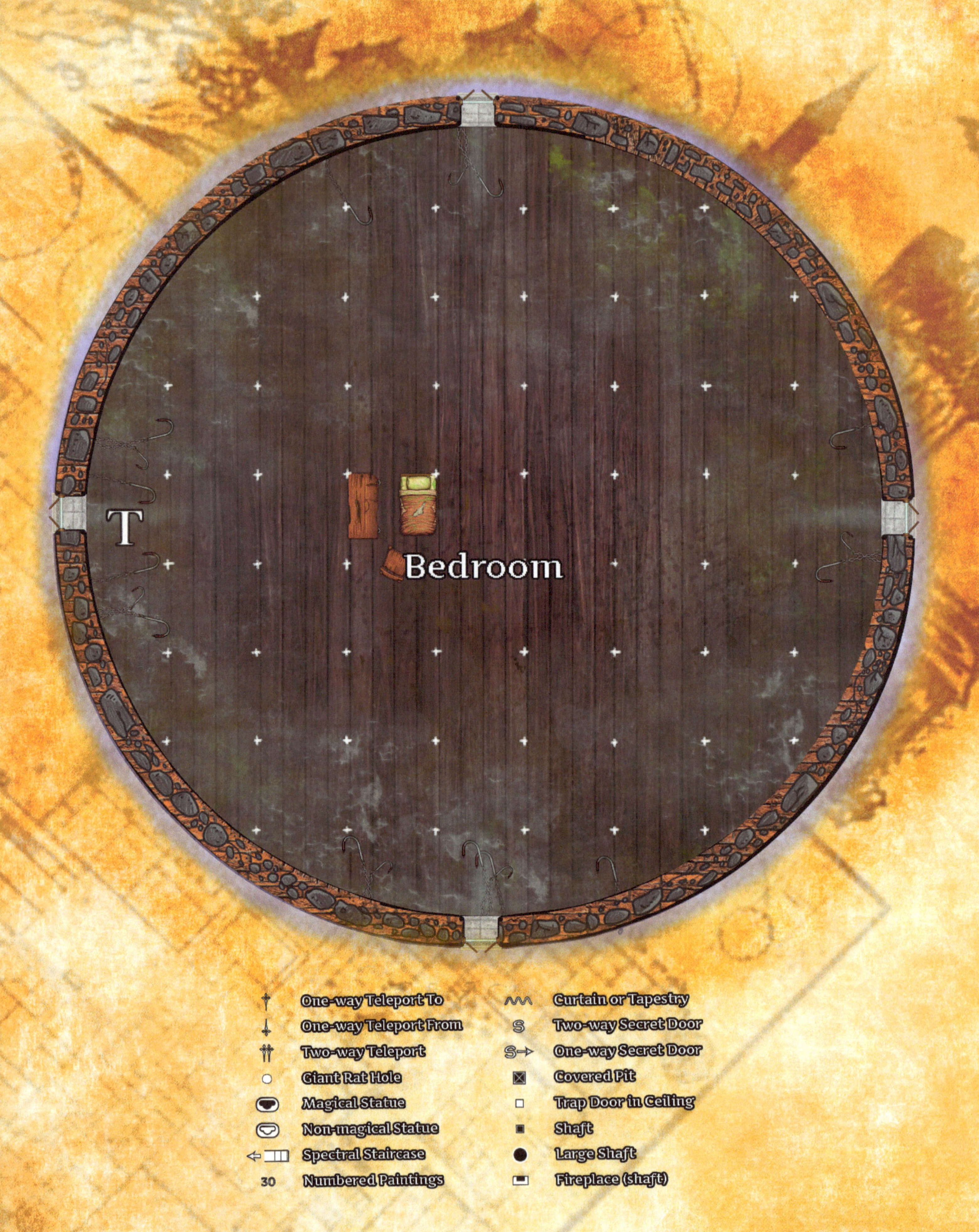
T
Bedroom
One-way Teleport To
One-way Teleport From
Two-way Teleport
Giant Rat Hole
Magical Statue
Non-magical Statue
Spectral Staircase
30 Numbered Paintings
Curtain or Tapestry
Two-way Secret Door
One-way Secret Door
Covered Pit
Trap Door in Ceiling
Shaft
Large Shaft
Fireplace (shaft)

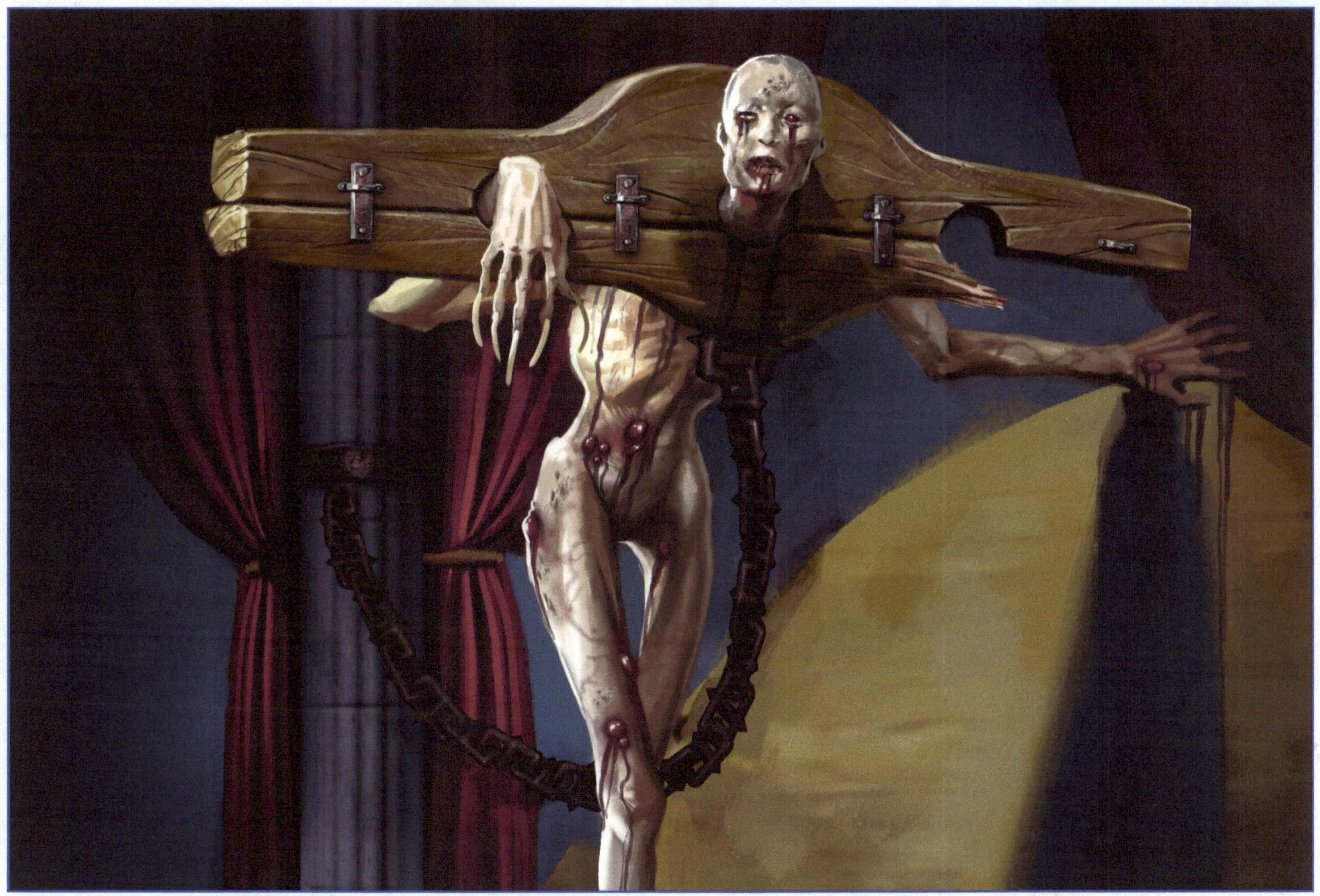

Moonwort Scrowle

Wondrous item, very rare

This cursed magic item is a venerable and mostly useless relic left behind by an insane wizard. It constantly reads itself and conjures hostile homunculi out of thin air. Up to three minor monstrosities may be in existence at one time. The homunculi are armed with poison-tipped spears and don't use their bites. The scroll is AC 12 and has 11 hp. It is immune to psychic and poison damage.

poison-tipped iron "spears" emerge from their hiding place below the bed and fly at intruders (add *poison dart. melee weapon attack:* +4 to hit, one target within 5 ft. *Hit*: 4 [1d4 + 2] piercing damage and target must succeed on a DC 11 Constitution saving throw or be poisoned for one minute. While poisoned, the target is also paralyzed and takes 1d4 poison damage per round. A poisoned creature may attempt a new saving throw at the end of its turn, ending the effect on a success.). Slain homunculi are immediately replaced by the *Moonwort Scrowle*.

O3. Fourth Story: Zoo

Hundreds of stuffed animals line the outer walls of the tower, in between four alien-looking statues. Starting with a small mouse and ending with a giraffe, the preserved creatures increase in size as they circle the room. Most of the stuffed animals are either dusty or have broken open, releasing their stuffing onto the floor. However, four creatures look to be newly stuffed: a grotesque **giant frog**, a **giant beaver**[II], a giant otter (as **giant weasel** with swimming speed of 30 ft.), and four **monkeys**[II] seem almost real. An examination of the lineup reveals that two of the animals are out of size order — a raccoon and a gorilla have been switched. If the two creatures are returned to their rightful place in the line, a golden crown materializes on the skull of the skeletal remains that sits upon the throne in the southwestern portion of the area (see below).

The four identical statues are impossible to identify as they are not from this world. Each has four arms ending with hooks, a smallish head with three overly large eyes, and short stunted legs. A small stubby tail can be found at the base of their spine. The northern statue is magical; if touched or manipulated, it emits a blast of high-pitched noise. All within 20 feet of it who can hear must succeed on a DC 18 Wisdom saving throw or take 7 (2d6) psychic damage and be unable to cast spells until he or she completes a long rest. After its attack, the statue becomes inert for 1d10 minutes.

A giant skeleton sits upon a large stone throne in the southwestern part of the area. If the characters switched the two creatures in line (above), it also has a golden crown upon its yellowed skull. If the golden crown is placed upon a character's head while sitting on the throne, the character is transported to the Hunter's Room of the East Wing (**J4**). The crown stays with this throne, either returning to the skeleton's head if still upon the throne or to the seat if not (the teleported character arrives in the East Wing without the crown). Note that returning to this floor from the East Wing is possible only if the two creatures are switched out of order again. The crown strongly emanates magic but cannot be removed from the room.

Zoo
J4
One-way Teleport To __
One-way Teleport From
Two-way Teleport
Giant Rat Hole
Magical Statue
Non-magical Statue
Spectral Staircase
30   Numbered Paintings
Curtain or Tapestry
Two-way Secret Door
One-way Secret Door
Covered Pit
Trap Door in Ceiling
Shaft
Large Shaft
Fireplace (shaft)

✝	One-way Teleport To	∿∿∿	Curtain or Tapestry
✝	One-way Teleport From	S	Two-way Secret Door
✝✝	Two-way Teleport	S→	One-way Secret Door
○	Giant Rat Hole	⊠	Covered Pit
⬬	Magical Statue	▢	Trap Door in Ceiling
⬮	Non-magical Statue	▪	Shaft
←▥	Spectral Staircase	●	Large Shaft
30	Numbered Paintings	⬛	Fireplace (shaft)

O4. Fifth Story: Brother's Tower

In order to open the trapdoor leading to this level, the characters need to succeed on a DC 16 Strength check: a heavy human corpse lies on it, accompanied by two others within arm's reach. They were once adventurers, as evidenced by their chainmail armor and rotted backpacks (these contain iron rations, coils of rope, and similar items). One of them carries a sack of loot: 170 gp, three golden candlesticks (60 gp each), and a shattered glass vial.

Instantly, the characters smell the foul scent of disease and decay that seems to emanate from behind semitransparent curtains that split the room into two sections. On the trapdoor side of the silken barrier, the characters find three unlit braziers, blackened but empty of coals. Dozens of wilted flower stems have been laid near the braziers. A small golden idol (worth 750 gp) stands on a marble pedestal between the three braziers — the statuette is of an overweight, balding man with arms outstretched, strangely grinning an open-mouthed smile.

Movement can be detected beyond the curtains — a frail man in a loincloth lies on the cold floor. His legs are shackled and an iron collar around his neck is secured to the eastern wall by a five-foot length of sturdy chain. If he detects movement on the other side of the curtains, he pleads for help. The sickly man claims he's been kidnapped by unknown assailants. However, he's really been left here to die, as he is stricken with a severe case of a fungal disease. The man is a carrier and although he will eventually die from his disorder, his purpose while alive is to host the disease and spread it to all he comes in contact with. He is **Brother**[II], the owner of the tower, and he has been here in this state for untold years. He attempts to lure characters within the five-foot reach of his chain, grabbing the closest of them as soon as he can. Brother breathes a fungal mold into the face of his victims, infecting them with his horrible disease.

The curtains are magical, acting as two **rugs of smothering** as characters try to pass through them. Working in tandem with Brother, they allow the first character to pass unharmed before assaulting the next to pass.

In addition to Brother and the curtains, there are two things of interest in the room. The first is the portrait of Rodip the Rationalist (**NPC #60**). The second is within the curtained area. A plain altar serving an unknown god is pushed up against the outer wall of the tower. Several unfired ceramic containers are lined up in front of the altar. A duplicate idol of the one in the opposite area sits atop the altar; however, the idol's expression is much different — instead of smiling and welcoming others with open arms, the bald man's features are twisted into hateful anger and its arms reach forward as if to try to strangle an unseen victim. A plain clay jar with seven gold rings (78 gp each), five silver rings (9 gp each), and 12 copper rings (1 gp each) lies on the altar. The idol radiates weak magic but does nothing: adding rings to the jar, removing one or all, or even taking the idol itself (value 1,260 gp) has no noticeable effect.

P – Wizard's Tower

Seven stories of magically protected limestone rise above the manor to form a circular tower that narrows as it ascends. Its blackened exterior stands out in the sunlight but blends into the darkness of the night. Perched upon a second-story ledge, 36 grinning **gargoyles** circle the tower in their never-ending watch for intruders. They remain motionless until summoned by the ringing of the great silver bell in the belfry above. Undead within the tower are highly resistant to foes — they may save versus attacks with Advantage.

P1. Second Story: Guardroom

The inner stairwell within the Lich's Laboratory (**L6**) ends in the second story of the tower. Eleven silhouettes of humanoids line the outer wall of the level, incorrectly hinting at mounted displays of shiny chainmail. As the last member of the group reaches the top step, 10 **ghouls** and a **wight** burst into action, screaming a deafening war cry that startles all but the most steely-nerved characters. They attack the living with devilish ferocity, and permanently fall only if slain outside the room and on the stairs. During the battle, there is a 1-in-4 chance each round that a "slain" ghoul rises and re-enters the battle. A trapdoor in the ceiling is the only way to access the third level from this room.

P2. Third Story: Conservatory

The stairs from the manor proper arrive here. A trapdoor leads down, while a set of circular stairs climbs up to the fifth level, bypassing the Lich's Quarters (**P3**), the latter being accessible through a shaft in the ceiling. The statue of a hooded skeleton peers on the scene with a cynical half-smile.

This level is filled by 14 huge, thick glass tubes containing an opaque, odorless gas that obscures creatures held in suspended animation. Only the fact that something dark is inside may be ascertained. Three tubes are empty; the rest have one creature each. All tubes have AC 15 and 20 hit points. Once freed, it takes 1d4 rounds for the prisoners to regain consciousness and for the gas to escape.

Glass Tube Prisoners

Glass Tube #1: Corleth the Elf Lord (**eldritch archer**[II] with AC 17 from *elven studded leather*), an inquisitive and honest adventurer, was exploring the manor seeking powerful magic items. He was captured by the lich's minions in the Laboratory (**L6**) while he was searching for Ridwik's greatest treasures. He is well versed in melee combat as well as casting spells. He is willing to join up with a group; however, he leaves the party if he finds one of the lich's great treasures.

Corleth has *elven studded leather*[VI], a *+1 sickle*, a *potion of healing*, a coil of elven rope, elven rations, a lantern, a spellbook with all his known spells, and a spell component pouch.

Glass Tube #2: Brand (**preacher**[II] with AC 20 from plate and shield) a dwarven cleric of Thor, is trapped in this glass prison. He was separated from his group elsewhere in the manor. After taking a few wrong turns, he found himself face to face with Ridwik in the Laboratory (**L6**). He has been detained for far too long and wishes only to leave this vile place. If escorted to an exterior exit, he promises to repay the group by leaving a *scroll of resurrection* with the local temple for their use.

Brand has plate armor, a large metal shield, a round silver helm, a warhammer, a holy symbol of Thor, a leather bag of iron nails, a hammer, a crowbar, torches, iron rations, and three bottles of holy water.

Glass Tube #3: The harpies (**P6**) lured a **griffon** to the tower, and it was captured after a brief scuffle with a few of the gargoyles. Characters who make a successful DC 18 Wisdom (Animal Handling) check may be able to keep the disoriented and angry creature from attacking the group.

Glass Tube #4: A **wyvern** is trapped in this glass tube. It attacks if released.

Glass Tube #5: An angry **chimera** is trapped in this tube and attacks when released. The chimera is wounded (80 hit points) and may (50% chance) try to flee instead of attacking the characters.

Glass Tube #6: A **dire weasel**[II] is held within this glass prison. It leaps at the characters when it is released.

Glass Tube #7: A **gorgon** is trapped inside this tube. The furious creature attacks immediately.

Glass Tube #8: This tube is empty.

Glass Tube #9: The harpies in the belfry (**P6**) were once a trio before one of them tried to deceive their master. Ridwik confined the lying **harpy** to the ninth glass tube for some time now. The harpy is now quite insane and unpredictable. When released, she may try to return to her sisters above or attack the group.

Glass Tube #10: This tube contains a dimwitted and gullible **troll**. He believes most anything he's told until he's figured out he's being deceived or made fun of. He is quite ferocious and once angered, does not quit trying to kill and eat his prey until he himself is dead.

Symbol	Meaning	Symbol	Meaning
	One-way Teleport To		Curtain or Tapestry
	One-way Teleport From	S	Two-way Secret Door
	Two-way Teleport	S→	One-way Secret Door
	Giant Rat Hole		Covered Pit
	Magical Statue		Trap Door in Ceiling
	Non-magical Statue		Shaft
	Spectral Staircase		Large Shaft
30	Numbered Paintings		Fireplace (shaft)

Conservatory
One-way Teleport To
One-way Teleport From
Two-way Teleport
Giant Rat Hole
Magical Statue
Non-magical Statue
Spectral Staircase
30 Numbered Paintings
Curtain or Tapestry
Two-way Secret Door
One-way Secret Door
Covered Pit
Trap Door in Ceiling
Shaft
Large Shaft
Fireplace (shaft)

One-way Teleport To		Curtain or Tapestry	
One-way Teleport From		Two-way Secret Door	
Two-way Teleport		One-way Secret Door	
Giant Rat Hole		Covered Pit	
Magical Statue		Trap Door in Ceiling	
Non-magical Statue		Shaft	
Spectral Staircase		Large Shaft	
Numbered Paintings		Fireplace (shaft)	

Glass Tube #11: This glass tube is empty.

Glass Tube #12: A weakened **dryad**, stripped of her powers and rendered mute, is the unfortunate prisoner within the 12th glass tube. She tries to get the group to help her escape so she can return to her magical home to regain her strength. If assisted, she gifts the characters 1d4 magical scrolls and/or potions.

Glass Tube #13: This tube is empty.

Glass Tube #14: The last prisoner is Liana (**incantor**[II] with AC 15 from *bracers of defense*) an evil enchantress. She had hoped to lure Ridwik into her trust by using her incredible beauty and intellect to seduce him. Alas, she was bested by the powerful lich and captured. When released, she thinks only of revenge and does not hesitate to trick the group into helping her achieve her new goal — the destruction of Ridwik! If the group catches on to her trickery or refuses to help her in her quest, she attempts to destroy them with her spells.

Liana has a dagger, *bracers of defense*, a spellbook with all her known spells, and a spell component pouch, a *spell scroll* with *stinking cloud*, *water breathing*, and *dimension door*, a *wand of secrets*, and a black cloak and robes.

P3. Fourth Story: Lich's Quarters

On the ceiling visible from the shaft below, an intricate rune glows with radiant light: a *symbol of fear* (DC 15 spell save). The room is rather plain and may trick characters into passing it by instead of giving it a thorough search. Much of the furniture lies in a large moldering pile next to the stairway that passes through (but doesn't open into) this level. A foul smell, combining rotting flesh and animal excrement, emanates from somewhere within the level, though it is hard to pinpoint the exact location.

A simple desk is hidden in the shadows, partially concealed by the curve of the staircase. Piles of books, tomes, scrolls, loose parchments, and discarded writing utensils cover the entire top of the small desk. The stacks are clearly disorganized and precariously piled — any change in their position may cause several piles to fall upon unsuspecting searchers. Although most of the writings are either the lesser works of insignificant wizards or the mindless blathering of an insane sorcerer, an interesting tome can be found within the piles

The Demon's Dark Lullaby

Wondrous item, legendary

Rumored to be constructed from the tears of demons and the skin of damned children, *The Demon's Dark Lullaby* at first appears to be a simple children's poetry book. However, each page of poetry has a different result when fully read aloud. Each of the 10 poems has a devastating effect that often leads to the demise of the reader, his or her friends, and sometimes, absolute strangers. The pages are made with thick, unrefined vellum, and inked with a flowing yet chaotic hand.

Poems

Page	Poem Name	Effect
1	*This Little Doggy*	Summons a **hell hound** to arrive within 100 feet of the reader, 50% chance searching for the reader.
2	*Monkey See, Monkey Do*	Summons a **gibbon demon**[II] to the reader's family home latest residence.
3	*What's in the Dark?*	A random person within 20 feet of the reader must succeed on a DC 15 Charisma saving throw or switch places with a **trickster demon**[II]. Killing the demon banishes the switched person to the Abyss forever.
4	*Ten Little Stitches*	A **flesh golem** appears directly behind the reader, looking to replace a missing limb with one of the reader's limbs.
5	*Here Kitty, Kitty*	The next time the reader is outdoors, a **manticore** appears to attack them and any of his or her companions.

Page	Poem Name	Effect
6	*Short Tail, Long Tail*	The reader (50% chance) or a random person within 20 feet (50% chance) must make a DC 14 Wisdom saving throw. If they fail the saving throw, they grow a short tail. If they fail the saving throw, their race is changed to tiefling. Either change can be undone with *greater restoration*.
7	*Silly, Sticky, Slimy*	Summons a **gelatinous cube** or a **black pudding** to appear within 20 feet of the reader.
8	*Washy Your Face and Hands*	The reader and anyone within 10 feet must succeed on a DC 14 Charisma saving throw or be transported to a locale inhabited by an **otyugh**.
9	*Tiny Hands*	A random target within 20 feet of the reader (including the reader) must succeed on a DC 14 Wisdom saving throw or be cursed with tiny hands — their hands reduce to one-tenth their normal size.
10	*Far Away Places*	The reader and 1d4 other random targets within 20 feet must succeed on a DC 12 Wisdom saving throw or be transported to the Abyss.

Although most of the effects of the poems appear to negatively impact the reader, any time a full poem is read, the reader is given a +3 bonus to skill checks and Advantage to all attack rolls, skill checks, and saving throws until completing a long rest. Additionally, the poems have a 10% chance to deposit a powerful magical item within 20 feet of the reader.

After each poem is read, its effects are erased (no repeating) until all 10 poems are activated. The book restores all the poems 24 hours after the last one is read. The effects do not manifest unless the entire poem is read aloud.

after a careful and thorough search: *The Demon's Dark Lullaby* is a priceless, one-of-a-kind tome highly sought after by the most powerful magicians in any land.

There is a one-way teleporter in the room. It is activated by pulling a heavy iron lever on the east wall. Pulling the lever transports everyone within 10 feet to **DL2E**.

P4. Fifth Story: Store

The middle of the tower is pierced by a large circular shaft that ascends to the Wizard's Belfry (**P6**) on the top. During the day, some light filters in from above; however, much of it is blocked by the huge silver bell hanging in the sixth story. Circular stairs lead down into the darkness.

Dusty crates, boxes, and barrels fill the level, giving the impression of a forgotten storeroom at best, or a hoarder's treasure trove at worst. Anything of value has long since evaporated or deteriorated — lamps are dry, barrels of rum are sadly empty, and crates of spices are filled with moldy remnants. Racks of clothes are motheaten, and a dilapidated weapon rack has nothing but brittle steel swords and dulled spears. A magical trap has been placed on the weapon rack. When activated (by touch), the weapons fly around the room, striking at everyone on the floor for a full minute. Each round a creature starts its turn in the area or enters it, the creature must succeed on a DC 16 Dexterity saving throw or take 2 (1d4) slashing and bludgeoning damage.

A rust-covered chest is found at the center of the disorganized mess. The chest is the lair of 6 **shadows**, whereas the trunk is full of lanterns resting atop a single dagger.

P5. Sixth Story: Belfry

A huge silver bell dominates the level. It is a true monstrosity, worth some 17,985 gp. The bell gently sways and resonates at all times, producing a distant chiming sound. This is due to the **bat swarm** dwelling inside. The bats emerge if their nest is disturbed. There is a 50% possibility the **harpies** on the seventh story likewise come to investigate any loud noise.

In addition to being an object of extraordinary value, the bell is also the lich's phylactery. It has 160 hit points, AC 18, and a damage threshold of 10. It is immune to psychic and poison damage. It can be broken with a successful DC 30 Strength check. Attacking it produces a loud peal, and the bell begins to toll — once every 10 rounds, or whenever damage is inflicted on the bell. On the first toll, nothing happens. On the second, a deep sigh emerges from the whole tower. On the third toll, the 36 **gargoyles** squatting on the tower's supporting pillars animate and take wing to do away with the intruders. On the fourth toll, **Ridwik**[1] himself is alerted to the commotion and *teleports* in unless he had previously been incapacitated. There is also a 75% chance that he brings help in the form of 1d4 Rumps rolled for on the family tree. If the roll indicates someone already laid to rest, treat it as a "no result." Destroying the bell does away with Ridwik of the Relic on a permanent basis.

A secret door in the west wall leads outside to an iron ladder that climbs up to the narrow walk around the Wizard's Belfry (**P6**).

†	One-way Teleport To	∿	Curtain or Tapestry
↓	One-way Teleport From	S	Two-way Secret Door
††	Two-way Teleport	S→	One-way Secret Door
○	Giant Rat Hole	⊠	Covered Pit
⬮	Magical Statue	□	Trap Door in Ceiling
⬯	Non-magical Statue	■	Shaft
←▭	Spectral Staircase	●	Large Shaft
30	Numbered Paintings	▭	Fireplace (shaft)

✝	One-way Teleport To	⋀⋀⋀	Curtain or Tapestry
⊥	One-way Teleport From	S	Two-way Secret Door
�	Two-way Teleport	S→	One-way Secret Door
○	Giant Rat Hole	⊠	Covered Pit
⬬	Magical Statue	☐	Trap Door in Ceiling
⬭	Non-magical Statue	▪	Shaft
⟵▭▭	Spectral Staircase	●	Large Shaft
30	Numbered Paintings	▱	Fireplace (shaft)

One-way Teleport To		Curtain or Tapestry	
One-way Teleport From		Two-way Secret Door	
Two-way Teleport		One-way Secret Door	
Giant Rat Hole		Covered Pit	
Magical Statue		Trap Door in Ceiling	
Non-magical Statue		Shaft	
Spectral Staircase		Large Shaft	
30 Numbered Paintings		Fireplace (shaft)	

P6. SEVENTH STORY: WIZARD'S BELFRY

A huge copper bell hangs above the silver one below. It is worth 2,200 gp for the metal, although it is almost impossible to transport, let alone disassemble. Two **harpies** have been chained to the bell with 50-foot lengths of chain. They act as guards against someone who would approach the tower by flight. Their nest is full of filth and feathers. The sole treasure is a broken telescope hidden in the refuse that can be found with a successful DC 16 Wisdom (Perception) check. The brass tripod it was originally mounted on remains visible. Not much more is to be seen in this place.

Q – OTHER BUILDINGS

This section encompasses all areas not detailed previously, including inner and outer courtyards, side buildings, etc. The Family Graveyard, however, is described in the Wilderness chapter (area **HH**.)

Q1. GAZEBO

This is a little retreat made of painted wood that offers pleasant shade and comfortable seats. The structure looks somewhat battle scarred, as if someone had tried to hack it apart at one point. There is even a single *+3 arrow* sticking out of a wall. However, it is disappointingly inanimate. The same can't be said of the **vampire vine**[II] that grows on the latticework: Its pointed leaves and innocent-looking crimson blossoms mask the true horror of its 10 tendrils that strangle and suffocate the unwary.

Q2. HERMITAGE

This small and modest building once housed the family hermit, an unpleasant old fellow with a mean disposition. Keeping hermits has long gone out of fashion, but this one decided to stick around as a **wraith**. Looking like a disheveled old man, he hurls mugs at intruders, accompanied by vile curses and insults. If he is turned or attacked, he turns white and sinks through the floor. In no way does he attack physically unless cornered or unless he can sneak up on an unsuspecting party member — and if he does, he flees immediately.

Aside from a bunk bed, a crude wooden table, and a fireplace, the building is empty. Lying on a rotted leather sack in the southwest corner is a yellow wedge of cheese. Predictably, there is a bear trap underneath that springs if the bait is bothered. A short flight of stairs leads to a cellar containing chopped firewood and a rusty hatchet. The trap can be noted with a successful DC 15 Wisdom (Perception) trap and disabled without a check. A creature who triggers the trap while within its square must succeed on a DC 18 Dexterity saving throw or take 7 (2d6) bludgeoning damage and be restrained. Opening the trap requires a successful DC 15 Strength check.

Q3. CISTERN

Foul water fills only the very bottom of the tank. A leak in the foundation thankfully allows water to seep into the surrounding ground. A pile of bones at the bottom of the well peeks above the waterline. Hundreds of corpses have been tossed into this well for many years. The water is diseased and makes anyone very sick who drinks it and then fails a DC 19 Constitution saving throw. Flesh-eating bugs crawl over the bones, awaiting their next meal.

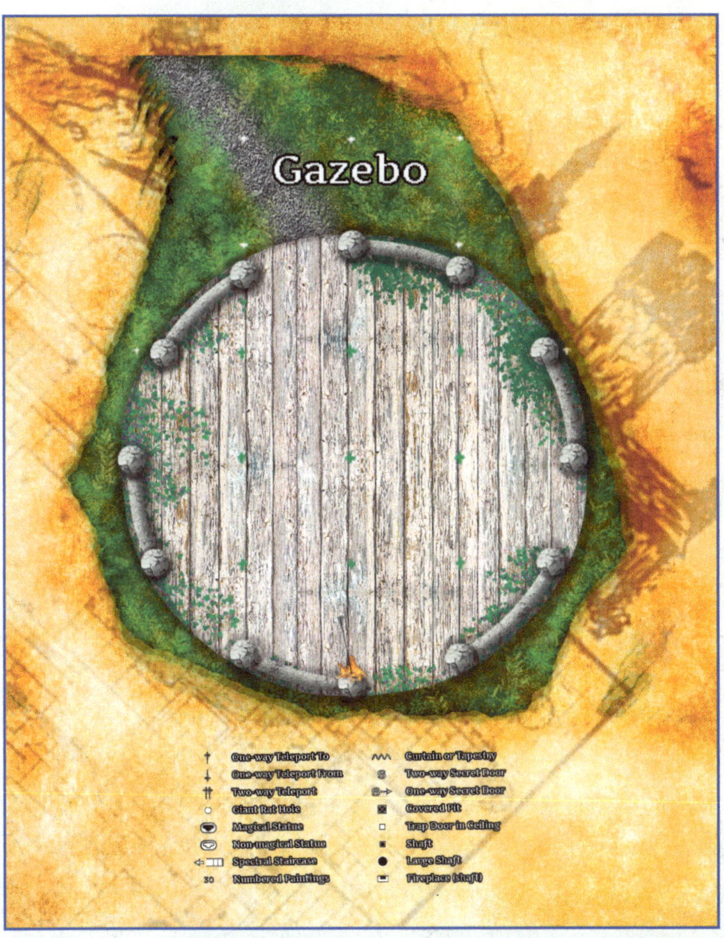

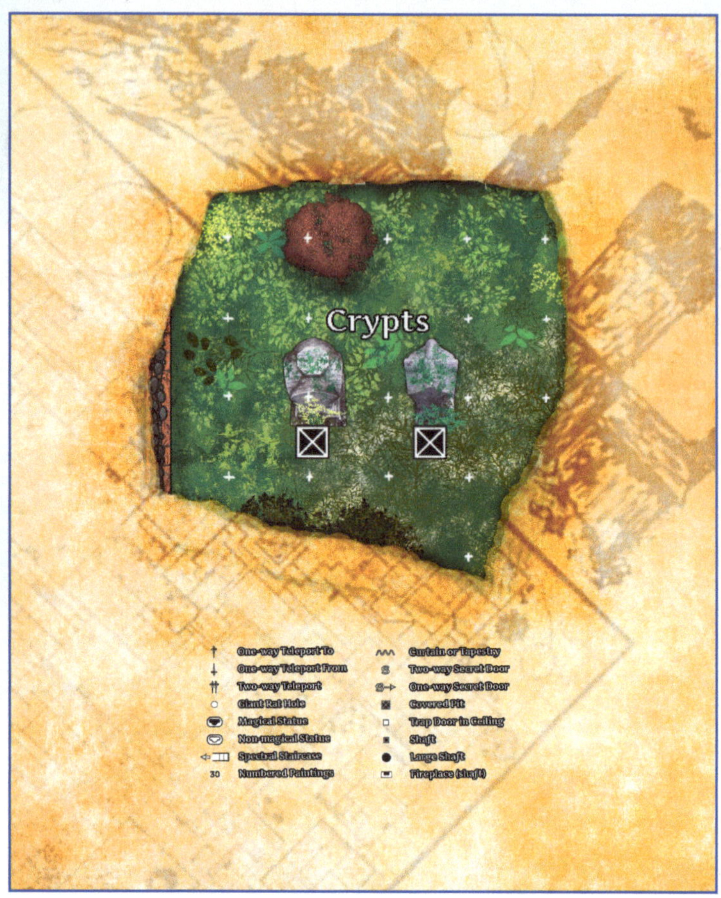

Q4. Crypts

Two large marble sarcophagi stand by the manor's walls. Their moss-covered inscriptions are too worn to decipher. Both sepulchers hide secret trapdoors that can be found with a successful DC 18 Wisdom (Perception) check. The one to the left leads to **DL2H** (10-foot shaft, 20-foot steps down to the north). The one to the right leads to **DL3B** (10-foot shaft, 230-foot crawlway north-northwest, 20-foot drop through cobweb-concealed ceiling shaft).

Q5. Outhouse

Just what the name implies, this building is inhabited by a **black pudding** that covers a pile of putrid clothes. It flows out sluggishly to envelop its next prey.

Q6. Vestibule

This courtyard is enclosed on three sides, leaving a flagstone path to the south. Someone constructed an elaborate rock garden here. Thorny plants cling to the soil in the gaps of rock piles, and stunted treelets bear miniature fruits. Three extraordinarily ugly statues depicting wrinkled giant foo dogs gaze upon the scene with empty eyes. The one to the east holds a plaque in its paws, reading: *"The strength of rocks is within."* The giant foo dog statue is animated (Huge fortified anamlistic **animated object**[II]) and defends itself capably. If it is destroyed, a gemstone may be found where the creature's heart would be.

Opening the double doors to the west results in a loud thunderclap — immediately roll for 1d3 random encounters to see if anyone is attracted to the noise.

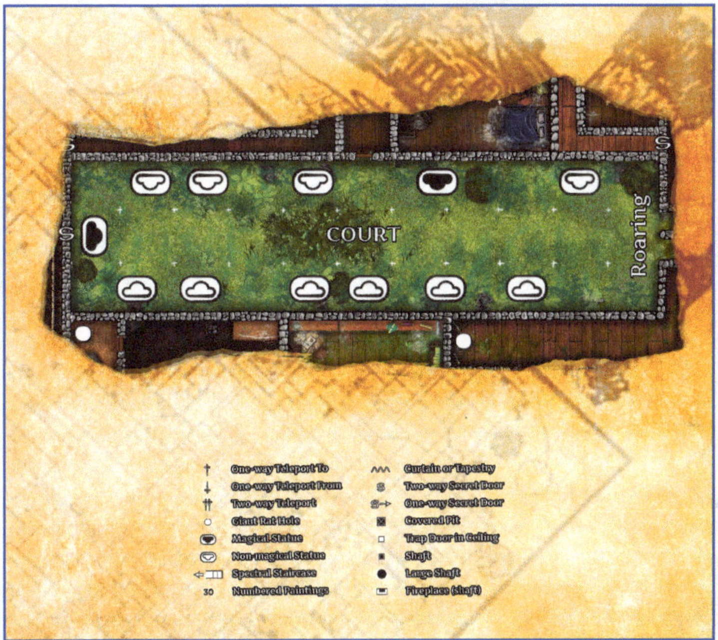

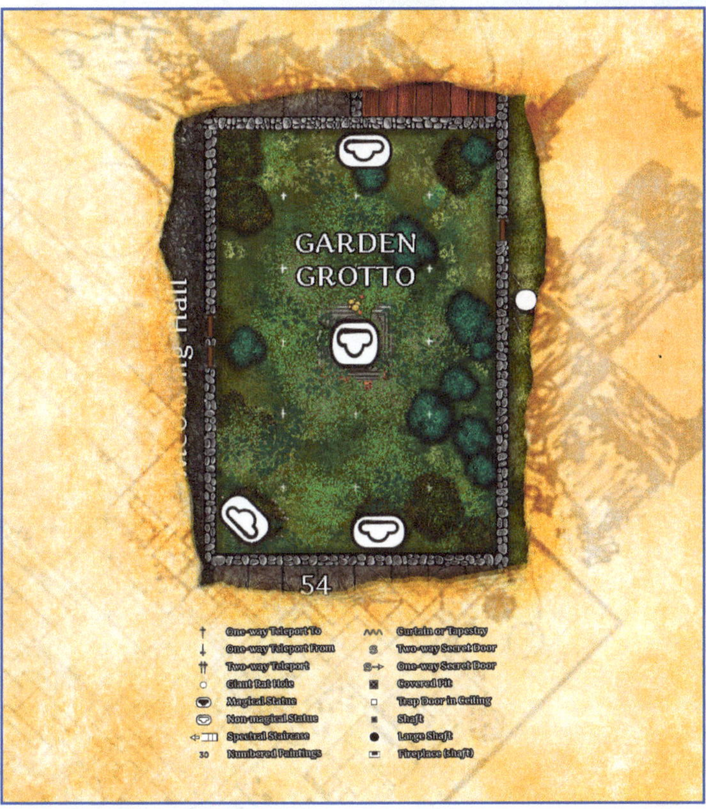

ROCK GEM

Wondrous item, legendary

This rough multifaceted gemstone is worth 5,000 gp. It resists all attempts to break, chip, or cut its surface. A character grasping the stone must succeed on a DC 22 Constitution saving throw or be permanently *polymorphed* into a stone giant (the stone crumbles to dust as soon as the transformation takes place). If the save is successful, the gem remains — it may be used 10 times to give the character (and only that character!) 23 Strength for an hour at a time. When all charges are exhausted, the gem crumbles as above.

Q7. COURT

This once beautiful inner garden has been overgrown with hardy weeds. Statues depicting noble gentlemen and fine ladies stand by the walls. Most of them have been so badly defaced by weather and some sort of corrosive that they look like mere stone pillars. Only two remain in fine shape. There is also a huge heap of offal in the court. It contains a multitude of glistening eggs and 3 **giant bombardier beetles**[II]. The beetles emerge to attack if their nest is disturbed. Unless the eggs are destroyed, the next time the party visits this area, there will be 4d6 of the critters! A thorough search with a successful DC 18 Wisdom (Perception) check of the offal also uncovers a stone hand belonging to the western statue.

The intact statues are both magical. The statue in the western end of the courtyard is that of a robed figure that holds a set of measuring scales in one hand and a book in the other. Placing two evenly valued items in the scale trays animates the statue for a brief moment as the statue thrusts the transformed book toward the characters. The characters have five seconds to view the open book and possibly catch a glimpse of the manor floorplan. Once the time passes, the statue returns to its original pose and cannot be activated again for 24 hours. If two unevenly valued items are placed in the scale's trays, one of them disappears and is transported to a random room of the manor. This effect is not limited by the 24-hour rule.

The other statue by the northern doorway is of a smiling old woman who looks to be offering a large-petaled flower to an invisible patron. If the stone flower is grasped, it curses the character with 12 hours of Disadvantage on all attack rolls, saving throws, and ability checks. The statue laughs for 10 seconds before returning to her original position.

Q8. GARDEN GROTTO

Lush vegetation chokes the dark garden grotto where broken bits of statuary stand on empty pedestals. The remains of a fountain are dry and empty in the middle of the grotto. The sole inhabitant of the place is a small black kitten named **Rustle**[II] that hides from the party — only its yellow eyes visible among the leaves give it away. The cat can be spotted with a successful DC 14 Wisdom (Perception) check. If this cute little thing is frightened, it changes into a giant cat and follows mercilessly.

CHAPTER 5: WITHIN THE VAULTS

INTRODUCTION

The dungeons beneath Tegel Manor are a series of limestone vaults connected by narrow tunnels. They are damp and moldy, exhaling an unpleasant, sickly smell that is always mixed with the stench of the grave. It is also cold down there. The silence is occasionally broken by the sound of dripping water or a gust of wind racing down long halls and blowing out unshielded light sources (accompanied by a quick random encounter check, of course!). Each level except the first conforms to these general characteristics. Of the four levels, the first lies 10 feet below the manor proper. All the others are roughly an additional 20 feet from the surface — 30 feet, 50 feet and 70 feet, respectively.

RANDOM ENCOUNTERS

Except for Level One (which has its own chart), use the standard manor encounter guidelines. However, only roll once per hour, since few undead venture down into the dungeons, and all of them avoid the caverns (**DL2B-C.**, **DL3F-G.**, **DL4C**). If the party finds a reasonably out of the way retreat, they may rest peacefully without worrying about interruptions.

GENERAL GUIDELINES

Rooms and Doors: dungeon rooms are usually either vaulted or rough-hewn, reaching their indicated height in the middle. The stonework is decayed and mottled by the ever-present mold, especially in the lowest chambers. Using potent destruction spells such as *fireball* has a 1% chance per damage die of causing a minor cave-in. If a minor cave-in occurs, each creature within 30 feet of the center of the cause of the cave-in must succeed on a DC 14 Dexterity saving throw or suffer 7 (2d6) bludgeoning damage from falling rocks.

Doors are just like those found in the manor, although slightly thicker and more decayed at the same time. Secret doors, unless specified otherwise, open by pushing a stone, moving a torch holder, or manipulating a similar fixture nearby. A standard wooden door has an AC of 15 and 15 hp, and is immune to cold, necrotic, poison, and psychic damage. It can be broken open with a DC 17 Strength check. Secret doors have AC of 17 and 30 hp, and are immune to cold, necrotic, poison, and psychic damage. They can be broken open with a DC 22 Strength check. A secret door can be found with a successful DC 20 Wisdom (Perception) check, and the operating mechanism with a DC 18 Intelligence (Investigation) check.

Continuous Effects: all undead in the dungeon have +1 on Wisdom saving throws to resist Channel Divinity effects (except for on Level Four, where they gain +2). Additionally, Rump family members cannot be destroyed or commanded by Channel Divinity, although they can be turned.

DUNGEON LEVEL ONE

Once down a rat hole, Characters find that all of Level One is a maze of rat tunnels, 3 feet wide by 3 feet high. Medium creatures must squeeze to pass through them and the entire area is considered difficult terrain for Small and Medium creatures (other than rats). At best, two humanoid creatures can crawl abreast in these tunnels. Encumbered characters, or those wearing bulky plate type armor may find it nigh impossible to progress without getting stuck while making turns and may not make a 180° turn in any case. At each corner, a Medium creature in heavy armor must make a successful DC 16 Strength (Athletics) or Dexterity (Acrobatics) check to avoid getting stuck.

A creature who fails such a check may attempt a new check at the end of their turn each subsequent round until they succeed, at which point they are no longer stuck. Stuck creatures are restrained. Rats, of course, may attack unhindered, and up to two can fight abreast.

Naturally, a lot of rats are found in the tunnels. Unlike simple unintelligent rodents, these possess a feral cunning and a mean demeanor. They wage a constant war against each other — this being the only activity that keeps their population in check. Rat lairs are foul places to visit, with piles of filth, rocks, linen shreds, table scraps, and a modest treasure trove, to boot! However, the respective headquarters of each rival rodent fraction possesses a higher-grade treasure like gems and jewelry. Usually, a good portion of the rats are out scavenging for goods or shiny baubles.

RAT TUNNEL ENCOUNTERS

No rat tunnel would be complete without hordes of ravenous giant rats. Roll for random encounters every 10 minutes. A 1 on an 1d6 (1d8 east of area H) indicates an encounter has occurred. Roll 1d8 below to determine type and number:

1d8	Encounter
1–5	3d6 lesser giant rats[II]
6	2d6 giant rats
7	1d6 greater giant rats[II]
8	1d6 superior giant rats[II]

DL1A. OUTPOST

Being a peripheral chamber of the tunnel network, only a few low level rats are found here. There are 3 **lesser giant rats**[II] and 2 **giant rats**.

DL1B. INCOMING TELEPORT ROOM

A group of 2 **lesser giant rats**[II], 1 **giant rat**, and 1 **greater giant rat**[II] is eating or snoozing in this cramped little nook. They live on the scraps they can steal from the werewolf pack living above them. The chamber is between the first and second stories of the Southwest Wing. It is also the destination of the teleport in **A2**. At your discretion, excessive weight may result in the floor giving away and dumping everyone — rat, human — into the Master Gallery (**B4.**). There are 1d3 x 10 silver pieces scattered about the lair.

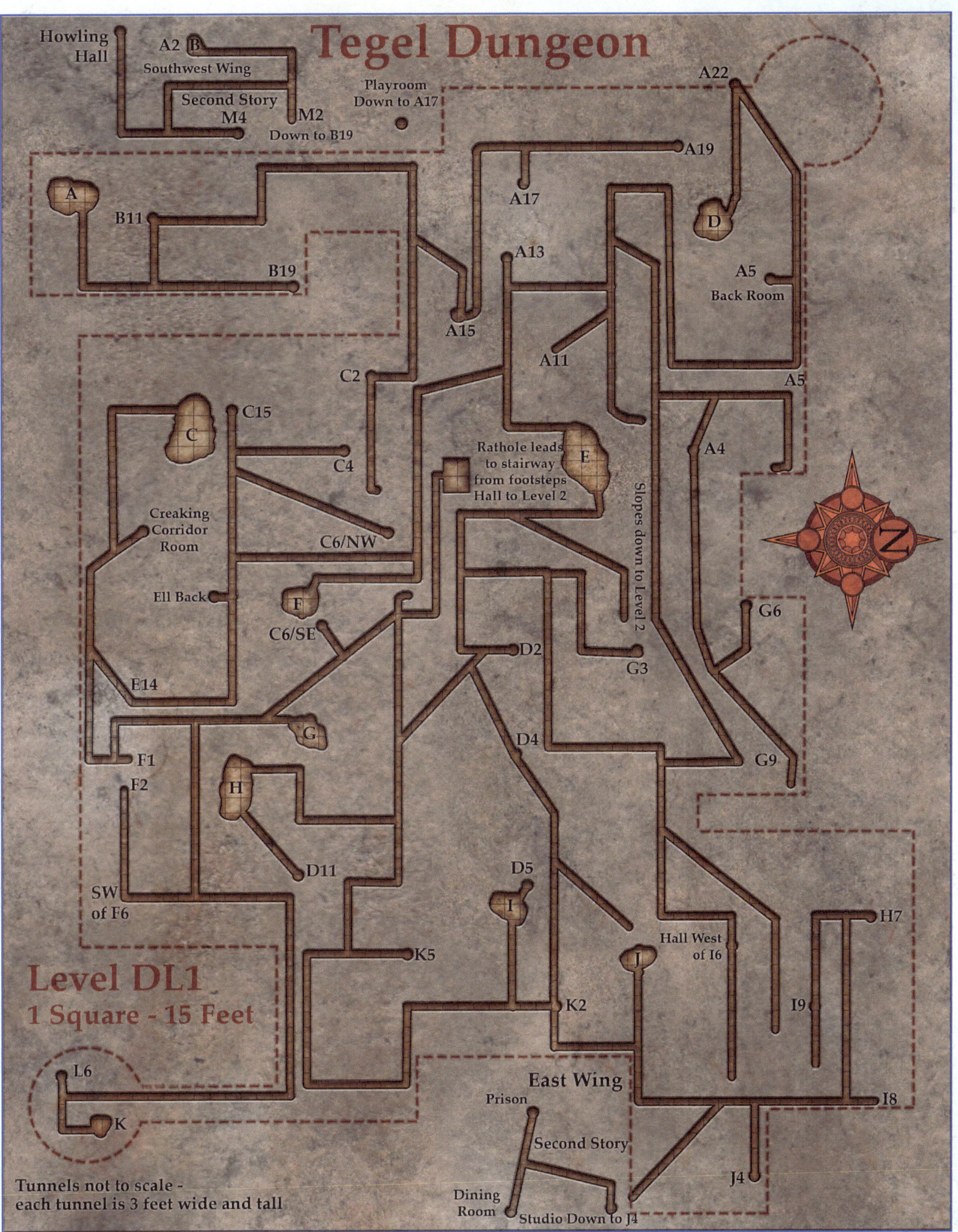

Tegel Dungeon
Howling Hall
A2 B
Southwest Wing
Second Story
M4
M2
Down to B19
Playroom Down to A17
A22
A19
A17
D
A5
Back Room
A13
A5
A
B11
A11
A4
B19
A15
C2
G6
C15
C
Rathole leads to stairway from footsteps Hall to Level 2
E
Slopes down to Level 2
Creaking Corridor Room
C4
C6/NW
Ell Back
F
G3
G9
C6/SE
D2
E14
D4
G
D11
F1
F2
D5
H7
H
I
SW of F6
Hall West of I6
J
I9
Level DL1
K5
K2
I8
1 Square - 15 Feet
L6
East Wing
Prison
K
Second Story
J4
Tunnels not to scale - each tunnel is 3 feet wide and tall
Dining Room
Studio Down to J4

DL1C. Rat HQ

This is the headquarters of the weaker faction. There are always 16 **giant rats** here, half of them **lesser**[II], the rest distributed among the other types. They are ruled by a **King Rat**[II], a nasty, fat rodent with gleaming red eyes who is present 60% of the time. Their hoard includes 1400 sp and 500 gp.

The following treasures are also hidden in the king's nest and can be found with a DC 16 Wisdom (Perception) check: four gems (13 gp turquoise, 11 gp achate, 170 gp bloodstone, 66 gp topaz) and two pieces of jewelry — a 140 gp golden comb and a 330 gp armband.

DL1D. Outpost

Another chamber off the beaten trail, only 8 **lesser giant rats**[II] types occupy this area. A small crate of six empty glass vials lies in a corner.

DL1E. Rat HQ

The lair of the stronger faction is also less defensible, as its central location makes it vulnerable to attacks from all directions. There are 24 **giant rats** present, 12 of the Lesser type and three each of the rest. Their king (as **King Rat**[II], except with 39 (6d8+12) hp) is an albino with a 70% probability of being present. The faction's horde includes 1100 cp, 500 sp, 640 gp and a golden rat statue with tiny ruby eyes, the "great artifact" the rats war over (1900 gp).

Underneath a large pile of rocks lies an enchanted *+2 longsword* complete with gem-encrusted golden scabbard worth 4000 gp. The sword loses its magic if separated from the scabbard for more than a day. The sword's location can be noted with a DC 23 Wisdom (Perception) check, but the sword still has to be uncovered.

DL1F. Lair

This lair usually contains 7 **giant rats**. Due to a recent battle, there are eight dead as well — most of them already half consumed.

DL1G. Lair

Thirteen rats are found here, 5 **lesser giant rats**[II], 6 **giant rats**, and 2 **greater giant rats**[II]. A careful search and a DC 22 Wisdom (Perception) check uncovers *pipes of the sewers* in a hard to reach nook.

DL1H. Outpost

Only five brave rats dare to stay so close to their mortal enemies, the weasels. There are 4 **lesser giant rats**[II] and 1 **greater giant rat**[II] here.

DL1I. Weasel Lair

This is the lair of 8 **giant weasels** (though only two are present 75% of the time). The weasels were introduced some time ago in an attempt to exterminate the giant rats. There are heaps of rat bones scattered about.

DL1J. Retreat

Unlike the other chambers, this room is clearly inhabited by an intelligent being: there is a modest bed and a wooden table here, along with a stool, a lantern and a copper drinking vessel filled with clear water. There is a 40% chance that the creature in question, the **wererat** (with *+2 dagger*) Haredric, is present. Not easily surprised and possessing acute hearing and vision, he often poses as a bewildered hermit and attempts to appear harmless — leading the party away from his treasure, contained in an invisible chest! Finding the chest, short of accidentally bumping into it, requires a DC 25 Intelligence (Investigation) check. It can be unlocked with a DC 25 Dexterity check with thieves' tools or a DC 22 Strength check. If the latter option is used, the *potion* within undoubtedly breaks. The treasure consists of 680 gp, a silver mirror wrapped in black velvet (22 gp), a *potion of healing* and a shortsword.

DL1K. Outpost

Only 2 **superior giant rats**[II] live beneath the Wizard's Tower, but they are both tough. Their most precious treasure is a copper ball that radiates a pleasant warmth and glows with a faint coppery light (*summer sphere*). They belong to neither faction, devouring everything that gets in their way.

Dungeon Level Two

DL2A. Empty Chamber

This rough hewn room looks half finished, as if construction had been abandoned and never resumed. A deep, narrow crack spans the stone floor. Wedged into the crack is a rusty chisel, left here by a long dead worker.

DL2B. Ogre Lair

Being below the Torture Chamber (**G3.**), the **ogre** here does little more than wait for what's dropped to him through the open pit (or catch a goblin who has wandered far from its tribe). As no victims have been coming through for a while, he is hungry and irritated. The rough-hewn chambers to the west are cold and empty except for the last, where the ogre keeps its flea-ridden furs it sleeps on, a bucket of water and a shelf of goblin and human skulls.

An observant character traversing the halls between the pit room and the ogre's sleeping chamber may notice odd fissures in the walls with something gleaming within. They are seen with a DC 18 Wisdom (Perception) check. Excavation reveals that the objects in question are sizable slabs of sea-green glass, with shadowy, humanoid skeletal forms frozen under their smooth surface. There are five slabs in all and they radiate magic and evil. No magic or weapon can penetrate the glass, but "listening" to the thoughts of the skeletons with *detect thoughts* or similar powers broadcasts such fear and shrieking pain that the character has to make a DC 14 Wisdom saving throw or go permanently insane.

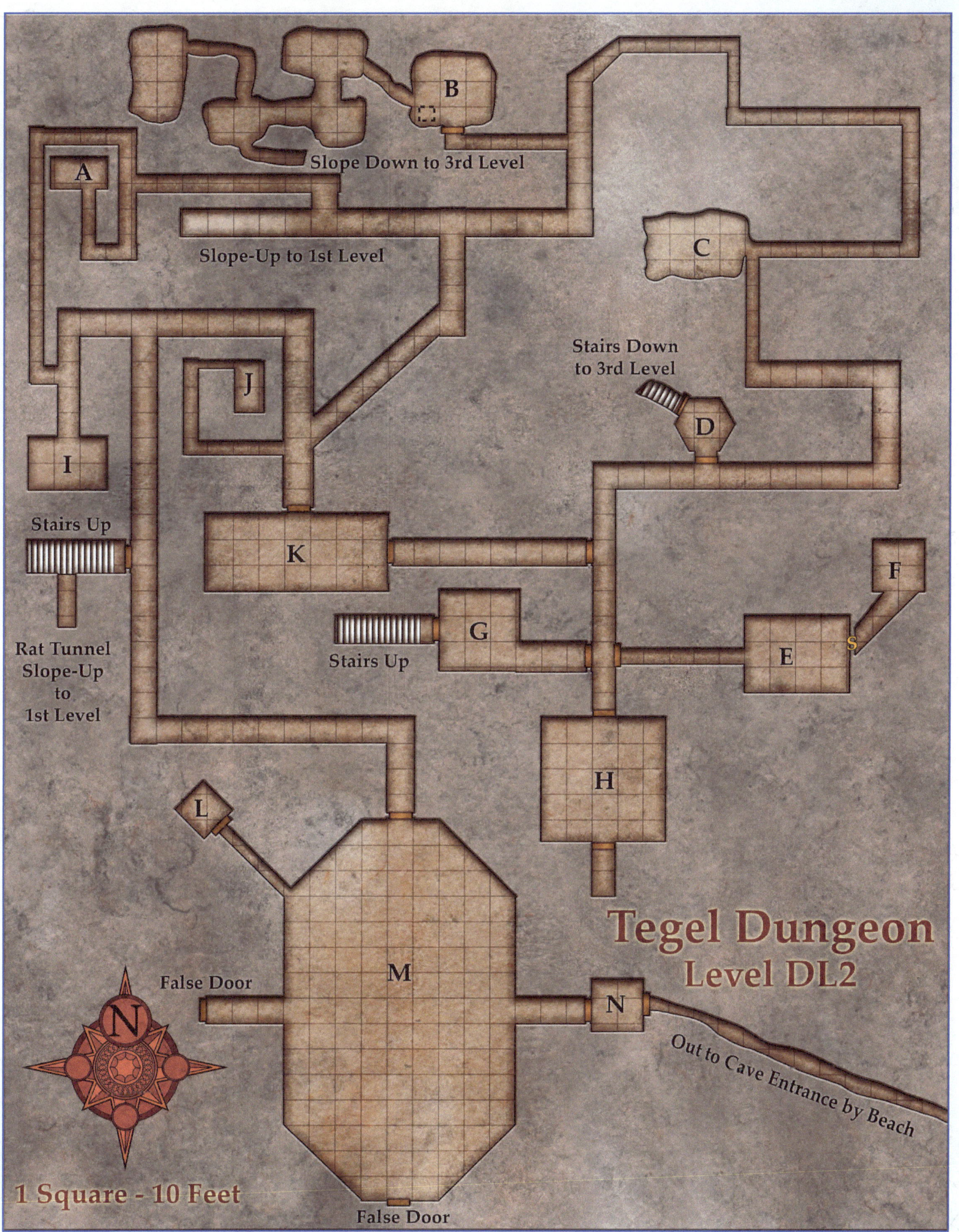

B
Slope Down to 3rd Level
A
Slope-Up to 1st Level
C
Stairs Down to 3rd Level
D
J
I
Stairs Up
F
E
S
K
G
Stairs Up
Rat Tunnel Slope-Up to 1st Level
H
L
Tegel Dungeon
Level DL2
False Door
M
N
Out to Cave Entrance by Beach
N
1 Square - 10 Feet
False Door

DL2C. Ranorek's Lair

This rocky cavern is the living quarters for **Ranorek Rump**[I] (**NPC #99**), a missing link relative. This gentle caveman shields his greatclub with animal skins to only inflict subdual damage. With the exception of a gold-plated horned helmet (valued at 250 gp), Ranorek has traded off any treasure coming his way for several large hamhocks, his favorite food, to the guards down the hall (**DL2K.**). Unless attacked, Ranorek proves extremely friendly if a bit dim — although not above clubbing an unsuspecting party member to carry home as a misguided gesture of friendship.

DL2D. Room of the Oracle

Black marble walls inlaid with geometric lapis ornaments meet above the room to form a hexagonal dome over a low pedestal. Two copper doors graven with mysterious glyphs proclaim this place to be the Oracle of Ormandula. The glyphs can be understood with a DC 17 Intelligence (Arcana) check. The Oracle herself is a stone head wearing a golden diadem. She sleeps most of the time and is so drowsy that she usually asks one riddle before falling asleep for several weeks. Her favorite riddle poses the question of the alchemist who presented his king with a vial of liquid that would eat through any substance known to man, but the king immediately had him put to death. The answer to this puzzling action, is that the man had to be a liar or the liquid would have eaten through the vial. The first character to answer correctly (and within half a minute!) has one random ability score permanently raised by one.

Any character touching the Oracle or her pedestal must make a DC 18 Constitution saving throw or be stunned for 1d6 minutes. Touching a second time inflicts 38 (7d10) non-lethal force damage on the victim and puts him or her into a coma unless a DC 18 Constitution saving throw is successful. Offensive spells either prove ineffective or are reflected back on the caster (your choice).

DL2E. Empty Room

This vault is empty most of the time (90% probability), being the incoming teleport room from the Lich's Quarters (**Q3.**). Thick sheets of cobwebs hang from the ceiling, their white shot through with filaments of sickly gray-green mold. Characters who fail a DC 12 Constitution saving throw are as poisoned due to coughing as long as they remain in here.

The secret door to the east is harder to find than usual, requiring a DC 22 Wisdom (Perception) check to find, and it is also locked. A small keyhole is hidden under a stone nearby. Picking the lock requires a DC 20 Dexterity check with thieves' tools. The 30-foot passage beyond the secret door is even more moldy than the outer chamber. Any movement disturbs a huge cloud of spores. Creatures that fail a DC 16 Constitution saving throw are poisoned as long as they remain in the passage and for 1d4 + 1 minutes afterwards. Three skeletons lie in the passage, having fallen prey to now defunct spear traps in the walls. They are covered with a thick crust of moldy growth, and still seem to be *somewhat* alive, emitting wheezing, gasping noises if they are moved or disturbed. The stout and mold-covered oak door at the end seems to have lain undisturbed for several years (indeed, Ridwik enters through the keyhole in gaseous form most of the time). It is *arcane locked* and hard to penetrate. Breaking it down requires a DC 25 Strength check.

DL2F. Storage

The cramped cubicle is a well-stocked storehouse for a large hoard of 13,000 copper pieces and weapons, used when the lich has a need of raising a small force. It is also where his spellbooks are kept safe from meddlers — by magical traps and physical guardians in the form of three extraordinarily ugly **gargoyles** slumbering in wall niches. The monsters activate if the treasures are disturbed or they themselves are touched.

There are 10 shortswords, 60 scimitars, 60 maces, 10 flails, 18 longswords, 30 battle axes and 70 spears in unruly stacks. Only two of the weapons are magical: a *lycanthrope-bane*[VI] and a *+1 flail* (both look identical to the others in the hoard).

In one of the niches (hidden behind a gargoyle) is a larger stone slab engraved with an open eye. It can be found with a DC 18 Wisdom (Perception) check. Touching the slab activates the trap — a *circle of death* spell going off in the room. All creatures that are not undead within 60 feet of the slab must make a DC 20 Constitution saving throw. Those who fail take 28 (8d6) necrotic damage, while those who succeed take half this amount. Only an undead creature can safely pull out the slab, which turns on hinges to reveal a cavity containing a black iron box. The box, in turn, is protected by a *glyph of warding*. The *glyph* is explosive runes. Touching the box triggers the runes. All creatures within 20 feet must make a DC 20 Dexterity saving throw. Those who fail take 27 (6d8) fire damage while those who succeed take half this amount. Therein are the Lich's spellbooks, slightly mold-eaten black tomes of weird dweomer.

Book #1: 0th — acid splash, chill touch, light, mage hand, ray of frost; 1st — alarm, burning hands, comprehend languages, feather fall, identify, magic missile, shield, unseen servant; 2nd — acid arrow, arcane lock, continual flame, darkness, flaming sphere, hold person, levitate, locate object, magic mouth, mirror image; 3rd — animate dead, dispel magic, fear, nondetection.

Book #2: 1st — fog cloud; 2nd — detect thoughts, see invisibility, suggestion; 3rd — animate dead, fireball, gaseous form, glyph of warding, haste, nondetection; 4th — black tentacles, confusion, dimension door, fire shield; 5th — dominate person; 6th — circle of death, Lankwiler's prismatic missile (see **L6.**), magic jar.

Book #3: 3rd — animate dead, clairvoyance, fireball, lightning bolt; 4th — polymorph, wall of fire; 5th — cloudkill, dominate person, telepathic bond, teleportation circle, wall of stone; 6th — create undead, disintegrate, guards and wards, magic jar, wall of ice.

DL2G. Wine Cellar

The walls of the damp cellar are black with mold. Ancient oak barrels full of wine stand in wall niches and orderly stacks. Some of them are still full, and three crystal bottles — worth 105 gp for their antiquity and workmanship — in a small, locked wooden case contain an excellent vintage equivalent to *potions healing*. All three bottles are marked with the sigil of someone with "R. R." for initials.

DL2H. Crypt

The secret stairs from the sarcophagi outside the manor lead down to this burial vault. Two barriers consisting of thick iron bars separate it into three sections, although the doors allowing passage through them are all wide open. There are signs of a previous battle: soot-blackened stones, broken arrows and weapons, smashed bones and split shields. If the characters enter the middle area and climb or descend the stairs, both doors slam and lock, while an evil voice chuckles in glee. Unlocking the doors requires a DC 18 Dexterity check with thieves' tools, and they require a DC 25 Strength check to break down. Beyond the bars, a faint apparition of a wild-eyed phantom in billowing robes, clutching an ebon staff and displaying a gem-set ring murmurs unknown words of power as the lights dim and an unnatural silence falls on the scene. The phantom is a mere illusion of no substance; however, the iron bars have been enchanted to reflect 50% of the spells cast at, or through them. Seeing through the illusion requires a DC 18 Intelligence (Investigation) check.

Various tombs are found in the vault: sarcophagi to the south, niches in the walls and slabs of stone in the floor. Many have been looted and broken into, but one still contains the intact body of a young lady — but that, too, falls apart with a moan in a shower of dust if touched. Finding the untouched tomb requires a DC 16 Intelligence (Investigation) check.

DL2I. Crypt

This crypt has never been broken into, as intact seals on the door indicate. The seals also warn the living not to disturb those who have lost their lives in the Red Death.

Beyond the grim reminder lies a chamber with nine simple, hastily constructed sarcophagi. Three of them contain mere corpses; the others are occupied by 4 **skeletons** and 2 **wights**, who animate when any of the lids is raised. These undead possess a skeletal visage mottled with patches of reddish mold, and cackle madly as they join the fray. They have no treasure, save for clothes suggestive of minor nobility.

DL2J. Statue Room

This oblong room is unoccupied, and contains four niches with a small statue in each: a bear, a serpent, a monkey and a peacock. When the statue of the monkey is touched, all characters in the room are teleported to **DL3K.** Upon touching any other statue, the monkey emits a fiendish laughter.

DL2K. Dungeon

This dank and foul-smelling prison is manned by 3 jailers (use **bandit** with AC 13 and 16 [3d8 + 3] hit points), unscrupulous sorts in the employ of the Rump family. They rarely leave their dimly lit dwelling, and tend to pass the time playing cards around a wooden table. They have a large cask of water, several large hamhocks against the wall and little else. They currently have eight prisoners, all but three captured by raiding goblins. Each jailer has studded leather armor and a longsword, and one of them has a deck of marked playing cards.

Prisoner #1 is Morton the Elf (as **scout**, with darkvision 60 feet and Fey Ancestry), better known as "the Hand" for the member he displays on his (fake) coat of arms. Morton is wanted in three towns for forgery and fraud. He denies all rumors as fabrications and scurrilous slander.

Prisoner #2 and **#3** are Frederik and Carolus, seasoned **veterans** looking for adventure. Both are rather dim, but likable that way.

Prisoners #4, #5 and **#6** are 3 **goblins**. These members of the tribe at **DL2M.** were thrown into the cells for insubordination and are currently awaiting their eventual fate.

Prisoner #7 is Xor of Un (as **thug** with AC 18 if rejoined with his armor), a thoroughly Chaotic Evil swordsman, prefers black plate armor and has a hollow, menacing voice. Predictably, his first deed once freed is betraying the party: whether to the Evil High Priest Sarthoggus, the Pirates, or someone else is immaterial.

Prisoner #8 is Vilis Mil, (as **scout**) Amazon worshipper of Athena. She has a concealed dagger in one of her leather boots, and isn't afraid to use it if a good opportunity presents itself.

DL2L. Hidden Tomb

This is the final resting place of Prince Choaxtl, warlord and conqueror in the last days of the Orichalan Dragon Kings. During Tegel Manor's construction, the architects discovered the outer chamber of his tomb — however, they never discovered the well hidden burial chamber itself. Much later, a resourceful fighter happened upon its hidden door, but fell victim to the cursed sword still prominently displayed in Choaxtl's grasp.

The tomb is a simple room, decorated with a few ornamental patterns on its walls, and the following glyphs: *"Thief, defiler / great wrath / run fast / [illegible line]/ Choaxtl is here"*. The message in the glyphs can be determined with a DC 18 Intelligence check. There are six desiccated corpses in antique bronze banded mail propped against the wall here. They are **zombies** who animate if the tomb's contents are disturbed. They surround a stone bier where a mummy in

Choaxtl's Sword

Weapon (longsword), legendary (requires attunement by a character proficient with longsword)

You gain a +3 bonus to attack and damage rolls with this weapon.

Spellcasting. You can use the sword to cast *hold person* on one person (DC 16 spell save DC), *see invisibility*, and *levitate* on yourself. Once you have cast one of these spells three times in a day, you cannot cast that spell again until the following midnight.

Sentience. The sword has an Intelligence of 14, a Wisdom of 12, and a Charisma of 15. The sword is extremely vain and vindictive, stopping at nothing to mercilessly destroy the "thief" who took it from its rightful owner. You must make a DC 15 Wisdom saving throw immediately upon attunement. If you fail the saving throw, you immediately enter a berserk rage. While in a rage, you attack the nearest conscious creature you can see. The rage lasts until you are knocked unconscious or 10 minutes have passed. In addition, if you do not pass the saving throw, each time that day that you attempt to use the sword to cast a spell, you must succeed on a DC 15 Wisdom saving throw or enter a berserk rage. Every day at midnight, you must make another DC 15 Wisdom saving throw with the same consequences for failure. If you succeed on five consecutive saving throws against the weapon's mental assault, Choaxtl's sword allows you to use its powers and you no longer have to make saving throws... as long as your superiority remains unquestionable. Choaxtl's sword speaks Ancient Orichalan and nothing else.

In the hands of an evil Orichalan character, it remains *reasonably* loyal — that is, it merely tries to control the character instead of causing utter destruction.

bronze half-plate slumbers. The mummy holds a heavy bastard sword made of some unknown bluish metal. It is inanimate, although it has been treated with enchanted oils, making it resistant to all sorts of physical and magical harm. Next to Choaxtl's stone bier lies the body of the fighter who originally tried to steal the sword. He has a suit of chainmail, a *Choaxtl's sword*[N1], a large metal shield, a torch, a coil of rope and a bag with 60 sp and 95 gp.

The only other treasure is hidden on the enchanted sword itself: a treasure map wrapped around the hilt reveals the resting place of a magic item not far from the manor. What it is and how it is guarded is left for you to develop.

DL2M. Goblin Tribe

It is immediately apparent that this huge room is unlike the rest of the dungeon; from the cyclopean stone blocks used in its construction to the bizarre abstract patterns adorning its walls, it looks like a relic from an eldritch past. A successful DC 20 Intelligence (History) check reveals it to be of ancient Orichalan make. This vault (along with rooms **DL2L.** and **DL2N.**) is the tomb of Prince Choaxtl (see area **DL2L.** for details). The large hall used to hold a funerary barge with a great number of valuable offerings. None of this survives: the Rumps looted the treasury long ago.

The hall's current inhabitants are a tribe of 60 **goblins** (with 12 hit points), who are employed by the manor for "odd jobs" including kidnappings, burglary, arson and general vandalism. Therefore, they are hardier than usual (hence the maximum hit points) and possess good combat training. They wear distinctive black felt clothing with a large red "R" embroidered on it. Their leader, Garstang (**hobgoblin** with AC 20 from *+1 chainmail* and a *+1 shield*, and a *+1 spear*), is a personal servant of the Lich Ridwik.

The two false stone doors leading out of the hall bear the markings of several pickaxes. The true door, however, is out of sight: a carefully hidden secret door in the northwest wall allows access to Prince Choaxtl's burial chamber. It can be located with a DC 22 Wisdom (Perception) check.

DL2N. Goblin Outpost

This small stone chamber is manned by 3 **goblins** who stand watch by the tunnel leading to the sea cliffs (hex 4931). They report any disturbances to their leader.

The chamber's walls are made of sizable stone blocks without a bit of mortar, yet the gaps are so small that not even a dagger's blade could slip through. Ancient and faded glyphs in Ancient Orichalan declare: *"This is the [going under] of Prince Choaxtl / he was the [final one] / sailed three times six, sailed four times four [great water] / alas, the world is no more / [unworthy] live now and forever."* A character that speaks Orichalan can decipher the glyphs with a DC 17 Intelligence check.

Dungeon Level Three

DL3A. Shadow Gallery

This room is crisscrossed with several shadows forming a sort of web or grid that fills the entire area. A character crossing the room must make a DC 16 Dexterity (Acrobatics) check to avoid touching the shadows 1d3 times. *Gaseous form* provides advantage on the checks. Each touch is like the touch of a **shadow**. A character reduced to 0 Strength becomes a part of the shadowy web. The DC for avoiding touching the shadow web increases by 1 for each character added to it.

Characters accompanied by *daylight* or its equivalent are unaffected. If a character attempts to channel divinity to turn undead against the shadows, the shadows make the saving throw with a +5 on the roll. If the shadow web fails the saving throw, it is driven back for 1d6 minutes. Casting *dispel evil and good* or *holy aura* destroys them permanently (along with all absorbed characters, regrettably).

DL3B. Crypt

Slime and mold coat the walls of the crypt, creating an atmosphere of wet miasma. What at first sounds like faint whispering turns out to be an air current — it comes from the cobweb-concealed shaft above, which climbs 20 feet and opens into a low passage leading outside the manor (**R4.**). The six sarcophagi in the room have all been looted. A huge trunk with two golden handles (20 gp each) is full of human bones. A stained leather cape and a shattered helm are concealed behind the trunk. They can be found with a successful DC 12 Intelligence (Investigation) check.

DL3C. Circular Room

The bricks of the decaying wall in this domed chamber have started to fall and the whole structure is on the brink of collapse. Every time the walls are disturbed, there is a 50% probability that a large section caves in. Creatures within 20 ft of the disturbance must make a DC 18 Dexterity saving throw. Those that fail take 21 (6d6) bludgeoning damage, while those that succeed take half this amount. Hidden behind beardlike growths of putrid mold, 3 **ghouls** wait patiently to leap at intruders. They are covered in the stuff — hopefully, none of the PCs are allergic! In addition to the ghouls, there is a grotesque skeleton in the middle of the room. This strange, deformed being was a giant hog; however, it *does* look disturbingly humanoid on first glance, reinforced by the rusty dagger the misshapen runt clutches in one of its … hands?

DL3D. Webbed Chamber

Yet more webs and mold fill this chamber. This time, however, the webs are occupied: a small **spider** drops on unsuspecting (and preferably solitary) prey.

A bricked-up niche concealed by a layer of wispy and mold-shot webs is the source of shuffling noises and occasional coughing. It can be located with a DC 14 Intelligence (Investigation) check. If the characters first succeed on a DC 15 Wisdom (Perception) check to hear the sounds, they should get advantage on the check. Walled in is a moldering corpse who falls outward with a dull thud if the brickwork is removed. It still grasps a sizable bundle of rotted parchment maps describing a multi-level dungeon complex, complete with key and notations. The parchments crumble into filth no matter how delicately they are handled. In pace requiescat!

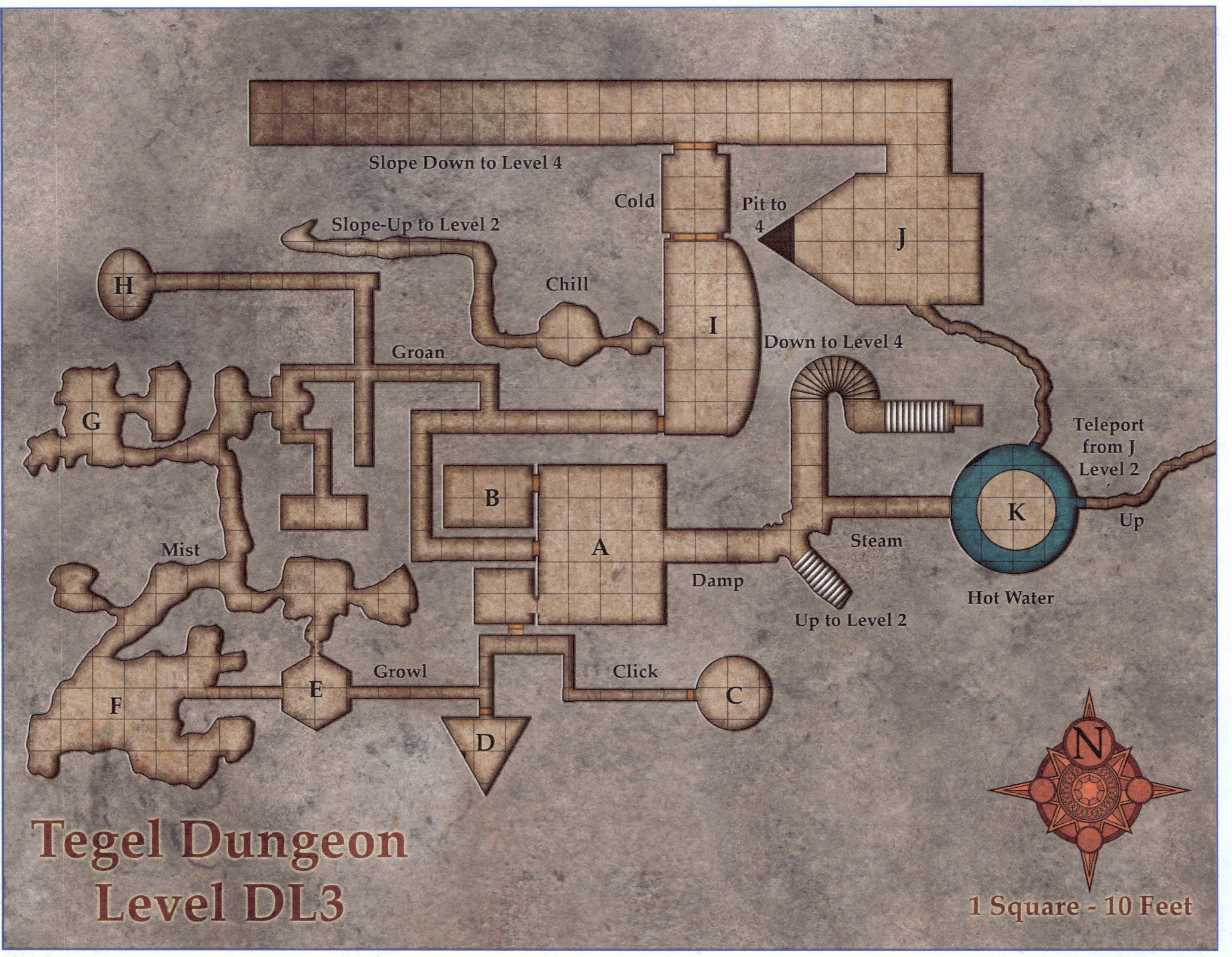

Tegel Dungeon
Level DL3
Slope Down to Level 4
Slope-Up to Level 2
Cold
Pit to 4
J
Chill
I
Down to Level 4
H
Groan
G
Teleport from J Level 2
Up
K
Steam
B
Damp
Hot Water
A
Up to Level 2
Mist
Growl
Click
C
F
E
D
N
1 Square - 10 Feet

DL3E. Hexagonal Vault

The growling heard before entering the chamber turns out to come from a **hell hound**; the monster is accompanied by a solitary **wight**. Standing by the walls are six unmarked stone coffins. The bones inside are gnarled and twisted. Some skulls have more than two eye sockets; others have small horns or bumpy protrusions of some other sort. One of the coffins contains diseased grave dust. A character who opens the coffin must succeed on a DC 18 Constitution saving throw or contract an extremely virulent form of Tsathoggan Rotting Disease. This rot is extremely fast, with a mere 1-hour incubation period and ability loss every two hours thereafter.

DL3F. The Mines

Rough, irregular chambers and treacherous, rubble filled passages make up this section of the level. Originally intended to be converted into more crypts, the mines were abandoned instead when the Rumps descended into madness and even worse fates. Not even the undead visit its solitude, and only the dripping of water — and the fluttering of tiny bats — breaks the silence. This doesn't mean the place is empty: hiding behind a pile of rocks is a **slithering tracker**[II]. This amorphous horror stalks and kills in complete silence and may follow a party for a long time before striking. It usually feeds on the bats, but only usually: it is time for something different!

DL3G. Silver Cavern

Separated from the rest of the mines by a narrow gap, this natural cavern is a garden of crystalline wonders. Perhaps less obvious, but much more valuable, is the huge silver vein in the north wall: it is possible to mine it in five hours (assuming six party members with mining equipment), resulting in 14,800 sp worth of raw silver. A remarkably fat **rust monster** — too bloated to even fit through the exit passage — has made its lair in the cavern.

DL3H. Abandoned Vampire Lair

Four **skeletons** armed with swords guard a dirt filled coffin. The coffin has not been used in ages, as its inhabitant was slain by adventurers. A corroded brass lantern suspended from the ceiling burns with a magical flame. It is hot to the touch (2 [1d4] fire damage per round of contact) and if its light is extinguished, continual *darkness* falls on the room — this inky black veil may not be removed short of *dispel magic* cast against a 6th level spell effect.

DL3I. Rubble Hall

Large mounds of crushed stone fill this spacious chamber — a deposit for the mine to the west. It was once used for religious purposes — a group of supplicants in hooded robes is still visible on a faded fresco. An upturned mine cart is the nest of a **giant constrictor snake**; the serpent has just hatched eight leathery eggs and defends its domain furiously. Characters fighting on the rubble must succeed on a DC 12 Dexterity saving throw each round or slip and fall.

DL3J. Domain of the Giant Hogs

Steaming hot water from **DL3K.** creates a fetid atmosphere in the hall. Slime and fungus covers the floor and walls, thriving on the wet rot. The floor is slippery from mud — characters running or fighting must succeed on a DC 12 Dexterity saving throw or fall down.

The inhabitants of this place are 5 **giant hogs**[II], currently munching on two giant rats. Created by bizarre alchemical experiments in an attempt to create the perfect servant race, the result was a repulsive swine-human hybrid; more porcine than humanoid. Still, these creatures do possess a simple (and hateful) mind, wear rotted leather rags and can communicate in guttural growls. They move with a shambling gait and like to capture victims, sacrificing them by hurling them down their 20 foot pit. They obey their high priest (**DL4A.**) and come to his aid if they are summoned.

DL3K. Hot Spring

A 10-foot-wide moat full of boiling water surrounds a central island — the incoming platform from the teleporter in **DL2J.** Hot water from the depths of the earth feeds the moat, supplying the manor's baths and greenhouses. A thick pipe exits to the west, eventually dividing into numerous lead vessels; a 4 foot diameter overflow leads north.

The heated steam in here is so bad that characters soon start to boil alive, taking 3 (1d6) fire damage every minute they remain. Add one additional point of damage per minte if they wear heavy clothing or armor. Metal armor is subject to *heat metal* after five minutes. To jump the 10 ft across the moat requires a DC 12 Strength (Athletics) check due to the slippery footing. Characters in heavy armor or who are encumbered have disadvantage on the check. Full immersion in the water deals 21 (6d6) fire damage per round. The moat is 10 feet deep. There may already be a cooked adventurer or two in there if you so desire…

Dungeon Level Four

DL4A. Abandoned Temple

Slimy, green-gray clumps of mold cling to the ceiling. The walls are adorned with an endless throng of dancing figures, contorted and repulsive. The procession ends in the inner shrine to the west, where the bloated frog-idol of Tsathoggus squats on a huge slab of transparent lime green crystal, flanked by two heavy golden candelabra (800 gp each, but tainted and evil). There is a permanent evil *hallow* effect radiating from the idol. All undead gain advantage on saving throws to resist effects of channel divinity and +2 to attack rolls, plus 2 temporary hit points per HD.

This temple beyond the beaten bronze gates was the gathering place of the Rumps, their shameful secret and the source of the family's corruption. Little did their subjects suspect that their overlords served the very evil they were supposed to protect the village from!

Fortunately, the place is mostly abandoned. Its only caretaker is a **giant hog**[II] (with *staff of withering*). This misshapen mongrel is clad

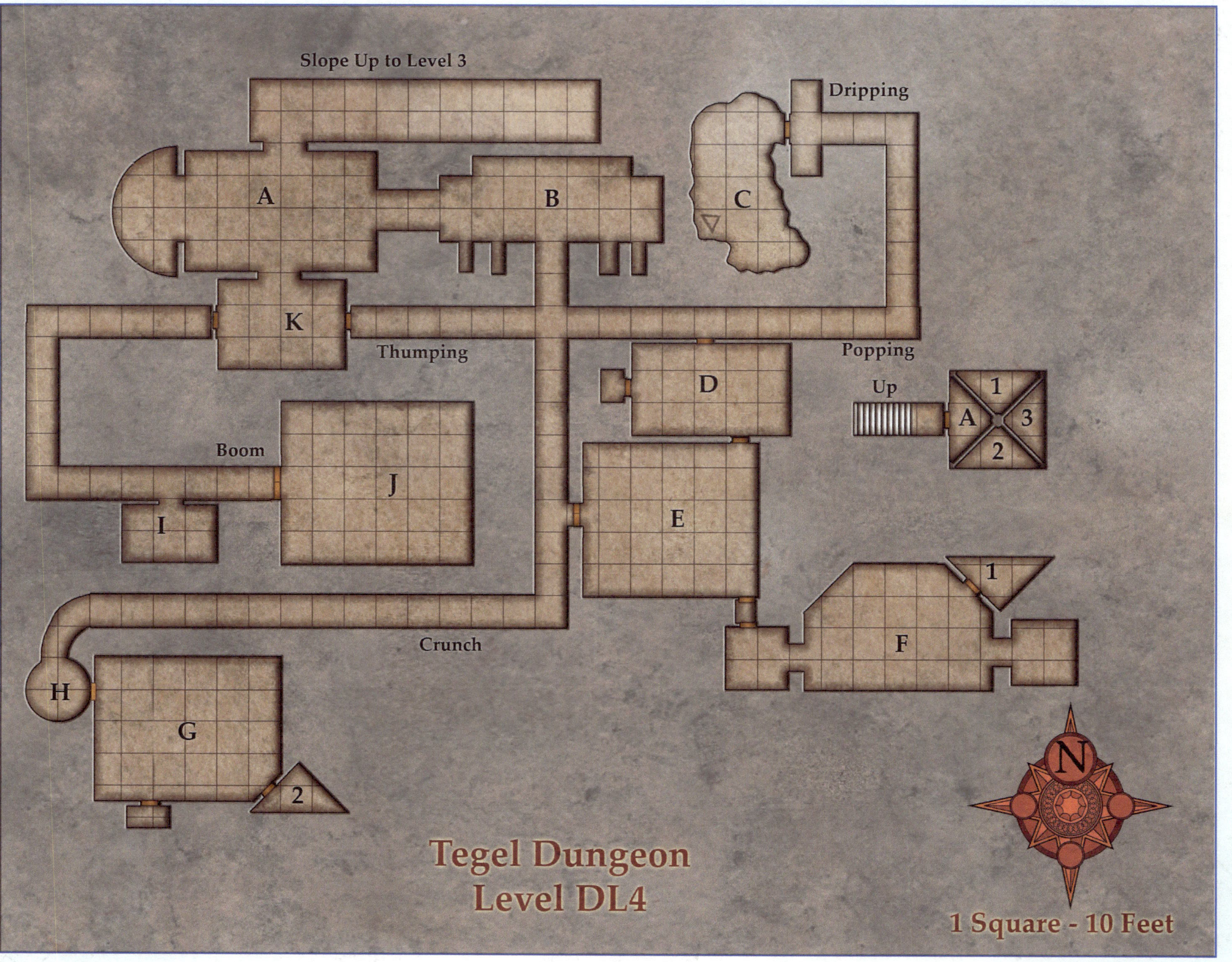

Slope Up to Level 3
Dripping
A
B
C
K
Thumping
Popping
D
Up
A
1
3
2
Boom
J
E
I
1
Crunch
F
H
G
2
N
Tegel Dungeon
Level DL4
1 Square - 10 Feet

Slimy Doom

Slimy Doom is caught from contact with the remains of a creature that dies of Tsathoggan Rotting Disease. For each round of contact with dissolved flesh of such a victim, a creature must succeed on a DC 16 Constitution saving throw or succumb to the disease with no initial incubation period. Slimy doom turns a person into goo from the inside out. Each day, the victim must pass a DC 16 Constitution saving throw or lose 1d4 points of their constitution. At 0 constitution, they are nothing more than a fleshy bag of pus and bloody foam. Those who are cured by spell or who pass two daily saving throws in a row, must make one additional saving throw for each day they took constitution damage. If these saving throws fail, the victim has permanently lost a point of constitution per failed saving throw.

in the grotesque garments of a High Priest and clutches the symbol of its station, a heavy brass staff studded with green gemstone "eyes" and "warts". This is a cursed *staff of withering* which is worth at least 10,000 gp as a grotesque curiosity alone (not to mention its value to Sarthoggus, or other frog-cultists). Alas, an unbeliever who holds the staff contracts slimy doom with no saving throw; such is the power of the rod that the wasting disease incubates in a minute and causes ability damage every ten minutes rather than every day! A character immediately renouncing the staff after the disease manifests may roll a DC 16 Constitution saving throw to avoid further harm.

The high priest may summon its companions from **DL3J.** with a bellowing cry: there is a 65% chance they hear his call and obey. The high priest and his cohorts occasionally raid the surface world for new captives to sacrifice; at other times, they bargain with the goblins on Level Two for the same.

DL4A123. Teleport Chamber

The entrance door is rusted and hot to the touch. A DC 16 Strength check is necessary to open it due to high pressure inside! The portal opens to reveal a steam-filled room full of rusty pipes transporting hot water from the depths. The steam makes the area lightly obscured and deals 3 (1d6) fire damage every minute. This is also a teleportation room: 1d6 rounds after entering the chamber, the entrance shuts and the transporter is activated. Characters standing in quadrants "1" and "2" are sent to the corresponding locations on this level; those in "3" are rotated to 2. All teleports are one way. The process repeats again in 1d6 rounds. Prying open the entrance from the inside requires another DC 16 Strength check.

DL4B. Hall of Entombment

At one time, a small number of frog-cultists, including four under-priests, rebelled against their demonic master, forsaking their perverted ways. Alas, the revolt was short-lived and the priests were placed in this former ante-chamber in perpetual imprisonment. Four barred niches, too low to stand up or move comfortably, contain the corpses of the priests. They remain as 4 **wraiths**, envious of the living.

Crystal Basilisk Blood

Wondrous item, very rare

The blood of a crystal basilisk imbues a gemstone worth at least 50 gp with rainbow radiance. If a gemstone is soaked in one gallon of crystal basilisk blood for 24 hours, the gemstone becomes a *gem of brightness* with 50 charges. A successful DC 15 Dexterity or Intelligence check using alchemist's supplies harvests 1 gallon of blood from a freshly-slain crystal basilisk. If the check succeeds by 5 or more, the harvested amount increases to 2 gallons. The blood congeals after it imbues a gemstone with radiance and can't be used to make another gemstone.

DL4C. Crystal Vault

Sparkling like the interior of a geode, light in this cavern is reflected a thousandfold from smooth surfaces and sharp angles. Crystalline columns, sheets and outcroppings in a dozen colors are glowing with an inner light. Excavating it all would fetch a ransom — 6000 gp, maybe even more. However, the beauty of the vault is broken by a motley collection of five crystal statues, including two stoned hobbits at the entrance. This is the work of a **crystal basilisk**[II], whose gaze turns mortal flesh into stone and stone into crystal. Crystal statues are roughly 500 gp each — not too valuable, but certainly fancy. The beast's hide, a sparkling shield of gemstones, is worth 600 gp; its blood imbues normal gems with a rainbow radiance.

DL4D. Sword Tomb

Rusty swords — 56 in number — hang from the walls in a neat order. They all point towards the wrought iron gate to the west, which bears the Rump insignia. The gate is locked and requires a DC 18 Dexterity check with thieves' tools to open. This is the tomb of a **vampiric warrior**[II] and his 6 **zombie** (AC 16 from chain mail, and add halberd attack, +3 to hit, reach 10 ft., one target, *hit*: 6 [1d10 + 1] slashing damage) minions. The vampire used to be a great lord, and is still clad in the full plate of his station.

Beyond the gate lies the coffin of the vampire. Therein are ashes mixed with earth, and a gold-and-platinum diadem (worth 1200 gp). Buried seven feet under his coffin are four large chests with 2000 gp each.

DL4E. Crypt

Rows upon rows of decaying wooden coffins fill this crypt. The chill in the air is accompanied by moaning and shuffling sounds — coming from a **specter** and its 2 **zombie** minions. The rest of the dead are inanimate. A niche in the east wall contains a mound of glistening, slime covered skulls flanked by four tallow candles. If the candles are lit, fire flares in the hollow eye sockets and the skulls shriek, possibly attracting more undead (roll four times).

DL4F. Amber Death

Enchanted phosphorescence glows in a 6-foot-deep pool of hazy amber liquid. It illuminates twelve moss-covered statues along the north wall. The statues are humanoid, being from 10 feet to 18 feet tall. The centermost is a figure of a six-armed human. One of its arms points at the tall brass doors to the northeast (this leads to the incoming teleport chamber from **DL4A123.**).

The inhabitants of the strange shrine are 4 **harpies**, foul bird demons nesting on ledges in the eastern chamber. They usually hide among the statues if they hear someone approach, and start singing to lure unsuspecting PCs into the amber pool. The thick liquid therein is paralytic and dissolves flesh at the rate of 6 (1d12) acid damage per round. A creature that starts its turn in contact or who comes into contact with the pool must make a DC 14 Constitution saving throw or be paralyzed until the beginning of its next turn. Inorganic materials are unaffected. Once a sufficient number of PCs are in the pool, the harpies rush the remaining heroes to tear them limb from limb.

Lying on the bottom of the pool are an iron flask, a finely carved dagger and 70 gold coins. The flask contains rough brandy.

DL4G. Laboratory

The chamber beyond the narrow opening from the circular room is the hidden laboratory of Rasping Rashuak, the *other* **Lich** of Tegel Manor (15% chance of being present). Six sarcophagi contain 3 animated **mummies** and three dead bodies (the latter are spares for Rashuak's use). The largest mummy wears a *ring of spell turning* and uses a *+2 longsword*. The rest are unarmed. They emerge from their resting places if any of the doors into the laboratory are opened.

This collection of the arcane and the unusual resembles a cluttered storeroom. Everywhere one turns, there are shelves of dusty glass implements, ceramic containers, boxes, dried homunculi, mummy wrappings, spices and so forth. 3d6 containers still hold active ingredients. There are also great trunks full of crumbling garments, heavy laboratory equipment, ruined components and bottles of barely potent acid. Six heavy bars of a silvery metal (mithral) are hidden under moldering rags in one of the trunks. A character who is searching can find the Mithril with a DC 17 Intelligence (Investigation) check. The mithral is sufficient for one suit of chain armor for a Medium creature.

The entrance to the southern closet is concealed behind one of the shelves. It can be located with a DC 20 Wisdom (Perception) check. The shelf turns on hinges to reveal a wall of swirling blue mist obscuring the entrance. The mist radiates cold. Anyone passing through suffers 100 points of cold damage (no save), and is likely frozen solid (50% fall and shatter). 50 points of fire damage in one round brings the curtain down for 2d6 rounds; protective spells may offer complete or partial resistance to the effects of the cold.

The closet beyond the prismatic wall contains a number of enchanted items, including the Lich's spellbooks. The items are: a *+2 mace*, a *ring of telekinesis*, a *globe of devious entrapment*, and a *prism of separation*. A **guardian demon**[II] protects the items, appearing immediately if any of them are touched. It tries to push its opponents into the wall if it has already been reactivated. The spellbooks contain the following spells:

Book #1: 0th — dancing lights, light, mage hand, ray of frost, shocking grasp; 1st — burning hands, charm person, detect magic, hold person, identify, mage armor, magic missile, suggestion; 2nd — detect thoughts, fear, levitate, locate object, mirror image, web; 3rd — fireball, lightning bolt; 4th — arcane eye, dimension door, wall of fire.

Book #2: 1st — detect magic, floating disk, unseen servant; 2nd — arcane lock, gust of wind, magic aura; 3rd — animate dead, bestow curse, clairvoyance, fear, fly, glyph of warding, lightning bolt; 4th — banishment, phantasmal killer, stoneskin; 5th — dismissal, planar binding, teleportation circle.

Globe of Devious Entrapment (oB-DL2U)

Wondrous item, rare

This item looks like a 1 foot diameter glass orb filled with water. Its surface is cool to the touch. If you maintain contact for more than a round you must make a DC 16 Charisma saving throw. If you fail, you shrink and are drawn into the orb. The water inside the orb is a gate to the Plane of Water, where you are sent.

The globe has AC 20 and takes 30 hit points of damage to crack. It is immune to acid, necrotic, poison, psychic, and radiant damage and vulnerable to bludgeoning, force, and thunder damage. If it is cracked within 3 rounds of trapping a character, the character within reappears in the nearest unoccupied square.

Prism of Separation

Wondrous item, very rare

This glass object separates light like any other prism, but may also be used to reduce the effectiveness of ray spells if worn openly. If you are targeted with a ray attack, it does not affect you. In addition, there is a 10% chance that a ray spell that would have hit you is reflected back to its source. If the source was a creature that can see, it must succeed on a DC 16 Constitution saving throw or be blinded for 1d4 rounds. If you hurl the *prism* at a *prismatic wall*, it destroys it, but then loses its powers permanently, turning into a 3,000 gp gem.

Book #3: 5th — cloudkill, geas, passwall, telekinesis; 6th — chain lightning, disintegrate, freezing sphere, globe of invulnerability, magic jar, wall of ice.

Book #4: 7th — delayed blast fireball, etherealness, finger of death, reverse gravity, sword; 8th — clone, maze.

DL4H. Circular Antechamber

Strings of skulls hang from the ceiling, surrounding the entrance to Rasping Rashuak's underground hideout. Each skull (there are 100 in all) has a single gold piece in its mouth, except one, which has a large sunstone gem instead. This last can be seen with a DC 19 Wisdom (Perception) check. This gemstone appears to be worth 5,000 gp as a valuable; however, it is also the Lich's phylactery! The phylactery is warded by permanent versions of *magic aura* (making it appear nonmagical) and *nondetection*. The gem has an AC of 18 and 40 hit points. It is immune to acid, fire, lightning, necrotic, poison, psychic and radiant damage, and vulnerable to bludgeoning damage.

DL4I. Storage

In a macabre display, ten dead elves are hanging upside down from the ceiling. The bodies appear fresh, as they are still dripping with blood. Blood splatters the dusty religious paraphernalia left here: sooty braziers, velvet drapes, incense burners and a collapsed podium. A large trunk covered by these odds and ends is full of 560 daggers, which in turn cover a mace with a golden head (90 gp). Discovering the mace requires a successful DC 15 Wisdom (Perception) check.

DL4J. Clerics' Quarters

Broken furniture has been piled up in the middle of the room. What used to be beds, chairs and a table are but firewood now. Even the large chandelier has been torn from the ceiling, its wax candles thrown on the ground. The only item seemingly left intact is a crimson tapestry to the east. It covers the wall, depicting monks bowing before a high priest who bears the staff of Tsathoggus (the gem-studded *rod of withering* now found in **DL4A.**). If a character approaches the tapestry, two crazed **werewolves** in black robes spring forward in a maddened rage. These monsters got lost while exploring the dungeons as their lanterns ran out of oil.

DL4K. Frog-pits

Those unfortunates who died before the loathsome idol of Tsathoggus were disposed of in the deep pits in this side chamber. At other times, they were thrown alive among the carnivorous giant frogs to be devoured screaming. Sustained by foul magic and the occasional sacrifice, the giant frogs under three round pits (which open into the same reservoir below) live on undisturbed. The smaller specimens subsist on scraps of meat and each other; the huge, bloated elders generally hibernate and only awaken if large prey is in reach.

The chamber above the pits is a bare, simple place. Three round openings are covered with iron grilles. These are corroded and weakened by age: there is a 50% chance they break under weight. A system of winches and pulleys used to lower victims is in the same sorry state: it appears sturdy on a casual observation (sturdy enough to climb down on its chains), but a more careful study and a successful DC 16 Intelligence (Investigation) check reveal the weaknesses which would send any foolhardy character down into the depths.

The pits are 50 feet deep. Since the fall is cushioned by water and mud, no damage is taken. The pits lead into a wet cavern full of slime, brackish water and the smell of vile feces and rot. Slimy eggs stick to the walls and glowing fungi provide sparse illumination. Most of the mire is only 2 feet deep, but there are places where it reaches 15 feet or more. Treat these places as quicksand. Determining this without sinking in requires a DC 14 Wisdom (Survival) or Intelligence (Nature) check. Moreover, the entire area is difficult terrain.

Anyone spending more than ten minutes in the unwholesome miasma must roll a DC 14 Constitution saving throw or contract Tsathoggan Rotting Disease. Of more immediate concern are the swarms of giant frogs eager to devour anyone and anything venturing into their cavern. There are 18 **killer frogs**[II] and 2 **giant dire abyssal frogs**[II]. Their sole treasure is a magical *+1 trident* in one of the deep sinkholes. Only *detect magic* reveals the item's location.

Quicksand

A creature who enters an area covered by quicksand sinks 1d4 + 1 feet into the quicksand. At the beginning of each turn after sinking into quicksand, the creature will sink another 1d4 feet. A creature that is completely submerged can't breathe. Provided the creature is not completely submerged, it can use its action to escape from the quicksand with a successful Strength check. The Strength check has a base DC of 10, which increases by one for each foot the creature has sunk. If the creature has sunk 5 feet, the DC of the Strength check would be 15.

A creature can pull another creature out of quicksand with a Strength check. The base DC for the Strength check is 5 and increases in the same manner mentioned previously — for each foot the target has sunk, the DC increases by 1.

APPENDIX I: RUMP FAMILY TREE
LYCANTHROPE-BANE

The following pages list the various personalities found in Tegel Manor. The Family Tree's primary function is to serve as a random encounter table. It also doubles as a list of the various magical portraits that may be encountered in galleries and other rooms. Entries are listed with names first, followed by the location of the associated portrait, creature type, note on appearance, tactics or personality, and the magical effects of the picture. The magical effect is listed with the required saving throw and the effect on a failure. In the case of some NPCs, their lair is also indicated in square brackets.

Magical portraits tend to have a limited consciousness. Some are barely sentient, others are good (if occasionally deranged) conversationalists, and yet others are bothersome louts. The GM should exploit their potential for entertainment and add a touch of (even more) chaos to the campaign through their use.

1. SIR RUNIC RUMP (B3.)

Male human **holy knight**[II]: see Tegel Village, area **R.** for details.
Note: Very cowardly, Sir Runic is usually accompanied by his coterie of lackeys. Unless reassured of good intentions (or he had previously encountered the party), he flees on sight.
Picture: No effect.

2. RECKLESS RORY (B3.)

Skeleton (replace shortsword and shortbow with greatsword +2 to hit, 7 (2d6) slashing damage).
Picture: DC 14 Wisdom, Reckless bravery. While you have this effect, you make all melee attacks with advantage and all creatures receive advantage on attacks against you. You may repeat the saving throw at the end of your turn, ending the effect on you on a success.

3. RIALTO THE RIFFRAFF (B3.)

Zombie
Note: A common vagrant of filthy aspect, putrid clothes, and a toothless grin.
Picture: DC 15 Dexterity within 5 feet. Viewer infected with lice.

4. RANTING REX (B3.)

Ghoul
Note: Cusses and rants constantly, hurling invectives and insults.
Picture: DC 14 Wisdom. Viewer talks in screaming curses for 2d6 x 10 minutes.

5. RAMBLING RAGNIRAK (B4.)

Ghoul
Picture: None. Pivots to room behind, dumping characters standing on square into the Altar Nook (**B7.**).

6. RUSTRUM THE RABID (B4.)

Wraith
Note: A massive monster of a man with bristling hair all over his face; has bushy beard and a mean disposition.
Picture: DC 14 Constitution. Viewer foams at the mouth for 2d4 rounds.

7. RANK RUMPULA (B4.) [D2.–D4.]

Vampiric Wizard
Note: Countess Rumpula is the wife of Radu (**NPC #46**) and usually haunts near the Throne Room. Unless ambushed, she raises a *fire shield* and opens combat with two *fireballs*. If brought to half her total hit points, she turns gaseous and retreats, returning to harass the party with *gust of wind* on their torches, summoning bats, etc. She has a red velvet gown and a 350 gp golden ring with a sapphire.
Picture: None. Warns of werewolves "above the Southwest Wing."

8. Randver the Rancid (B4.)

Wraith
Picture: DC 14 Constitution. Nausea for 1d8 x 10 minutes. Treat nauseated characters as poisoned.

9. Raps Redaxe (B4.)

Doppelganger
Note: Appears as a wounded Skandik barbarian, joins party to slay them in their sleep. The picture bears the same image but is garbed in the finery of Skandik royalty.
Picture: Offers a *+2 battleaxe* for the body of Runic Rump.

10. Raw Ribby (B4.)

Skeleton
Note: Face looks suspiciously like a fish.
Picture: Poses riddle ("A Lord who never leaves his palace, yet always travels across the land." [snail]), +1 permanent adjustment to constitution for correct answer, −1 for an incorrect one.

11. Radif the Reprobate (B4.)

Shadow
Note: His shadow drags heavy chains, slowing his movement to 30 ft.
Picture: No effect, has been stabbed several times.

12. Racy Rawley (B4.)

Mummy (with Speed of 50 ft. and advantage on initiative rolls)
Note: Poncy nobleman, fond of bets and bragging. Wears plumed hat, carries walking stick. Mummy is lightning quick.
Picture: Offers treasure trove to race winner from one end of Master Gallery to the other. The treasure in question is a large sack of gold (870 gp).

13. Ronahr the Repellent (B4.)

Specter

Note: Extremely ugly, with long bulbous nose, bulging eyes, and buck teeth. Specter sobs silently as it attacks.

Picture: If characters compliment his appearance, Ronahr offers to teleport them to the Library (**M12.**).

14. Racktor the Rash (B4.)

Skeleton

Note: Wears the black robes of a Judge, bears golden scales in one hand. Piercing gaze and contemptuous expression. Inscription: "Step forward and ask for your judgement."

Picture: Causes a rash on characters who lie before him. Succeed on a DC 18 constitution saving throw or be sickened (as poisoned) for 1d12 days, very good at settling confusing legal cases or simple differences of opinion.

15. Racketeer Retok (B4.)

Ghoul

Note: Cunning expression, fine clothes with fur trimmings, pets black cat.

Picture: Demands protection money "or else" (at least 100 gp — otherwise summons random Rump).

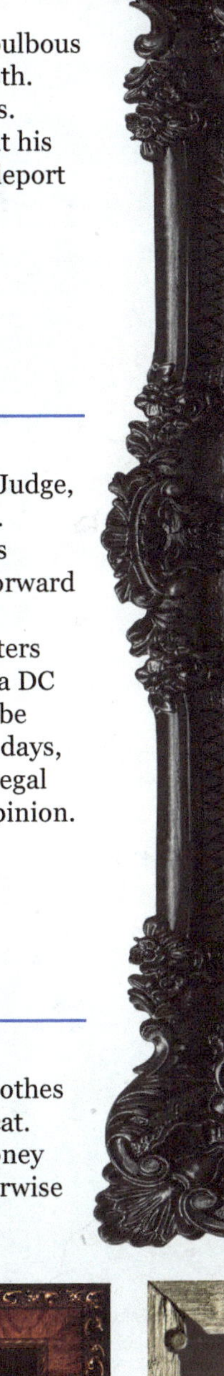

16. RETAKANG RAGELOT (B4.)

Skeleton (with Strength 16, replace shortsword with flail at +5 to hit, 7 [1d8 + 3] bludgeoning):
Note: Looks constantly angry; refuses to speak but eyes follow party with evident dislike.
Picture: No effect.

17. RAVING RINDAT (B4.)

Wight
Note: Insane, wild eyed madman, paranoid ravings.
Picture: No effect.

18. RIGAT THE RABBLE ROUSER (B4.)

Specter
Note: Skilled demagogue, slimy personality; leads lynch mob of 3d6 **skeletons**.
Picture: None. Offers viewer 1 gp to strike viewer's companion.

19. REOT OF THE RAGING RIVER (B4.)

Shadow
Note: Outdoorsman depicted in front of a mountain stream.
Picture: No effect.

20. RASCAL ROWING (B4.)

Greater Ghost[II] (despicable)
Note: Older, portly nobleman, half-smile under graying moustache.
Picture: No effect.

21. REPTILAKIS RUMP (B4.)

Water Naga
Note: Approaches party invisibly and extorts valuables with vague threats. Prefers subtle tactics but isn't afraid of combat. Portrait is of a smiling man with yellow snake eyes and greenish, scaly skin.
Picture: Teleports viewer to the Crying Hall (north of **E1.**).

22. RANCOROUS RIMY (B4.)

Zombie
Picture: No effect.

23. RAPID RITHIENA (B4.) [E14.]

Headless female human **Vampire** (with no vision, bite, or charm, with Speed of 50 ft.).
Note: Clad in unpleasant and moldy clothes, Rapid Rithiena's appearance is made worse by the cheap perfumes she sprinkles herself with. Being headless, she is blind as a bat, and may easily be distracted or avoided by a cautious party. Obviously, Rithiena cannot drain blood, charm or summon helpers, which

makes her extremely frustrated — alas, the sole way to express
this discomfort is the gurgling noises she emits. On the other
hand, she can move with blinding speed if necessary, and is a
frightful combatant.
Picture: Teleports party to **E12**.

24. RUMMY RORY (B3.)

Wraith
Note: Dread Pirate Rory was the captain of the Seaborn Saber.
He is depicted in his pirate regalia, and his wraith may be
recognized by his billowing black beard.
Picture: DC 14 Constitution. Drunkenness in viewer for 1d6+2 x
10 minutes.

25. RAUCOS (B3.)

Male human **Bandit Captain** (with AC 25 from *+3 plate* and *+2
shield*, and a *+1 longsword*):
Note: The lesser known brother of Roughneck Rump the Rotund.
His armaments are a prized family heirloom (and of the same
design Sir Runic and Roughneck wear).
Picture: No effect.

26. RANTING REDURN (B3.)

Greater Ghost[II] (fearful, repulsive):
Note: Thin and leathery skin, reminisces about the old days in a
stream of complaints.
Picture: No effect.

27. SIR RITARK THE RAT-HEARTED (B3.)

Ghost
Note: Noncombatant, flees in terror with a piercing scream!
Picture: Offers to teleport viewers to the Spectral Staircase (the
entrance to the second story of Southwest Wing) to prove their
bravery.

28. RICIENNA THE RAVENOUS (B3.)

Greater Ghost[II] (fearful, withered)
Note: Emaciated, feral expression of hunger despite noble
clothes. Almost impossible to drive away once attached to a
character — returns to haunt him or her again and again.
Picture: No effect.

29. ROCKY THE ROGUE (B3.)

Zombie
Picture: No effect.

30. RINSEL THE RAVISHING (B3.)

Greater Ghost[II] (cold-blooded, corrupt)
Note: A regular Adonis, displaying a winning smile. Wears a
plumed hat, extremely courteous. Ghost excuses self if ladies are
in the party and leaves through the wall.

Picture: DC 13 Charisma saving throw. Permanently changes Charisma by +1 if passed, −1 if failed, once per character — has a soft spot for comely women.

31. Retreat Rumplast (B3.)

Ghoul (with AC 16 from torn chain mail)
Note: Limping movement, he wears a badly damaged suit of chainmail with several arrows and a sword sticking out of the back! On the painting, he appears in the same clothes, grinning while he twirls his moustache.
Picture: No effect.

32. Reydd the Razor (A18.)

Wight
Note: Portrait is seen clutching a map.
Picture: The map reveals the way to area **D1**.

33. Ready Rhydreg (A18.)

Skeleton
Note: A wiry little fellow with long, nimble fingers.
Picture: 30% probability of permanent +1 to viewer's Dexterity, once per viewer.

34. Risque Roschar (A18.)

Mummy
Picture: No effect.

35. Rosienna the Romancer (A18.)

Specter
Note: A flirty dame with a sensuous expression. Specter likes to attack through walls and retreats immediately.
Picture: Teleports viewers to area **B14**.

36. Reipsik the Rapt (A18.)

Shadow
Picture: No effect.

37. Rozet the Seriberiter (A18.)

Shadow
Note: His coat-of-arms has been painted black to reflect his expulsion from the family.
Picture: Permanent +1 to Wisdom if viewer is Neutral (LN, N, CN), once per viewer.

38. Radaw the Rebel (A18.)

Zombie
Picture: Levitates viewer for 2d4 rounds.

39. Rasping Rashuak (A18.) [DL4G.]

Lich (with *ring of spell turning*)
Note: Rasping Rashuak is the dreaded "Man in Scarlet," the most powerful being in Tegel Manor. He was among the first in the noble Rump line, and although he was never a faithful adherent of Tsathoggus, his ruthlessness was legendary nonetheless. Rashuak's experiments into alchemy have finally yielded him insight into planes beyond our own, and knowledge unfit for mortal men. He and his younger brother Ridwik became immortal in their own way, casting aside life as a mere cloak. However, in unlife, the two brothers pursued alternate paths: Ridwik was more tied to the living world and quite interested in conquest, while Rashuak's mind wandered yet unseen dimensions. Today, he has mostly abandoned this world altogether. His mortal form — a single skull atop a scarlet robe with heavy golden embroidery — wanders the corridors of Tegel Manor without aim or purpose, while his mind is far, far away. Thus, an encounter with this undead lord is not necessarily fatal: he mostly ignores everyone unless attacked. But if he is, he doesn't rest until the nuisance is dead — or simply teleports away to avoid lengthy confrontations (25% chance).
Picture: DC 14 Wisdom. Viewer becomes hoarse, able to speak only in a rasping whisper. While hoarse, spells cast that require a verbal component have a 20% chance of failing. The hoarseness is cured with a long rest or *lesser restoration*.

40. Rushrat the Rainmaker (A1.)

Shadow
Picture: Miniature raincloud follows viewer for 2d6 x 10 minutes.

41. Relang the Racker (A1.)

Wight
Note: A giant of a man with a vacuous expression.
Picture: No effect.

42. Rumpus Rundel the Rover (A1.)

Greater Ghost[II] (corrupt, iniquitous, carries a spiritual sabre)
Note: Incredibly tall, thin as a log.
Picture: DC 14 Constitution. Itching feet for 2d6 x 10 minutes, causing −2 to all attack rolls due to discomfort.

43. Rivona the Radiant (A1.)

Wight (with Charisma 18)
Note: A fair lady of incredible beauty.
Picture: A DC 14 Wisdom. Casts *charm person* at viewer, who is obsessed with finding this heavenly apparition and throws self into the arms of the undead monster willingly if they ever meet!

44. Rorkad the Rare (A1.)

Doppelganger
Note: A young and handsome nobleman.
Picture: Warns, *"Beware the Great Hall!"*

45. Radical Roman (A1.)

Skeleton
Picture: Eyes follow viewers.

46. Count Radu Rumpula (A1.)

Vampire
Note: The stereotypical vampire: well-mannered, jovial, and thoroughly evil. He appears as a man in his fifties, always impeccably elegant. He doesn't lower himself to fighting mere commoners if he can help it. Instead, he summons a wolf pack (3d6) and watches the fray in gaseous form. Radu has a billowing black cloak, a valuable golden brooch (1200 gp), and a diamond ring (1200 gp).
Picture: DC 17 Wisdom. Viewer drops everything carried and flees for 1d4 + 1 rounds.

47. Sir Rankling (A1.)

Greater Ghost[II] (with 30 hp, cold-blooded, withered)
Note: Frail and venerable gentleman with long white moustache and feathered cap, playing a golden harp. Ghost is friendly if portrait has been talked to previously. Ghost has Neutral alignment
Picture: Answers a question once per day; well versed in lore and fond of telling tales.

48. Raging Raktor (A1.)

Skeleton
Picture: DC 14 Wisdom Enrages viewer for 2d4 rounds. Viewer attacks everyone in range.

49. Raphod the Reaper (A1.)

Wraith
Note: Towering barbarian lord in black armor and furs, holds a scythe in his hand.
Picture: Scythe swings at viewer with melee weapon attack at +8 to hit. Does 11 (2d4+6) slashing damage on a hit.

50. Roparoc the Raider (West of E8.)

Greater Ghost[II] (corrupt, iniquitous, carries spiritual cutlass, repulsive)
Note: Bleeds from a hundred wounds.
Picture: No effect.

51. Rembard the Rake (West of E6.)

Wraith
Picture: 20% probability of teleporting viewers to area **C2.**

52. Ramatic Rumpula (L5.)

Ghoul
Note: Hunchback with mischievous grin. Cackles maniacally as he attacks.
Picture: No effect.

53. Roderik the Righteous (L5.)

Greater Ghost[II] (with Strength of 17, AC 22 from *+2 plate* and *+2 shield*, corrupt, iniquitous, carries spiritual longsword)
Note: Armored knight with a stern expression. Ghost challenges strongest character to a one-on-one duel in corporeal form — winner gets loser's suit of armor (Roderik has *+2 plate*).
Picture: DC 14 Wisdom. Lawfully aligned viewer enraged; seeks out foes immediately.

54. Ransack Rosco (South of Garden Grotto)

Wight
Note: Haughty, grizzled veteran grasping a battleaxe in one hand and a sack of stolen gold in the other. Has 110 gp stuffed into pockets.
Picture: No effect.

55. Radded Rufus (J5.)

Zombie
Note: Lonesome and extremely bored, desires the company of the other portraits.
Picture: 30% probability of a ripping viewer's sack or backpack. Damaged item is noticed with a DC 15 Wisdom (Perception) check. 50% chance every 10 minutes of lost item moving about.

56. Rarin the Rearguard (I11.)

Mummy
Picture: 30% probability of panic (as *fear* spell, DC 17).

57. Rattlepate Remalda (West of H13.)

Wight
Note: Obese matron in simple black clothes and silver jewelry, fond of stern lectures.
Picture: DC 8 Wisdom. Rattling voice in viewer.

58. Reldor the Ransomer (H6.)

Doppelganger
Note: Poses as cowardly halfling, follows party to village and robs them blind. Ransom note leads to the portrait; offers to sell back various valuables at a "very advantageous price."
Picture: No effect.

59. Railler Rolandil (H6.)

Zombie
Note: Bloated, decaying body smells of foul water and seaweed.
Picture: No effect.

60. Rodip the Rationalist (O4.)

Wight (with innate spellcaster, *charm person* and *suggestion* three times each per day with spell save DC of 15)
Note: A skilled demagogue. Rodip stays silent as long as Brother (q.v.) is alive. Thereafter, he tries to win the favor of the group and persuade them to remove him from the wall and use him as a guide to the manor. He hints at his extensive knowledge of the place and basically tells the characters what they want to hear. Thereafter, he tries to sow discord in the ranks, using his *charm person* or *suggestion* ability if necessary.
Picture: DC 15 Wisdom. Discord in viewers — *magic symbol* (discord) and a bit of demagogy.

61. Rahad the Random (D1.)

Zombie (with 126 hp)
Note: Can't dish it out, but sure can take it — keeps on coming and coming. Portrait is of a real tough fellow with a grin flexing his beefy arms.
Picture: No effect.

62. Ricochet Remnar (D1.)

Skeleton
Picture: No effect.

63. Rigorn the Recruit (D1.)

Zombie (with Dexterity of 8 and AC 15 from chainmail, uses mace attack at +4 to hit for 7 [1d8 + 3] bludgeoning damage)
Note: Wears shining chainmail and holds a heavy mace.
Picture: No effect.

64. Rebounding Reydahl (D1.)

Will-o'-wisp
Note: Lures party toward the nearest pit trap and attacks those who try to climb out.
Picture: No effect.

65. Rongo the Router (D1.)

Ghoul
Note: Middle-aged aristocrat counting money on a table.
Picture: DC 14 Constitution. Paralysis on touch lasts 2d6 hours.

66. Rellah the Rebuker (D1.)

Ghoul
Note: A frowning young woman with no sense of humor.
Picture: No saving throw. 3 (1d6) lightning damage on touch.

67. Rebut Roridok (D1.)

Wight
Note: Jovial, overweight old man.
Picture: No effect.

68. Rimout the Reviver (D1.)

Mummy (with *cloak of resistance* [radiant], as *ring of resistance*)
Note: Saintly expression, white robes. Incessant preaching.
Picture: 15% probability of *resurrection* spell — if needed.

69. Ryth the Recanter (D1.)

Specter
Note: Grossly overweight monk and a firm believer in Tsathoggus. Jovial but lecherous and foul-mouthed.
Picture: No effect.

70. Retort Rowanter (L6.)

Specter
Picture: No effect.

71. Reciting Ralfrid (N1.)

Wight
Note: This poncy bard constantly recites horrendously bad poetry if he has an audience — doing the same in undead form. Only threats of violence or a quick sword strike to the throat shut him up.
Picture: 30% probability of a poem sung off key and attracting a random monster.

72. Rufienna the Reckless (N1.)

Greater Ghost[II] (corrupt, fearful)
Note: Attacks with a cry but retreats as soon as she takes a few wounds — unless clearly winning.
Picture: No effect.

73. RABURY THE RECLUSE (N1.)

Wight
Note: Miserly old man with a sour attitude.
Picture: Shouts: *"Go away!"*

74. RHUBART THE RECONDITE (N1.)

Skeleton (with 1 hp)
Note: Grim, bearded knight. His undead form is weighed down by heavy iron chains that he can barely drag down the corridors. Shuffling noises.
Picture: Turns face from viewer.

75. REGENERATING RODARK (A4.)

Wight (regenerates 5 hp at the start of its turn unless in direct sunlight or at 0 hp)
Picture: No effect.

76. REELING RIHORN (A4.)

Wraith
Note: Hypnotist with a long black beard, bushy eyebrows, and enigmatic stare.
Picture: Spins viewer around.

77. RIGORMORTIS RUMPULA (A4.)

Wraith
Note: Old, rickety man with a long face and thin limbs.
Picture: DC 8 Constitution. Stiffness: Disadvantage on all Dexterity checks and saving throws for 80 minutes.

78. ROZETTA RUMPULA (A4.)

Ghoul
Note: An old spinster who still wears her lace wedding gown despite the fact that no one ever proposed to her. Hates all females.
Picture: No effect.

79. LADY RUBIENNA RUMPULA (A4.) [F1.]

Vampire (with *+1 dagger* [poisoned] and Sneak Attack once per turn: deals an extra 14 [4d6] damage when it hits a target with a weapon attack and has advantage on the attack roll, or when the target is within 5 feet of an ally of the vampire that isn't Incapacitated and the vampire doesn't have disadvantage on the attack roll.)
Possessions: *+1 dagger* with deathblade poison (creature struck by poison must make a DC 18 Constitution saving throw. Target that fails loses 2d6 Constitution until after a long rest while a target that succeeds loses 1d6 Constitution), red gown, ruby necklace (800 gp).
Note: Lady Rubienna was well known in her life as a poisoner, and not much has changed since. Although frail in melee, her deadly poison and seductive skills make her a formidable opponent. She prefers to kidnap handsome young men (keeping the rest of the party at bay with wolves until she *dominates* her new prey) and turn them into her servants — vampire spawn, probably even a vampire. Such slaves are always devoid of all free will and obey the lady without a question.
Picture: None. 5% chance per level of viewer of teleporting viewer to area **F1**.

80. RIVEN THE REFECTED (A4.)

Specter
Picture: Cries a *potion of mind reading*.

81. RUANG THE RIPPER (B14.)

Assassin
Note: Ruang the Ripper, assassin extraordinaire, lives in room **B12**. He prowls the wilderness most of the time but may occasionally be encountered in the manor. Unless surprised, he never engages a full party (and even then, he flees to safety), preferring to target separated characters from ambush.
Picture: No effect.

82. REVELER ROTCHAR (M5.)

Ghoul
Note: Comes a-cackling, increasing to hysterical howling as he gets close. Wears jester's outfit, mouth crawling with maggots.
Picture: Laughs at viewer.

83. RABRIAL THE RELENTLESS (M5.)

Greater Ghost[II] (with maximum hit points, cold-blooded, corrupt, repulsive, ruthless, immune to being turned)
Note: Never, ever retreats. May not be turned, either.
Picture: No effect.

84. RUDLONG THE REVENGER (SOUTHWEST WING, HOWLING HALL)

Wraith
Note: Crazed grin, paranoid as hell.
Picture: Forewarns of next random encounter — 100% veracity.

85. RIDWIK OF THE RELIC (SOUTHWEST WING, HOWLING HALL)

Lich
Possessions: bracers of superior defense, ring of greater protection[I], *slippers of levitation* (as *boots of levitation*).
Note: The lich of Tegel Manor lives and experiments in the treacherous Wizard's Tower, which was built according to his own designs. Ridwik's solitary nature didn't endear him to others in the family — but, together with Rasping Rashuak, he obtained the key to a limited form of immortality. Having become one of the undead, Ridwik started planning the eventual conquest of the land. Tegel village would just be the first step in his campaign, but he still fears the cult of Tsathoggus, just as he desires to know the secrets of creating cauldron-born zombies. Thus, he waits patiently for a good opportunity — a weakness, or maybe potential allies even going so far as to offer a suitably unscrupulous group an offer that they cannot refuse.
Picture: Moans, "Come to the Wizard's Tower!"

86. REMONGER THE REMORSEFUL (SOUTHWEST WING, HOWLING HALL)

Greater Ghost[II] (fearful, repulsive)
Note: Utters sobbing prayers to atone for past sins as he drifts down corridors. Rotted, decomposing visage.
Picture: No effect.

87. RESPLENDENT RAMBERT (SOUTHWEST WING, HOWLING HALL)

Ghoul
Note: Followed by intense glowing aura.
Picture: DC 10 Dexterity. Blinding light that causes blindness for 3d6.

88. RINBAK THE RICH (NORTH OF E9., CREAKING CORRIDOR)

Zombie
Note: Grossly fat, scatters gold coins while walking — has 1d100 gp stuffed into pockets.
Picture: 40% chance of bribe (1d100 gp) to sneak into next room to off the portraits there.

89. RELVIDOR THE RENOWNED (NORTH OF E9.)

Wight
Note: Grumpy veteran, reeks of alcohol. Righteous attitude and hurt feelings.
Picture: No effect.

90. Restless Ralome (North of E9.)

Doppelganger
Note: Another veteran, berates "the youth of today" for their insolence. A raging hypocrite demanding deference and granting none in turn. As a doppelganger, he masquerades as a dwarf and mixes his *potion of poison* into someone's water rations.
Picture: Slaps a character — melee weapon attack at +5 to hit, on a hit the target takes 4 (1d6+1) bludgeoning damage and must succeed on a DC16 Constitution saving throw or be stunned for 1d6 rounds.

91. Rickety Ridmand (D5.)

Shadow
Note: All skin and bones, as ancient as the manor itself. Dodders about past victories and heroic deeds that never were.
Picture: Knocks helm off of non-viewer within 15 feet.

92. Rourdan the Repressor (D5.)

Greater Ghost[II] (corrupt, iniquitous, carries a cat-o'-nine tails, withered)
Note: Attacks with ghostly cat-o'-nine-tails.
Picture: No effect.

93. Riddles Rellwod (D5.)

Wight
Picture: Offers unimaginable riches for solving his riddle ("A vast army that guards the sea, yet without their ward, they escape from your grasp." [sand]), gives 2d6 gp.

94. Ribbonsor the Rider (D5.)

Greater Ghost[II] (cold-blooded, corrupt, repulsive)
Note: A brightly clothed character with a rather long face. Possessed character neighs and bolts.
Picture: DC 16 Wisdom. *Polymorphs* a viewer into a horse.

95. Ritzy Rutorn (D5.)

Skeleton
Note: Skeleton wears 300 gp golden necklace, three 160 gp rings.

96. Roughneck Rump the Rotund (D4.)

Knight (with AC 21 [*+1 plate armor, +3 large metal shield*])
Possessions: *+1 plate armor, +3 large metal shield, +1 longsword, potion of gaseous form*, 80 gp.
Note: One of the few Rumps still alive and kicking, Roughneck and his band of 12 tough **goblins** (as **goblin** with maximum hit points) are terrorizing the countryside. He is extraordinarily ugly and not too bright, but he knows the value of an ambush and never engages a clearly superior foe. He still has his family heirlooms — magical weaponry and a potion he once got from Ridwik — on his person. He stores his ill-gotten gains in a goblin cave (Wilderness, **BB.**).
Picture: Shouts, *"Stand and deliver!"*

97. Redbud Rump (D3.)

Scout (with AC 15 [chain loincloth and halter], 35 hp, Strength 14, replace shortsword with longsword at +4 to hit, 6 [1d8 + 2] slashing damage, and innate ability to cast *speak with animals* once per day)
Possessions: longsword, chain loincloth & halter, large metal shield, cape.
Note: Strikingly beautiful, sensuous, flirts constantly — she wears Amazon armor, a red cape, and little else. If questioned, she avoids talking about the family, whom she describes as a bit eccentric and unused to strangers, but basically likable and warmhearted. If she is suitably impressed by a handsome warrior, she may reveal a few secrets about the manor.
Picture: Invites viewer to "her place." This could be any room in the manor, and there is a 35% probability Redbud Rump is encountered there.

98. Raoul the Reformer

Priest (with AC 18 [half-plate and shield] and *inflict wounds* in place of *cure wounds*)

Possessions: half-plate, small wooden shield, flail, unholy symbol of Tsathoggus (golden frog with emerald eyes [400 gp]), holy symbol of Mitra, plain white robes, prayer book, 130 gp, *amulet of proof against detection and location.*

Note: Founder and sole member of the Reformed Cult of Tsathoggus. This faction of the faith believes that sacrifices to the demon lord should be killed by strangling instead of the sacrificial dagger, as no precious blood is spilled this way. Raoul has the appearance of a traveling priest of Mitra, holy symbol and prayer book included. Appearing as a saintly priest, he intends to manipulate characters to his cause — which is, first and foremost, killing as many of the *other* frog-priests as possible. Thereafter, he may try to slay them or use them as pawns in his bid for power against the rest of the family — all heretics and unbelievers.

Picture: No effect.

99. Ranorek (D2.)

Ranorek Rump[II]

Possessions: cushioned greatclub (does only non-lethal damage), filthy hides, stone knife, bone carving.

Note: This gentle primitive lives in area **DL2C.** and occasionally ventures upstairs to raid the pantries. The "missing link relative" in the family, Ranorek proves extremely friendly if a bit dim unless attacked — although not above clubbing an unsuspecting party member to carry home as a misguided gesture of friendship.

Picture: No effect.

100. Ramshackle Riparian (D2.)

Veteran (with AC 11 [no armor], replace short- and longswords with poisoned cane sword [as rapier] +5 to hit, 7 [1d8 + 3] piercing damage and target must make DC 18 Constitution saving throw. On a failure, target loses 2d6 Constitution until after a long rest, and on a success 1d6)

Possessions: Courtier's outfit, cane sword with deathblade poison concealed in walking stick, snuff box.

Note: Impeccably elegant and diplomatic. Doesn't reveal confidential information in any case. In combat, he relies on feints and his envenomed sword hidden in an ornate walking stick.

Picture: Offers to serve *writ of habeas corpus* when needed . . . for a modest fee (1d10 x 100 gp).

The Esteemed BelDarius "Beady" Rump (Dave Derocha)

He looks rather shabby, wearing fashionable clothing that is just not maintained. A small pair of spectacles perch precariously on his nose, looking like they might fly off at any moment (the small chain must have saved the day at least once). He has the countenance of one who always seems to have his head cocked as if listening to something that no one else can hear. Those who stare might notice that his right eye twinkles a bit in an orangey color, unlike his blue left eye.

Once a deep practitioner of forbidden mysteries of the mind, he contacted an alien presence that began overtaking his mind. He managed to segment off his left brain with a mental barrier, preserving the cold logic of his human self. His emotional side has been described by his detractors (and his admirers) as unearthly to the extreme.

BelDarius Rump

Medium humanoid (human), neutral

Armor Class 12
Hit Points 117 (18d8 + 36)
Speed 30 ft.

STR	DEX	CON	INT	WIS	CHA
11 (+0)	14 (+2)	15 (+2)	18 (+4)	8 (−1)	14 (+2)

Saving Throws Con +6, Int +8, Wis +3
Skills Arcana +8, Medicine +3, Nature +8
Senses passive Perception 9
Languages Aboleth, Common, Elder Thing, Mi-Go, Yithian
Challenge 10 (5,900 XP)

Double-Minded. BelDarius has advantage on saving throws against being charmed or frightened, and his mind cannot be read by magic.

Mutant Form (1/long rest). BelDarius can use an action to imbibe a special magical elixir of his own devising. No other creature can benefit from drinking the elixir. When he drinks it, BelDarius gains the following features for 1 minute:

- His Strength score becomes 17 (+3), and his Intelligence score becomes 16 (+3).
- He has resistance to bludgeoning, piercing, and slashing damage from nonmagical attacks
- His Armor Class is 16.

- He has a Bite and Claw attack, and can make one Bite attack and two Claw attacks when he takes the Attack action.

Spellcasting. BelDarius is a 12th-level spellcaster. His spellcasting ability is Intelligence (spell save DC 16, +8 to hit with spell attacks; spell save DC 15, +7 to hit if in mutant form). He has the following wizard spells prepared.

Cantrips (at will): *acid splash, light, mending, ray of frost, shocking grasp*
1st level (4 slots): *detect magic, false life, magic missile, shield*
2nd level (3 slots): *enhance ability, enlarge/reduce, invisibility*
3rd level (3 slots): *dispel magic, fireball, fly, haste*
4th level (3 slots): *arcane eye, banishment, fabricate*
5th level (2 slots): *animate objects, contact other plane*
6th level (1 slot): *disintegrate*

Actions

Multiattack. While in mutant form, BelDarius can make one Bite attack and two Claw attacks.

***Bite* (mutant form only).** *Melee Weapon Attack:* +7 to hit, reach 5 ft., one creature. *Hit:* 8 (1d10 + 3) piercing damage.

***Claw* (mutant form only).** *Melee Weapon Attack:* +7 to hit, reach 5 ft., one target. *Hit:* 7 (1d8 + 3) slashing damage.

ANGELA (JOHN WILS)

Angela is an attractive, charming, and self-deprecating forty something seer who roams the sea coast road in her black wagon with her large pet spider, Mr. Flibble. Widely read, a source for local lore, and a reader of tarot, her intelligent and highly perceptive mind reveals much to her about those she meets.

Angela, however, possesses a powerful gift and curse. She can predict the future unerringly to any who ask, yet anyone who hears that prediction will believe it to be the truth. These predictions most often occur as a warning. If the recipient of this prediction acts in disbelief, the event will transpire as predicted. Should the creature try to take advantage of or avoid the prediction, fate ensures that the prediction will bear fruit regardless. Angela rarely bears ill will; this is simply her gift and her curse.

ANGELA

Medium humanoid (human), neutral

Armor Class 10 (13 with *mage armor*)
Hit Points 27 (5d8 + 5)
Speed 30 ft.

STR	DEX	CON	INT	WIS	CHA
8 (−1)	10 (+0)	12 (+1)	15 (+2)	14 (+2)	18 (+4)

Saving Throws Con +3, Cha +6
Skills Arcana +4, History +4, Insight +4, Nature +4, Perception +4
Senses passive Perception 14
Languages Celestial, Common, Elven, Gnome, Halfling
Challenge 4 (1,100 XP)

Innate Spellcasting. Angela's innate spellcasting ability is Charisma (spell save DC 14). She can cast the following spells, requiring no material components:

At will: *guidance*
3/day each: *bane, bless, find familiar*

Spellcasting. Angela is a 5th-level spellcaster. He spellcasting ability is Charisma (spell save DC 14, +6 to hit with spell attacks). She knows the following sorcerer spells.

Cantrips (at will): *acid splash, fire bolt, mage hand, message, shocking grasp*
1st level (4 slots): *detect magic, mage armor, thunderwave*
2nd level (3 slots): *shatter, suggestion*
3rd level (2 slots): *lightning bolt*

***Swift Casting* (3/day).** Whenever Angela uses an action to cast a cantrip or spell, she can cast a cantrip as a bonus action.

Actions

Dagger. *Melee or Ranged Weapon Attack:* +2 to hit, reach 5 ft. or range 20/60 ft., one target. *Hit:* 2 (1d4) piercing damage.

***Predict Future* (1/day).** Angela predicts a future for one willing creature of her choice. Until the creature next takes a long rest, the creature can replace a d20 roll of their choice with an automatic success before or after they roll it, but before any results of that roll are applied.

However, before the creature's next long rest, up to 3 d20 rolls of the Game Master's choice are failures, regardless of the final result and regardless of whether or not the creature uses their automatic successes.

SOLOMON DRAKE (TRAVIS DRAKE)

Solomon Drake was a surgeon and doctor serving in the army. He was recognized for his calm and reserved demeanor when dealing with the physical tragedies of war. He returned home after the war and continued to practice medicine and alchemy. He married into the Rump family and seemed at home in Tegel Manor. He was never a physical man but always had slim arms and legs and a bit of a gut that grew slowly as he aged. It wasn't until after his passing that anyone realized the extent of his fascination with the dead and dying. There were many tomes dealing with necromancy found hidden in his study, though the family kept this a secret. There is no knowing what else he collected over his long life.

Solomon Drake uses the statistics of a **neophyte lich**, save that he has the following additional ability:

Hide in False Flesh **(1/day).** Until Solomon takes a long rest or ends this effect as a bonus action on his turn, his undead flesh is masked from both magical and mundane senses. Visually he appears as an elderly male human. All spells and other magical effects or class features register Solomon as a human, rather than an undead. Creatures that have truesight can pierce the transmutation of Solomon's flesh and reveal his true form. While in this form, Solomon cannot use his paralyzing touch attack or his legendary actions; if he does so, this effect immediately ends.

RAUL RUMP (JOHN E BALL) (CJ)

Raul's insatiable desire to explore and discover arcane secrets drove him to travel the world. He amassed significant wealth and created numerous magical wonders. The greatest of these were the Eyes of Raul. These arcane tattoos, applied below the eyes, conferred increasing benefits to the recipient as they advanced in rank and allowed Raul to share their senses. Using this network, Raul built a merchant empire and prospered until the deed to Tegel Manor found him. Raul continued to live vicariously through his agents but this was not enough. . . Delving into the dark secrets of the Manor, Raul found ways to use the link forged by the Eyes of Raul to gain control of the recipients' minds, enhancing his own mental abilities. Raul's body may no longer draw breath but his mind now spans a network of hosts; can he ever be said to truly die?

The hosts of Raul Rump have the **Raul Rump Hive Mind** template applied to them (see below).

RAUL RUMP HIVE MIND TEMPLATE

THE HIVE MIND

The hive mind of Raul Rump shares much of the same desires and knowledge that the living Rump had. The hive mind cannot be targeted by attacks or magical effects other than an *antimagic field*; a host that begins its turn within an *antimagic field* is rendered incapacitated (see Freeing a Host below).

Traits. The hive mind is chaotic evil, has a proficiency bonus of +5, and it has Intelligence 20 (+5), Wisdom 18 (+4), and Charisma 10 (+0). Abilities that the hive mind provides to a host use the hive mind's Ability Scores to determine saving throw DCs and spell attack modifiers.

Skills. The hive mind also has proficiency in the Arcana (+10), History (+10), Insight (+9), Investigation (+10), Nature (+10), Perception (+9), and Religion (+10) skills.

Senses. The hive mind shares all the senses of the host.

Languages. The hive mind can speak and understand all languages. It can speak these languages through all hosts.

Actions. The hive mind can take no actions of its own. It is limited by the actions of its hosts. If a host has class levels or other features, such as innate spellcasting, the hive mind can use the features of that host, but each host only has its normal action and reaction, and possible bonus action.

TARGETS

The hive mind of Raul Rump requires a sufficiently complex mind to become a viable host. Humanoids of any type and beasts whose Intelligence score is 10 or greater are viable hosts. Another host must convert the target creature over the course of 8 hours' worth of work, after which time the target creature gains the features below.

FEATURES

A host of the hive mind of Raul Rump gains the following features.

Alignment. The creature's alignment changes to chaotic evil to match the hive mind's alignment.

Challenge Rating. The host's Challenge Rating increases by 1.

Eyes of Raul. The creature's eyes have faint lines atop their eyelids or around their eye sockets. This is the only outward sign of a creature's possession in the hive mind, and is the only way to infest another creature and add it to the hive mind.

Shared Senses. The hive mind is aware of anything that happens to a host, no matter its location, and it is immune to magic that would read its thoughts. Magic such as *antimagic field* can suppress this effect, which frees the host from the hive mind as long as it remains within the area of the spell.

Immunities. A hive mind host is immune to the charmed and frightened condition, is immune to psychic damage, and cannot be possessed.

Innate Spellcasting. The host's innate spellcasting ability is the hive mind's Intelligence (spell save DC 18, +10 to hit with spell effects). It can cast the following spells, requiring no material components:

At will: *acid splash, dancing lights, detect magic, fire bolt, identify, mage hand, prestidigitation*

3/day each: *alter self, arcanist's magic aura, detect thoughts, hold person, suggestion*

hive mind's Intelligence (spell save DC 18, +10 to hit with spell effects). It can cast the following spells, requiring no material components:

At will: *acid splash, dancing lights, detect magic, fire bolt, identify, mage hand, prestidigitation*

3/day each: *alter self, arcanist's magic aura, detect thoughts, hold person, suggestion*

1/day each: *counterspell, dispel magic, hypnotic pattern*

Shared Senses. The hive mind is aware of anything that happens to a host, no matter its location. Magic such as *antimagic field* can suppress this effect, which frees the host from the hive mind as long as it remains within the area of the spell.

Actions

Multiattack. The veteran makes two Longsword attacks. If it has a shortsword drawn, it can also make a Shortsword attack.

Longsword. *Melee Weapon Attack:* +5 to hit, reach 5 ft., one target. *Hit:* 7 (1d8 + 3) slashing damage, or 8 (1d10 + 3) slashing damage if used with two hands.

Shortsword. *Melee Weapon Attack:* +5 to hit, reach 5 ft., one target. *Hit:* 6 (1d6 + 3) piercing damage.

Heavy Crossbow. *Ranged Weapon Attack:* +3 to hit, range 100/400 ft., one target. *Hit:* 6 (1d10 + 1) piercing damage.

Liam Von Rump (William Steffen)

Liam was renowned as a sorcerer since casting his first spell at age 6. Growing up in the wealthy manor festered somewhat of a haughty streak in him, however, and his studies soon turned to evocation and the darker arts. As an adult, he gained a reputation for seducing the daughters of noblemen up and down the coast, but was never actually caught in the act due to his sorcerous power. Despite all of this, he was an avid patron of the temple of Thor.

He was known to have had several bloody run-ins with the clergy of Tsathoggus, always coming out the victor. He was rumored to have disappeared after performing a dreadful ritual to summon an outer entity to combat Tsathoggus. His empty grave has a memorial stone engraved in draconic: "No Body Lies Within, For Still I Roam"

Liam Von Rump

Medium undead, chaotic good

Armor Class 11
Hit Points 104 (16d8 + 32)
Speed 0 ft., fly 40 ft. (hover)

STR	DEX	CON	INT	WIS	CHA
7 (−2)	13 (+1)	14 (+2)	15 (+2)	12 (+1)	17 (+3)

Saving Throws Con +5, Cha +6
Skills Arcana +5, History +5, Nature +5
Damage Resistances acid, fire, lightning, thunder; bludgeoning, piercing, and slashing from nonmagical attacks
Damage Immunities cold, necrotic, poison
Condition Immunities charmed, exhaustion, frightened, grappled, paralyzed, petrified, poisoned, prone, restrained
Senses darkvision 60 ft., passive Perception 11
Languages Common
Challenge 7 (2,900 XP)

Ethereal Sight. Liam can see 60 feet into the Ethereal Plane when he is on the Material Plane, and vice versa.

Incorporeal Movement. Liam can move through other

1/day each: *counterspell, dispel magic, hypnotic pattern*

Ending the Hive

Freeing a Host. A host can be freed if a creature begins its turn within the area of an *antimagic field* and has *greater restoration* cast on it.

Destroying the Hive. There is no centralized hive. If each creature that is a member of the hive is destroyed or has the hive mind removed from it, the hive is destroyed.

Veteran Host

Medium humanoid (human), chaotic evil

Armor Class 17 (splint)
Hit Points 58 (9d8 + 18)
Speed 30 ft.

STR	DEX	CON	INT	WIS	CHA
16 (+3)	13 (+1)	14 (+2)	20 (+5)	18 (+4)	10 (+0)

Skills Athletics +5, Perception +6
Damage Immunities psychic
Condition Immunities charmed, frightened
Senses passive Perception 16
Languages all
Challenge 4 (1,100 XP)

Eyes of Raul. The creature's eyes have faint lines atop their eyelids or around their eye sockets. This is the only outward sign of a creature's possession in the hive mind, and is the only way to infest another creature and add it to the hive mind.

Innate Spellcasting. The host's innate spellcasting ability is the

restoration spell, but only within 24 hours of it occurring.

Possession (recharge 6). One humanoid that Liam can see within 5 feet of him must succeed on a DC 14 Charisma saving throw or be possessed by the ghost; Liam then disappears, and the target is incapacitated and loses control of its body. Liam now controls the body but doesn't deprive the target of awareness. Liam can't be targeted by any attack, spell, or other effect, except ones that turn undead, and he retains his alignment, Intelligence, Wisdom, Charisma, and immunity to being charmed and frightened. He otherwise uses the possessed target's statistics, but doesn't gain access to the target's knowledge, class features, or proficiencies.

The possession lasts until the body drops to 0 hit points, Liam ends it as a bonus action, or Liam is turned or forced out by an effect like the *dispel evil and good* spell. When the possession ends, Liam reappears in an unoccupied space within 5 feet of the body. The target is immune to Liam's Possession for 24 hours after succeeding on the saving throw or after the possession ends.

LIGHTNING SPIKE

Evocation cantrip
Casting Time: 1 action
Range: 120 feet
Components: V, S
Duration: Instantaneous

You hurl a bolt of lightning at a creature within range. Make a ranged spell attack against the target. On a hit, the target takes 1d8 lightning damage. If the target is wearing metal armor, you can reroll the damage and take the higher of the two results.

This spell's damage increases by 1d8 when you reach 5th level (2d8), 11th level (3d8), and 17th level (4d8).

JEFFREY THE JADED RUMP (JEFF SCIFERT)

Jeffrey "the Jaded" Rump was a consummate mage and manipulator who infiltrated high society's ranks to charm and influence the powerful into furthering his goals. A master of disguise, he adopted new personas as easily as others slip on a pair of boots, able to disappear if his plans were uncovered, only to reappear under a new persona elsewhere to continue his schemes. His pastime was eugenics, manipulating bloodlines to breed magically-gifted individuals who were loyal to him. His cultists still exist today, hidden within the ranks of society waiting to enact their nefarious leader's plans. Because of the Rump curse and a failed dark ritual, Jeffrey is now a lich shade, haunting Tegel Manor as an Unsettled Rump. Jeffrey is relatively passive and flees obvious danger, unless a spellcaster is present, in which case he flies into a violent rage, attacking without remorse or concern for his safety.

LICH SHADE

Medium undead, neutral evil

Armor Class 16 (natural armor)
Hit Points 85 (9d8 + 45)
Speed 30 ft.

STR	DEX	CON	INT	WIS	CHA
11 (+0)	16 (+3)	20 (+5)	18 (+4)	16 (+3)	13 (+1)

Skills Arcana +7, History +7, Insight +6, Perception +6

---

creatures and objects as if they were difficult terrain. He takes 5 (1d10) force damage if he ends his turn inside an object.

Spellcasting. Liam is a 6th-level spellcaster. His spellcasting ability is Charisma (spell save DC 14, +6 to hit with spell attacks). He knows the following sorcerer spells:

Cantrips (at will): *lightning spike, mage hand, mending, minor illusion, shocking grasp*

1st level (4 slots): *detect magic, magic missile, shield, thunderwave*

2nd level (3 slots): *gust of wind, shatter*

3rd level (2 slots): *lightning bolt*

Swift Casting (3/day). Whenever Liam uses an action to cast a cantrip or a spell, he can cast a cantrip as a bonus action.

Actions

Withering Touch. *Melee Weapon Attack:* +6 to hit, reach 5 ft., one target. *Hit:* 17 (4d6 + 3) necrotic damage.

Etherealness. Liam enters the Ethereal Plane from the Material Plane, or vice versa. He is visible on the Material Plane while he is in the Border Ethereal, and vice versa, yet he can't affect or be affected by anything on the other plane.

Horrifying Visage. Each non-undead creature within 60 feet of Liam that can see him must succeed on a DC 14 Wisdom saving throw or be frightened for 1 minute. If the save fails by 5 or more, the target also ages 1d4 × 10 years. A frightened target can repeat the saving throw at the end of each of its turns, ending the frightened condition on itself on a success. If a target's saving throw is successful or the effect ends for it, the target is immune to Liam's Horrifying Visage for the next 24 hours. The aging effect can be reversed with a *greater*

Damage Resistances cold, lightning, poison; bludgeoning, piercing, and slashing damage from nonmagical attacks
Damage Immunities necrotic
Condition Immunities charmed, exhaustion, frightened, paralyzed, poisoned
Senses darkvision 60 ft., passive Perception 16
Languages Common, Infernal, plus up to four other languages
Challenge 8 (3,900 XP)

Death Throes. When the lich shade drops to 0 hit points, it explodes in a cloud of dust in a 10-foot radius. Creatures within this area must make a DC 16 Constitution saving throw. On a failed saving throw, the creature takes 22 (4d10) necrotic damage, and the creature's maximum hit points are reduced by the same amount. If a creature's maximum hit points are reduced to 0, it dies. Magic such as *greater restoration* is necessary to cure this effect. On a successful saving throw, the creature takes half damage and is poisoned for 1 minute, but its maximum hit points are unaffected.

Magic Resistance. The lich shade has advantage on saving throws against spells and other magical effects.

Magic Weapon. The lich shade's weapon attacks are magical.

Actions

Multiattack. The lich shade makes two Claw attacks.

Claw. *Melee Weapon Attack:* +6 to hit, reach 5 ft., one target. *Hit:* 12 (2d8 + 3) slashing damage plus 11 (2d10) cold damage.

Reactions

Spell Leech. When a creature the lich shade can see within 30 feet of it casts a spell of 1st level or higher, the lich shade can counter the spell, as if the lich shade had cast *counterspell*. If the lich shade attempts to leech a spell of 4th level or higher, it must make an Intelligence ability check. The DC for this check is 10 + the spell's level.

If the spell leech is successful, the lich shade absorbs the magical energy and can use it only on its next turn in one of the following ways:

Cast. The lich shade can cast the spell as an action on its turn, using the original caster's spell save DC and spell attack modifier.

Eldritch Bolt. The lich shade chooses one creature it can see within 60 feet of it as an action. That creature must make a DC 16 Dexterity saving throw, taking 22 (4d10) force damage on a failed saving throw, or half as much damage on a successful one.

Heal. The lich shade uses an action to regain 22 (4d10) hit points, up to its maximum hit points.

If the lich shade does not use the absorbed magic, it fades at the end of its next turn.

Rhona Rump (Kim George)

A white witch who wielded the silver hammer of Bahm. She fought many years against the encroaching evil of the old family estate before finally succumbing to its evils. Her afterlife malevolence is in keeping with the haunts of the home, though the goodness that was her living self shines through in many cases and she often merely stands to warn away trespassers or provide helpful hints to those who have become lost in the manor's twisting corridors.

Rhona Rump

Medium undead, neutral evil

Armor Class 11
Hit Points 104 (16d8 + 32)
Speed 0 ft., fly 40 ft. (hover)

STR	DEX	CON	INT	WIS	CHA
7 (−2)	13 (+1)	14 (+2)	16 (+3)	12 (+1)	17 (+3)

Saving Throws Con +5, Cha +6
Skills Arcana +6, History +6, Medicine +7, Nature +6
Damage Resistances acid, fire, lightning, thunder; bludgeoning, piercing, and slashing from nonmagical attacks
Damage Immunities cold, necrotic, poison
Condition Immunities charmed, exhaustion, frightened, grappled, paralyzed, petrified, poisoned, prone, restrained
Senses darkvision 60 ft., passive Perception 11
Languages Common, Dwarven, Elven, Gnome, Halfling
Challenge 7 (2,900 XP)

Ethereal Sight. Rhona can see 60 feet into the Ethereal Plane when she is on the Material Plane, and vice versa.

Incorporeal Movement. Rhona can move through other creatures and objects as if they were difficult terrain. She takes 5 (1d10) force damage if she ends her turn inside an object.

Innate Spellcasting. Rhona's innate spellcasting ability is Charisma (spell save DC 14). She can cast the following spells, requiring no material components:

At will: *resistance*

3/day each: *bless, cure wounds, lesser restoration*

Spellcasting. Rhona is a 6th-level spellcaster. Her spellcasting ability is Charisma (spell save DC 14, +6 to hit with spell attacks). She knows the following sorcerer spells.

Cantrips (at will): *fire bolt, guidance, mage hand, message, minor illusion*

1st level (4 slots): *burning hands, cure wounds, detect magic,*

2nd level (3 slots): *blindness/deafness, hold person*

3rd level (3 slots): *bestow curse, remove curse*

Swift Casting (3/day). Whenever Rhona uses an action to cast a cantrip or a spell, she can cast a cantrip as a bonus action.

Actions

Withering Touch. *Melee Weapon Attack:* +6 to hit, reach 5 ft., one target. *Hit:* 17 (4d6 + 3) necrotic damage.

Etherealness. Rhona enters the Ethereal Plane from the Material Plane, or vice versa. She is visible on the Material Plane while she is in the Border Ethereal, and vice versa, yet she can't affect or be affected by anything on the other plane.

Horrifying Visage. Each non-undead creature within 60 feet of Rhona that can see her must succeed on a DC 14 Wisdom saving throw or be frightened for 1 minute. If the save fails by 5 or more, the target also ages 1d4 × 10 years. A frightened target can repeat the saving throw at the end of each of its turns, ending the frightened condition on itself on a success. If a target's saving throw is successful or the effect ends for it, the target is immune to Rhona's Horrifying Visage for the next 24 hours. The aging effect can be reversed with a *greater restoration* spell, but only within 24 hours of it occurring.

Possession (recharge 6). One humanoid that Rhona can see within 5 feet of her must succeed on a DC 14 Charisma saving throw or be possessed by the ghost; Rhona then disappears, and the target is incapacitated and loses control of its body. Rhona now controls the body but doesn't deprive the target of awareness. Rhona can't be targeted by any attack, spell, or other effect, except ones that turn undead, and she retains her alignment, Intelligence, Wisdom, Charisma, and immunity to being charmed and frightened. She otherwise uses the possessed target's statistics, but doesn't gain access to the target's knowledge, class features, or proficiencies.

The possession lasts until the body drops to 0 hit points, Rhona ends it as a bonus action, or Rhona is turned or forced out by an effect like the *dispel evil and good* spell. When the possession ends, Rhona reappears in an unoccupied space within 5 feet of the body. The target is immune to Rhona's Possession for 24 hours after succeeding on the saving throw or after the possession ends.

KERION D'ARCANGELI (STEPHEN "GUPPY" GETTY)

Kerion D'arcangeli was an eccentric among eccentrics. He placed great weight on the phrase, "If you look too long into the Abyss, the Abyss also looks into you." As such, he removed his eyes and replaced them with electric blue glowing permanent *wizard's eyes* that could be upgraded with protective magics as needed. Although this helped his arcane planar studies immensely, many people found it unnerving. As such, when in public, he wore eye covers of his own design. This didn't really make people feel better around him; if anything, the blue glow around the edges only made people more uneasy.

KERION D'ARCANGELI

Medium humanoid (human), neutral

Armor Class 12 (15 with *mage armor*)
Hit Points 84 (13d8 + 26)
Speed 30 ft.

STR	DEX	CON	INT	WIS	CHA
10 (+0)	14 (+2)	14 (+2)	20 (+5)	13 (+1)	8 (−1)

Saving Throws Con +6, Int +9, Wis +5
Skills Arcana +9, History +9, Religion +9
Senses darkvision 60 ft., passive Perception 11
Languages Aboleth, Abyssal, Aklo, Aquan, Auran, Celestial, Common, Daemonic, Draconic, Elder Thing, Ignan, Infernal, Mi-Go, Protean, Shae, Sylvan, Terran, Yithian
Challenge 10 (5,900 XP)

Special Equipment. Kerion has replaced his eyes with the magic item *wizard's eyes*. In addition, he wears a *ring of alien geometries*.

Conjurer. Kerion always succeeds on saving throws to maintain concentration on a conjuration spell.

Innate Spellcasting. Kerion's innate spellcasting ability is Intelligence (spell save DC 17). He can cast the following spells, requiring no material components.

At will: *acid splash*

2/day: *misty step*

1/day: *banishment, conjure minor elementals**

Spellcasting. Kerion is a 13th-level spellcaster. His spellcasting ability is Intelligence (spell save DC 17, +9 to hit with spell attacks). He has the following wizard spells prepared.

Cantrips (at will): *dancing lights, mage hand, mending, ray of*

and darkvision out to a distance of 60 feet. In addition, you can cast *detect magic* at will, and the *true seeing* spell. Once you have cast *true seeing*, you cannot do so again until you finish a long rest.

If the eyes are suppressed by another effect, such as *antimagic field*, they do not function and you are blinded while in the area of the effect. The eyes can be removed with another DC 20 Wisdom (Medicine) check, at which point you reduce your maximum hit points by 20 until you take a long rest and you lose the magic item's benefits.

Rings of Alien Geometries

Ring, rare (requires attunement)

This magic ring is actually two crystal rings carved in a maddening number of facets. Connecting both is a very short silver chain, short enough that the rings cannot be worn save on adjacent fingers.

You can use an action to cast the *dimension door* spell. Each time you do, you have a cumulative 20 percent chance the alien dimensions you travel through when casting the spell deal you 14 (4d6) psychic damage. Once you take damage, the chance returns to 0.

Undead Orchard Keeper (Scott Kehl)

The orchard keeper is a hunched undead covered in fine vines and leaves that appear as if they were the hair that the corpse once had. Slung over its back is a knapsack that is filled with magical fruits and bizarre fungi, and the orchard keeper keeps which is which to himself. The undead appears wild and eccentric, almost as if possessed of a bizarre affinity for the perverse nature that it seems to sprout wherever it decides to take up residence.

While it carries a staff, it shares some similarities with ghasts in that its claws can paralyze its foes. There, however, the similarities end.

Undead Orchard Keeper

Medium undead, neutral evil

Armor Class 15 (natural armor)
Hit Points 71 (11d8 + 22)
Speed 40 ft., fly 60 ft.

STR	DEX	CON	INT	WIS	CHA
17 (+3)	14 (+2)	15 (+2)	11 (+0)	13 (+1)	18 (+4)

Skills Athletics +6, Nature +6, Perception +4, Stealth +5, Survival +4
Damage Immunities poison
Condition Immunities exhaustion, poison
Senses darkvision 60 ft., passive Perception 14
Languages Abyssal, Common, Necronomus
Challenge 6 (2,300 XP)

Special Equipment. The undead orchard keeper carries a magical knapsack that functions as a *wand of wonder*. Only the orchard keeper can attune to it.

Innate Spellcasting. The orchard keeper's innate spellcasting ability is Charisma (spell save DC 15). It can cast the following spells without material components:

At will: *chill touch, prestidigitation*

3/day each: *alter self, charm person, insect plague, plant growth*

Turning Defiance. The undead orchard keeper has advantage on saving throws against effects that turn undead.

---

frost, shocking grasp
1st level (4 slots): *detect magic, grease*, mage armor, magic missile, shield*
2nd level (3 slots): *acid arrow, darkvision, detect thoughts, flaming sphere*, web**
3rd level (3 slots): *dispel magic, lightning bolt, stinking cloud**
4th level (3 slots): *black tentacles*, dimension door*, faithful hound**
5th level (2 slots): *conjure elemental*, legend lore*
6th level (1 slot): *instant summons*
7th level (1 slot): *teleport*
* Conjuration spell

Actions

Quarterstaff. *Melee Weapon Attack:* +3 to hit, reach 5 ft., one target. *Hit:* 2 (1d6 − 1) bludgeoning damage, or 3 (1d8 − 1) bludgeoning damage if wielded with two hands.

Wizard's Eyes

Wondrous item, very rare

These small orbs are just over 1 inch in diameter and glow a dim blue. They are etched with miniscule and tightly packed arcane runes. In order to use this set of magic items, you must surgically remove your eyes and then you or another creature must make a DC 20 Wisdom (Medicine) check to implant these orbs in their place. On a failed check, the surgery does not work and you reduce your maximum hit points by 20 until you take a long rest. On a successful check, the orbs replace your eyes.

While you continue to possess the eyes, you have normal vision

Actions

Multiattack. The orchard keeper makes one Bite attack and two Claw attacks.

Bite. *Melee Weapon Attack:* +6 to hit, reach 5 ft., one creature. *Hit:* 12 (2d8 + 3) piercing damage.

Claw. *Melee Weapon Attack:* +6 to hit, reach 5 ft., one target. *Hit:* 10 (2d6 + 3) slashing damage. If the target is a creature other than an undead, it must succeed on a DC 13 Constitution saving throw or be paralyzed for 1 minute. The target can repeat the saving throw at the end of each of its turns, ending the effect on itself on a success.

Ragged Kew Rump (Kyle Walker)

Purveyor of puns and pranks, Ragged often both entertained and annoyed other Rump family members. His fondness for stuffed toys encouraged hours of recreation in the playroom until the unpleasant "biting toy" incident. After that, the pranks worsened and his fate remains unknown to this date but a boy's giggling or guffawing, possibly his, can still be heard in nearby proximity to the playroom.

Ragged Kew Rump

Small undead, neutral evil

Armor Class 13 (natural armor)
Hit Points 44 (8d6 + 16)

Speed 20 ft.

STR	DEX	CON	INT	WIS	CHA
9 (−1)	14 (+2)	15 (+2)	11 (+0)	13 (+1)	17 (+3)

Skills Deception +7, Stealth +4
Damage Immunities poison
Condition Immunities charmed, exhaustion, poisoned
Senses darkvision 60 ft., passive Perception 11
Languages Common, plus 4 random languages
Challenge 3 (700 XP)

Aura of Sobs. Any creature that starts its turn within 10 feet of Ragged Kew must succeed on a DC 13 Wisdom saving throw. On a failed saving throw, the creature is frightened of Kew for 1 minute. While frightened, it has disadvantage on attack rolls and skill checks. On a successful saving throw, the creature is immune to Kew's Aura of Sobs for 24 hours.

Actions

Bite. *Melee Weapon Attack:* +4 to hit, reach 5 ft., one creature. *Hit:* 9 (2d6 + 2) piercing damage and the target must make a DC 12 Constitution saving throw or be incapacitated until the end of its next turn.

Steal Voice. One creature that is not an undead or construct within 5 feet of Ragged Kew must make a DC 13 Charisma saving throw. On a failed saving throw, the creature loses its voice for 1 hour. That creature cannot cast spells that require vocal components or use abilities that require them to speak. A *remove curse* spell can return the creature's voice to normal.

If Ragged Kew steals a creature's voice, it can mimic that voice at any time, even if the creature's voice returns. Kew can speak the languages that the creature knew. A creature that hears the mimicry can tell they are imitations with a successful DC 15 Wisdom (Insight) check.

Roka Rump (Terry Demeter)

Adorned in ancient, battle-scarred armor emblazoned with the Rump Family crest and brandishing a large, spiked flail upon his right shoulder, the noble features of this rather long-haired gentleman known as Roka Rump, may at first glance appear to be sincere and charming.

However, the deep chestnut eyes, the thick coarse mustache, and goatee do very little to hide an obvious, maniacal penchant for fiendish brutality and perverse might.

Closer inspection of the portrait for this particularly loathsome member of the Rump family (who was disavowed on several occasions after his numerous "atrocities" were exposed), reveals vicious, almost canine-like teeth and devilish eyes that threaten to pull the viewer into the abyss itself.

Those casting their gaze upon the painting are left with a tangible sense that Roka Rump may have actually been devoid of anything resembling true humanity, and most likely would have loved nothing more than to dominate, destroy, and devour the very heart and soul of anyone whose shadow crossed his dreadful path.

Roka Rump

Medium undead, chaotic evil

Armor Class 19 (+1 plate armor)
Hit Points 78 (12d8 + 24)
Speed 30 ft.

STR	DEX	CON	INT	WIS	CHA
18 (+4)	12 (+1)	14 (+2)	12 (+1)	16 (+3)	18 (+4)

Saving Throws Wis +6, Cha +7
Skills Athletics +7, Medicine +4, Persuasion +7, Religion +4
Damage Resistances bludgeoning, piercing, and slashing from nonmagical attacks
Damage Immunities acid, cold, lightning
Condition Immunities charmed, exhaustion, frightened
Senses darkvision 60 ft., passive Perception 13
Languages Common
Challenge 8 (3,900 XP)

Special Equipment. Roka wears a set of *+1 plate armor*.
Unholy Smite. When Roka hits with a melee weapon attack, he can expend a spell slot to deal additional necrotic damage to the target, in addition to the weapon's damage. The extra damage is 9 (2d8) for a 1st-level spell slot, plus 4 (1d8) for each spell level higher than 1st, to a maximum of 21 (5d8). The damage increases by 4 (1d8) if the target is a celestial.
Unholy Resilience. Roka is immune to disease, and cannot be charmed or frightened. He has a +4 bonus to any saving throw he makes. These benefits cease to function if Roka is unconscious or slain.
Spellcasting. Roka is a 12th-level spellcaster. His spellcasting ability is Charisma (spell save DC 15). He has the following paladin spells prepared.

1st level (4 slots): *bane, divine favor, protection from evil and good, sanctuary, shield of faith*
2nd level (3 slots): *aid, lesser restoration, hold person, silence*
3rd level (3 slots): *bestow curse, dispel magic, protection from energy*

Actions

Multiattack. Roka makes two Flail attacks.
Flail. *Melee Weapon Attack:* +7 to hit, reach 5 ft., one target. *Hit:* 8 (1d8 + 4) bludgeoning damage.
Lay on Hands. Roka has a pool of 60 hit points to use with his Lay on Hands ability. He regains spent hit points from this pool when he takes a long rest. He can use this ability to cause a creature within 5 feet of him or itself to regain any number of hit points, up to its hit point maximum or Roka's pool of hit points is reduced to 0.
Unholy Weapon (1/short or long rest). Roka adds +4 to his attack and damage rolls for 1 minute, and his weapon is considered magical for the purposes of damage resistances.

Ryhlen Rump (Douglas Zielsdorf)

Born the illegitimate son of a Tegel scion, Ryhlen was deposited upon the steps of the Manor shortly before his mother hung herself from a nearby tree limb. Never properly acknowledged, though unquestionably accepted, he drifted on the periphery of the Rump family for the entirety of his lifetime. Never known to utter a solitary word in more than 3 decades of life, Ryhlen earned the nickname of

Innate Spellcasting. Ryhlen's innate spellcasting ability is Intelligence (spell save DC 18). He can cast the following spells, requiring no material components:

At will: *blur, creation, detect thoughts, dream, sleep*

3/day each: *gaseous form, invisibility, phantasmal killer, sleep* (9th-level version), *suggestion*

1/day each: *feeblemind, modify memory, plane shift* (from the material plane to the dimension of dreams or vice versa only)

Master of the Mind. Ryhlen always succeeds on Constitution saving throws to maintain concentration on enchantment and illusion spells. Whenever Ryhlen casts an enchantment or illusion spell, he can use a bonus to force a target to reroll their saving throw, taking the lower of the two results.

Magic Resistance. Ryhlen has advantage on saving throws against spells and other magical effects.

Nightmare Lord. Ryhlen Rump has no need of sleep and suffers no penalties from not doing so. He is immune to magic that would put him to sleep.

Regeneration. Ryhlen regains 5 hit points at the start of his turns as long as he has at least 1 hit point. If Ryhlen takes radiant damage or damage from a silvered attack, this trait doesn't function at the start of Ryhlen's next turn.

Spellcasting. Ryhlen is a 13th-level spellcaster. His spellcasting ability is Intelligence (spell save DC 18, +10 to hit with spell attacks). He has the following wizard spells prepared.

Cantrips (at will): *chill touch, mage hand, message, minor illusion, ray of frost*

1st level (4 slots): *detect magic, expeditious retreat, mage armor, magic missile, shield*

2nd level (3 slots): *blindness/deafness, hold person, shatter*

3rd level (3 slots): *bestow curse, dispel magic, lightning bolt*

4th level (3 slots): *banishment, greater invisibility, phantasmal killer*

5th level (2 slots): *contact other plane, telekinesis*

6th level (1 slot): *eyebite*

7th level (1 slot): *etherealness*

Actions

Psychic Blast. Ryhlen releases a psychic blast in a 30-foot cone. Creatures in the area must make a DC 18 Intelligence saving throw. On a failed saving throw, the target takes 27 (4d10 + 5) psychic damage and is stunned until the end of the target's next turn. On a successful saving throw, the target takes half damage and is not stunned.

Frightful Presence. Each creature of Ryhlen's choice that is within 120 feet of him and aware of him must succeed on a DC 18 Wisdom saving throw or become frightened for 1 minute. A creature can repeat the saving throw at the end of each of its turns, ending the effect on itself on a success. If a creature's saving throw is successful or the effect ends for it, the creature is immune to Ryhlen's Frightful Presence for the next 24 hours.

Incorporeal Form (1/day). Ryhlen can become an incorporeal phantom for up to 1 minute. While in this form, he has the following additional benefits:

• He has a flying speed of 30 feet.

• He has resistance to acid, fire, lightning, and thunder damage, as well as bludgeoning, piercing, and slashing damage from nonmagical attacks that aren't silvered.

• He has immunity to cold, necrotic, and poison damage, as well as the grappled, paralyzed, petrified, poisoned, prone, and restrained condition.

• He can move through other creatures and objects as if they were difficult terrain. He takes 5 (1d10) force damage if he ends his turn inside an object.

Ghost long before his disappearance. None however seemed shocked by his apt return, and his shade has been known to skulk through the halls of the Manor occasionally whispering dread secrets to some -- often in surreal nightmarish dreams.

Ryhlen Rump

Medium humanoid (human), chaotic evil

Armor Class 13 (16 with *mage armor*)
Hit Points 120 (16d8 + 48)
Speed 30 ft.

STR	DEX	CON	INT	WIS	CHA
7 (−1)	16 (+3)	16 (+3)	22 (+6)	17 (+3)	15 (+2)

Saving Throws Con +7, Int +10, Wis +7
Skills Arcana +10, History +10, Nature +10, Perception +7, Religion +10, Survival +7
Damage Resistances psychic
Senses darkvision 120 ft., passive Perception 17
Languages Aklo, Common, Elder Thing, Mi-go, Necronomus, Shadowtongue, Yithian; telepathy 120 ft.
Challenge 12 (8,400 XP)

Dream Slave. If Ryhlen kills a creature via psychic damage, the creature instead drops to 1 hit point and is charmed by Ryhlen, as if he had cast the *dominate monster* spell on the target. Ryhlen has no limit to the number of dream slaves he can possess.

The effect can be broken with *dispel magic* or an effect that ends the charmed condition on the target. If the target takes damage while under the effect, they can attempt a DC 18 Wisdom saving throw to end the effect early.

The Fiend (Michael Badalato)

This particular haunt of the manor is a devil straight out of hell. Quick to offer you a deal, he always promises a seafood buffet with broiled king crab, fresh oysters, clam strips, and swordfish but never manages to deliver on the deal. A collector of sorts, he is believed to be tied closely to the curse of Tegel manor itself, sent straight from hell to administrate the consumption and sale of souls trapped within its unholy walls.

Contract Devil

Medium fiend (devil), lawful evil

Armor Class 18 (natural armor)
Hit Points 136 (16d8 + 64)
Speed 30 ft.

STR	DEX	CON	INT	WIS	CHA
21 (+5)	19 (+4)	18 (+4)	16 (+3)	17 (+3)	19 (+4)

Saving Throws Con +8, Wis +7, Cha +8
Skills Arcana +7, Deception +12, History +7, Nature +7, Persuasion +12
Damage Resistances acid, cold; bludgeoning, piercing, and slashing from nonmagical attacks that aren't silvered
Damage Immunities fire, poison
Condition Immunities poisoned
Senses darkvision 60 ft., passive Perception 13
Languages Abyssal, Aklo, Aquan, Auran, Celestial, Common, Draconic, Dwarven, Elven, Giant, Gnome, Goblin, Gnoll, Halfling, Ignan, Infernal, Orc, Sylvan, Terran, Undercommon, telepathy 120 ft.
Challenge 11 (7,200 XP)

Devil's Sight. Magical darkness doesn't impede the devil's darkvision.
Innate Spellcasting. The contract devil's innate spellcasting ability is Charisma (spell save DC 16). It can cast the following spells without requiring material components.
At will: *detect magic, detect thoughts, fireball, identify, sending, tongues*
3/day each: *arcane eye, dimension door, hold person, locate person, silence*
1/day each: *contact other plane, banishment, plane shift*
Magic Resistance. The contract devil has advantage on saving throws against spells and other magical effects.

Actions

Multiattack. The contract devil makes three Binding Contract attacks. If the contract devil has at least one grappled creature it can make a Horns attack as a bonus action against each grappled creature.
Binding Contract. *Melee Spell Attack:* +8 to hit, reach 10 ft., one target. *Hit:* 13 (2d8 + 4) slashing damage, and the target is grappled (escape DC 17). A contract devil has no limit to the number of creatures it can have grappled at a time.
Horns. *Melee Weapon Attack:* +9 to hit, reach 5 ft., one target. *Hit:* 19 (4d6 + 5) piercing damage.

Loscann and "Mam" Dian

This mad couple is thought to be near the root of incursions by Tsathoggus's cult in the region. Their relations with the Rumps date back many centuries. They arrive with a bit of charm and wit, ply the locals with bread and wine. The next thing anyone knows the region is hip deep in frog cults, plagues and curses. The only thing anyone can say is that it's always fun while the good times last and a little less fun when you awaken to a horrible headache about to be sacrificed on a primordial altar out in the swamp.

Loscann and "Mam" Dian use the statistics of an **apostle**.

Apostle

Medium humanoid (any), chaotic evil

Armor Class 13 (natural armor)
Hit Points 97 (15d8 + 30)
Speed 30 ft.

STR	DEX	CON	INT	WIS	CHA
15 (+2)	12 (+1)	15 (+2)	13 (+1)	18 (+4)	9 (−1)

Saving Throws Wis +7, Cha +2
Skills Medicine +7, Religion +4
Damage Resistances necrotic, psychic
Senses passive Perception 14
Languages Common, Tsathar
Challenge 8 (3,900 XP)

Fetid Blessing. Whenever the apostle deals acid or poison damage, it ignores resistance to those damage types and deals an additional 7 (2d6) damage of the same type.
Spellcasting. The apostle is a 10th-level spellcaster. Its spellcasting ability is Wisdom (spell save DC 15, +7 to hit with spell attacks). It has the following cleric spells prepared.
Cantrips (at will): *acid splash, mending, poison spray, thaumaturgy*

1st level (4 slots): *bane, inflict wounds, protection from evil and good, shield of faith*
2nd level (3 slots): *acid arrow, hold person, lesser restoration, spiritual weapon*
3rd level (3 slots): *caustic burst, create food and water, dispel magic, tongue of the frog god*
4th level (3 slots): *blight, control water*
5th level (2 slots): *insect plague*

Actions

Mace. *Melee Weapon Attack:* +5 to hit, reach 5 ft., one target. *Hit:* 5 (1d6 + 2) bludgeoning damage.

***Plague of Frogs* (recharges after a short or long rest).** The apostle magically calls 1d4 **giant frogs**, provided that the apostle is within 100 feet of a body of water large enough to cover a Medium creature. The called creatures arrive within 1d4 rounds, acting as allies of the apostle, and obey its spoken commands. The beasts remain for 1 hour, until the apostle dies, or until the apostle dismisses them as a bonus action.

The Chu"Lich" Family

Beware their stare! Wete, the wicked Wizard impedes your movement through achy joints. Bom, the bearded barbarous Bard causes long hair growth over your entire body. Feter, the fearsome Father blisters your hands causing your weapon to drop. Malberta, mischievous Mom makes you glow like a beacon.

The Chu"Lich" family all use the same statistics, that of a **neophyte lich**. Each has an additional feature:

Wete Chu"Lich"

Wete has the following two new actions:

***Bolster Undead* (1/day).** Undead of Wete's choice within 30 feet of him have advantage on saving throws against being turned, and on attack rolls against other creatures, for one minute.

Boneshatter. One target of Wete's choice within 30 feet of him must make a DC 18 Constitution saving throw or be cursed for 1 minute. Whenever a cursed creature fails an attack roll or saving throw, they take 10 (3d6) bludgeoning damage as their bones crack from the stress. A cursed creature can repeat the saving throw at the end of each of its turns, ending the effect on itself on a success.

Bom Chu"Lich"

Bom has the following new action. When Bom uses an action to use its paralyzing touch or casts a spell, he can use this new ability as a bonus action:

Dance of the Dead. An undead of Bom's choice within 30 feet of him can use its reaction to make one melee or ranged attack against a creature that is within the undead's range.

Feter Chu"Lich"

Feter has the *heat metal* spell prepared, and has the following new action:

***Swarmcaller* (1/day).** Feter can magically summon 1d4 + 1 **insect swarms**. The swarms appear in an unoccupied space within 60 feet of Feter, remain for 1 minute, until they or Feter are slain, or until Feter takes an action to dismiss them.

Malberta Chu"Lich"

Malberta has this additional feature:

Innate Spellcasting. Malberta's innate spellcasting ability is Charisma (spell save DC 15). She can cast the following spells, requiring no material components:

At will: *guidance*
3/day each: *bane, bless*
1/day each: *blight, dream, geas*

Neophyte Lich

Medium undead, chaotic evil

Armor Class 17 (natural armor)
Hit Points 82 (11d8 + 33)
Speed 30 ft.

STR	DEX	CON	INT	WIS	CHA
8 (−1)	13 (+1)	17 (+3)	21 (+5)	14 (+2)	16 (+3)

Saving Throws Con +8, Int +10, Wis +7
Skills Arcana +10, History +10, Insight +7, Medicine +12, Perception +7
Damage Resistances cold, lightning, necrotic
Damage Immunities poison; bludgeoning, piercing, and slashing from nonmagical attacks
Condition Immunities charmed, exhaustion, frightened, paralyzed, poisoned
Senses truesight 120 ft., passive Perception 17

Languages Abyssal, Common, Daemonic, Draconic, Infernal, Necronomus
Challenge 14 (11,500 XP)

Legendary Resistance (3/day). If the neophyte lich fails a saving throw, it can choose to succeed instead.

Rejuvenation. If it has a phylactery and it is destroyed, the neophyte lich gains a new body in 1d10 days, regaining all its hit points and becoming active again. The new body appears within 5 feet of the phylactery.

Spellcasting. The neophyte lich is an 11th-level spellcaster. Its spellcasting ability is Intelligence (spell save DC 18, +10 to hit with spell attacks). It has the following wizard spells prepared:

Cantrips (at will): *acid splash, mage hand, prestidigitation, ray of frost, shocking grasp*

1st level (4 slots): *detect magic, magic missile, shield, thunderwave*

2nd level (3 slots): *acid arrow, detect thoughts, invisibility, mirror image*

3rd level (3 slots): *animate dead, counterspell, dispel magic, fireball*

4th level (3 slots): *blight, dimension door*

5th level (2 slots): *cloudkill, scrying*

6th level (1 slot): *disintegrate, globe of invulnerability*

Turn Resistance. The lich has advantage on saving throws against any effect that turns undead.

Actions

Paralyzing Touch. *Melee Spell Attack:* +10 to hit, reach 5 ft., one creature. *Hit:* 10 (3d6) cold damage. The target must succeed on a DC 16 Constitution saving throw or be paralyzed for 1 minute. The target can repeat the saving throw at the end of each of its turns, ending the effect on itself on a success.

Legendary Actions

The neophyte lich can take 3 legendary actions, choosing from the options below. Only one legendary action option can be used at a time and only at the end of another creature's turn. The neophyte lich regains spent legendary actions at the start of its turn.

Cantrip. The neophyte lich casts a cantrip.

Paralyzing Touch (costs 2 actions). The neophyte lich uses its Paralyzing Touch.

Frightening Gaze (costs 2 actions). The neophyte lich fixes its gaze on one creature it can see within 10 feet of it. The target must succeed on a DC 15 Wisdom saving throw against this magic or become frightened for 1 minute. The frightened target can repeat the saving throw at the end of each of its turns, ending the effect on itself on a success. If a target's saving throw is successful or the effect ends for it, the target is immune to neophyte lich's gaze for the next 24 hours.

Disrupt Life (costs 3 actions). Each living creature within 20 feet of the lich must make a DC 15 Constitution saving throw against this magic, taking 17 (5d6) necrotic damage on a failed save, or half as much damage on a successful one.

Appendix II: Creatures

Creatures

This appendix contains those creatures found in the halls and dungeons of the Tegel Manor adventures that are not also found in the Fifth Edition SRD. Hazards (Brown and Yellow Mold, for example) are listed with the rest of the creatures, and the various NPCs are also mixed in. There are two special section, one on animated objects and the other on greater ghosts. Both of these play important roles in Tegel Manor so we have some tools you can use to provide a variety pack of these two types of encounters.

Animated Objects

in Tegel Manor

Tegel Manor is filled with a variety of mundane and magical items. Some of these items have taken on a life of their own through long exposure to the latent magical energy in the manor or through purposeful experimentation by some of the manor's more powerful residents.

The rules for creating Tegel Manor's animated objects are listed below. Though not a comprehensive list of every possible object in the manor that could become animate, it should provide you with enough information to create objects of your own to throw at your unsuspecting players as they traverse the manor's halls.

Creating an Animated Object

When creating an animated object, you must first decide the size of the object. The five creature statistics listed below provide the foundation for an animated object of Tiny, Small, Medium, Large, or Huge size. Gargantuan objects, though possible to animate, are outside the scope of this adventure and are not included.

Tiny Animated Object

Tiny construct, unaligned

Armor Class 12
Hit Points 28 (8d4 + 8)
Speed 20 ft.

STR	DEX	CON	INT	WIS	CHA
10 (+0)	14 (+2)	13 (+1)	1 (−5)	5 (−3)	1 (−5)

Skills Perception −1
Damage Immunities poison, psychic
Condition Immunities blinded, charmed, deafened, exhaustion, frightened, paralyzed, petrified, poisoned
Senses blindsight 60 ft. (blind beyond this radius), passive Perception 9
Languages —
Challenge 1/2 (100 XP)

Antimagic Susceptibility. The animated object is incapacitated while in the area of an *antimagic field*. If targeted by *dispel magic*, the animated object must succeed on a Constitution saving throw against the caster's spell save DC or fall unconscious for 1 minute.
Constructed Nature. An animated object doesn't require air, food, drink, or sleep.
False Appearance. While the animated object remains motionless, it is indistinguishable from a normal object of its type.

Actions

Multiattack. The animated object makes two Slam attacks.
Slam. *Melee Weapon Attack:* +4 to hit, reach 5 ft., one target.
  Hit: 4 (1d4 + 2) bludgeoning damage.

Small Animated Object

Small construct, unaligned

Armor Class 12
Hit Points 44 (8d6 + 16)
Speed 25 ft.

STR	DEX	CON	INT	WIS	CHA
14 (+2)	14 (+2)	15 (+2)	1 (−5)	5 (−3)	1 (−5)

Skills Perception −1
Damage Immunities poison, psychic
Condition Immunities blinded, charmed, deafened, exhaustion, frightened, paralyzed, petrified, poisoned
Senses blindsight 60 ft. (blind beyond this radius), passive Perception 9
Languages —
Challenge 1 (200 XP)

Antimagic Susceptibility. The animated object is incapacitated while in the area of an *antimagic field*. If targeted by *dispel magic*, the animated object must succeed on a Constitution saving throw against the caster's spell save DC or fall unconscious for 1 minute.
Constructed Nature. An animated object doesn't require air, food, drink, or sleep.
False Appearance. While the animated object remains motionless, it is indistinguishable from a normal object of its type.

Actions

Multiattack. The animated object makes two Slam attacks.
Slam. *Melee Weapon Attack:* +4 to hit, reach 5 ft., one target.
  Hit: 5 (1d6 + 2) bludgeoning damage.

Medium Animated Object

Medium construct, unaligned

Armor Class 12
Hit Points 60 (8d8 + 24)
Speed 30 ft.

STR	DEX	CON	INT	WIS	CHA
16 (+3)	14 (+2)	17 (+3)	1 (−5)	5 (−3)	1 (−5)

Skills Perception −1
Damage Immunities poison, psychic
Condition Immunities blinded, charmed, deafened, exhaustion, frightened, paralyzed, petrified, poisoned
Senses blindsight 60 ft. (blind beyond this radius), passive Perception 9

Languages —
Challenge 2 (450 XP)

Antimagic Susceptibility. The animated object is
incapacitated while in the area of an *antimagic field*. If targeted
by *dispel magic*, the animated object must succeed on a
Constitution saving throw against the caster's spell save DC or
fall unconscious for 1 minute.

Constructed Nature. An animated object doesn't require air,
food, drink, or sleep.

False Appearance. While the animated object remains
motionless, it is indistinguishable from a normal object of its type.

Actions

Multiattack. The animated object makes two Slam attacks.

Slam. *Melee Weapon Attack:* +5 to hit, reach 5 ft., one target.
Hit: 7 (1d8 + 3) bludgeoning damage.

LARGE ANIMATED OBJECT

Large construct, unaligned

Armor Class 13
Hit Points 76 (8d10 + 32)
Speed 30 ft.

STR	DEX	CON	INT	WIS	CHA
18 (+4)	16 (+3)	19 (+4)	1 (−5)	5 (−3)	1 (−5)

Skills Perception −1
Damage Immunities poison, psychic
Condition Immunities blinded, charmed, deafened,
exhaustion, frightened, paralyzed, petrified, poisoned
Senses blindsight 60 ft. (blind beyond this radius), passive
Perception 9
Languages —
Challenge 3 (700 XP)

Antimagic Susceptibility. The animated object is
incapacitated while in the area of an *antimagic field*. If targeted
by *dispel magic*, the animated object must succeed on a
Constitution saving throw against the caster's spell save DC or
fall unconscious for 1 minute.

Constructed Nature. An animated object doesn't require air,
food, drink, or sleep.

False Appearance. While the animated object remains
motionless, it is indistinguishable from a normal object of its type.

Actions

Multiattack. The animated object makes two Slam attacks.

Slam. *Melee Weapon Attack:* +6 to hit, reach 5 ft., one target.
Hit: 9 (1d10 + 4) bludgeoning damage.

HUGE ANIMATED OBJECT

Huge construct, unaligned

Armor Class 13
Hit Points 92 (8d12 + 40)
Speed 40 ft.

STR	DEX	CON	INT	WIS	CHA
20 (+5)	16 (+3)	21 (+5)	1 (−5)	5 (−3)	1 (−5)

Skills Perception −1
Damage Immunities poison, psychic
Condition Immunities blinded, charmed, deafened,
exhaustion, frightened, paralyzed, petrified, poisoned
Senses blindsight 60 ft. (blind beyond this radius), passive
Perception 9
Languages —
Challenge 4 (1,100 XP)

Antimagic Susceptibility. The animated object is
incapacitated while in the area of an *antimagic field*. If targeted
by *dispel magic*, the animated object must succeed on a
Constitution saving throw against the caster's spell save DC or
fall unconscious for 1 minute.

Constructed Nature. An animated object doesn't require air,
food, drink, or sleep.

False Appearance. While the animated object remains
motionless, it is indistinguishable from a normal object of its type.

Actions

Multiattack. The animated object makes two Slam attacks.

Slam. *Melee Weapon Attack:* +7 to hit, reach 5 ft., one target.
Hit: 11 (1d12 + 5) bludgeoning damage.

THEMES

After you have chosen the size of the animated object, choose
a theme. Each theme adds a variety of features to the base
animated object, such as the ensnaring theme which gives the
animated object the Hard to Grasp trait, or adjusts features of
the object, such as the animalistic theme which modifies the
creature's method of locomotion.

Each animated object must have at least one theme, but it can
have more. Increase the animated object's challenge rating
by 1 for each theme you add to it beyond the first theme,
rounding down for Tiny animated objects. For example, a Small
animalistic ensnaring animated object would have a challenge
rating of 2 while a Tiny animalistic ensnaring animated object
would have a challenge rating of 1. If you use two themes that
replace or modify the same feature (such as animalistic and
paraphernalia which both modify the Slam attack), pick one
theme's modification and ignore the other theme's modification;
do not apply both modifications to the same creature.

An animated object uses its Constitution modifier when setting
the saving throw DC for its traits and actions (DC equal to 8 +
the object's proficiency bonus + its Constitution modifier).

ANIMALISTIC THEME

This theme applies to animated objects that look like animals, such
as figurines of griffons or children's toy animals. An animalistic
animated object retains its statistics except as noted below.

Speed. The animated object's method of locomotion changes.
Choose one of the following:

Increased Movement. The animated object's walking speed
increases by 20 feet.

Unique Movement. The animated object has a climbing, flying, or swimming speed of 30 feet.

New Action: Multiattack. The animated object's Multiattack action changes to: The animated object makes one Bite attack and two Claw attacks.

New Action: Bite. The animated object's Slam attack is replaced with a Bite attack. This attack deals the same damage as the Slam, except it deals piercing damage instead of bludgeoning damage.

New Action: Claw. The animated object has a Claw attack. This attack deals slashing damage, and its damage dice are half of the animated object's Slam damage dice (rounded down to the nearest damage die). Otherwise, this attack works like the animated object's Slam attack. For example, a Tiny object's claw attack would use a d2 (half of a d4) as its base damage die while Medium and Large objects would use a d4 (half of a d8 and d10, respectively).

ENSNARING THEME

This theme applies to animated objects that are used to tie or wrap objects, such as chains, rope, drapes, and blankets. An ensnaring animated object retains its statistics except as noted below.

Hard to Grasp. The animated object has advantage on ability checks and saving throws made to escape a grapple.

Skill Proficiency: Athletics. The animated object is proficient in Strength (Athletics) checks.

New Action: Smother. The animated object has the Smother action, wrapping itself around its target's throat, chest, or face. This action works like the animated object's Slam attack, except it deals double the Slam attack's damage dice to the target and the target is grappled (escape DC equal to 8 + the animated object's Athletics). Until this grapple ends, the target is restrained, blinded, and at risk of suffocating, and the animated object can't smother another target. The animated object can still use its Slam action while grappling a target. For example, a Tiny object's smother attack would have a base damage of 4d4 + 2 while a Large object would do 4d10 + 4.

FORTIFIED THEME

This theme applies to animated objects made of a sturdy material, such as stone statues or metal cauldrons. A fortified animated object retains its statistics except as noted below.

Armor Class. The animated object has Armor Class equal to 12 + its Dexterity modifier.

Damage Resistances. The animated object has resistance to bludgeoning, piercing, and slashing damage from nonmagical attacks.

Blunting Form. Any nonmagical piercing or slashing weapon made of metal that hits the animated object begins to dull. After dealing damage, the weapon takes a permanent and cumulative −1 penalty to damage rolls. If its penalty drops to −5, the weapon is too dull to deal damage and can't be used to deal damage again until a creature spends 10 minutes sharpening the weapon.

HUMANOID THEME

This theme applies to animated objects that are humanoid in shape, such as toy soldiers or dress mannequins. A humanoid animated object retains its statistics except as noted below.

Ability Score. The animated object's Intelligence increases to 6.

Skill Proficiency: Perception. The animated object's proficiency bonus is doubled for its Wisdom (Perception) checks.

Languages. The animated object understands Common but speaks only through the use of its Mimicry trait.

Mimicry. The animated object can mimic humanoid voices. A creature that hears the sounds can tell they are imitations with a successful Wisdom (Insight) check.

New Action: Multiattack. The animated object's Multiattack action changes to: The animated object makes two Slam attacks or two attacks with its chosen weapon. Alternatively, the animated object can make one Slam attack and one attack with its chosen weapon.

New Action: Weapon Attack. The animated object has one weapon suitable for a creature of its size and shape. It is proficient with that weapon.

MONSTROUS THEME

This theme applies to animated objects that are often monstrous in appearance, and they contain some substance that they unleash on their enemies, including objects such as a horrifying amalgam of cobbled-together parts that emits bursts of springs and gears, a barrel that spews ale on those nearby, or a wardrobe infested with thousands of spiders. A monstrous animated object retains its statistics except as noted below.

Contents. The animated object is filled with a substance that it can eject on its enemies. Choose one of the following damage types: acid, bludgeoning, cold, fire, lightning, piercing, poison, slashing, or thunder. The animated object deals this type of damage when a creature comes into contact with its contents.

Pervasive Contents. A creature that touches the animated object or hits it with a melee attack while within 5 feet of it takes half the animated object's Slam damage dice (rounded down to the nearest damage die) of the type related to its contents. If the animated object uses its Spew Contents, this trait doesn't function until the end of the animated object's next turn.

New Action: Spew Contents (recharge 6). The animated object spews its contents in a cone. Each creature in that area must make a Dexterity saving throw, taking quadruple the animated object's Slam damage dice of the type related to its contents on a failed save, or half as much damage on a successful one. The cone is 15 feet for Tiny, Small, and Medium animated objects, and it is 30 feet for Large and Huge animated objects.

PARAPHERNALIA THEME

This theme applies to animated objects that are objects in the most mundane sense, such as standard traveling equipment, kitchen cookware, or bedroom furniture. These objects often defy specificity and this theme serves as a catch-all theme for animated objects that don't fit into any of the other themes. Animated objects with this theme usually don't have other themes. A paraphernalia animated object retains its statistics except as noted below.

Speed. The animated object has a flying speed and it can hover. Its flying speed is 20 feet at Tiny and increases by 10 feet for each size above Tiny.

Ability Score. The animated object's Dexterity increases by 4.

Saving Throw. The animated object has proficiency in Dexterity saving throws.

Weaponized Form. The animated object's Slam attack deals bludgeoning, piercing, or slashing damage, your choice, each time it attacks as the object utilizes all aspects of its form to damage its enemies.

POSSESSED THEME

This theme applies to an animated object that has been possessed by some otherworldly force, such as an angel, demon, or devil. A possessed animated object can't be possessed by more than one entity and the entity possessing it must be good or evil. A possessed animated object retains its statistics except as noted below.

Alignment. The animated object's alignment is the same as the entity possessing it.

Type. The animated object is a construct but it counts as a celestial (if good) or a fiend (if evil) for spells and features, such as *protection from evil and good* and a paladin's Divine Sense.

Damage Immunities. The animated object is immune to necrotic damage (if evil) or radiant damage (if good).

Senses. The animated object has truesight with a radius of 30 feet.

Languages. The animated object knows the Abyssal, Celestial, and Infernal languages, and it has telepathy with a radius of 60 feet.

Magic Resistance. The animated object has advantage on saving throws against spells and other magical effects.

New Reaction: Otherworldly Presence. When a creature the animated object can see targets it with an attack, the animated object shows a glimpse of the entity possessing it. The attacker must succeed on a Wisdom saving throw or the attack misses, and the attacker is frightened until the end of its next turn.

EXAMPLE ANIMATED OBJECTS

Below are examples of some animated objects that inhabit Tegel Manor.

CHAIN

Medium construct, unaligned

Armor Class 12
Hit Points 60 (8d8 + 24)
Speed 30 ft.

STR	DEX	CON	INT	WIS	CHA
16 (+3)	14 (+2)	17 (+3)	1 (−5)	5 (−3)	1 (−5)

Skills Athletics +5, Perception −1
Damage Immunities poison, psychic
Condition Immunities blinded, charmed, deafened, exhaustion, frightened, paralyzed, petrified, poisoned
Senses blindsight 60 ft. (blind beyond this radius), passive Perception 9
Languages —
Challenge 2 (450 XP)

Animated Object Theme. The chain's theme is ensnaring.

Antimagic Susceptibility. The chain is incapacitated while in the area of an *antimagic field*. If targeted by *dispel magic*, the chain must succeed on a Constitution saving throw against the caster's spell save DC or fall unconscious for 1 minute.

Constructed Nature. An animated object doesn't require air, food, drink, or sleep.

False Appearance. While the chain remains motionless, it is indistinguishable from a normal chain.

Hard to Grasp. The chain has advantage on ability checks and saving throws made to escape a grapple.

Actions

Multiattack. The chain makes two Slam attacks.

Slam. *Melee Weapon Attack:* +5 to hit, reach 5 ft., one target. *Hit:* 7 (1d8 + 3) bludgeoning damage.

Smother. *Melee Weapon Attack:* +5 to hit, reach 5 ft., one target. *Hit:* 12 (2d8 + 3) bludgeoning damage, and the target is grappled (escape DC 13). Until this grapple ends, the target is restrained, blinded, and at risk of suffocating, and the chain can't smother another target. The chain can still use its Slam while grappling the target.

DEMON-POSSESSED DOLL

Tiny construct, chaotic evil

Armor Class 12
Hit Points 28 (8d4 + 8)
Speed 20 ft.

STR	DEX	CON	INT	WIS	CHA
10 (+0)	14 (+2)	13 (+1)	6 (−2)	5 (−3)	1 (−5)

Skills Perception +1
Damage Immunities necrotic, poison, psychic
Condition Immunities blinded, charmed, deafened, exhaustion, frightened, paralyzed, petrified, poisoned
Senses blindsight 60 ft. (blind beyond this radius), truesight 30 ft., passive Perception 9
Languages understands Common but speaks only through the use of its Mimicry trait
Challenge 1 (200 XP)

Animated Object Theme. The demon-possessed doll's themes are possessed and humanoid. As a possessed animated object, it counts as a fiend for spells and features, such as *protection from evil and good* and a paladin's Divine Sense.

Antimagic Susceptibility. The demon-possessed doll is incapacitated while in the area of an *antimagic field*. If targeted by *dispel magic*, the doll must succeed on a Constitution saving throw against the caster's spell save DC or fall unconscious for 1 minute.

Constructed Nature. An animated object doesn't require air, food, drink, or sleep.

False Appearance. While the demon-possessed doll remains motionless, it is indistinguishable from a normal doll.

Magic Resistance. The demon-possessed doll has advantage on saving throws against spells and other magical effects.

Mimicry. The demon-possessed doll can mimic humanoid voices. A creature that hears the sounds can tell they are imitations with a successful DC 11 Wisdom (Insight) check.

Actions

Multiattack. The demon-possessed doll makes two Slam attacks or two attacks with its Knife. Alternatively, the doll can make one Slam attack and one attack with its Knife.

Slam. *Melee Weapon Attack:* +4 to hit, reach 5 ft., one target. *Hit:* 4 (1d4 + 2) bludgeoning damage.

Knife. *Melee or Ranged Weapon Attack:* +4 to hit, reach 5 ft. or range 20/60 ft., one target. *Hit:* 4 (1d4 + 2) piercing damage.

Reactions

Otherworldly Presence. When a creature the demon-possessed doll can see targets it with an attack, the doll shows a glimpse of the demon possessing it. The attacker must succeed on a DC 11 Wisdom saving throw or the attack misses, and the attacker is frightened until the end of its next turn.

Giant Foo Dog Statue

Huge construct, unaligned

Armor Class 15 (natural armor)
Hit Points 92 (8d12 + 40)
Speed 60 ft.

STR	DEX	CON	INT	WIS	CHA
20 (+5)	16 (+3)	21 (+5)	1 (−5)	5 (−3)	1 (−5)

Skills Perception −1
Damage Resistances bludgeoning, piercing, and slashing from nonmagical attacks
Damage Immunities poison, psychic
Condition Immunities blinded, charmed, deafened, exhaustion, frightened, paralyzed, petrified, poisoned
Senses blindsight 60 ft. (blind beyond this radius), passive Perception 9
Languages —
Challenge 5 (1,800 XP)

Animated Object Theme. The giant foo dog statue's themes are animalistic and fortified.
Antimagic Susceptibility. The giant foo dog statue is incapacitated while in the area of an *antimagic field*. If targeted by *dispel magic*, the statue must succeed on a Constitution saving throw against the caster's spell save DC or fall unconscious for 1 minute.
Blunting Form. Any nonmagical piercing or slashing weapon made of metal that hits the giant foo dog statue begins to dull. After dealing damage, the weapon takes a permanent and cumulative −1 penalty to damage rolls. If its penalty drops to −5, the weapon is too dull to deal damage and can't be used to deal damage again until the creature spends 10 minutes sharpening the weapon.
Constructed Nature. An animated object doesn't require air, food, drink, or sleep.
False Appearance. While the giant foo dog statue remains motionless, it is indistinguishable from a normal statue of a foo dog.

Actions

Multiattack. The giant foo dog statue makes one Bite attack and two Claw attacks.
Bite. *Melee Weapon Attack:* +7 to hit, reach 5 ft., one target. *Hit:* 11 (1d12 + 5) piercing damage.
Claw. *Melee Weapon Attack:* +7 to hit, reach 5 ft., one target. *Hit:* 8 (1d6 + 5) slashing damage.

Jar

Tiny construct, unaligned

Armor Class 14
Hit Points 28 (8d4 + 8)
Speed 20 ft., fly 30 ft. (hover)

STR	DEX	CON	INT	WIS	CHA
10 (+0)	18 (+4)	13 (+1)	1 (−5)	5 (−3)	1 (−5)

Saving Throws Dex +5
Skills Perception −1
Damage Immunities poison, psychic
Condition Immunities blinded, charmed, deafened, exhaustion, frightened, paralyzed, petrified, poisoned
Senses blindsight 60 ft. (blind beyond this radius), passive Perception 9
Languages —
Challenge 1/2 (100 XP)

Animated Object Theme. The jar's theme is paraphernalia.
Antimagic Susceptibility. The jar is incapacitated while in the area of an *antimagic field*. If targeted by *dispel magic*, the jar must succeed on a Constitution saving throw against the caster's spell save DC or fall unconscious for 1 minute.
Constructed Nature. An animated object doesn't require air, food, drink, or sleep.
False Appearance. While the jar remains motionless, it is indistinguishable from a normal jar.

Actions

Multiattack. The jar makes two Slam attacks.
Slam. *Melee Weapon Attack:* +6 to hit, reach 5 ft., one target. *Hit:* 6 (1d4 + 4) bludgeoning, piercing, or slashing damage.

Miniature Red Dragon

Small construct, unaligned

Armor Class 12
Hit Points 44 (8d6 + 16)
Speed 25 ft., fly 30 ft.

STR	DEX	CON	INT	WIS	CHA
14 (+2)	14 (+2)	15 (+2)	1 (−5)	5 (−3)	1 (−5)

Skills Perception −1
Damage Immunities poison, psychic
Condition Immunities blinded, charmed, deafened, exhaustion, frightened, paralyzed, petrified, poisoned
Senses blindsight 60 ft. (blind beyond this radius), passive Perception 9
Languages —
Challenge 2 (450 XP)

Animated Object Theme. The miniature red dragon's themes are animalistic and monstrous.
Antimagic Susceptibility. The miniature red dragon is incapacitated while in the area of an *antimagic field*. If targeted by *dispel magic*, the dragon must succeed on a Constitution saving throw against the caster's spell save DC or fall unconscious for 1 minute.
Constructed Nature. An animated object doesn't require air, food, drink, or sleep.
False Appearance. While the miniature red dragon remains motionless, it is indistinguishable from a figurine of a dragon.
Fiery Contents. The miniature red dragon is filled with magical and chemical substances that keep its body searing to the touch and allow it to breathe fire.
Pervasive Fiery Contents. A creature that touches the miniature red dragon or hits it with a melee attack while within 5 feet of it takes 1 (1d2) fire damage. If the dragon uses its Spew Contents, this trait doesn't function until the end of its next turn.

Actions

Multiattack. The miniature red dragon makes one Bite attack and two Claw attacks.

Bite. *Melee Weapon Attack:* +4 to hit, reach 5 ft., one target. *Hit:* 5 (1d6 + 2) piercing damage.

Claw. *Melee Weapon Attack:* +4 to hit, reach 5 ft., one target. *Hit:* 2 (1d2 + 1) slashing damage.

Spew Contents (recharge 6). The miniature red dragon spews its contents in a 15-foot cone. Each creature in that area must make a DC 12 Dexterity saving throw, taking 14 (4d6) fire damage on a failed save, or half as much damage on a successful one.

Mossy Couch

Large construct, unaligned

Armor Class 13
Hit Points 76 (8d10 + 32)
Speed 30 ft.

STR	DEX	CON	INT	WIS	CHA
18 (+4)	16 (+3)	19 (+4)	1 (−5)	5 (−3)	1 (−5)

Skills Perception −1
Damage Immunities poison, psychic
Condition Immunities blinded, charmed, deafened, exhaustion, frightened, paralyzed, petrified, poisoned
Senses blindsight 60 ft. (blind beyond this radius), passive Perception 9
Languages —
Challenge 3 (700 XP)

Animated Object Theme. The mossy couch's theme is monstrous.

Antimagic Susceptibility. The mossy couch is incapacitated while in the area of an *antimagic field*. If targeted by *dispel magic*, the couch must succeed on a Constitution saving throw against the caster's spell save DC or fall unconscious for 1 minute.

Constructed Nature. An animated object doesn't require air, food, drink, or sleep.

False Appearance. While the mossy couch remains motionless, it is indistinguishable from a normal, moss-covered couch.

Pervasive Poisonous Contents. A creature that touches the mossy couch or hits it with a melee attack while within 5 feet of it takes 2 (1d4) poison damage. If the mossy couch uses its Spew Contents, this trait doesn't function until the end of its next turn.

Poisonous Contents. The mossy couch is filled with a variety of mosses and poisonous molds.

Actions

Multiattack. The mossy couch makes two Slam attacks.

Slam. *Melee Weapon Attack:* +6 to hit, reach 5 ft., one target. *Hit:* 9 (1d10 + 4) bludgeoning damage.

Spew Contents (recharge 6). The mossy couch spews its contents in a 30-foot cone. Each creature in that area must make a DC 14 Dexterity saving throw, taking 22 (4d10) poison damage on a failed save, or half as much damage on a successful one.

Annis Hag

Large fey, neutral evil

Armor Class 16 (natural armor)
Hit Points 119 (14d10 + 42)
Speed 30 ft.

STR	DEX	CON	INT	WIS	CHA
18 (+4)	10 (+0)	16 (+3)	14 (+2)	12 (+1)	16 (+3)

Skills Deception +9, Perception +4, Stealth +3
Senses darkvision 60 ft., passive Perception 14
Languages Common, Deep Speech
Challenge 5 (1,800 XP)

Innate Spellcasting. The annis hag's innate spellcasting ability is Charisma (spell save DC 14). She can innately cast the following spells, requiring no material components:

At will: *minor illusion, prestidigitation, vicious mockery*
2/day each: *invisibility, sleep*
1/day: *major image*

Warty Skin. The annis hag's warty skin is always present, though it changes with her form. Her warty skin might manifest as coarse, bumpy fur if she is an animal, as a hard and lumpy interior if she is a stuffed toy, or as a network of scratches or tarnish if she is an object like a candelabra. Whatever the form the hag takes, a creature that touches her immediately notices the bumpy or scratchy quality and knows the object or animal is not as it appears. Otherwise, a creature must take an action to visually inspect the hag's form and succeed on a DC 20 Intelligence (Investigation) check to discern that the hag is disguised.

Actions

Multiattack (hag form only). The annis hag makes two Claw attacks. She can use her Life Drain in place of one Claw attack.

Claws (hag form only). *Melee Weapon Attack:* +7 to hit, reach 5 ft., one target. *Hit:* 13 (2d8 + 4) slashing damage, and the target is grappled (escape DC 15). The hag has two claws, each of which can grapple only one target.

Life Drain. *Melee Spell Attack:* +6 to hit, reach 5 ft., one creature grappled by the hag. *Hit:* 13 (3d8) necrotic damage. The target must succeed on a DC 15 Constitution saving throw or its hit point maximum is reduced by an amount equal to the damage taken. This reduction lasts until the creature finishes a long rest. The target dies if this effect reduces its hit point maximum to 0.

Change Shape. The annis hag magically polymorphs into a Tiny or Small beast or object, usually a young animal or a child's toy, or back into her true form. Her statistics are the same in each form. Any equipment she is wearing or carrying isn't transformed. She reverts to her true form if she dies.

Apostle

Medium humanoid (any), chaotic evil

Armor Class 13 (natural armor)
Hit Points 97 (15d8 + 30)
Speed 30 ft.

STR	DEX	CON	INT	WIS	CHA
15 (+2)	12 (+1)	15 (+2)	13 (+1)	18 (+4)	9 (−1)

Saving Throws Wis +7, Cha +2
Skills Medicine +7, Religion +4
Damage Resistances necrotic, psychic
Senses passive Perception 14
Languages Common, Tsathar
Challenge 8 (3,900 XP)

Fetid Blessing. Whenever the evangelist deals acid or poison damage, it ignores resistance to those damage types and deals an additional 7 (2d6) damage of the same type.

Spellcasting. The apostle is a 10th-level spellcaster. Its spellcasting ability is Wisdom (spell save DC 15, +7 to hit with spell attacks). It has the following cleric spells prepared.

Cantrips (at will): *acid splash, mending, poison spray, thaumaturgy*
1st level (4 slots): *bane, inflict wounds, protection from evil and good, shield of faith*
2nd level (3 slots): *acid arrow, hold person, lesser restoration, spiritual weapon*
3rd level (3 slots): *caustic burst*[VI], *create food and water, dispel magic, tongue of the frog god*[VI]
4th level (3 slots): *blight, control water*
5th level (2 slots): *insect plague*

Actions

Mace. *Melee Weapon Attack:* +5 to hit, reach 5 ft., one target. *Hit:* 5 (1d6 + 2) bludgeoning damage.

Astral Ronin

Medium aberration, chaotic evil

Armor Class 17 (natural armor)
Hit Points 119 (14d8 + 56)
Speed 30 ft.

STR	DEX	CON	INT	WIS	CHA
18 (+4)	18 (+4)	15 (+2)	13 (+1)	13 (+1)	12 (+1)

Saving Throws Str +7, Con +5, Wis +4
Skills Athletics +6, Perception +3
Damage Resistances bludgeoning, piercing, and slashing from nonmagical attacks
Senses darkvision 60 ft., passive Perception 15
Languages Astral Ronin
Challenge 7 (2,900 XP)

Innate Spellcasting. The astral ronin's innate spellcasting ability is Intelligence (spell save DC 12, +4 to hit with spell attacks). It can innately cast the following spells, requiring no material components.

At will: *light, shocking grasp, true strike*
2/day each: *disguise self, shield, sleep*
1/day each: *darkness, detect thoughts, dimension door, plane shift, see invisibility*

Actions

Multiattack. The astral ronin makes two Longsword attacks. If it has its Shortsword drawn, it can make a Shortsword attack.
Longsword. *Melee Weapon Attack:* +7 to hit, reach 5 ft., one target. *Hit:* 8 (1d8 + 4) slashing damage, or 9 (1d10 + 4) slashing damage if wielded with two hands.
Shortsword. *Melee Weapon Attack:* +7 to hit, reach 5 ft., one target. *Hit:* 7 (1d6 + 4) piercing damage.

Baladar the Ranger

Medium humanoid (human), neutral good

Armor Class 15 (chain shirt)
Hit Points 91 (14d8 + 28)
Speed 30 ft.

STR	DEX	CON	INT	WIS	CHA
16 (+3)	18 (+4)	15 (+2)	8 (−1)	14 (+2)	9 (−1)

Saving Throws Dex +7
Skills Nature +5, Perception +5, Stealth +7, Survival +8
Senses passive Perception 15
Languages Common, Giant
Challenge 5 (1,800 XP)

Ambusher. Baladar has advantage on attack rolls against any creature he has surprised.

Hunter's Grace. If Baladar hits a creature with a ranged attack and then moves at least 10 feet straight toward the creature, Baladar can make one dagger attack against the creature as a bonus action.

Actions

Multiattack. Baladar makes three Longbow attacks. Alternatively, he can make three Longsword attacks. If all three Longsword attacks hit the same target, the target must succeed on a DC 15 Constitution saving throw or take an additional 9 (2d8) slashing damage.
Dagger. *Melee or Ranged Weapon Attack:* +7 to hit, reach 5 ft. or range 20/60 ft., one target. *Hit:* 6 (1d4 + 4) piercing damage.
Longsword. *Melee Weapon Attack:* +6 to hit, reach 5 ft., one target. *Hit:* 7 (1d8 + 3) slashing damage, or 8 (1d10 + 3) slashing damage if used with two hands.
Longbow. *Ranged Weapon Attack:* +7 to hit, range 150/600 ft., one target. *Hit:* 8 (1d8 + 4) piercing damage.

Bloody Bones

Medium undead, neutral evil

Armor Class 12
Hit Points 78 (12d8 + 24)
Speed 30 ft.

STR	DEX	CON	INT	WIS	CHA
17 (+3)	14 (+2)	15 (+2)	8 (−1)	12 (+1)	9 (−1)

Saving Throws Wis +3
Damage Immunities poison

Condition Immunities poisoned
Senses darkvision 60 ft., passive Perception 11
Languages the languages it knew in life
Challenge 4 (1,100 XP)

Bloody Regeneration. When the bloody bones doesn't have all of its hit points, it seeps blood from its pores. At the start of its turn if it is seeping blood from its pores, it regains 5 hit points. If the bloody bones takes radiant damage, this trait doesn't function at the start of the bloody bones' next turn. The bloody bones dies only if it starts its turn with 0 hit points and doesn't regenerate.

Undead Nature. A bloody bones doesn't require air, food, drink, or sleep.

Actions

Multiattack. The bloody bones makes two Bloody Fist attacks.

Bloody Fist. *Melee Weapon Attack:* +5 to hit, reach 5 ft., one target. *Hit:* 6 (1d6 + 3) bludgeoning damage plus 4 (1d8) poison damage.

Blood Spray (recharge 5–6). If the bloody bones doesn't have all of its hit points, it sprays blood in a 30-foot cone. Each creature in that area must make a DC 13 Dexterity saving throw. On a failure, a creature takes 18 (4d8) poison damage and is poisoned for 1 minute. On a success, a creature takes half the damage and isn't poisoned.

BRAIN OF AN IMPRISONED DEMON

Tiny fiend, chaotic evil

Armor Class 15 (natural armor)
Hit Points 103 (23d4 + 46)
Speed 5 ft.

STR	DEX	CON	INT	WIS	CHA
5 (−3)	16 (+3)	14 (+2)	21 (+5)	15 (+2)	17 (+3)

Saving Throws Con +5, Int +9, Wis +6
Skills Arcana +13, Deception +7, History +13, Persuasion +7
Damage Resistances cold, fire, lightning; bludgeoning, piercing, and slashing from nonmagical attacks
Damage Immunities poison
Condition Immunities poisoned
Senses blindsight 90 ft. (blind beyond this radius), passive Perception 12
Languages all, telepathy 120 ft.
Challenge 10 (5,900 XP)

Innate Spellcasting (psionics). The brain's innate spellcasting ability is Intelligence (spell save DC 17, +9 to hit with spell attacks). It can innately cast the following spells, requiring no components.

At will: *mage hand, levitate, prestidigitation, telekinesis*
3/day each: *arcane eye, confusion*
1/day: *dominate person*

Shielded Mind. The brain is immune to scrying and to any effect that would sense its emotions, read its thoughts, or detect its location.

Actions

Multiattack. The brain uses its Brain Lock and makes three Mental Blast attacks.

Mental Blast. *Ranged Spell Attack:* +9 to hit, range 90 ft., one target. *Hit:* 18 (4d8) psychic damage.

Brain Lock. The brain targets one creature it can see within 30 feet. That creature must succeed on a DC 17 Intelligence saving throw or its Intelligence score is reduced by 1d4. The target is incapacitated if this reduces its Intelligence to 0. Otherwise, the reduction lasts until the target finishes a short or long rest.

Concussion (recharge 5–6). The brain chooses a point it can see within 90 feet of it. Each creature within 10 feet of that point must make a DC 17 Dexterity saving throw, taking 45 (10d8) thunder damage on a failed save, or half as much damage on a successful one. If a creature fails the saving throw by 5 or more, it is also knocked prone.

BROTHER

Medium humanoid (human), chaotic neutral

Armor Class 9
Hit Points 84 (13d8 + 26)
Speed 20 ft.

STR	DEX	CON	INT	WIS	CHA
16 (+3)	8 (−1)	14 (+2)	7 (−2)	12 (+1)	13 (+1)

Saving Throws Con +3
Skills Athletics +5, Deception +5
Damage Immunities poison
Condition Immunities poisoned
Senses passive Perception 11
Languages Common
Challenge 4 (1,100 XP)

Shriveled Lung Carrier. A creature that touches Brother or hits him with a melee attack while within 5 feet of him takes 3 (1d6) necrotic damage and must succeed on a DC 13 Constitution saving throw or contract a disease. At the end of each hour, the diseased creature must succeed on a DC 13 Constitution saving throw or it takes 7 (2d6) necrotic damage as its lungs deteriorate from the inside out. The creature's hit point maximum is reduced by an amount equal to the damage taken. This reduction lasts until the disease is cured. When the diseased creature's hit point maximum is reduced to 10 or fewer, it begins to run out of breath and must hold its breath. While holding its breath, the diseased creature must succeed on a DC 13 Constitution saving throw at the end of each minute or reduce the remaining time it can hold its breath by 30 seconds. The creature is reduced to 0 hit points and is dying if it runs out of breath. The disease lasts until removed by the *lesser restoration* spell (or similar magic) or until the diseased target makes two consecutive successful saving throws.

Actions

Slam. *Melee Weapon Attack:* +5 to hit, reach 5 ft., one target. *Hit:* 6 (1d6 + 3) bludgeoning damage plus 10 (3d6) necrotic damage. If the target is a Medium or smaller creature, it is grappled (escape DC 13). Until this grapple ends, the target is restrained, and Brother can't use his slam attack against another target.

Breathe Death. Brother breathes in the face of a creature he is grappling. The target takes 14 (4d6) necrotic damage and must succeed on a DC 13 Constitution saving throw or become infected with the shriveled lung disease (see the Shriveled Lung Carrier trait).

Captain

Medium humanoid (any race), any alignment

Armor Class 18 (chain mail and shield)
Hit Points 65 (10d8+20)
Speed 30 ft.

STR	DEX	CON	INT	WIS	CHA
18 (+4)	10 (+0)	15 (+2)	12 (+1)	12 (+1)	16 (+3)

Saving Throws Str +6, Con +4
Skills Athletics +6, Perception +5, Intimidation +7
Senses passive Perception 15
Languages Common, Dwarven
Challenge 4 (1,100 XP)

Brave. The captain has advantage on all saving throws against fear.
Leadership (recharges after a short or long rest). For 1 minute, the captain can utter a special command or warning whenever a nonhostile creature that it can see within 30 feet of it makes an attack roll or a saving throw. The creature can add a d4 to its roll provided it can hear and understand the captain. A creature can benefit from only one Leadership die at a time. This effect ends if the captain is incapacitated.

Actions

Multiattack. The captain makes three melee attacks.
Longsword. *Melee Weapon Attack:* +6 to hit, reach 5 ft., one target. *Hit:* 8 (1d8 + 4) slashing damage, or 9 (1d10 + 4) if used with two hands.
Heavy Crossbow. *Ranged Weapon Attack:* +2 to hit, range 100/400, one target. *Hit:* 5 (1d10) piercing damage.

Coffer Corpse

Medium undead, neutral evil

Armor Class 13 (natural armor)
Hit Points 26 (4d8 + 8)
Speed 30 ft.

STR	DEX	CON	INT	WIS	CHA
15 (+2)	12 (+1)	14 (+2)	5 (−3)	8 (−1)	5 (−3)

Saving Throws Wis +1
Skills Perception +1
Damage Immunities poison
Condition Immunities poisoned
Senses darkvision 60 ft., passive Perception 11
Languages understands the languages it knew in life but can't speak
Challenge 1 (200 XP)

Blood Frenzy. The coffer corpse has advantage on melee attack rolls against any creature that doesn't have all its hit points.
Sense Blood. The coffer corpse can pinpoint, by scent, the location of creatures with blood within 60 feet of it.
Undead Nature. A coffer corpse doesn't require air, food, drink, or sleep.

Actions

Multiattack. The coffer corpse makes two attacks, only one of which can be a Bite attack.

Slam. *Melee Weapon Attack:* +4 to hit, reach 5 ft., one target. *Hit:* 5 (1d6 + 2) bludgeoning damage, and the target is grappled (escape DC 12). A coffer corpse can have only one creature grappled at a time.
Bite. *Melee Weapon Attack:* +4 to hit, reach 5 ft., one willing creature, or a creature that is grappled by the coffer corpse, incapacitated, or restrained. *Hit:* 4 (1d4 + 2) piercing damage plus 2 (1d4) necrotic damage. The target's hit point maximum is reduced by an amount equal to the necrotic damage taken. The reduction lasts until the target finishes a long rest. The target dies if this effect reduces its hit point maximum to 0.

Commoner, Greater

Medium humanoid (any), any

Armor Class 12
Hit Points 39 (6d8 + 12)
Speed 30 ft.

STR	DEX	CON	INT	WIS	CHA
16 (+3)	16 (+3)	14 (+2)	10 (+0)	12 (+1)	10 (+0)

Skills Athletics +5, Survival +3
Senses passive Perception 11
Languages Common
Challenge 1/2 (100 XP)

Actions

Multiattack. The greater commoner makes two Improvised Weapon attacks (either melee or ranged).
Improvised Melee Weapon. *Melee Weapon Attack:* +5 to hit, reach 5 ft., one target. *Hit:* 6 (1d6 + 3) bludgeoning, piercing, or slashing damage.
Improvised Ranged Weapon. *Ranged Weapon Attack:* +5 to hit, range 20 ft., one target. *Hit:* 5 (1d4 + 3) bludgeoning, piercing, or slashing damage.

Commoner, Hardy

Medium humanoid (any), any

Armor Class 12
Hit Points 22 (4d8 + 4)
Speed 30 ft.

STR	DEX	CON	INT	WIS	CHA
14 (+2)	14 (+2)	12 (+1)	10 (+0)	12 (+1)	10 (+0)

Skills Athletics +4, Survival +2
Senses passive Perception 11
Languages Common
Challenge 1/4 (50 XP)

Actions

Improvised Melee Weapon. *Melee Weapon Attack:* +4 to hit, reach 5 ft., one target. *Hit:* 5 (1d6 + 2) bludgeoning, piercing, or slashing damage.
Improvised Ranged Weapon. *Ranged Weapon Attack:* +4 to hit, range 20 ft., one target. *Hit:* 4 (1d4 + 2) bludgeoning, piercing, or slashing damage.

Crystal Basilisk

Medium monstrosity, unaligned

Armor Class 15 (natural armor)
Hit Points 112 (15d8 + 45)
Speed 20 ft.

STR	DEX	CON	INT	WIS	CHA
18 (+4)	8 (−1)	16 (+3)	2 (−4)	10 (+0)	7 (−2)

Saving Throws Dex +2
Damage Vulnerabilities thunder
Damage Resistances bludgeoning, piercing, and slashing damage from nonmagical attacks
Damage Immunities radiant
Condition Immunities blinded
Senses darkvision 60 ft., passive Perception 10
Languages —
Challenge 6 (2,300 XP)

Crystallizing Gaze. If a creature starts its turn within 30 feet of the crystal basilisk and the two of them can see each other, the crystal basilisk can force the creature to make a DC 14 Constitution saving throw if the crystal basilisk isn't incapacitated. On a failed save, the creature magically begins to turn to crystal and is restrained. It must repeat the saving throw at the end of its next turn. On a success, the effect ends. On a failure, the creature is petrified until freed by the *greater restoration* spell or other magic.

A creature that isn't surprised can avert its eyes to avoid the saving throw at the start of its turn. If it does so, it can't see the basilisk until the start of its next turn, when it can avert its eyes again. If it looks at the crystal basilisk in the meantime, it must immediately make the save.

Actions

Multiattack. The crystal basilisk makes two Bite attacks.
Bite. *Melee Weapon Attack:* +7 to hit, reach 5 ft., one target. *Hit:* 11 (2d6 + 4) piercing damage plus 3 (1d6) radiant damage.
Shard Breath (recharge 5–6). The crystal basilisk exhales crystal shards in a 30-foot cone. Each creature in that area must make a DC 15 Dexterity saving throw, taking 28 (8d6) piercing damage on a failed save, or half as much damage on a successful one.

Crystal Basilisk Blood

Wondrous item, very rare

The blood of a crystal basilisk imbues a gemstone worth at least 50 gp with rainbow radiance. If a gemstone is soaked in one gallon of crystal basilisk blood for 24 hours, the gemstone becomes a *gem of brightness* with 50 charges. A successful DC 15 Dexterity or Intelligence check using alchemist's supplies harvests 1 gallon of blood from a freshly-slain crystal basilisk. If the check succeeds by 5 or more, the harvested amount increases to 2 gallons. The blood congeals after it imbues a gemstone with radiance and can't be used to make another gemstone.

Reactions

Crystalline Hide. When a creature hits the crystal basilisk with a nonmagical metal weapon while within 5 feet of the crystal basilisk, the crystal basilisk can toughen its skin to crystalline hardness. The attacker must succeed on a DC 15 Dexterity saving throw or the crystal basilisk deflects the damage from the attack and the attacker is blinded until the end of its next turn as the weapon sparks on the basilisk's hide.

Demon, Cambion

Medium fiend (demon), chaotic evil

Armor Class 14 (natural armor)
Hit Points 45 (7d8 + 14)
Speed 30 ft.

STR	DEX	CON	INT	WIS	CHA
15 (+2)	13 (+1)	14 (+2)	13 (+1)	12 (+1)	14 (+2)

Damage Resistances acid, cold, fire
Damage Immunities lightning, poison
Condition Immunities poisoned
Senses darkvision 60 ft., passive Perception
Languages Abyssal, Common, telepathy 30 ft.
Challenge 2 (450 XP)

Innate Spellcasting. The cambion's innate spellcasting ability is Charisma (spell save DC 12). It can cast the following spells, requiring no material components.
3/day: *command*
1/day each: *charm person, enthrall*

Actions

Multiattack. The cambion makes two weapon attacks.
Claw. *Melee Weapon Attack:* +4 to hit, reach 5 ft., one target. *Hit:* 4 (1d4 + 2) slashing damage.
Scimitar. *Melee Weapon Attack:* +4 to hit, reach 5 ft., one target. *Hit:* 5 (1d6 + 2) slashing damage.
Longbow. *Melee Weapon Attack:* +3 to hit, range 150/600 ft., one target. *Hit:* 5 (1d8 + 1) piercing damage.

Demon, Geruzou

Small fiend (demon), chaotic evil

Armor Class 15 (natural armor)
Hit Points 31 (7d6 + 7)
Speed 30 ft., fly 50 ft.

STR	DEX	CON	INT	WIS	CHA
12 (+1)	15 (+2)	12 (+1)	8 (−1)	8 (−1)	10 (+0)

Skills Perception +1, Stealth +4
Damage Resistances cold, fire, lightning
Damage Immunities poison
Condition Immunities poisoned
Senses darkvision 60 ft., passive Perception 11
Languages Abyssal, common; telepathy 100 ft.
Challenge 2 (450 XP)

Innate Spellcasting. The demon's spellcasting ability is Charisma (spell save DC 10, +2 to hit with spell attacks). The demon can innately cast the following spells at will, requiring no material components: *darkness, detect evil and good, invisibility* (self only)

Magic Resistance. The demon has advantage on saving throws against spells and other magical effects.

Magic Weapons. The demon's weapon attacks are magical.

Slimy Hide. The demon's hide is extremely slick and oozes with slime. Creatures attempting to grapple the demon do so with disadvantage.

Actions

Multiattack. The demon makes one Bite attack and two Claw attacks. It can use its Spit Slime in place of the Bite.

Bite. *Melee Weapon Attack:* +4 to hit, reach 5 ft., one target. *Hit:* 5 (1d6 + 2) piercing damage.

Claw. *Melee Weapon Attack:* +4 to hit, reach 5 ft., one target. *Hit:* 5 (1d6 + 2) slashing damage.

Spit Slime. *Ranged Weapon Attack:* +4 to hit, range 20/60 ft., one target. *Hit:* 10 (3d6) acid damage and the target must succeed on a DC 13 Constitution saving throw or its speed is reduced by half until the end of the demon's next turn.

Teleport. The Geruzou magically teleports, along with any equipment it is wearing or carrying, up to 30 feet to an unoccupied space it can see.

DEMON, GIBBON

Medium fiend (demon), chaotic evil

Armor Class 14
Hit Points 52 (7d8 + 21)
Speed 30 ft., climb 40 ft.

STR	DEX	CON	INT	WIS	CHA
12 (+1)	18 (+4)	16 (+3)	8 (−1)	14 (+2)	8 (−1)

Saving Throws Dex +6
Skills Acrobatics +6, Perception +4
Damage Resistances cold, fire, lightning
Damage Immunities poison
Condition Immunities poisoned
Senses darkvision 120 ft., passive Perception 14
Languages Abyssal, telepathy 120 ft.
Challenge 4 (1,100 XP)

Innate Spellcasting. The gibbon demon's spellcasting ability is Wisdom (spell save DC 12). The gibbon demon can innately cast the following spells, requiring no material components:
At will: *detect magic, feather fall*
2/day each: *enlarge/reduce* (self only), *invisibility* (self only)
1/day: *spike growth*

Nimble Climber. While climbing, the demon can take the Dash or Disengage action as a bonus action on each of its turns.

Standing Leap. The gibbon's long jump is up to 20 feet and its high jump is up to 10 feet, with or without a running start.

Actions

Multiattack. The gibbon demon makes one attack with its Bite and two with its Fists.

Bite. *Melee Weapon Attack:* +6 to hit, reach 5 ft., one target. *Hit:* 9 (2d4 + 4) piercing damage.

Fist. *Melee Weapon Attack:* +6 to hit, reach 5 ft., one target. *Hit:* 7 (1d6 + 4) bludgeoning damage.

Putrid Roar (recharge 5–6). The gibbon demon expands its throat sac and roars in a 30-foot cone. Each creature in that area that can hear the gibbon demon must make a DC 14 Dexterity saving throw. On a failure, a creature takes 21 (6d6) thunder damage and is poisoned for 1 minute. On a success, a creature takes half the damage and isn't poisoned. A poisoned creature can repeat the saving throw at the end of each of its turns, ending the effect on itself on a success.

DEMON, GUARDIAN

Large fiend (demon), neutral evil

Armor Class 15 (natural armor)
Hit Points 85 (10d10 + 30)
Speed 30 ft.

STR	DEX	CON	INT	WIS	CHA
18 (+4)	12 (+1)	16 (+3)	12 (+1)	14 (+2)	14 (+2)

Skills Perception +5
Damage Resistances cold, fire, lightning
Damage Immunities poison
Condition Immunities poisoned
Senses darkvision 120 ft., passive Perception 15
Languages Abyssal, telepathy 120 ft.
Challenge 7 (2,900 XP)

Magic Resistance. The demon has advantage on saving throws against spells and other magical effects.

Magic Weapons. The demon's weapon attacks are magical.

Actions

Multiattack. The demon makes one Bite attack and two Claw attacks.

Bite. *Melee Weapon Attack:* +7 to hit, reach 5 ft., one target. *Hit:* 13 (2d8 + 4) piercing damage.

Claw. *Melee Weapon Attack:* +7 to hit, reach 5 ft., one target. *Hit:* 14 (3d6 + 4) slashing damage.

Flame Breath (recharge 5–6). The demon exhales fire in a 30-foot cone. Each creature in that area must make a DC 15 Dexterity saving throw, taking 28 (8d6) fire damage on a failed save, or half as much damage on a successful one.

DEMON, KYTHA

Medium fiend (demon), chaotic evil

Armor Class 16 (natural armor)
Hit Points 97 (15d8 + 30)
Speed 40 ft.

STR	DEX	CON	INT	WIS	CHA
17 (+3)	16 (+3)	15 (+2)	12 (+1)	15 (+2)	18 (+4)

Saving Throws Str +7, Con +6, Wis +6
Damage Resistances cold, fire, lightning; bludgeoning, piercing, and slashing from nonmagical attacks
Damage Immunities poison
Condition Immunities poisoned
Senses darkvision 120 ft., passive Perception 12
Languages Abyssal, Celestial, Draconic, telepathy 120 ft.
Challenge 9 (5,000 XP)

Keen Scent. The kytha has advantage on Wisdom (Perception) checks based on scent.

Innate Spellcasting. The kytha's innate spellcasting ability is Charisma (spell save DC 16). It can cast the following spells, requiring no material components.

At will: *darkness*

3/day: *silence*

1/day: *hold person*

Magic Resistance. The kytha has advantage on saving throws against spells and other magical effects.

Actions

Multiattack. The kytha makes two Claw attacks, and one Bite or Tongue attack.

Bite. *Melee Weapon Attack:* +7 to hit, reach 5 ft., one creature. *Hit:* 13 (3d6 + 3) piercing damage plus 10 (3d6) poison damage.

Claw. *Melee Weapon Attack:* +7 to hit, reach 5 ft., one target. *Hit:* 12 (2d8 + 3) slashing damage.

Tongue. *Melee Weapon Attack:* +7 to hit, reach 10 ft., one creature. *Hit:* 7 (1d8 + 3) bludgeoning damage plus 10 (3d6) poison damage.

Summon (1/day). The kytha has a 40% chance to summon 1d2 **vrock demons** or a 30% chance to summon 1 **kytha**[II]. The summoned demons appear in an unoccupied space within 60 feet of the summoner and can't summon other demons. The summoned creatures remain for 1 minute, until the summoner or the summoned demons are slain, or until the summoner takes an action to dismiss it.

DEMON, KIMARIS

Medium fiend (demon), chaotic evil

Armor Class 18 (natural armor)
Hit Points 157 (21d8 + 63)
Speed 30 ft., fly 60 ft.

STR	DEX	CON	INT	WIS	CHA
18 (+4)	17 (+3)	16 (+3)	20 (+5)	15 (+2)	18 (+4)

Saving Throws Str +9, Con +8, Int +10, Wis +7
Skills Arcana +10, History +10, Nature +10, Perception +12
Damage Resistances cold, fire, lightning; bludgeoning, piercing, and slashing from nonmagical attacks
Damage Immunities poison
Condition Immunities poisoned
Senses darkvision 120 ft., passive Perception 22
Languages Abyssal, Celestial, Draconic, telepathy 120 ft.
Challenge 13 (10,000 XP)

Flyby. The kimaris doesn't provoke opportunity attacks when it flies out of an enemy's reach.

Innate Spellcasting. The kimaris' innate spellcasting ability is Charisma (spell save DC 17). It can cast the following spells, requiring no material components.

At will: *detect magic, magic missile*

3/day each: *gust of wind, see invisibility*

1/day each: *dispel magic, plane shift* (self only)

Keen Hearing and Sight. The kimaris has advantage on Wisdom (Perception) checks that rely on hearing or sight.

Magic Resistance. The kimaris demon has advantage on saving throws against spells and other effects.

Spellcasting. The kimaris is a 10th-level spellcaster. Its spellcasting ability is Intelligence (spell save DC 18, +10 to hit with spell attacks). It has the following wizard spells prepared.

Cantrips (at will): *acid splash, mage hand, mending, ray of frost, shocking grasp*

1st level (4 slots): *comprehend languages, identify, shield, thunderwave*

2nd level (3 slots): *blindness/deafness, detect thoughts, shatter, suggestion*

3rd level (3 slots): *counterspell, lightning bolt, slow*

4th level (3 slots): *dimension door, ice storm*

5th level (2 slots): *cone of cold, legend lore*

Actions

Multiattack. The kimaris demon makes two Talon attacks.

Talons. *Melee Weapon Attack:* +9 to hit, reach 5 ft., one target. *Hit:* 11 (2d6 + 4) slashing damage.

DEMON, LESSER BALOR

Large fiend (demon), chaotic evil

Armor Class 16 (natural armor)
Hit Points 189 (18d10 + 90)
Speed 30 ft., fly 60 ft.

STR	DEX	CON	INT	WIS	CHA
22 (+6)	15 (+2)	20 (+5)	18 (+4)	16 (+3)	20 (+5)

Saving Throws Con +9, Wis +7
Damage Resistances cold, lightning; bludgeoning, piercing, and slashing from nonmagical attacks
Damage Immunities fire, poison
Condition Immunities poisoned
Senses truesight 60 ft., passive Perception 13
Languages Abyssal, telepathy 120 ft.
Challenge 11 (7,200 XP)

Fire Aura. At the start of each of the lesser balor's turns, each creature within 5 feet of it takes 10 (3d6) fire damage, and flammable objects in the aura that aren't being worn or carried ignite. A creature that touches the lesser balor or hits it with a melee attack while within 5 feet of it takes 10 (3d6) fire damage.

Magic Resistance. The lesser balor has advantage on saving throws against spells and other magical effects.

Magic Weapons. The lesser balor's weapon attacks are magical.

Actions

Multiattack. The lesser balor makes one Whip attack and one Longsword attack.

Whip. *Melee Weapon Attack:* +10 to hit, reach 20 ft., one target. *Hit:* 11 (2d4 + 6) slashing damage plus 10 (3d6) fire damage, and the target must succeed on a DC 18 Strength saving throw or be pulled up to 15 feet toward the lesser balor.

Longsword. *Melee Weapon Attack:* +10 to hit, reach 5 ft., one target. *Hit:* 15 (2d8 + 6) slashing damage, or 17 (2d10 + 6) slashing damage if used with two hands, plus 13 (3d8) lightning damage.

Summon Demon (1/day). The lesser balor has a 50 percent chance of summoning 1d4 gibbon demons, 1d2 trickster demons, or one hezrou.

Demon, Trickster

Medium fiend (demon), chaotic evil

Armor Class 15 (natural armor)
Hit Points 84 (13d8 + 26)
Speed 30 ft.

STR	DEX	CON	INT	WIS	CHA
8 (−1)	16 (+3)	14 (+2)	13 (+1)	10 (+0)	19 (+4)

Saving Throws Dex +6, Int +4, Wis +3
Skills Deception +7, Stealth +6
Damage Resistances cold, fire, lightning; bludgeoning, piercing, and slashing from nonmagical attacks
Damage Immunities poison
Condition Immunities charmed, poisoned
Senses darkvision 120 ft., passive Perception 10
Languages Abyssal, telepathy 120 ft.
Challenge 6 (2,300 XP)

Innate Spellcasting. The trickster demon's spellcasting ability is Charisma (spell save DC 15). The trickster demon can innately cast the following spells, requiring no material components:

At will: *charm person, mage hand, minor illusion*
2/day each: *alter self, mirror image, sleep*
1/day each: *major image, mislead*

Magic Resistance. The trickster demon has advantage on saving throws against spells and other magical effects.

Shadow Stealth. While in dim light or darkness, the trickster demon can take the Hide action as a bonus action.

Actions

Multiattack. The trickster demon makes two Disfiguring Touch attacks.

Disfiguring Touch. *Melee Weapon Attack:* +6 to hit, reach 5 ft., creature. *Hit:* 17 (4d6 + 3) necrotic damage, and the target's Charisma score is reduced by 1d4. The target is incapacitated if this reduces its Charisma to 0. Otherwise, the reduction lasts until the target finishes a short or long rest.

Reactions

Clumsy Advance. When a creature the trickster demon can see moves within 10 feet of the demon, the creature must succeed on a DC 15 Dexterity saving throw or be knocked prone as it trips over its own feet, over a sudden flaw in the ground where it walks, or experiences some other clumsy stumble as it moves toward the demon.

Demon Spider

Large beast, chaotic evil

Armor Class 16 (natural armor)
Hit Points 73 (6d10 + 18)
Speed 30 ft., climb 30 ft.

STR	DEX	CON	INT	WIS	CHA
10 (+0)	17 (+3)	16 (+3)	5 (−3)	12 (+1)	3 (−4)

Skills Stealth +9
Damage Immunities poison
Condition Immunities poisoned

Senses blindsight 10 ft., darkvision 60 ft., passive Perception 11
Languages —
Challenge 6 (2,300 XP)

Spider Climb. The spider can climb difficult surfaces, including upside down on ceilings, without needing to make an ability check.

Web Sense. While in contact with a web, the spider knows the exact location of any other creature in contact with the same web.

Web Walker. The spider ignores movement restrictions caused by webbing.

Actions

Bite. *Melee Weapon Attack:* +6 to hit, reach 5 ft., one creature. *Hit:* 12 (2d8 + 3) piercing damage, and the target must make a DC 14 Constitution saving throw, taking 28 (8d6) poison damage on a failed save, or half as much damage on a successful one. If the poison damage reduces the target to 0 hit points, the target is stable but poisoned for 1 hour, even after regaining hit points, and is paralyzed while poisoned in this way.

Web (recharge 5–6). *Ranged Weapon Attack:* +6 to hit, range 30/60 ft., one creature. *Hit:* The target is restrained by webbing. As an action, the restrained target can make a DC 14 Strength check, bursting the webbing on a success. The webbing can also be attacked and destroyed (AC 10; hp 5; vulnerability to fire damage; immunity to bludgeoning, poison, and psychic damage).

Dire Weasel

Large beast, unaligned

Armor Class 12
Hit Points 39 (6d10 + 6)
Speed 40 ft.

STR	DEX	CON	INT	WIS	CHA
16 (+3)	14 (+2)	13 (+1)	4 (−3)	12 (+1)	5 (−3)

Saving Throws Con +2
Skills Perception +3, Stealth +6

Senses darkvision 60 ft., passive Perception 13
Languages —
Challenge 2 (450 XP)

Keen Hearing and Smell. The dire weasel has advantage on Wisdom (Perception) checks that rely on hearing or smell.

Weasel Musk. Any creature that starts its turn within 5 feet of the dire weasel must succeed on a DC 11 Constitution saving throw or be poisoned until the start of its next turn. On a successful saving throw, the creature is immune to the dire weasel's Weasel Musk for 24 hours. Mongooses, weasels, and similar beasts are immune to this trait.

Actions

Multiattack. The dire weasel makes one attack with its Bite and one attack with its Claws.

Bite. *Melee Weapon Attack:* +5 to hit, reach 5 ft., one target. *Hit:* 8 (2d4 + 3) piercing damage.

Claws. *Melee Weapon Attack:* +5 to hit, reach 5 ft., one target. *Hit:* 5 (1d4 + 3) slashing damage.

DISCIPLE

Medium humanoid (any), any neutral alignment

Armor Class 16 (natural armor)
Hit Points 60 (11d8 + 11)
Speed 40 ft.

STR	DEX	CON	INT	WIS	CHA
10 (+0)	16 (+3)	13 (+1)	11 (+0)	16 (+3)	10 (+0)

Saving Throws Dex +5, Wis +5
Skills Acrobatics +5, History +2, Stealth +5
Senses passive Perception 13
Languages Common, plus 1 other language
Challenge 3 (700 XP)

Slow Fall. The disciple reduces any falling damage by 30. If it does not take damage from a fall, it does not drop prone.

Actions

Multiattack. The disciple can make two attacks with its dagger and one with its unarmed strike, or three attacks with its unarmed strike. It can use its Flurry of Blows ability in place of one of the unarmed strikes.

Quarterstaff. *Melee Weapon Attack:* +5 to hit, reach 5 ft., one target. *Hit:* 6 (1d6 + 3) bludgeoning damage, or 7 (1d8 + 3) bludgeoning damage if wielded with two hands.

Unarmed Strike. *Melee Weapon Attack:* +5 to hit, reach 5 ft., one target. *Hit:* 6 (1d6 + 3) bludgeoning damage.

Sling. *Ranged Weapon Attack:* +5 to hit, range 30/120 ft., one target. *Hit:* 6 (1d6 + 3) bludgeoning damage.

Flurry of Blows (3/day). *Melee Weapon Attack:* +5 to hit, reach 5 ft., one target. *Hit:* 13 (3d6 + 3) bludgeoning damage, and the target suffers one of the following effects of the disciple's choice:
• The target must succeed on a DC 13 Dexterity saving throw or be knocked prone.
• The target must make a DC 13 Strength saving throw or be pushed up to 15 feet away from the disciple.
• The target can't take reactions until the end of the disciple's next turn.

Reactions

Deflect Missiles. If the disciple has at least one hand free, it can use its reaction in response to being hit with a ranged weapon attack. It reduces the damage by 14 (1d10 + 8). If it reduces the damage to 0, it can catch the missile if it is small enough for it to hold with one hand.

ELDRITCH ARCHER

Medium humanoid (elf), neutral

Armor Class 16 (chain mail)
Hit Points 88 (16d8 + 16)
Speed 30 ft.

STR	DEX	CON	INT	WIS	CHA
12 (+1)	20 (+5)	13 (+1)	16 (+3)	16 (+3)	12 (+1)

Saving Throws Dex +8, Int +6
Skills Perception +6, Stealth +8, Survival +6
Senses darkvision 60 ft., passive Perception 16
Languages Common, Elven
Challenge 7 (2,900 XP)

Eldritch Arrow. Once per turn, the eldritch archer can apply an eldritch effect to an arrow fired from its longbow. The eldritch effect does 4 (1d8) damage. The damage type can be either acid, cold, fire, lightning, or poison.

Fey Ancestry. The elf has advantage on saving throws against being charmed, and magic can't put the elf to sleep.

Keen Hearing and Sight. The elf has advantage on Wisdom (Perception) checks related to hearing or sight.

Spellcasting. The eldritch archer is a 5th-level spellcaster. Its spellcasting ability is Intelligence (spell save DC 14, +6 to hit with spell attacks). It can cast the following spells:
Cantrips (at will): *fire bolt, mage hand, mending, prestidigitation*
1st level (4 slots): *burning hands, expeditious retreat, shield*
2nd level (3 slots): *darkness, enhance ability, silence*
3rd level (2 slots): *blink, gaseous form*

Actions

Multiattack. The eldritch archer makes two melee or three ranged weapon attacks.

Rapier. *Melee Weapon Attack:* +8 to hit, reach 5 ft., one target. *Hit:* 9 (1d8 + 5) piercing damage.

+2 Longbow. *Ranged Weapon Attack:* +10 to hit, range 150/600 ft., one target. *Hit:* 11 (1d8 + 7) piercing damage.

ENORMOUS CENTIPEDE

Medium beast, unaligned

Armor Class 13 (natural armor)
Hit Points 38 (7d8 + 7)
Speed 30 ft., climb 30 ft.

STR	DEX	CON	INT	WIS	CHA
16 (+3)	14 (+2)	12 (+1)	1 (−5)	7 (−2)	3 (−4)

Skills Stealth +4
Damage Resistances poison
Condition Immunities poisoned
Senses blindsight 60 ft., passive Perception 8

Languages —
Challenge 2 (450 XP)

Ambusher. The enormous centipede has advantage on attack
rolls against any creature it has surprised.

Actions

Bite. *Melee Weapon Attack:* +5 to hit, reach 5 ft., one creature.
Hit: 8 (2d4 + 3) piercing damage, and the target must succeed
on a DC 12 Constitution saving throw or take 10 (3d6) poison
damage. If the poison damage reduces the target to 0 hit points,
the target is stable but poisoned for 1 hour, even after regaining
hit points, and is paralyzed while poisoned in this way.

Hundred Leg Grab (recharge 6). The enormous centipede
wraps itself around creatures within 5 feet of it. Each creature
in that area must make a DC 12 Dexterity saving throw. On
a failure, a creature takes 14 (4d6) piercing damage and, if
it is Medium or smaller, it is grappled (escape DC 13). Until
this grapple ends, the target is restrained, and the enormous
centipede can automatically hit the target with its bite. On a
success, a creature takes half the damage and isn't grappled.

Evangelist

Medium humanoid (any), chaotic evil

Armor Class 12 (natural armor)
Hit Points 60 (11d8 + 11)
Speed 30 ft.

STR	DEX	CON	INT	WIS	CHA
14 (+2)	11 (+0)	12 (+1)	11 (+0)	16 (+3)	9 (−1)

Saving Throws Wis +6, Cha +2
Skills Medicine +6, Religion +3
Damage Resistances necrotic, psychic
Senses passive Perception 13
Languages Common, Tsathar
Challenge 5 (1,800 XP)

Fetid Blessing. Whenever the evangelist deals acid or poison
damage, it ignores resistance to those damage types and deals
an additional 7 (2d6) damage of the same type.

Spellcasting. The evangelist is an 8th-level spellcaster. Its
spellcasting ability is Wisdom (spell save DC 14, +6 to hit with
spell attacks). The evangelist has the following cleric spells
prepared.

Cantrips (at will): *acid splash, mending, poison spray,
thaumaturgy*
1st level (4 slots): *bane, inflict wounds, protection from evil and
good, shield of faith*
2nd level (3 slots): *acid arrow, hold person, lesser restoration,
spiritual weapon*
3rd level (2 slots): *caustic burst*[VI]*, create food and water, dispel
magic, tongue of the frog god*[VI]
4th level (2 slots): *control water*

Actions

Mace. *Melee Weapon Attack:* +5 to hit, reach 5 ft., one target.
Hit: 5 (1d6 + 2) bludgeoning damage.

Plague of Frogs (recharges after a short or long rest). The
evangelist magically calls 1d4 **giant frogs**, provided that the
evangelist is within 100 feet of a body of water large enough to
cover a Medium creature. The called creatures arrive within 1d4

rounds, acting as allies of the evangelist, and obeying its spoken
commands. The beasts remain for 1 hour, until the evangelist
dies, or until the evangelist dismisses them as a bonus action.

Flying Skull

Tiny undead, chaotic evil

Armor Class 13
Hit Points 30 (12d4)
Speed 0 ft., fly 30 ft. (hover)

STR	DEX	CON	INT	WIS	CHA
5 (−3)	16 (+3)	10 (+0)	7 (−2)	13 (+1)	8 (−1)

Saving Throws Wis +3
Skills Perception +5, Stealth +5
Damage Immunities fire, poison
Condition Immunities poisoned, prone
Senses darkvision 60ft., passive Perception 15
Languages the languages it knew in life
Challenge 2 (450 XP)

Master's Spy. Flying skulls are often created by spellcasters
for use as spies or guardians. The flying skull's creator can
communicate with the skull telepathically and can use an action
to see through the skull's eyes and hear what it hears until the
start of the creator's next turn, gaining the benefits of the skull's
darkvision. During this time, the creator is deaf and blind with
regard to its own senses. The creator can sense through the
flying skull in this way only if the two are on the same plane of
existence.

Actions

Bite. *Melee Weapon Attack:* +5 to hit, reach 5 ft., one target. *Hit:*
6 (1d6 + 3) bludgeoning damage plus 7 (2d6) fire damage.

Spark Shower (recharge 5–6). The flying skull exhales searing
sparks in a 15-foot cone. Each creature in that area must make a
DC 13 Dexterity saving throw, taking 14 (4d6) fire damage on a
failed save, or half as much damage on a successful one.

Footman

Medium humanoid (any race), any alignment

Armor Class 15 (studded leather, shield)
Hit Points 38 (7d8 + 7)
Speed 30 ft.

STR	DEX	CON	INT	WIS	CHA
14 (+2)	12 (+1)	12 (+1)	10 (+0)	10 (+0)	10 (+0)

Senses passive Perception 10
Languages Common
Challenge 1 (200 XP)

Actions

Multiattack. The footman makes two Spear attacks or two
Longsword attacks.

Spear. *Melee or Ranged Weapon Attack:* +4 to hit, reach 5 ft. or
range 20/60 ft., one target. *Hit:* 5 (1d6 + 2) piercing damage, or
6 (1d8 + 2) piercing damage if used with two hands.

Longsword. *Melee Weapon Attack:* +4 to hit, reach 5 ft., one target. *Hit:* 6 (1d8 + 2) slashing damage, or 7 (1d10 + 2) piercing damage if used with two hands.

Light Crossbow. *Ranged Weapon Attack:* +3 to hit, range 80/320 ft., one target. *Hit:* 5 (1d8 + 1) piercing damage.

GARGANTUAN DIRE WOLF OF GARM

Gargantuan monstrosity, lawful evil

Armor Class 18 (natural armor)
Hit Points 250 (20d20 + 40)
Speed 60 ft.

STR	DEX	CON	INT	WIS	CHA
26 (+8)	17 (+3)	15 (+2)	5 (−3)	13 (+1)	6 (−2)

Skills Perception +6, Stealth +8
Damage Resistances bludgeoning, piercing, and slashing from nonmagical attacks
Senses passive Perception 16
Challenge 15 (13,000 XP)

Keen Hearing and Smell. The gargantuan dire wolf has advantage on Wisdom (Perception) checks that rely on hearing or smell.
Magic Resistance. The gargantuan dire wolf has advantage on saving throws against spells and other magical effects.

Actions

Bite. *Melee Weapon Attack:* +13 to hit, reach 5 ft., one target. *Hit:* 29 (6d6 + 8) piercing damage. If the target is a Medium or smaller creature, the creature must make a DC 21 Strength saving throw or be swallowed. While swallowed, the creature is blinded and restrained, it has total cover against attacks and other effects outside the gargantuan dire wolf, and it takes 35 (10d6) acid damage at the start of each of the gargantuan dire wolf's turns. If the dire wolf takes 30 damage or more on a single turn from a creature inside it, the dire wolf must succeed on a DC 25 Constitution saving throw at the end of that turn or regurgitate all swallowed creatures, which fall prone in a space within 10 feet of the dire wolf. If the gargantuan dire wolf dies, a swallowed creature is no longer restrained by it and can escape from the corpse using 15 feet of movement, exiting prone.
Teleport (1/day). The gargantuan dire wolf magically teleports up to 60 feet to an unoccupied space it can see.

GREATER GHOSTS OF TEGEL MANOR

The powerful ghosts of Tegel Manor are in some ways the stars and the hosts of the manor. Each of these greater ghosts has its own personality, desires, and story to tell for those willing to listen.

The rules for creating the greater ghosts of Tegel Manor are listed below. Greater ghosts have the same base statistics, but many have differing traits and actions based on the events surrounding their deaths. Though not a comprehensive list of every possible way a creature can die and become a greater ghost, the below themes should provide you with enough information to create the greater ghosts of Tegel Manor or make variant greater ghosts of your own. Note that like in the rest of the adventure, some options may prove a little more hazardous to your players than others.

GHOST, GREATER

Medium undead, any alignment

Armor Class 11
Hit Points 90 (20d8)
Speed 0 ft., fly 40 ft. (hover)

STR	DEX	CON	INT	WIS	CHA
7 (−2)	13 (+1)	10 (+0)	10 (+0)	16 (+3)	20 (+5)

Skills Deception +9, Stealth +6
Damage Resistances acid, fire, lightning, thunder
Damage Immunities cold, necrotic, poison; bludgeoning, piercing, and slashing from nonmagical attacks
Condition Immunities charmed, exhaustion, frightened, grappled, paralyzed, petrified, poisoned, prone, restrained
Senses darkvision 60 ft., passive Perception 13
Languages any languages it knew in life
Challenge 10 (5,900 XP)

Ethereal Sight. The greater ghost can see 60 feet into the Ethereal Plane when it is on the Material Plane, and vice versa.
Incorporeal Movement. The greater ghost can move through other creatures and objects as if they were difficult terrain. It takes 5 (1d10) force damage if it ends its turn inside an object.
Undead Nature. A greater ghost doesn't require air, food, drink, or sleep.

Actions

Multiattack. The greater ghost makes two Draining Touch attacks.
Draining Touch. *Melee Weapon Attack:* +9 to hit, reach 5 ft., one creature. *Hit:* 19 (4d6 + 5) necrotic damage. The target must succeed on a DC 15 Constitution saving throw or its hit point maximum is reduced by an amount equal to the damage taken. This reduction lasts until the creature finishes a long rest. The target dies if this effect reduces its hit point maximum to 0.
A humanoid slain by this attack rises 24 hours later as a ghost under the greater ghost's control, unless the humanoid is restored to life or its body is destroyed. The greater ghost can have no more than three ghosts under its control at one time.
Etherealness. The greater ghost enters the Ethereal Plane from the Material Plane, or vice versa. It is visible on the Material Plane while it is in the Border Ethereal, and vice versa, yet it can't affect or be affected by anything on the other plane.

THEMES

When creating a greater ghost, choose a theme that represents how the creature died. Each theme adds a variety of features to the base greater ghost or adjusts current features of it. Each greater ghost must have at least one theme, but it can have more. Increase the greater ghost's challenge rating by 1 for each theme you add to it beyond the first theme. If you use two themes that replace or modify the same feature, pick one theme's modification and ignore the other theme's modification; do not apply both modifications to the same creature.

A greater ghost with four or more themes is of a sufficient challenge rating for an increase in its proficiency bonus. Such a greater ghost uses its Wisdom modifier when setting the saving throw DC for its traits and actions (DC equal to 8 + the greater ghost's proficiency bonus + its Wisdom modifier).

COLD-BLOODED

This theme applies to creatures that were killed in cold blood or suddenly without warning or provocation. Such a greater ghost always feels disoriented by its death and seeks the warmth of the living. A cold-blooded greater ghost retains its statistics except as noted below.

Sense Warmth. The greater ghost is drawn to warm places and creatures. It can pinpoint the location of a warm-blooded creature or other source of warmth such as a match or a campfire within 60 feet.

New Action: Possession (recharge 6). One humanoid that the greater ghost can see within 5 feet of it must succeed on a DC 15 Charisma saving throw or be possessed by the ghost; the ghost then disappears, and the target is incapacitated and loses control of its body. The ghost now controls the body but doesn't deprive the target of awareness. The ghost can't be targeted by any attack, spell, or other effect, except ones that turn undead, and it retains its alignment, Intelligence, Wisdom, Charisma, and immunity to being charmed and frightened . It otherwise uses the possessed target's statistics, but doesn't gain access to the target's knowledge, class features, or proficiencies.

The possession lasts until the body drops to 0 hit points, the ghost ends it as a bonus action, or the ghost is turned or forced out by an effect like the *dispel evil and good* spell. When the possession ends, the ghost reappears in an unoccupied space within 5 feet of the body. The target is immune to this ghost's Possession for 24 hours after succeeding on the saving throw or after the possession ends.

CORRUPT

This theme applies to creatures that were despicable individuals in life, and their deaths were caused by their own deplorable actions. Such a greater ghost died with wickedness lodged like a stone in its heart. A corrupt greater ghost retains its statistics except as noted below.

Alignment. The greater ghost's alignment is evil.

New Action: Multiattack. The greater ghost's Multiattack action changes to: The greater ghost makes two attacks, only one of which can be with its Corrupting Gaze.

New Action: Corrupting Gaze. *Ranged Spell Attack:* +9 to hit, range 60 ft., one creature. *Hit:* 18 (4d8) psychic damage, and the target's Charisma score is reduced by 1d4. The target is incapacitated if this reduces its Charisma to 0. Otherwise, the reduction lasts until the target finishes a short or long rest.

FEARFUL

This theme applies to creatures who died while experiencing something truly terrifying. Such a greater ghost wails its terror at any creature it encounters, sharing its pain as it perpetually relives its death. A fearful greater ghost retains its statistics except as noted below.

Condition Immunities. The greater ghost can be frightened, but it can't fall unconscious, cursed to never have reprieve from its death.

New Action: Terrifying Moan (recharge 5–6). The greater ghost releases a terrifying moan into the minds of creatures in a 30-foot cone. Each creature in the area with an Intelligence of 3 or higher must make a DC 15 Wisdom saving throw. On a failure, the creature takes 35 (10d6) psychic damage and is frightened for 1 minute. On a success, the creature takes half the damage and isn't frightened. If the saving throw fails by 5 or more, the target is instead paralyzed for 1 minute. A frightened or paralyzed creature can repeat the saving throw at the end of each of its turns, ending the condition on itself on a success.

INIQUITOUS

This theme applies to creatures who died armed and armored but who were killed in an unfair combat, such as overwhelming odds or the secret use of poison in an honorable duel. Such a greater ghost wears and carries spectral versions of the armor and weaponry that it was wearing when it died. An iniquitous greater ghost retains its statistics except as noted below.

Armor Class. The greater ghost's armor class changes as if it is wearing the armor it wore in life. Though the armor it wears is a spectral version of the original armor, it provides the same bonuses and penalties of a suit of armor of its type. For example, an iniquitous greater ghost who died while wearing plate has an armor class of 18. When the greater ghost dies, the spectral armor disappears with it, unless the armor is magical, in which case the armor falls to the ground in the exact state it was when the greater ghost originally died (fresh bloodstains and all).

New Action: Multiattack. The greater ghost's Multiattack changes to: The greater ghost makes three attacks, only one of which can be with its Draining Touch.

New Action: Weapon Attack. The greater ghost carries the spectral version of one weapon it was proficient with in life. It is also proficient with that weapon in death, and, when it attacks with the weapon, it uses its Charisma modifier, instead of Strength or Dexterity, for attack and damage rolls with that weapon. When the greater ghost dies, the spectral weapon disappears with it, unless the weapon is magical, in which case the weapon falls to the ground in the exact state it was when the greater ghost originally died (as dull or sharp as it was in the greater ghost's original life).

REPULSIVE

This theme applies to creatures who died in a gruesome or grisly way. Such a greater ghost is permanently marred or disfigured by its killing blow, vexing the ghost's fragile vanity. A repulsive greater ghost retains its statistics except as noted below.

Condition Immunities. The greater ghost can be charmed.

Horrific Presence. When a creature that can see the greater ghost's wound starts its turn within 30 feet of the greater ghost, the greater ghost can force it to make a DC 15 Wisdom saving throw if the greater ghost isn't incapacitated and can see the creature. If the saving throw fails by 5 or more, the target ages 1d4 x 10 years. Otherwise, a creature that fails the save is stunned until the start of its next turn.

Unless surprised, a creature can avert its eyes to avoid the saving throw at the start of its turn. If the creature does so, it can't see the greater ghost until the start of its next, when it can avert its eyes again. If the creature looks at the greater ghost in the meantime, it must immediately make the save.

The aging effect of the greater ghost's Horrific Presence can be reversed with a *greater restoration* spell, but only within 24 hours of it occurring.

Vain. The greater ghost has disadvantage on ability checks and saving throws made to avoid being charmed by a creature that complimented it within the last 1 minute.

Ruthless

This theme applies to creatures who were killed surreptitiously by someone they trusted or held dear. Such a greater ghost despises all beings who use their physical or magical strength to aid or protect others. A ruthless greater ghost retains its statistics except as noted below.

Ruthless. The greater ghost has advantage on melee attack rolls against any creature that has used the Help action, restored hit points to another creature, or aided another creature through a feature, such as Bardic Inspiration, or magic, such as the *longstrider* or *aid* spells, within the last 1 minute. This trait doesn't give the greater ghost advantage on melee attack rolls against creatures who have features or traits that passively aid others, such as a paladin's Aura of Protection or a wolf's Pack Tactics.

New Action: Multiattack. The greater ghost's Multiattack changes to: The greater ghost makes two Enfeebling Touch attacks.

New Action: Enfeebling Touch. The greater ghost replaces its Draining Touch action with the following action:

Enfeebling Touch. *Melee Weapon Attack:* +9 to hit, reach 5 ft., one creature. *Hit:* 19 (4d6 + 5) necrotic damage, and the target's Strength, Intelligence, or Wisdom score (your choice) is reduced by 1d4. The target dies if this reduces its Strength to 0. The target is incapacitated if this reduces its Intelligence or Wisdom to 0. Otherwise, the reduction lasts until the target finishes a short or long rest.

Withered

This theme applies to creatures who died from extreme exposure to necrotic damage or from an effect that drains the life out of its target. This theme can also apply to a greater ghost that has existed for a considerable period of time. Such a greater ghost appears more insubstantial than most ghosts and spectral pieces of it perpetually flake off in its wake. A withered greater ghost retains its statistics except as noted below.

Innate Spellcasting. The greater ghost's innate spellcasting ability is Charisma. It can innately cast *telekinesis* at will.

New Action: Draining Touch. The greater ghost's Draining Touch action can age its target. Add the following to the end of the Draining Touch action:

Instead of reducing the target's hit point maximum, the greater ghost can increase the target creature's age by 2d4 years. The aging effect can be reversed with a *greater restoration* spell, but only within 24 hours of it occurring.

Giant Beaver

Medium beast, unaligned

Armor Class 11
Hit Points 32 (5d8 + 10)
Speed 20 ft., swim 40 ft.

STR	DEX	CON	INT	WIS	CHA
17 (+3)	13 (+1)	14 (+2)	2 (−4)	12 (+1)	5 (−3)

Saving Throws Dex +3
Skills Perception +3
Senses passive Perception 13

Languages —
Challenge 1 (200 XP)

Hold Breath. The giant beaver can hold its breath for 30 minutes.

Keen Hearing and Smell. The giant beaver has advantage on Wisdom (Perception) checks that rely on hearing or smell.

Wood-Eater. The giant beaver deals double damage to creatures, objects, and structures made of wood.

Actions

Bite. *Melee Weapon Attack:* +5 to hit, reach 5 ft., one target. *Hit:* 7 (1d8 + 3) slashing damage.

Tail Slap (recharge 4–6). *Melee Weapon Attack:* +5 to hit, reach 10 ft., one target. *Hit:* 10 (2d6 + 3) bludgeoning damage. If the target is a creature, it must succeed on a DC 12 Strength saving throw or be knocked prone.

Giant Bombardier Beetle

Small beast, unaligned

Armor Class 15 (natural armor)
Hit Points 18 (4d6 + 4)
Speed 30 ft., burrow 15 ft.

STR	DEX	CON	INT	WIS	CHA
10 (+0)	15 (+2)	12 (+1)	1 (−5)	9 (−1)	3 (−4)

Skills Stealth +4
Damage Resistances acid
Senses darkvision 60 ft., passive Perception 9
Languages —
Challenge 1/2 (100 XP)

Forest Camouflage. The bombardier beetle has advantage on Dexterity (Stealth) checks made to hide in forest terrain.

Actions

Bite. *Melee Weapon Attack:* +4 to hit, reach 5 ft., one target. *Hit:* 5 (1d6 + 2) piercing damage.

Acid Spray (recharge 6). The bombardier beetle expels heated acid in a 15-foot cone. Each creature in that area must make a DC 12 Dexterity saving throw, taking 5 (2d4) acid damage on a failed save, or half as much damage on a successful one.

Giant Dire Abyssal Frog

Large elemental, chaotic evil

Armor Class 16 (natural armor)
Hit Points 105 (10d10 + 50)
Speed 30 ft., swim 30 ft.

STR	DEX	CON	INT	WIS	CHA
20 (+5)	18 (+4)	20 (+5)	5 (−3)	10 (+0)	10 (+0)

Saving Throws Dex +7, Con +8
Skills Stealth +7, Perception +6
Damage Resistances acid, cold; bludgeoning, piercing and slashing from nonmagical weapons
Damage Immunities poison
Condition Immunities exhaustion, grappled, paralyzed,

petrified, poisoned, prone, restrained, unconscious
Senses darkvision 60 ft., passive Perception 16
Languages —
Challenge 6 (2,300 XP)

Amphibious. The frog can breathe air and water.
Keen Smell. The frog has advantage on Wisdom (Perception)
checks that rely on smell.
Poison Hide. A creature that touches the giant dire Abyssal
frog or hits it with an unarmed or natural weapon attack takes
10 (3d6) poison damage from the milky, poisonous slime that
oozes from its hide.
Standing Leap. The frog's long jump is up to 30 feet and its
high jump is up to 20 feet, with or without a running start.

Actions

Multiattack. The giant dire Abyssal frog makes three attacks:
one with its bite, one with its claws, and one with its tongue.
Bite. *Melee Weapon Attack:* +8 to hit, reach 5 ft., one target. *Hit:*
14 (2d8 + 5) piercing damage, and the target is grappled (escape
DC 16). Until this grapple ends, the target is restrained and the
frog can't bite another target.
Claws. *Melee Weapon Attack:* +8 to hit, reach 5 ft., one target.
Hit: 15 (3d6 + 5) slashing damage.
Tongue. *Melee Weapon Attack:* +8 to hit, reach 15 ft., one target.
Hit: 18 (2d12 + 5) slashing damage, and the target must succeed
on a DC 16 Strength saving throw or be pulled up to 10 feet
toward the giant dire Abyssal frog.
Swallow. The giant dire Abyssal frog makes one bite attack
against a Large or smaller target it is grappling. If the attack
hits, the target is swallowed, and the grapple ends. The
swallowed target is blinded and restrained, it has total cover
against attacks and other effects outside the giant dire Abyssal
frog, and it takes 14 (4d6) acid damage at the start of each of the
giant dire Abyssal frog's turns. The giant dire Abyssal frog can
only swallow one target at a time.
If the giant dire Abyssal frog dies, a swallowed creature is no
longer restrained by it and can escape from the corpse using 5
feet of movement, exiting prone.

Giant Hog

Medium monstrosity, neutral evil

Armor Class 13 (natural armor)
Hit Points 39 (6d8 + 12)
Speed 30 ft.

STR	DEX	CON	INT	WIS	CHA
17 (+3)	12 (+1)	14 (+2)	6 (−2)	7 (−2)	5 (−3)

Saving Throws Con +4
Skills Athletics +5
Senses passive Perception 8
Languages Common
Challenge 2 (450 XP)

Charge. If the giant hog moves at least 15 feet straight toward a
target and then hits it with a tusk attack on the same turn, the
target takes an extra 3 (1d6) slashing damage. If the target is a
creature, it must succeed on a DC 12 Strength saving throw or
be knocked prone.
Relentless (recharges after a short or long rest). If the
giant hog takes 10 damage or less that would reduce it to 0 hit

points, it is reduced to 1 hit point instead.

Actions

Multiattack. The giant hog makes one Tusk attack and one
Greatclub attack.
Tusk. *Melee Weapon Attack:* +5 to hit, reach 5 ft., one target.
Hit: 6 (1d6 + 3) slashing damage.
Greatclub. *Melee Weapon Attack:* +5 to hit, reach 5 ft., one
target. *Hit:* 7 (1d8 + 3) bludgeoning damage.
Squeal (recharge 6). The giant hog releases a deafening squeal
in a 15-foot cone. Each creature in that area that can hear the
giant hog must make a DC 12 Constitution saving throw. On
a failure, a creature takes 10 (3d6) thunder damage and is
deafened for 1 minute. On a success, a creature takes half the
damage and isn't deafened.

Giant Leech

Medium beast (aquatic), unaligned

Armor Class 11
Hit Points 26 (4d8 + 8)
Speed 5 ft., swim 20 ft.

STR	DEX	CON	INT	WIS	CHA
11 (+0)	12 (+1)	14 (+2)	2 (−4)	10 (+0)	1 (−5)

Senses blindsight 30 ft., passive Perception 10
Languages —
Challenge 1 (200 XP)

Vulnerability to Salt. A handful of salt burns a giant leech as if
it were a flask of acid, causing 1d6 acid damage per use.

Actions

Blood Drain. *Melee Weapon Attack:* +3 to hit, reach 5 ft.
one creature. Hit: 4 (1d6 + 1) piercing damage, and the leech
attaches to the target. While attached, the leech doesn't attack.
Instead, at the start of the leech's turns, the target loses 5 (1d8 +
1) hit points due to blood loss.
The leech can detach itself by spending 5 feet of its movement.
It does so after it drains 25 hit points of blood from the target
or the target dies. A creature, including the target, can use its
action to make a DC 10 Strength check to rip the leech off and
make it detach.

Giant Stag Beetle

Medium beast, unaligned

Armor Class 15 (natural armor)
Hit Points 52 (8d8 + 16)
Speed 40 ft., climb 20 ft., fly 15 ft.

STR	DEX	CON	INT	WIS	CHA
17 (+3)	12 (+1)	15 (+2)	1 (−5)	10 (+0)	3 (−4)

Saving Throws Con +4
Skills Athletics +5
Senses darkvision 60 ft., passive Perception 10
Languages —
Challenge 3 (700 XP)

Sure-Footed. The giant stag beetle has advantage on Strength and Dexterity saving throws made against effects that would knock it prone.

Actions

Multiattack. The giant stag beetle makes two attacks with its Mandibles.

Mandibles. *Melee Weapon Attack:* +5 to hit, reach 5 ft., one target. *Hit:* 8 (1d10 + 3) slashing damage and the target is grappled (escape DC 13). Until this grapple ends, the creature is restrained, and the giant stag beetle can't make mandible attacks against another target.

Pinch (recharge 6). One creature grappled by the giant stag beetle must make a DC 13 Strength saving throw. On a failure, a creature takes 19 (3d10 + 3) bludgeoning damage and is incapacitated until the end of its next turn. On a success, a creature takes half the damage and isn't incapacitated.

GIANT TICK

Small beast, unaligned

Armor Class 13 (natural armor)
Hit Points 10 (3d6)
Speed 10 ft., climb 20 ft.

STR	DEX	CON	INT	WIS	CHA
11 (+0)	10 (+0)	11 (+0)	2 (−4)	10 (+0)	2 (−4)

Senses darkvision 60 ft., passive Perception 10
Languages —
Challenge 1/4 (50 XP)

Keen Smell. The tick has advantage on Wisdom (Perception) checks that rely on smell.

Red Ache. Creatures bitten by a giant tick must make a DC 15 Constitution saving throw or become infected with this disease. Within 4 hours of infection, the infected creature will develop red welts that are hot to the touch all over its skin. Its joints will swell and its bones will ache painfully. While infected, the creature has disadvantage on Strength checks, Strength saving throws, and attack rolls that use Strength. The saving throw can be repeated after every long rest and if successful in 2 consecutive tries (two long rests in a row), the creature is cured and the effects of the disease end. A *greater restoration* spell will also cure the disease.

Actions

Blood Drain. *Melee Weapon Attack:* +2 to hit, reach 5 ft., one target. *Hit:* 2 (1d4) piercing damage and the tick attaches to the target. While attached, the tick doesn't attack. Instead, at the start of each of the ticks's turns, the target loses 2 (1d4) hit points due to blood loss.

The tick can detach itself by spending 5 feet of its movement. It does so after it drains 10 hit points of blood from the target or the target dies. A creature, including the target, can use its action to detach the tick.

GIANT WATER BUG

Small beast, unaligned

Armor Class 13 (natural armor)
Hit Points 22 (5d6 + 5)
Speed 20 ft., swim 40 ft.

STR	DEX	CON	INT	WIS	CHA
15 (+2)	10 (+0)	12 (+1)	1 (−5)	9 (−1)	3 (−4)

Skills Perception +1, Stealth +2
Senses darkvision 60 ft., passive Perception 11
Languages —
Challenge 1/2 (100 XP)

Hold Breath. The giant water bug can hold its breath for 15 minutes.

Spider Climb. The giant water bug can climb difficult surfaces, including upside down on ceilings, without needing to make an ability check.

Actions

Bite. *Melee Weapon Attack:* +4 to hit, reach 5 ft., one target. *Hit:* 5 (1d6 + 2) piercing damage and the target must make a DC 11 Constitution saving throw, taking 5 (2d4) poison damage on a failed save, or half as much damage on a successful one.

Reactions

Play Dead. When the giant water bug is reduced to 10 hit points or fewer, it can use its reaction to become prone and leak a blood-like fluid, appearing dead. A creature that sees this reaction can tell the giant water bug was not actually slain with a successful DC 12 Wisdom (Insight) check. If a creature believes the giant water bug is dead and ends its turn within 5 feet of the giant water bug, the bug can use this reaction to leap up and attack the creature. If it hits, the attack deals an extra 3 (1d6) piercing damage.

GREEN SLIME

Green slime is corrosive, slick, and adhesive, sticking to anything it comes into contact with. Metal, flesh, organic material is especially vulnerable to the corrosive properties of the slime. It is often found in warm, humid caverns and ruins, and will be noticeable as it clings to ceilings, walls, and covers floors, usually in 5-foot squares.

Green slime can detect movement within 30 feet and will drop on unsuspecting victims when they are below it; it is unable to move so much depend on unwitting prey. If a creature is aware of the presence of the slime, they can attempt to avoid the hazard by succeeding on a DC 10 Dexterity saving throw.

The green slime secretes acid and does 5 (1d10) acid damage to any creature it comes into contact with. This damage continues on each of the creature's turns until it uses an action to remove or destroy the slime. Much like its more evolved ooze relatives, the green slime is doubly caustic to nonmagical wood and metal, doing 11 (2d10) acid damage against objects of these types.

Green slime is vulnerable to and will be destroyed by fire, cold, radiant damage, sunlight or any disease curing magic.

Grotesque Plant

Large plant, unaligned

Armor Class 15 (natural armor)
Hit Points 90 (12d10 + 24)
Speed 10 ft., climb 20 ft.

STR	DEX	CON	INT	WIS	CHA
18 (+4)	10 (+0)	15 (+2)	4 (−3)	13 (+1)	4 (−3)

Skills Perception +3, Stealth +4
Damage Vulnerabilities fire
Damage Immunities poison
Condition Immunities blinded, charmed, deafened, paralyzed, poisoned
Senses blindsight 60 ft. (blind beyond this radius), passive Perception 13
Languages —
Challenge 4 (1,100 XP)

False Appearance. While the grotesque plant remains motionless, it is indistinguishable from a normal, vine-covered plant.

Actions

Multiattack. The grotesque plant makes two Spiked Vine attacks, uses Reel, and makes one Beak attack.

Spiked Vine. *Melee Weapon Attack:* +6 to hit, reach 20 ft., one target. *Hit:* 6 (1d4 + 4) piercing damage. If the target is a Medium or smaller creature, it is grappled (escape DC 14). Until this grapple ends, the target is restrained. The grotesque plant has four spiked vines, each of which can grapple only one target.

Beak. *Melee Weapon Attack:* +6 to hit, reach 5 ft., one target. *Hit:* 8 (1d8 + 4) piercing damage plus 7 (2d6) poison damage.

Reel. The grotesque plant pulls each creature grappled by it up to 15 feet straight toward it.

Reactions

Recoil. When the grotesque plant takes fire damage, it stops grappling any creatures and wraps itself in its large leaves and seeps a sickly-sweet fluid. If a creature touches the grotesque plant or hits it with a melee attack while within 5 feet of it before the end of the plant's next turn, the creature takes 3 (1d6) poison damage. Until the start of its next turn, its Armor Class is increased by 2.

Holy Knight

Medium humanoid (any), any alignment

Armor Class 20 (plate, shield)
Hit Points 65 (10d8 + 20)
Speed 30 ft.

STR	DEX	CON	INT	WIS	CHA
16 (+3)	11 (+0)	14 (+2)	11 (+0)	11 (+0)	15 (+2)

Saving Throws Wis +2, Cha +4
Skills Insight +2, Religion +2
Senses passive Perception 10
Languages Common, plus one other language
Challenge 4 (1,100 XP)

Divine Blessings. The holy knight has advantage on saving throws against being frightened, and is immune to disease.

Divine Smite. When the holy knight hits with a melee weapon attack, it can expend a spell slot to deal additional radiant damage to the target, in addition to the weapon's damage. The extra damage is 9 (2d8) for a 1st-level spell slot, plus 4 (1d8) for each spell level higher than 1st, to a maximum of 21 (5d8). The damage increases by 4 (1d8) if the target is a fiend or undead.

Spellcasting. The holy knight is a 5th-level spellcaster. Its spellcasting ability is Charisma (spell save DC 12). It has the following paladin spells.

1st level (4 slots): *bless, divine favor, protection from evil and good, sanctuary, shield of faith*

2nd level (2 slots): *aid, lesser restoration, protection from poison, zone of truth*

Actions

Multiattack. The holy knight makes two Longsword attacks.

Longsword. *Melee Weapon Attack:* +5 to hit, reach 5 ft., one target. *Hit:* 7 (1d8 + 3) slashing damage, or 8 (1d10 + 3) slashing damage if used with two hands to make a melee attack.

Lay on Hands. The holy knight has a pool of 25 hit points to use with its Lay on Hands ability. It regains spent hit points from this pool when it takes a long rest. It can use this ability to cause a creature within 5 feet of it or itself to regain any number of hit points, up to its hit point maximum or its pool of hit points is reduced to 0.

Incantor

Medium humanoid (any), any alignment

Armor Class 13 (16 with *mage armor*)
Hit Points 91 (14d8 + 28)
Speed 30 ft.

STR	DEX	CON	INT	WIS	CHA
10 (+0)	16 (+3)	14 (+2)	20 (+5)	15 (+2)	14 (+2)

Saving Throws Int +9, Wis +6
Skills Arcana +13, Nature +9, Perception +6
Senses darkvision 120 ft., passive Perception 16
Languages Common, Elvish, Ignan, Undercommon
Challenge 9 (5,900 XP)

Dual Enchantment. If the incantor casts an enchantment spell that would normally target one creature, it can have it target two.

Redirect (recharge 4–6). When a creature within 40 feet of the incantor attacks it, it can use its reaction to redirect the attack. The attacking creature must succeed on a DC 17 Wisdom saving throw or target another creature of the incantor's choice within range of the attack. Creatures that can't be charmed are immune to this effect.

Spellcasting. The incantor is a 14th level spellcaster. The incantor's spellcasting ability is Intelligence (spell save DC 17, +9 to hit with spell attacks). It has the following spells prepared:

Cantrips (at will): *dancing lights, fire bolt, mage hand, poison spray, prestidigitation*

1st level (4 slots): *mage armor, enlarge/reduce, hideous laughter, magic missile, sleep*

2nd level (3 slots): *arcane lock, hold person, mirror image, suggestion*

3rd level (3 slots): *counterspell, glyph of warding, sleet storm*

4th level (3 slots): *confusion, fire shield, greater invisibility*

5th level (2 slots): *dispel evil and good, dominate person, flame strike, passwall*

6th level (1 slot): *disintegrate, mass suggestion*

7th level (1 slot): *forcecage*

Sunlight Sensitivity. While in sunlight, the incantor has disadvantage on attack rolls, as well as on Wisdom (Perception) checks that rely on sight.

Actions

Dagger. *Melee Weapon Attack:* +7 to hit, reach 5 ft., one target. *Hit:* 6 (1d4 + 3) piercing damage.

Hand Crossbow. *Ranged Weapon Attack* +7 to hit, range 30/120 ft., one target. *Hit:* 6 (1d6 + 3) piercing damage, and the target must succeed on a DC 13 Constitution saving throw or be poisoned for 1 hour. If the saving throw fails by 5 or more, the target is also unconscious while poisoned in this way. The target wakes up if it takes damage or if another creature takes an action to shake it awake.

Bonus Actions

Hypnosis. The incantor uses its charming voice to hypnotize one creature within 15 feet of it who can hear and understand it. The creature must succeed on a DC 17 Wisdom saving throw or be charmed until the end of the incantor's next turn. A hypnotized creature is incapacitated and does nothing but gaze at the incantor. The effect ends for a hypnotized creature if that creature takes damage or is more than 15 feet from the incantor.

INITIATE

Medium humanoid (any), any neutral alignment

Armor Class 16 (natural armor)
Hit Points 49 (9d8 + 9)
Speed 40 ft.

STR	DEX	CON	INT	WIS	CHA
10 (+0)	16 (+3)	13 (+1)	11 (+0)	16 (+3)	10 (+0)

Saving Throws Dex +5, Wis +5
Skills Acrobatics +5, Stealth +5
Senses passive Perception 13
Languages Common, plus 1 other language
Challenge 2 (450 XP)

Slow Fall. The initiate reduces any falling damage by 30. If it does not take damage from a fall, it does not fall prone.

Actions

Multiattack. The initiate makes two attacks with its Quarterstaff, Sling, or its Unarmed Strike. It can use its Flurry of Blows ability in place of one of the attacks.

Quarterstaff. *Melee Weapon Attack:* +5 to hit, reach 5 ft., one target. *Hit:* 6 (1d6 + 3) bludgeoning damage, or 7 (1d8 + 3) bludgeoning damage if wielded with two hands.

Unarmed Strike. *Melee Weapon Attack:* +5 to hit, reach 5 ft., one target. *Hit:* 6 (1d6 + 3) bludgeoning damage.

Sling. *Ranged Weapon Attack:* +5 to hit, range 30/120 ft., one target. *Hit:* 6 (1d6 + 3) bludgeoning damage.

Flurry of Blows (3/day). *Melee Weapon Attack:* +5 to hit, reach 5 ft., one target. *Hit:* 13 (3d6 + 3) bludgeoning damage, and the target suffers one of the following effects of the ascetic's choice:

- The target must succeed on a DC 14 Dexterity saving throw or be knocked prone.
- The target must make a DC 14 Strength saving throw or be pushed up to 15 feet away from it.
- The target can't take reactions until the end of it's next turn.

Reactions

Deflect Missiles. If it has one hand free, it can use its reaction in response to being hit with a ranged weapon attack. It reduces the damage by 11 (1d10 + 6). If it reduces the damage to 0, it can catch the missile if it is small enough for it to hold with one hand.

Intellect Devourer

Tiny aberration, lawful evil

Armor Class 13
Hit Points 36 (8d4 + 16)
Speed 40 ft.

STR	DEX	CON	INT	WIS	CHA
4 (−3)	16 (+3)	14 (+2)	12 (+1)	14 (+2)	20 (+5)

Skills Stealth +5
Damage Resistances bludgeoning, piercing, and slashing from nonmagical weapons
Condition Immunities blinded, exhaustion, frightened, paralyzed, poisoned
Senses blindsight 60 ft., passive Perception 12
Languages understands Deep Speech but can't speak, telepathy 60 ft.
Challenge 3 (700 XP)

Mindsense. The intellect devourer is aware of the presence of creatures within 300 feet of it that have an Intelligence of 3 or higher. It knows the relative distance and direction of each creature, regardless of physical barriers. Creatures under the effects of magic that protects the mind cannot be detected by the intellect devourer.

Actions

Multiattack. The intellect devourer makes one attack with its claws and uses Consume Mind.

Claws. *Melee Weapon Attack:* +5 to hit, reach 5 ft., one target. *Hit:* 6 (1d6 + 3) slashing damage.

Consume Mind. The intellect devourer chooses one creature it can see within 30 feet of it that has an Intelligence of 3 or higher. The target must succeed on a DC 13 Intelligence saving throw or take 16 (3d10) psychic damage. If the target fails the saving throw by 5 or more, its Intelligence score is reduced to 0. The target is incapacitated until it regains at least 1 point of Intelligence (either from completing a long rest or from a *lesser restoration* spell).

Body Snatcher. The intellect devourer chooses one incapacitated creature within 5 feet of it and engages it in a contest of Intelligence. The intellect devourer overpowers the creature's mental defenses if it beats the target on a contested Intelligence check. The intellect devourer magically consumes the creature's brain and teleports into its skull, taking full control of the target's body. While inside the creature's skull, the intellect devourer has total cover against attacks and other effects outside of the host. The intellect devourer retains its Intelligence, Wisdom, and Charisma scores, as well as its comprehension of language, its telepathy, and its traits. Otherwise, it inherits the target's statistics, memories and knowledge, including spells and languages.

If the host body drops to 0 hit points, the intellect devourer must leave the host. It can also be magically forced from the host's body by means of a *protection from evil and good* spell being cast on the host. If the host's devoured brain is restored (only possibly with a *wish* spell), the intellect devourer is forced out of the host. The intellect devourer can choose to leave the host at any time by spending 5 feet of its movement and then teleporting to an unoccupied space within 15 feet of the target. Unless its brain is restored within 1 round, the body dies.

Jackalwere

Medium humanoid (shapechanger), chaotic evil

Armor Class 14
Hit Points 26 (4d8 + 8)
Speed 30 ft.

STR	DEX	CON	INT	WIS	CHA
15 (+2)	18 (+4)	15 (+2)	12 (+1)	12 (+1)	10 (+0)

Skills Deception +4, Perception +5, Stealth +6
Damage Immunities bludgeoning, piercing, and slashing from nonmagical attacks not made with silver
Senses passive Perception 15
Languages Common (can't speak in jackal form)
Challenge 2 (450 XP)

Keen Smell. The jackalwere has advantage on Wisdom (Perception) checks that rely on smell.

Pack Tactics. The jackalwere has advantage on an attack roll against a creature if at least one of the jackalwere's allies is within 5 ft. of the creature and the ally isn't incapacitated.

Rampage (jackal or hybrid form only). When the jackalwere reduces a creature to 0 hit points with a melee attack on its turn, the jackalwere can take a bonus action to move up to half its speed and make a bite attack.

Shapechanger. The jackalwere can use its action to polymorph into a specific Medium human or a jackal-humanoid hybrid, or back into its true form, which is a Small jackal. Its statistics, other than its size, are the same in each form. Any equipment it is wearing or carrying isn't transformed. It reverts to its true form if it dies.

Actions

Multiattack (jackal or hybrid form only). The jackalwere makes two melee weapon attacks.

Bite (jackal or hybrid form only). *Melee Weapon Attack:* +6 to hit, reach 5 ft., one target. *Hit:* 8 (1d8 + 4) piercing damage.

Battleaxe (humanoid or hybrid form only). *Melee Weapon Attack:* +4 to hit, reach 5 ft., one target. *Hit:* 6 (1d8 + 2) slashing damage, or 7 (1d10 + 2) slashing damage if used with two hands.

Sleep Gaze. The jackalwere gazes at one creature it can see within 30 feet of it. The target must make a DC 13 Wisdom saving throw. On a failed save, the target succumbs to a magical slumber, falling unconscious for 10 minutes or until someone uses an action to shake the target awake. A creature that successfully saves against the effect is immune to this jackalwere's gaze for the next 24 hours. Undead and creatures immune to being charmed aren't affected by it.

Ki-rin

Medium celestial, neutral good

Armor Class 15 (natural armor)
Hit Points 45 (6d8 + 18)
Speed 40 ft., fly 60 ft.

STR	DEX	CON	INT	WIS	CHA
18 (+4)	17 (+3)	16 (+3)	15 (+2)	20 (+5)	19 (+4)

Saving Throws Wis +7, Cha +6
Skills History +4, Insight +7, Religion +4
Damage Resistances radiant; bludgeoning, piercing, and slashing from nonmagical attacks
Damage Immunities fire, poison
Condition Immunities charmed, poisoned
Senses truesight 120 ft., passive Perception 15
Languages all, telepathy 60 ft.
Challenge 3 (700 XP)

Innate Spellcasting. The ki-rin's innate spellcasting ability is Charisma (spell save DC 14, +6 to hit with spell attacks). It can innately cast the following spells, requiring only verbal components:

At will: *detect evil and good, detect thoughts*
3/day each: *bless, heroism, sanctuary*
1/day: *dispel evil and good*

Magic Resistance. The ki-rin has advantage on saving throws against spells and other magical effects.

Magic Weapons. The ki-rin's weapon attacks are magical.

Actions

Multiattack. The ki-rin makes one attack with its Horn and one attack with its Hooves.

Horn. *Melee Weapon Attack:* +6 to hit, reach 5 ft., one target. *Hit:* 8 (1d8 + 4) piercing damage.

Hooves. *Melee Weapon Attack:* +6 to hit, reach 5 ft., one target. *Hit:* 9 (2d4 + 4) bludgeoning damage.

Divine Breath (recharge 5–6). The ki-rin exhales divine fire in a 15-foot cone. Each creature in that area must make a DC 13 Dexterity saving throw, taking 10 (3d6) fire damage and 10 (3d6) radiant damage on a failed save, or half as much damage on a successful one.

Killer Frog

Small beast, unaligned

Armor Class 12 (natural armor)
Hit Points 11 (2d6 + 4)
Speed 30 ft., swim 30 ft.

STR	DEX	CON	INT	WIS	CHA
12 (+1)	13 (+1)	14 (+2)	2 (−4)	9 (−1)	6 (−2)

Skills Perception +3
Senses passive Perception 13
Languages —
Challenge 1/4 (50 XP)

Amphibious. The killer frog can breathe air and water.

Keen Smell. The killer frog has advantage on Wisdom (Perception) checks that rely on smell.

Standing Leap. The killer frog's long jump is up to 15 feet and its high jump is up to 10 feet, with or without a running start.

Actions

Multiattack. The killer frog makes one Bite attack and one with its Claws.

Bite. *Melee Weapon Attack:* +3 to hit, reach 5 ft., one target. *Hit:* 3 (1d4 + 1) piercing damage.

Claws. *Melee Weapon Attack:* +3 to hit, reach 5 ft., one target. *Hit:* 3 (1d4 + 1) slashing damage.

Killer Shrew

Small beast, unaligned

Armor Class 13
Hit Points 44 (8d6 + 16)
Speed 20 ft., burrow 30 ft.

STR	DEX	CON	INT	WIS	CHA
11 (+0)	16 (+3)	14 (+2)	2 (−4)	10 (+0)	4 (−3)

Skills Stealth +5
Damage Resistances poison
Senses blindsight 30 ft., passive Perception 10
Languages —
Challenge 2 (450 XP)

Energetic. The killer shrew can take the Dash action as a bonus action on each of its turns.

Keen Hearing. The killer shrew has advantage on Wisdom (Perception) checks that rely on hearing.

Actions

Bite. *Melee Weapon Attack:* +5 to hit, reach 5 ft., one target. *Hit:* 6 (1d6 + 3) piercing damage, and the target must make a DC 12 Constitution saving throw, taking 9 (2d8) poison damage on a failed save, or half as much damage on a successful one. If the poison damage reduces the target to 0 hit points, the target is stable but poisoned for 1 hour, even after regaining hit points, and is paralyzed while poisoned in this way.

King Rat

Medium beast, unaligned

Armor Class 13
Hit Points 44 (8d8 + 8)
Speed 30 ft., climb 10 ft.

STR	DEX	CON	INT	WIS	CHA
10 (+0)	17 (+3)	13 (+1)	5 (−3)	12 (+1)	4 (−3)

Skills Stealth +5
Senses darkvision 60 ft., passive Perception 11
Languages —
Challenge 2 (450 XP)

Horde Empathy. The king rat can communicate simple ideas and emotions with rats of its horde within 100 feet of it.

Keen Smell. The king rat has advantage on Wisdom (Perception) checks that rely on smell.

Pack Tactics. The king rat has advantage on an attack roll against a creature if at least one of the king rat's allies is within 5 feet of the creature and the ally isn't incapacitated.

Actions

Multiattack. The king rat makes one attack with its Bite and one attack with its Claws.

Bite. *Melee Weapon Attack:* +5 to hit, reach 5 ft., one target. *Hit:* 6 (1d6 + 3) piercing damage. If the target is a creature, it must succeed on a DC 11 Constitution saving throw or contract a disease. Until the disease is cured, the target can't regain hit points except by magical means, and the target's hit point maximum decreases by 3 (1d6) every 24 hours. If the target's hit point maximum drops to 0 as a result of this disease, the target dies.

Claws. *Melee Weapon Attack:* +5 to hit, reach 5 ft., one target. *Hit:* 5 (1d4 + 3) slashing damage.

Tail Sweep **(recharge 6).** The king rat sweeps its tail in an arc around it. Each creature within 10 feet of the king rat must make a DC 13 Dexterity saving throw. On a failure, a creature takes 14 (4d6) bludgeoning damage and is knocked prone. On a success, a creature takes half the damage and isn't knocked prone.

LURKER ABOVE

Huge aberration, neutral

Armor Class 13
Hit Points 68 (8d12 + 16)
Speed 10 ft., climb 5 ft., fly 40 ft.

STR	DEX	CON	INT	WIS	CHA
18 (+4)	16 (+3)	15 (+2)	2 (−4)	15 (+2)	9 (−1)

Skills Athletics +7, Stealth +6
Damage Resistances cold, fire; bludgeoning, piercing, and slashing from nonmagical weapons
Senses darkvision 60 ft., passive Perception 12
Languages —
Challenge 7 (2,900 XP)

Damage Transfer. While it is grappling a creature, the lurker above takes only half the damage dealt to it, and the creature grappled by the lurker above takes the other half.

Keen Scent. The lurker above has advantage on Wisdom (Perception) checks based on scent.

Sunlight Sensitivity. While in sunlight, the lurker above has disadvantage on attack rolls, as well as on Wisdom (Perception) checks that rely on sight.

Actions

Slam. *Melee Weapon Attack:* +7 to hit, reach 5 ft., one target. *Hit:* 17 (3d8 + 4) bludgeoning damage and the target is grappled (escape DC 15) and the lurker above cannot grapple or use its Slam attack on another target.

Smother. The lurker above wraps itself around one grappled creature of Large size or smaller, completely enclosing it. The grappled target is restrained, blinded, no longer able to speak or use spells with verbal components, and at risk of suffocating. At the start of each of the target's turns, the target takes 17 (3d8 + 4) bludgeoning damage.

MASTER KANDASTO

Medium humanoid (human), lawful evil

Armor Class 19 (natural armor)
Hit Points 135 (18d8 + 54)
Speed 60 ft.

STR	DEX	CON	INT	WIS	CHA
18 (+4)	20 (+5)	16 (+3)	17 (+3)	20 (+5)	15 (+2)

Saving Throws Str +9, Dex +10, Con +8, Int +8, Wis +10, Cha +7
Skills Acrobatics +10, Athletics +9, History +8, Perception +10, Religion +8, Stealth +10

Condition Immunities charmed, frightened
Senses passive Perception 20
Languages all
Challenge 13 (10,000 XP)

Special Equipment. Master Kandasto carries the *monk's tri-color sash.*

Evasion. If Master Kandasto is subjected to an effect that allows him to make a Dexterity saving throw to take only half damage, he instead takes no damage if he succeeds on the saving throw, and only half damage if he fails.

Magical Weapons. Master Kandasto's attacks count as magical for the purposes of damage resistances and immunities.

Martial Arts Master. Once per turn, Master Kandasto can deal an additional 13 (3d8) bludgeoning damage when he hits a creature with a weapon attack.

Slow Fall. Master Kandasto reduces all falling damage by 30. If he does not take damage from a fall, he does not drop prone.

Actions

Multiattack. Master Kandasto makes three attacks with his Quarterstaff or Unarmed Strike. He can use his Flurry of Blows or Stunning Strike in place of one of either the Quarterstaff or Unarmed Strike attacks.

Tri-Color Sash. *Melee Weapon Attack:* +12 to hit, reach 10 ft., one target. *Hit:* 10 (1d10 + 7) slashing damage, and the target must make a DC 18 Strength saving throw or be grappled (escape DC 18).

Quarterstaff. *Melee Weapon Attack:* +10 to hit, reach 5 ft., one target. *Hit:* 10 (1d10 + 5) bludgeoning damage.

Unarmed Strike. *Melee Weapon Attack:* +10 to hit, reach 5 ft., one target. *Hit:* 10 (1d10 + 5) bludgeoning damage.

Flurry of Blows (3/day). *Melee Weapon Attack:* +10 to hit, reach 5 ft., one target. *Hit:* 21 (3d10 + 5) bludgeoning damage, and the target suffers one of the following effects of Kandasto's choice:

* The target must succeed on a DC 18 Dexterity saving throw or be knocked prone.
* The target must make a DC 18 Strength saving throw or be pushed up to 15 feet away from Master Kandasto.
* The target can't take reactions until the end of Master Kandasto's next turn.

Stunning Strike (3/day). *Melee Weapon Attack:* +10 to hit, reach 5 ft., one target. *Hit:* 10 (1d10 + 5) bludgeoning damage, and the target must succeed on a DC 18 Constitution saving throw or be stunned until the end of Master Kandasto's next turn.

Reactions

Deflect Missiles. If Master Kandasto has one hand free, he can use his reaction in response to being hit with a ranged weapon attack. He reduces the damage by 28 (1d10 + 23). If he reduces the damage to 0, he can catch the missile if it is small enough for him to hold with one hand.

MEDOOZA

Large ooze, unaligned

Armor Class 7
Hit Points 153 (18d10 + 54)
Speed 30 ft., climb 30 ft.

STR	DEX	CON	INT	WIS	CHA
18 (+4)	5 (−3)	16 (+3)	1 (−5)	6 (−2)	1 (−5)

Damage Resistances bludgeoning, piercing, and slashing from nonmagical attacks
Damage Immunities acid, cold, fire
Condition Immunities blinded, charmed, deafened, exhaustion, frightened, prone
Senses blindsight 60 ft. (blind beyond this radius), passive Perception 8
Languages —
Challenge 10 (5,900 XP)

Corrosive Form. A creature that touches or hits the medooza with a melee attack while within 5 feet of it takes 4 (1d8) acid damage. Any nonmagical weapon made of metal or wood that hits the medooza corrodes. After dealing damage, the weapon takes a permanent and cumulative −1 penalty to damage rolls. If its penalty drops to −5, the weapon is destroyed. Nonmagical ammunition made of metal or wood that hits the medooza is destroyed after dealing damage. The medooza can eat through 2-inch-thick, nonmagical wood or metal in 1 round.

Actions

Multiattack. The medooza makes two Pseudopod attacks.

Pseudopod. *Melee Weapon Attack:* +8 to hit, reach 5 ft., one target. *Hit:* 13 (2d8 + 4) bludgeoning damage plus 18 (4d8) acid damage. In addition, nonmagical armor worn by the target is partly dissolved and takes a permanent and cumulative −1 penalty to the AC it offers. The armor is destroyed if the penalty reduces its AC to 10.

Petrifying Gaze. One creature that can see the medooza and is within 60 feet of it must make a DC 15 Constitution saving throw. If the saving throw fails by 5 or more, the creature is instantly petrified and turned to unrefined iron. Otherwise, a creature that fails the saving throw begins to change and is restrained. The restrained creature must repeat the saving throw at the end of its next turn, becoming petrified on a failure or ending the effect on a success. The petrification lasts until the creature is freed by the *greater restoration* spell or other magic.

MENDICANT

Medium humanoid (any), any neutral alignment

Armor Class 18 (natural armor)
Hit Points 82 (15d8 + 15)
Speed 45 ft.

STR	DEX	CON	INT	WIS	CHA
12 (+1)	18 (+4)	13 (+1)	11 (+0)	18 (+4)	14 (+2)

Saving Throws Dex +7, Wis +7
Skills Acrobatics +7, History +3, Insight +7, Perception +7, Stealth +7
Senses passive Perception 17
Languages Common, plus 1 other language
Challenge 5 (1,800 XP)

Magical Weapons. All of the mendicant's attacks count as magical for the purposes of damage resistances and immunities.

Slow Fall. The mendicant reduces all falling damage by 30. If it does not take damage from a fall, it does not drop prone.

Actions

Multiattack. The mendicant can make two attacks with its Quarterstaff and one attack with its Unarmed Strike, or makes three attacks with its Unarmed Strike. It can use its Flurry of Blows or Stunning Strike ability in place of one of the unarmed strikes.

Quarterstaff. *Melee Weapon Attack:* +7 to hit, reach 5 ft., one target. *Hit:* 7 (1d6 + 4) bludgeoning damage, or 8 (1d8 + 4) bludgeoning damage is used with two hands to make a melee attack.

Unarmed Strike. *Melee Weapon Attack:* +7 to hit, reach 5 ft., one target. *Hit:* 7 (1d6 + 4) bludgeoning damage.

Sling. *Ranged Weapon Attack:* +5 to hit, range 30/120 ft., one target. *Hit:* 6 (1d6 + 3) bludgeoning damage.

Flurry of Blows (3/day). *Melee Weapon Attack:* +7 to hit, reach 5 ft., one target. *Hit:* 13 (3d6 + 4) bludgeoning damage, and the target suffers one of the following effects of the master ascetic's choice:
• The target must succeed on a DC 15 Dexterity saving throw or be knocked prone.
• The target must make a DC 15 Strength saving throw or be pushed up to 15 feet away from the mendicant.
• The target can't take reactions until the end of the mendicant's next turn.

Stunning Strike (3/day). *Melee Weapon Attack:* +7 to hit, reach 5 ft., one target. *Hit:* 7 (1d6 + 4) bludgeoning damage, and the target must succeed on a DC 15 Constitution saving throw or be stunned until the end of the mendicant's next turn.

Reactions

Deflect Missiles. If the mendicant has one hand free, it can use its reaction in response to being hit with a ranged weapon attack. It reduces the damage by 15 (1d10 + 10). If it reduces the damage to 0, it can catch the missile if it is small enough for it to hold with one hand.

MOLD, BROWN

Brown mold is an ectotherm and feeds on the warmth of the environment surrounding it. When within 30 feet of brown mold, the temperature is noticeably colder, often to the point of freezing depending on the size of the brown mold patch. It is common for brown mold to cover a 10-foot square, but it isn't unusual for patches to be much larger.

Creatures that come within 10 feet of brown mold, or start their turn within 10 feet of the mold must succeed on a DC 12 Constitution saving throw. A failed save results in 22 (4d10) cold damage, or half as much on a successful saving throw.

Exposure to fire causes the brown mold to rapidly expand and grow in the direction of the fire. Exposure to cold will instantly destroy brown mold.

MOLD, YELLOW

Patches of yellow mold are most commonly encountered in dark, damp locations, and grows in 5-foot square and larger patches. If disturbed, the yellow mold releases a cloud of spores in a 10-foot radius around itself. Creatures caught in the spore cloud take 11 (2d10) poison damage and must succeed on a DC 15 Constitution saving throw or be poisoned for 1 minute. The creature takes an additional 5 (1d10) poison damage at the start of each of their turns and can repeat the saving throw at the end of each of their turns, ending the effect ton itself on a successful save.

Yellow mold is instantly destroyed by fire damage or sunlight.

MONKEY

Tiny beast, unaligned

Armor Class 12
Hit Points 5 (2d4)
Speed 30 ft., climb 30 ft.

STR	DEX	CON	INT	WIS	CHA
4 (−3)	15 (+2)	10 (+0)	3 (−4)	12 (+1)	5 (−3)

Skills Acrobatics +4, Perception +3
Senses passive Perception 13
Languages —
Challenge 1/8 (25 XP)

Actions

Bite. *Melee Weapon Attack:* +4 to hit, reach 5 ft., one target. *Hit*: 1 piercing damage.

MUDBOG OOZE

Large ooze, unaligned

Armor Class 9
Hit Points 51 (6d10 + 18)
Speed 10 ft., swim 10 ft.

STR	DEX	CON	INT	WIS	CHA
20 (+5)	8 (−1)	17 (+3)	1 (−5)	10 (+0)	3 (−4)

Skills Stealth +1
Senses blindsight 60 ft. (blind beyond this radius), passive Perception 10
Damage Resistances fire
Damage Immunities acid, psychic
Condition Immunities blinded, charmed, deafened, exhaustion, frightened, prone
Languages —
Challenge 2 (450 XP)

Acid. A mudbog secretes a digestive acid that quickly dissolves organic material, but not metal or stone. A creature that attacks the mudbog takes 3 (1d6) acid damage. Any wood or other organic material that touches the mudbog is pitted. Wooden weapons suffer a cumulative −1 penalty to damage rolls made with it unless it is magical. When this penalty reaches −5, the weapon is destroyed.

Amorphous. The ooze can move through a space as narrow as 1 inch wide without squeezing.

False Appearance. The mudbog, while not moving, is indistinguishable from a muddy puddle.

Actions

Engulf. The mudbog moves up to its speed. While doing so, it can enter Medium or smaller creatures' spaces. Whenever the mudbog enters a creature's space, the creature must make a DC13 Dexterity saving throw.

On a successful save, the creature can choose to be pushed 5 feet back or to the side of the mudbog. A creature that chooses not to be pushed suffers the consequences of a failed saving throw. On a failed save, the creature is engulfed and the mudbog enters the creature's space. The creature takes 10 (3d6) acid damage. The engulfed creature can't breathe, is restrained, and takes 21 (6d6) acid damage at the start of each of the ooze's turns. When the mudbog moves, the engulfed creature moves with it.

An engulfed creature can try to escape by taking an action to make a DC13 Strength check. On a success, the creature escapes and enters a space of its choice within 5 feet of the ooze.

Pandemule the Pandemagisticator

Medium humanoid (human), chaotic neutral

Armor Class 12 (15 with *mage armor*)
Hit Points 81 (18d8)
Speed 30 ft.

STR	DEX	CON	INT	WIS	CHA
7 (−2)	14 (+2)	11 (+0)	20 (+5)	10 (+0)	9 (−1)

Saving Throws Con +3, Wis +3
Skills Arcana +8, History +8
Senses passive Perception 10
Languages Abyssal, Celestial, Common, Draconic, Elvish, Infernal
Challenge 8 (3,900 XP)

Bibliophile Frenzy. Pandemule has advantage on attack rolls against any creature that has damaged a book, scroll, or other object containing written words since the end of Pandemule's last turn.

Magic Resistance. Pandemule has advantage on saving throws against spells and other magical effects.

Split Mind. Pandemule can concentrate on two spells at once, but only one can be active at a time. At the start of each of his turns, he can decide which concentration spell is active and which is dormant. That maximum duration of each spell doesn't change and the spell ends as normal when its duration is up. If an effect forces Pandemule to make a Constitution saving throw to maintain concentration, he has disadvantage on the check if he is concentrating on two spells at once. If he fails to maintain his concentration, both spells end.

Spellcasting. Pandemule is an 12th-level spellcaster. His spellcasting ability is Intelligence (spell save DC 16, +8 to hit with spell attacks). He has the following wizard spells prepared:

Cantrips (at will): *chill touch, light, mage hand, mending, ray of frost*
1st level (4 slots): *comprehend languages, magic missile, mage armor, shield*
2nd level (3 slots): *blur, hold person, misty step*
3rd level (3 slots): *counterspell, slow, vampiric touch*
4th level (3 slots): *black tentacles, greater invisibility, stoneskin*
5th level (2 slots): *cloudkill, dominate person*
6th level (1 slot): *disintegrate, globe of invulnerability*

Actions

Dagger. *Melee or Ranged Weapon Attack:* +5 to hit, reach 5 ft. or range 20/60 ft., one target. *Hit:* 4 (1d4 + 2) piercing damage.

Pennagalen

Medium undead, neutral evil

Armor Class 13
Hit Points 45 (7d8 + 14)
Speed 0 ft., fly 40 ft. (hover)

STR	DEX	CON	INT	WIS	CHA
12 (+1)	16 (+3)	14 (+2)	6 (−2)	12 (+1)	10 (+0)

Saving Throws Wis +3
Damage Immunities poison
Condition Immunities frightened, poisoned, prone
Senses darkvision 60 ft., passive Perception 11
Languages Common
Challenge 3 (700 XP)

Exit Host. As a bonus action, the pennagalen exits its host body. Each creature within 20 feet of it that can see it must succeed on a DC 13 Wisdom saving throw or be frightened for 1 minute. A frightened creature can repeat the saving throw at the end of each of its turns, ending the effect on itself on a success. If a creature's saving throw is successful or the effect ends for it, the creature is immune to this feature for the next 24 hours.

Poisonous Blood. When a pennagalen or its empty host body takes piercing or slashing damage, each creature within 5 feet of it must succeed on a DC 13 Dexterity saving throw or take 4 (1d8) poison damage. A creature that fails its saving throw by 5 or more is also poisoned for 1 minute.

Regeneration (host form only). The pennagalen regains 2 hit points at the start of its turn if it has at least 1 hit point.

Sunlight Sensitivity (true form only). While in sunlight, the pennagalen has disadvantage on attack rolls, as well as on Wisdom (Perception) checks that rely on sight.

Undead Nature. A pennagalen doesn't require air, food, drink, or sleep.

Actions

Club (host form only). *Melee Weapon Attack:* +3 to hit, reach 5 ft., one target. *Hit:* 3 (1d4 + 1) bludgeoning damage.

Draining Bite (true form only). *Melee Weapon Attack:* +5 to hit, reach 5 ft., one target. *Hit:* 13 (3d6 + 3) necrotic damage. The target must succeed on a DC 13 Constitution saving throw or its hit point maximum is reduced by an amount equal to the damage taken. This reduction lasts until the creature finishes a long rest. The target dies if this effect reduces its hit point maximum to 0.

A humanoid slain by this attack rises 24 hours later as a pennagalen under this pennagalen's control, unless the humanoid is restored to life, its body is destroyed, or the pennagalen uses the body as a host body. The pennagalen can have only one pennagalen under its control at a time. If another humanoid rises as a pennagalen, the control of the previous pennagalen ends.

Inhabit Host (true form only). The pennagalen inhabits its bonded host body if the body is within 5 feet of it. Its statistics remain the same while inhabiting its host body. Any equipment it is wearing or carrying falls to the ground within 5 feet of the host body. While connected to its host body, the pennagalen doesn't detect as undead when under the scrutiny of features such as a paladin's Divine Sense or spells such as *detect evil and good*. In addition, it slowly regains lost hit points, it loses its Sunlight Sensitivity trait, and it can't use its Draining Bite when inhabiting its host body. While it is outside its host body, the host body is a hollow lump of dead flesh which can be attacked and destroyed (AC 10; hp 20; resistance to bludgeoning damage; immunity to psychic damage). If the pennagalen's host body is destroyed while it is outside of the body, it can bind itself to a new host body by spending 2 hours consuming the head and entrails of a dead humanoid.

Pirate Lieutenant

Medium humanoid (human), any non-lawful alignment

Armor Class 14 (studded leather)
Hit Points 26 (4d8 + 8)
Speed 30 ft.

STR	DEX	CON	INT	WIS	CHA
14 (+2)	15 (+2)	14 (+2)	13 (+1)	11 (+0)	12 (+1)

Saving Throws Dex +4
Skills Acrobatics +4, Deception +3, Perception +2
Senses passive Perception 12
Languages any two languages
Challenge 1 (200 XP)

Scallywag. The pirate lieutenant has advantage on Strength and Dexterity saving throws made against effects that would knock it prone, and it has advantage on Wisdom (Perception) checks that rely on sight.

Actions

Multiattack. The pirate lieutenant makes one attack with its Scimitar and one with its Dagger.
Scimitar. *Melee Weapon Attack:* +4 to hit, reach 5 ft., one target. *Hit:* 5 (1d6 + 2) slashing damage.
Dagger. *Melee or Ranged Weapon Attack:* +4 to hit, reach 5 ft. or range 20/60 ft., one target. *Hit:* 4 (1d4 + 2) piercing damage.
Light Crossbow. *Ranged Weapon Attack:* +4 to hit, range 80/320 ft., one target. *Hit:* 6 (1d8 + 2) piercing damage.

Reactions

Hornswoggle. When a creature the pirate lieutenant can see targets it with an attack, the pirate lieutenant feigns in an attempt to avoid the attack. The attacker must succeed on a DC 12 Wisdom saving throw or the attack misses.

Plant Goblin

Tiny plant, neutral

Armor Class 11
Hit Points 10 (4d4)
Speed 20 ft., climb 20 ft.

STR	DEX	CON	INT	WIS	CHA
5 (−3)	12 (+1)	10 (+0)	6 (−2)	8 (−1)	5 (−3)

Skills Stealth +3
Damage Vulnerabilities fire
Damage Immunities poison
Condition Immunities poisoned
Senses darkvision 60 ft., passive Perception 9
Languages understands Sylvan but can't speak
Challenge 1/8 (25 XP)

Mobile Seeds. When the plant goblin dies, it explodes in a burst of vegetation, sap, and thorns. Each creature within 5 feet of it must make a DC 11 Dexterity saving throw, taking 5 (2d4) piercing damage on a failed save, or half as much damage on a successful one. If in a location of ample soil and not burned, the remains meld into the soil within 24 hours and enrich the plant life within 30 feet for 1 month. The plants yield twice the normal amount of food when harvested.
Pack Tactics. The plant goblin has advantage on an attack roll against a creature if at least one of the goblin's allies is within 5 feet of the creature and the ally isn't incapacitated.

Actions

Thorned Fist. *Melee Weapon Attack:* +3 to hit, reach 5 ft., one target. *Hit:* 3 (1d4 + 1) piercing damage.
Spit Thorn. *Ranged Weapon Attack:* +3 to hit, range 20/60 ft., one target. *Hit:* 1 piercing damage plus 2 (1d4) poison damage.

Ranorek Rump

Medium humanoid (human), chaotic good

Armor Class 12
Hit Points 65 (10d8 + 20)
Speed 30 ft.

STR	DEX	CON	INT	WIS	CHA
17 (+3)	14 (+2)	15 (+2)	7 (−2)	11 (+0)	13 (+1)

Saving Throws Con +4
Skills Athletics +5, Survival +2
Senses passive Perception 10
Languages Common
Challenge 2 (450 XP)

Bravest of the Tribe. Ranorek has advantage on saving throws against being frightened if at least one of Ranorek's allies is within 30 feet of him and he can see the ally.
Reckless. At the start of his turn, Ranorek can gain advantage on all melee weapon attack rolls during that turn, but attack rolls against him have advantage until the start of his next turn.

Actions

Multiattack. Ranorek makes two attacks with his Greatclub.
Greatclub. *Melee Weapon Attack:* +5 to hit, reach 5 ft., one target. *Hit:* 7 (1d8 + 3) bludgeoning damage.
Spear. *Melee or Ranged Weapon Attack:* +5 to hit, reach 5 ft. or range 20/60 ft., one target. *Hit:* 6 (1d6 + 3) piercing damage, or 7 (1d8 + 3) piercing damage if used with two hands to make a melee attack.
Bear Roar (recharge 4–6). Ranorek Rump roars like a cave bear in a 15-foot cone. Each creature in that area that can hear Ranorek must make a DC 13 Wisdom saving throw or be frightened until the end of its next turn.

Preacher

Medium humanoid (any race), any alignment

Armor Class 16 (chain shirt, shield)
Hit Points 78 (12d8 + 24)
Speed 30 ft.

STR	DEX	CON	INT	WIS	CHA
16 (+3)	12 (+1)	14 (+2)	13 (+1)	20 (+5)	17 (+3)

Saving Throws Con +5, Wis +8
Skills History +4, Performance +6, Persuasion +9, Religion +4
Senses passive Perception 15

Languages any three languages
Challenge 8 (3,900 XP)

Spellcasting. The preacher is a 10th-level spellcaster. Its
spellcasting ability is Wisdom (spell save DC 16, +8 to hit with
spell attacks). The preacher has the following cleric spells
prepared:

Cantrips (at will): *guidance, light, resistance, sacred flame,
thaumaturgy*
1st level (4 slots): *bane, bless, command, cure wounds, inflict wounds*
2nd level (3 slots): *aid, hold person, spiritual weapon*
3rd level (3 slots): *beacon of hope, mass healing word, tongues*
4th level (3 slots): *freedom of movement, locate creature*
5th level (2 slots): *flame strike, geas*

Unshakeable Faith. The preacher has advantage on Wisdom and
Charisma saving throws.

Actions

Multiattack. The preacher uses its Speech and makes three
melee attacks.

Morningstar. *Melee Weapon Attack:* +6 to hit, reach 5 ft., one
target. *Hit:* 7 (1d8 + 3) piercing damage.

Speech. The preacher makes one of the following speeches; it
can't use the same speech two rounds in a row:

Condemning Speech. The preacher speaks words of
condemnation at one target within 30 feet of it. The target
must make a DC 16 Wisdom saving throw. On a failure, the
target takes 28 (8d6) thunder damage and is frightened for
1 minute. On a success, the target takes half the damage and
isn't frightened. A frightened creature can repeat the saving
throw at the end of each of its turns, ending the effect on itself
on a success. If the creature's saving throw is successful or
the effect ends for it, the creature is immune to the preacher's
Condemning Speech for the next 24 hours.

Inspiring Speech. The preacher targets up to three creatures
it can see within 30 feet of it and speaks words of inspiration.
Each target has advantage on its next attack roll, saving throw,
or ability check.

Swaying Speech. The preacher speaks persuasively to one target
within 30 feet of it. The target must make a DC 16 Wisdom
saving throw. On a failure, the target takes 28 (8d6) psychic
damage and is charmed for 1 minute. On a success, the target
takes half the damage and isn't charmed. A charmed creature
can repeat the saving throw at the end of each of its turns,
ending the effect on itself on a success. If a creature's saving
throw is successful or the effect ends for it, the creature is
immune to the preacher's Swaying Speech for the next 24 hours.

Rats, Superior, Greater,
and Lesser Giant

A lesser giant rat is as a **giant rat** except with 3 (1d6) hit points.
A greater giant rat is as a giant rat except with 13 (3d6 + 3) hit
points, Constitution 12, and a bite that does 5 (1d6 + 2) piercing
damage on a hit. A superior giant rat is as a greater giant rat
except with 18 (4d6 + 4) hit points. All the rats have *Filth Fever*,
and a creature bitten by one must make a DC 14 Constitution
saving throw to avoid contracting it.

Rot Grubs

Rot grubs are nauseating parasites that feed on flesh and nest in
corpses. Generally, a handful of the grubs infest a single corpse
at a time. A DC 10 Wisdom (Perception) check is enough to
notice and avoid the grubs. If the grubs go unnoticed, contact
with the corpse results in 1d6 grubs bursting from the corpse
and beginning to burrow into the creature's flesh. The creature
must succeed on a DC 12 Dexterity saving throw or take 1
piercing damage from each grub and be infested with rot grubs.
Within 4 hours, the grubs will have started to burrow toward
the host's heart, brain, and other internal organs, eventually
killing the host.

The host must succeed on a DC 15 Constitution saving throw
every 4 hours or take 3 (1d6) necrotic damage and the target's
Constitution score is reduced by 1d4 points. The target dies if
this reduces their Constitution to 0. Otherwise, the reduction
lasts until the infestation is cured.

The rot grub infestation can be mitigated by applying fire for 3
turns to the point of entry, causing a combined 13 (3d8) fire
damage to the host, or by succeeding on a DC 15 Wisdom
(Medicine) check and cutting the grubs out with a sharp
instrument, causing an additional 14 (4d6) piercing damage
to the host. A *greater restoration* or *heal* spell will destroy the
grubs, ending the infestation and restoring the lost Constitution.

Rustle (Giant Cat)

Tiny monstrosity, unaligned

Armor Class 13
Hit Points 49 (11d4 + 22)
Speed 40 ft., climb 20 ft.

STR	DEX	CON	INT	WIS	CHA
13 (+1)	16 (+3)	14 (+2)	3 (−4)	12 (+1)	7 (−2)

Saving Throws Str +3
Skills Perception +3, Stealth +7
Senses darkvision 60 ft., passive Perception 13
Languages —
Challenge 3 (700 XP)

Keen Smell. Rustle has advantage on Wisdom (Perception)
checks that rely on smell.

Pounce (lynx form only). If Rustle moves at least 20 feet
straight toward a creature and then hits it with a claw attack on
the same turn, that target must succeed on a DC 13 Strength
saving throw or be knocked prone. If the target is prone, Rustle
can make one bite attack against it as a bonus action.

Shadow Stealth (true form only). While in dim light or
darkness, Rustle can take the Hide action as a bonus action.

Shapechanger. Rustle can use his action to polymorph into a
Small, black lynx or back into his true form. His statistics are
the same in each form. Any equipment he is wearing or carrying
isn't transformed. He reverts to his true form if he dies.

Actions

Multiattack. Rustle makes one Bite attack and two Claw attacks.

Bite. *Melee Weapon Attack:* +5 to hit, reach 5 ft., one target. *Hit:*
6 (1d6 + 3) piercing damage.

Claw. *Melee Weapon Attack:* +5 to hit, reach 5 ft., one target.
Hit: 8 (2d4 + 3) slashing damage. ***Frightening Hiss.*** Rustle
targets up to three creatures that he can see within 30 feet of
him and hisses. If the target can hear Rustle, it must succeed on
a DC 13 Wisdom saving throw or become frightened until the
end of its next turn.

Sarthoggus

Medium humanoid (human), chaotic evil

Armor Class 17 (*robe of the devoted*[VI])
Hit Points 150 (20d8 + 60)
Speed 30 ft.

STR	DEX	CON	INT	WIS	CHA
11 (+0)	16 (+3)	17 (+3)	16 (+3)	22 (+6)	18 (+4)

Saving Throws Con +9, Wis +12, Cha +10
Skills Arcana +9, Insight +12, Medicine +12, Nature +9, Perception +12
Damage Resistances acid; bludgeoning, piercing, and slashing from nonmagical attacks
Damage Immunities poison, psychic
Condition Immunities frightened, poisoned
Senses darkvision 60 ft., passive Perception
Languages Abyssal, Common, Infernal, Undercommon, Tsathar
Challenge 20 (25,000 XP)

Special Equipment. Sarthoggus wears a *robe of the devoted*[VI], and carries a *staff of the frog*[VI] and *wand of painful anguish*[VI].

Amphibious. Sarthoggus can breathe air and water.

Fetid Blessing. Whenever Sarthoggus deals acid or poison damage, he ignores resistance to those damage types and deals an additional 7 (2d6) damage of the same type.

Legendary Resistances (1/day). If Sarthoggus fails a saving throw, he can choose to succeed instead.

Magic Resistance. Sarthoggus has advantage on saving throws against spells and other magical effects.

Spellcasting. Sarthoggus is a 20th-level spellcaster. His spellcasting ability is Wisdom (spell save DC 20, +12 to hit with spell attacks). He has the following cleric spells prepared.

Cantrips (at will): *acid splash, guidance, mending, resistance, poison spray, thaumaturgy*
1st level (4 slots): *command, inflict wounds, protection from evil and good, shield of faith*
2nd level (3 slots): *acid arrow, aid, hold person, lesser restoration, silence, spiritual weapon*
3rd level (3 slots): *caustic burst*[VI]*, create food and water, dispel magic, tongue of the frog god*[VI]
4th level (3 slots): *banishment, blight, control water*
5th level (3 slots): *contagion, insect plague*
6th level (2 slots): *harm*
7th level (2 slots): *divine word, plane shift*
8th level (1 slot): *feeblemind*
9th level (1 slot): *power word kill*

Actions

Quarterstaff. *Melee Weapon Attack:* +6 to hit, reach 5 ft., one target. *Hit:* 5 (1d6 + 2) bludgeoning damage, or 6 (1d8 + 2) bludgeoning damage if wielded with two hands, plus 9 (2d8) poison damage.

Touch of Filth (recharge 5–6). *Melee Spell Attack:* +12 to hit, reach 5 ft., one target. *Hit:* 33 (5d10 + 6) necrotic damage, and the target's hit point maximum is reduced by an equal amount. If the creature drops to 0 hit points because of this damage, its body is reduced to a puddle of retch and filth, and nothing short of *true resurrection* or *wish* can return the creature to life.

Summon (1/day). Sarthoggus has a 60% chance to summon 1 **kytha demon**. The summoned creature appears in an unoccupied space within 60 feet of Sarthoggus, and can't summon other creatures. It remains for 1 minute, until it or Sarthoggus is slain, or until Sarthoggus takes an action to dismiss it.

Legendary Actions

Sarthoggus can take 3 legendary actions, choosing from the options below. Only one legendary action option can be used at a time and only at the end of another creature's turn. Sarthoggus regains spent legendary actions at the start of his turn.

Cantrip. Sarthoggus casts a cantrip.

Spew Slime (costs 2 actions). Sarthoggus spews a spray of slime

Sarthoggus' Spells

Caustic Burst

3rd-level evocation
Casting Time: 1 action
Range: 60 feet
Components: V, S, M (an acid pitted ruby worth 5 gp)
Duration: Instantaneous

You launch a ball of viscous acid from your open hand which lands at a point you choose within range and then splashes in a 10-foot radius. Each creature in the area centered on that point must make a Dexterity saving throw. A target takes 6d4 acid damage on a failed saving throw, or half as much damage on a successful saving throw. If a target took acid damage, it takes an additional 3d4 acid damage at the start of its next turn.

At Higher Levels. When you cast this spell using a spell slot of 4th level or higher, the damage increases by 1d4 for each slot level above 3rd.

Tongue of the Frog God

3rd-level transmutation
Casting Time: 1 bonus action
Range: Self
Components: V, S, M (the tongue of a poisonous frog)
Duration: Concentration, up to 1 minute

This spell conjures a long, swollen tongue that grows from the mouth of the caster. This tongue can be used as a whiplike appendage. You can use an action to make a melee spell attack with the tongue which has a range of 20 feet. It deals 1d8 bludgeoning damage on a hit, and the creature is grappled. The escape DC is equal to your spellcasting DC. While grappled, the creature makes a Constitution saving throw at the start of each of its turns, taking 2d10 poison damage on a failed save, or half as much on a successful one.

The tongue can be attacked, has AC 15 and hit points equal to half your hit point maximum. When the tongue is destroyed, it dissolves into nothing and the caster's tongue returns to normal. It does not impede the casting of other spells with verbal components.

***Summon Infestation* (costs 3 actions).** Sarthoggus summons a scourge of insects, which functions as if he had cast the *insect plague* spell. He does not have to concentrate on this effect, and it ends at the end of his next turn.

SEVERED HAND

Tiny undead, neutral evil

Armor Class 12
Hit Points 10 (4d4)
Speed 30 ft., climb 10 ft.

STR	DEX	CON	INT	WIS	CHA
8 (−1)	15 (+2)	10 (+0)	6 (−2)	8 (−2)	5 (−3)

Skills Acrobatics +4
Damage Immunities poison
Condition Immunities blinded, deafened, poisoned
Senses blindsight 30 ft. (blind beyond this radius), passive Perception 8
Languages understands the languages it knew in life but can't speak
Challenge 1/8 (25 XP)

Pack Tactics. The severed hand has advantage on an attack roll against a creature if at least one of the hand's allies is within 5 feet of the creature and the ally isn't incapacitated.
Standing Leap. The severed hand's long jump is up to 20 feet and its high jump is up to 10 feet, with or without a running start.
Weapons Specialist. The severed hand is proficient with one-handed finesse weapons and can use its action to make an attack roll with such a weapon in place of its Slam attack.
Undead Nature. A severed hand doesn't require air, food, drink, or sleep.

Actions

Slam. *Melee Weapon Attack:* +4 to hit, reach 5 ft., one target. *Hit:* 4 (1d4 + 2) bludgeoning damage.

SEVERED HEAD

Tiny undead, neutral evil

Armor Class 12
Hit Points 10 (4d4)
Speed 30 ft.

STR	DEX	CON	INT	WIS	CHA
6 (−2)	14 (+2)	11 (+0)	10 (+0)	12 (+1)	8 (−1)

Skills Perception +3
Damage Immunities poison
Condition Immunities poisoned
Senses darkvision 60 ft., passive Perception 13
Languages any languages it knew in life
Challenge 1/8 (25 XP)

Incessant Blathering. A creature that casts a spell with a verbal component while within 10 feet of the severed head must succeed on a DC 10 Constitution saving throw or fail to cast the spell, losing the action but not the spell slot.
Keen Sight. The severed head has advantage on Wisdom (Perception) checks that rely on sight.

Undead Nature. A severed head doesn't require air, food, drink, or sleep.

Actions

Bite. *Melee Weapon Attack:* +4 to hit, reach 5 ft., one target. *Hit:* 4 (1d4 + 2) piercing damage.

SKELETON, GIANT LIZARD

Large undead, lawful evil

Armor Class 13 (natural armor)
Hit Points 45 (6d10 + 12)
Speed 30 ft., climb 30 ft.

STR	DEX	CON	INT	WIS	CHA
16 (+3)	13 (+1)	14 (+2)	2 (−4)	10 (+0)	5 (−3)

Saving Throws Wis +2
Skills Athletics +5
Damage Vulnerabilities bludgeoning
Damage Immunities poison
Condition Immunities exhaustion, poisoned
Senses darkvision 60 ft., passive Perception 10
Languages Abyssal
Challenge 1 (200 XP)

Undead Nature. A giant lizard skeleton doesn't require air, food, drink, or sleep.

Actions

Bite. *Melee Weapon Attack:* +5 to hit, reach 5 ft., one target. *Hit:* 7 (1d8 + 3) piercing damage.
Tail. *Melee Weapon Attack:* +5 to hit, reach 10 ft., one target. *Hit:* 5 (1d4 + 3) bludgeoning damage, and the target is grappled (escape DC 13). Until this grapple ends, the target is restrained, and the giant lizard skeleton can't use its tail attack on another target. If the target's check to escape the grapple succeeds by 5 or more, the giant lizard skeleton's tail breaks and it can't use its tail again until it finishes a long rest.

SKELETON, NOBLE

Medium undead, lawful evil

Armor Class 13
Hit Points 71 (11d8 + 22)
Speed 30 ft.

STR	DEX	CON	INT	WIS	CHA
10 (+0)	17 (+3)	15 (+2)	11 (+0)	8 (−1)	16 (+3)

Saving Throws Wis +1
Skills Deception +5, History +2, Persuasion +5
Damage Vulnerabilities bludgeoning
Damage Immunities poison
Condition Immunities exhaustion, poisoned
Senses darkvision 60 ft., passive Perception 9
Languages any languages it knew in life
Challenge 4 (1,100 XP)

Air of Nobility. Skeletons of CR 1 or lower within 15 feet of the noble skeleton obey the noble's verbal commands to the

best of their abilities. If a skeleton is under the control of another creature, the controller must succeed on a contested Charisma check with the noble skeleton each time the controller commands the skeleton to act or the skeleton doesn't obey its controller.

Turning Defiance. The noble skeleton and any skeletons within 15 feet of it have advantage on saving throws against effects that turn undead.

Undead Nature. A noble skeleton doesn't require air, food, drink, or sleep.

Actions

Multiattack. The noble skeleton makes three attacks, only one of which can be with its Broken Mirror.

Scepter. *Melee Weapon Attack:* +5 to hit, reach 5 ft., one target. *Hit:* 7 (1d8 + 3) bludgeoning damage.

Hairpin. *Ranged Weapon Attack:* +5 to hit, range 20/60 ft., one target. *Hit:* 5 (1d4 + 3) piercing damage.

Broken Mirror. *Melee Weapon Attack:* +5 to hit, reach 5 ft., one target. *Hit:* 10 (2d6 + 3) piercing damage and the target must make a DC 13 Dexterity saving throw. On a failure, a shard of the mirror breaks off and sticks in the target's flesh. The target takes 3 (1d6) piercing damage at the start of each of its turns as long as the mirror shard remains lodged in its flesh. A creature, including the target, can take its action to remove the shard by succeeding on a DC 13 Wisdom (Medicine) check. The shard also falls out if the target receives magical healing.

SLITHERING TRACKER

Small ooze, unaligned

Armor Class 9
Hit Points 75 (10d6 + 40)
Speed 20 ft., climb 10 ft.

STR	DEX	CON	INT	WIS	CHA
14 (+2)	8 (−1)	18 (+4)	2 (−4)	7 (−2)	2 (−4)

Skills Stealth +3
Damage Resistances acid
Condition Immunities blinded, charmed, deafened, exhaustion, frightened, prone
Senses blindsight 60 ft. (blind beyond this radius), passive Perception 8
Languages —
Challenge 4 (1,100 XP)

Amorphous. The slithering tracker can move through a space as narrow as 1 inch wide without squeezing.

Ooze Nature. The slithering tracker doesn't require sleep.

Spider Climb. The slithering tracker can climb difficult surfaces, including upside down on ceilings, without needing to make an ability check.

Transparent. Even when the slithering tracker is in plain sight, it takes a successful DC 14 Wisdom (Perception) check to spot a slithering tracker that has neither moved nor attacked. A creature that tries to enter the slithering tracker's space while unaware of the tracker is surprised by the tracker.

Silent Stalker. The slithering tracker has advantage on stealth checks while moving.

Actions

Pseudopod. *Melee Weapon Attack:* +4 to hit, reach 5 ft., one target. *Hit:* 5 (1d6 + 2) bludgeoning damage plus 14 (4d6) acid damage, and the target must succeed on a DC 14 Wisdom saving throw or be incapacitated for 1 minute. A creature can repeat the saving throw at the end of each of its turns, ending the effect on itself on a success.

Cling. *Melee Weapon Attack:* +4 to hit, reach 5 ft., one willing creature, or a creature that is incapacitated or restrained. *Hit:* 14 (4d6) acid damage, and the slithering tracker attaches to the target. While attached, the slithering tracker doesn't attack. Instead, at the start of each of the slithering tracker's turns, the target loses 14 (4d6) hit points due to blood loss.

The slithering tracker can detach itself by spending 5 feet of its movement. It does so after it drains 30 hit points of blood from the target or the target dies. A creature, including the target, can use its action to detach the slithering tracker.

STONE DELVER

Large monstrosity, chaotic evil

Armor Class 19 (natural armor)
Hit Points 114 (12d10 + 48)
Speed 30 ft., burrow 30 ft.

STR	DEX	CON	INT	WIS	CHA
21 (+5)	14 (+2)	18 (+4)	7 (−2)	10 (+0)	9 (−1)

Senses darkvision 120 ft., tremorsense 120 ft., passive Perception 10

Languages Stone Delver
Challenge 7 (2,900 XP)

Six Limb Charge. If the stone delver moves at least 20 feet straight towards a target and then hits it with a claw attack on the same turn, the target takes an extra 10 (3d6) slashing damage. If the target is a creature, it must succeed on a DC 16 Strength saving throw or be knocked prone.

If the stone delver hit its initial target on the same turn and knocked it prone, it can use a bonus action to make up to four claw attacks against targets that are adjacent to the initial target.

Tunneler. The stone delver can burrow through solid stone at half its burrowing speed and leaves a 5 foot wide, 10 foot high tunnel in its wake.

Actions

Multiattack. The stone delver makes three Claw attacks.
Claw. *Melee Weapon Attack:* +8 to hit, reach 10 ft., one target. *Hit:* 10 (1d10+5) slashing damage.

Swarm of Green Frogs

Medium swarm of Tiny beasts, unaligned

Armor Class 14
Hit Points 38 (7d8 + 7)
Speed 30 ft., swim 30 ft.

STR	DEX	CON	INT	WIS	CHA
6 (−2)	18 (+4)	12 (+1)	2 (−4)	10 (+0)	3 (−4)

Saving Throws Con +3
Damage Resistances bludgeoning, piercing, slashing
Damage Immunities poison
Condition Immunities charmed, frightened, grappled, paralyzed, petrified, poisoned, prone, restrained, stunned
Senses darkvision 60 ft., passive Perception 10
Languages —
Challenge 2 (450 XP)

Amphibious. The swarm of green frogs can breathe air and water.
Poisonous Skin. A creature that touches the swarm, hits it with a melee attack while within 5 feet of it, or that ends its turn in the same space as the swarm takes 4 (1d8) poison damage.

Swarm. The swarm can occupy another creature's space and vice versa, and the swarm can move through any opening large enough for a Tiny frog. The swarm can't regain hit points or gain temporary hit points.

Actions

Bite. *Melee Weapon Attack:* +6 to hit, reach 0 ft., one creature in the swarm's space. *Hit:* 14 (4d6) piercing damage, or 7 (2d6) piercing damage if the swarm has half of its hit points or fewer.
Many-Legged Kick (recharge 6). The frogs in the swarm kick at the same time. Each creature in the swarm's space must succeed on a DC 14 Dexterity saving throw or be knocked prone. If a creature is prone in the swarm's space, it takes 9 (2d8) poison damage.

Swarm of Miniature Mermaids

Large swarm of Small humanoids (merfolk), neutral

Armor Class 13
Hit Points 60 (11d10)
Speed 10 ft., swim 40 ft.

STR	DEX	CON	INT	WIS	CHA
12 (+1)	16 (+3)	10 (+0)	8 (−1)	14 (+2)	17 (+3)

Skills Perception +4
Damage Resistances bludgeoning, piercing, slashing
Condition Immunities charmed, frightened, grappled, paralyzed, petrified, prone, restrained, stunned
Senses passive Perception 14
Languages Aquan, Common
Challenge 3 (700 XP)

Amphibious. The swarm can breathe air and water.
Smothering Embrace. While in water, a creature in the swarm's space is at risk of suffocating. It must succeed on a DC 13 Constitution saving throw to hold its breath or begin choking. A choking creature can survive a number of rounds equal to its Constitution modifier (minimum of 1 round) before dropping to 0 hit points and dying.
Swarm. The swarm can occupy another creature's space and vice versa, and the swarm can move through any opening large enough for a Small mermaid. The swarm can't regain hit points or gain temporary hit points.

Actions

Bites. *Melee Weapon Attack:* +5 to hit, reach 0 ft., one creature in the swarm's space. *Hit:* 21 (6d6) piercing damage, or 10 (3d6) piercing damage if the swarm has half of its hit points or fewer.
Haunting Melody (recharge 6). The voices of the dozens of miniature mermaids harmonize into a haunting melody. Each creature within 30 feet of the swarm that can hear it must succeed on a DC 13 Charisma saving throw or be charmed by the swarm for 1 minute. A creature can repeat the saving throw at the end of each of its turns, ending the effect on itself on a success. If a creature's saving throw is successful or the effect ends for it, the creature is immune to the swarm's Haunting Melody for the next 24 hours.

Theurgist

The Theurgist of Tsathoggus uses the statistics of a **priest**,
save that its Divine Eminence ability deals poison damage
instead of radiant, it has resistance to necrotic and
psychic damage, and speaks Common and Tsathar. It has
the following cleric spells prepared:

Cantrips (at will): *acid splash, mending, poison spray*
1st level (4 slots): *inflict wounds, protection from evil and
good, shield of faith*
2nd level (3 slots): *acid arrow, lesser restoration, spiritual
weapon*
3rd level (2 slots): *caustic burst, dispel magic, tongue of the
frog god*

Troll Warlord

The troll warlord uses the statistics of a **troll**, except for the
following changes:

- Its Challenge Rating is 8 (3,900 XP).
- It has 136 (13d10 + 65) hit points, and its Armor Class is 16
  (natural armor).
- Its Speed is 40 ft.
- Its Strength score is 20 (+5), and it has a +8 to hit with its Bite
  and Claw attacks. The Bite attack deals 8 (1d6 + 5) piercing
  damage and the Claw attack deals 12 (2d6 + 5) slashing
  damage.
- It has resistance to bludgeoning, piercing, and slashing
  damage from nonmagical attacks.
- It has proficiency in Strength (+8), Dexterity (+4), and
  Constitution (+8) saving throws.
- It has the following new feature:

Reckless. At the start of its turn, the troll warlord can gain
advantage on all melee weapon attack rolls during that turn, but
attack rolls against it have advantage until the start of its next turn.

Tsathar

Medium monstrosity, chaotic evil

Armor Class 13 (leather armor)
Hit Points 16 (3d8 + 3)
Speed 30 ft., swim 30 ft.

STR	DEX	CON	INT	WIS	CHA
13 (+1)	14 (+2)	12 (+1)	12 (+1)	12 (+1)	10 (+0)

Skills Athletics +3, Stealth +4
Senses darkvision 60 ft., passive Perception 11
Languages Abyssal, Tsathar
Challenge 1/2 (100 XP)

Amphibious. The tsathar can breathe air and water.
Keen Smell. The tsathar has advantage on Wisdom (Perception)
checks that rely on smell.
Slimy. Tsathar continuously cover themselves with muck and
slime. Creatures attempting to grapple a tsathar do so with
disadvantage.
Standing Leap. The tsathar's long jump is up to 20 feet and its
high jump is up to 10 feet, with or without a running start.

Actions

Multiattack. The tsathar makes one attack with its Spear and one
attack with its Bite, or one attack with its Bite and one with its Claws.

Spear. *Melee Weapon Attack:* +3 to hit, reach 5 ft. or
20/60 ft., one target. *Hit:* 4 (1d6 + 1) piercing damage, or 5 (1d8
+1) piercing damage if used with two hands to make the melee
attack.
Bite. *Melee Weapon Attack:* +4 to hit, reach 5 ft., one target. *Hit:*
4 (1d4 + 2) piercing damage.
Claws. *Melee Weapon Attack:* +4 to hit, reach 5 ft., one target.
Hit: 4 (1d4 + 2) slashing damage
***Implant* (1/day).** The tsathar uses its tongue to implant one
incapacitated creature with a tsathar egg. The target must make
a DC 13 Constitution saving throw or contract the tsathar egg
infestation disease.

Tsathar, Hellbender

Large aberration, chaotic evil

Armor Class 18 (natural armor)
Hit Points 76 (8d10 + 32)
Speed 20 ft., burrow 20 ft.

STR	DEX	CON	INT	WIS	CHA
20 (+5)	12 (+1)	19 (+4)	5 (−3)	9 (−1)	5 (−3)

Damage Resistances acid, poison; bludgeoning, piercing, and
slashing damage from nonmagical attacks
Damage Immunities fire

Hit: 10 (1d10 + 5) slashing damage plus 7 (2d6) fire damage.

Fiery Pulse (recharge 5-6). The hellbender releases a burst of fire from its small pores in its skin in a 10-foot radius. Each creature in the area must make a DC 15 Dexterity saving throw, taking 28 (8d6) fire damage on a failed saving throw, or half as much damage on a successful saving throw.

Implant (1/day). The hellbender tsathar uses its tongue to implant one incapacitated creature with a tsathar egg. The target must make a DC 13 Constitution saving throw or contract the tsathar egg disease.

TSATHAR, SACERDOTAL

Medium monstrosity, chaotic evil

Armor Class 14 (hide armor)
Hit Points 112 (15d8 + 45)
Speed 30 ft., swim 30 ft.

STR	DEX	CON	INT	WIS	CHA
15 (+2)	14 (+2)	17 (+3)	14 (+2)	17 (+3)	12 (+1)

Saving Throws Wis +6, Cha +4
Skills Nature +5, Perception +6, Religion +5
Damage Resistances poison
Senses darkvision 60 ft., passive Perception 16
Languages Abyssal, Tsathar
Challenge 6 (2,300 XP)

Amphibious. The tsathar priest can breathe air and water.

Fetid Strike. Once on each of the tsathar priest's turns when it hits a creature with a weapon attack, it can cause the attack to deal an extra 4 (1d8) poison damage to the target.

Keen Smell. The tsathar priest has advantage on Wisdom (Perception) checks that rely on smell.

Slimy. Tsathar continuously cover themselves with muck and slime. Creatures attempting to grapple a tsathar do so with disadvantage.

Senses darkvision 60 ft., passive Perception 9
Languages Ignan
Challenge 7 (2,900 XP)

Actions

Multiattack. The hellbender can make two Claw attacks and one Bite attack.

Bite. Melee Weapon Attack: +8 to hit, reach 5 ft., one target. Hit: 1d6 + 5 piercing damage, plus 7 (2d6) fire damage.

Claw. *Melee Weapon Attack:* +8 to hit, reach 5 ft., one target.

NEW DISEASE: TSATHAR EGG INFESTATION

Tsathar are sexless, reproducing by injecting eggs into living hosts. An egg can be implanted only into a helpless host creature. The host must be of Small size or larger. Giant frogs, bred for this very purpose, are the most common host.

The symptoms of the infestation manifest when the creature next takes a long rest. The infected creature suffers one level of exhaustion. While it has any levels of exhaustion, it is paralyzed, does not benefit from a long rest, and cannot regain hit points from any source save for magic. At the end of each long rest, an infected creature must make a DC 15 Constitution saving throw. On a failed saving throw, the creature gains one level of exhaustion. When an infected creature dies, the young tsathar emerges.

A *lesser restoration* spell rids the victim of any implanted egg. In addition, another creature can attempt a DC 20 Wisdom (Medicine) check to remove an implanted egg surgically. Each attempt made deals 4 (1d8) slashing damage to a creature.

The type of creature and the implanting tsathar determines what type of tsathar emerges upon the death of the victim:

• If the implanting creature is any type of tsathar and the victim is any type of beast, the emerging egg is a tsathar.

• If the implanting creature is a sacerdotal tsathar and the victim is a humanoid, roll a d6. On a 1-3, the egg is a tsathar; a 4-5, the resulting egg is a sacerdotal tsathar. On a 6, it is instead a hellbender tsathar.

• If the implanting creature is a hellbender tsathar and the victim is humanoid, roll a d6. On a 1-4, the egg is a tsathar. On a 5-6, the egg is a hellbender tsathar.

Standing Leap. The tsathar priest's long jump is up to 20 feet and its high jump is up to 10 feet, with or without a running start.

Spellcasting. The tsathar priest is an 8th-level spellcaster. Its spellcasting ability is Wisdom (spell save DC 14, +6 to hit with spell attacks). It has the following cleric spells prepared:

Cantrips (at will): *guidance, poison spray, resistance, thaumaturgy*

1st level (4 slots): *bane, bless, cure wounds, detect magic, inflict wounds*

2nd level (3 slots): *acid arrow, calm emotions, hold person, silence*

3rd level (3 slots): *bestow curse, dispel magic, stinking cloud*

4th level (2 slots): *control water, guardian of faith*

Actions

Multiattack. The tsathar makes one attack with its Kukri and one attack with its Bite, or one attack with its Bite and one with its Claws.

Kukri. *Melee Weapon Attack:* +5 to hit, reach 5 ft., one target. *Hit:* 5 (1d6 + 2) slashing damage.

Bite. *Melee Weapon Attack:* +5 to hit, reach 5 ft., one target. *Hit:* 5 (1d6 + 2) piercing damage.

Claws. *Melee Weapon Attack:* +5 to hit, reach 5 ft., one target. *Hit:* 4 (1d4 + 2) slashing damage

Implant (1/day). The tsathar uses its tongue to implant one incapacitated creature with a tsathar egg. The target must make a DC 13 Constitution saving throw or contract the tsathar egg infestation disease.

Unmasked Priest of Tsathoggus

Medium humanoid (human), chaotic evil

Armor Class 17 (+1 scale mail)
Hit Points 127 (17d8 + 51)
Speed 30 ft., swim 30 ft.

STR	DEX	CON	INT	WIS	CHA
16 (+3)	12 (+1)	16 (+3)	14 (+2)	18 (+4)	8 (−2)

Saving Throws Wis +8, Cha +2
Skills Medicine +8, Religion +6
Damage Resistances necrotic, psychic
Senses darkvision 60 ft., passive Perception 14
Languages Common, Tsathar
Challenge 10 (5,900 XP)

Special Equipment. The unmasked priest of Tsathoggus wears a set of green *+1 scale mail* and wields a black enameled *unholy mace*[VI].

Amphibious. The unmasked priest can breath air and water.

Fetid Blessing. Whenever the evangelist deals acid or poison damage, it ignores resistance to those damage types and deals an additional 7 (2d6) damage of the same type.

Spellcasting. The unmasked priest is a 12th-level spellcaster. Its spellcasting ability is Wisdom (spell save DC 15, +7 to hit with spell attacks). It has the following cleric spells prepared.

Cantrips (at will): *acid splash, guidance, mending, poison spray, thaumaturgy*

1st level (4 slots): *bane, inflict wounds, protection from evil and good, shield of faith*

2nd level (3 slots): *acid arrow, hold person, lesser restoration, spiritual weapon*

3rd level (3 slots): *caustic burst*[VI], *create food and water, dispel magic, tongue of the frog god*[VI]

4th level (3 slots): *blight, control water*

5th level (2 slots): *insect plague*

6th level (1 slot): *harm*

Actions

Unholy Mace. *Melee Weapon Attack:* +8 to hit, reach 5 ft., one target. *Hit:* 7 (1d6 + 4) bludgeoning damage. If the target is good-aligned, it takes an additional 3 (1d6) poison damage.

Unholy Mace

Weapon (mace), uncommon (requires attunement)

This black-iron mace seems to glow with a very dim, sickly green light, and its head is adorned with curved, almost thorn-like spikes. You have a +1 bonus to attack and damage rolls made with the *unholy mace*. In addition, if you strike a good-aligned creature, you deal an additional 1d6 poison damage.

Vali

Small celestial, neutral good

Armor Class 17
Hit Points 190 (20d6 +120)
Speed 50 ft.

STR	DEX	CON	INT	WIS	CHA
20 (+5)	25 (+7)	22 (+6)	18 (+4)	21 (+5)	23 (+6)

Saving Throws Str +10, Int +9, Wis +10
Skills Acrobatics +12, History +9, Insight +10, Perception +10
Damage Resistances bludgeoning, piercing, and slashing from nonmagical attacks
Damage Immunities necrotic, radiant
Condition Immunities charmed, exhaustion, frightened
Senses truesight 120 ft., passive Perception 20
Languages all, telepathy 120 ft.
Challenge 15 (13,000 XP)

Expert Archer. Vali's attacks with a bow don't have disadvantage when he is within 5 feet of a hostile creature or when he is shooting at long range.

Imbued Arrows. As a bonus action, Vali can imbue one arrow he fires from a bow that turn with one of the following.
- **Fell the Mighty.** The attack deals an extra 21 (6d6) thunder damage, and, if the target is Large or larger, it must succeed on a DC 19 Dexterity saving throw or be knocked prone.
- **Lightning.** The attack deals an extra 14 (4d6) lightning damage, and each creature within 10 feet of the target must succeed on a DC 19 Constitution saving throw or be stunned until the end of its next turn.
- **Slaying.** If the target is a creature that has 50 hit points or fewer, it must succeed on a DC 13 Constitution saving throw or die.
- **Valhalla's Light.** The attack deals an extra 14 (4d6) radiant damage, and each creature in a 5-foot-wide line between Vali and the target must succeed on a DC 19 Dexterity saving throw or be blinded until the end of its next turn.

Immortal Nature. Vali doesn't require food, drink, or sleep.

Legendary Resistance (3/day). If Vali fails a saving throw, he can choose to succeed instead.

Magic Weapons. Vali's weapon attacks are magical.

Master of Missiles. When Vali is targeted by an attack or spell that requires a ranged attack roll, the attacker must succeed on a DC 19 Charisma saving throw or the attack fails. If the attack fails, the action or spell slot is still expended.

Actions

Multiattack. Vali makes three Shortbow attacks or three Battleaxe attacks.

Battleaxe. *Melee Weapon Attack:* +10 to hit, reach 5 ft., one target. *Hit:* 9 (1d8 + 5) slashing damage, or 10 (1d10 + 5) slashing damage if used with two hands.

Shortbow. *Ranged Weapon Attack:* +12 to hit, range 80/320 ft., one target. *Hit:* 10 (1d6 + 7) piercing damage.

Legendary Actions

Vali can take 3 legendary actions, choosing from the options below. Only one legendary action can be used at a time and only at the end of another creature's turn. Vali regains spent legendary actions at the start of its turn.

Shortbow. Vali makes one Shortbow attack.
Move. Vali moves up to his speed without provoking opportunity attacks.
Rain of Arrows (costs 3 actions). Vali chooses a point on the ground he can see within 100 feet of him and shoots arrows into the air. Each creature within 10 feet of that point must make a DC 19 Dexterity saving throw. On a failure, a creature takes 18 (4d8) piercing damage and is restrained until the end of its next turn. On a success, a creature takes half the damage and isn't restrained.

Vampire Bat

Small beast, unaligned

Armor Class 12
Hit Points 22 (4d6 + 8)
Speed 10 ft., fly 40 ft.

STR	DEX	CON	INT	WIS	CHA
10 (+0)	15 (+2)	14 (+2)	2 (−4)	12 (+1)	6 (−2)

Saving Throws Con +4
Skills Stealth +4
Senses blindsight 60 ft., passive Perception 11
Languages —
Challenge 1/4 (50 XP)

Echolocation. The vampire bat can't use its blindsight while deafened.

Keen Hearing. The vampire bat has advantage on Wisdom (Perception) checks that rely on hearing.

Actions

Blood Drain. *Melee Weapon Attack:* +4 to hit, reach 5 ft., one creature. *Hit:* 5 (2d4) necrotic damage, and the vampire bat attaches to the target. While attached, the vampire bat doesn't attack. Instead, at the start of each of the vampire bat's turns, the target loses 5 (2d4) hit points due to blood loss. The vampire bat regains hit points equal to the hit points the target loses.

The vampire bat can detach itself by spending 5 feet of its movement. It does so after it drains 15 hit points of blood from the target or the target dies. A creature, including the target, can use its action to detach the vampire bat by succeeding on a DC 12 Strength check.

Vampire Vine

Large plant, unaligned

Armor Class 15 (natural armor)
Hit Points 112 (15d10 + 30)
Speed 15 ft., climb 30 ft.

STR	DEX	CON	INT	WIS	CHA
13 (+1)	19 (+4)	14 (+2)	4 (−3)	11 (+0)	5 (−3)

Skills Stealth +7
Damage Vulnerabilities fire
Damage Resistances necrotic
Condition Immunities blinded, charmed, deafened, paralyzed, poisoned
Senses blindsight 60 ft. (blind beyond this radius), passive Perception 10

Languages —
Challenge 5 (1,800 XP)

Blood Frenzy. The vampire vine has advantage on melee attack rolls against any creature that doesn't have all of its hit points.

False Appearance. While the vampire vine remains motionless, it is indistinguishable from a vine covered in crimson flowers.

Actions

Multiattack. The vampire vine makes two Thorned Tendril attacks. If both attacks hit a Medium or smaller target, the target is grappled (escape DC 15) and begins to suffocate.

Thorned Tendril. *Melee Weapon Attack:* +7 to hit, reach 10 ft., one target. *Hit:* 7 (1d8 + 3) piercing damage plus 7 (2d6) necrotic damage. The target's hit point maximum is reduced by an amount equal to the necrotic damage taken, and the vampire vine regains hit points equal to that amount. The reduction lasts until the target finishes a long rest. The target dies if this effect reduces its hit point maximum to 0.

Pointed Leaves. *Ranged Weapon Attack:* +7 to hit, range 60 ft., one target. *Hit:* 8 (2d4 + 3) piercing damage.

VAMPIRIC WARRIOR

Medium undead, neutral evil

Armor Class 18 (plate)
Hit Points 102 (12d8 + 48)
Speed 30 ft.

STR	DEX	CON	INT	WIS	CHA
18 (+4)	15 (+2)	19 (+4)	11 (+0)	10 (+0)	12 (+1)

Saving Throws Con +7, Wis +3
Skills Athletics +7, Perception +3
Damage Resistances necrotic; bludgeoning, piercing, and slashing from nonmagical attacks
Condition Immunities exhaustion, frightened
Senses darkvision 60 ft., passive Perception 13
Languages any languages it knew in life
Challenge 8 (3,900 XP)

Regeneration. The vampiric warrior regains 10 hit points at the start of its turn if it has at least 1 hit point and isn't in sunlight or running water. If the vampiric warrior takes radiant damage or damage from holy water, this trait doesn't function at the start of the vampiric warrior's next turn.

Turning Defiance. The vampiric warrior and any zombies or skeletons within 15 feet of it have advantage on saving throws against effects that turn undead.

Vampire Weaknesses. The vampiric knight has the following flaws:

Forbiddance. The vampiric warrior can't enter a residence without an invitation from one of the occupants.

Harmed by Running Water. The vampiric knight takes 20 acid damage when it ends its turn in running water.

Stake to the Heart. The vampiric knight is destroyed if a piercing weapon made of wood is driven into its heart while it is incapacitated in its resting place.

Sunlight Hypersensitivity. The vampiric warrior takes 20 radiant damage when it starts its turn in sunlight. While in sunlight, it has disadvantage on attack rolls and ability checks.

Undead Nature. A vampiric warrior doesn't require air.

Actions

Multiattack. The vampiric warrior makes four Greatsword attacks.

Greatsword. *Melee Weapon Attack:* +7 to hit, reach 5 ft., one target. *Hit:* 11 (2d6 + 4) slashing damage.

Heavy Crossbow. *Ranged Weapon Attack:* +5 to hit, range 100/400 ft., one target. *Hit:* 7 (1d10 + 2) piercing damage.

Bite. *Melee Weapon Attack:* +7 to hit, reach 5 ft., one willing creature, or a creature that is grappled by the vampiric warrior, incapacitated, or restrained. *Hit:* 7 (1d6 + 4) piercing damage plus 10 (3d6) necrotic damage. The target's hit point maximum is reduced by an amount equal to the necrotic damage taken, and the vampiric warrior regains hit points equal to that amount. The reduction lasts until the target finishes a long rest. The target dies if this effect reduces its hit point maximum to 0.

Reactions

Parry. The vampiric warrior adds 2 to its AC against one melee attack that would hit it. To do so, the vampiric warrior must see the attacker and be wielding a melee weapon.

VAMPIRIC WIZARD

Medium undead, neutral evil

Armor Class 13 (16 with *mage armor*)
Hit Points 110 (17d8 + 34)
Speed 30 ft.

STR	DEX	CON	INT	WIS	CHA
14 (+2)	16 (+3)	14 (+2)	20 (+5)	12 (+1)	18 (+4)

Saving Throws Int +9, Wis +5
Skills Arcana +9, Perception +5, Persuasion +8
Damage Resistances necrotic; bludgeoning, piercing, and slashing from nonmagical attacks
Condition Immunities charmed
Senses darkvision 60 ft., passive Perception 11
Languages any languages it knew in life
Challenge 10 (5,900 XP)

Legendary Resistance (3/day). If the vampiric wizard fails a saving throw, it can choose to succeed instead.

Regeneration. A vampiric wizard regains 10 hit points at the start of its turn if it has at least 1 hit point and isn't in sunlight or running water. If it takes radiant damage or damage from holy water, this trait doesn't function at the start of its next turn.

Spellcasting. A vampiric wizard is a 7th-level spellcaster. Its spellcasting ability is Intelligence (spell save DC 17, +9 to hit with spell attacks). A vampiric wizard has the following wizard spells prepared:

Cantrips (at will): *chill touch, mage hand, ray of frost, shocking grasp*
1st level (4 slots): *burning hands, charm person, mage armor, magic missile, shield*
2nd level (3 slots): *detect thoughts, gust of wind, levitate*
3rd level (3 slots): *fireball, gaseous form, glyph of warding*
4th level (1 slot): *fire shield*

Spider Climb. A vampiric wizard can climb difficult surfaces, including upside down on ceilings, without needing to make an ability check.

Vampire Weaknesses. A vampiric wizard has the following flaws:

Forbiddance. A vampiric wizard can't enter a residence without an invitation from one of the occupants.

Harmed by Running Water. A vampiric wizard takes 20 acid damage when it ends its turn in running water.

Stake to the Heart. A vampiric wizard is destroyed if a piercing weapon made of wood is driven into her heart while it is incapacitated in its resting place.

Sunlight Hypersensitivity. A vampiric wizard takes 20 radiant damage when it starts its turn in sunlight. While in sunlight, it has disadvantage on attack rolls and ability checks.

Undead Nature. A vampiric wizard doesn't require air.

Actions

Multiattack. A vampiric wizard makes two attacks, only one of which can be a Bite attack.

Unarmed Strike. *Melee Weapon Attack:* +7 to hit, reach 5 ft., one target. *Hit:* 7 (1d8 + 3) bludgeoning damage. Instead of dealing damage, a vampiric wizard can grapple the target (escape DC 14).

Bite. *Melee Weapon Attack:* +7 to hit, reach 5 ft., one willing creature, or a creature that is grappled by the vampiric wizard, incapacitated, or restrained. *Hit:* 6 (1d6 + 3) piercing damage plus 10 (3d6) necrotic damage. The target's hit point maximum is reduced by an amount equal to the necrotic damage taken, and the vampiric wizard regains hit points equal to that amount. The reduction lasts until the target finishes a long rest. The target dies if this effect reduces its hit point maximum to 0.

Legendary Actions

A vampiric wizard can take 3 legendary actions, choosing from the options below. Only one legendary action can be used at a time and only at the end of another creature's turn. A vampiric wizard regains spent legendary actions at the start of its turn.

Cantrip. The vampiric wizard casts a cantrip.

Move. The vampiric wizard moves up to her speed without provoking opportunity attacks.

Bite (costs 2 actions). The vampiric wizard makes one Bite attack.

Mesmerizing Gaze (costs 2 actions). The vampiric wizard fixes its gaze on one creature it can see within 10 feet of it. The target must succeed on a DC 16 Charisma saving throw or be incapacitated for 1 minute. If the saving throw fails by 5 or more, the creature is instead stunned for 1 minute as it can't take its eyes away from the vampire's beautiful face. The incapacitated or stunned target can repeat the saving throw at the end of each of its turns, ending the effect on itself on a success. If a target's saving throw is successful or the effect ends for it, the target is immune to the vampiric wizard's Mesmerizing Gaze for the next 24 hours.

Water Naga

Large monstrosity, neutral

Armor Class 15 (natural armor)
Hit Points 58 (9d10 + 9)
Speed 20 ft., swim 40 ft.

STR	DEX	CON	INT	WIS	CHA
19 (+4)	16 (+3)	13 (+1)	15 (+2)	14 (+2)	17 (+3)

Saving Throws Dex +6, Con +5, Cha +7
Skills Deception +7, Perception +5
Damage Immunities poison
Condition Immunities charmed, poisoned
Senses darkvision 60 ft., passive Perception 15
Languages Aquan, Common
Challenge 6 (2,300 XP)

Amphibious. The water naga can breathe air and water.

Rejuvenation. If it dies, the water naga returns to life in 1d10 days and regains all its hit points. Only a *wish* spell can prevent this trait from functioning.

Spellcasting. The naga is an 8th-level spellcaster. Its spellcasting ability is Charisma (spell save DC 14, +6 to hit with spell attacks), and it needs only verbal components to cast its spells. It has the following wizard spells prepared:

Cantrips (at will): *chill touch, dancing lights, minor illusion, ray of frost*
1st level (4 slots): *charm person, detect magic, fog cloud, thunderwave*
2nd level (3 slots): *blindness/deafness, gust of wind, ray of enfeeblement*
3rd level (3 slots): *counterspell, sleet storm*
4th level (2 slots): *control water, ice storm*

Actions

Bite. *Melee Weapon Attack:* +7 to hit, reach 10 ft., one creature. *Hit:* 7 (1d6 + 4) piercing damage, and the creature must make a DC 12 Constitution saving throw, taking 22 (5d8) poison damage on a failed save, or half as much damage on a successful one.

Reactions

Canceling Cascade. If a creature casts a spell within 60 feet of it, the water naga can command water within 30 feet of the spellcaster to rise up and splash against the spellcaster. The spellcaster must succeed on a DC 14 Constitution saving throw or it fails to cast the spell, losing its action for the turn but not its a spell slot.

WEREWOLF, YOUNG

Small humanoid (human, shapechanger), chaotic evil

Armor Class 12 in humanoid form, 13 (natural armor) in hybrid form
Hit Points 22 (5d6 + 5)
Speed 30 ft.

STR	DEX	CON	INT	WIS	CHA
10 (+0)	15 (+2)	12 (+1)	10 (+0)	11 (+0)	10 (+0)

Skills Perception +4, Stealth +4
Damage Resistances bludgeoning, piercing, and slashing from nonmagical attacks not made with silver
Senses passive Perception 14
Languages Common
Challenge 1 (200 XP)

Keen Hearing and Smell. The young werewolf has advantage on Wisdom (Perception) checks that rely on hearing or smell.
Pack Tactics. The young werewolf has advantage on an attack roll against a creature if at least one of the werewolf's allies is within 5 feet of the creature and the ally isn't incapacitated.
Shapechanger. The young werewolf can use its action to polymorph into a wolf-humanoid hybrid or back into its true form, which is humanoid. Its statistics, other than its AC, are the same in each form. Any equipment it is wearing or carrying isn't transformed. It reverts to its true form if it dies.

Actions

Multiattack. The young werewolf makes one attack with its Bite and one with its Claws.
Bite. *Melee Weapon Attack:* +4 to hit, reach 5 ft., one target. *Hit:* 5 (1d6 + 2) piercing damage.
Claws. *Melee Weapon Attack:* +4 to hit, reach 5 ft., one target. *Hit:* 4 (1d4 + 2) slashing damage.

ZOMBIE, CAULDRON-BORN

Medium undead, neutral evil

Armor Class 8
Hit Points 30 (4d8 + 12)
Speed 20 ft.

STR	DEX	CON	INT	WIS	CHA
14 (+2)	6 (−2)	16 (+3)	3 (−4)	6 (−2)	5 (−3)

Saving Throws Con +5, Wis +0
Damage Immunities acid, poison
Condition Immunities poisoned
Senses darkvision 60 ft., passive Perception 8
Languages understands the languages it knew in life but can't speak
Challenge 1/2 (100 XP)

Cauldron-Born. A cauldron-born zombie is created through a complex, magical process that involves injecting the corpse with a variety of alchemical substances. By some quirk of its creation, a cauldron-born zombie is more connected to its creator than the average zombie. A cauldron-born zombie's hit point maximum is reduced by 1d4 for each mile of distance between it and its creator. If this reduces the zombie's hit point maximum to 0, it is destroyed.
Undead Nature. A cauldron-born zombie doesn't require air, food, drink, or sleep.
Unstable Components. When the cauldron-born zombie dies, it explodes in a burst of unstable, alchemical substances. Each creature within 5 feet of it must succeed on a DC 12 Dexterity saving throw or take 4 (1d8) acid damage.

Actions

Slam. *Melee Weapon Attack:* +4 to hit, reach 5 ft., one target. *Hit:* 5 (1d6 + 2) bludgeoning damage.

ZOMBIE, GIANT OCTOPUS

Huge undead, neutral evil

Armor Class 13 (18 if attacked through its bowl)
Hit Points 138 (12d12 + 60)
Speed 10 ft., swim 50 ft.

STR	DEX	CON	INT	WIS	CHA
20 (+5)	16 (+3)	20 (+5)	2 (−4)	8 (−1)	5 (−3)

Skills Perception +3, Stealth +7
Damage Resistances cold; bludgeoning from nonmagical attacks
Damage Immunities poison
Condition Immunities exhaustion, poisoned
Senses darkvision 60 ft., passive Perception 13
Languages —
Challenge 11 (7,200 XP)

Protective Bowl. The giant octopus zombie lives in an extremely durable 10-foot diameter, 10-foot tall glass bowl. It has an Armor Class of 18 against almost all physical attacks made against it from outside its bowl. Attacks directed at the giant octopus zombie from above or from within the bowl use its normal Armor Class of 13.
Turn Resistance. The giant octopus zombie has advantage on saving throws against any effect that turns undead.
Undead Fortitude. If damage reduces the giant octopus zombie to 0 hit points, it must make a Constitution saving throw with a DC of 5 + the damage taken, unless the damage is radiant or from a critical hit. On a success, the giant octopus zombie drops to 1 hit point instead.

Actions

Multiattack. The giant octopus zombie makes eight Tentacle attacks and one Bite attack. Reduce the number of Tentacle attacks by one for each creature the giant octopus zombie has grappled.
Bite. *Melee Weapon Attack:* +9 to hit, reach 5 ft., one grappled target. *Hit:* 15 (3d6 + 5) piercing damage.
Tentacle. *Melee Weapon Attack:* +9 to hit, reach 20 ft., one target. *Hit:* 12 (2d6 + 5) bludgeoning damage. If the target is a creature, it is grappled (escape DC 17). Until this grapple ends, the target is restrained.
Ink Spray (recharges after a short or long rest). A 20-foot-radius cloud of ink extends all around the giant octopus zombie if it is underwater. The area is heavily obscured for 1 minute, although a significant current can disperse the ink. After releasing the ink, the giant octopus zombie can use its bonus action to Dash. If used while the giant octopus zombie is out of

water (or against targets out of water), the giant octopus zombie sprays a 30-foot cone of black ink. All creatures in the cone must succeed on a DC 17 Dexterity saving throw or be blinded and poisoned for 1 minute. Each affected creature may make a DC 17 Constitution saving throw at the end of each of its turns, ending the effects on itself on a success.

Reactions

Don't Tap the Glass. When a creature hits the giant octopus zombie (or its bowl) with a melee attack or moves within 10 feet of its bowl, it may use its reaction to make one Tentacle attack against the creature, unless all of its tentacles are occupied grappling creatures.

ZOMBIE, PYRE

Medium undead, neutral evil

Armor Class 8
Hit Points 39 (6d8 + 12)
Speed 20 ft.

STR	DEX	CON	INT	WIS	CHA
15 (+2)	6 (−2)	14 (+2)	3 (−4)	6 (−2)	5 (−3)

Saving Throws Wis +0
Damage Immunities fire, poison
Condition Immunities poisoned
Senses darkvision 60 ft., passive Perception 8
Languages understands the languages it knew in life but can't speak
Challenge 1 (200 XP)

Flaming Death. When the pyre zombie dies, it explodes in a burst of rotten flesh and fire. Each creature within 5 feet of it must make a DC 12 Dexterity saving throw, taking 7 (2d6) fire damage on a failed save, or half as much damage on a successful one. Flammable objects that aren't being worn or carried in that area are ignited.

Undead Nature. A pyre zombie doesn't require air, food, drink, or sleep.

Actions

Fiery Slam. *Melee Weapon Attack:* +4 to hit, reach 5 ft., one target. *Hit:* 5 (1d6 + 2) bludgeoning damage plus 3 (1d6) fire damage.

Belch Fire **(recharge 6).** The pyre zombie belches fire in a 15-foot cone. Each creature in that area must make a DC 12 Dexterity saving throw, taking 10 (3d6) fire damage on a failed save, or half as much damage on a successful one. If the saving throw fails by 5 or more, the target is coated in some of the zombie's burning bile and takes 3 (1d6) fire damage on the next round.

ZOMBIE, STRANGLING

Medium undead, neutral evil

Armor Class 10
Hit Points 32 (5d8 + 10)
Speed 30 ft., climb 20 ft.

STR	DEX	CON	INT	WIS	CHA
16 (+3)	10 (+0)	14 (+2)	3 (−4)	6 (−2)	5 (−3)

Saving Throws Wis +0
Skills Athletics +5
Damage Resistances fire
Damage Immunities poison
Condition Immunities poisoned
Senses darkvision 60 ft., passive Perception 8
Languages understands the languages it knew in life but can't speak
Challenge 1/2 (100 XP)

Undead Fortitude. If damage reduces the strangling zombie to 0 hit points, it must make a Constitution saving throw with a DC of 5 + the damage taken, unless the damage is radiant or from a critical hit. On a success, the zombie drops to 1 hit point instead.

Undead Nature. A strangling zombie doesn't require air, food, drink, or sleep.

Actions

Slam. *Melee Weapon Attack:* +5 to hit, reach 5 ft., one target. *Hit:* 6 (1d6 + 3) bludgeoning damage and the target is grappled (escape DC 13).

Strangle. One creature grappled by the strangling zombie must succeed on a DC 12 Constitution saving throw or take 7 (2d6) bludgeoning damage and be unable to breathe until the grapple ends.

Appendix III: Startling Statues

Several statues are already described in this work, but the you may desire to replace them with others or imbue yet more with some kind of enchantment. The first table below provides a general subject of the statue by rolling a 4-sided die to choose a column and an 8-sided die for the row. Upon encountering a magical statue, use the second table and roll a 12-sided die for the horizontal column and an 8-sided die for the vertical column and cross-index. Most statues function only one time. If combat stats are needed, they are roughly equivalent to **animated armor** but can be adjusted to have more hit points for large statues or whatever else feels appropriate.

Startling Statues

(Roll 1d4 for category and 1d8 for appearance)

1d8	Appearance			
	Human	Animal	Monster	Grotesque
1	Knight	Canine	Griffon	Hunchback
2	Priest	Feline	Humanoid	Skeletal
3	Lady	Reptile	Giant class	Zombie
4	Nobleman	Frog type	Draconic	Gargoyle
5	Wizard	Ape	Centaur	Jester
6	Hermit	Ursine	Demon	Defaced
7	Man-at-arms	Rodent	Sphinx	Extra limbs/eyes
8	Nude	Avian	Harpy	Contorted

1d12	
1	Raises[1]
2	Lowers[1]
3	Casts Spell of[4]
4	Gives Scroll of[4]
5	Advises
6	Asks
7	Shape changes to[5]
8	Polymorphs character to[6]
9	Points Towards
10	Gives Map of
11	Part Missing[7]
12	Casts Curse on

[1] Permanent.
[2] 25% of sum needed for next level.
[3] Proficiency in one skill.
[4] Using minimum possible spell slot level , DC 13 + spell level.
[5] Average creature as per the **5eSRD**.
[6] *Polymorph*, DC 17.
[7] Finding and restoring a missing part of the statue results in the following actions (1d6):

1	Shape changes and serves replacer for 1d20 days.
2	Attacks replacer.
3	Casts spell at replacer (as per column 3.).
4	Gives replacer 1d10 pieces of jewelry, valued at 1d4 x 100 gp apiece.
5	Destroys replacer's most precious carried or worn item (avoid with DC 19 Dexterity saving throw).
6	Grants replacer one *wish*.

1d8	Raises/ Lowers	Casts Spell of/ Gives Scroll of	Advises/ Asks	Polymorph character to	Points Towards/ Gives Map of	Part Missing/ Casts Curse on
1	Strength	Sleep	Location	Orc	Treasure	Eye
2	Dexterity	Fear	Name	Troll	Monster	Nose
3	Constitution	Enhance Ability (strength)	Class	Stone Giant	Village	Ear
4	Intelligence	Lightning Bolt	Purpose	Efreeti	Trap	Hand
5	Wisdom	Suggestion	Origin	Giant Frog	Exit	Foot
6	Charisma	Geas	Riddle	Blink Dog	Sea	Arm
7	Experience[2]	Hold Person	Poem	Stone Golem	Passage	Leg
8	Skill[3]	Raise Dead	Directions	Giant Weasel	Random	Finger

APPENDIX IV: TERRIBLE TRAPS

Traps may be encountered at several locations as indicated on the GM's map of the manor. Those found in keyed rooms are usually given a description. The rest can be rolled for on the table below (1d20) or chosen as appropriate.

1d20	Type
1	**Crossbow Trap** *Mechanical trap* When a creature steps on a pressure plate with more than 20 lbs of force, or trips another type of proximity trigger, 1d6 crossbows make a ranged attack at +8 to hit at random creatures within a 10 foot by foot area around the trigger. A target that is hit takes 4 (1d8) piercing damage per hit. The crossbows are hidden in the walls and usually concealed by wooden paneling. The DC to spot them is 16. Locating the trigger requires a DC 18 Intelligence (Investigation) check. The trap can be disabled by wedging the pressure plate or blocking the bolt holes.
2	**Falling Stone Blocks** *Mechanical trap* When a creature steps on a pressure plate with more than 20 lbs of force (or, in the case of weak construction, causes a large vibration by, for example, casting *thunder wave*), several stone blocks fall from the ceiling in a 10-foot radius around the creature. Each creature within the circle must make a DC 15 Dexterity saving throw. Those who fail the saving throw take 18 (4d8) bludgeoning damage while those who succeed take half this amount. The unstable state of the ceiling can be identified with a successful DC 14 Intelligence (Investigation) check. Finding the pressure plate requires a DC 15 Wisdom (Perception) check.
3	**Scything Blade** *Mechanical trap* Typically released by a trip wire, the scything blade can also be swung by a suit of armor. When the trigger is released, the scythe makes a melee weapon attack against a creature within 5 feet at +6 to hit. On a successful hit, it does 6 (1d8 + 2) slashing damage. The trip wire can be noted with a DC 14 Wisdom (Perception) check and the trap can be disarmed by carefully cutting the wire. This requires a DC 12 Dexterity check and failing the check by five or more triggers the trap
4	**Swinging Block** *Mechanical trap* When, after placing more than 20 lbs of force on a pressure plate, a creature removes its weight from the plate, a large stone block swings across on metal chains. Any creature within 5 feet of the trigger must make a DC 15 Dexterity saving throw. On a failed saving throw, the creature takes 21 (6d6) bludgeoning damage. A creature that is moving normally feels the plate shift with a DC 18 Wisdom (Perception) check. If a creature is dashing when it steps on the plate, it has disadvantage on the check. Disarming the trap once the trigger is detected requires a DC 18 Dexterity check with thieves' tools.

1d20	Type
5	**Moving Executioner Statue** *Mechanical trap* If a creature comes within 5 feet of the statue without depressing the bypass switch to disarm it, the statue makes a melee attack at +10 to hit against it. On a hit, the target takes 15 (2d6 + 8) slashing damage. The statue continues to make attacks as long as a target is within range and the statue has not been destroyed or disarmed. The bypass switch can be located with a successful DC 18 Wisdom (Perception) check. The statue is destroyed if it takes 25 points of damage. It has an AC of 15. The statue may guard a pedestal with small gemstones of little value, or stand in a room resembling a shrine or temple.
6	**Green Slime**[II] Green slime may hang from the ceiling, fall from half-eaten furniture, be concealed in large ceramic pots, a fountain or disguised as a potion in a chest, etc.
7	**Brown Mold**[II] Mold is usually hidden in decaying garbs, on a decomposing corpse, a chest, a tapestry covering a wormeaten wardrobe, etc.
8	**Yellow Mold**[II] Mold is usually hidden in decaying garbs, on a decomposing corpse, a chest, a tapestry covering a wormeaten wardrobe, etc.
9	**Hypnotic Brazier** *Magic trap* This brazier may stand in something resembling an elaborate ritual chamber – with candles, diagrams, tapestries and idols. Its magical flames create a hypnotic pattern. Any creature that looks upon it must succeed on a DC 16 Wisdom saving throw or be hypnotized by the brazier. A hypnotized creature may attempt a new saving throw at the end of each its turns. Once it has succeeded on a saving throw, the creature is immune to the brazier's hypnosis for 24 hours. A hypnotized creature makes every effort to get amidst the brazier's flames as quickly as possible. Each round that a creature spends in the fire it takes 27 (6d8) fire damage. *Dispel magic* cast with a level 4 spell slot dampens the hypnotic pattern for 1 round, giving any creatures needing to make a saving throw advantage.
10	**Fire Breathing Suit of Armor** *Magic trap* When a creature comes within fifteen feet of the armor, the armor releases a 15-foot cone of fire. Each creature within the cone must make a DC 16 Dexterity saving throw. Those that fail take 17 (4d6) damage while those that succeed take half as much. The trap recharges on a 5 or 6 on 1d6. A variant of this trap is a fireplace breathing sparks instead.

Disembodied Hands with Chilling Touch
Magical trap

11 — When a creature enters a room being guarded by this trap, a pair of spectral hands appear and target it. Up to six pairs of hands may appear, one per creature in the area. On initiative 20, the hands move up to 50 feet to follow their target as long as the target is within the room, and make a spell attack against their target if they are within 10 feet of the target. The attack is made at +7 to hit. On a successful hit, the target takes 3 (1d6) cold damage and, on a failed DC 15 Constitution saving throw, loses 1 point of Strength until completing a long rest.

Disembodied Hands with Vampiric Touch
Magical trap

12 — When a creature enters a room being guarded by this trap, a pair of spectral hands appear and target it. Up to six pairs of hands may appear, one per creature in the area. On initiative 20, the hands move up to 50 feet to follow their target as long as the target is within the room, and make a spell attack against their target if they are within 10 feet of the target. The attack is made at +7 to hit. On a successful hit, the target takes 14 (4d6) necrotic damage and cannot regain hit points until the start of the next round.

***Animate Objects* Trap**
Magical trap

13 — When one or more creatures enter the trapped region, up to 11 small or 5 medium weapons animate and attack them. On initiative 10, each weapon moves up to 30 feet towards a target and makes a melee weapon attack against a target within 5 feet at +6 to hit. Small weapons do 5 (1d6 + 2) slashing or piercing (as appropriate) damage on a hit while medium ones do 8 (1d10 + 3). Each weapon has AC 14 and is destroyed if it takes 18 hit points of damage. They are immune to necrotic, poison, and psychic damage. Casting *dispel magic* on a weapon causes it to revert to an inanimate state for one hour.

Rot Grubs[II] in Decaying Bodies

14 — The bodies may be dead adventurers with a few useful items still on their bodies (20% probability), villagers or just random corpses.

Animated Fresco
Magical trap

15 — A horrible fresco animates, causing all who can see it to make a DC 18 Wisdom saving throw. Those who fail drop whatever they are holding and become frightened for up to one minute. While frightened, a creature must take the dash action and move away from the fresco by the safest available route, unless there is nowhere to move. A creature who ends its turn in a location where it does not have line of sight to the fresco may make a DC 18 Wisdom saving throw, ending the effect on a success. After animating, the fresco cannot animate again for 24 hours.

Commanding Visage
Magical trap

16 — When a creature approaches within 10 feet of large stone visage, it commands the creature to drink the *potion of poison* lying on pedestal. The target of the command must make a successful DC 16 Wisdom saving throw or attempt to comply with it. A creature that succeeds on the saving throw is immune from further commands from this face. There is a 50% probability that the stone face has 100 gp gems for eyes.

Magic Mouth
Magical trap

17 — When a creature comes within 30 feet of the *magic mouth*, it cries loudly for help. Make three random monster checks. The *magic mouth* then becomes inactive for one hour. A variant of this trap also casts *arcane lock* on all exits, increasing the DC to break them down or unlock them by 10.

Room Full of Diseased Corpses

18 — The corpses all have Slimy Doom (see **DL4A**). The disease can be recognized with a successful DC 15 Wisdom (Medicine) check. The corpses may be just piled up, or placed elaborately in wooden thrones, hung on hooks, sitting in plush chairs or any other arrangement. They are usually moldy and putrid, but some (25% probability) possess 1d3 pieces of jewelry, value 2d8 x 10 gp. Finding any treasure requires a DC 14 Wisdom (perception) check (and probably touching the corpses).

Malevolent Mirage
Magical trap

19 — A wondrous hypnotic illusion appears. Any creature seeing the illusion must make a DC 16 Wisdom saving throw or use its movement and make the dash action to enter its area. Within the area covered by the illusion may be spiked pits, fire, or any other form of dangerous area. The illusion can be seen through with a successful DC 18 Intelligence (Investigation) check. The mirage could originate from an idol, fresco, statue, gemstone (1d3 x 100 gp), etc.

Rapid Rot
Magical trap

20 — A creature who touches the objet protected by this trap must make a successful DC 14 Charisma saving throw or it and all objects it is wearing or carrying instantly age 1000 years. For most creatures, this means instant death, leaving only grey, moldy dust remaining. Detecting the trap requires a successful DC 18 Intelligence (Arcana) check. Once the trap has triggered, it cannot do so again for 24 hours.

Note: This trap is always linked to an item of great worth (1d6 x 500 gp), usually prominently displayed and surrounded by grim reminders of death and decay. E.g. a solid gold bowl in a room full of graven stone skulls, dust and moldy cobwebs, held by the statue of Death personified.

Appendix V: Eldritch Experiments

In a well-stocked laboratory, it is only natural that inquisitive characters are going to try their hands at alchemy, even if they lack the necessary knowledge. Since no less than five such places are described in this work (**B16.**, **E9.**, **L6.**, **DL4G.** and **X11.** in the Wilderness), the following guidelines are provided.

Roll on the **Alchemical Substance Characteristics Table** below to determine substance parameters. A successful DC 17 Intelligence (Arcana) check identifies its general effects. Mixing two or more substances requires a roll on the **Miscibility Table**. Again, a successful DC 20 Intelligence (Arcana) check before making an attempt gives the character a good idea about the results. Although the mixtures created this way may be potent, 80% of them are also rather unstable and become ineffective in 1d6 x 10 minutes.

Alchemical Substance Characteristics

1d10	Contained In	State	Color	Activity[1]	Effect
1	vial	liquid	chromatic	inert	harmless
2	tube	powdered	pastel	inert	harmless
3	globe	crystalline	compound	inert	foul taste/smell
4	jar	solid	white	bubbling	irritant
5	bowl	paste	black	fizzy	poison[2]
6	pan	(semi)gaseous	metallic	sparkling	disease
7	alembic	granular	transparent	flowing	pigment[3]
8	box	oily	hazy	churning	corrosive[4]
9	beaker	hardened	radiant	evaporating	beneficial[5]
10	flask	gelatinous	1d3 colors	melting	magical[6]

[1] If appropriate.
[2] Determine application method and effect.
[3] Strong colorative effect on items/members in contact.
[4] 40% mild acid (1d3), 40% normal acid (1d6), 20% potent acid (4d6), 1d4 doses.
[5] This could be anything, e.g. minor curative effect (1d4 hp), smoke generation when burnt, heightening/extending potions when mixed, neutralizing mild poisons, etc.
[6] Roll on the potion table. Application is typically ingested, inhaled or topical. Alternatively, you may invent new effects, e.g. growing the character's ears to double size or making a metal item rustproof. Since these aren't genuine magical mixtures, feel free to add a side effect or reduce effectiveness.

Miscibility Table

1d10	Result	Remains Effective	Catastrophe[3]
1	inert mixture	one remains	fire
2	inert mixture	both/all remains	explosion (3d6)
3	inert mixture	new effects (1d3)	explosion (6d6)
4	remains effective	increased duration	poison gas
5	remains effective	increased potency	*sleep gas*[4]
6	ruins equipment	reduced potency	*stinking cloud*
7	ruins materials	side effect	*acid fog*
8	catastrophe	changes state	*cloudkill*
9	magical, unstable[1]	changes color	rust gas[5]
10	magical, stable[2]	changes activity	demon summoned[6]

[1] Turns inert in 2d10 minutes unless used.
[2] Permanent item. You may make up something entirely new – such as a nugget of silvery material that turns a pool of water into glass, a balm that ignites when mixed with blood, dust which causes cold damage, etc.
[3] Generally, spell effects are at the lowest possible levels. Saving throw DCs are 14.
[4] Equivalent to *sleep*.
[5] All iron items in a 20 foot area need to roll a generic DC 14 saving throw or rust to uselessness. Creatures carrying or wearing such items may make a DC 14 Dexterity saving throw for their items.
[6] Guardian Demons[II] are highly recommended.

Appendix VI: New Magic Items & Spells

Magic Items

Blade of Two Sides

Weapon (shortsword), rare

You have a +1 bonus to attack and damage rolls made with the *blade of two sides*. In addition, when you make an attack roll with the weapon, you can grant yourself a +5 bonus to the attack roll. Once you've done so, the next attack roll you make has a –5 penalty.

Book of Madness

Wondrous item, artifact (requires attunement)

Rivaling the *Book of Dark Vileness* in power and rarity, the *Book of Madness* was lost for centuries of epic struggles between powerful wizards and priests. The artifact's power is as legendary as its maddening corruption of the minds of the weak. All but the greatest intellects and strongest of wills fail to resist the eventual destruction of sanity, succumbing to permanent mental collapse. Unfortunately, the maddened possessor continues to use the powers of the *Book of Madness* to wreak havoc on their enemies and any who seek to tear the artifact from their grasp.

A creature that gazes upon the closed *Book of Madness* even for a moment must make a DC 20 Wisdom saving throw. On a failed saving throw, the target is frightened of the *Book of Madness* for 1 hour. During that time, the creature must use its actions to flee from the tome in abject terror. A creature that touches the tome must make another DC 20 Wisdom saving throw. On a successful saving throw, the target takes 4d10 psychic damage, but is able to grasp the tome. On a failed saving throw, the target gains a form of short-term madness for 1d10 minutes. If the saving throw fails by 10 or more, it instead gains a form of long-term madness. Short and long-term madness can be temporarily suppressed with a *calm emotions* spell, or permanently cured with *lesser restoration* or *greater restoration*.

Finally, a creature who succeeds on the above and open the *Book of Madness* to gaze upon its contents must make a DC 20 Wisdom saving throw. On a successful saving throw, the target takes 8d10 psychic damage. On a failed saving throw, the target is struck with a form of indefinite madness, which can only be cured with magic such as *greater restoration*.

Detections. The *Book of Madness* cannot be targeted by divination magic, including magic such as *identify*, *detect magic*, or *locate object*. A creature with truesight recognizes that the *Book of Madness* truly is, however, a mind-twisting creation.

Attunement. To attune to the *Book of Madness*, you must spend 7 days studying the book. After each 7 day period, you must make a DC 20 Intelligence saving throw. On a failed saving throw, you gain a form of indefinite madness. Once you have accumulated three successful saving throws, you have attuned to the *Book of Madness*.

After attuning to the book, you cannot willingly let your attunement lapse. Magic such as *greater restoration* is required to end the attunement to the item. In addition, you age one full year for every month that passes. This aging is permanent, even if your attunement to the *Book of Madness* ends. Finally, you gain the following flaw: *"I cannot bear to let the* Book of Madness *from my sight, or to allow another to touch it."*

Adjusted Ability Scores. After you spend the requisite amount of time studying the tome, your Wisdom and Intelligence scores increase by 2, to a maximum of 22. However, your Constitution score decreases by 2, to a minimum of 3. If your attunement to the *Book of Madness* ends, your scores return to normal after you take a long rest.

Spells. Packed within the pages of the *Book of Madness* are all the spells on the Wizard spell list. You merely need to think of a Wizard spell and turn to any page to find it within the shifting pages. The spells listed within can easily be copied into another spellbook. When turning to the spell, if the spell's level is 5th or lower, you can use your action to cast the spell. When you do, make a DC 20 Intelligence saving throw. On a successful saving throw, you can't use the *Book of Madness* to cast another spell until you take a long rest. On a failed saving throw, you gain a form of Indefinite madness and the *Book of Madness* regains the ability to cast another Wizard spell.

Each time you use the *Book of Madness* to cast a spell, there is a cumulative 1% chance that a lawfully aligned deity will take notice and send a **deva**. The deva shares the deity's alignment and goals, and will attempt to take the *Book of Madness* from you. Once the celestial has been summoned, the chance of summoning another does not reset, making it much more likely that the deity will take further measures.

Destruction. The *Book of Madness* is entirely immune to all damage and cannot be permanently destroyed. If the *Book of Madness* is brought to a lawful deity, that deity can rip the pages from the book to temporarily disperse it across the planes. However, after a few years or decades, it will reappear on another plane of existence.

Bracers of the Master Pugilist

Wondrous item, rare

These seemingly simple cloth hand and wrist wrappings are a light brown in color, mottled with red specks. When you first grasp them, the wrappings immediately wrap themselves around your wrists and hands, until both are wrapped tightly to you. You can use an action to unwrap them. You are incapable of wielding a weapon while wearing the wraps, but you have a +2 bonus to attack and damage rolls made with your unarmed strikes.

Charismatic Sickle

Weapon (sickle), very rare

When you wield this weapon, you gain a +2 bonus to attack and damage rolls. In addition, if you are a cleric or a druid, you gain +1 to your Charisma score while carrying this weapon.

Choaxtl's Sword

Weapon (longsword), legendary
(requires attunement by a character proficient with longsword)

You gain a +3 bonus to attack and damage rolls with this weapon.

Spellcasting. You can use the sword to cast *hold person* on one person (DC 16 spell save DC), *see invisibility*, and *levitate* on yourself. Once you have cast one of these spells three times in a day, you cannot cast that spell again until the following midnight.

Sentience. The sword has an Intelligence of 14, a Wisdom of 12, and a Charisma of 15. The sword is extremely vain and vindictive, stopping at nothing to mercilessly destroy the "thief" who took it from its rightful owner. You must make a DC 15 Wisdom saving throw immediately upon attunement. If you fail the saving throw, you immediately enter a berserk rage. While in a rage, you attack the nearest conscious creature you can see. The rage lasts until you are knocked unconscious or 10 minutes have passed. In addition, if you do not pass the saving throw, each time that day that you attempt to use the sword to cast a spell, you must succeed on a DC 15 Wisdom saving throw or enter a berserk rage. Every day at midnight, you must make another DC 15 Wisdom saving throw with the same consequences for failure. If you succeed on five consecutive saving throws against the weapon's mental assault, Choaxtl's sword allows you to use its powers and you no longer have to make saving throws… as long as your superiority remains unquestionable. Choaxtl's sword speaks Ancient Orichalan and nothing else.

In the hands of an evil Orichalan character, it remains *reasonably* loyal — that is, it merely tries to control the character instead of causing utter destruction.

DUST OF APPEARANCE

Wondrous item, uncommon

Found in a small tin, this powder resembles fine chalk dust. There is enough of it for one use. When you use an action to throw the dust into the air, any invisible or ethereal creature in a 10-foot-cube adjacent to you becomes visible. A normally invisible creature remains visible for 1 minute while a creature that used an action, spell, or similar means of becoming so must do so again before becoming invisible again. The dust is consumed when its magic takes effect.

DUST OF UNDEAD PROTECTION

Wondrous item, rare

Found in a small pouch, this powder resembles ground quartz. There is enough of it for one use. When you use an action to throw the dust into the air, you and each creature within 10 feet of you becomes protected from undead for 1 minute. Undead creatures attacking a protected creature have disadvantage. The dust is consumed when its magic takes effect.

ELVEN STUDDED LEATHER

Armor (studded leather), very rare

You are considered proficient with this armor even if you lack proficiency with light armor. While wearing this armor, you are considered proficient in Stealth. If you are already proficient in Stealth, you are considered to have expertise.

ENDLESS ROPE

Wondrous item, rare

This lock of golden hair is, in its default state, a 3-inch strand of woven hair. You can use an action to extend the *endless rope* up to 500 feet long. The *endless rope* has 30 hit points, AC 18, and can be burst with a successful DC 23 Strength check.

FRIGGA'S INFLUENCE

Weapon, legendary (requires attunement)

The golden mace acts as a *mace of disruption* with the following additional features: You have a +1 bonus to attack and damage rolls with this weapon. Against undead and fiends, the bonus is +2. Additionally, if you are a disciple of Frigga, you can use the mace to case *heal* once per week.

GLOVE OF EXSANGUINATION

Wondrous item, very rare
(requites attunement by a neutral evil or chaotic evil creature)

This is a single left-hand glove made of black leather, cut from the back of an ebony demon. When you attune to the item, it grows or shrinks to fit your hand like a second skin. While wearing it, you can use your action to touch a creature within 5 feet of you. That creature must make a DC 17 Dexterity saving throw. On a failed saving throw, a spectral copy of the glove attaches to the creature. While the spectral glove is attached, the creature must make a DC 17 Constitution saving throw at the beginning of each of its turns. On a successful saving throw, the target is freed from the spectral glove. On a failed saving throw, the target takes 4d6 necrotic damage and you regain hit points equal to the amount of damage dealt, up to your hit point maximum.

A *remove curse* or *dispel magic* can end the effect early. Once you have used the *glove of exsanguination*, you cannot do so again until you take a short or long rest.

GOLDEN PLATE ARMOR OF THOR

Armor (plate), legendary (requires attunement)

Worn by a chosen paladin of the order of Thor during the destruction of the frog god's original temple in the area, this gilded suit of plate armor was stored in a secret vault after the warrior's death. It is to be used again if needed to fight the return of the frog god, worn by another chosen of Thor or one of his trusted priests.

While wearing this armor, you have a +2 bonus to AC. The armor is wrought to weigh only 30 pounds and requires only Strength 13 to wear.

Blessing of Thor. You can use your action to beg for the blessing of Thor. For 10 minutes, you have immunity to lightning and thunder damage, your Strength score becomes 19 if it was not higher, and you have advantage on saving throws against spells and other magical effects.

LYCANTHROPE-BANE

Weapon (shortsword), very rare

You gain a +1 bonus to attack and damage rolls with this weapon. If you attack a lycanthrope with it, you gain a +2 bonus to attack and damage rolls. On a hit, the creature must succeed on a DC 15 Wisdom saving throw or revert to its natural form.

MONK'S COLORED SASHES

Wondrous item, rarity varies (requires attunement by a monk)

These long sashes are made of enchanted silk and are potent weapons when wielded by a monk. They are martial weapons with finesse and a 10-foot reach that deal 1d6 slashing damage on a hit, and *sashes* of rare or higher have a bonus to attack and damage rolls made with the weapon. If you are a monk, it is considered a monk weapon for you. In addition, each *colored sash* has the following additional ability: when you hit with an attack using the *monk's colored sash*, you can force the target must make a Strength saving throw against your ki save DC. On a failed saving throw, the target is grappled by you.

If the target is grappled at the start of your next turn, you can use your bonus action to use one of the other abilities of your *sash*. Each rarity has two abilities, save for the *tri-colored sash*, which possesses all of them. If an ability requires a saving throw, the DC to resist the effect is equal to your ki save DC. Once you've used an ability, you can't do so again until you take a short or long rest.

Color	Rarity	Abilities	Bonus
Yellow	Uncommon	Inflict Pain, Paralyze	+0
Red	Rare	Heat, Fatigue	+1
Blue	Very Rare	Freeze, Stun	+1
Tri-Colored	Legendary	All	+2

Inflict Pain. Until the end of the target's next turn, it has disadvantage on Intelligence, Wisdom, and Charisma saving throws.

Paralyze. The target makes a Constitution saving throw. On a failed saving throw, the target is paralyzed for 1 minute. A paralyzed creature can repeat the saving throw at the end of each of its turns, ending the effect on a success.

Heat. The target makes a Constitution saving throw. On a failed saving throw, the target takes 3d6 fire damage, or half as much damage on a successful saving throw.

Fatigue. The target must make a Constitution saving throw. On a failed saving throw, the target is weakened for 1 minute. While weakened, the target deals only half damage with weapon attacks that use Strength. A weakened target can repeat the saving throw at the end of each of its turns, ending the effect on a success.

Freeze. The target must make a Constitution saving throw. On a failed saving throw, the target takes 4d6 cold damage, or half as much damage on a successful saving throw.

Stun. The target must make a Constitution saving throw. On a failed saving throw, the target is stunned for 1 minute. The stunned target can repeat the saving throw on each of its turns, ending the effect on a success.

NECKLACE OF STRANGULATION

Wondrous item, uncommon

When you put this necklace on, it constricts about your neck, preventing you from breathing. You immediately begin to suffocate. The necklace can be broken with a successful DC 18 Strength check or relaxed for 1 minute with *dispel magic*. *Remove curse* allows the necklace to be removed and the wearer is forever immune to that particular *necklace of strangulation*.

POTION OF INVULNERABILITY

Potion, legendary

This potion glows dimly and within floats a single bead of white light, from which the glow originates. When you drink the potion, you have immunity to bludgeoning, piercing, and slashing damage for 1 minute.

POTION OF PARALYSIS

Potion, rare

When you drink this potion, you must succeed DC 16 Constitution saving throw or be paralyzed for 1 hour. The effect can be removed with *dispel magic* or *remove curse*.

RING OF PROTECTION

Wondrous item, rarity varies (requires attunement)

While wearing this ring, you gain a bonus to your AC and saving throws. The amount of the bonus depends on the ring's rarity.

Ring of...	Rarity	Bonus
Protection	rare	+1
Greater protection	very rare	+2
Superior protection	legendary	+3

QUILL OF ACCURATE WRITING

Wondrous item, uncommon

This magical quill never needs ink and allows you to write mistake-free messages simply by dictating. You can also provide an empty book or scroll and a book or scroll you wish to copy, and the *quill of accurate writing* will copy it in 1 hour. The *quill of accurate writing* cannot copy *spell scrolls* or magical books such as a *tome of understanding*.

ROBE OF THE DEVOTED

Wondrous item, very rare
(requires attunement by a cleric or druid)

The *robes of the devoted* are magically enchanted robes made of simple-looking but exquisite cloth and often adorned with a holy symbol. You gain these benefits while wearing the robe:
- If you aren't wearing armor, your base Armor Class is 14 + your Dexterity modifier.
- You have resistance to bludgeoning, piercing, and slashing damage from nonmagical attacks.
- You can use an action to cast the *commune* spell. Once you have done so, you can't use the robe to cast the spell again until you finish a long rest.
- You are immune to the effects of spells that would cause you to act against your deity or sacred oath.

ROD OF RESURRECTION

Rod, very rare
(requires attunement by a cleric, druid, or paladin)

This 1-foot-tall rod is made of silver and glows dimly with white light. Etched into the rod is a detailed scene; when dipped in ink and rolled onto canvas, it shows a beautiful, middle-aged woman tending to the sick and wounded that lie around a large hearth. The *rod of resurrection* has 10 charges. While holding it, you can use an action to expend 1 or more of its charges to cast one of the following spells from it, with a spellcasting ability modifier of +3: *cure wounds* (1 charge per spell level, up to 4th), *lesser restoration* (2 charges), *mass cure wounds* (5 charges), or *resurrection* (7 charges). The rod regains 1d6 + 4 expended charges daily at dawn. If you expend the last charge, roll a d20. On a 1, the staff vanishes in a flash of light, lost forever.

ROD OF THE PROTECTOR

Rod, very rare (requires attunement)

This simple steel rod has an emblem of a shield on it. You can use an action to cast one of the following spells: *protection from energy, protection from evil and good, protection from poison,* or *sanctuary*. You may cast each of these spells once, regaining the ability to cast it again when you finish a short rest. In addition, you may cast the spell *antimagic field*. Once you've cast this spell, you may not do so again until you finish a long rest.

SACERDOTAL SCEPTER

Wondrous item, rare (requires attunement)

This scepter is just over a foot long, made of blackened iron topped with a green frog head with two glowing red eyes. You have a +1 bonus to your AC while you wield the *sacerdotal scepter*, and you add a +1 bonus to spell attack rolls.

SCEPTER OF AGONIZING TORMENT

Wondrous item, legendary
(requires attunement by a neutral evil or chaotic evil creature)

This 2-foot-long scepter is wrought of steel and infused with chunks of meteorite, giving it a blending of gray, silver, and black. The whorls seem to shape a suggestion of faces trapped within the scepter. You have a +1 bonus to your Armor Class while attuned to the *scepter of agonizing torment*, and you gain access to the following abilities.

Torment. You can use an action to target one creature and cause it to make a DC 17 Dexterity saving throw. On a failed saving throw, the target takes 2d12 necrotic damage and is stunned until the end of its next turn.

Spells. The *scepter of agonizing torment* has 35 charges. The *scepter* regains 4d6 charges each night at midnight. You can expend charges to *animate dead* and *create dead*. When you do so, the casting time of each spell is 1 action instead of each spell's normal casting time, and you can expend additional charges to cast the spells at a higher level: *animate dead* requires 3 charges, and you can expend 1 additional charge for each spell level above 3rd; and *create undead* requires 7 charges, and you can expend 1 additional charge for each spell level above 7th.

Rejuvenation. If you die your attunement doesn't end and the *scepter of agonizing torment* vanishes to a location that you determine when you attune to the item. At the next midnight, you regain 1 hit point as long as your body wasn't completely destroyed when you died.

SPEAR OF FRIGGA

Weapon (spear), very rare (requires attunement)

This is a beautifully wrought, solid gold spearhead, carved with depictions of snow fall and the first spring thaw. The spearhead is preternaturally sharp and indestructible. You can attach the spearhead to any suitable haft with 1 minute's work. You have a +2 bonus to attack and damage rolls made with the *spear of Frigga*, and you deal an additional 2d6 damage to fiends or undead. In addition, you can use the *spear of Frigga* as a holy symbol if you are a cleric of Frigga. If you do, the *spear* adds its +2 bonus to spell attack rolls that you make while holding the *spear of Frigga*.

STAFF OF THE FROG

Staff, rare (requires attunement)

This green staff has the head of a bloated frog at its tip, and emanates a faint mist from the figurehead's eyes. This staff can be wielded as a magic quarterstaff that grants a +2 bonus to attack and damage rolls made with it. The staff has 10 charges. While holding the staff, you can use an action to expend charges and cast one of the following spells: *giant insect* (4 charges), *insect plague* (5 charges), or *heal* (6 charges).

You can also use an action to cast the *jump* spell at will without expending charges, and you have resistance to poison damage and advantage on saving throws against poison.

THE WAY OF THE WARRIOR

Wondrous item, very rare

This book contains combat exercises and conditioning, and its words are charged with magic. If you spend 48 hours over a period of 6 days or fewer studying the book's contents and practicing its guidelines, your Strength or Dexterity score (your choice) increases by 2 to a maximum of 20, and you gain proficiency in martial weapons, shields, medium armor, and heavy armor. The book then loses its magic, but regains it in a century.

UNHOLY MACE

Weapon (mace), uncommon (requires attunement)

This black-iron mace seems to glow with a very dim, sickly green light, and its head is adorned with curved, almost thorn-like spikes. You have a +1 bonus to attack and damage rolls made with the *unholy mace*. In addition, if you strike a good-aligned creature, you deal an additional 1d6 poison damage.

WAND OF PAINFUL ANGUISH

Wand, very rare (requires attunement by a spellcaster)

This black wood wand is unadorned, but carries an aura of menace. The wand has 5 charges. While holding it, you can expend 1 charge and target one creature. That creature must make a Constitution saving throw against your spell save DC. On a failed saving throw, the creature is cursed. While it is cursed, the target has disadvantage on Wisdom saving throws, and takes 2d10 necrotic damage at the beginning of each of its turns. A cursed creature remains cursed until magic such as *remove curse* is used to end the effect early.

The wand regains 1d4 + 1 expended charges daily at midnight. If you expend the wand's last charge, roll a d20. On a 1, the wand crumbles into ashes and is destroyed.

SPELLS

CAUSTIC BURST

3rd-level evocation
Casting Time: 1 action
Range: 60 feet
Components: V, S, M (an acid pitted ruby worth 5 gp)
Duration: Instantaneous

You launch a ball of viscous acid from your open hand which lands at a point you choose within range and then splashes in a 10-foot radius. Each creature in the area centered on that point must make a Dexterity saving throw. A target takes 6d4 acid damage on a failed saving throw, or half as much damage on a successful saving throw. If a target took acid damage, it takes an additional 3d4 acid damage at the start of its next turn.

At Higher Levels. When you cast this spell using a spell slot of 4th level or higher, the damage increases by 1d4 for each slot level above 3rd.

TONGUE OF THE FROG GOD

3rd-level transmutation
Casting Time: 1 bonus action
Range: Self
Components: V, S, M (the tongue of a poisonous frog)
Duration: Concentration, up to 1 minute

This spell conjures a long, swollen tongue that grows from the mouth of the caster. This tongue can be used as a whiplike appendage. You can use an action to make a melee spell attack with the tongue which has a range of 20 feet. It deals 1d8 bludgeoning damage on a hit, and the creature is grappled. The escape DC is equal to your spellcasting DC. While grappled, the creature makes a Constitution saving throw at the start of each of its turns, taking 2d10 poison damage on a failed save, or half as much on a successful one.

The tongue can be attacked, has AC 15 and hit points equal to half your hit point maximum. When the tongue is destroyed, it dissolves into nothing and the caster's tongue returns to normal. It does not impede the casting of other spells with verbal components.

LEGAL APPENDIX

Designation of Product Identity: The following items are hereby designated as Product Identity as provided in section 1(e) of the Open Game License: Any and all material or content that could be claimed as Product Identity pursuant to section 1(e), below, is hereby claimed as product identity, including but not limited to: **1.** The name "Frog God Games" as well as all logos and identifying marks of Frog God Games, LLC, including but not limited to the Frog God logo and the phrase "Adventures worth winning," as well as the trade dress of Frog God Games products; **2.** The product name "The Lost Lands," "Tegel Manor" as well as any and all Frog God Games product names referenced in the work; **3.** All artwork, illustration, graphic design, maps, and cartography, including any text contained within such artwork, illustration, maps or cartography; **4.** The proper names, personality, descriptions and/or motivations of all artifacts, characters, races, countries, geographic locations, plane or planes of existence, gods, deities, events, magic items, organizations and/or groups unique to this book, but not their stat blocks or other game mechanic descriptions (if any), and also excluding any such names when they are included in monster, spell or feat names. **5.** Any other content previously designated as Product Identity is hereby designated as Product Identity and is used with permission and/or pursuant to license.

This printing is done under version 1.0a of the Open Game License, below.

Notice of Open Game Content: This product contains Open Game Content, as defined in the Open Game License, below. Open Game Content may only be Used under and in terms of the Open Game License.

Designation of Open Game Content: Subject to the Product Identity Designation herein, the following material is designated as Open Game Content. (1) all monster statistics, descriptions of special abilities, and sentences including game mechanics such as die rolls, probabilities, and/or other material required to be open game content as part of the game rules, or previously released as Open Game Content, (2) all portions of spell descriptions that include rules-specific definitions of the effect of the spells, and all material previously released as Open Game Content, (3) all other descriptions of game-rule effects specifying die rolls or other mechanic features of the game, whether in traps, magic items, hazards, or anywhere else in the text, (4) all previously released Open Game Content, material required to be Open Game Content under the terms of the Open Game License, and public domain material anywhere in the text.

Use of Content from *The Tome of Horrors Complete*: This product contains or references content from *The Tome of Horrors Complete* and/or other monster *Tomes* by Frog God Games. Such content is used by permission and an abbreviated Section 15 entry has been approved. Citation to monsters from *The Tome of Horrors Complete* or other monster *Tomes* must be done by citation to that original work.

OPEN GAME LICENSE Version 1.0a The following text is the property of Wizards of the Coast, Inc. and is Copyright 2000 Wizards of the Coast, Inc. ("Wizards"). All Rights Reserved.

1. Definitions: (a) "Contributors" means the copyright and/or trademark owners who have contributed Open Game Content; (b) "Derivative Material" means copyrighted material including derivative works and translations (including into other computer languages), potation, modification, correction, addition, extension, upgrade, improvement, compilation, abridgment or other form in which an existing work may be recast, transformed or adapted; (c) "Distribute" means to reproduce, license, rent, lease, sell, broadcast, publicly display, transmit or otherwise distribute; (d) "Open Game Content" means the game mechanic and includes the methods, procedures, processes and routines to the extent such content does not embody the Product Identity and is an enhancement over the prior art and any additional content clearly identified as Open Game Content by the Contributor, and means any work covered by this License, including translations and derivative works under copyright law, but specifically excludes Product Identity; (e) "Product Identity" means product and product line names, logos and identifying marks including trade dress; artifacts; creatures; characters; stories, storylines, plots, thematic elements, dialogue, incidents, language, artwork, symbols, designs, depictions, likenesses, formats, poses, concepts, themes and graphic, photographic and other visual or audio representations; names and descriptions of characters, spells, enchantments, personalities, teams, personas, likenesses and special abilities; places, locations, environments, creatures, equipment, magical or supernatural abilities or effects, logos, symbols, or graphic designs; and any other trademark or registered trademark clearly identified as Product identity by the owner of the Product Identity, and which specifically excludes the Open Game Content; (f) "Trademark" means the logos, names, mark, sign, motto, designs that are used by a Contributor to identify itself or its products or the associated products contributed to the Open Game License by the Contributor; (g) "Use", "Used" or "Using" means to use, Distribute, copy, edit, format, modify, translate and otherwise create Derivative Material of Open Game Content; (h) "You" or "Your" means the licensee in terms of this agreement.

2. The License: This License applies to any Open Game Content that contains a notice indicating that the Open Game Content may only be Used under and in terms of this License. You must affix such a notice to any Open Game Content that you Use. No terms may be added to or subtracted from this License except as described by the License itself. No other terms or conditions may be applied to any Open Game Content distributed using this License.

3. Offer and Acceptance: By Using the Open Game Content You indicate Your acceptance of the terms of this License.

4. Grant and Consideration: In consideration for agreeing to use this License, the Contributors grant You a perpetual, worldwide, royalty-free, non-exclusive license with the exact terms of this License to Use, the Open Game Content.

5. Representation of Authority to Contribute: If You are contributing original material as Open Game Content, You represent that Your Contributions are Your original creation and/or You have sufficient rights to grant the rights conveyed by this License.

6. Notice of License Copyright: You must update the COPYRIGHT NOTICE portion of this License to include the exact text of the COPYRIGHT NOTICE of any Open Game Content You are copying, modifying or distributing, and You must add the title, the copyright date, and the copyright holder's name to the COPYRIGHT NOTICE of any original Open Game Content you Distribute.

7. Use of Product Identity: You agree not to Use any Product Identity, including as an indication as to compatibility, except as expressly licensed in another, independent Agreement with the owner of each element of that Product Identity. You agree not to indicate compatibility or co-adaptability with any Trademark or Registered Trademark in conjunction with a work containing Open Game Content except as expressly licensed in another, independent Agreement with the owner of such Trademark or Registered Trademark. The use of any Product Identity in Open Game Content does not constitute a challenge to the ownership of that Product Identity. The owner of any Product Identity used in Open Game Content shall retain all rights, title and interest in and to that Product Identity.

8. Identification: If you distribute Open Game Content You must clearly indicate which portions of the work that you are distributing are Open Game Content.

9. Updating the License: Wizards or its designated Agents may publish updated versions of this License. You may use any authorized version of this License to copy, modify and distribute any Open Game Content originally distributed under any version of this License.

10. Copy of this License: You MUST include a copy of this License with every copy of the Open Game Content You Distribute.

11. Use of Contributor Credits: You may not market or advertise the Open Game Content using the name of any Contributor unless You have written permission from the Contributor to do so.

12. Inability to Comply: If it is impossible for You to comply with any of the terms of this License with respect to some or all of the Open Game Content due to statute, judicial order, or governmental regulation then You may not Use any Open Game Material so affected.

13. Termination: This License will terminate automatically if You fail to comply with all terms herein and fail to cure such breach within 30 days of becoming aware of the breach. All sublicenses shall survive the termination of this License.

14. Reformation: If any provision of this License is held to be unenforceable, such provision shall be reformed only to the extent necessary to make it enforceable.

15. COPYRIGHT NOTICE

Open Game License v 1.0a © 2000, Wizards of the Coast, Inc.

System Reference Document © 2000. Wizards of the Coast, Inc; Authors Jonathan Tweet, Monte Cook, Skip Williams, based on material by E. Gary Gygax and Dave Arneson.

System Reference Document 5.1 © 2016. Wizards of the Coast, Inc; Authors Mike Mearls, Jeremy Crawford, Chris Perkins, Rodney Thompson, Peter Lee, James Wyatt, Robert J. Schwalb, Bruce R. Cordell, Chris Sims, and Steve Townshend, based on material by E. Gary Gygax and Dave Arneson.

Tome of Horrors © 2018, Frog God Games, LLC; Authors: Kevin Baase, Erica Balsley, John "Pexx" Barnhouse, Christopher Bishop, Casey Christofferson, Jim Collura, Andrea Costantini, Jayson 'Rocky' Gardner, Zach Glazar, Meghan Greene, Scott Greene, Lance Hawvermale, Travis Hawvermale, Ian S. Johnston, Bill Kenower, Patrick Lawinger, Rhiannon Louve, Ian McGarty, Edwin Nagy, James Patterson, Nathan Paul, Patrick N. Pilgrim, Clark Peterson, Anthony Pryor, Greg Ragland, Robert Schwalb, G. Scott Swift, Greg A. Vaughan, and Bill Webb

Tegel Manor © 2019, Frog God Games, LLC; Authors: Bill Webb & Thom Wilson with additional material by Gabor Lux